GEORGE R. R. MARTIN

STARPORT

A GRAPHIC NOVEL

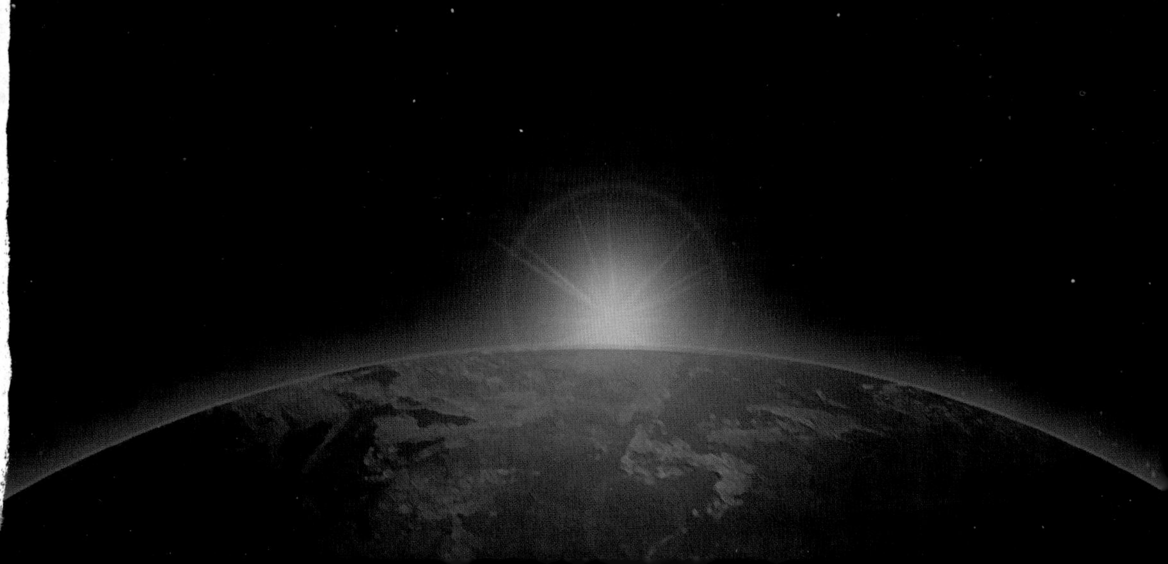

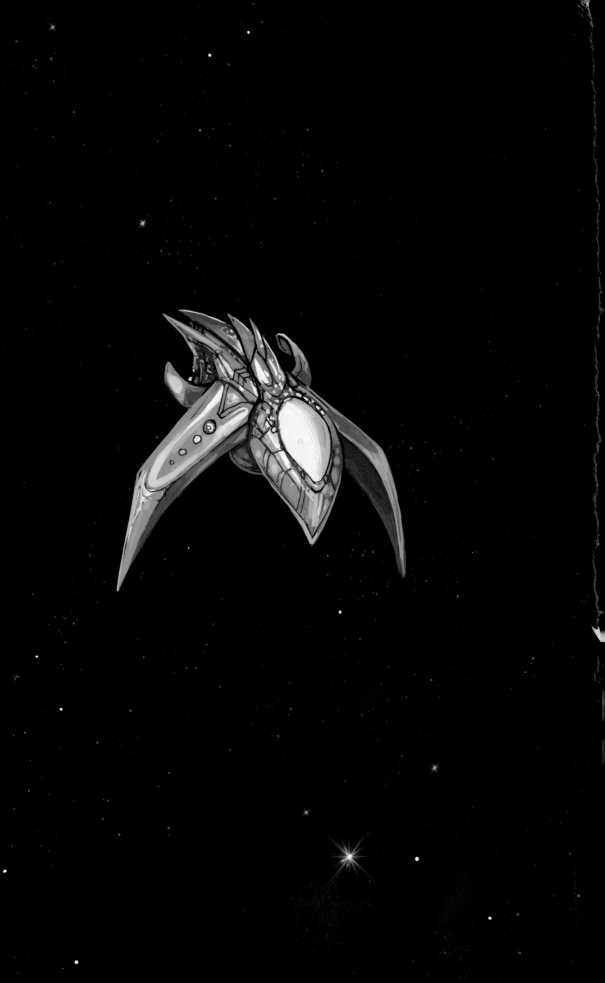

GEORGE R. R. MARTIN
STARPORT

A GRAPHIC NOVEL

WRITTEN BY
George R. R. Martin

ART AND ADAPTATION BY
Raya Golden

COLORING BY
Rachel Hilley

LETTERING BY
Bill Tortolini

BANTAM BOOKS
NEW YORK

Starport is a work of fiction. Names, characters, places, and incidents are the products of the author's imagination or are used fictitiously. Any resemblance to actual events, locales, or persons, living or dead, is entirely coincidental.

Copyright © 2019 by George R. R. Martin

All rights reserved.

Published in the United States by Bantam Books, an imprint of Random House, a division of Penguin Random House LLC, New York.

BANTAM BOOKS and the HOUSE colophon are registered trademarks of Penguin Random House LLC.

All characters featured in this book, and the distinctive names and likenesses thereof, and all related indicia are trademarks of George R. R. Martin.

ISBN 978-1-101-96504-7
Ebook ISBN 978-1-101-96505-4

Printed in China

randomhousebooks.com

2 4 6 8 9 7 5 3 1

Graphic novel interior design by Bill Tortolini

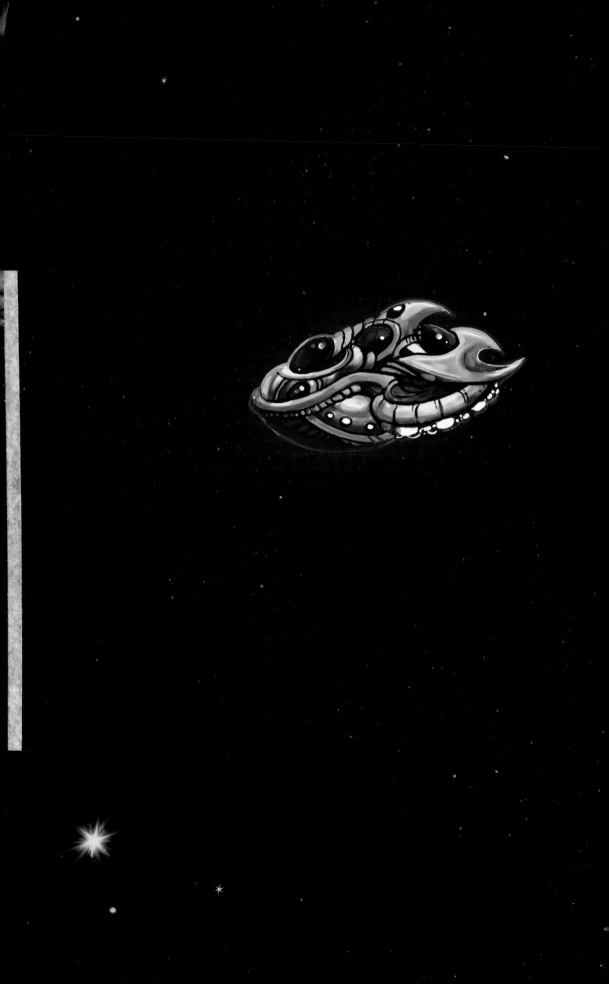

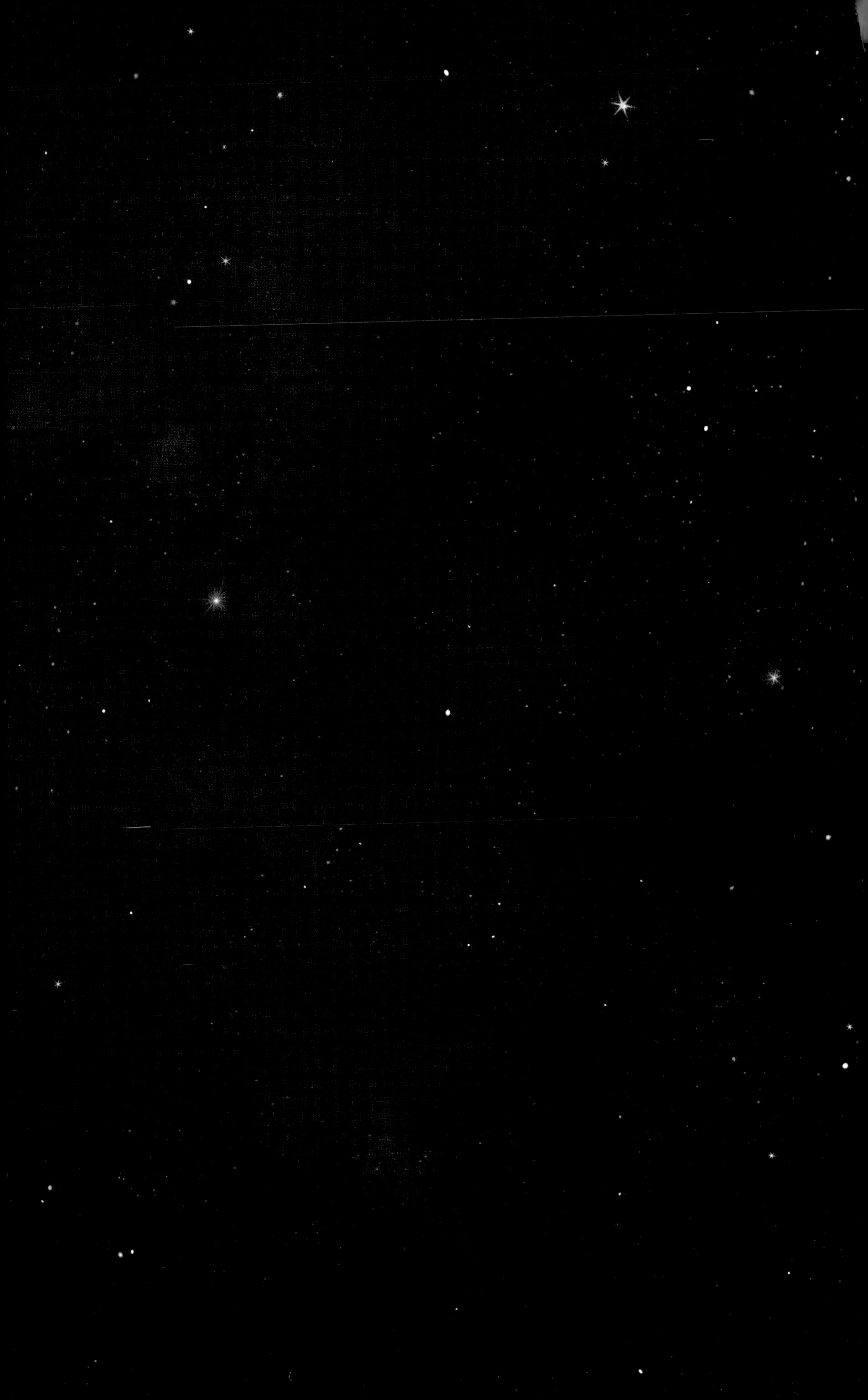

PROLOGUE

A decade ago, something amazing happened: Aliens discovered Earth. Three Chaseen ships landed, all randomly searching for active sports stadiums, looking to make a real entrance. The first ship landed in Singapore during the AFF Tiger Cup Championship. The second landed in Denmark at the Parken Stadium during a New Firm local rivalry pregame and unfortunately caused a small stampede of university students—which was indeed an entrance, although maybe not the one that particular pilot was looking for. The third landed at one other notable stadium on the other side of the planet, but more on that later.

Thankfully, they didn't come to rule over us or anything dramatic like that. Instead, humanity got to join the 314 other species within the Harmony of Worlds. With the help of three main pilgrim species—the Lohb, the Nhar, and the founding Chaseen—Earth began to construct three intergalactic treaty ports: one in Singapore, the first to open, six years after the landing; one in Copenhagen, which opened the following year ...and one plagued with delays and all sorts of intrigue, opening two years after that...

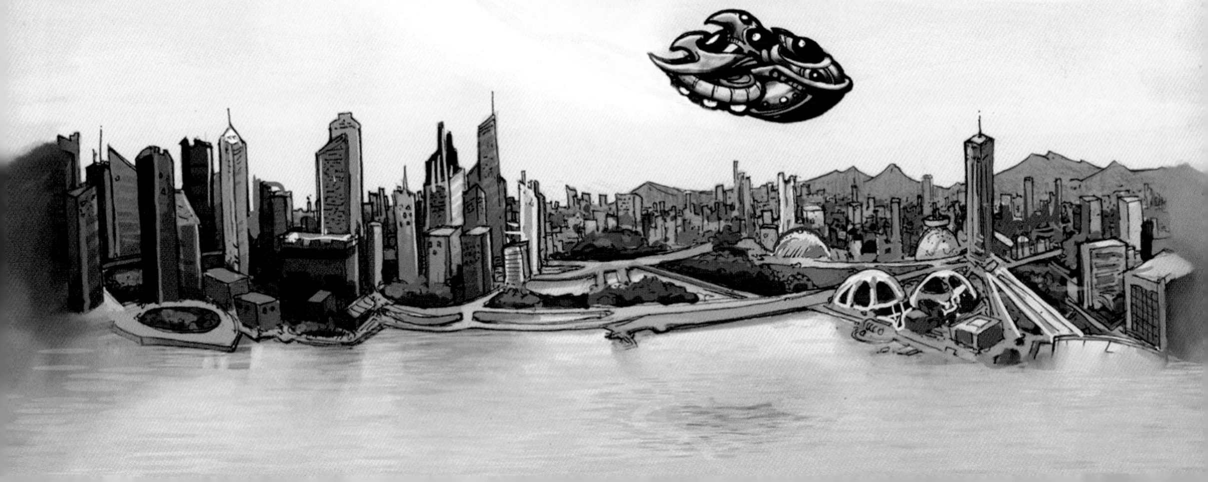

CHAPTER ONE

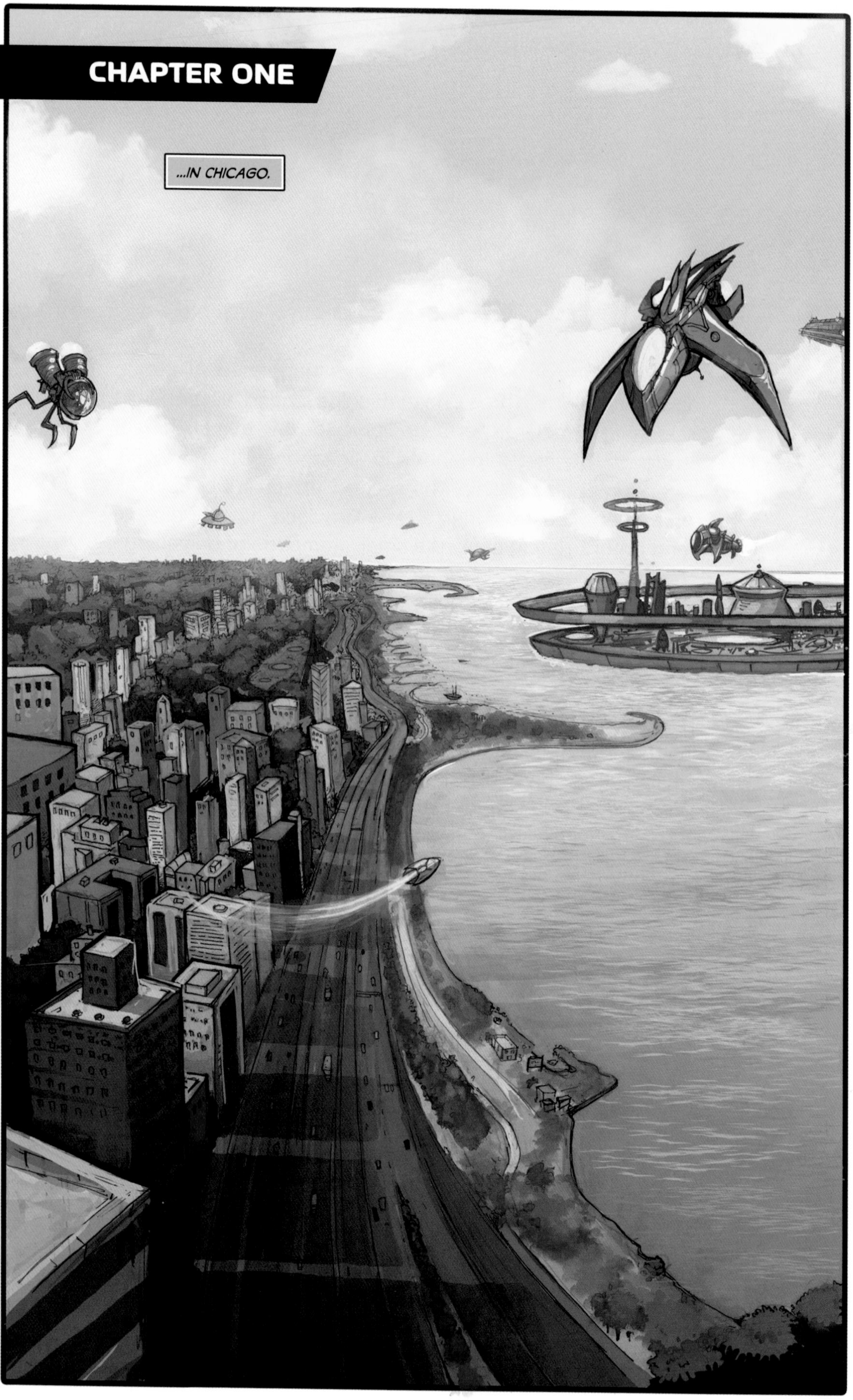
...IN CHICAGO.

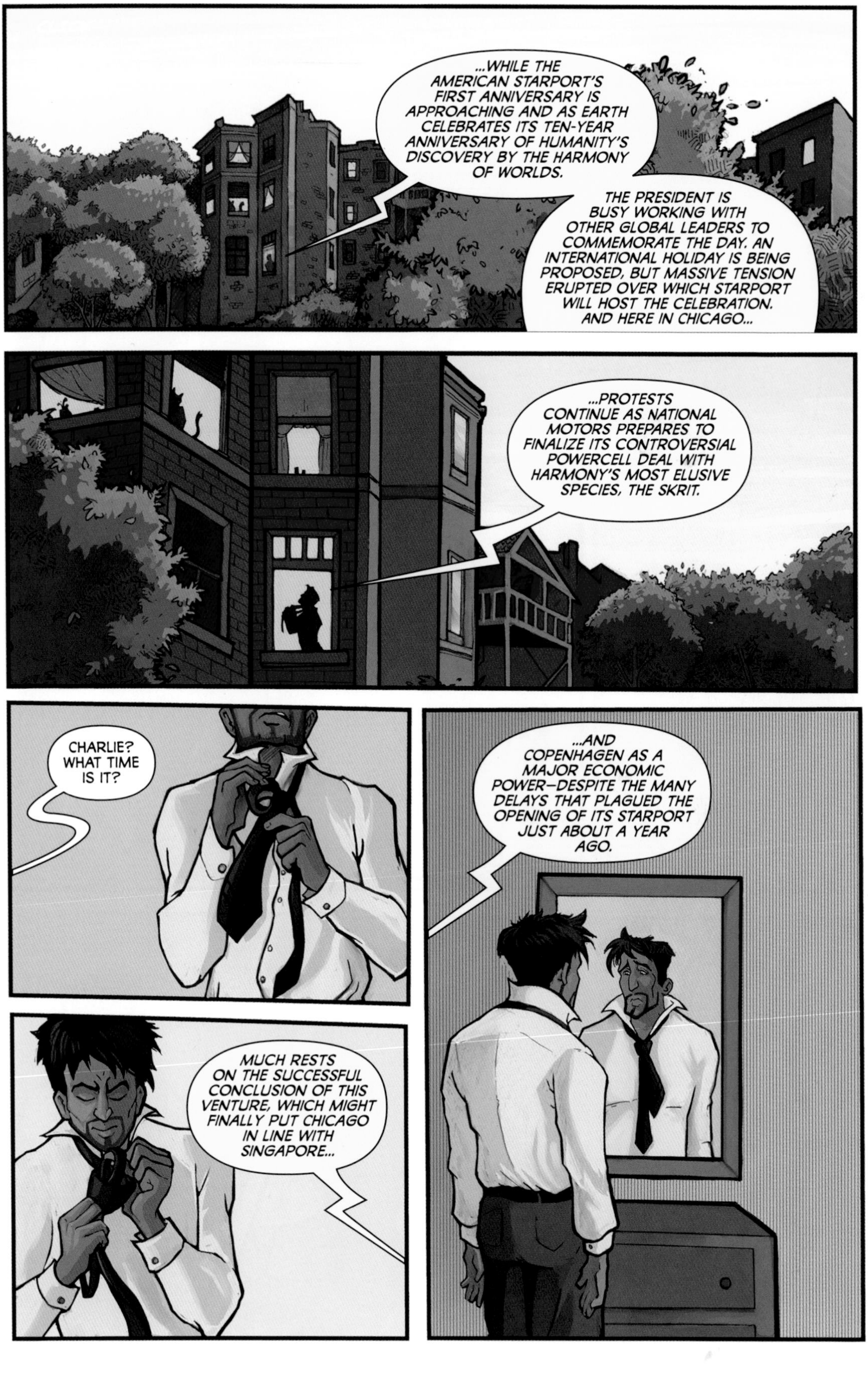
...WHILE THE AMERICAN STARPORT'S FIRST ANNIVERSARY IS APPROACHING AND AS EARTH CELEBRATES ITS TEN-YEAR ANNIVERSARY OF HUMANITY'S DISCOVERY BY THE HARMONY OF WORLDS.
THE PRESIDENT IS BUSY WORKING WITH OTHER GLOBAL LEADERS TO COMMEMORATE THE DAY. AN INTERNATIONAL HOLIDAY IS BEING PROPOSED, BUT MASSIVE TENSION ERUPTED OVER WHICH STARPORT WILL HOST THE CELEBRATION. AND HERE IN CHICAGO...
...PROTESTS CONTINUE AS NATIONAL MOTORS PREPARES TO FINALIZE ITS CONTROVERSIAL POWERCELL DEAL WITH HARMONY'S MOST ELUSIVE SPECIES, THE SKRIT.
CHARLIE? WHAT TIME IS IT?
MUCH RESTS ON THE SUCCESSFUL CONCLUSION OF THIS VENTURE, WHICH MIGHT FINALLY PUT CHICAGO IN LINE WITH SINGAPORE...
...AND COPENHAGEN AS A MAJOR ECONOMIC POWER—DESPITE THE MANY DELAYS THAT PLAGUED THE OPENING OF ITS STARPORT JUST ABOUT A YEAR AGO.

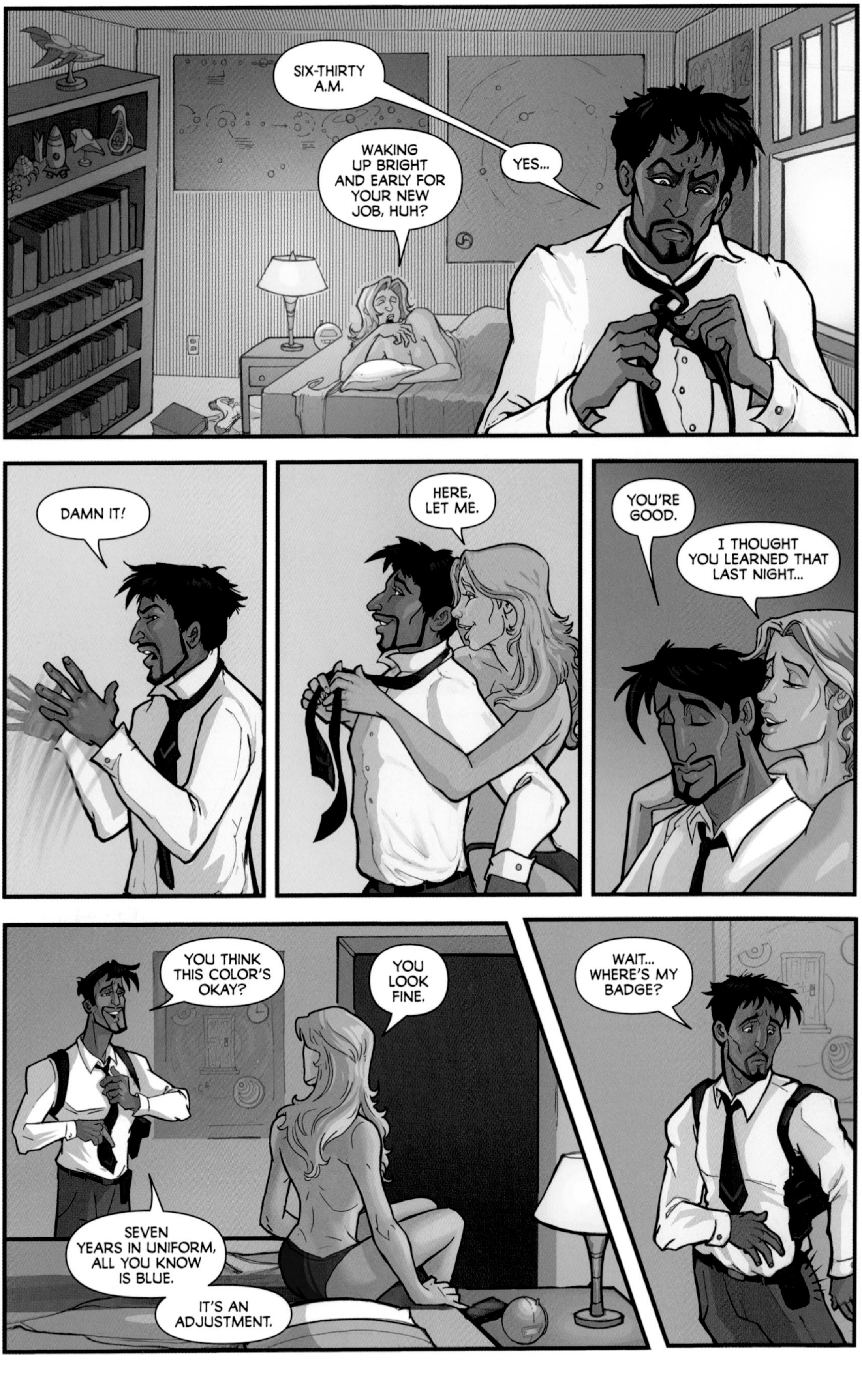
SIX-THIRTY A.M.
WAKING UP BRIGHT AND EARLY FOR YOUR NEW JOB, HUH?
YES...
DAMN IT!
HERE, LET ME.
YOU'RE GOOD.
I THOUGHT YOU LEARNED THAT LAST NIGHT...
YOU THINK THIS COLOR'S OKAY?
YOU LOOK FINE.
SEVEN YEARS IN UNIFORM, ALL YOU KNOW IS BLUE.
IT'S AN ADJUSTMENT.
WAIT... WHERE'S MY BADGE?

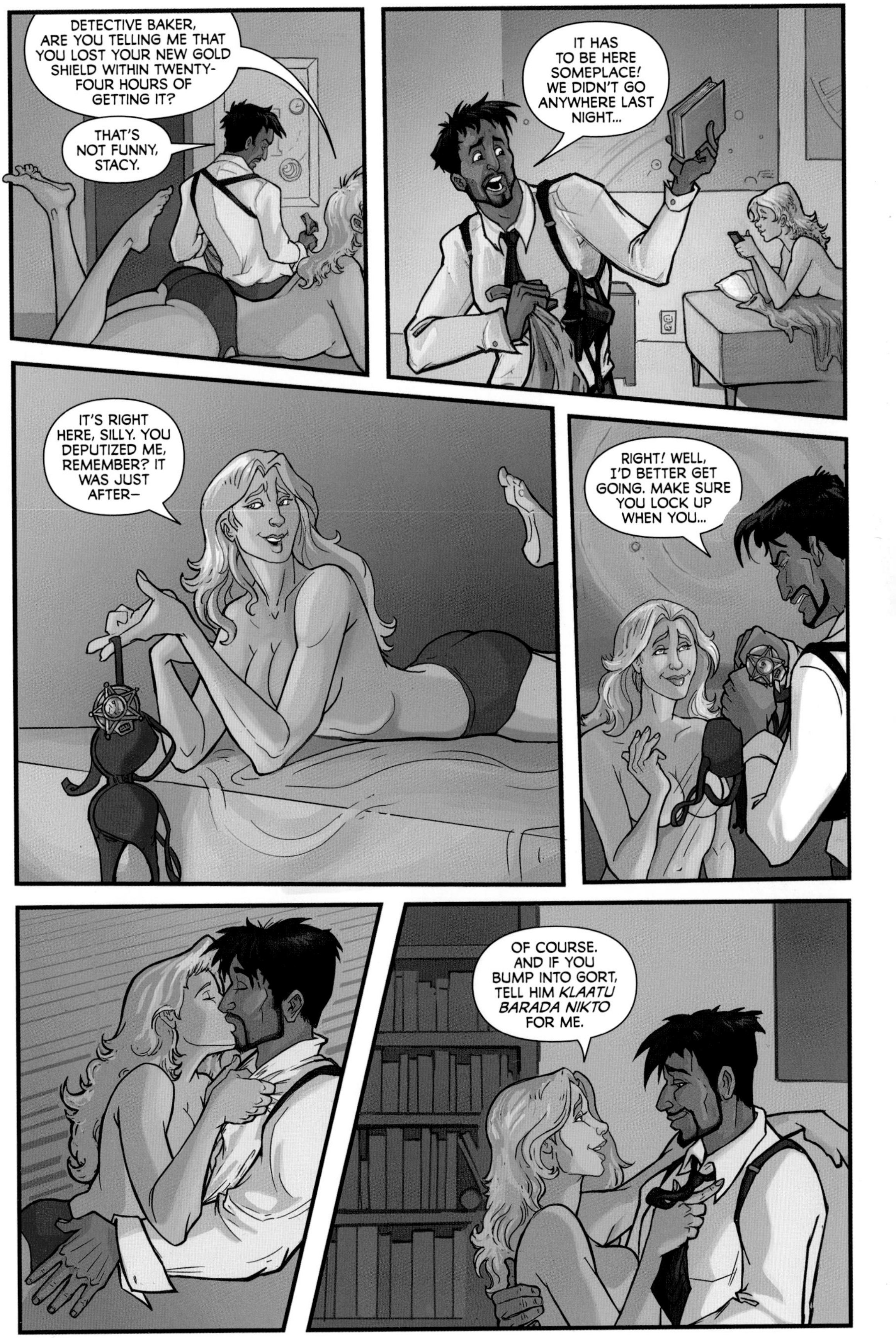
DETECTIVE BAKER, ARE YOU TELLING ME THAT YOU LOST YOUR NEW GOLD SHIELD WITHIN TWENTY-FOUR HOURS OF GETTING IT?
THAT'S NOT FUNNY, STACY.
IT HAS TO BE HERE SOMEPLACE! WE DIDN'T GO ANYWHERE LAST NIGHT...
IT'S RIGHT HERE, SILLY. YOU DEPUTIZED ME, REMEMBER? IT WAS JUST AFTER–
RIGHT! WELL, I'D BETTER GET GOING. MAKE SURE YOU LOCK UP WHEN YOU...
OF COURSE. AND IF YOU BUMP INTO GORT, TELL HIM *KLAATU BARADA NIKTO* FOR ME.

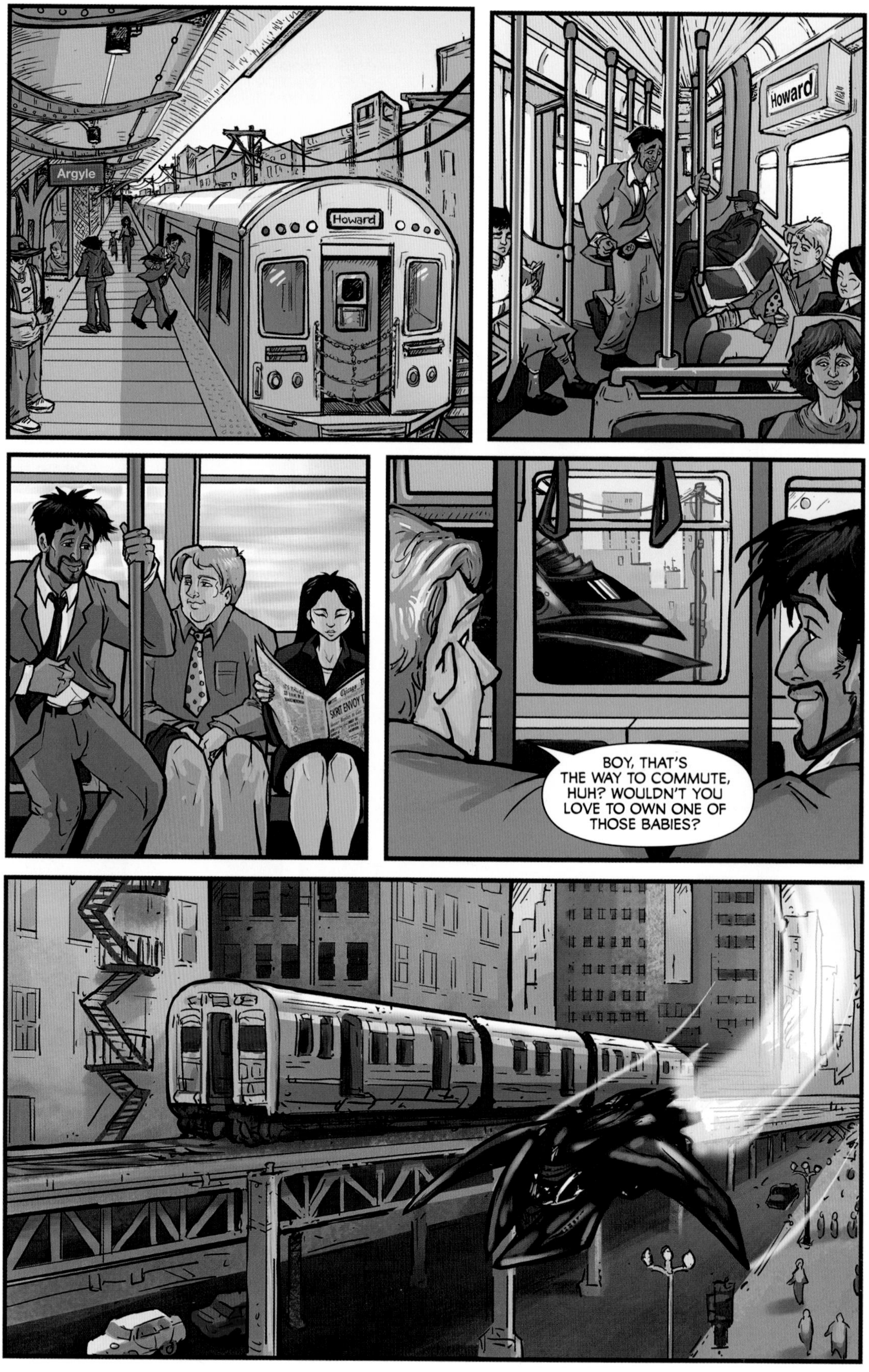
Argyle
Howard
Howard
SKRT ENVOY
BOY, THAT'S THE WAY TO COMMUTE, HUH? WOULDN'T YOU LOVE TO OWN ONE OF THOSE BABIES?

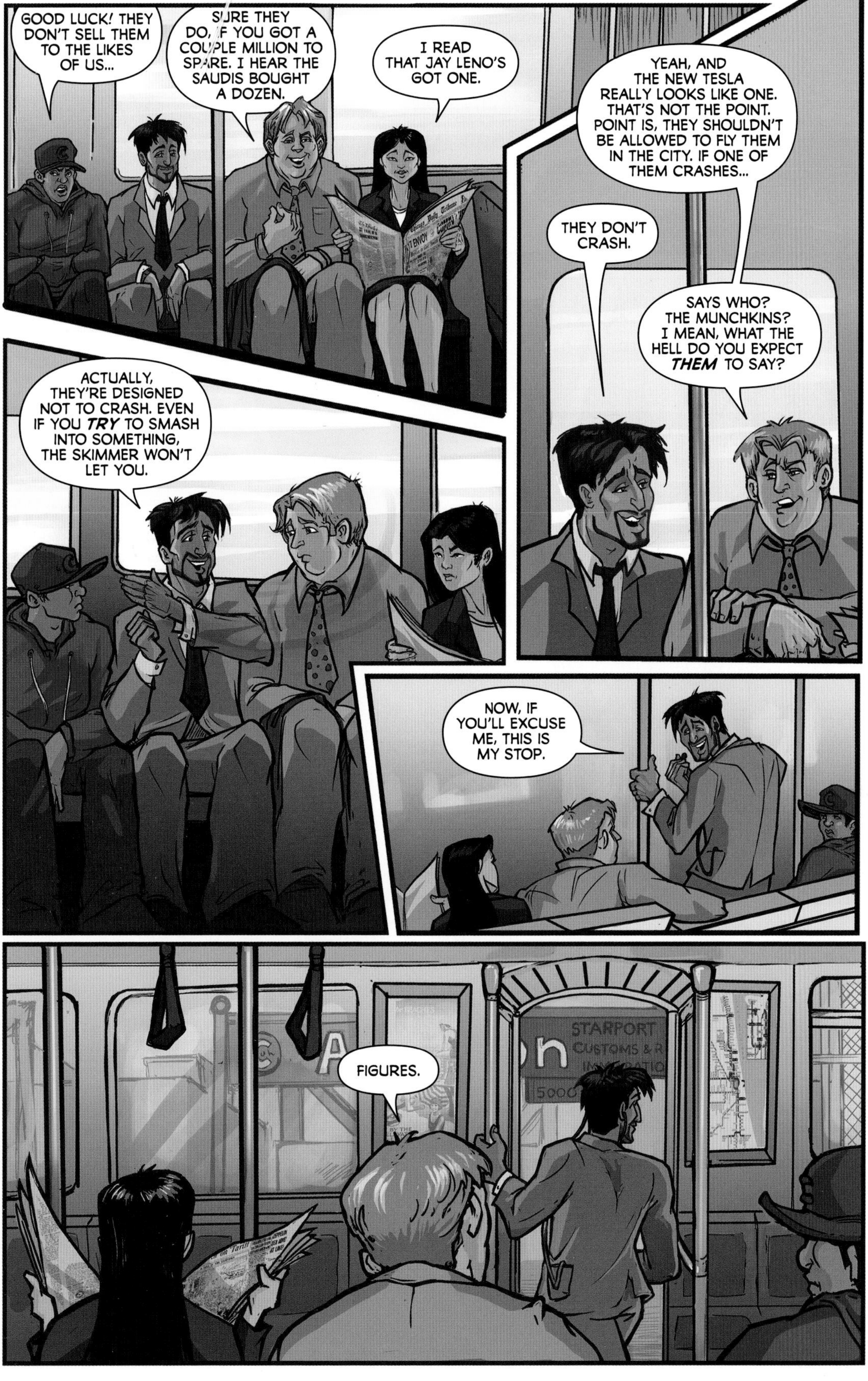
GOOD LUCK! THEY DON'T SELL THEM TO THE LIKES OF US...
SURE THEY DO, IF YOU GOT A COUPLE MILLION TO SPARE. I HEAR THE SAUDIS BOUGHT A DOZEN.
I READ THAT JAY LENO'S GOT ONE.
YEAH, AND THE NEW TESLA REALLY LOOKS LIKE ONE. THAT'S NOT THE POINT. POINT IS, THEY SHOULDN'T BE ALLOWED TO FLY THEM IN THE CITY. IF ONE OF THEM CRASHES...
THEY DON'T CRASH.
SAYS WHO? THE MUNCHKINS? I MEAN, WHAT THE HELL DO YOU EXPECT *THEM* TO SAY?
ACTUALLY, THEY'RE DESIGNED NOT TO CRASH. EVEN IF YOU *TRY* TO SMASH INTO SOMETHING, THE SKIMMER WON'T LET YOU.
NOW, IF YOU'LL EXCUSE ME, THIS IS MY STOP.
STARPORT
FIGURES.

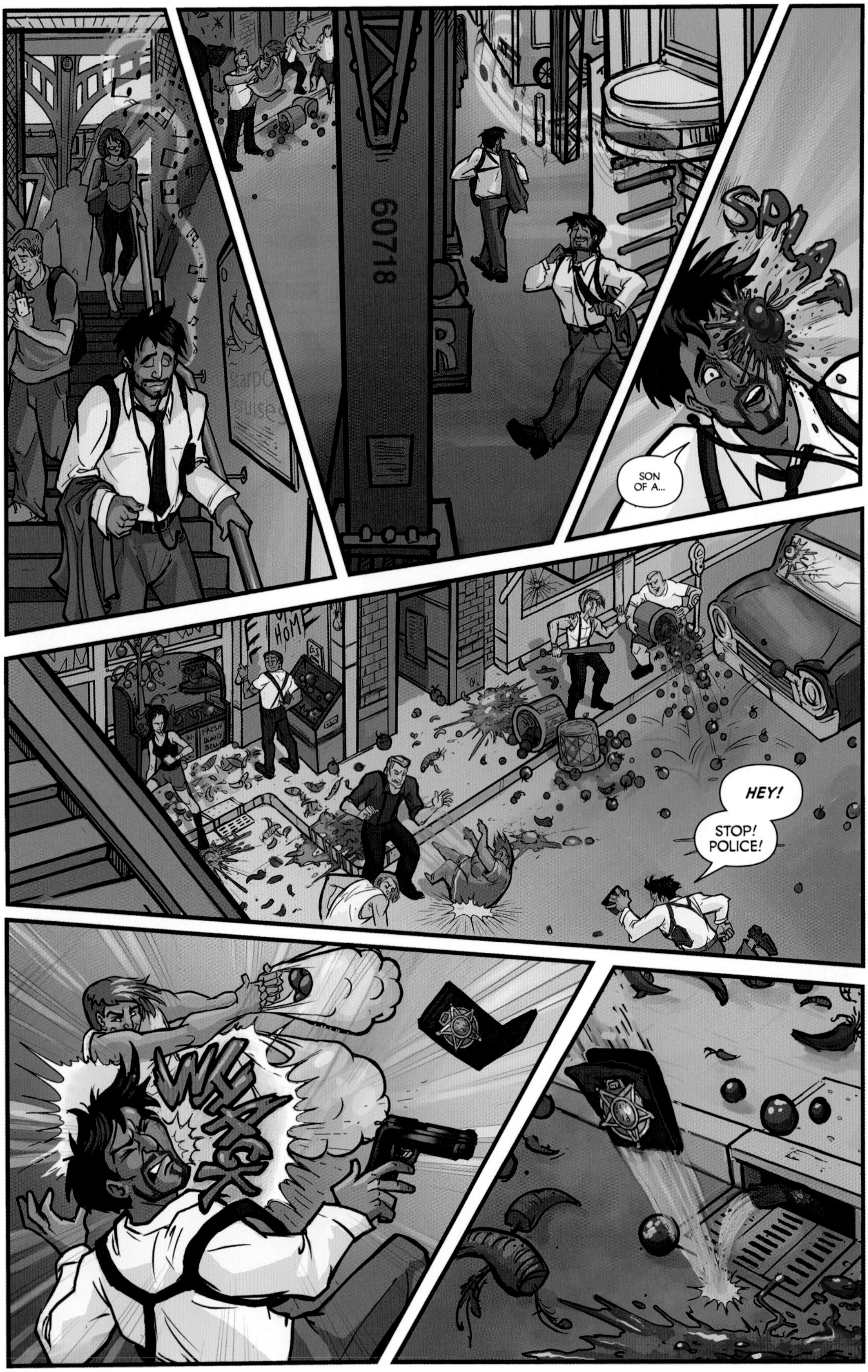

60718
SPLAT
SON OF A...
HEY!
STOP! POLICE!
WHACK

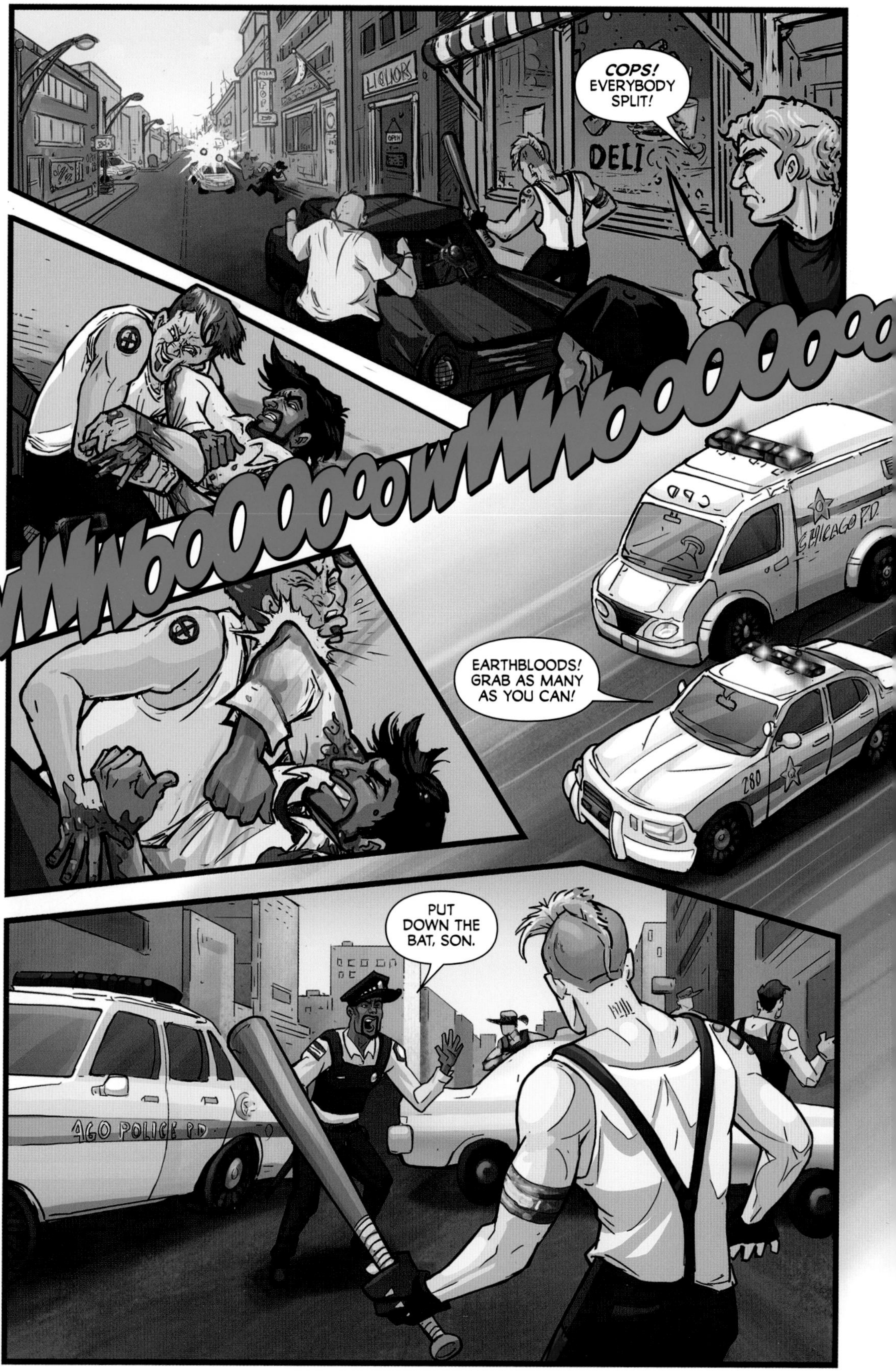
LIQUORS
OPEN
DELI
COPS! EVERYBODY SPLIT!
wWWooOOOooowWWooOOOooo
CPD
CHICAGO P.D.
280
EARTHBLOODS! GRAB AS MANY AS YOU CAN!
AGO POLICE PD
PUT DOWN THE BAT, SON.

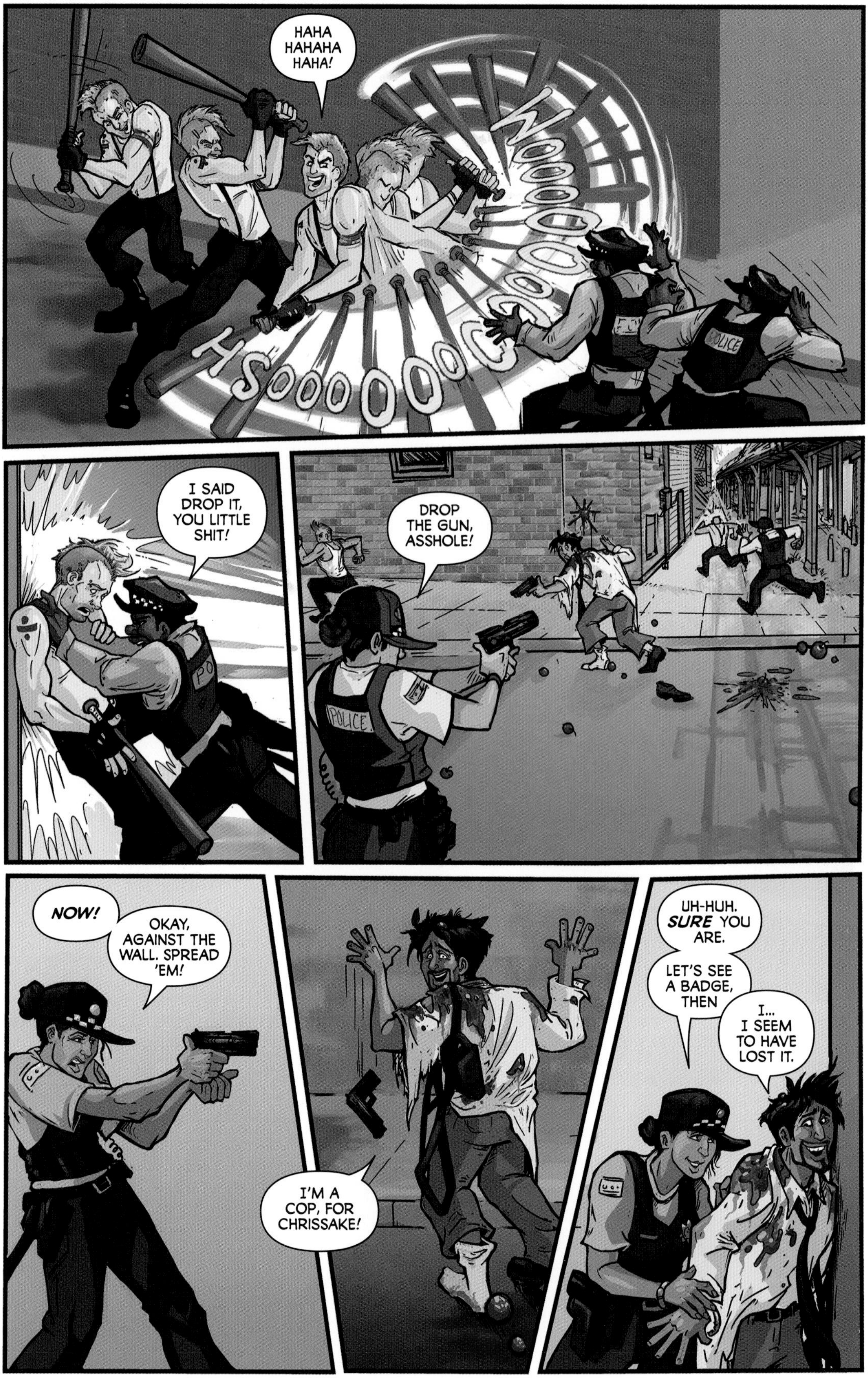
HAHA HAHAHA HAHA!
I SAID DROP IT, YOU LITTLE SHIT!
DROP THE GUN, ASSHOLE!
NOW!
OKAY, AGAINST THE WALL. SPREAD 'EM!
I'M A COP, FOR CHRISSAKE!
UH-HUH. SURE YOU ARE.
LET'S SEE A BADGE, THEN
I... I SEEM TO HAVE LOST IT.

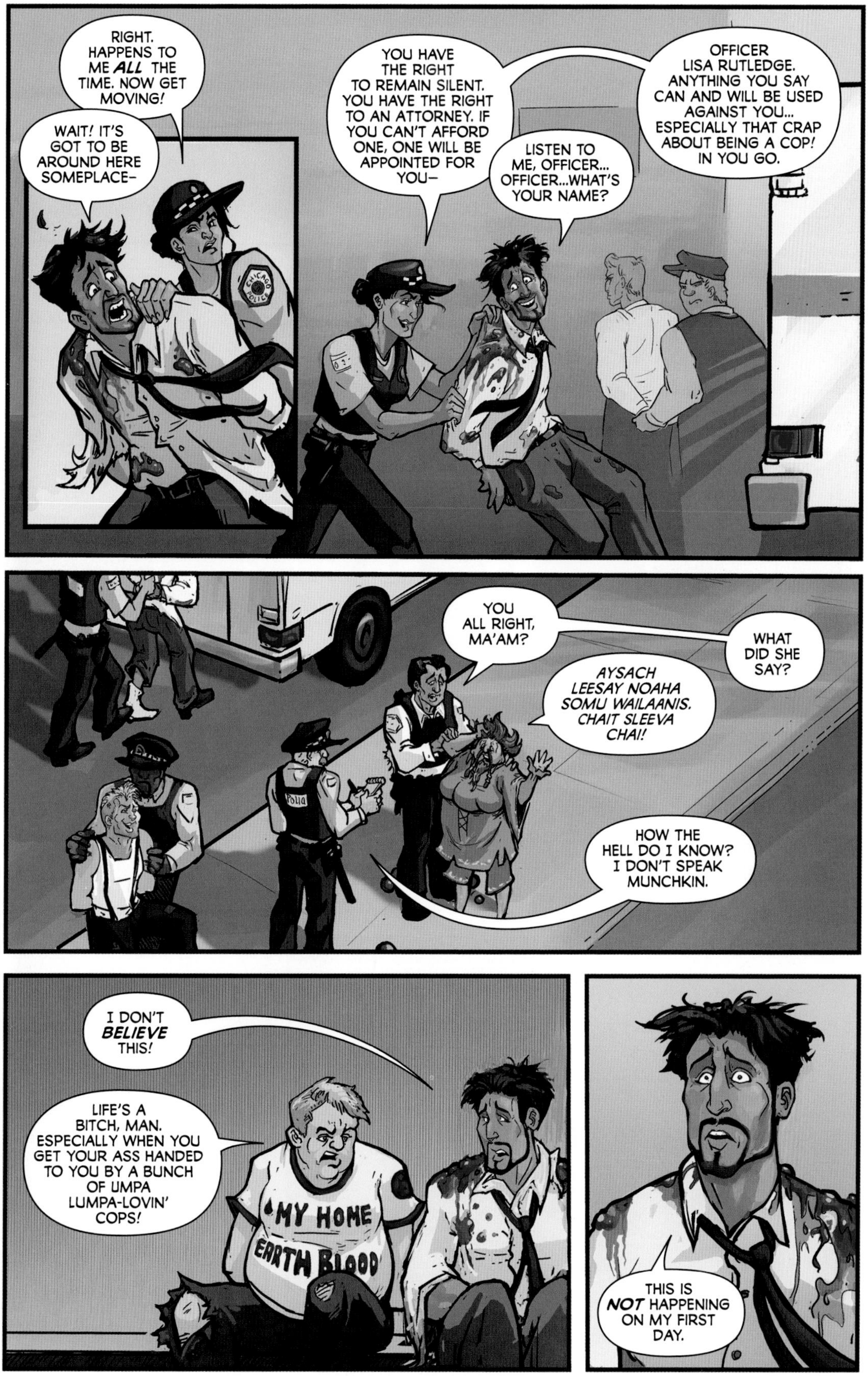
WAIT! IT'S GOT TO BE AROUND HERE SOMEPLACE–
RIGHT. HAPPENS TO ME *ALL* THE TIME. NOW GET MOVING!
YOU HAVE THE RIGHT TO REMAIN SILENT. YOU HAVE THE RIGHT TO AN ATTORNEY. IF YOU CAN'T AFFORD ONE, ONE WILL BE APPOINTED FOR YOU–
LISTEN TO ME, OFFICER... OFFICER...WHAT'S YOUR NAME?
OFFICER LISA RUTLEDGE. ANYTHING YOU SAY CAN AND WILL BE USED AGAINST YOU... ESPECIALLY THAT CRAP ABOUT BEING A COP! IN YOU GO.
YOU ALL RIGHT, MA'AM?
AYSACH LEESAY NOAHA SOMU WAILAANIS. CHAIT SLEEVA CHAI!
WHAT DID SHE SAY?
HOW THE HELL DO I KNOW? I DON'T SPEAK MUNCHKIN.
I DON'T *BELIEVE* THIS!
LIFE'S A BITCH, MAN. ESPECIALLY WHEN YOU GET YOUR ASS HANDED TO YOU BY A BUNCH OF UMPA LUMPA-LOVIN' COPS!
MY HOME EARTH BLOOD
THIS IS *NOT* HAPPENING ON MY FIRST DAY.

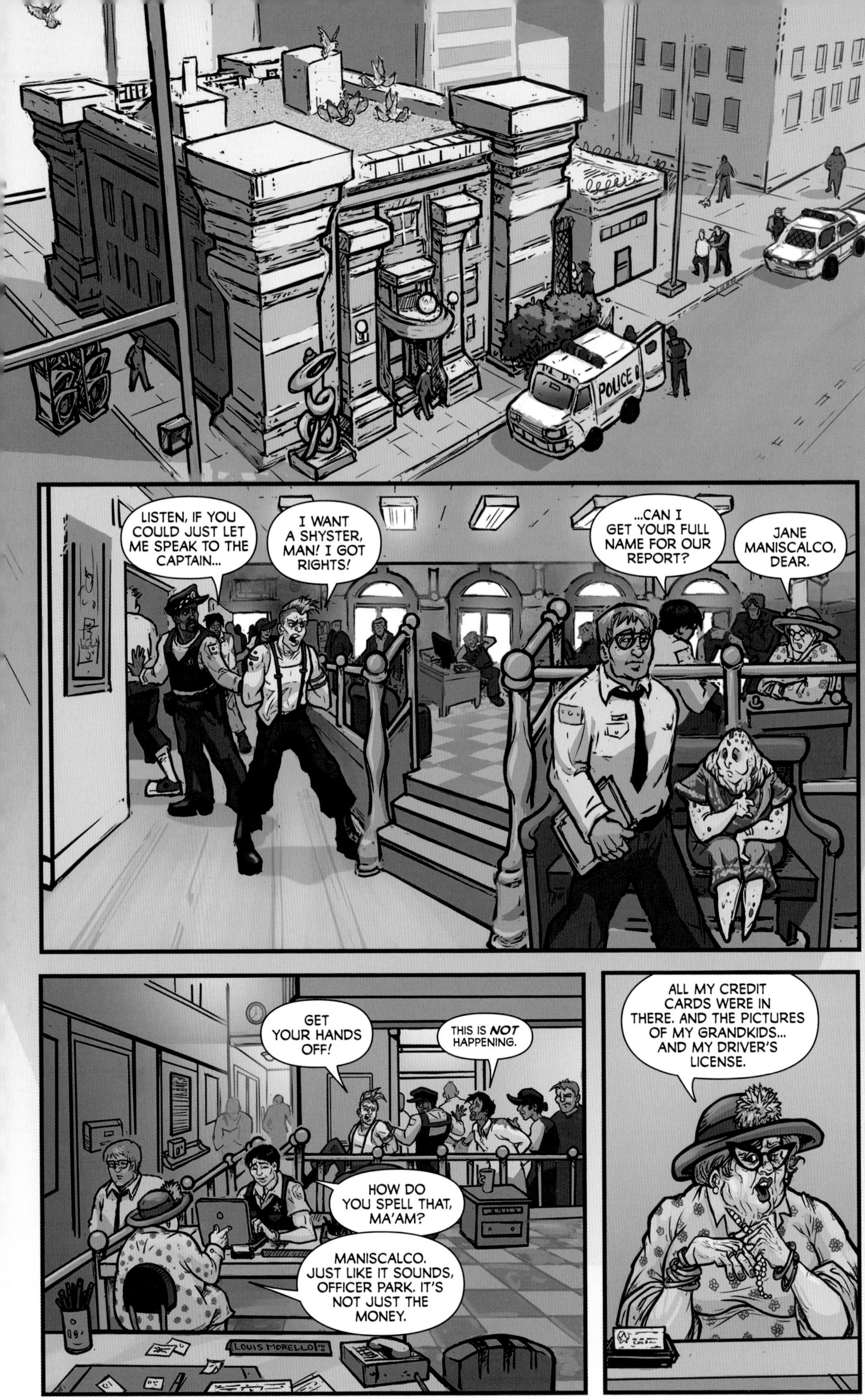
POLICE
LISTEN, IF YOU COULD JUST LET ME SPEAK TO THE CAPTAIN...
I WANT A SHYSTER, MAN! I GOT RIGHTS!
...CAN I GET YOUR FULL NAME FOR OUR REPORT?
JANE MANISCALCO, DEAR.
GET YOUR HANDS OFF!
THIS IS ***NOT*** HAPPENING.
HOW DO YOU SPELL THAT, MA'AM?
MANISCALCO. JUST LIKE IT SOUNDS, OFFICER PARK. IT'S NOT JUST THE MONEY.
LOUIS MORELLO
ALL MY CREDIT CARDS WERE IN THERE. AND THE PICTURES OF MY GRANDKIDS... AND MY DRIVER'S LICENSE.

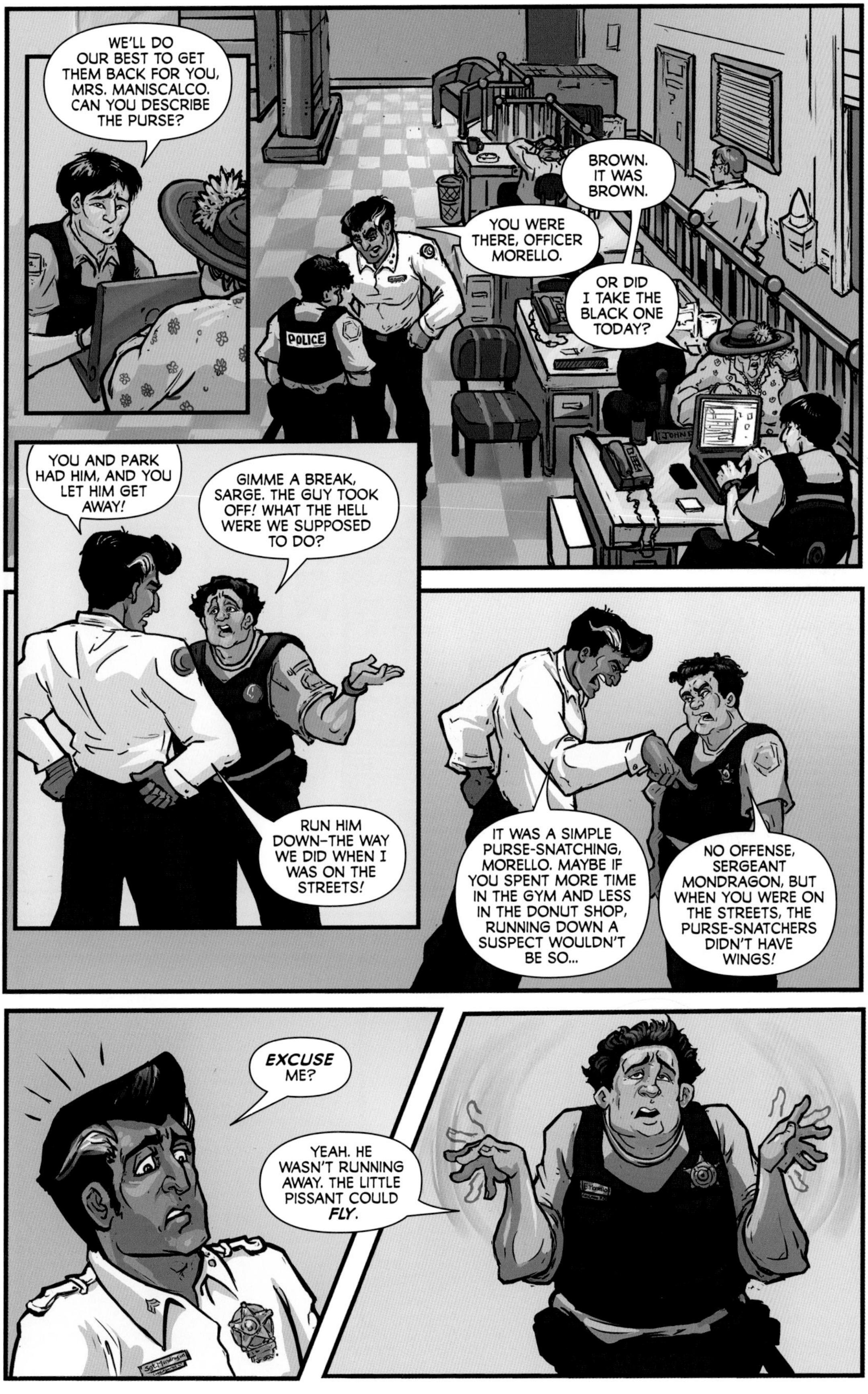

WE'LL DO OUR BEST TO GET THEM BACK FOR YOU, MRS. MANISCALCO. CAN YOU DESCRIBE THE PURSE?
BROWN. IT WAS BROWN.
OR DID I TAKE THE BLACK ONE TODAY?
YOU WERE THERE, OFFICER MORELLO.
POLICE
YOU AND PARK HAD HIM, AND YOU LET HIM GET AWAY!
GIMME A BREAK, SARGE. THE GUY TOOK OFF! WHAT THE HELL WERE WE SUPPOSED TO DO?
RUN HIM DOWN–THE WAY WE DID WHEN I WAS ON THE STREETS!
IT WAS A SIMPLE PURSE-SNATCHING, MORELLO. MAYBE IF YOU SPENT MORE TIME IN THE GYM AND LESS IN THE DONUT SHOP, RUNNING DOWN A SUSPECT WOULDN'T BE SO...
NO OFFENSE, SERGEANT MONDRAGON, BUT WHEN YOU WERE ON THE STREETS, THE PURSE-SNATCHERS DIDN'T HAVE WINGS!
EXCUSE ME?
YEAH. HE WASN'T RUNNING AWAY. THE LITTLE PISSANT COULD *FLY*.

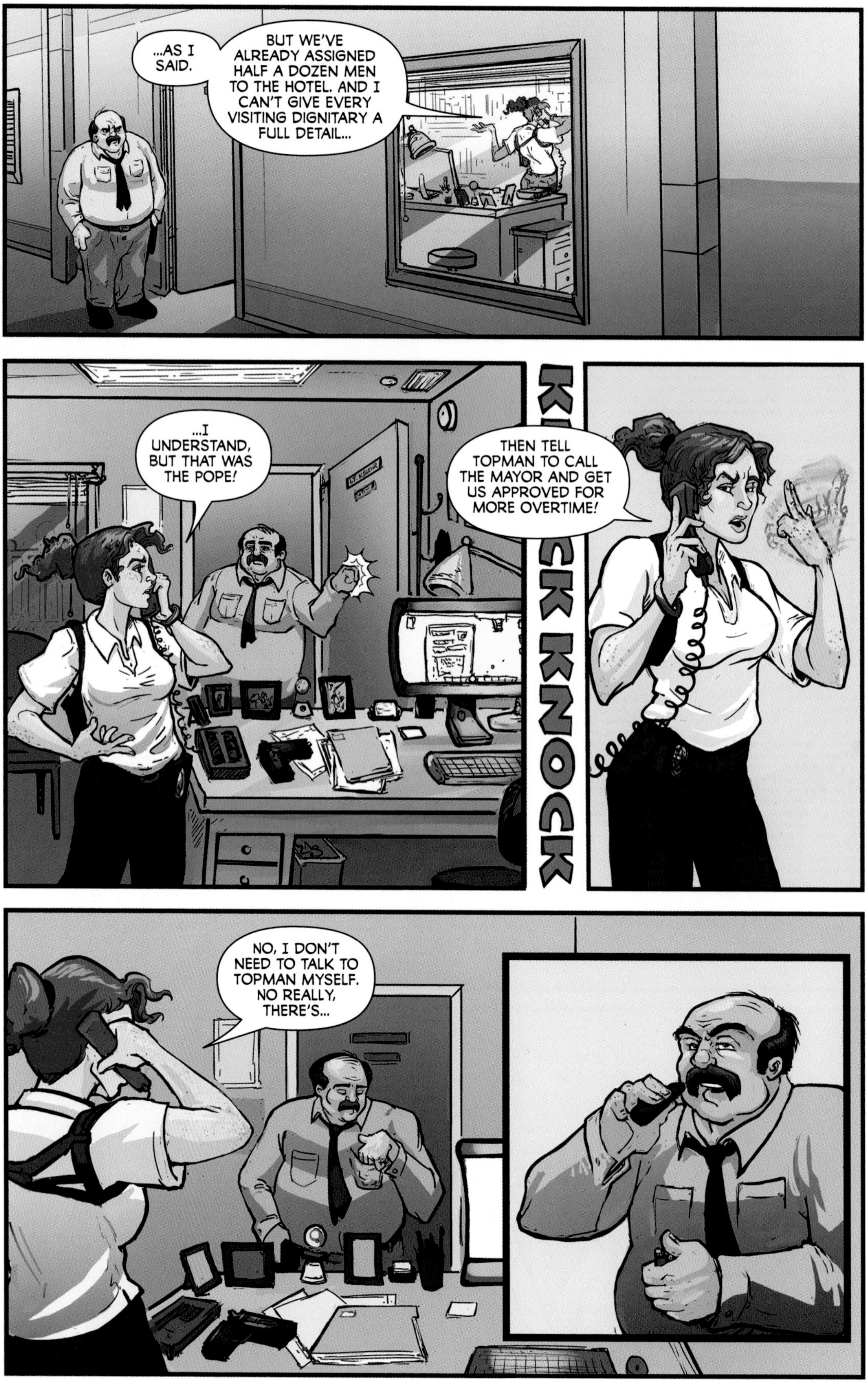
...AS I SAID.
BUT WE'VE ALREADY ASSIGNED HALF A DOZEN MEN TO THE HOTEL. AND I CAN'T GIVE EVERY VISITING DIGNITARY A FULL DETAIL...
...I UNDERSTAND, BUT THAT WAS THE POPE!
KNOCK KNOCK
THEN TELL TOPMAN TO CALL THE MAYOR AND GET US APPROVED FOR MORE OVERTIME!
NO, I DON'T NEED TO TALK TO TOPMAN MYSELF. NO REALLY, THERE'S...

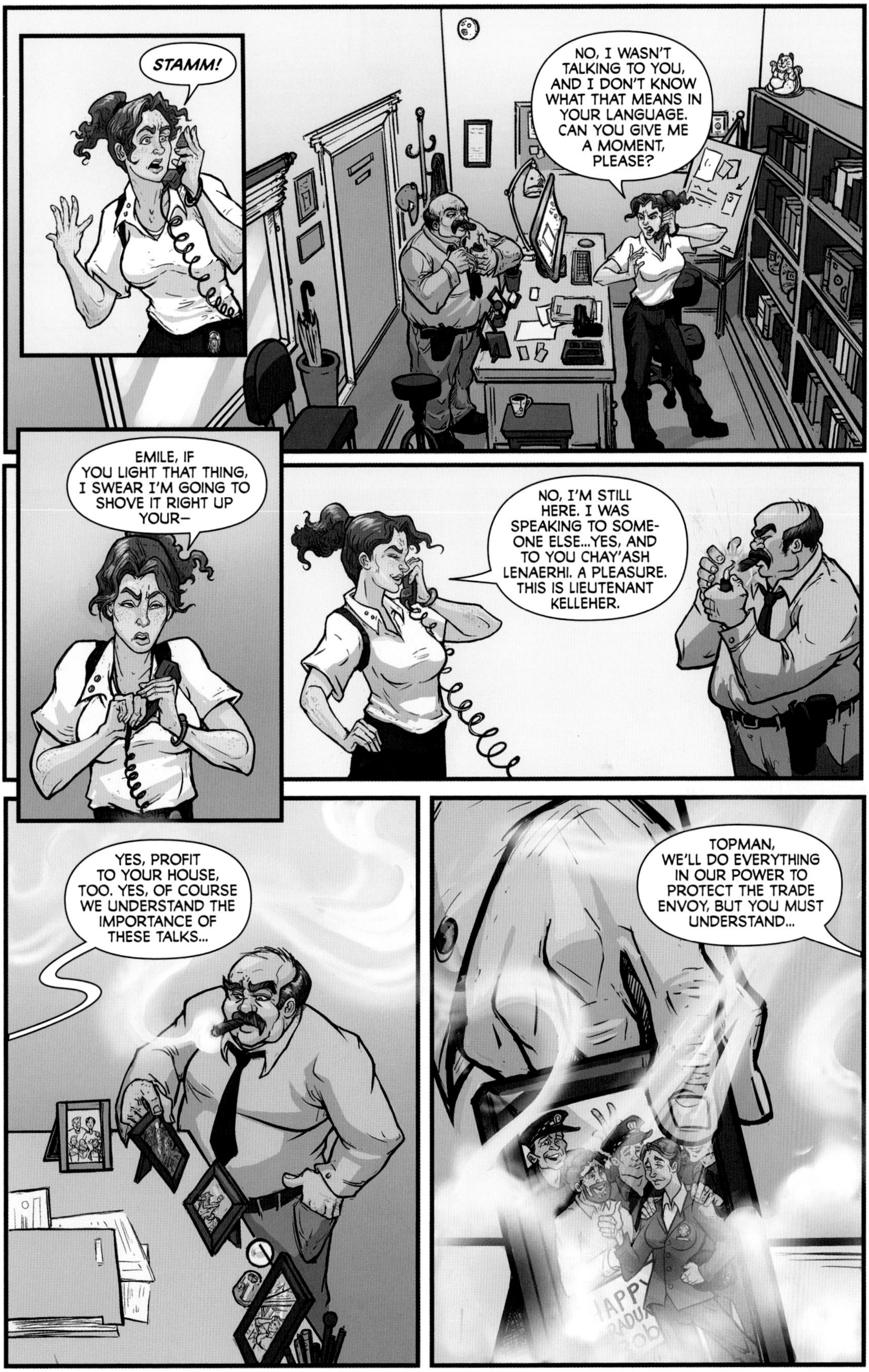
STAMM!
NO, I WASN'T TALKING TO YOU, AND I DON'T KNOW WHAT THAT MEANS IN YOUR LANGUAGE. CAN YOU GIVE ME A MOMENT, PLEASE?
EMILE, IF YOU LIGHT THAT THING, I SWEAR I'M GOING TO SHOVE IT RIGHT UP YOUR–
NO, I'M STILL HERE. I WAS SPEAKING TO SOME-ONE ELSE...YES, AND TO YOU CHAY'ASH LENAERHI. A PLEASURE. THIS IS LIEUTENANT KELLEHER.
YES, PROFIT TO YOUR HOUSE, TOO. YES, OF COURSE WE UNDERSTAND THE IMPORTANCE OF THESE TALKS...
TOPMAN, WE'LL DO EVERYTHING IN OUR POWER TO PROTECT THE TRADE ENVOY, BUT YOU MUST UNDERSTAND...

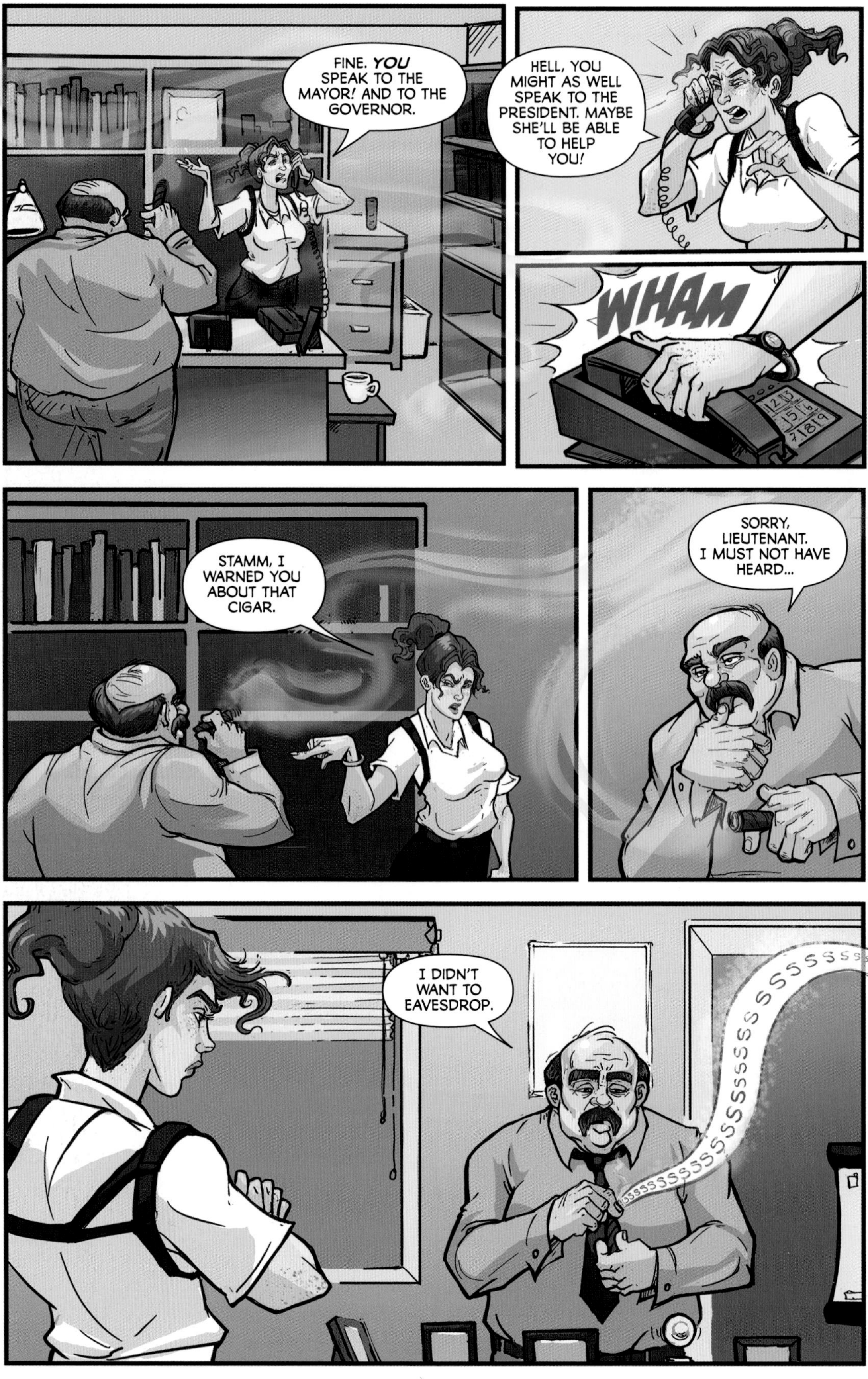
FINE. *YOU* SPEAK TO THE MAYOR! AND TO THE GOVERNOR.
HELL, YOU MIGHT AS WELL SPEAK TO THE PRESIDENT. MAYBE SHE'LL BE ABLE TO HELP YOU!
WHAM
STAMM, I WARNED YOU ABOUT THAT CIGAR.
SORRY, LIEUTENANT. I MUST NOT HAVE HEARD...
I DIDN'T WANT TO EAVESDROP.
SSSSSSSSSSSSSSSSSSSSSSSSSSSSSSS

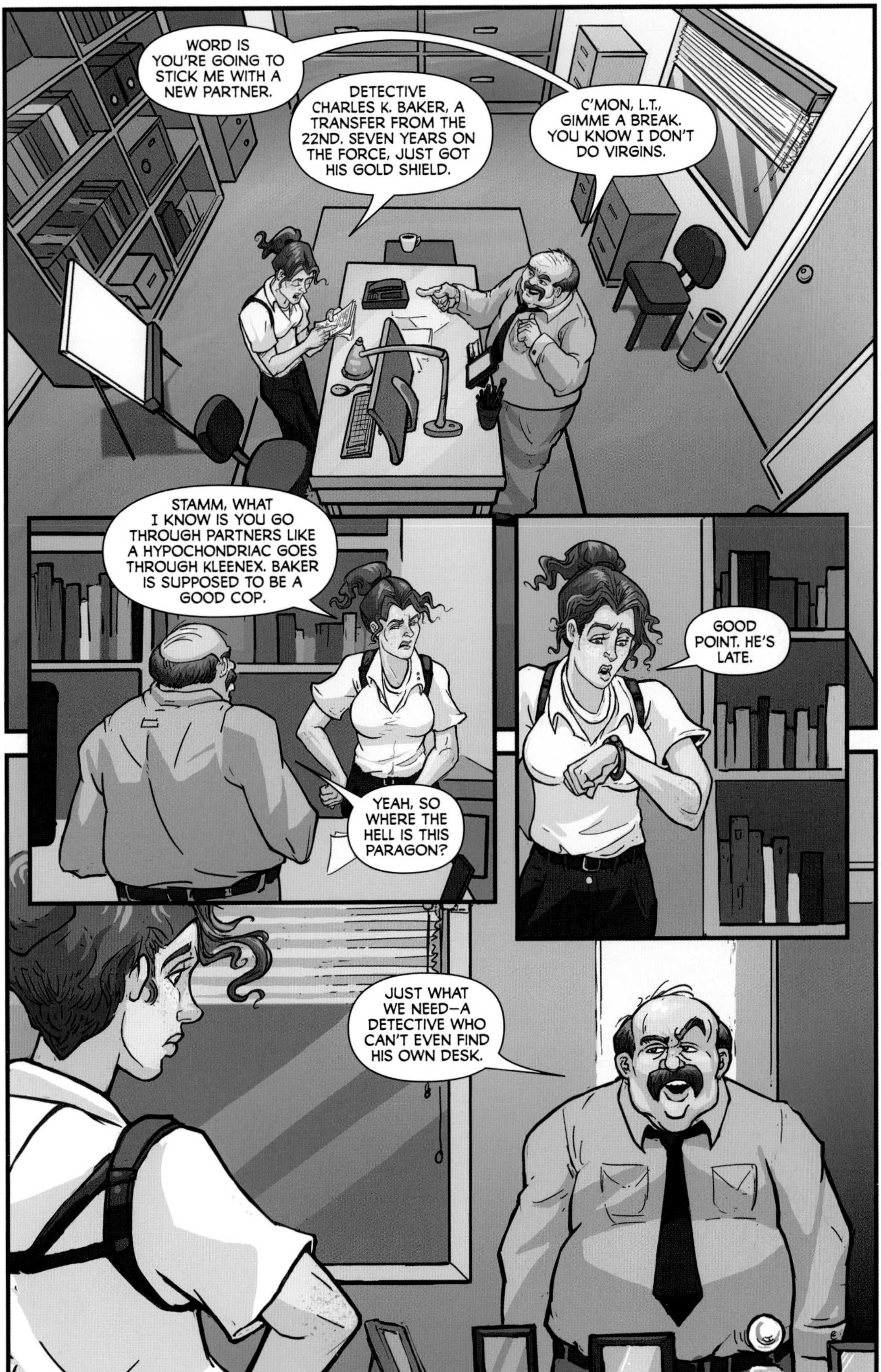
WORD IS YOU'RE GOING TO STICK ME WITH A NEW PARTNER.
DETECTIVE CHARLES K. BAKER, A TRANSFER FROM THE 22ND. SEVEN YEARS ON THE FORCE, JUST GOT HIS GOLD SHIELD.
C'MON, L.T., GIMME A BREAK. YOU KNOW I DON'T DO VIRGINS.
STAMM, WHAT I KNOW IS YOU GO THROUGH PARTNERS LIKE A HYPOCHONDRIAC GOES THROUGH KLEENEX. BAKER IS SUPPOSED TO BE A GOOD COP.
YEAH, SO WHERE THE HELL IS THIS PARAGON?
GOOD POINT. HE'S LATE.
JUST WHAT WE NEED—A DETECTIVE WHO CAN'T EVEN FIND HIS OWN DESK.

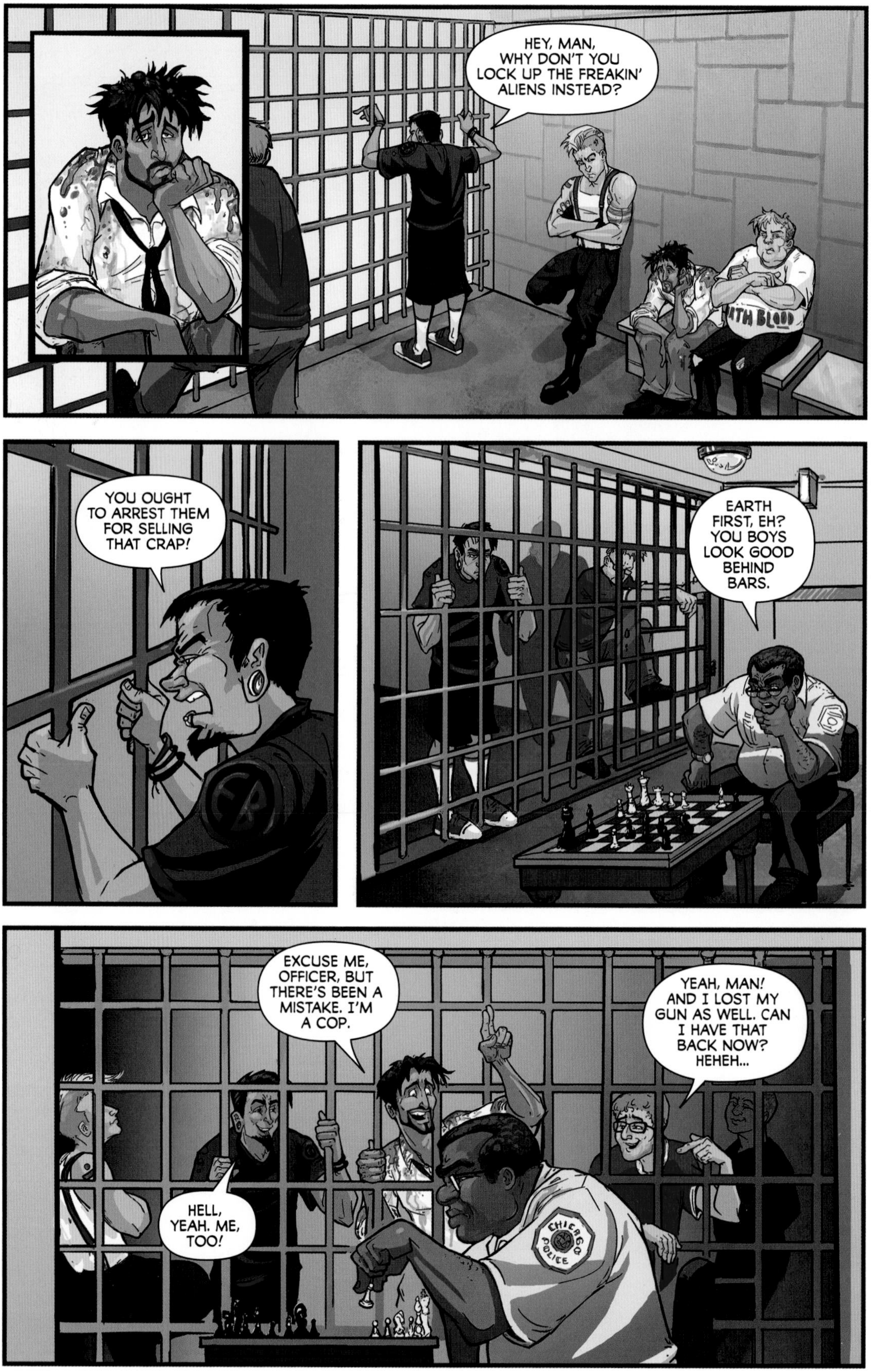
HEY, MAN, WHY DON'T YOU LOCK UP THE FREAKIN' ALIENS INSTEAD?
YOU OUGHT TO ARREST THEM FOR SELLING THAT CRAP!
EARTH FIRST, EH? YOU BOYS LOOK GOOD BEHIND BARS.
EXCUSE ME, OFFICER, BUT THERE'S BEEN A MISTAKE. I'M A COP.
YEAH, MAN! AND I LOST MY GUN AS WELL. CAN I HAVE THAT BACK NOW? HEHEH...
HELL, YEAH. ME, TOO!

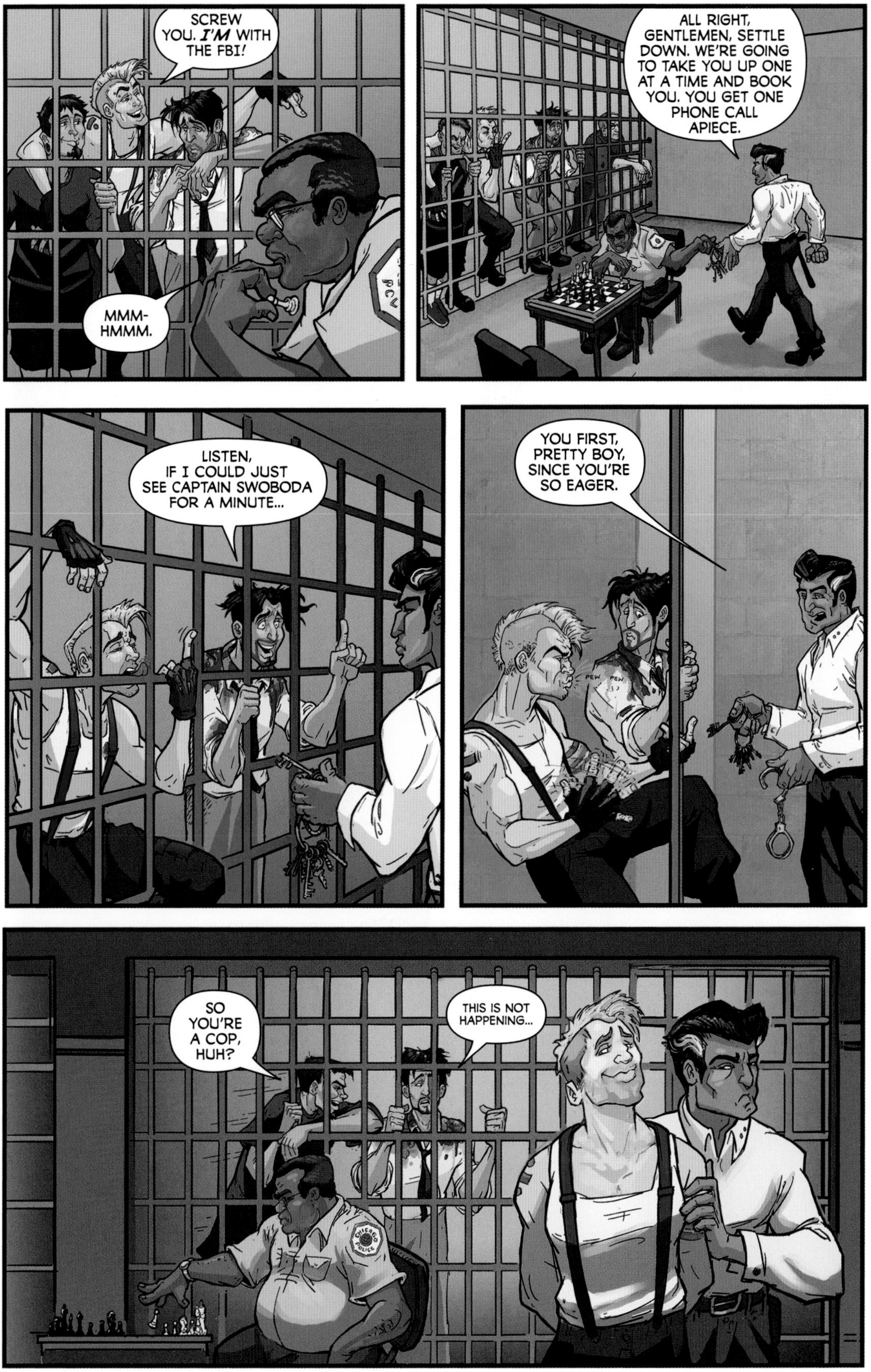
SCREW YOU. *I'M* WITH THE FBI!
MMM-HMMM.
ALL RIGHT, GENTLEMEN, SETTLE DOWN. WE'RE GOING TO TAKE YOU UP ONE AT A TIME AND BOOK YOU. YOU GET ONE PHONE CALL APIECE.
LISTEN, IF I COULD JUST SEE CAPTAIN SWOBODA FOR A MINUTE...
YOU FIRST, PRETTY BOY, SINCE YOU'RE SO EAGER.
SO YOU'RE A COP, HUH?
THIS IS NOT HAPPENING...

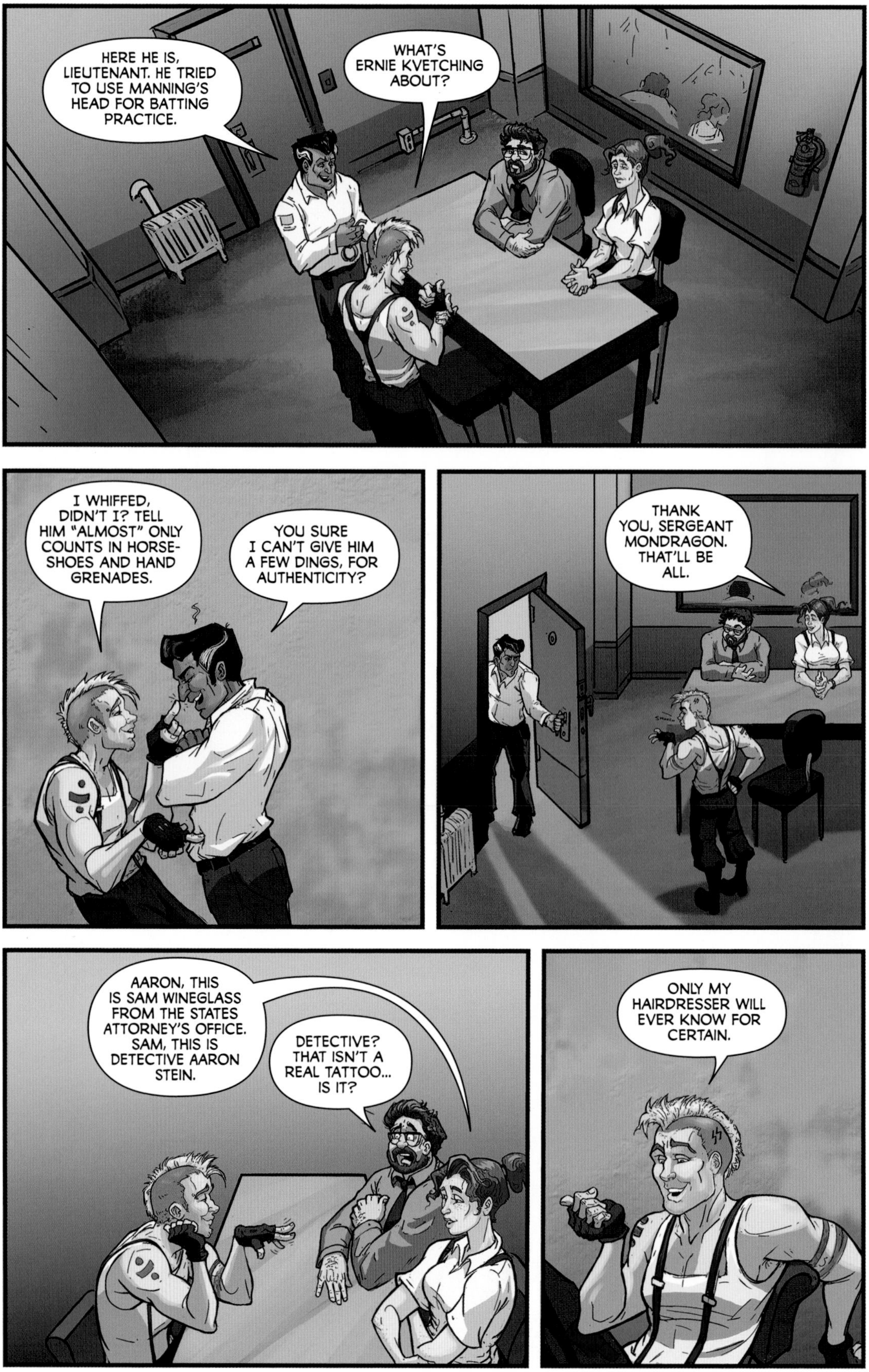
HERE HE IS, LIEUTENANT. HE TRIED TO USE MANNING'S HEAD FOR BATTING PRACTICE.
WHAT'S ERNIE KVETCHING ABOUT?
I WHIFFED, DIDN'T I? TELL HIM "ALMOST" ONLY COUNTS IN HORSE-SHOES AND HAND GRENADES.
YOU SURE I CAN'T GIVE HIM A FEW DINGS, FOR AUTHENTICITY?
THANK YOU, SERGEANT MONDRAGON. THAT'LL BE ALL.
AARON, THIS IS SAM WINEGLASS FROM THE STATES ATTORNEY'S OFFICE. SAM, THIS IS DETECTIVE AARON STEIN.
DETECTIVE? THAT ISN'T A REAL TATTOO... IS IT?
ONLY MY HAIRDRESSER WILL EVER KNOW FOR CERTAIN.

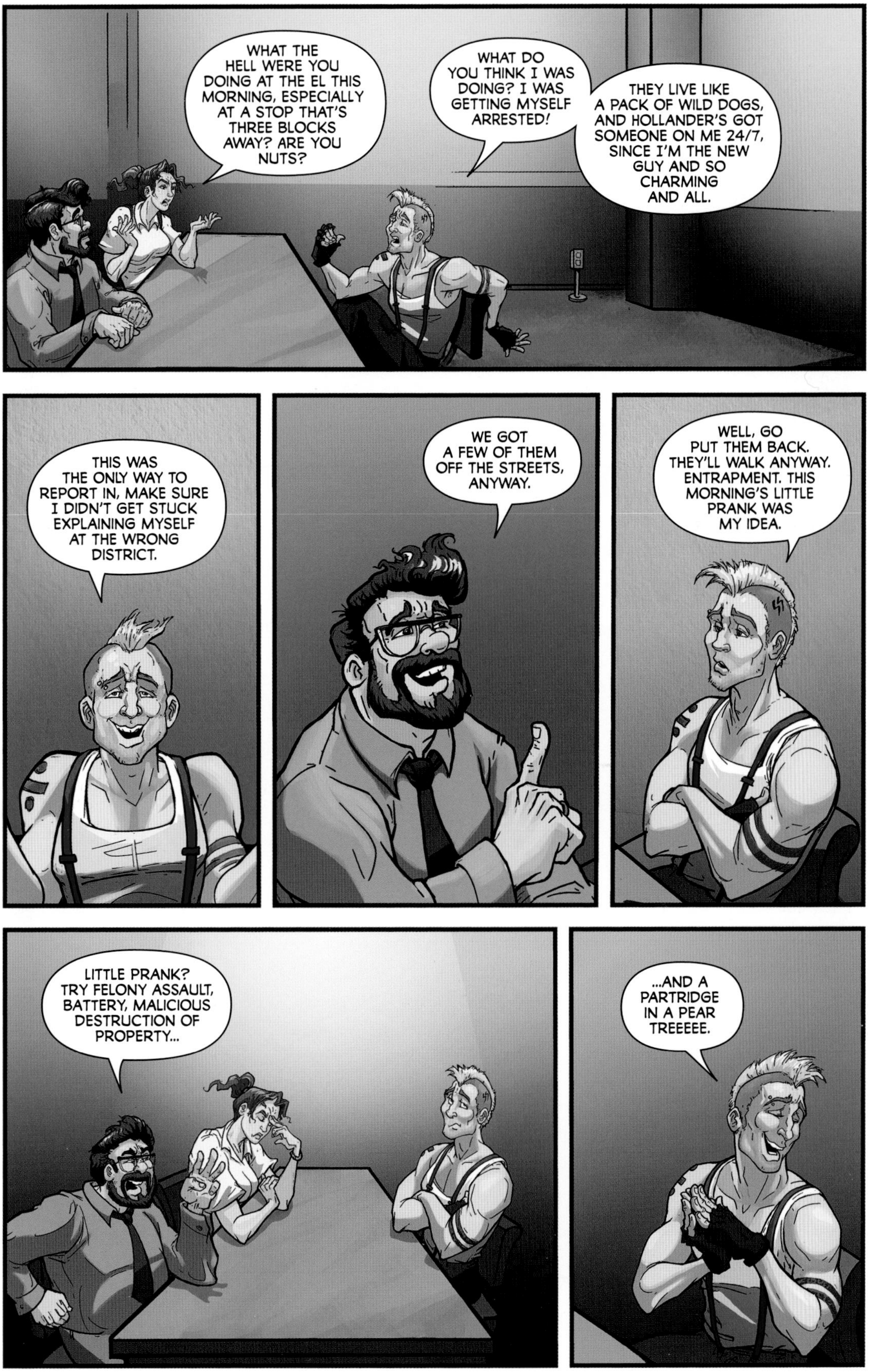
WHAT THE HELL WERE YOU DOING AT THE EL THIS MORNING, ESPECIALLY AT A STOP THAT'S THREE BLOCKS AWAY? ARE YOU NUTS?
WHAT DO YOU THINK I WAS DOING? I WAS GETTING MYSELF ARRESTED!
THEY LIVE LIKE A PACK OF WILD DOGS, AND HOLLANDER'S GOT SOMEONE ON ME 24/7, SINCE I'M THE NEW GUY AND SO CHARMING AND ALL.
THIS WAS THE ONLY WAY TO REPORT IN, MAKE SURE I DIDN'T GET STUCK EXPLAINING MYSELF AT THE WRONG DISTRICT.
WE GOT A FEW OF THEM OFF THE STREETS, ANYWAY.
WELL, GO PUT THEM BACK. THEY'LL WALK ANYWAY. ENTRAPMENT. THIS MORNING'S LITTLE PRANK WAS MY IDEA.
LITTLE PRANK? TRY FELONY ASSAULT, BATTERY, MALICIOUS DESTRUCTION OF PROPERTY...
...AND A PARTRIDGE IN A PEAR TREEEEE.

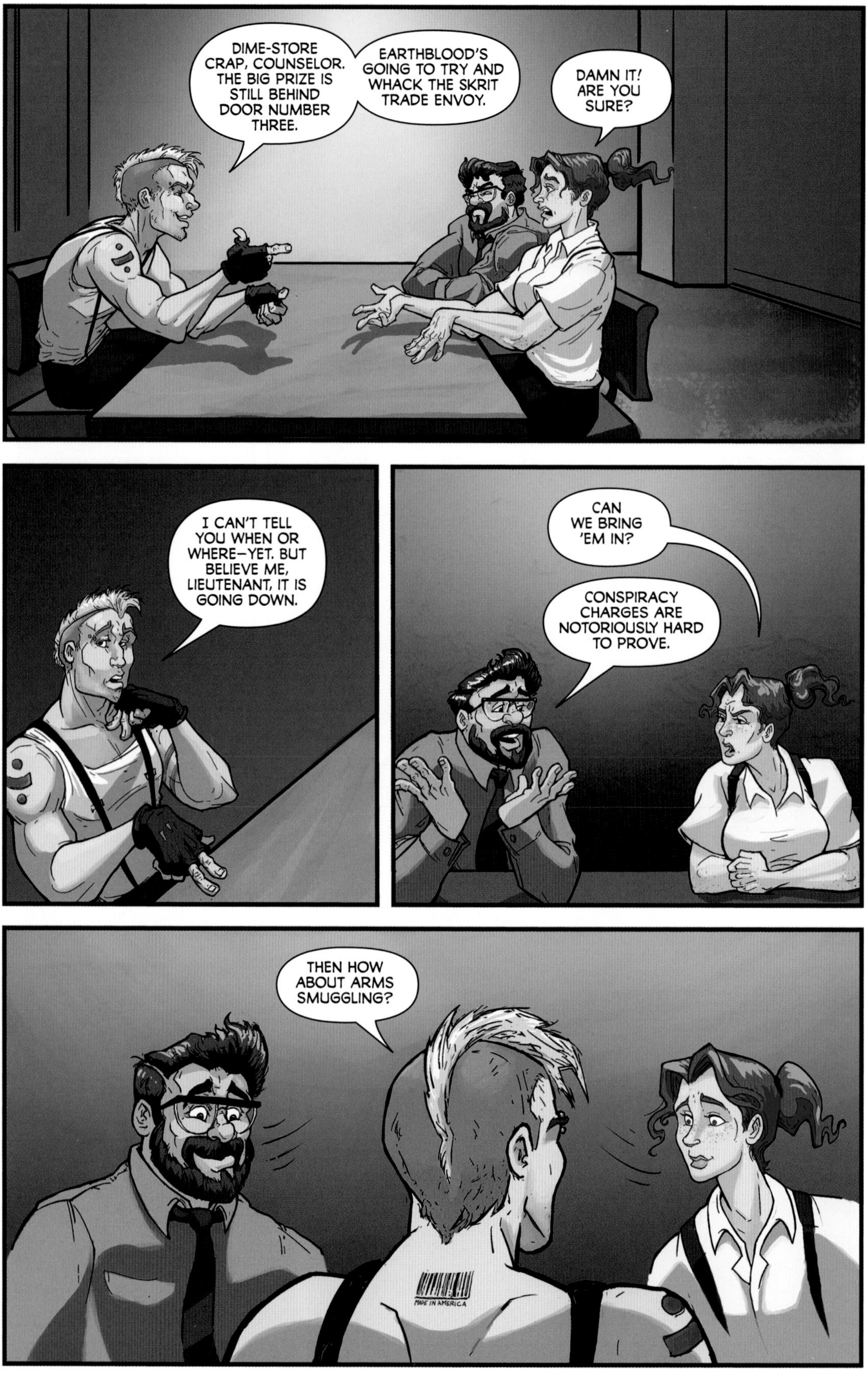
DIME-STORE CRAP, COUNSELOR. THE BIG PRIZE IS STILL BEHIND DOOR NUMBER THREE.
EARTHBLOOD'S GOING TO TRY AND WHACK THE SKRIT TRADE ENVOY.
DAMN IT! ARE YOU SURE?
I CAN'T TELL YOU WHEN OR WHERE—YET. BUT BELIEVE ME, LIEUTENANT, IT IS GOING DOWN.
CAN WE BRING 'EM IN?
CONSPIRACY CHARGES ARE NOTORIOUSLY HARD TO PROVE.
THEN HOW ABOUT ARMS SMUGGLING?
MADE IN AMERICA

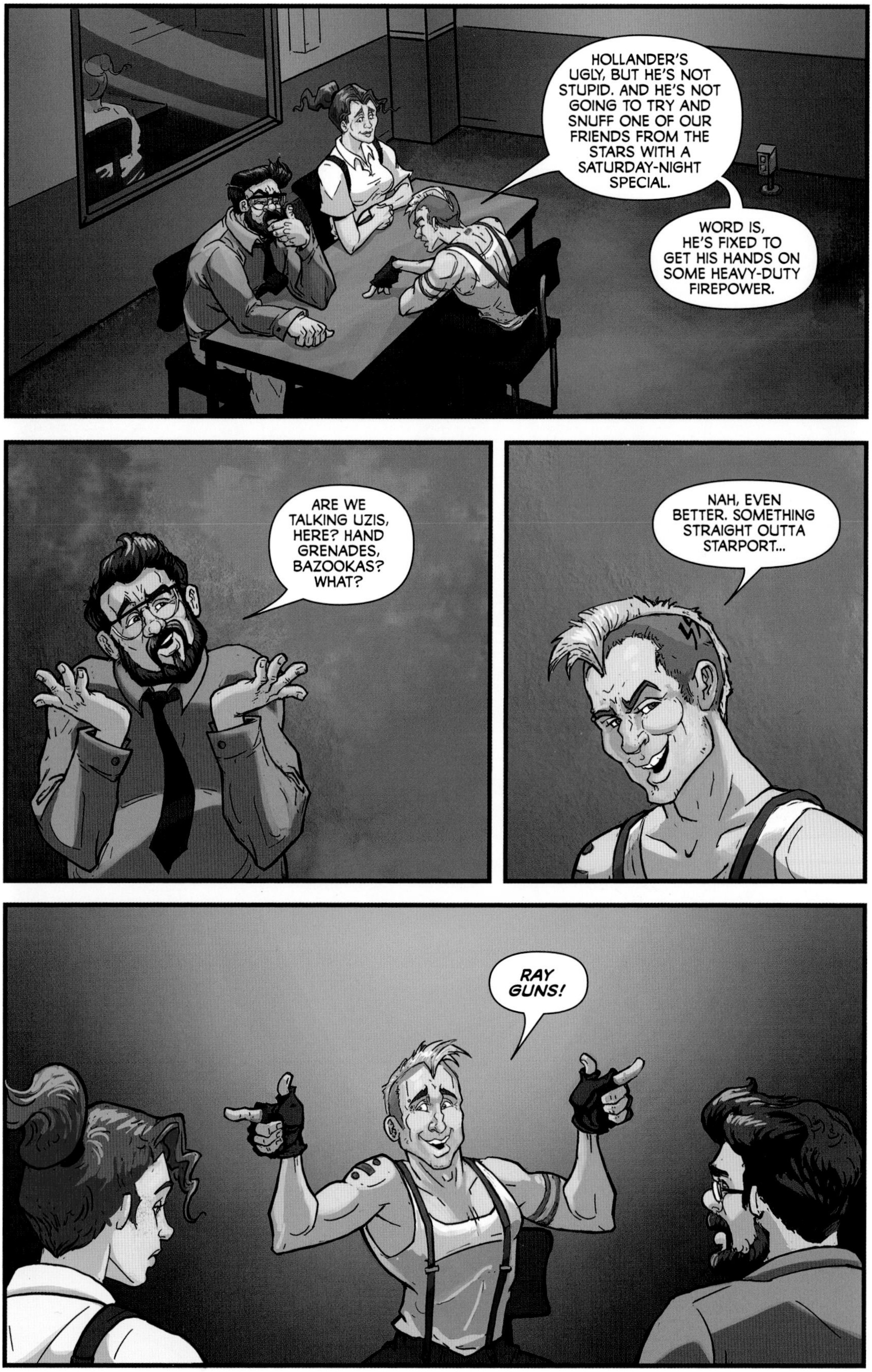
HOLLANDER'S UGLY, BUT HE'S NOT STUPID. AND HE'S NOT GOING TO TRY AND SNUFF ONE OF OUR FRIENDS FROM THE STARS WITH A SATURDAY-NIGHT SPECIAL.
WORD IS, HE'S FIXED TO GET HIS HANDS ON SOME HEAVY-DUTY FIREPOWER.
ARE WE TALKING UZIS, HERE? HAND GRENADES, BAZOOKAS? WHAT?
NAH, EVEN BETTER. SOMETHING STRAIGHT OUTTA STARPORT...
RAY GUNS!

CHAPTER TWO

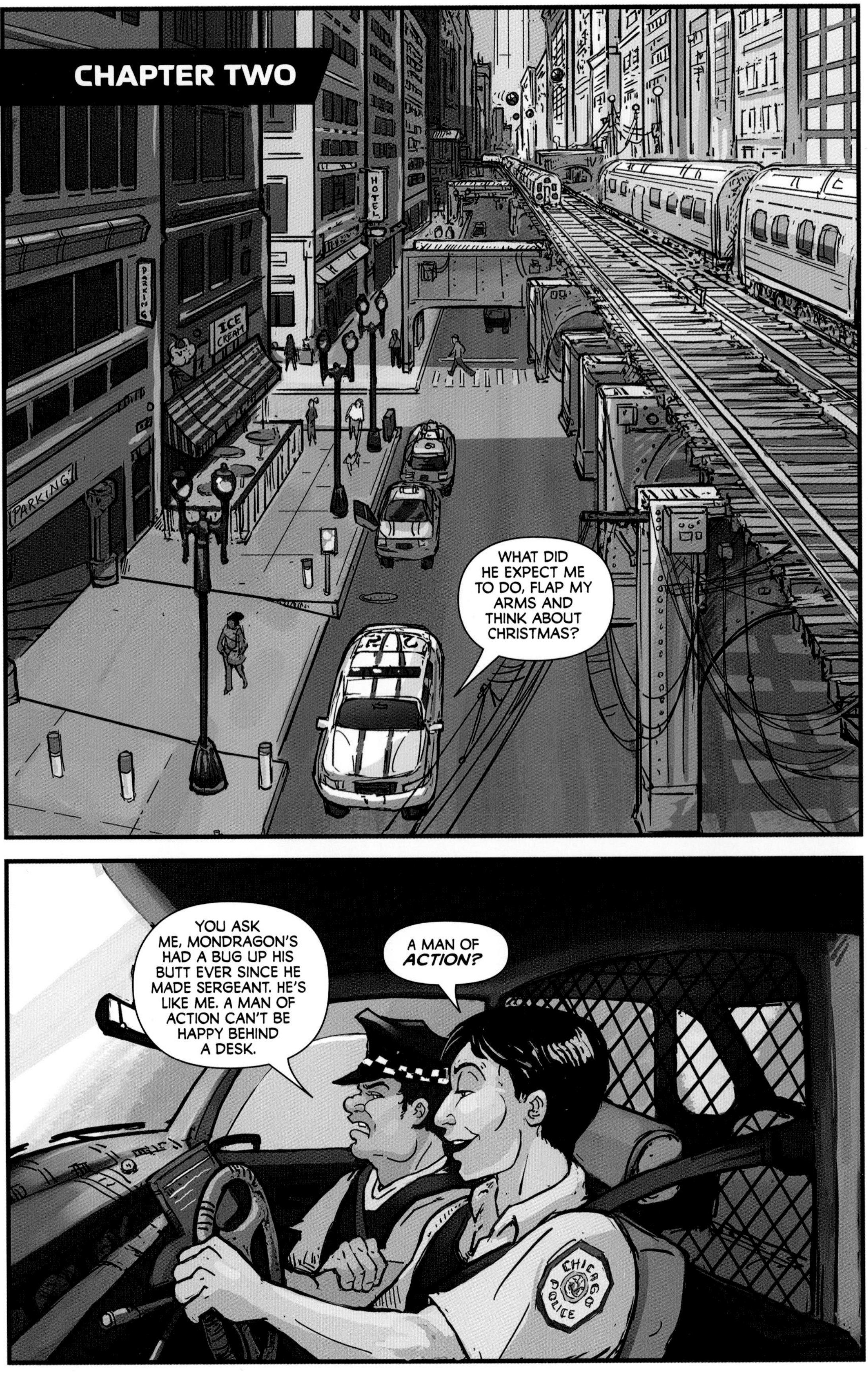
WHAT DID HE EXPECT ME TO DO, FLAP MY ARMS AND THINK ABOUT CHRISTMAS?
YOU ASK ME, MONDRAGON'S HAD A BUG UP HIS BUTT EVER SINCE HE MADE SERGEANT. HE'S LIKE ME. A MAN OF ACTION CAN'T BE HAPPY BEHIND A DESK.
A MAN OF *ACTION?*

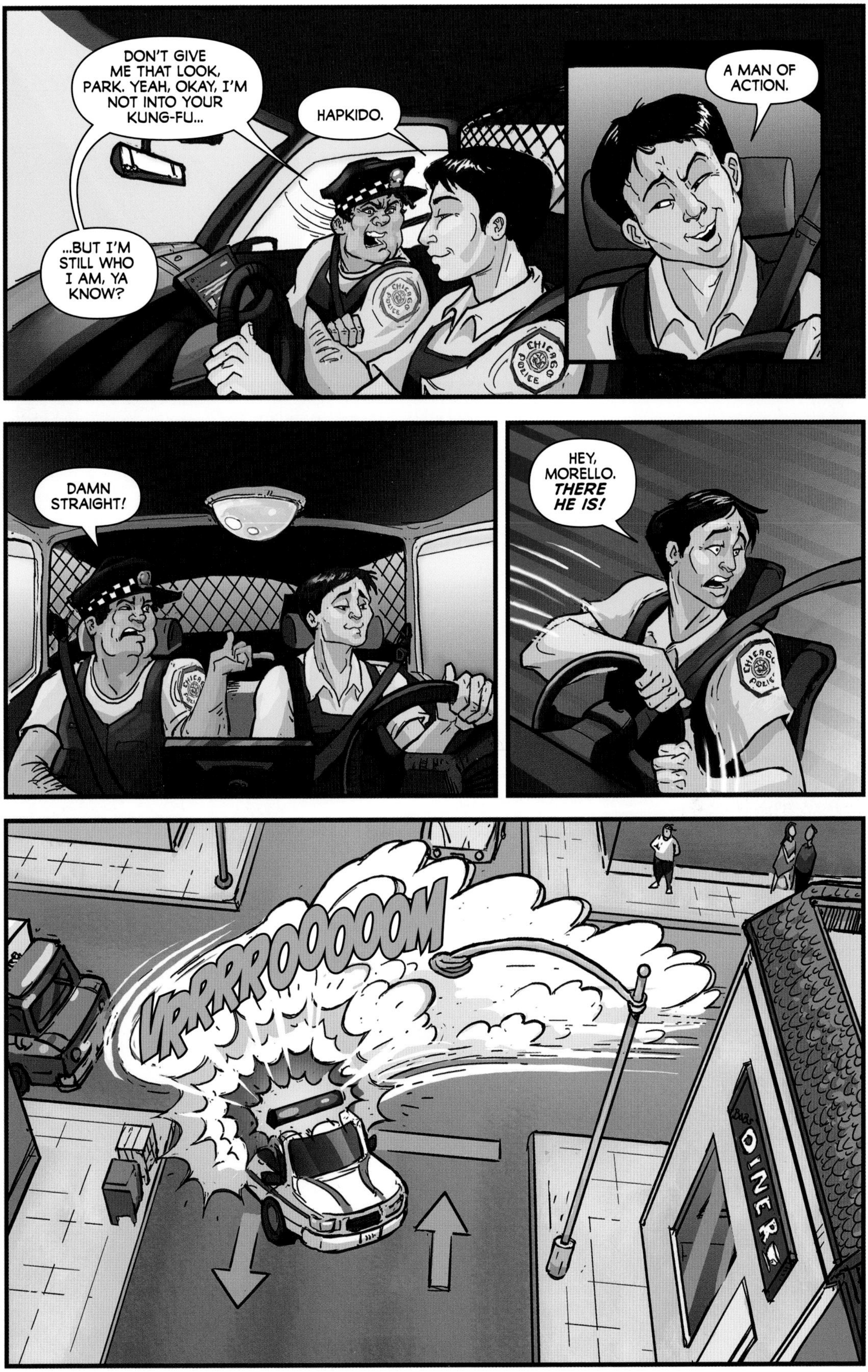
DON'T GIVE ME THAT LOOK, PARK. YEAH, OKAY, I'M NOT INTO YOUR KUNG-FU...
HAPKIDO.
...BUT I'M STILL WHO I AM, YA KNOW?
A MAN OF ACTION.
DAMN STRAIGHT!
HEY, MORELLO. THERE HE IS!
VRRRROOOOOOM
DINER

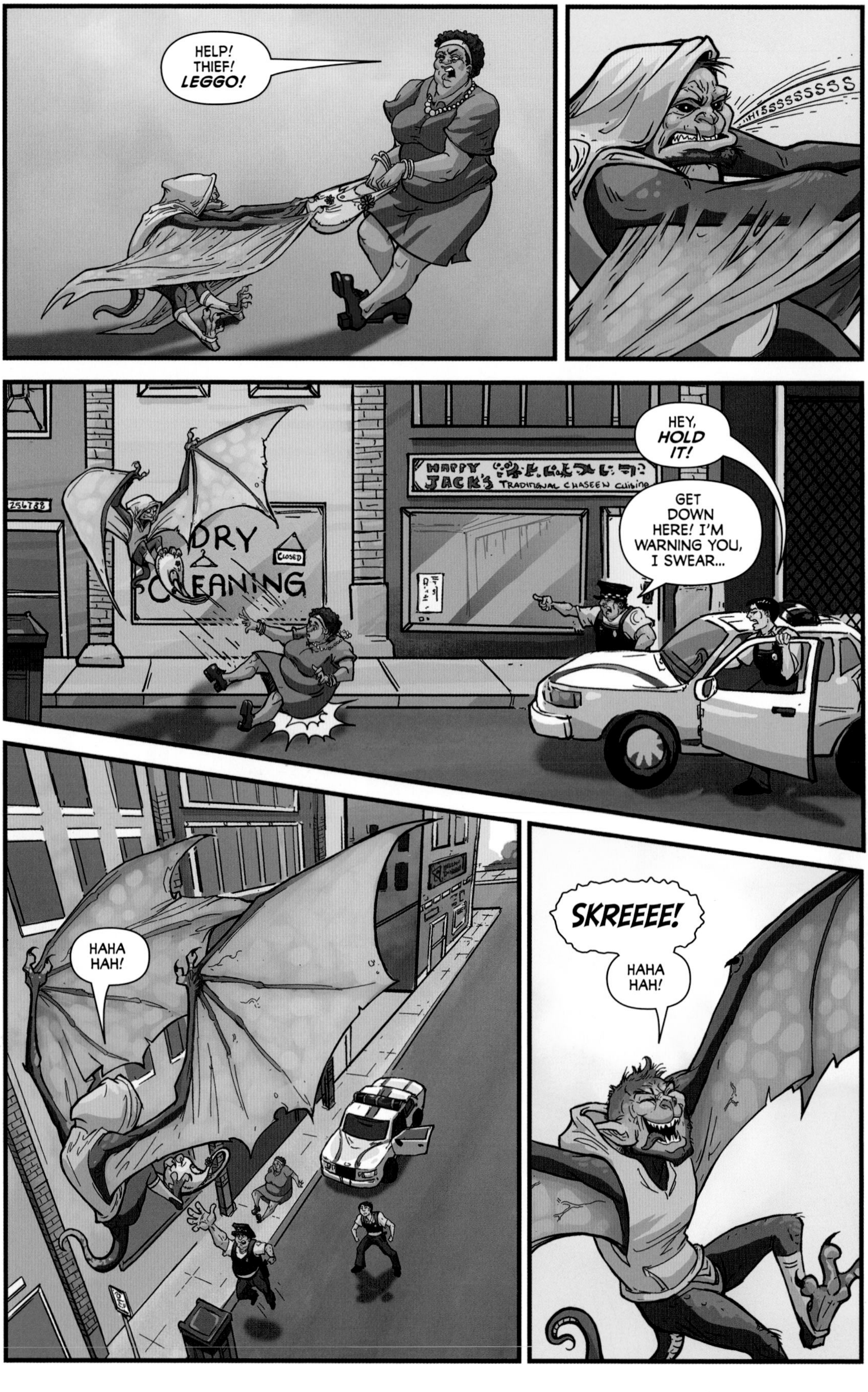
HELP! THIEF! *LEGGO!*
HISSSSSSSSS
DRY CLEANING
CLOSED
HAPPY JACK'S TRADITIONAL CHASEEN Cuisine
HEY, *HOLD IT!*
GET DOWN HERE! I'M WARNING YOU, I SWEAR...
HAHA HAH!
SKREEEE!
HAHA HAH!

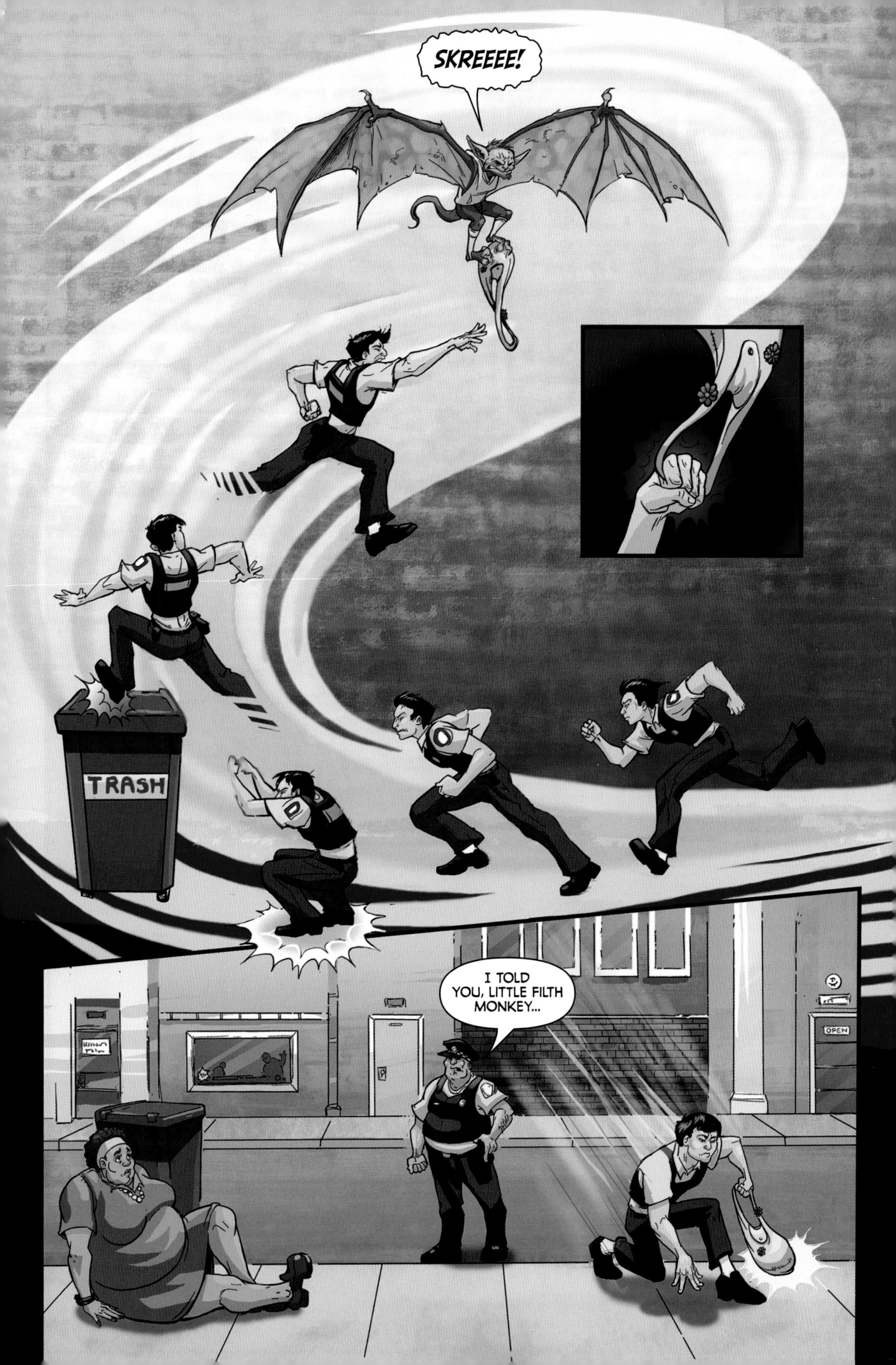
SKREEEE!
TRASH
I TOLD YOU, LITTLE FILTH MONKEY...
OPEN

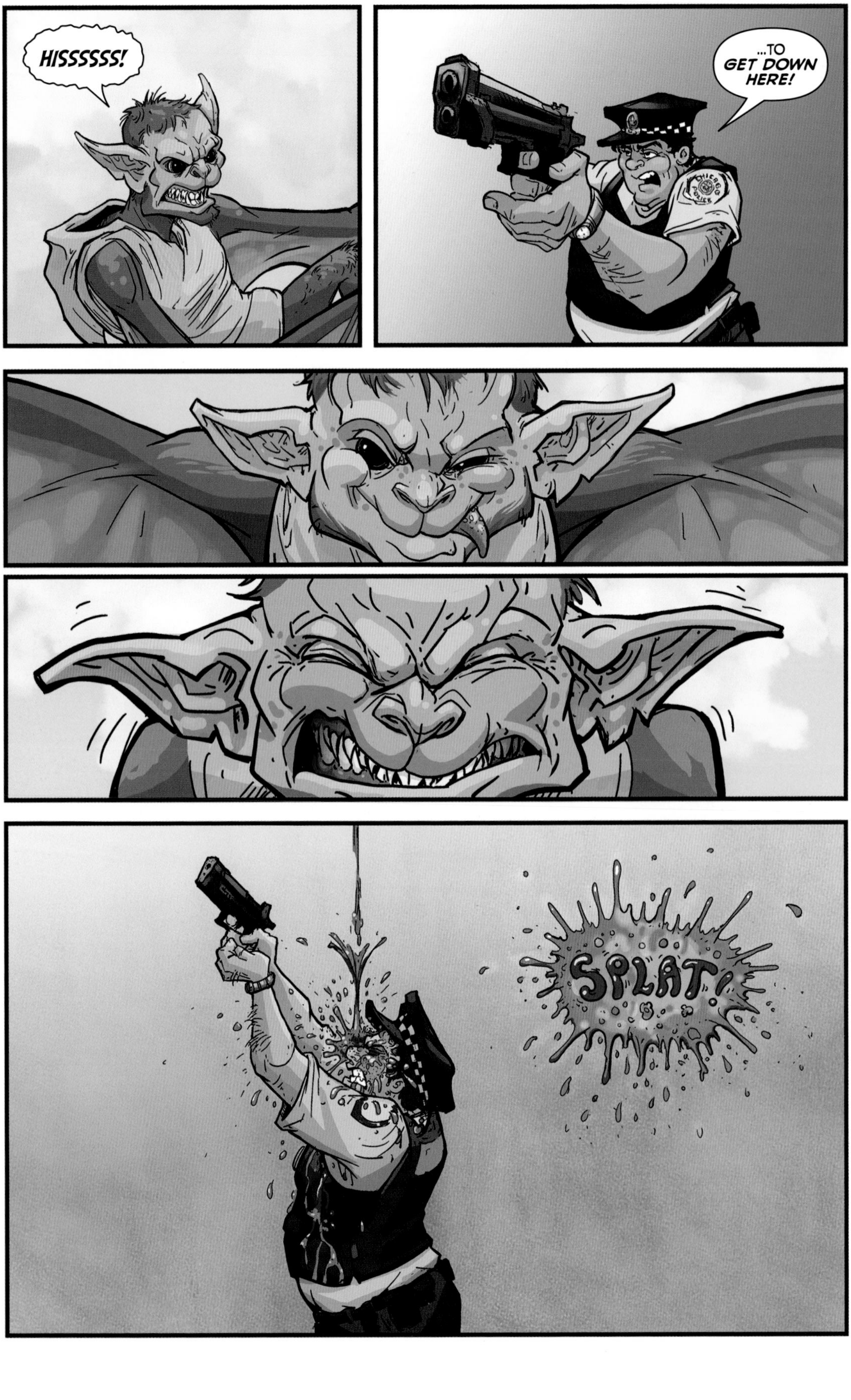
HISSSSSS!
...TO GET DOWN HERE!
SPLAT!

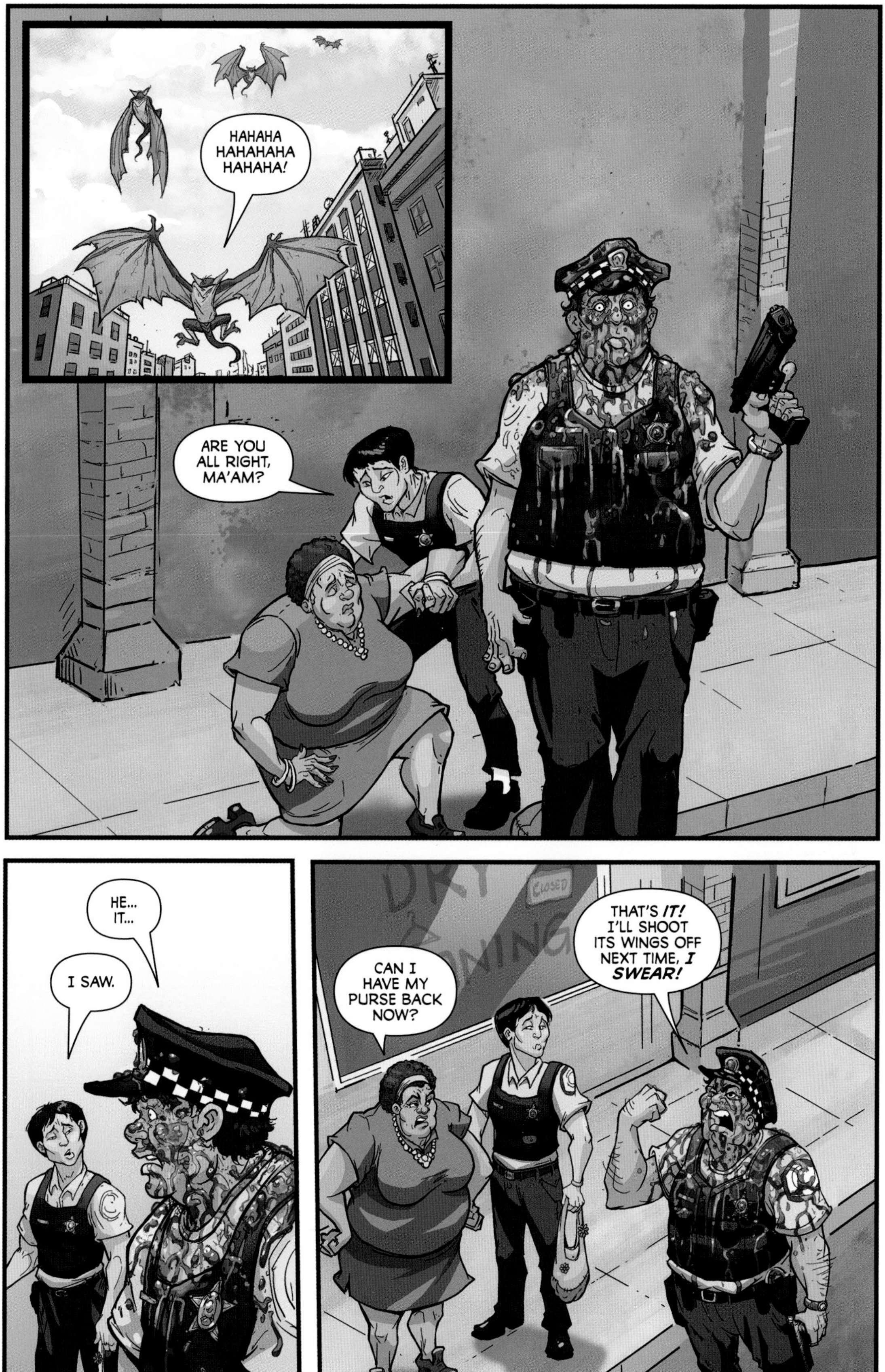
HAHAHA
HAHAHAHA
HAHAHA!
ARE YOU ALL RIGHT, MA'AM?
HE... IT...
I SAW.
CLOSED
CAN I HAVE MY PURSE BACK NOW?
THAT'S *IT!* I'LL SHOOT ITS WINGS OFF NEXT TIME, ***I SWEAR!***

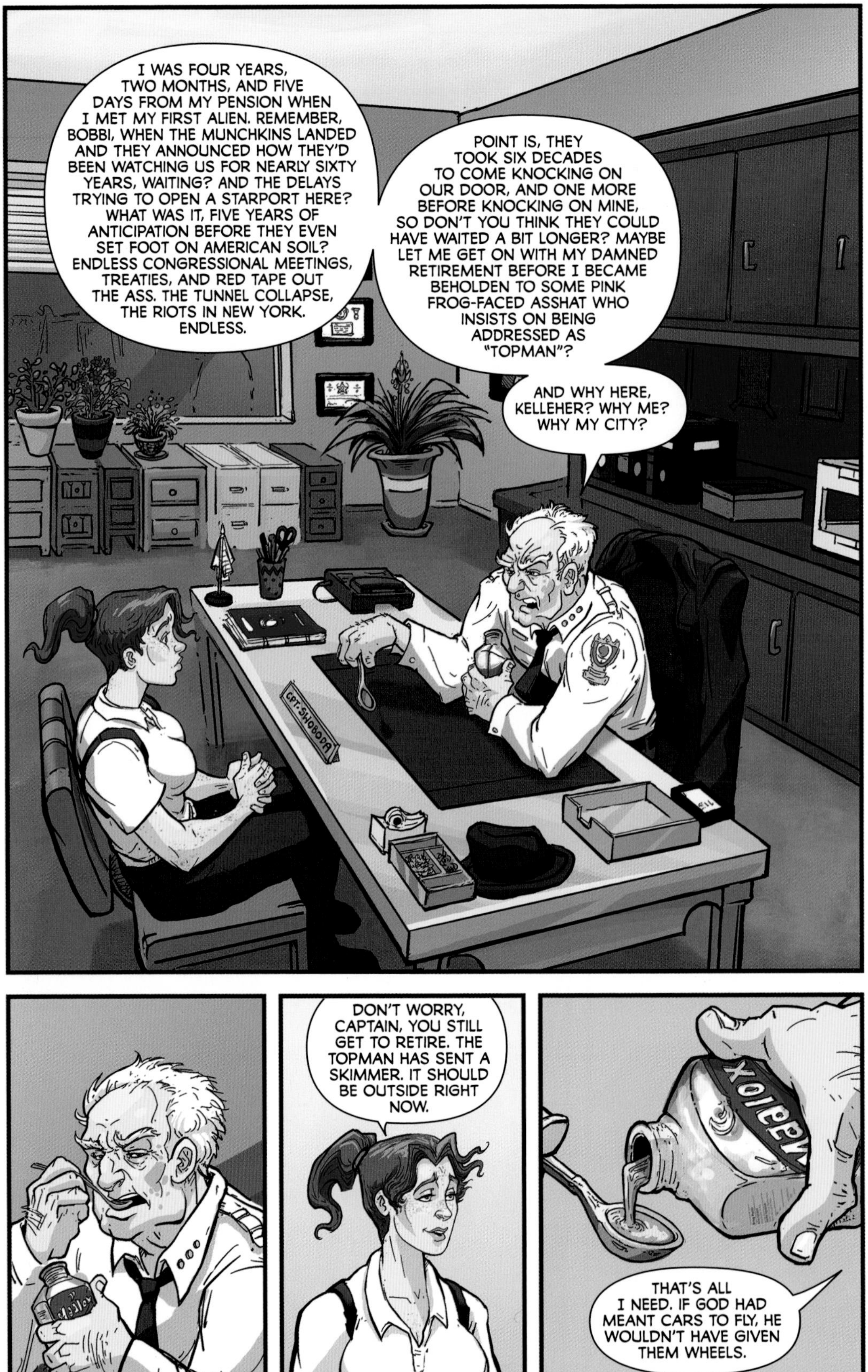
I WAS FOUR YEARS, TWO MONTHS, AND FIVE DAYS FROM MY PENSION WHEN I MET MY FIRST ALIEN. REMEMBER, BOBBI, WHEN THE MUNCHKINS LANDED AND THEY ANNOUNCED HOW THEY'D BEEN WATCHING US FOR NEARLY SIXTY YEARS, WAITING? AND THE DELAYS TRYING TO OPEN A STARPORT HERE? WHAT WAS IT, FIVE YEARS OF ANTICIPATION BEFORE THEY EVEN SET FOOT ON AMERICAN SOIL? ENDLESS CONGRESSIONAL MEETINGS, TREATIES, AND RED TAPE OUT THE ASS. THE TUNNEL COLLAPSE, THE RIOTS IN NEW YORK. ENDLESS.
POINT IS, THEY TOOK SIX DECADES TO COME KNOCKING ON OUR DOOR, AND ONE MORE BEFORE KNOCKING ON MINE, SO DON'T YOU THINK THEY COULD HAVE WAITED A BIT LONGER? MAYBE LET ME GET ON WITH MY DAMNED RETIREMENT BEFORE I BECAME BEHOLDEN TO SOME PINK FROG-FACED ASSHAT WHO INSISTS ON BEING ADDRESSED AS "TOPMAN"?
AND WHY HERE, KELLEHER? WHY ME? WHY MY CITY?
DON'T WORRY, CAPTAIN, YOU STILL GET TO RETIRE. THE TOPMAN HAS SENT A SKIMMER. IT SHOULD BE OUTSIDE RIGHT NOW.
THAT'S ALL I NEED. IF GOD HAD MEANT CARS TO FLY, HE WOULDN'T HAVE GIVEN THEM WHEELS.

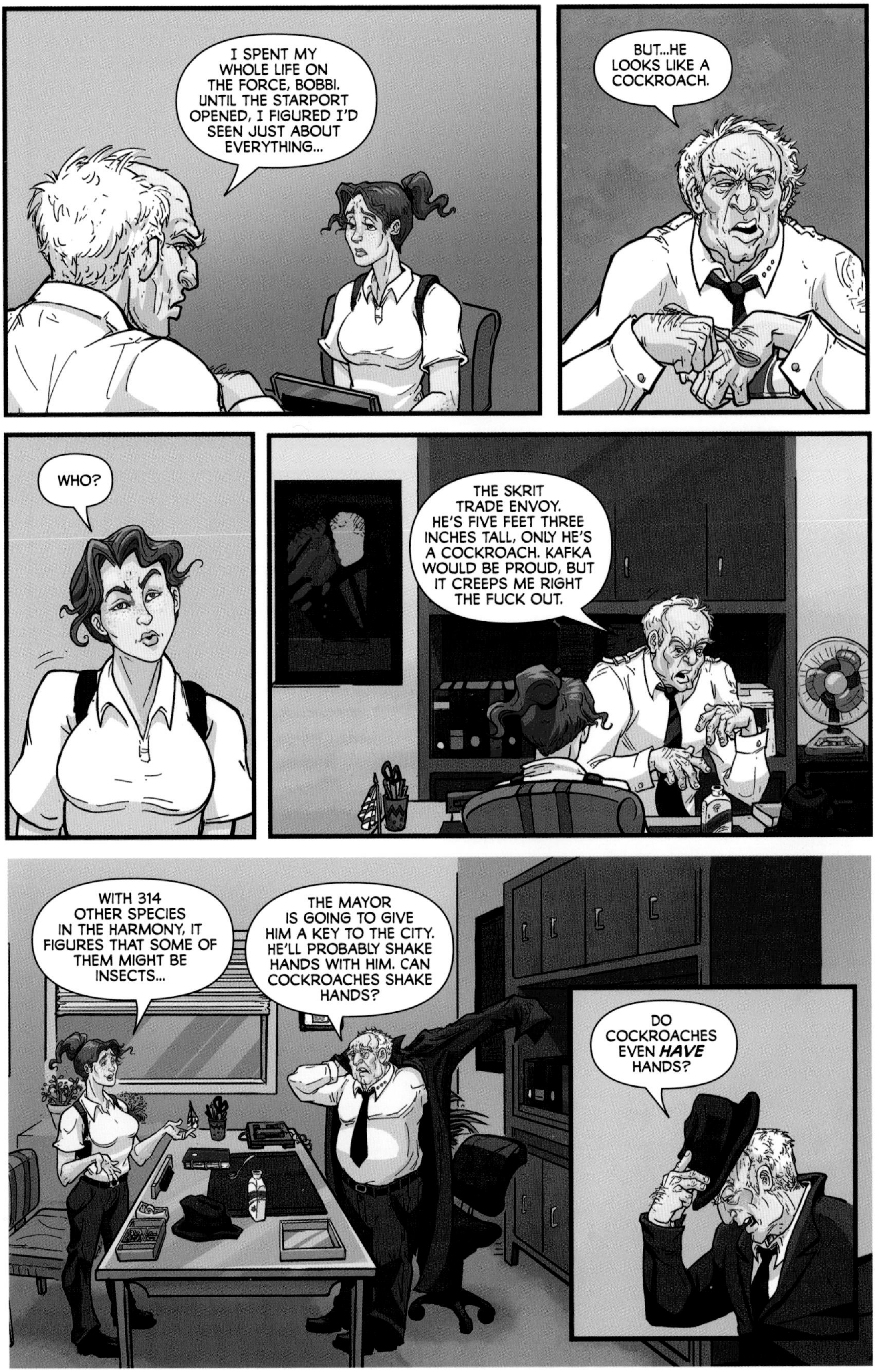
I SPENT MY WHOLE LIFE ON THE FORCE, BOBBI. UNTIL THE STARPORT OPENED, I FIGURED I'D SEEN JUST ABOUT EVERYTHING...
BUT...HE LOOKS LIKE A COCKROACH.
WHO?
THE SKRIT TRADE ENVOY. HE'S FIVE FEET THREE INCHES TALL, ONLY HE'S A COCKROACH. KAFKA WOULD BE PROUD, BUT IT CREEPS ME RIGHT THE FUCK OUT.
WITH 314 OTHER SPECIES IN THE HARMONY, IT FIGURES THAT SOME OF THEM MIGHT BE INSECTS...
THE MAYOR IS GOING TO GIVE HIM A KEY TO THE CITY. HE'LL PROBABLY SHAKE HANDS WITH HIM. CAN COCKROACHES SHAKE HANDS?
DO COCKROACHES EVEN ***HAVE*** HANDS?

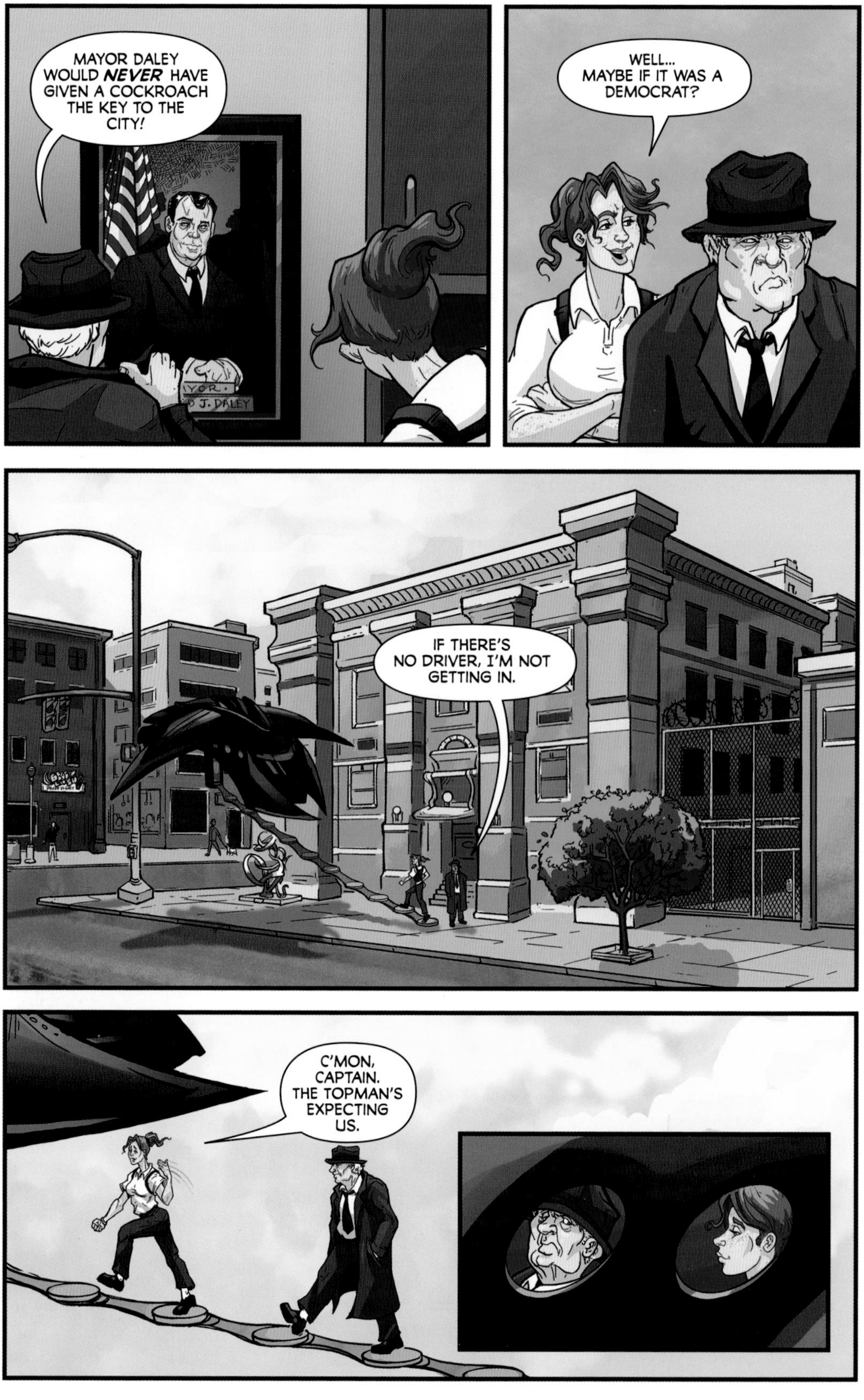
MAYOR DALEY WOULD ***NEVER*** HAVE GIVEN A COCKROACH THE KEY TO THE CITY!
WELL... MAYBE IF IT WAS A DEMOCRAT?
IF THERE'S NO DRIVER, I'M NOT GETTING IN.
C'MON, CAPTAIN. THE TOPMAN'S EXPECTING US.

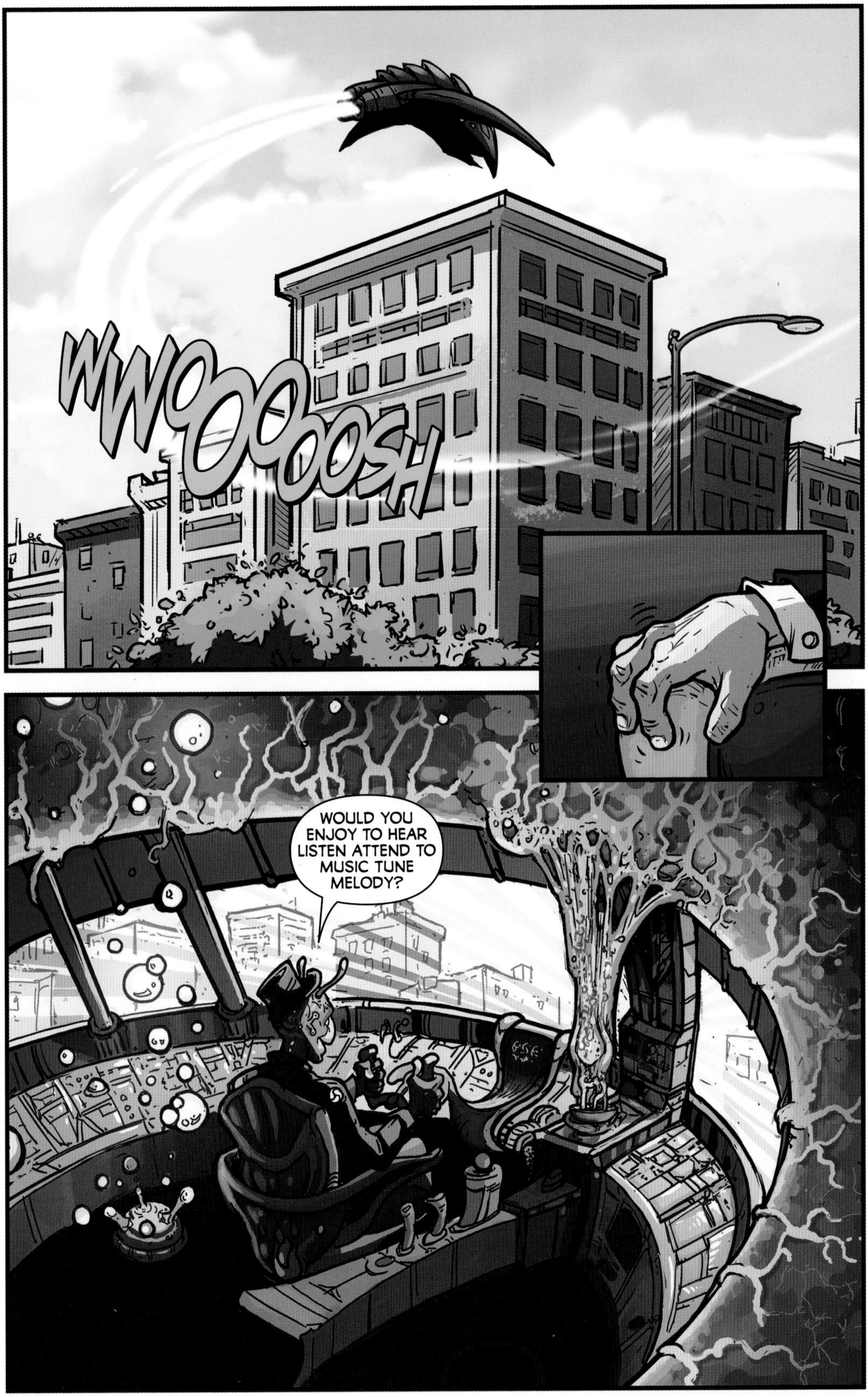
WWOOOOOSH
WOULD YOU ENJOY TO HEAR LISTEN ATTEND TO MUSIC TUNE MELODY?

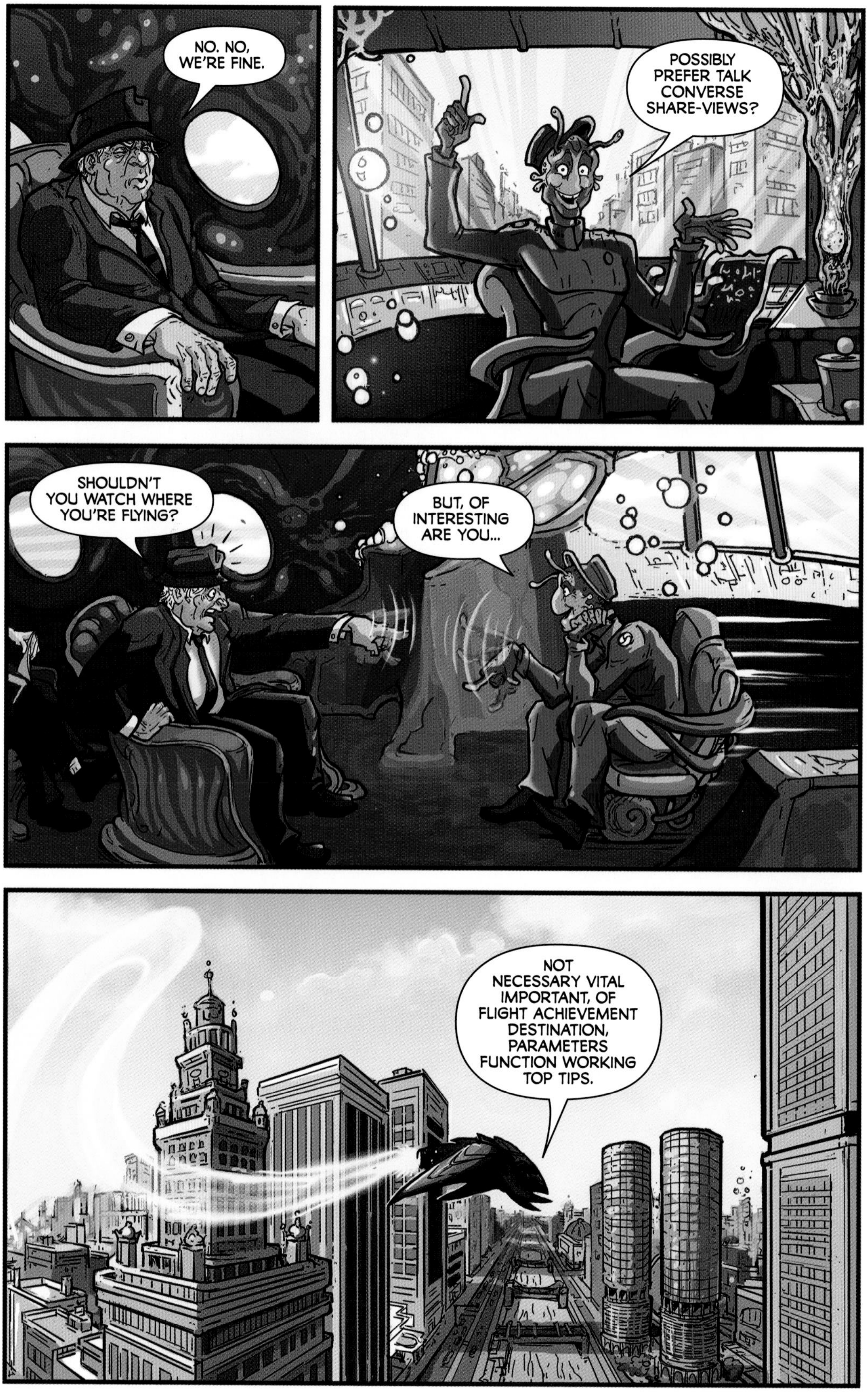
NO. NO, WE'RE FINE.
POSSIBLY PREFER TALK CONVERSE SHARE-VIEWS?
SHOULDN'T YOU WATCH WHERE YOU'RE FLYING?
BUT, OF INTERESTING ARE YOU...
NOT NECESSARY VITAL IMPORTANT, OF FLIGHT ACHIEVEMENT DESTINATION, PARAMETERS FUNCTION WORKING TOP TIPS.

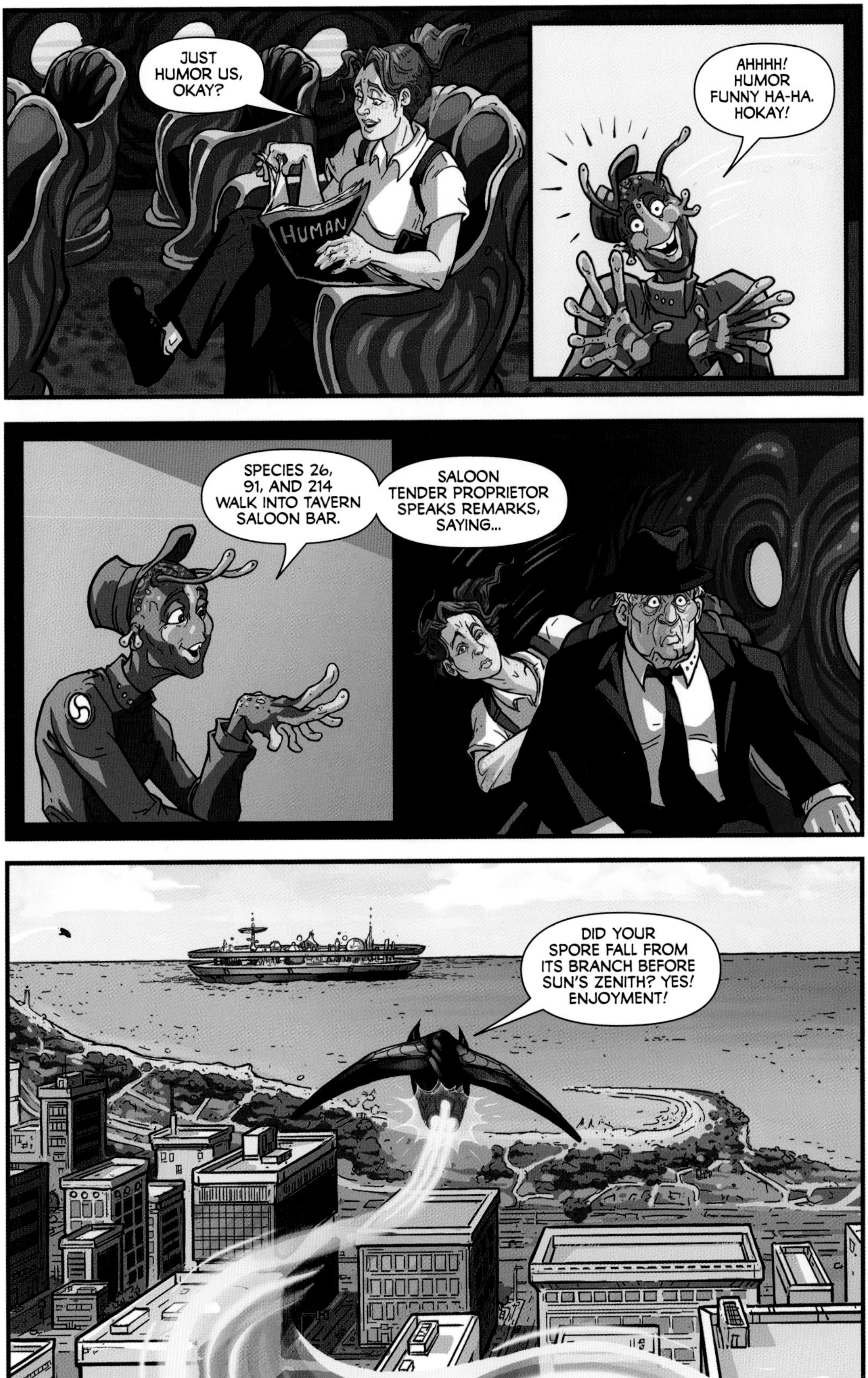
JUST HUMOR US, OKAY?
HUMAN
AHHHH! HUMOR FUNNY HA-HA. HOKAY!
SPECIES 26, 91, AND 214 WALK INTO TAVERN SALOON BAR.
SALOON TENDER PROPRIETOR SPEAKS REMARKS, SAYING...
DID YOUR SPORE FALL FROM ITS BRANCH BEFORE SUN'S ZENITH? YES! ENJOYMENT!

THE POLICE ARE HERE!
STEP ASIDE, PLEASE. MOVE ASIDE.
WHAT'S THE PROBLEM?
WHAT THE HELL TOOK YOU SO LONG?
THE POLICE... THANK YOU, JESUS!
UH-OH. ANGELS.
WORSE. MAROON CADRE.
POLICE

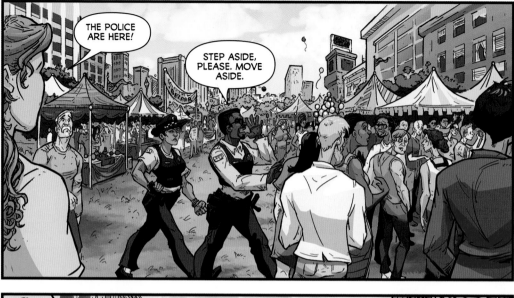

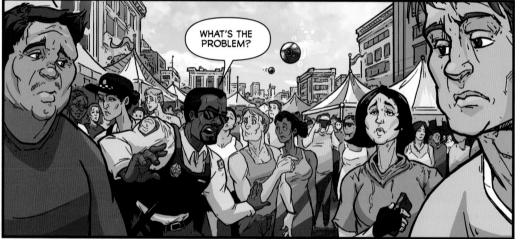

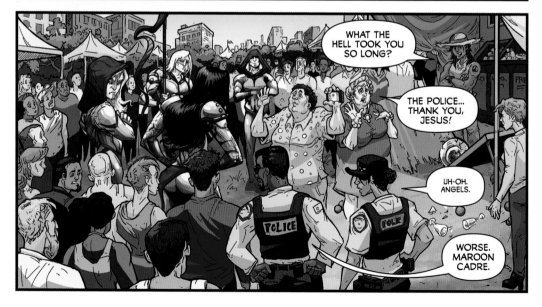

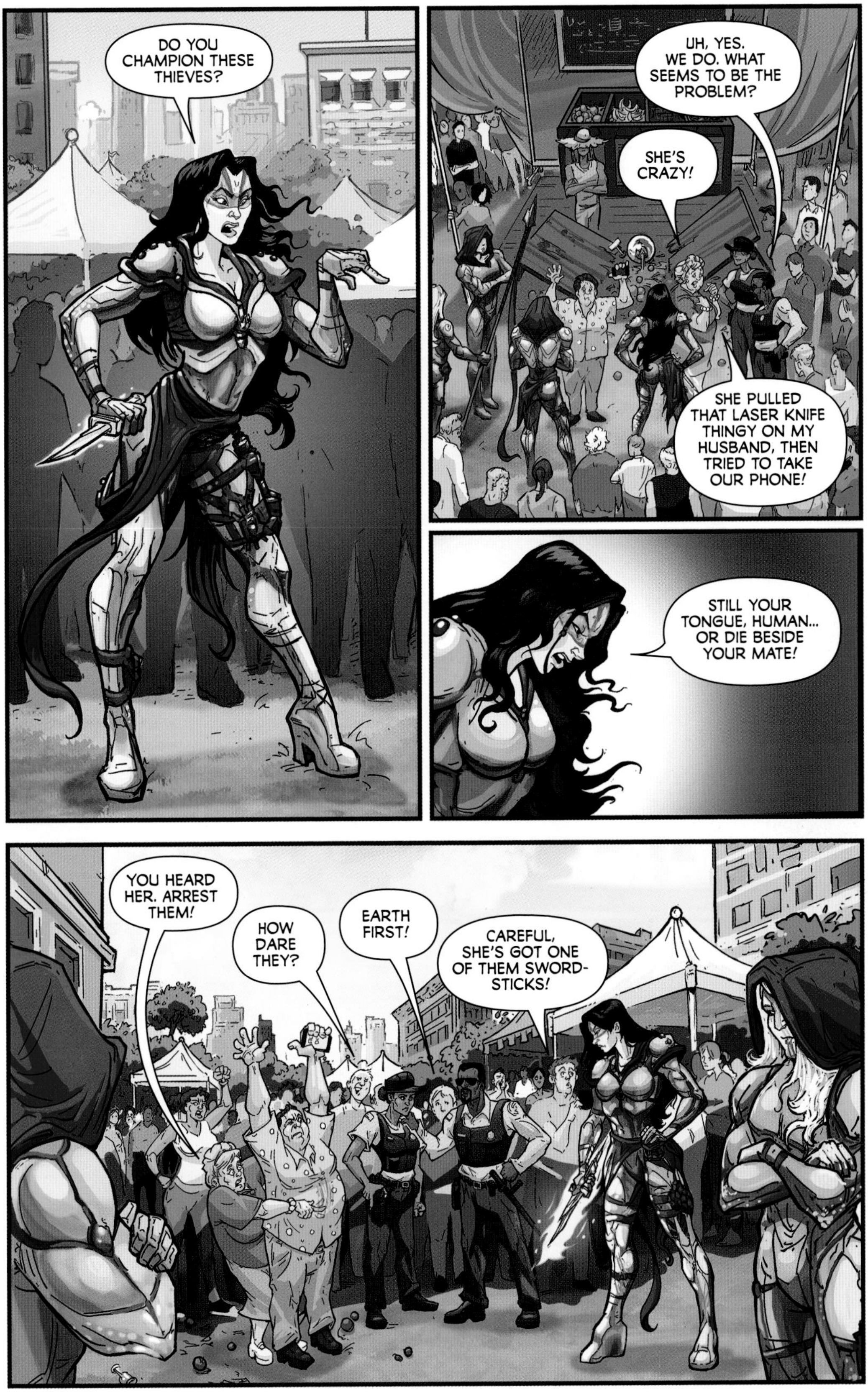
DO YOU CHAMPION THESE THIEVES?
UH, YES. WE DO. WHAT SEEMS TO BE THE PROBLEM?
SHE'S CRAZY!
SHE PULLED THAT LASER KNIFE THINGY ON MY HUSBAND, THEN TRIED TO TAKE OUR PHONE!
STILL YOUR TONGUE, HUMAN... OR DIE BESIDE YOUR MATE!
YOU HEARD HER. ARREST THEM!
HOW DARE THEY?
EARTH FIRST!
CAREFUL, SHE'S GOT ONE OF THEM SWORD-STICKS!

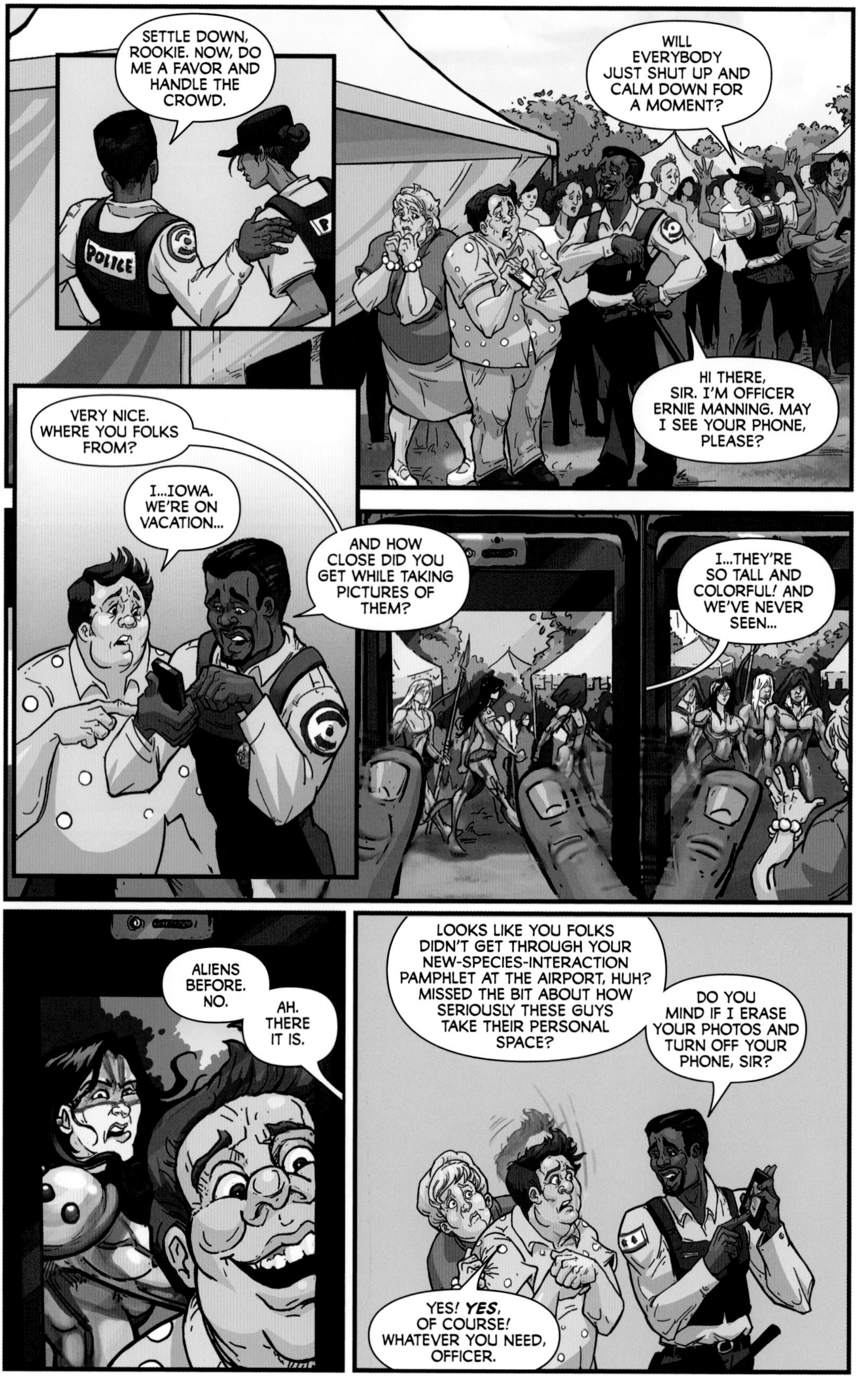
SETTLE DOWN, ROOKIE. NOW, DO ME A FAVOR AND HANDLE THE CROWD.
POLICE
WILL EVERYBODY JUST SHUT UP AND CALM DOWN FOR A MOMENT?
HI THERE, SIR. I'M OFFICER ERNIE MANNING. MAY I SEE YOUR PHONE, PLEASE?
VERY NICE. WHERE YOU FOLKS FROM?
I...IOWA. WE'RE ON VACATION...
AND HOW CLOSE DID YOU GET WHILE TAKING PICTURES OF THEM?
I...THEY'RE SO TALL AND COLORFUL! AND WE'VE NEVER SEEN...
ALIENS BEFORE. NO.
AH. THERE IT IS.
LOOKS LIKE YOU FOLKS DIDN'T GET THROUGH YOUR NEW-SPECIES-INTERACTION PAMPHLET AT THE AIRPORT, HUH? MISSED THE BIT ABOUT HOW SERIOUSLY THESE GUYS TAKE THEIR PERSONAL SPACE?
DO YOU MIND IF I ERASE YOUR PHOTOS AND TURN OFF YOUR PHONE, SIR?
YES! *YES*, OF COURSE! WHATEVER YOU NEED, OFFICER.

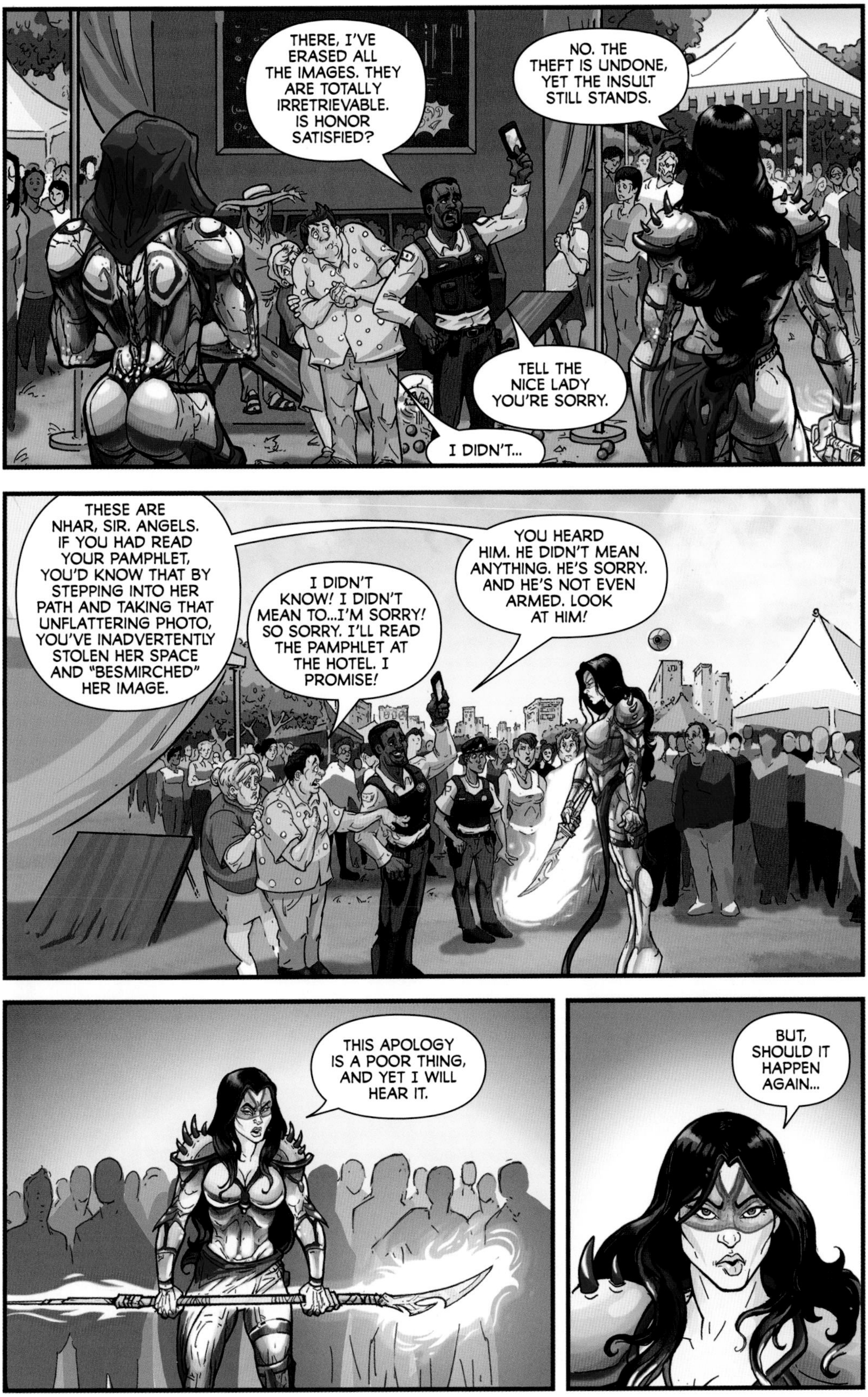
THERE, I'VE ERASED ALL THE IMAGES. THEY ARE TOTALLY IRRETRIEVABLE. IS HONOR SATISFIED?
NO. THE THEFT IS UNDONE, YET THE INSULT STILL STANDS.
TELL THE NICE LADY YOU'RE SORRY.
I DIDN'T...
THESE ARE NHAR, SIR. ANGELS. IF YOU HAD READ YOUR PAMPHLET, YOU'D KNOW THAT BY STEPPING INTO HER PATH AND TAKING THAT UNFLATTERING PHOTO, YOU'VE INADVERTENTLY STOLEN HER SPACE AND "BESMIRCHED" HER IMAGE.
I DIDN'T KNOW! I DIDN'T MEAN TO...I'M SORRY! SO SORRY. I'LL READ THE PAMPHLET AT THE HOTEL. I PROMISE!
YOU HEARD HIM. HE DIDN'T MEAN ANYTHING. HE'S SORRY. AND HE'S NOT EVEN ARMED. LOOK AT HIM!
THIS APOLOGY IS A POOR THING, AND YET I WILL HEAR IT.
BUT, SHOULD IT HAPPEN AGAIN...

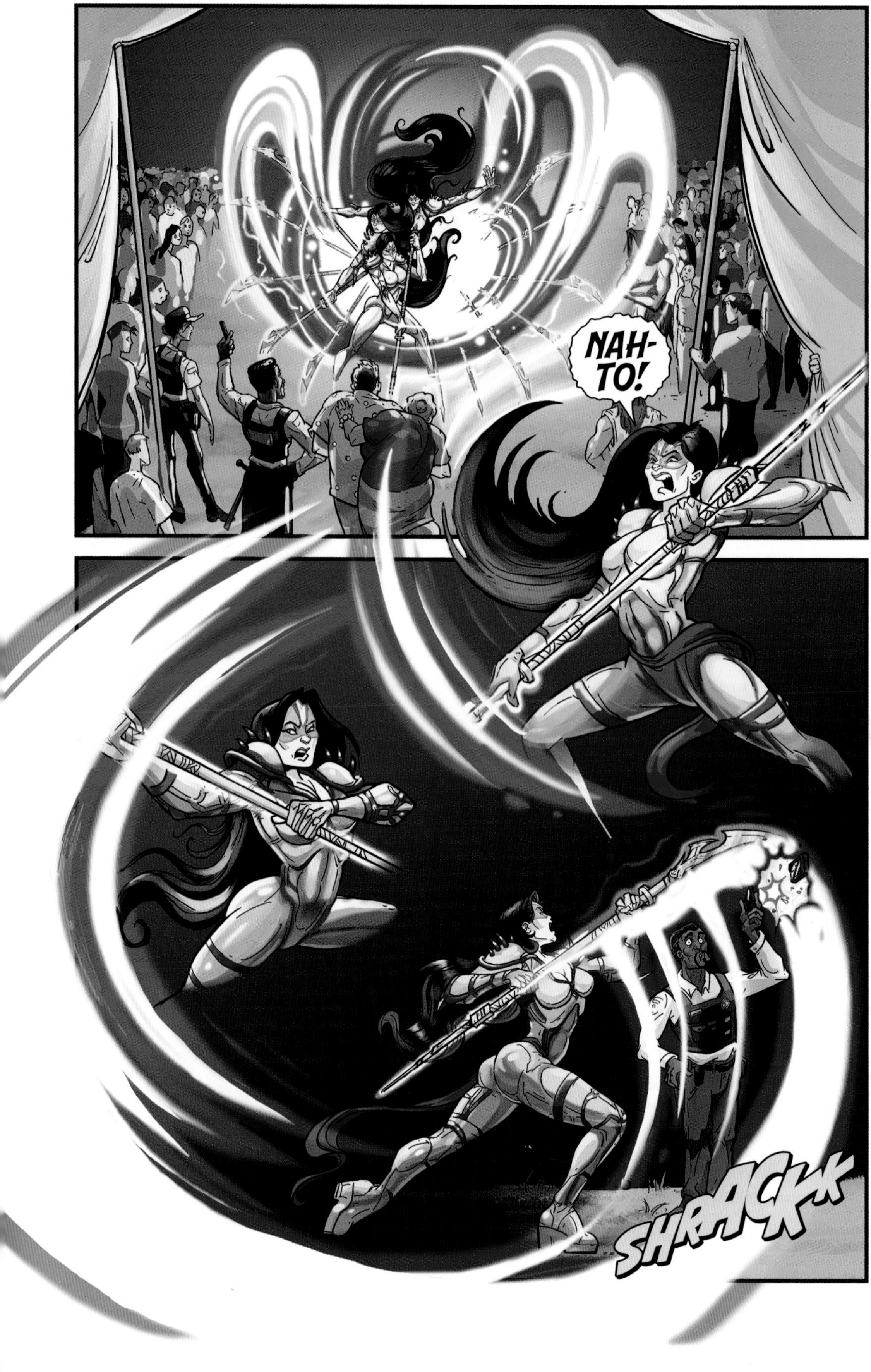
NAH-TO!
SHRACKK

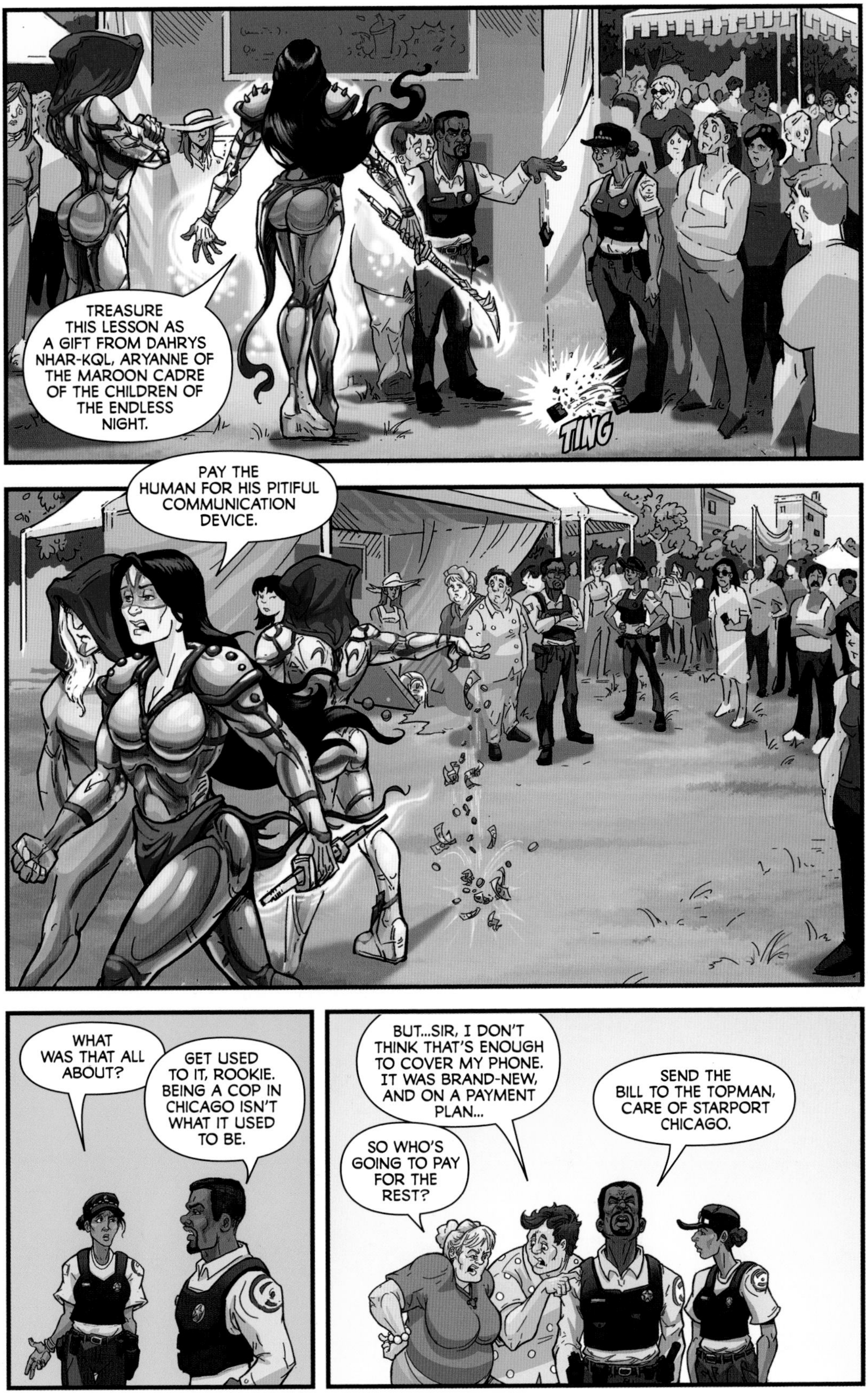
TREASURE THIS LESSON AS A GIFT FROM DAHRYS NHAR-KQL, ARYANNE OF THE MAROON CADRE OF THE CHILDREN OF THE ENDLESS NIGHT.
TING
PAY THE HUMAN FOR HIS PITIFUL COMMUNICATION DEVICE.
WHAT WAS THAT ALL ABOUT?
GET USED TO IT, ROOKIE. BEING A COP IN CHICAGO ISN'T WHAT IT USED TO BE.
BUT...SIR, I DON'T THINK THAT'S ENOUGH TO COVER MY PHONE. IT WAS BRAND-NEW, AND ON A PAYMENT PLAN...
SO WHO'S GOING TO PAY FOR THE REST?
SEND THE BILL TO THE TOPMAN, CARE OF STARPORT CHICAGO.

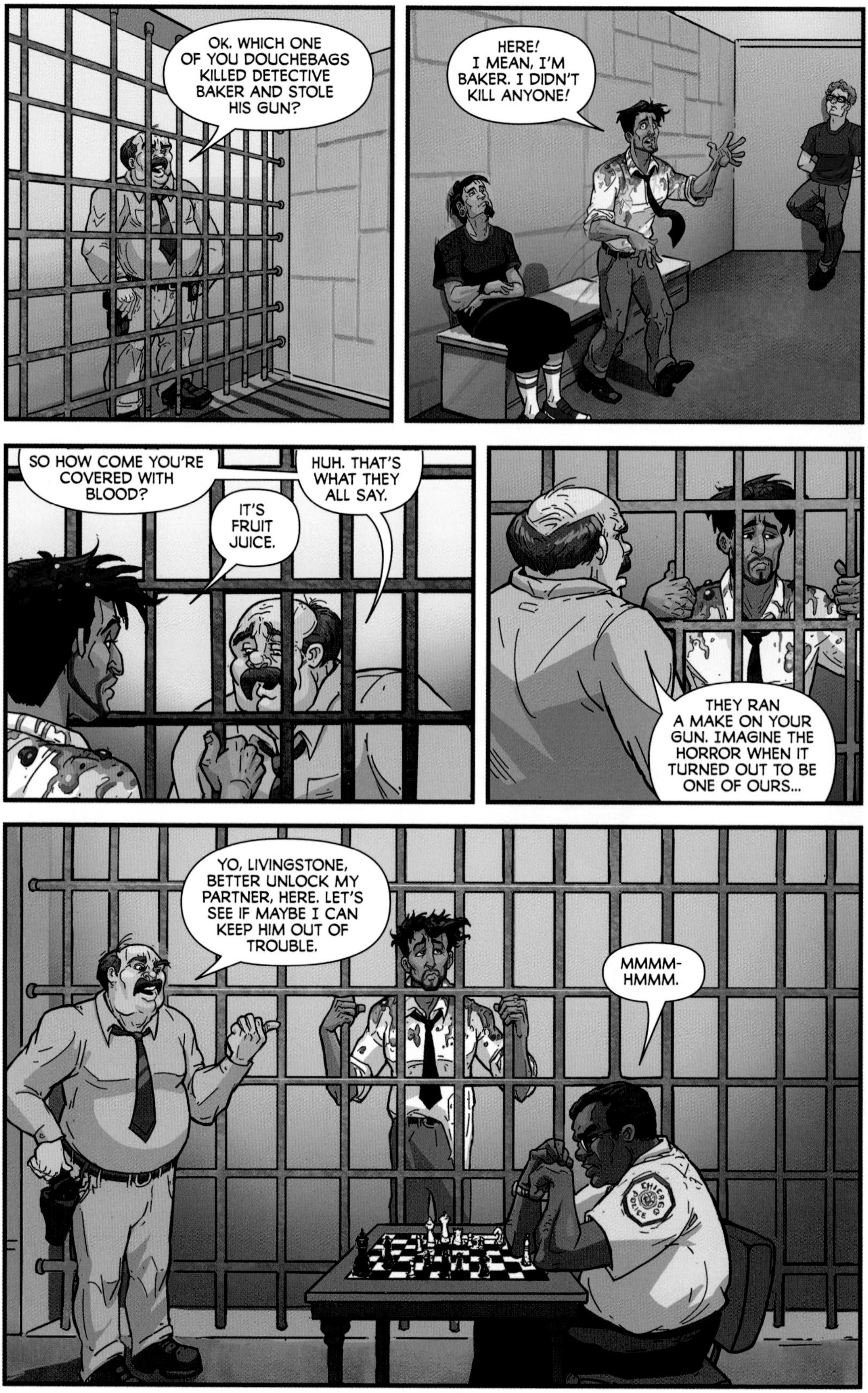

OK. WHICH ONE OF YOU DOUCHEBAGS KILLED DETECTIVE BAKER AND STOLE HIS GUN?
HERE! I MEAN, I'M BAKER. I DIDN'T KILL ANYONE!
SO HOW COME YOU'RE COVERED WITH BLOOD?
IT'S FRUIT JUICE.
HUH. THAT'S WHAT THEY ALL SAY.
THEY RAN A MAKE ON YOUR GUN. IMAGINE THE HORROR WHEN IT TURNED OUT TO BE ONE OF OURS...
YO, LIVINGSTONE, BETTER UNLOCK MY PARTNER, HERE. LET'S SEE IF MAYBE I CAN KEEP HIM OUT OF TROUBLE.
MMMM-HMMM.

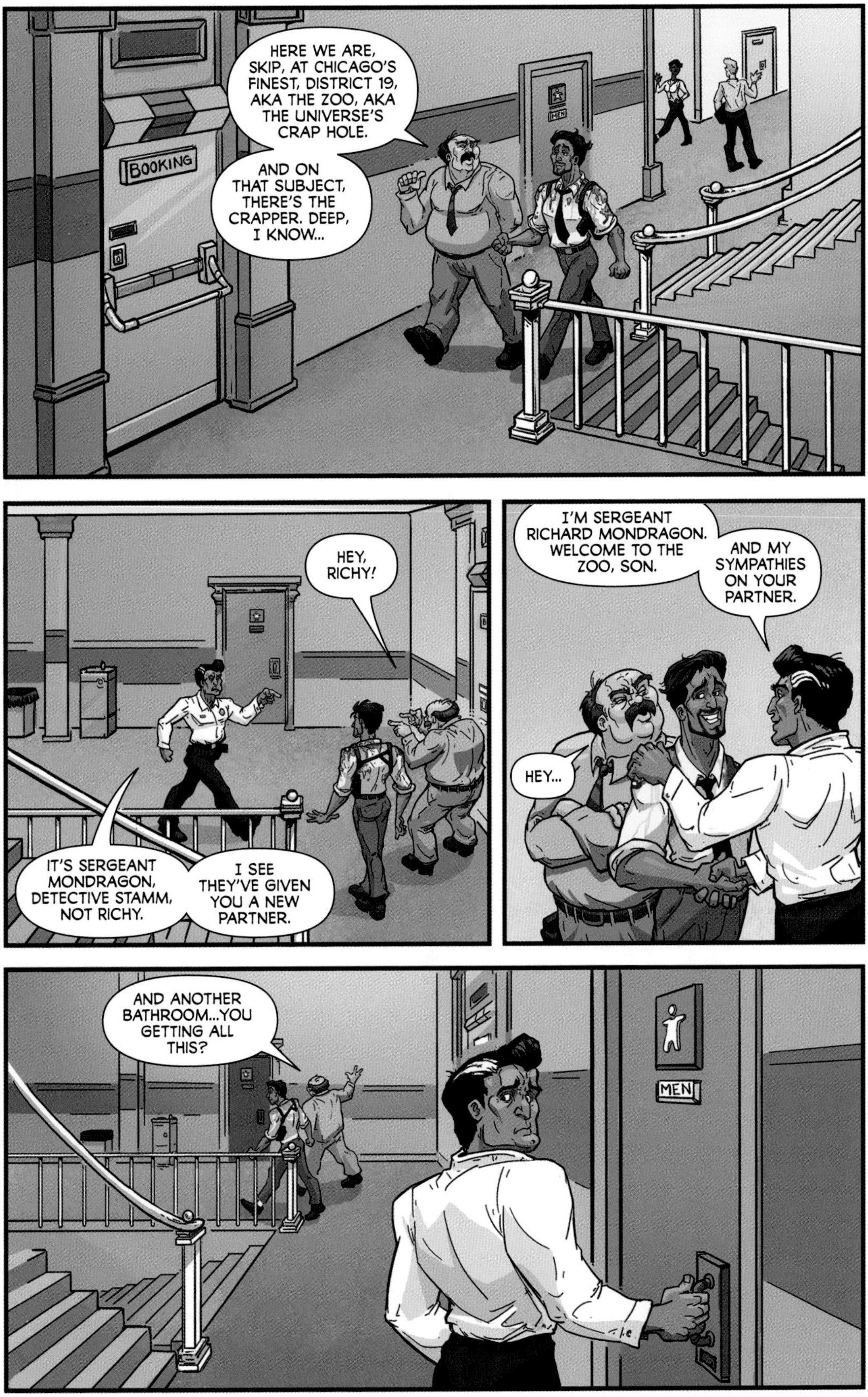
HERE WE ARE, SKIP, AT CHICAGO'S FINEST, DISTRICT 19, AKA THE ZOO, AKA THE UNIVERSE'S CRAP HOLE.
BOOKING
MEN
AND ON THAT SUBJECT, THERE'S THE CRAPPER. DEEP, I KNOW...
HEY, RICHY!
IT'S SERGEANT MONDRAGON, DETECTIVE STAMM, NOT RICHY.
I SEE THEY'VE GIVEN YOU A NEW PARTNER.
I'M SERGEANT RICHARD MONDRAGON. WELCOME TO THE ZOO, SON.
AND MY SYMPATHIES ON YOUR PARTNER.
HEY...
AND ANOTHER BATHROOM...YOU GETTING ALL THIS?
MEN

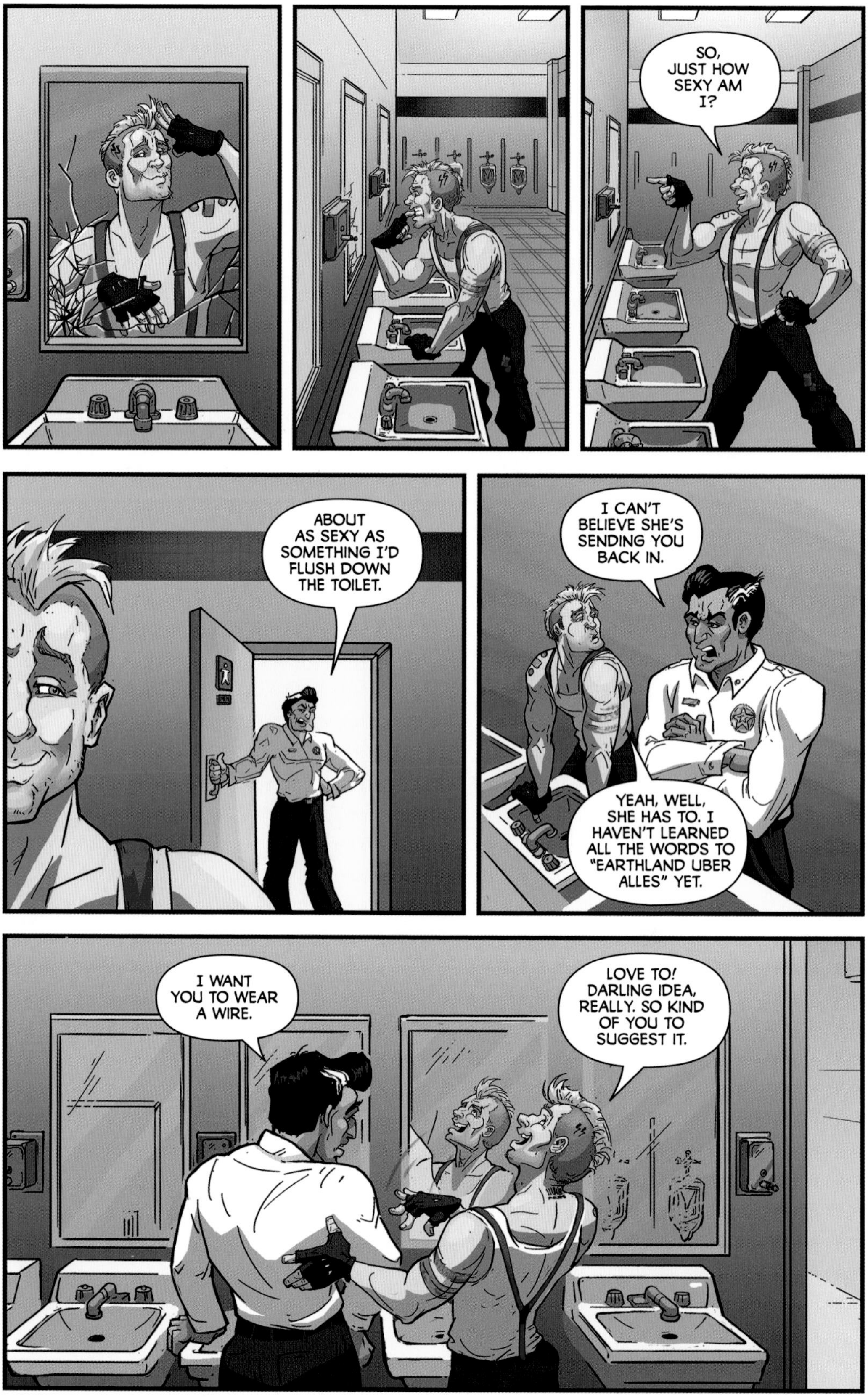
SO, JUST HOW SEXY AM I?
ABOUT AS SEXY AS SOMETHING I'D FLUSH DOWN THE TOILET.
I CAN'T BELIEVE SHE'S SENDING YOU BACK IN.
YEAH, WELL, SHE HAS TO. I HAVEN'T LEARNED ALL THE WORDS TO "EARTHLAND UBER ALLES" YET.
I WANT YOU TO WEAR A WIRE.
LOVE TO! DARLING IDEA, REALLY. SO KIND OF YOU TO SUGGEST IT.

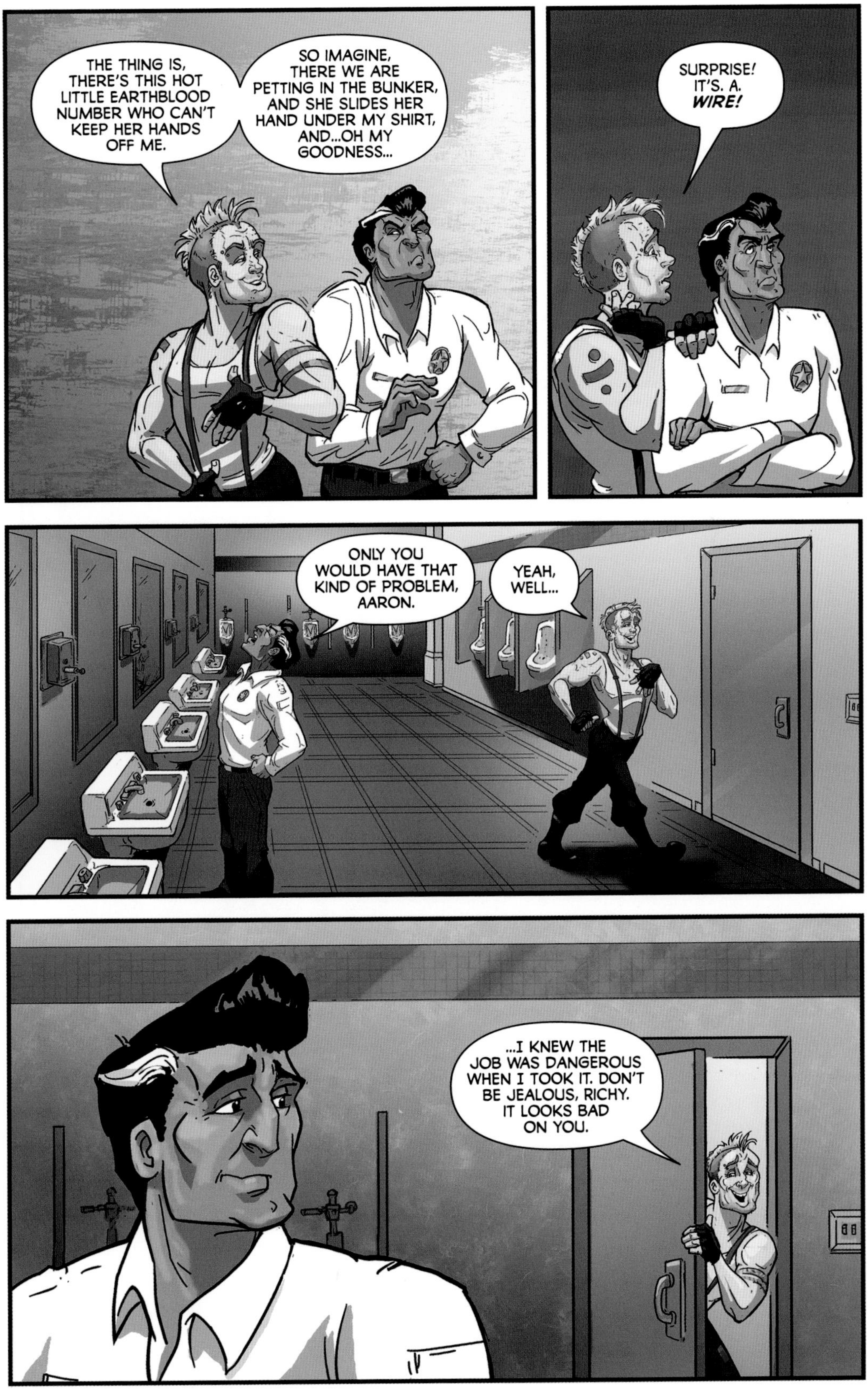
THE THING IS, THERE'S THIS HOT LITTLE EARTHBLOOD NUMBER WHO CAN'T KEEP HER HANDS OFF ME.
SO IMAGINE, THERE WE ARE PETTING IN THE BUNKER, AND SHE SLIDES HER HAND UNDER MY SHIRT, AND...OH MY GOODNESS...
SURPRISE! IT'S. A. *WIRE!*
ONLY YOU WOULD HAVE THAT KIND OF PROBLEM, AARON.
YEAH, WELL...
...I KNEW THE JOB WAS DANGEROUS WHEN I TOOK IT. DON'T BE JEALOUS, RICHY. IT LOOKS BAD ON YOU.

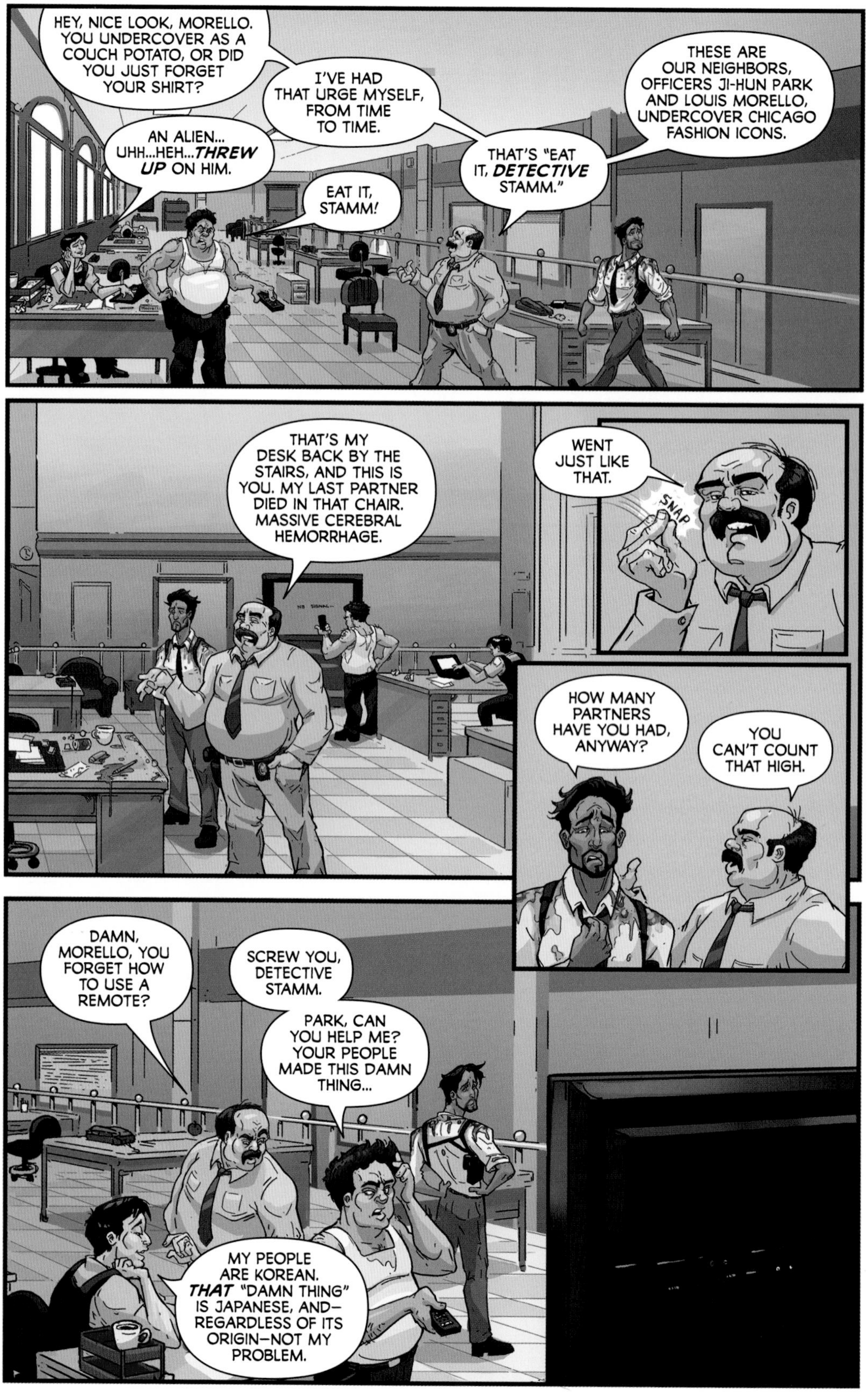
HEY, NICE LOOK, MORELLO. YOU UNDERCOVER AS A COUCH POTATO, OR DID YOU JUST FORGET YOUR SHIRT?
AN ALIEN... UHH...HEH...THREW UP ON HIM.
I'VE HAD THAT URGE MYSELF, FROM TIME TO TIME.
EAT IT, STAMM!
THAT'S "EAT IT, DETECTIVE STAMM."
THESE ARE OUR NEIGHBORS, OFFICERS JI-HUN PARK AND LOUIS MORELLO, UNDERCOVER CHICAGO FASHION ICONS.
THAT'S MY DESK BACK BY THE STAIRS, AND THIS IS YOU. MY LAST PARTNER DIED IN THAT CHAIR. MASSIVE CEREBRAL HEMORRHAGE.
WENT JUST LIKE THAT.
SNAP
HOW MANY PARTNERS HAVE YOU HAD, ANYWAY?
YOU CAN'T COUNT THAT HIGH.
DAMN, MORELLO, YOU FORGET HOW TO USE A REMOTE?
SCREW YOU, DETECTIVE STAMM.
PARK, CAN YOU HELP ME? YOUR PEOPLE MADE THIS DAMN THING...
MY PEOPLE ARE KOREAN. THAT "DAMN THING" IS JAPANESE, AND—REGARDLESS OF ITS ORIGIN—NOT MY PROBLEM.

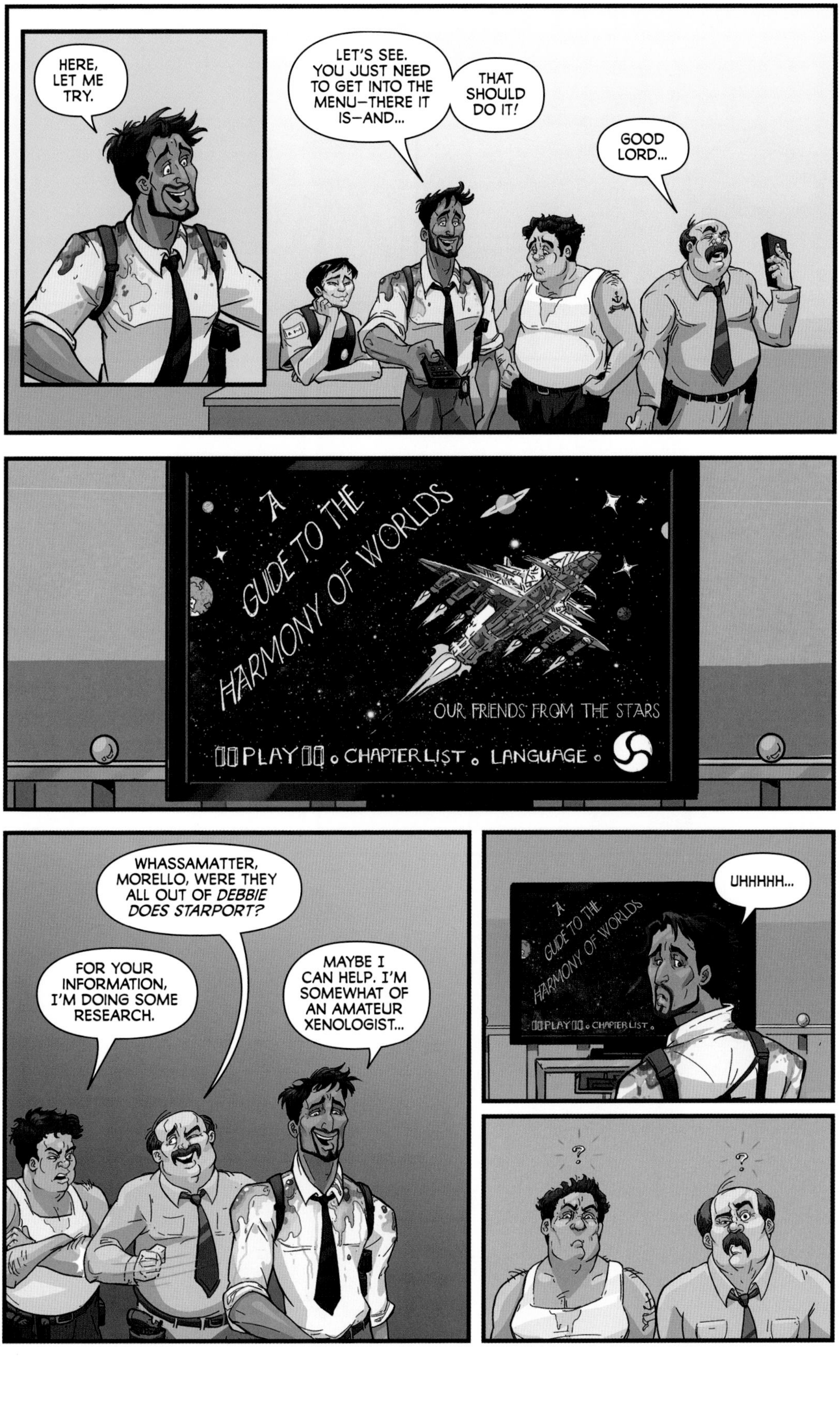
HERE, LET ME TRY.
LET'S SEE. YOU JUST NEED TO GET INTO THE MENU—THERE IT IS—AND...
THAT SHOULD DO IT!
GOOD LORD...
A GUIDE TO THE HARMONY OF WORLDS
OUR FRIENDS FROM THE STARS
PLAY CHAPTER LIST LANGUAGE
WHASSAMATTER, MORELLO, WERE THEY ALL OUT OF *DEBBIE DOES STARPORT?*
FOR YOUR INFORMATION, I'M DOING SOME RESEARCH.
MAYBE I CAN HELP. I'M SOMEWHAT OF AN AMATEUR XENOLOGIST...
A GUIDE TO THE HARMONY OF WORLDS
PLAY CHAPTER LIST
UHHHHH...
?
?

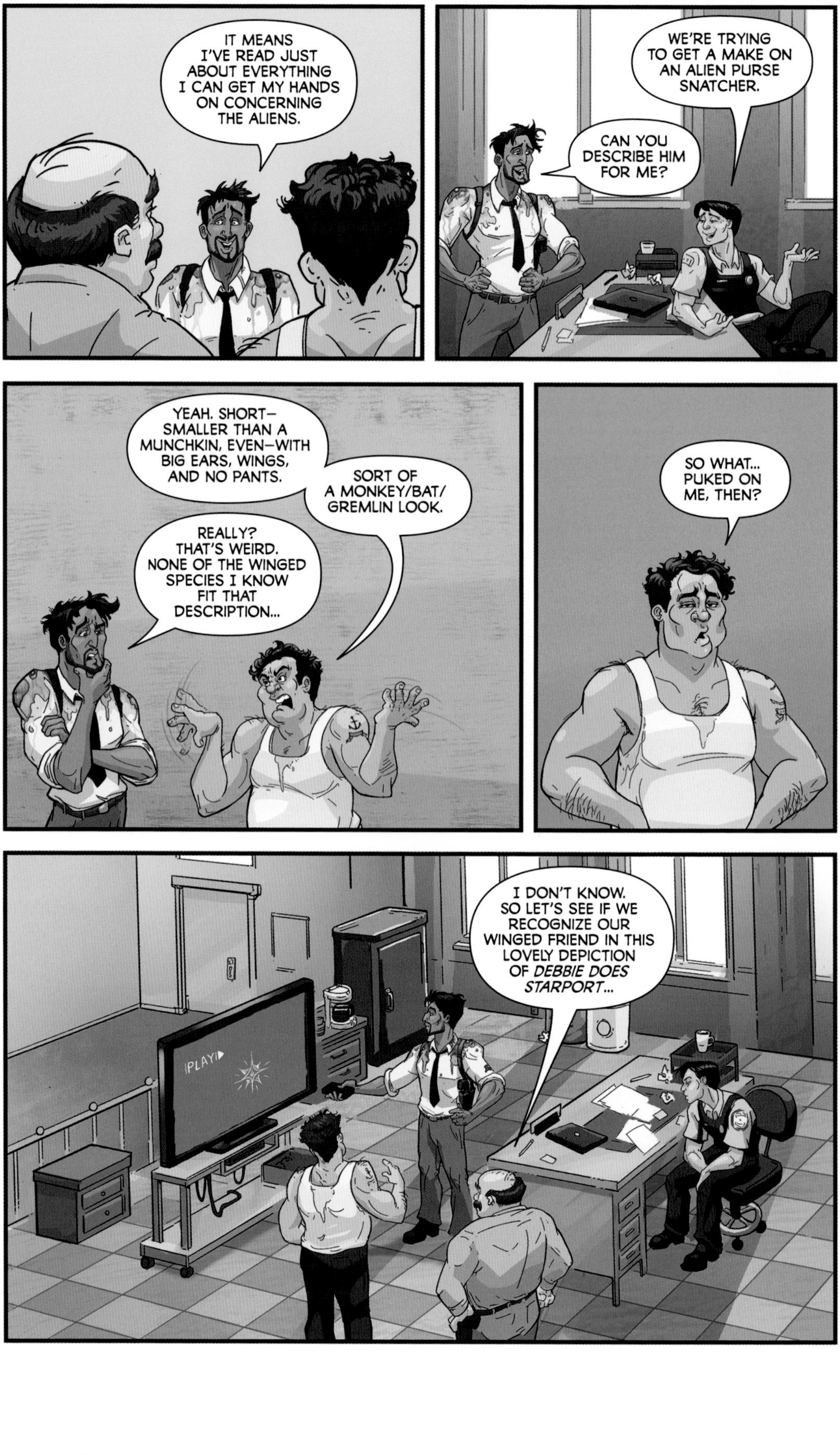
IT MEANS I'VE READ JUST ABOUT EVERYTHING I CAN GET MY HANDS ON CONCERNING THE ALIENS.
WE'RE TRYING TO GET A MAKE ON AN ALIEN PURSE SNATCHER.
CAN YOU DESCRIBE HIM FOR ME?
YEAH. SHORT—SMALLER THAN A MUNCHKIN, EVEN—WITH BIG EARS, WINGS, AND NO PANTS.
SORT OF A MONKEY/BAT/GREMLIN LOOK.
REALLY? THAT'S WEIRD. NONE OF THE WINGED SPECIES I KNOW FIT THAT DESCRIPTION...
SO WHAT... PUKED ON ME, THEN?
I DON'T KNOW. SO LET'S SEE IF WE RECOGNIZE OUR WINGED FRIEND IN THIS LOVELY DEPICTION OF *DEBBIE DOES STARPORT*...
PLAY

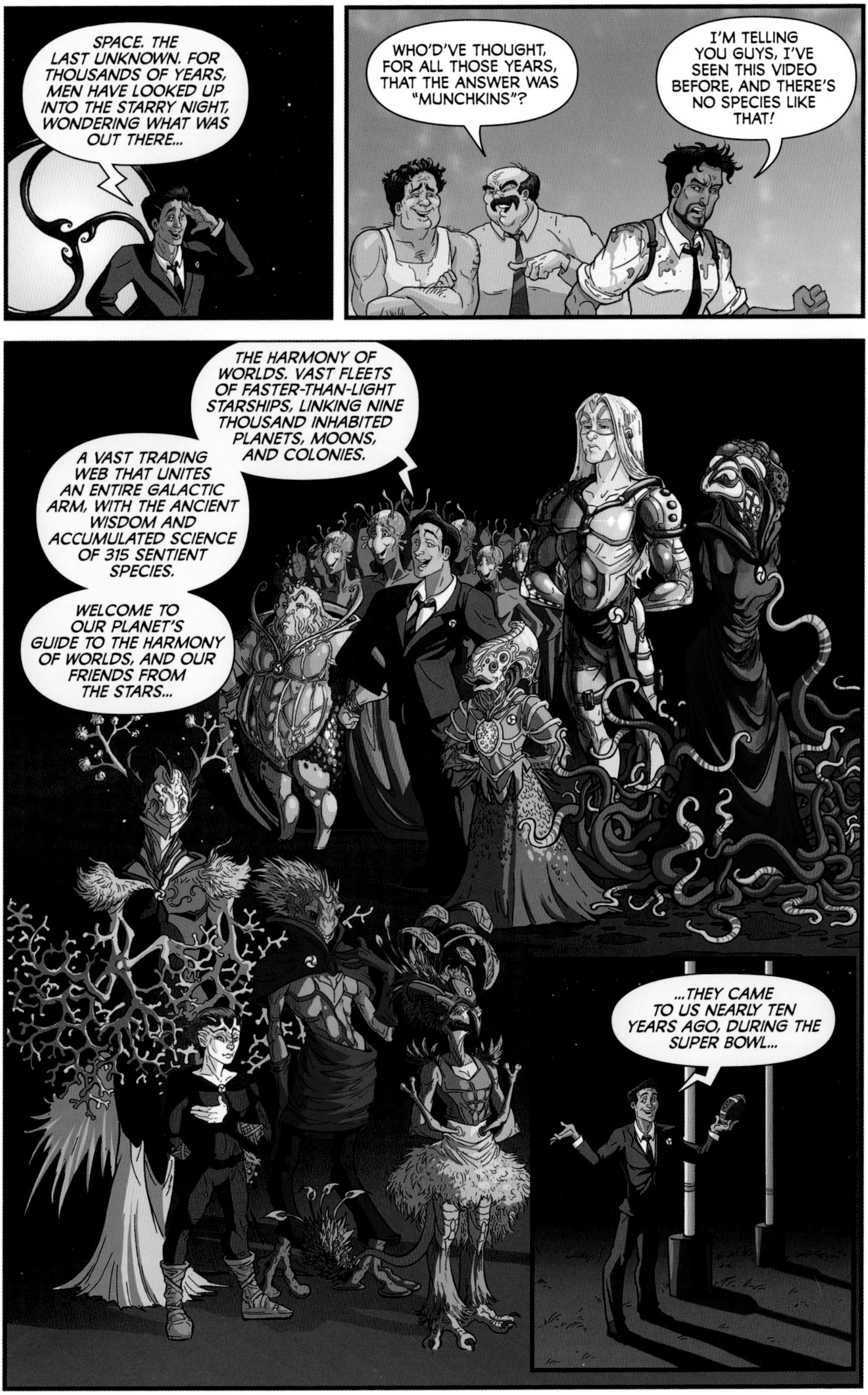
SPACE. THE LAST UNKNOWN. FOR THOUSANDS OF YEARS, MEN HAVE LOOKED UP INTO THE STARRY NIGHT, WONDERING WHAT WAS OUT THERE...
WHO'D'VE THOUGHT, FOR ALL THOSE YEARS, THAT THE ANSWER WAS "MUNCHKINS"?
I'M TELLING YOU GUYS, I'VE SEEN THIS VIDEO BEFORE, AND THERE'S NO SPECIES LIKE THAT!
THE HARMONY OF WORLDS. VAST FLEETS OF FASTER-THAN-LIGHT STARSHIPS, LINKING NINE THOUSAND INHABITED PLANETS, MOONS, AND COLONIES.
A VAST TRADING WEB THAT UNITES AN ENTIRE GALACTIC ARM, WITH THE ANCIENT WISDOM AND ACCUMULATED SCIENCE OF 315 SENTIENT SPECIES.
WELCOME TO OUR PLANET'S GUIDE TO THE HARMONY OF WORLDS, AND OUR FRIENDS FROM THE STARS...
...THEY CAME TO US NEARLY TEN YEARS AGO, DURING THE SUPER BOWL...

CHAPTER THREE

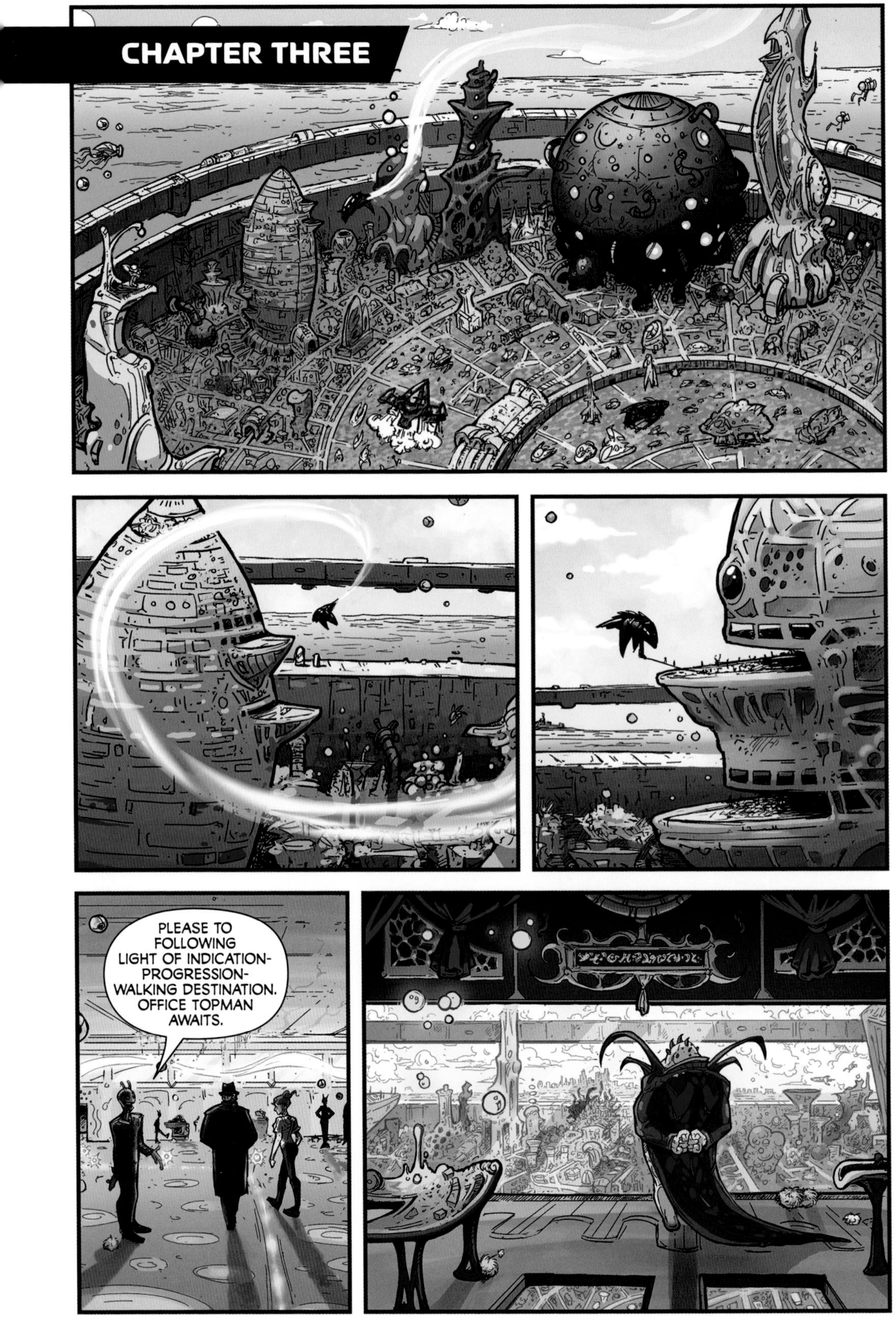
PLEASE TO FOLLOWING LIGHT OF INDICATION-PROGRESSION-WALKING DESTINATION. OFFICE TOPMAN AWAITS.

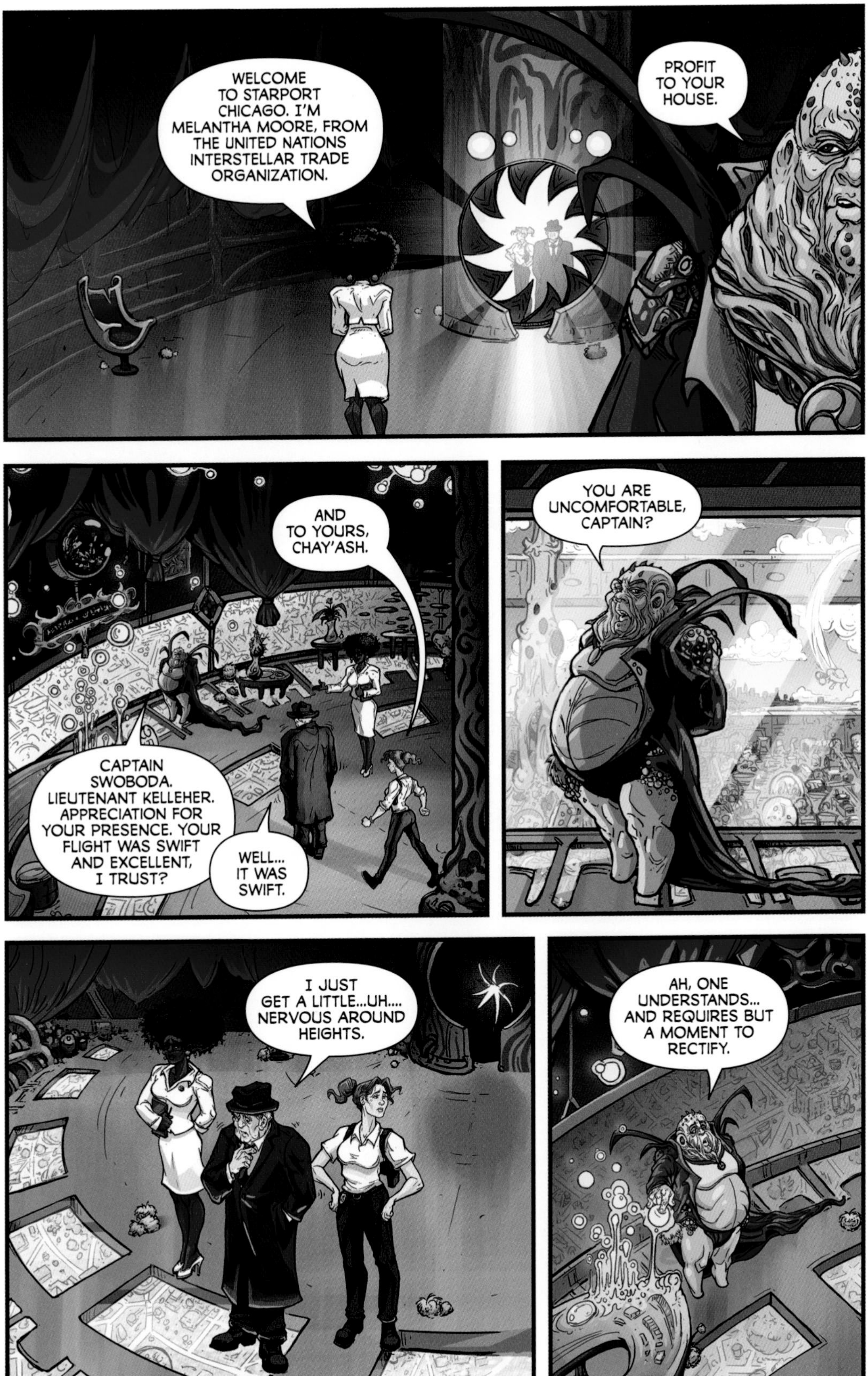
WELCOME TO STARPORT CHICAGO. I'M MELANTHA MOORE, FROM THE UNITED NATIONS INTERSTELLAR TRADE ORGANIZATION.
PROFIT TO YOUR HOUSE.
AND TO YOURS, CHAY'ASH.
CAPTAIN SWOBODA. LIEUTENANT KELLEHER. APPRECIATION FOR YOUR PRESENCE. YOUR FLIGHT WAS SWIFT AND EXCELLENT, I TRUST?
WELL... IT WAS SWIFT.
YOU ARE UNCOMFORTABLE, CAPTAIN?
I JUST GET A LITTLE...UH.... NERVOUS AROUND HEIGHTS.
AH, ONE UNDERSTANDS... AND REQUIRES BUT A MOMENT TO RECTIFY.

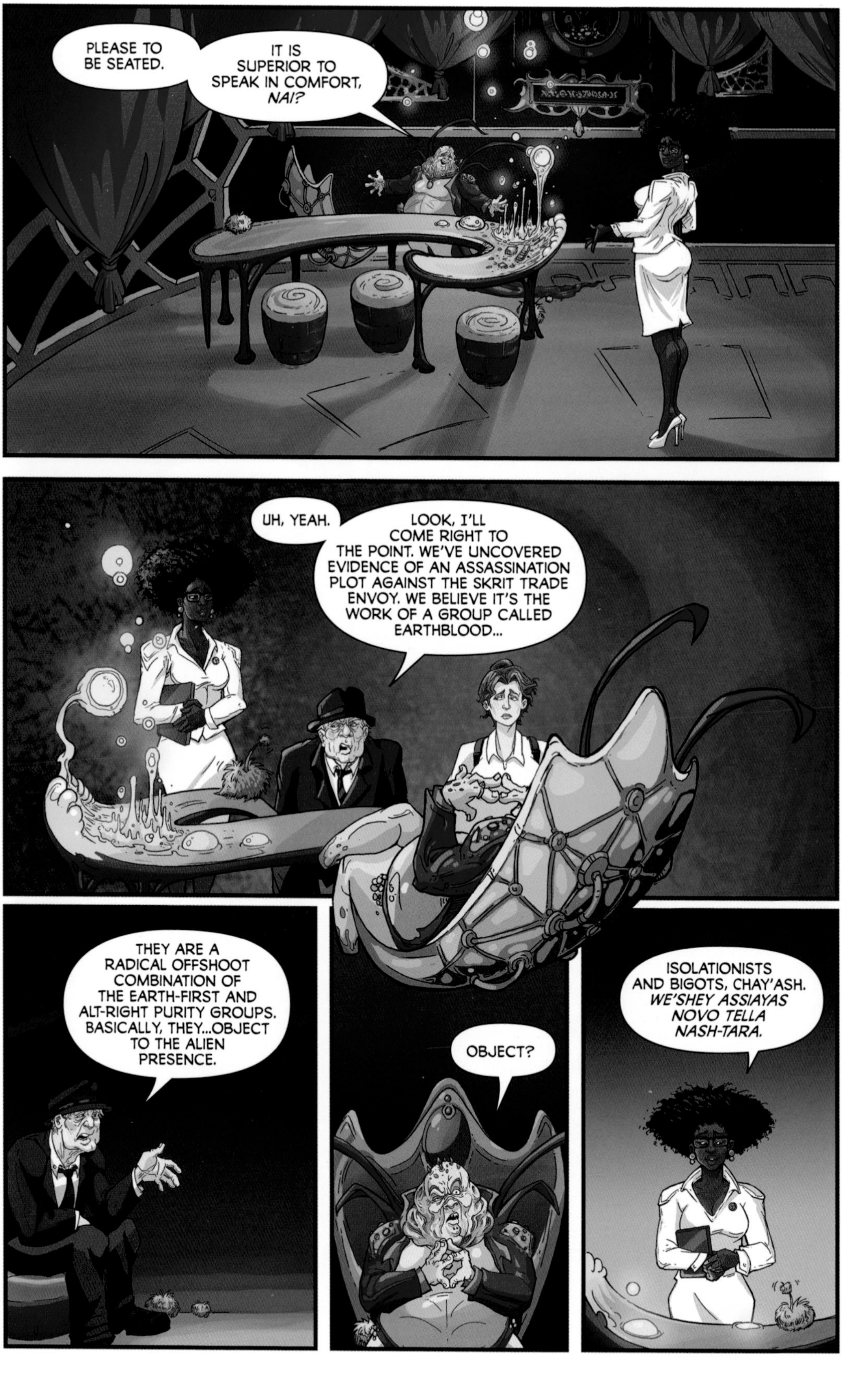
PLEASE TO BE SEATED.
IT IS SUPERIOR TO SPEAK IN COMFORT, *NAI?*
UH, YEAH.
LOOK, I'LL COME RIGHT TO THE POINT. WE'VE UNCOVERED EVIDENCE OF AN ASSASSINATION PLOT AGAINST THE SKRIT TRADE ENVOY. WE BELIEVE IT'S THE WORK OF A GROUP CALLED EARTHBLOOD...
THEY ARE A RADICAL OFFSHOOT COMBINATION OF THE EARTH-FIRST AND ALT-RIGHT PURITY GROUPS. BASICALLY, THEY...OBJECT TO THE ALIEN PRESENCE.
OBJECT?
ISOLATIONISTS AND BIGOTS, CHAY'ASH. *WE'SHEY ASSIAYAS NOVO TELLA NASH-TARA.*

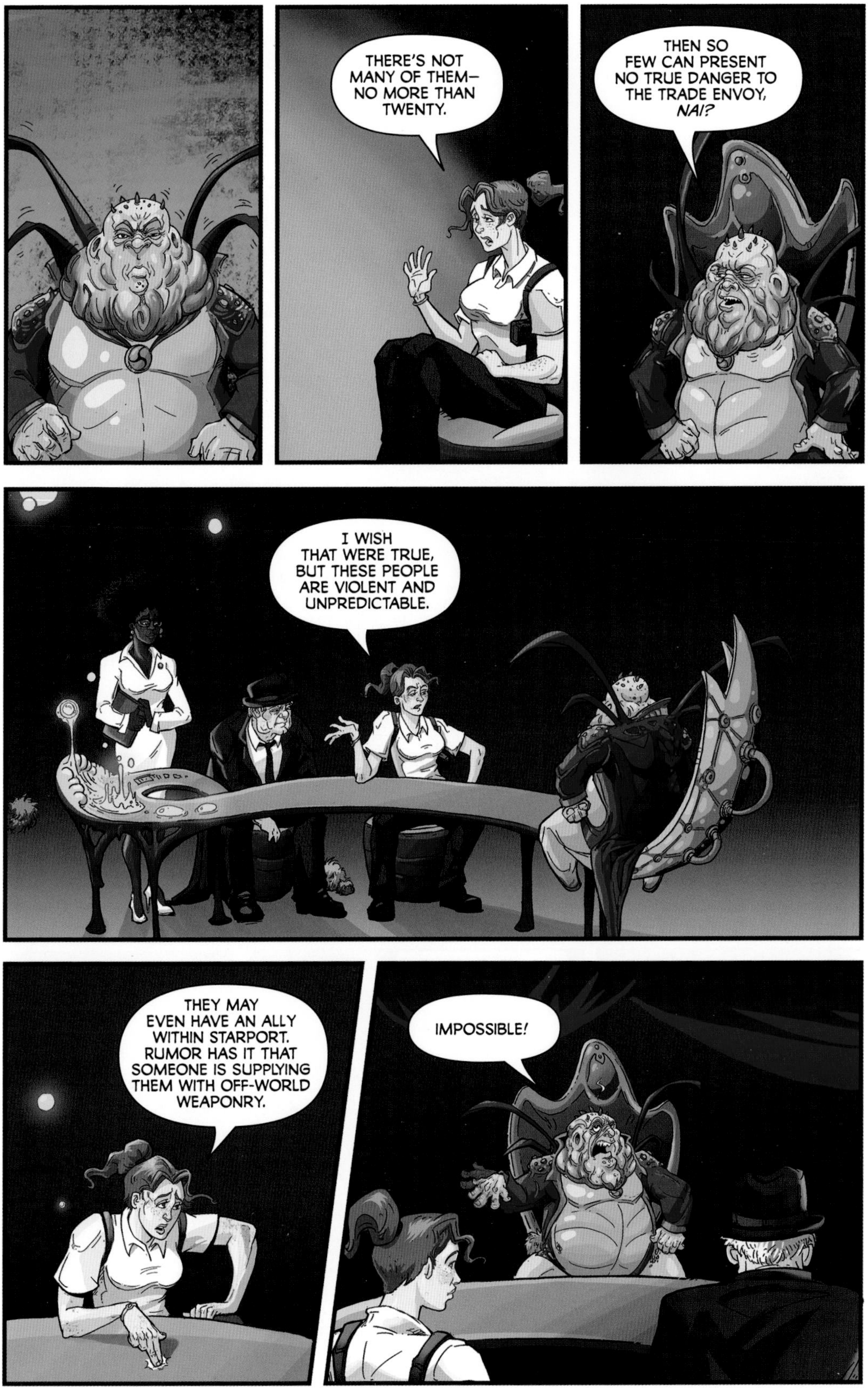
THERE'S NOT MANY OF THEM— NO MORE THAN TWENTY.
THEN SO FEW CAN PRESENT NO TRUE DANGER TO THE TRADE ENVOY, *NAI?*
I WISH THAT WERE TRUE, BUT THESE PEOPLE ARE VIOLENT AND UNPREDICTABLE.
THEY MAY EVEN HAVE AN ALLY WITHIN STARPORT. RUMOR HAS IT THAT SOMEONE IS SUPPLYING THEM WITH OFF-WORLD WEAPONRY.
IMPOSSIBLE!

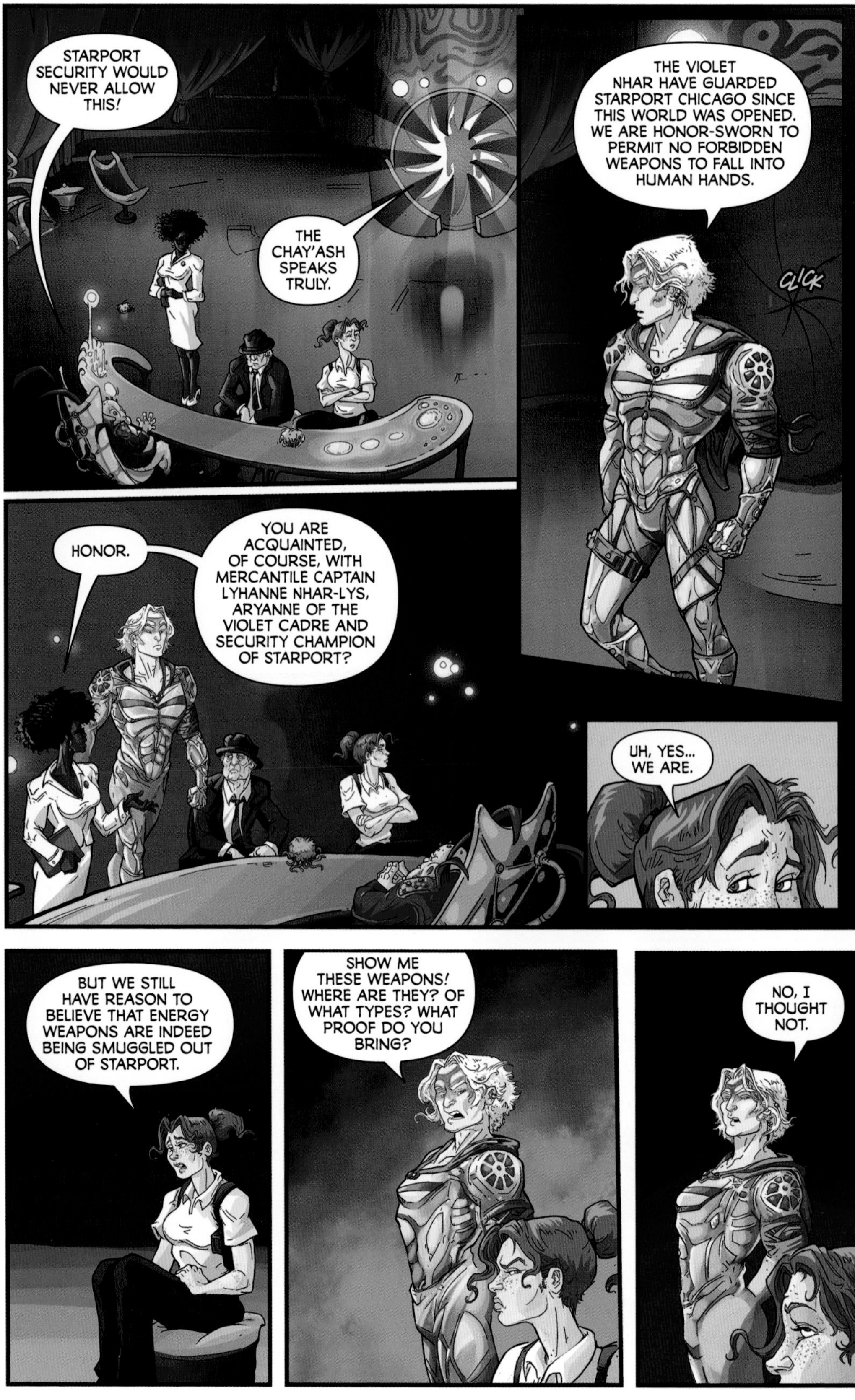
STARPORT SECURITY WOULD NEVER ALLOW THIS!
THE CHAY'ASH SPEAKS TRULY.
THE VIOLET NHAR HAVE GUARDED STARPORT CHICAGO SINCE THIS WORLD WAS OPENED. WE ARE HONOR-SWORN TO PERMIT NO FORBIDDEN WEAPONS TO FALL INTO HUMAN HANDS.
CLICK
HONOR.
YOU ARE ACQUAINTED, OF COURSE, WITH MERCANTILE CAPTAIN LYHANNE NHAR-LYS, ARYANNE OF THE VIOLET CADRE AND SECURITY CHAMPION OF STARPORT?
UH, YES... WE ARE.
BUT WE STILL HAVE REASON TO BELIEVE THAT ENERGY WEAPONS ARE INDEED BEING SMUGGLED OUT OF STARPORT.
SHOW ME THESE WEAPONS! WHERE ARE THEY? OF WHAT TYPES? WHAT PROOF DO YOU BRING?
NO, I THOUGHT NOT.

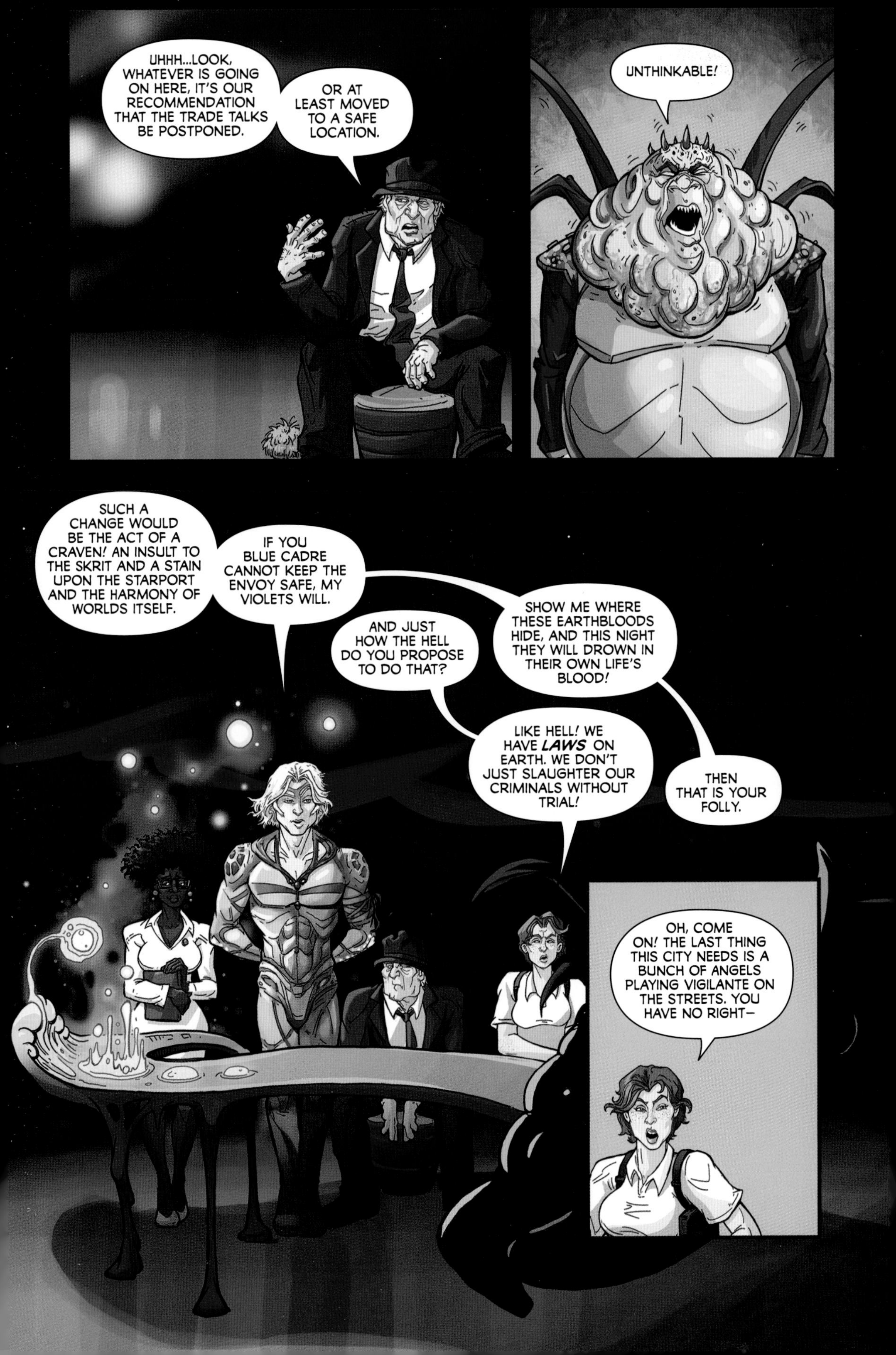

UHHH...LOOK, WHATEVER IS GOING ON HERE, IT'S OUR RECOMMENDATION THAT THE TRADE TALKS BE POSTPONED.
OR AT LEAST MOVED TO A SAFE LOCATION.
UNTHINKABLE!
SUCH A CHANGE WOULD BE THE ACT OF A CRAVEN! AN INSULT TO THE SKRIT AND A STAIN UPON THE STARPORT AND THE HARMONY OF WORLDS ITSELF.
IF YOU BLUE CADRE CANNOT KEEP THE ENVOY SAFE, MY VIOLETS WILL.
AND JUST HOW THE HELL DO YOU PROPOSE TO DO THAT?
SHOW ME WHERE THESE EARTHBLOODS HIDE, AND THIS NIGHT THEY WILL DROWN IN THEIR OWN LIFE'S BLOOD!
LIKE HELL! WE HAVE *LAWS* ON EARTH. WE DON'T JUST SLAUGHTER OUR CRIMINALS WITHOUT TRIAL!
THEN THAT IS YOUR FOLLY.
OH, COME ON! THE LAST THING THIS CITY NEEDS IS A BUNCH OF ANGELS PLAYING VIGILANTE ON THE STREETS. YOU HAVE NO RIGHT–

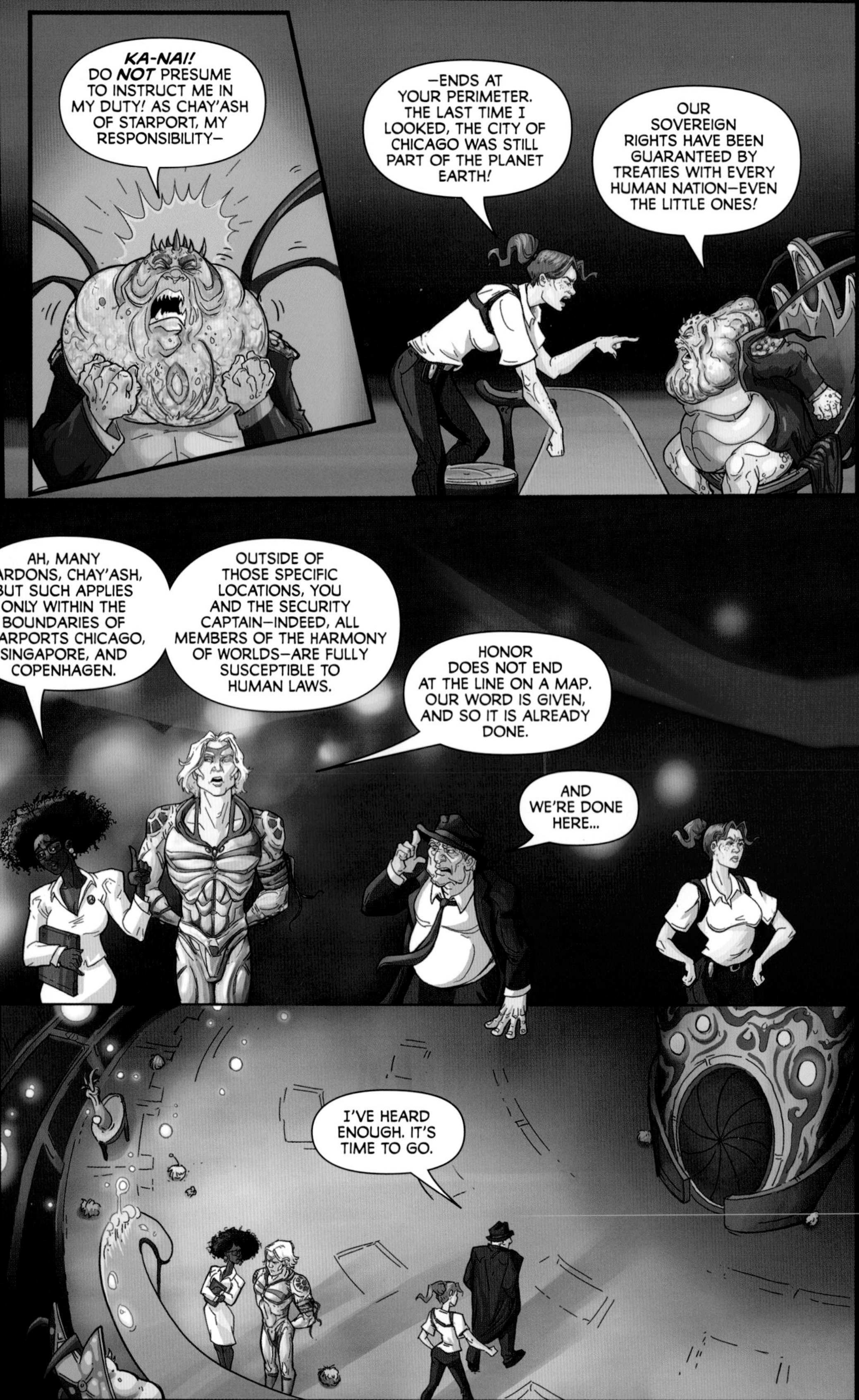
KA-NAI! DO NOT PRESUME TO INSTRUCT ME IN MY DUTY! AS CHAY'ASH OF STARPORT, MY RESPONSIBILITY–
–ENDS AT YOUR PERIMETER. THE LAST TIME I LOOKED, THE CITY OF CHICAGO WAS STILL PART OF THE PLANET EARTH!
OUR SOVEREIGN RIGHTS HAVE BEEN GUARANTEED BY TREATIES WITH EVERY HUMAN NATION–EVEN THE LITTLE ONES!
AH, MANY PARDONS, CHAY'ASH, BUT SUCH APPLIES ONLY WITHIN THE BOUNDARIES OF STARPORTS CHICAGO, SINGAPORE, AND COPENHAGEN.
OUTSIDE OF THOSE SPECIFIC LOCATIONS, YOU AND THE SECURITY CAPTAIN–INDEED, ALL MEMBERS OF THE HARMONY OF WORLDS–ARE FULLY SUSCEPTIBLE TO HUMAN LAWS.
HONOR DOES NOT END AT THE LINE ON A MAP. OUR WORD IS GIVEN, AND SO IT IS ALREADY DONE.
AND WE'RE DONE HERE...
I'VE HEARD ENOUGH. IT'S TIME TO GO.

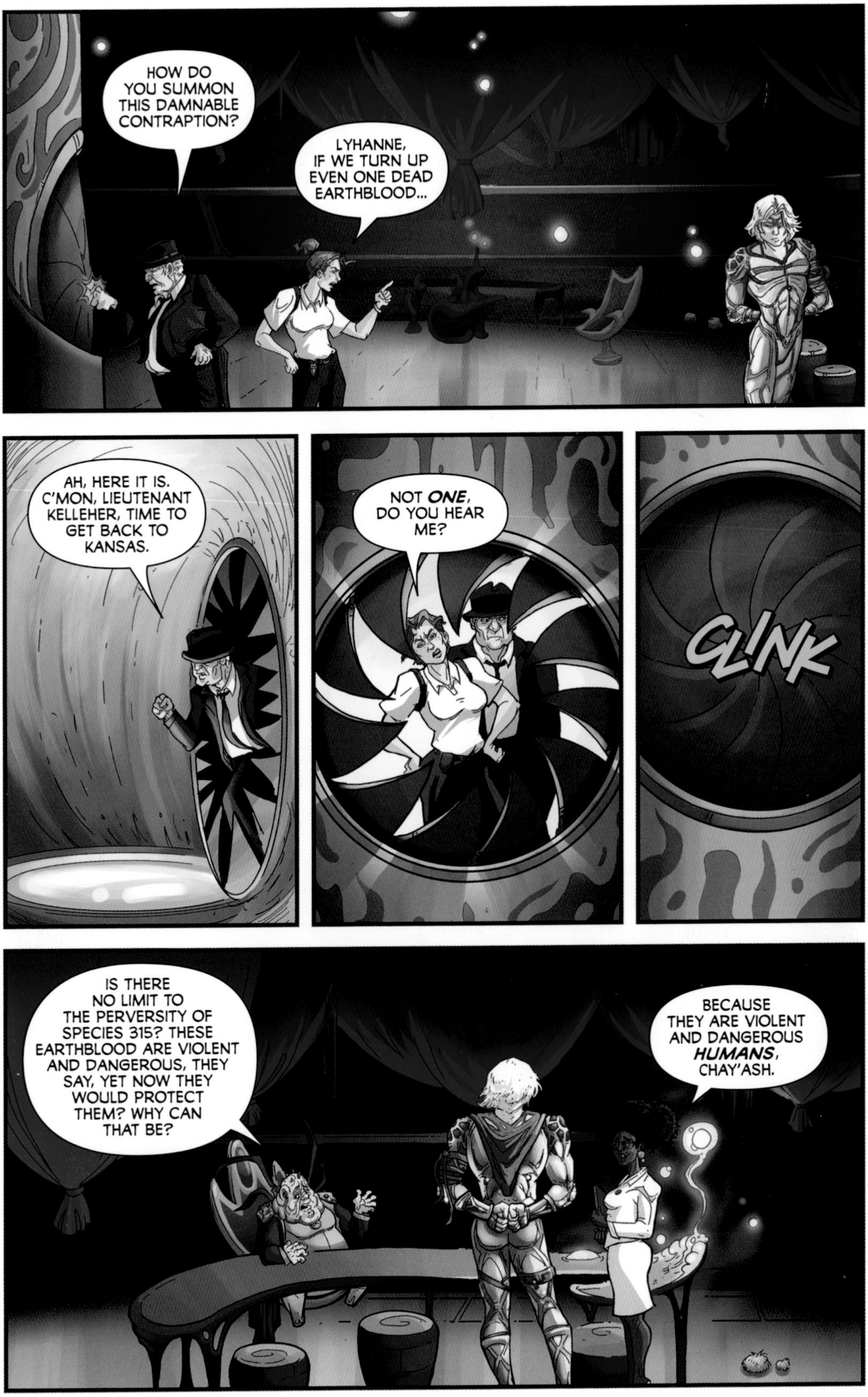
HOW DO YOU SUMMON THIS DAMNABLE CONTRAPTION?
LYHANNE, IF WE TURN UP EVEN ONE DEAD EARTHBLOOD...
AH, HERE IT IS. C'MON, LIEUTENANT KELLEHER, TIME TO GET BACK TO KANSAS.
NOT *ONE*, DO YOU HEAR ME?
CLINK
IS THERE NO LIMIT TO THE PERVERSITY OF SPECIES 315? THESE EARTHBLOOD ARE VIOLENT AND DANGEROUS, THEY SAY, YET NOW THEY WOULD PROTECT THEM? WHY CAN THAT BE?
BECAUSE THEY ARE VIOLENT AND DANGEROUS ***HUMANS***, CHAY'ASH.

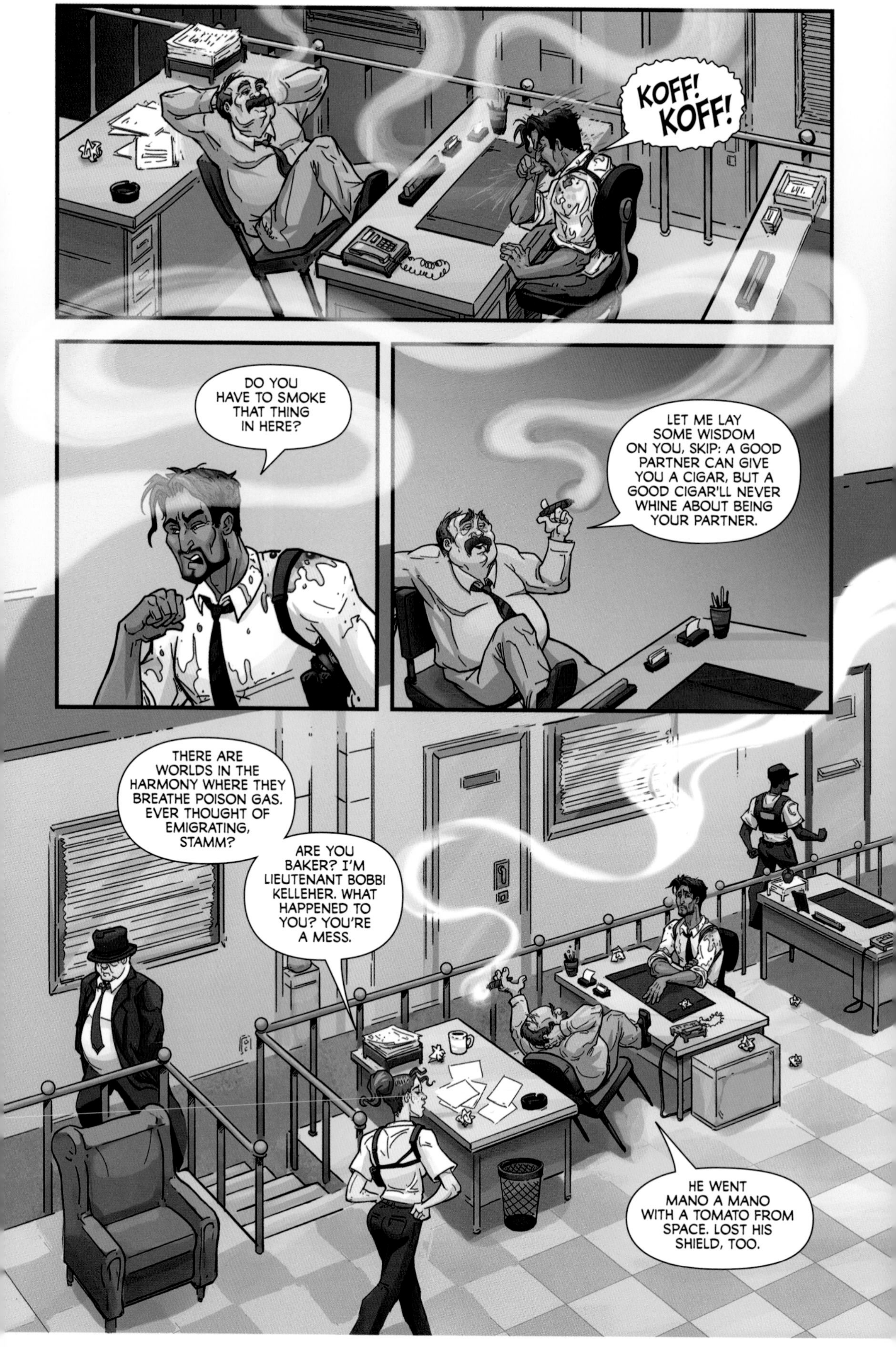
KOFF! KOFF!
DO YOU HAVE TO SMOKE THAT THING IN HERE?
LET ME LAY SOME WISDOM ON YOU, SKIP: A GOOD PARTNER CAN GIVE YOU A CIGAR, BUT A GOOD CIGAR'LL NEVER WHINE ABOUT BEING YOUR PARTNER.
THERE ARE WORLDS IN THE HARMONY WHERE THEY BREATHE POISON GAS. EVER THOUGHT OF EMIGRATING, STAMM?
ARE YOU BAKER? I'M LIEUTENANT BOBBI KELLEHER. WHAT HAPPENED TO YOU? YOU'RE A MESS.
HE WENT MANO A MANO WITH A TOMATO FROM SPACE. LOST HIS SHIELD, TOO.

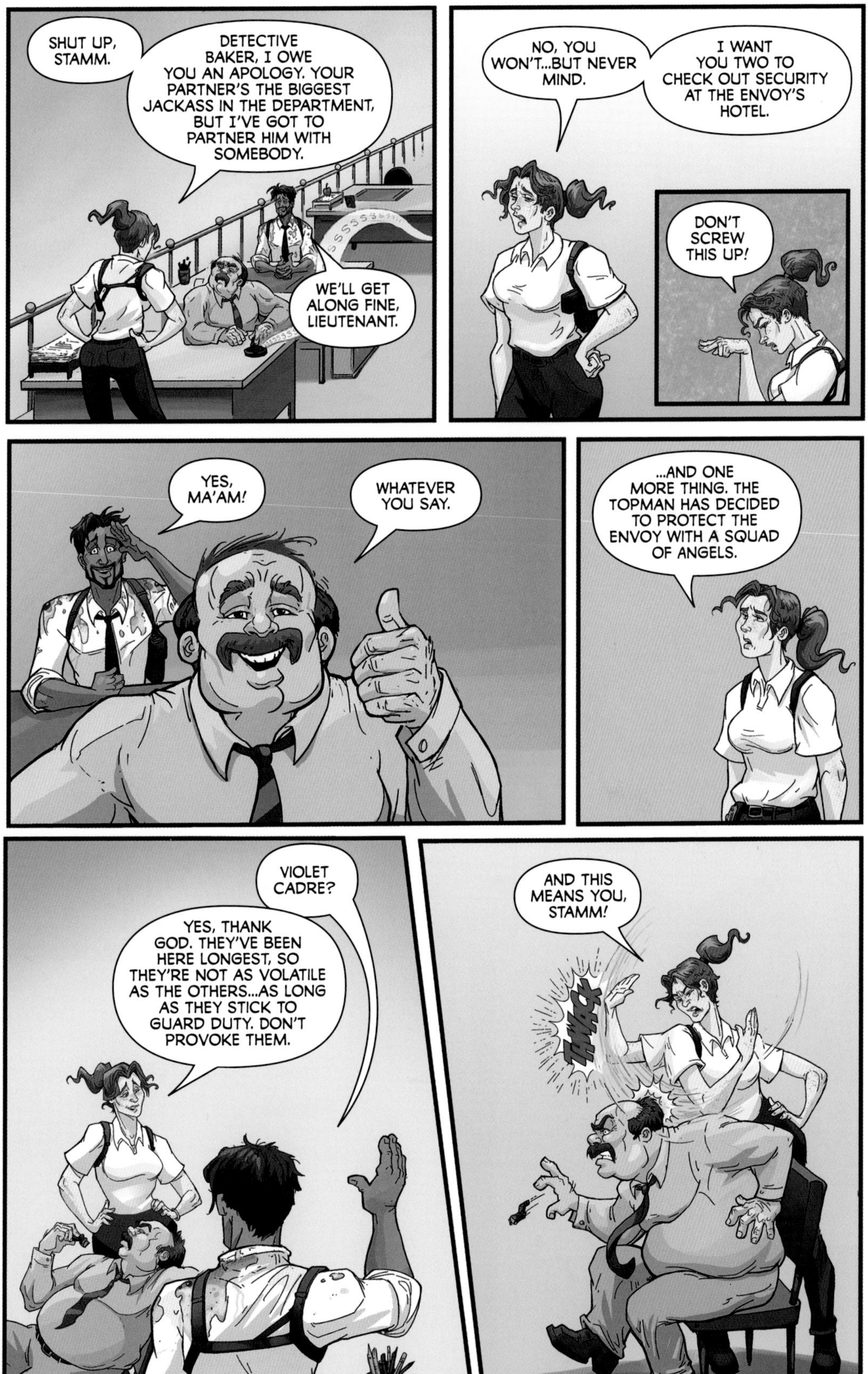
SHUT UP, STAMM.
DETECTIVE BAKER, I OWE YOU AN APOLOGY. YOUR PARTNER'S THE BIGGEST JACKASS IN THE DEPARTMENT, BUT I'VE GOT TO PARTNER HIM WITH SOMEBODY.
WE'LL GET ALONG FINE, LIEUTENANT.
NO, YOU WON'T...BUT NEVER MIND.
I WANT YOU TWO TO CHECK OUT SECURITY AT THE ENVOY'S HOTEL.
DON'T SCREW THIS UP!
YES, MA'AM!
WHATEVER YOU SAY.
...AND ONE MORE THING. THE TOPMAN HAS DECIDED TO PROTECT THE ENVOY WITH A SQUAD OF ANGELS.
VIOLET CADRE?
YES, THANK GOD. THEY'VE BEEN HERE LONGEST, SO THEY'RE NOT AS VOLATILE AS THE OTHERS...AS LONG AS THEY STICK TO GUARD DUTY. DON'T PROVOKE THEM.
AND THIS MEANS YOU, STAMM!
THWACK

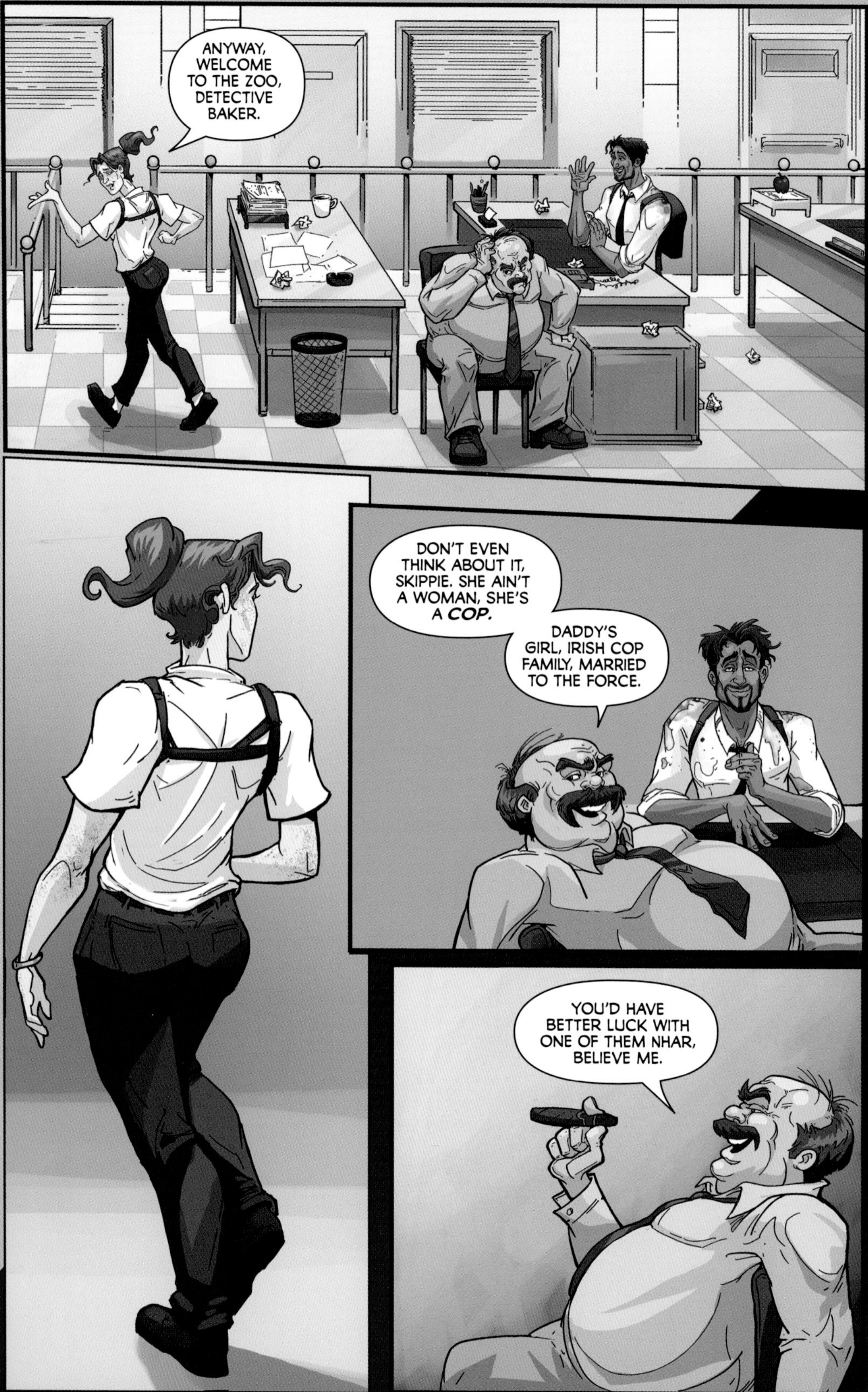
ANYWAY, WELCOME TO THE ZOO, DETECTIVE BAKER.
DON'T EVEN THINK ABOUT IT, SKIPPIE. SHE AIN'T A WOMAN, SHE'S A *COP.*
DADDY'S GIRL, IRISH COP FAMILY, MARRIED TO THE FORCE.
YOU'D HAVE BETTER LUCK WITH ONE OF THEM NHAR, BELIEVE ME.

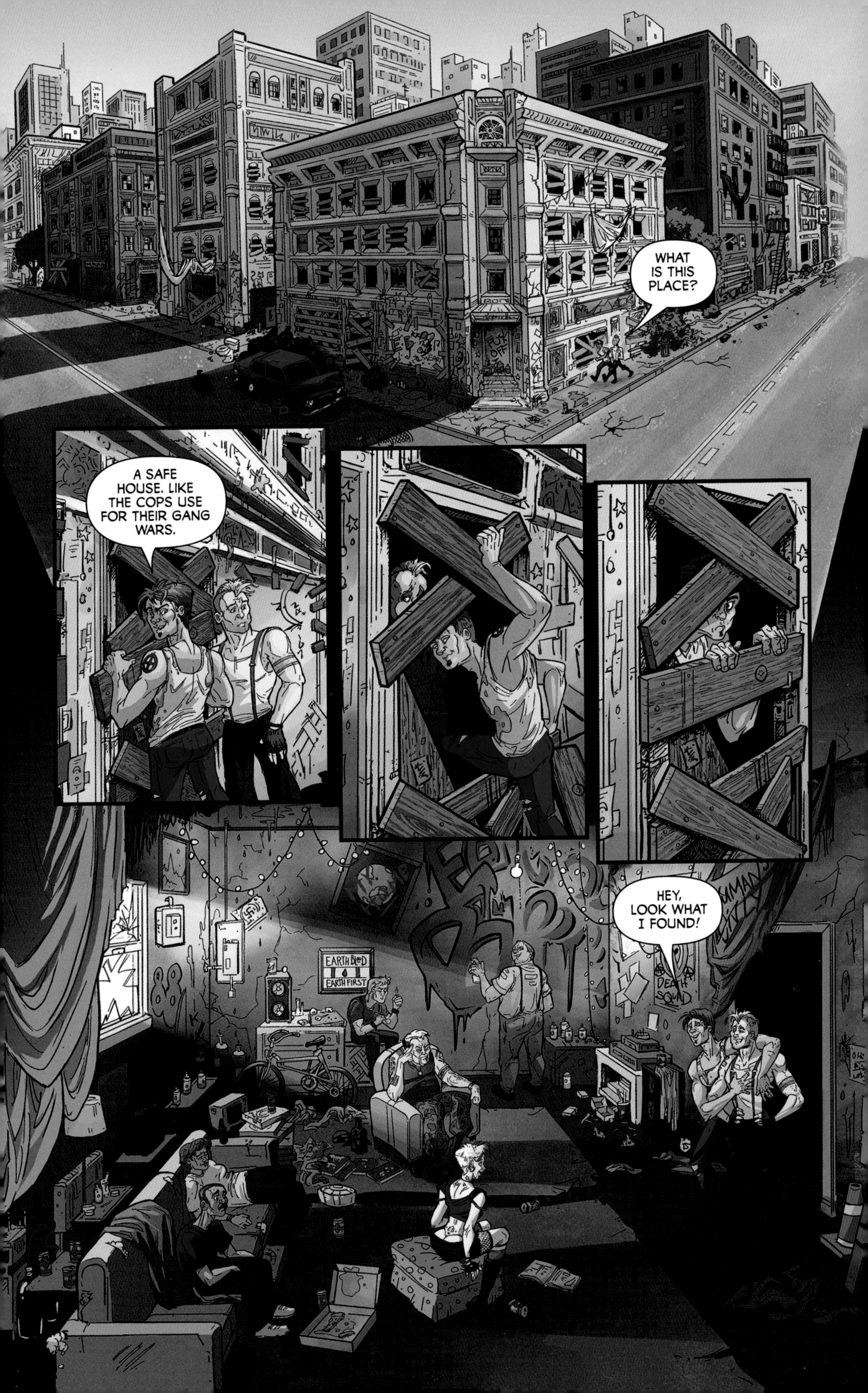
WHAT IS THIS PLACE?
A SAFE HOUSE. LIKE THE COPS USE FOR THEIR GANG WARS.
HEY, LOOK WHAT I FOUND!

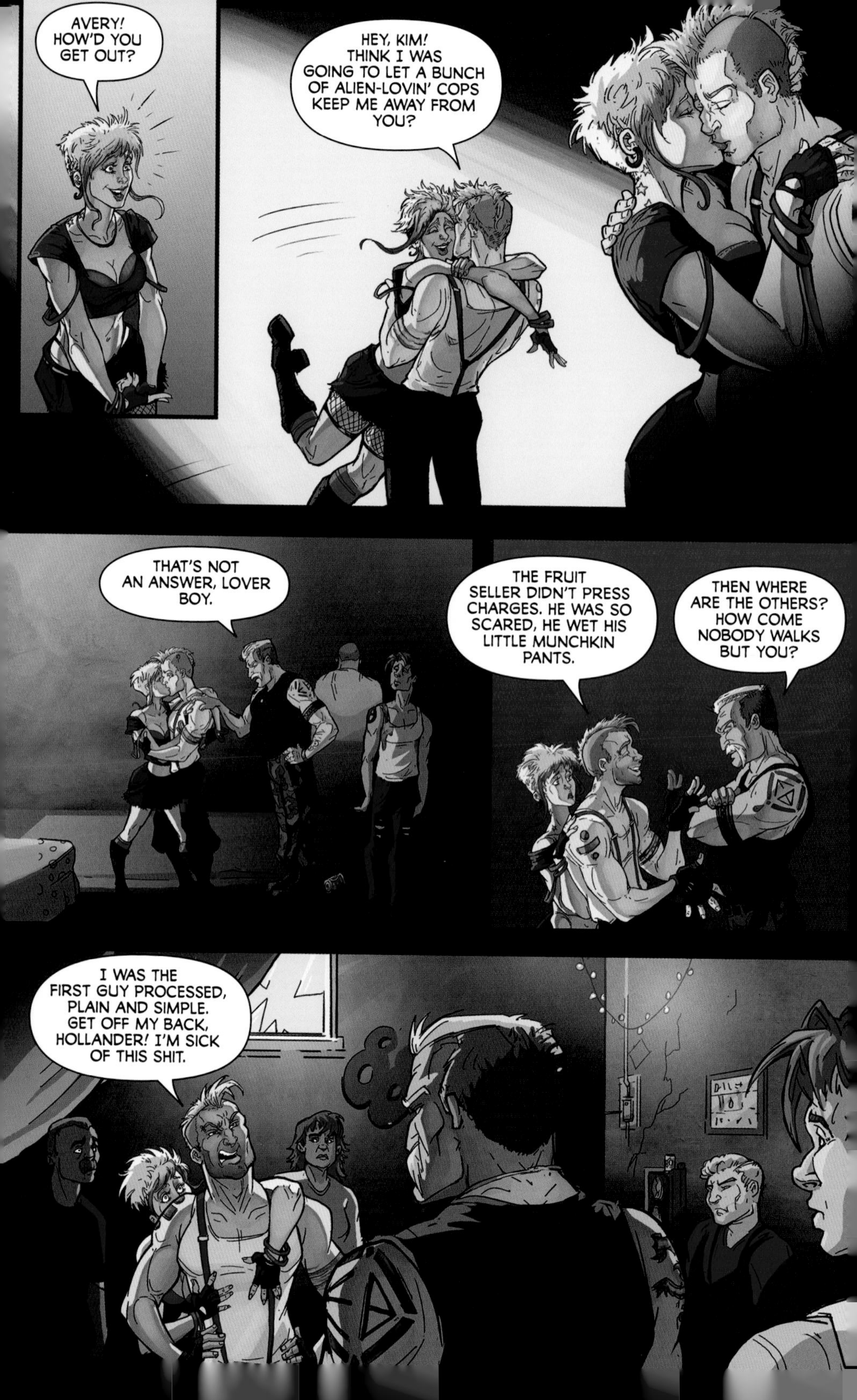
AVERY! HOW'D YOU GET OUT?
HEY, KIM! THINK I WAS GOING TO LET A BUNCH OF ALIEN-LOVIN' COPS KEEP ME AWAY FROM YOU?
THAT'S NOT AN ANSWER, LOVER BOY.
THE FRUIT SELLER DIDN'T PRESS CHARGES. HE WAS SO SCARED, HE WET HIS LITTLE MUNCHKIN PANTS.
THEN WHERE ARE THE OTHERS? HOW COME NOBODY WALKS BUT YOU?
I WAS THE FIRST GUY PROCESSED, PLAIN AND SIMPLE. GET OFF MY BACK, HOLLANDER! I'M SICK OF THIS SHIT.

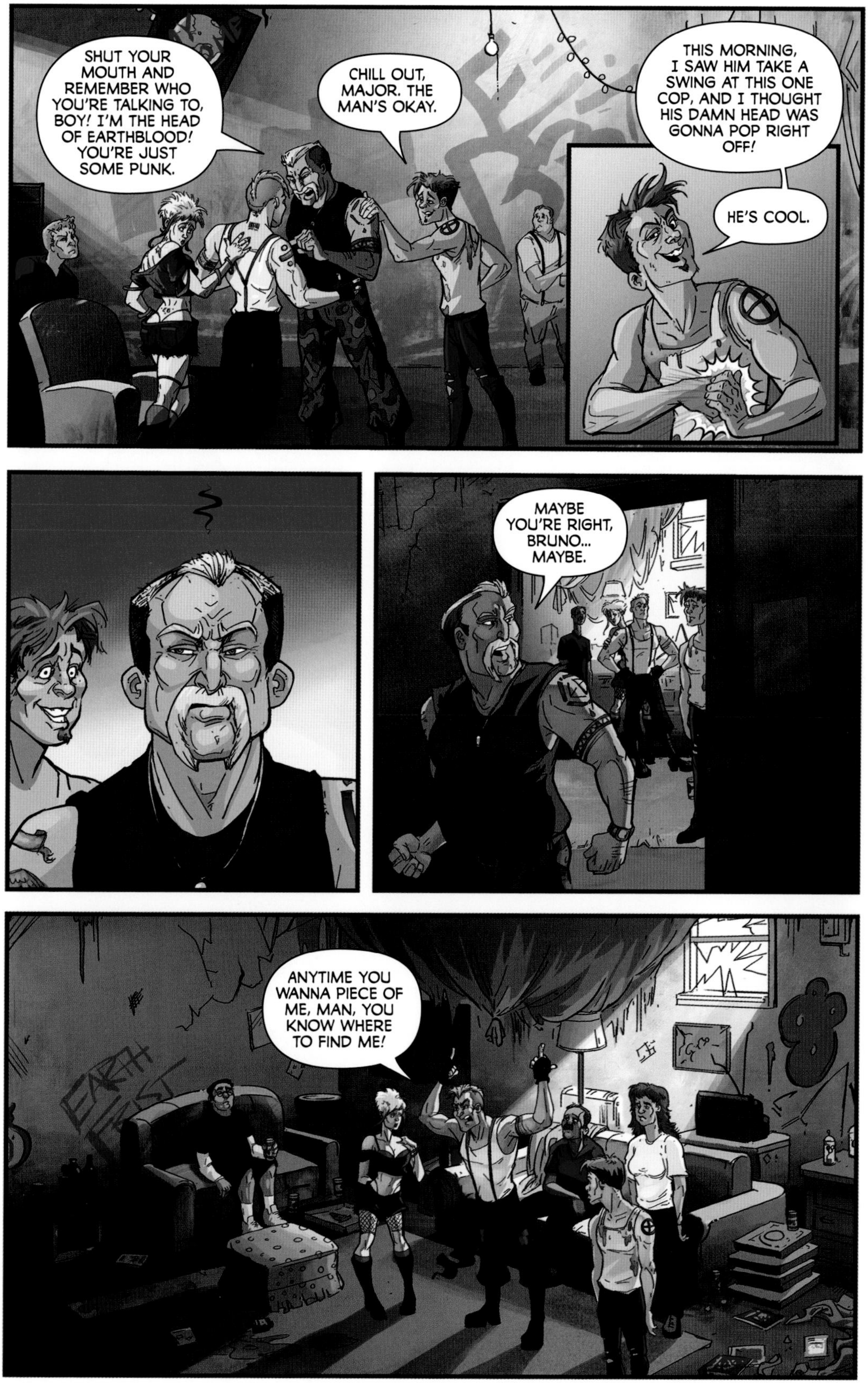

SHUT YOUR MOUTH AND REMEMBER WHO YOU'RE TALKING TO, BOY! I'M THE HEAD OF EARTHBLOOD! YOU'RE JUST SOME PUNK.
CHILL OUT, MAJOR. THE MAN'S OKAY.
THIS MORNING, I SAW HIM TAKE A SWING AT THIS ONE COP, AND I THOUGHT HIS DAMN HEAD WAS GONNA POP RIGHT OFF!
HE'S COOL.
MAYBE YOU'RE RIGHT, BRUNO... MAYBE.
ANYTIME YOU WANNA PIECE OF ME, MAN, YOU KNOW WHERE TO FIND ME!
EARTH FIRST

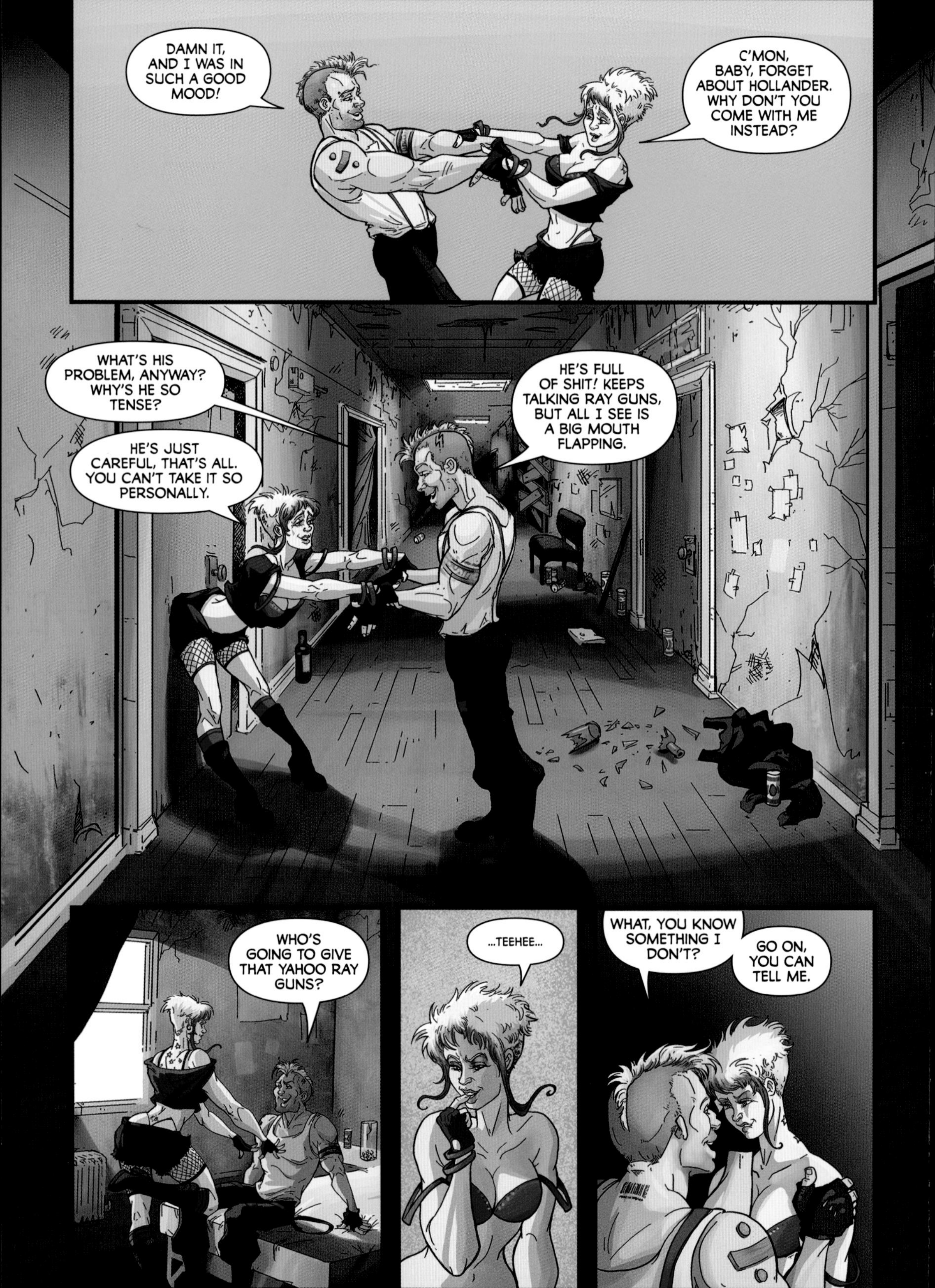
DAMN IT, AND I WAS IN SUCH A GOOD MOOD!
C'MON, BABY, FORGET ABOUT HOLLANDER. WHY DON'T YOU COME WITH ME INSTEAD?
WHAT'S HIS PROBLEM, ANYWAY? WHY'S HE SO TENSE?
HE'S JUST CAREFUL, THAT'S ALL. YOU CAN'T TAKE IT SO PERSONALLY.
HE'S FULL OF SHIT! KEEPS TALKING RAY GUNS, BUT ALL I SEE IS A BIG MOUTH FLAPPING.
WHO'S GOING TO GIVE THAT YAHOO RAY GUNS?
...TEEHEE...
WHAT, YOU KNOW SOMETHING I DON'T?
GO ON, YOU CAN TELL ME.

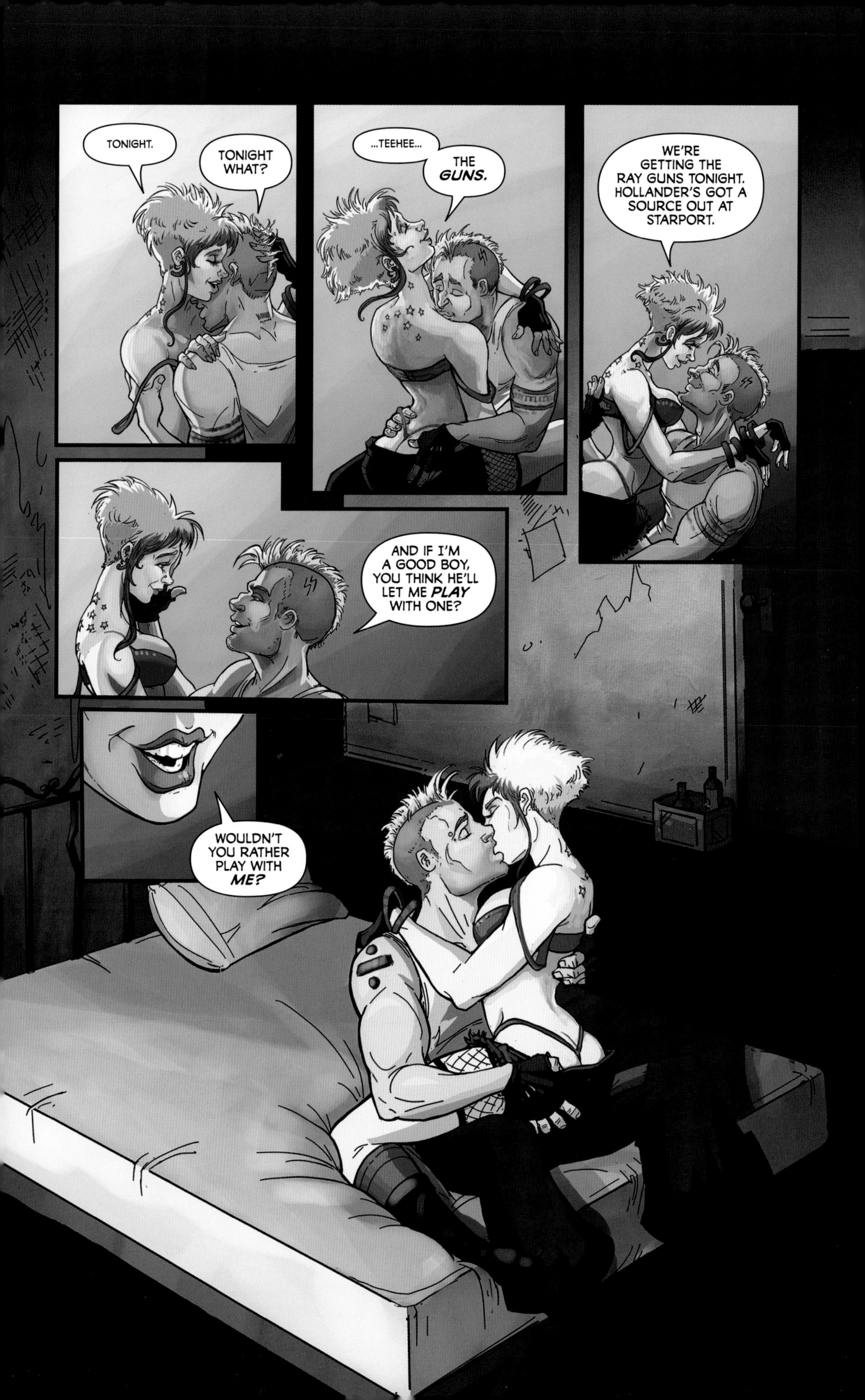
TONIGHT.
TONIGHT WHAT?
...TEEHEE...
THE GUNS.
WE'RE GETTING THE RAY GUNS TONIGHT. HOLLANDER'S GOT A SOURCE OUT AT STARPORT.
AND IF I'M A GOOD BOY, YOU THINK HE'LL LET ME PLAY WITH ONE?
WOULDN'T YOU RATHER PLAY WITH ME?

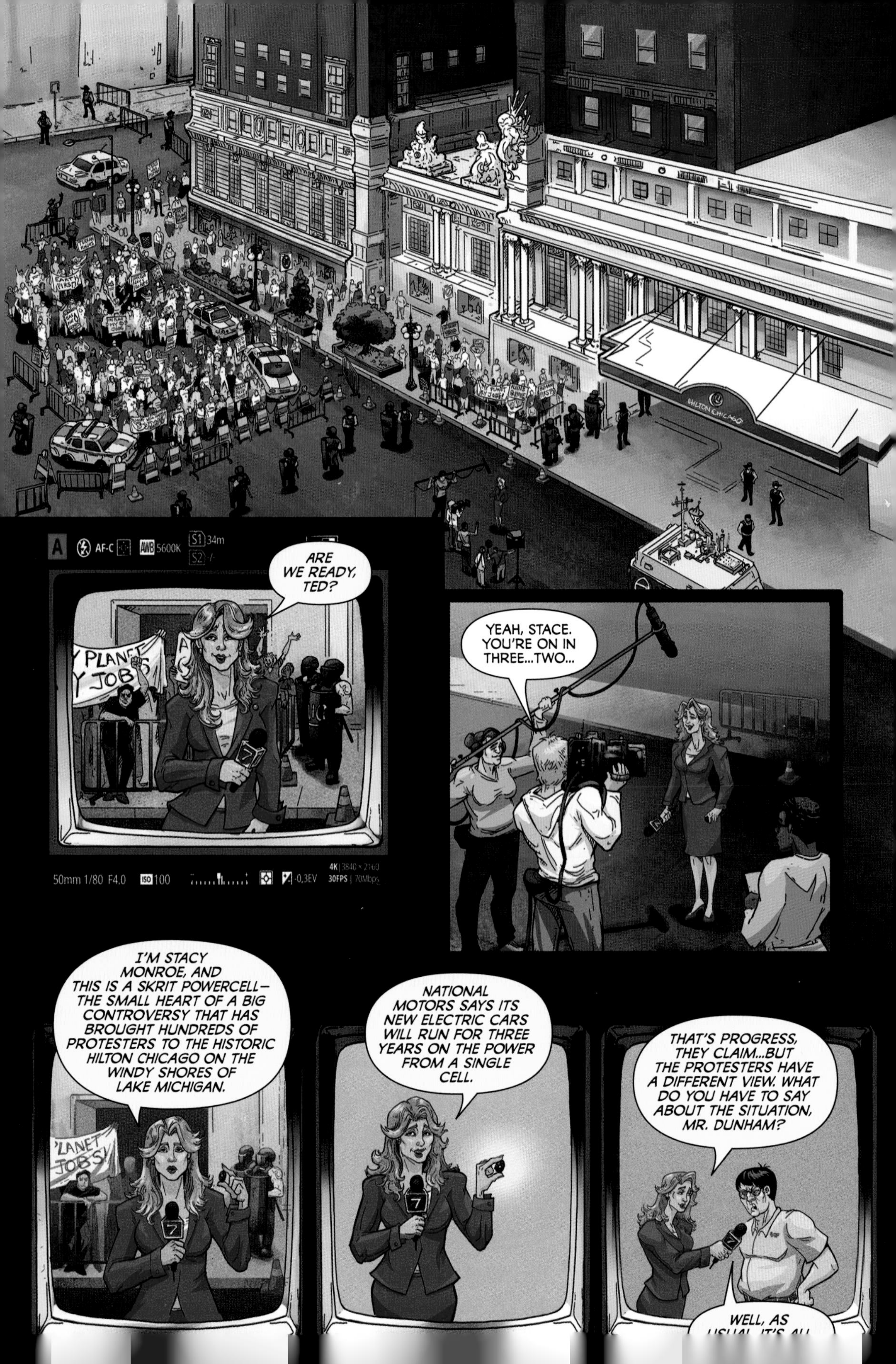
A AF-C AWB 5600K S1 34m S2 -/-
ARE WE READY, TED?
50mm 1/80 F4.0 ISO 100 -0,3EV
4K | 3840 × 2160 30FPS | 70Mbps
YEAH, STACE. YOU'RE ON IN THREE...TWO...
I'M STACY MONROE, AND THIS IS A SKRIT POWERCELL— THE SMALL HEART OF A BIG CONTROVERSY THAT HAS BROUGHT HUNDREDS OF PROTESTERS TO THE HISTORIC HILTON CHICAGO ON THE WINDY SHORES OF LAKE MICHIGAN.
NATIONAL MOTORS SAYS ITS NEW ELECTRIC CARS WILL RUN FOR THREE YEARS ON THE POWER FROM A SINGLE CELL.
THAT'S PROGRESS, THEY CLAIM...BUT THE PROTESTERS HAVE A DIFFERENT VIEW. WHAT DO YOU HAVE TO SAY ABOUT THE SITUATION, MR. DUNHAM?
WELL, AS

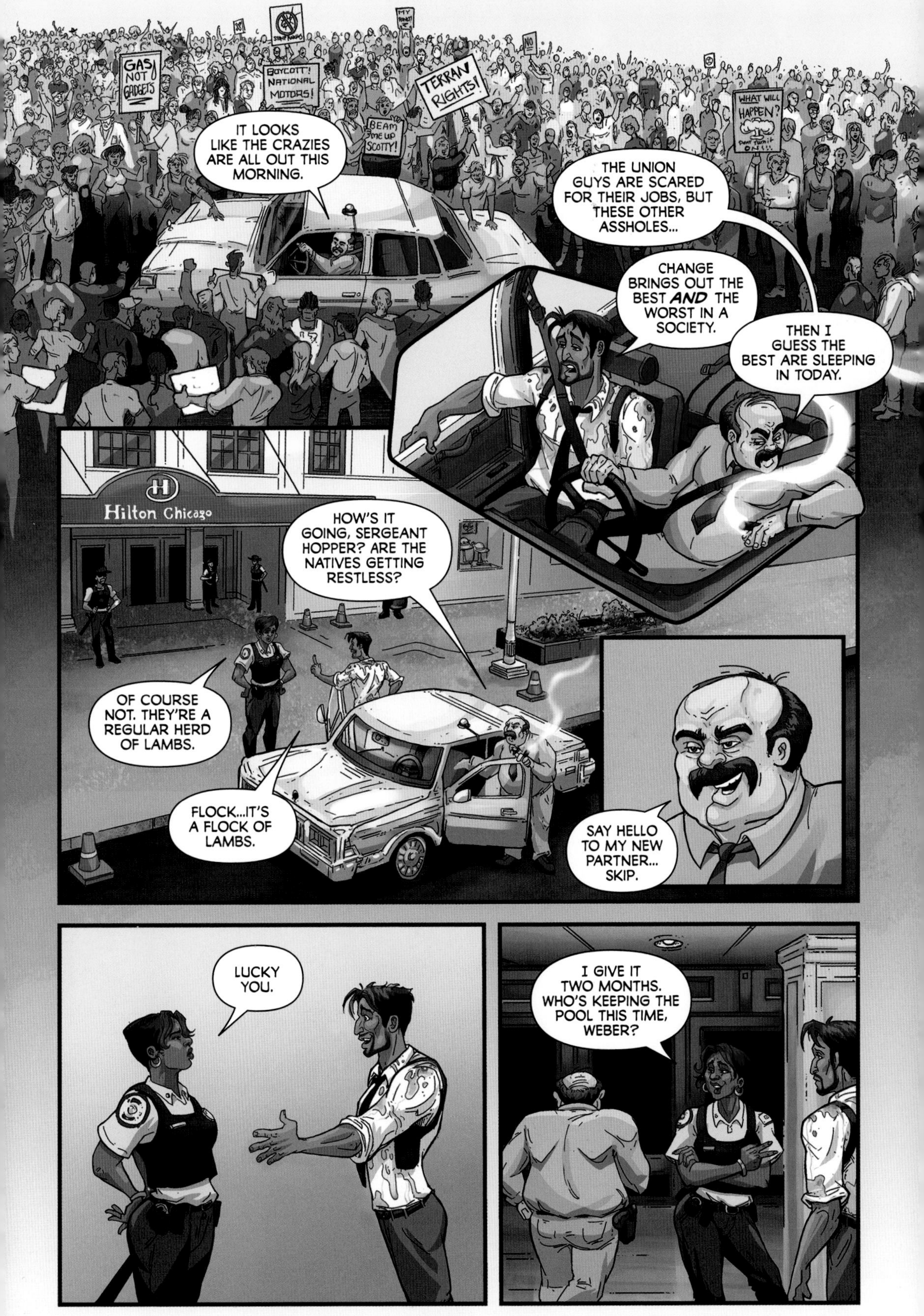
GAS NOT GADGETS
BOYCOTT! NATIONAL MOTORS!
TERRAN RIGHTS!
BEAM me UP SCOTTY!
WHAT WILL HAPPEN?
IT LOOKS LIKE THE CRAZIES ARE ALL OUT THIS MORNING.
THE UNION GUYS ARE SCARED FOR THEIR JOBS, BUT THESE OTHER ASSHOLES...
CHANGE BRINGS OUT THE BEST AND THE WORST IN A SOCIETY.
THEN I GUESS THE BEST ARE SLEEPING IN TODAY.
Hilton Chicago
HOW'S IT GOING, SERGEANT HOPPER? ARE THE NATIVES GETTING RESTLESS?
OF COURSE NOT. THEY'RE A REGULAR HERD OF LAMBS.
FLOCK...IT'S A FLOCK OF LAMBS.
SAY HELLO TO MY NEW PARTNER... SKIP.
LUCKY YOU.
I GIVE IT TWO MONTHS. WHO'S KEEPING THE POOL THIS TIME, WEBER?

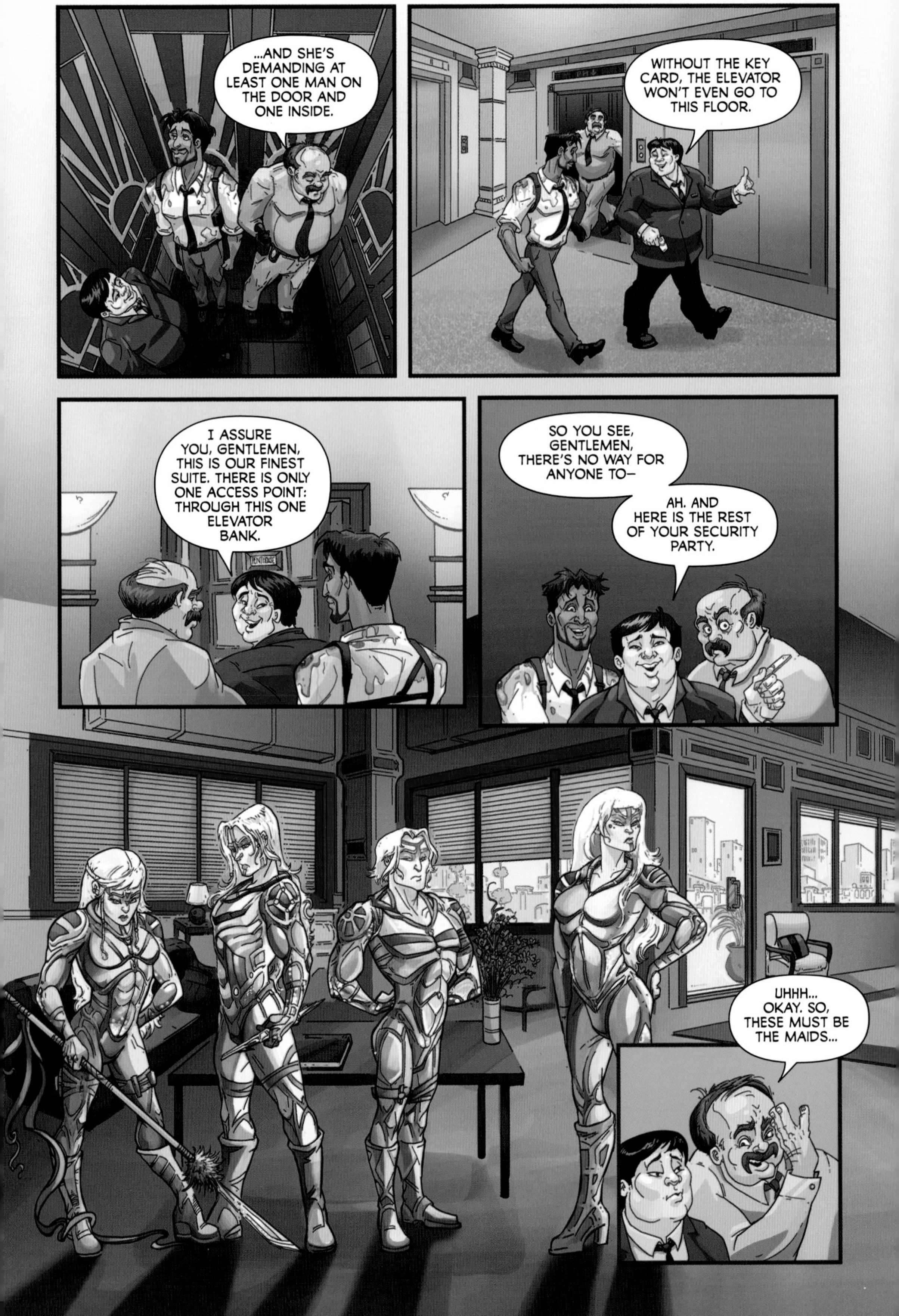
...AND SHE'S DEMANDING AT LEAST ONE MAN ON THE DOOR AND ONE INSIDE.
WITHOUT THE KEY CARD, THE ELEVATOR WON'T EVEN GO TO THIS FLOOR.
I ASSURE YOU, GENTLEMEN, THIS IS OUR FINEST SUITE. THERE IS ONLY ONE ACCESS POINT: THROUGH THIS ONE ELEVATOR BANK.
PENTHOUSE
SO YOU SEE, GENTLEMEN, THERE'S NO WAY FOR ANYONE TO—
AH. AND HERE IS THE REST OF YOUR SECURITY PARTY.
UHHH... OKAY. SO, THESE MUST BE THE MAIDS...

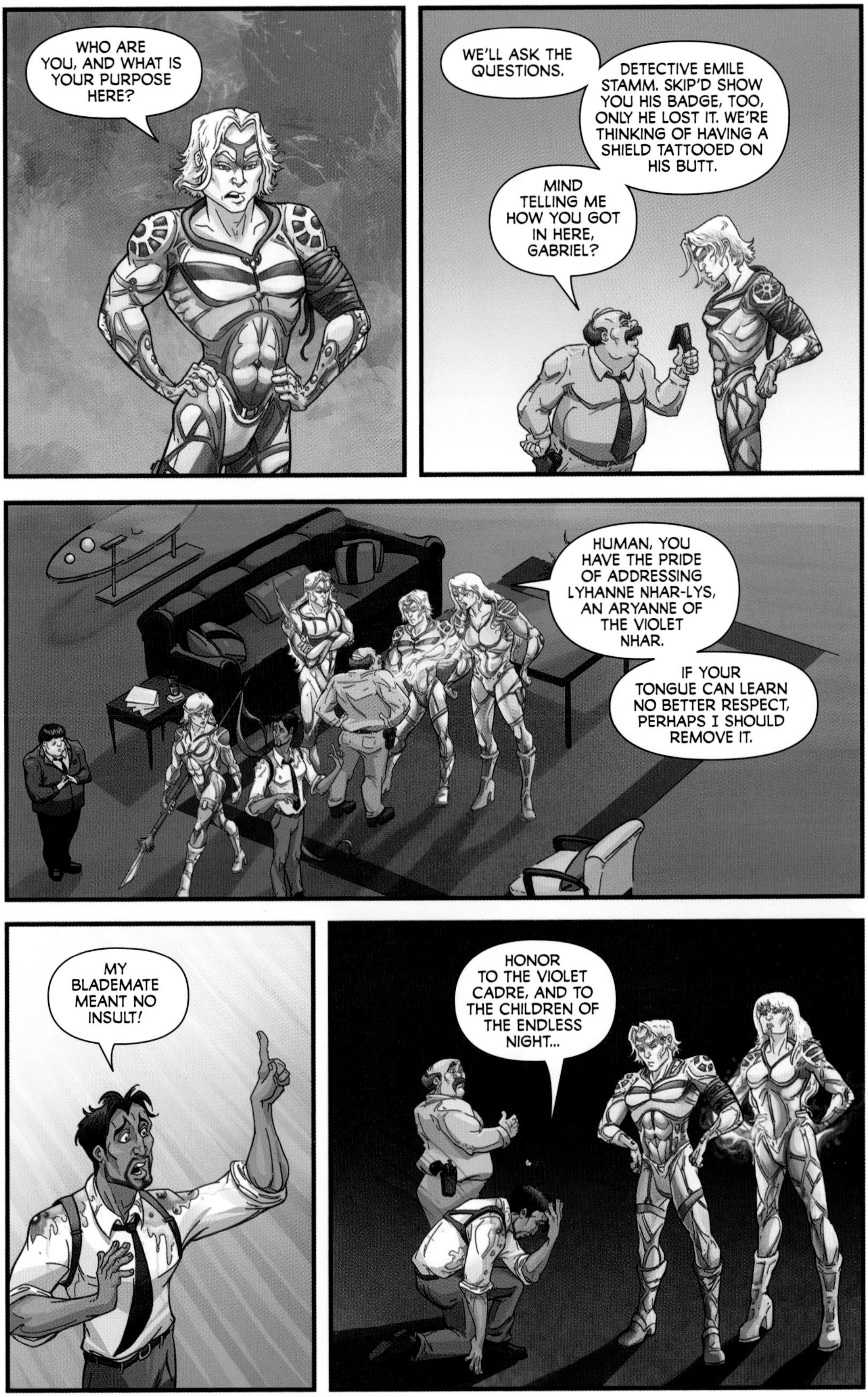
WHO ARE YOU, AND WHAT IS YOUR PURPOSE HERE?
WE'LL ASK THE QUESTIONS.
DETECTIVE EMILE STAMM. SKIP'D SHOW YOU HIS BADGE, TOO, ONLY HE LOST IT. WE'RE THINKING OF HAVING A SHIELD TATTOOED ON HIS BUTT.
MIND TELLING ME HOW YOU GOT IN HERE, GABRIEL?
HUMAN, YOU HAVE THE PRIDE OF ADDRESSING LYHANNE NHAR-LYS, AN ARYANNE OF THE VIOLET NHAR.
IF YOUR TONGUE CAN LEARN NO BETTER RESPECT, PERHAPS I SHOULD REMOVE IT.
MY BLADEMATE MEANT NO INSULT!
HONOR TO THE VIOLET CADRE, AND TO THE CHILDREN OF THE ENDLESS NIGHT...

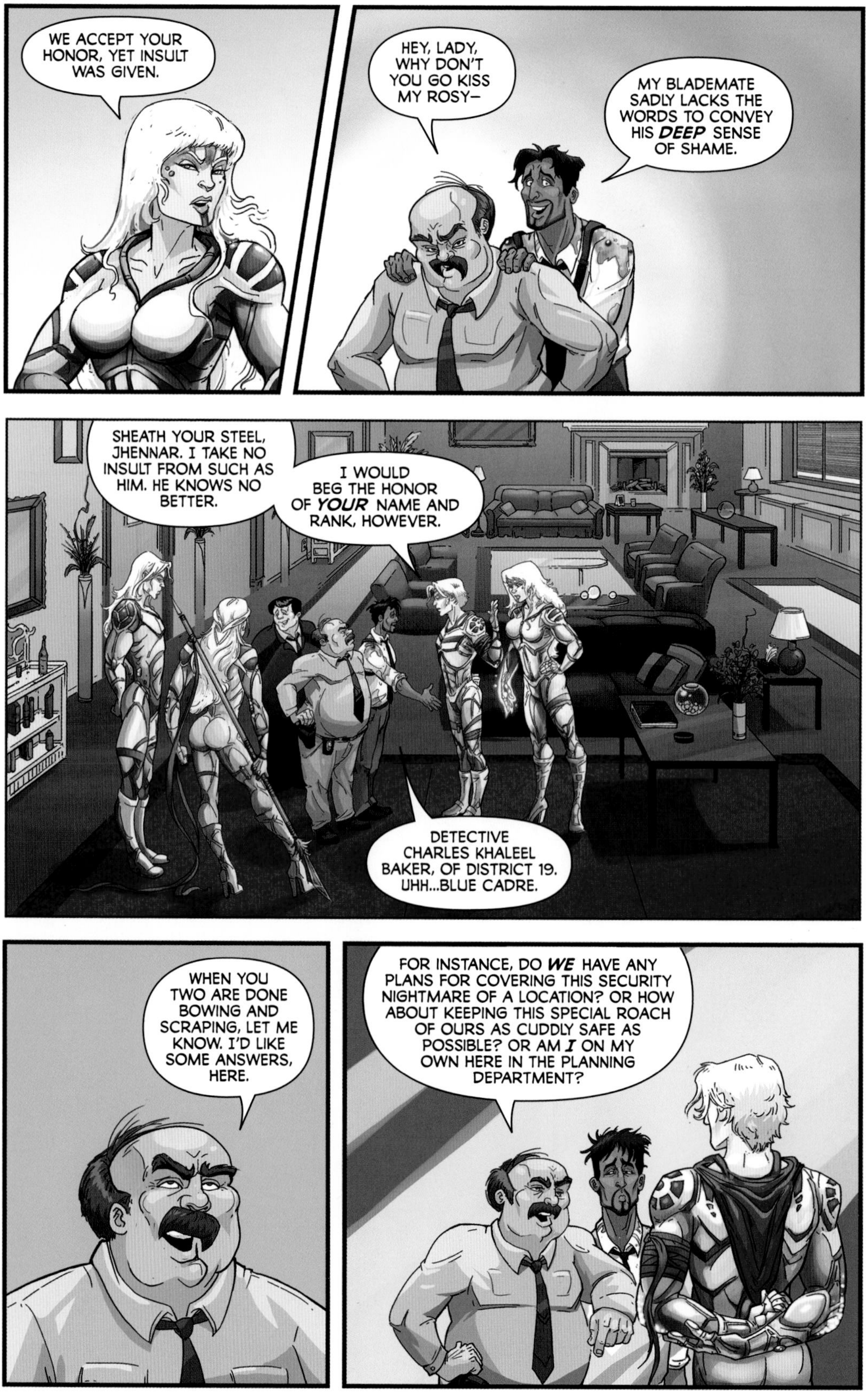
WE ACCEPT YOUR HONOR, YET INSULT WAS GIVEN.
HEY, LADY, WHY DON'T YOU GO KISS MY ROSY—
MY BLADEMATE SADLY LACKS THE WORDS TO CONVEY HIS ***DEEP*** SENSE OF SHAME.
SHEATH YOUR STEEL, JHENNAR. I TAKE NO INSULT FROM SUCH AS HIM. HE KNOWS NO BETTER.
I WOULD BEG THE HONOR OF ***YOUR*** NAME AND RANK, HOWEVER.
DETECTIVE CHARLES KHALEEL BAKER, OF DISTRICT 19. UHH...BLUE CADRE.
WHEN YOU TWO ARE DONE BOWING AND SCRAPING, LET ME KNOW. I'D LIKE SOME ANSWERS, HERE.
FOR INSTANCE, DO ***WE*** HAVE ANY PLANS FOR COVERING THIS SECURITY NIGHTMARE OF A LOCATION? OR HOW ABOUT KEEPING THIS SPECIAL ROACH OF OURS AS CUDDLY SAFE AS POSSIBLE? OR AM ***I*** ON MY OWN HERE IN THE PLANNING DEPARTMENT?

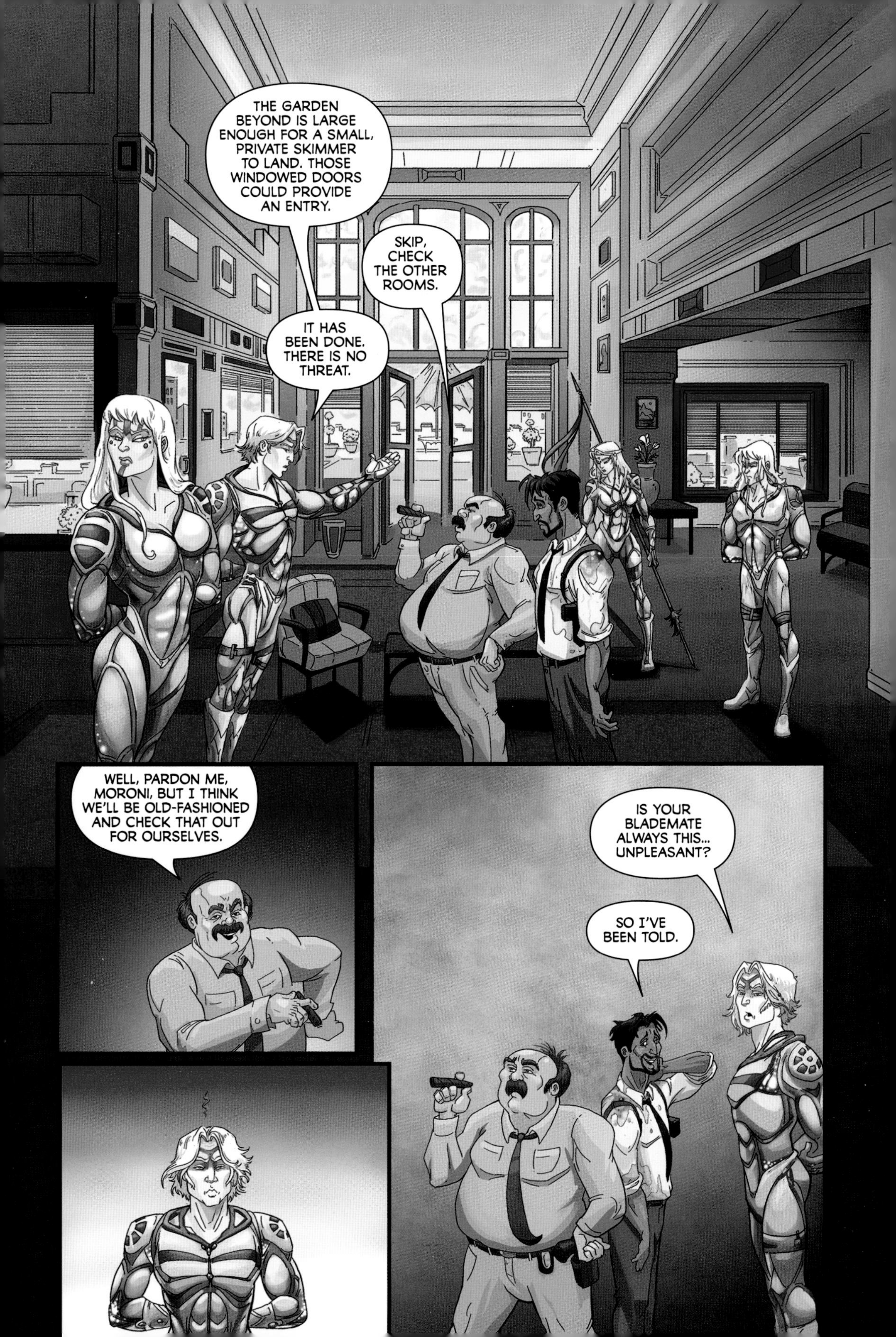
THE GARDEN BEYOND IS LARGE ENOUGH FOR A SMALL, PRIVATE SKIMMER TO LAND. THOSE WINDOWED DOORS COULD PROVIDE AN ENTRY.
SKIP, CHECK THE OTHER ROOMS.
IT HAS BEEN DONE. THERE IS NO THREAT.
WELL, PARDON ME, MORONI, BUT I THINK WE'LL BE OLD-FASHIONED AND CHECK THAT OUT FOR OURSELVES.
IS YOUR BLADEMATE ALWAYS THIS... UNPLEASANT?
SO I'VE BEEN TOLD.

CHAPTER FOUR

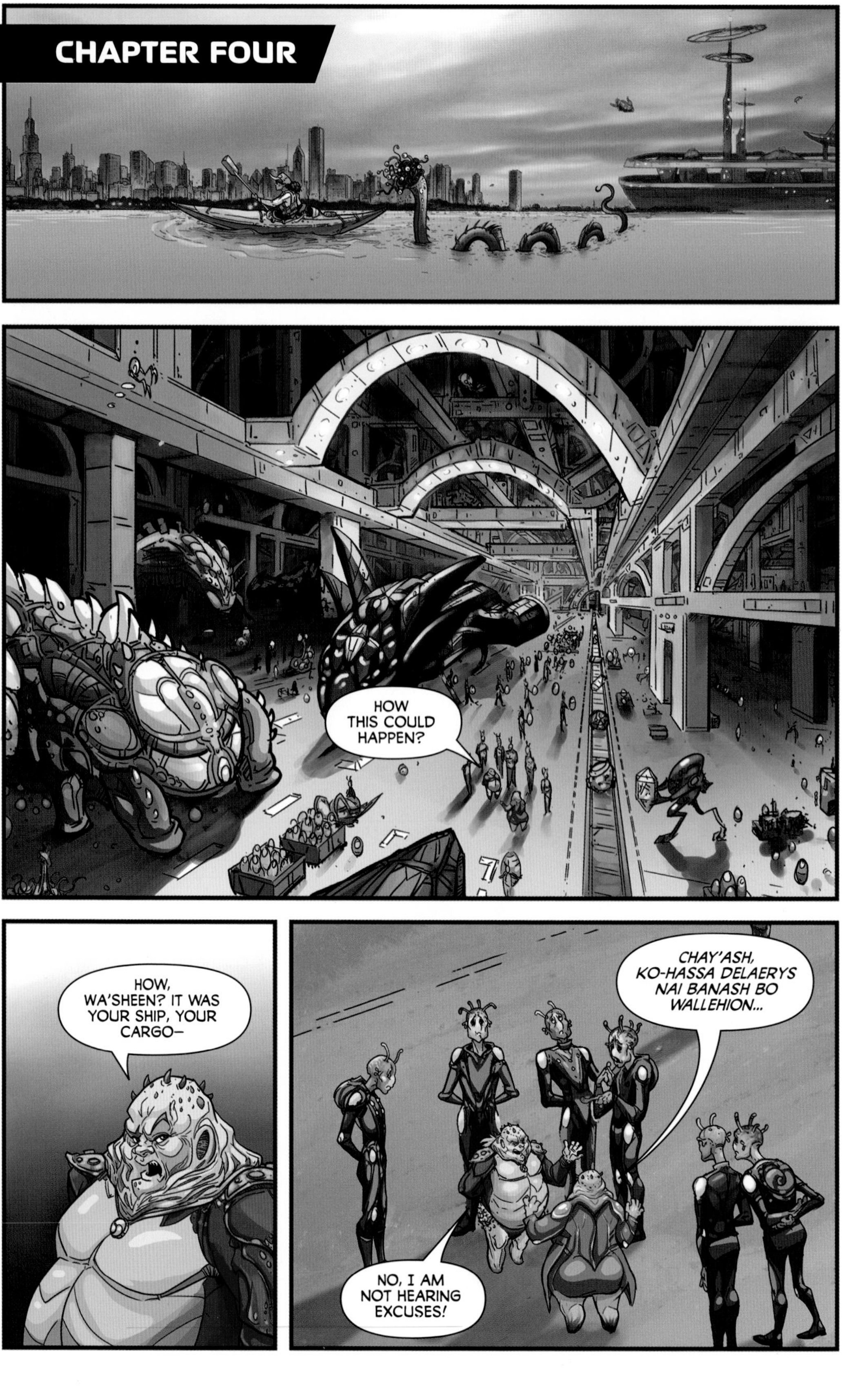
HOW THIS COULD HAPPEN?
HOW, WA'SHEEN? IT WAS YOUR SHIP, YOUR CARGO–
CHAY'ASH, KO-HASSA DELAERYS NAI BANASH BO WALLEHION...
NO, I AM NOT HEARING EXCUSES!

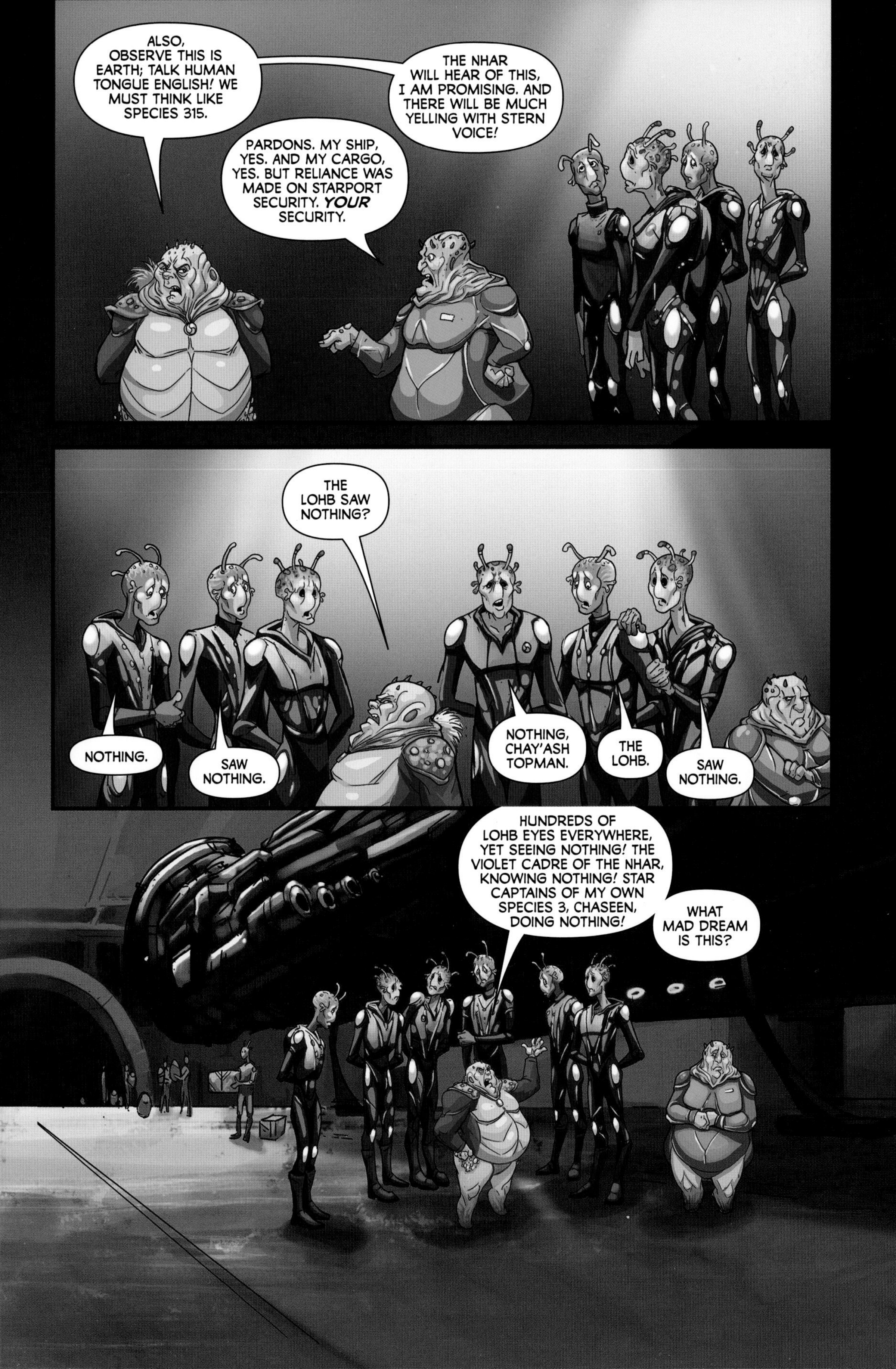
ALSO, OBSERVE THIS IS EARTH; TALK HUMAN TONGUE ENGLISH! WE MUST THINK LIKE SPECIES 315.
THE NHAR WILL HEAR OF THIS, I AM PROMISING. AND THERE WILL BE MUCH YELLING WITH STERN VOICE!
PARDONS. MY SHIP, YES. AND MY CARGO, YES. BUT RELIANCE WAS MADE ON STARPORT SECURITY. ***YOUR*** SECURITY.
THE LOHB SAW NOTHING?
NOTHING.
SAW NOTHING.
NOTHING, CHAY'ASH TOPMAN.
THE LOHB.
SAW NOTHING.
HUNDREDS OF LOHB EYES EVERYWHERE, YET SEEING NOTHING! THE VIOLET CADRE OF THE NHAR, KNOWING NOTHING! STAR CAPTAINS OF MY OWN SPECIES 3, CHASEEN, DOING NOTHING!
WHAT MAD DREAM IS THIS?

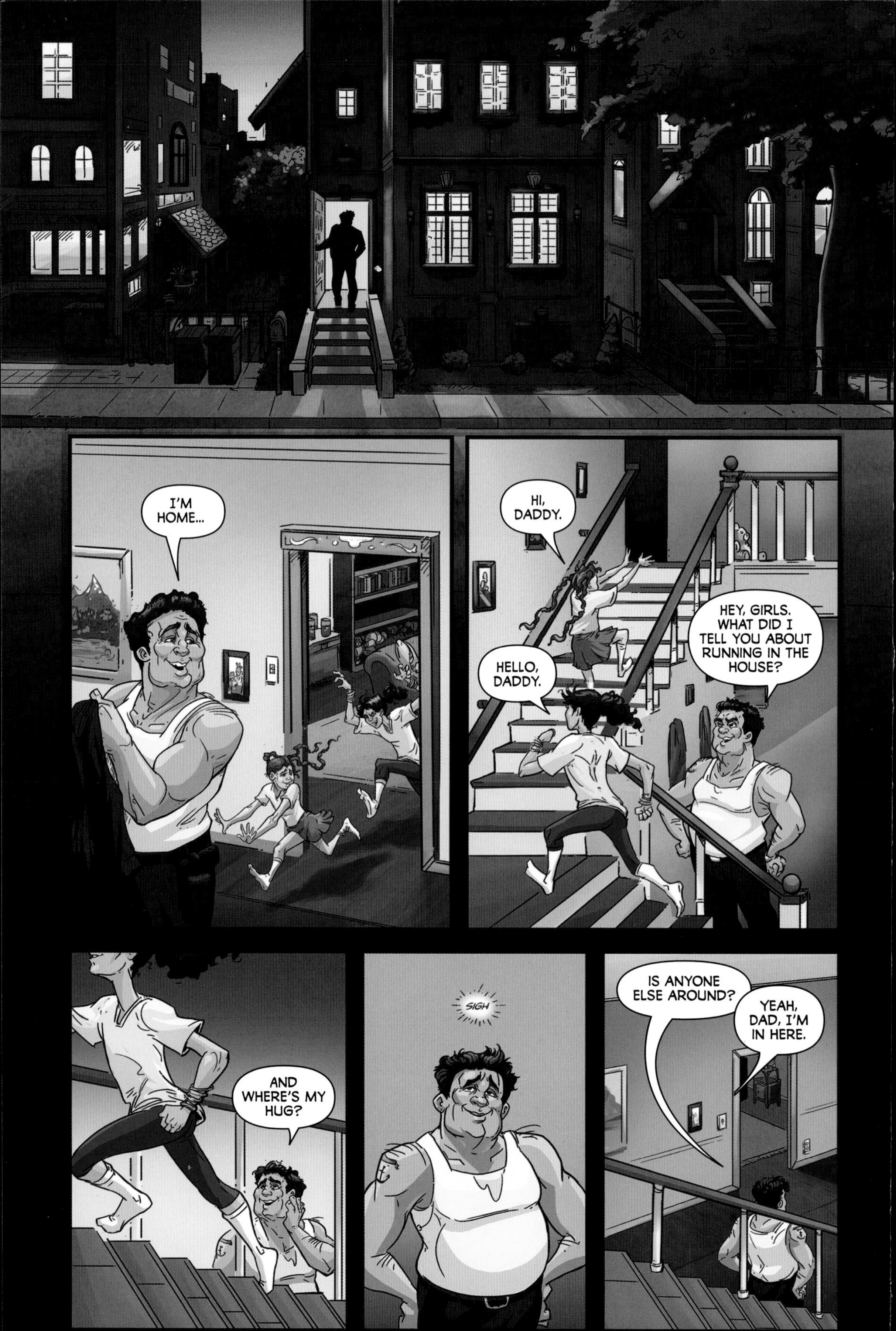
I'M HOME...
HI, DADDY.
HELLO, DADDY.
HEY, GIRLS. WHAT DID I TELL YOU ABOUT RUNNING IN THE HOUSE?
AND WHERE'S MY HUG?
SIGH
IS ANYONE ELSE AROUND?
YEAH, DAD, I'M IN HERE.

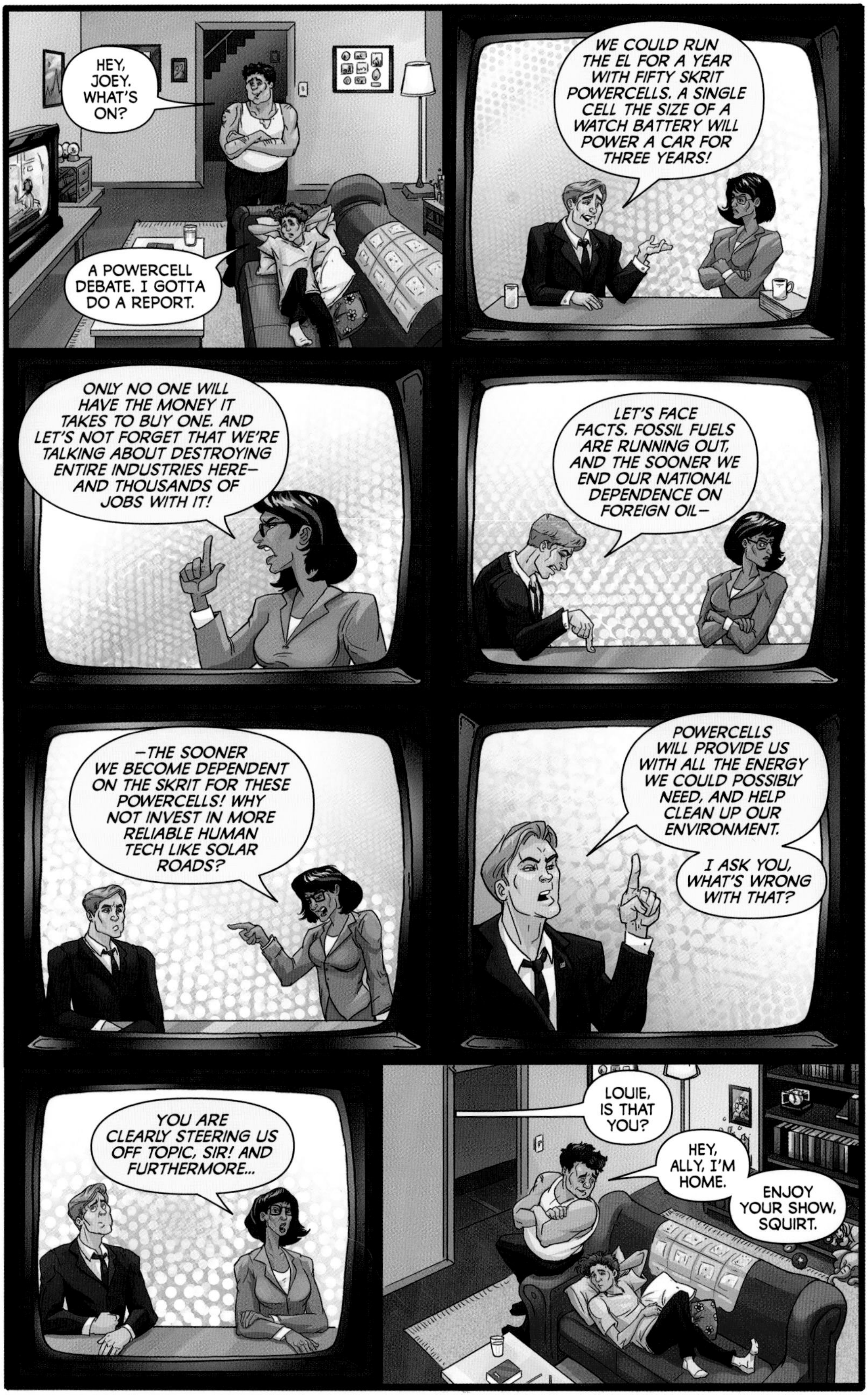
HEY, JOEY. WHAT'S ON?
A POWERCELL DEBATE. I GOTTA DO A REPORT.
WE COULD RUN THE EL FOR A YEAR WITH FIFTY SKRIT POWERCELLS. A SINGLE CELL THE SIZE OF A WATCH BATTERY WILL POWER A CAR FOR THREE YEARS!
ONLY NO ONE WILL HAVE THE MONEY IT TAKES TO BUY ONE. AND LET'S NOT FORGET THAT WE'RE TALKING ABOUT DESTROYING ENTIRE INDUSTRIES HERE—AND THOUSANDS OF JOBS WITH IT!
LET'S FACE FACTS. FOSSIL FUELS ARE RUNNING OUT, AND THE SOONER WE END OUR NATIONAL DEPENDENCE ON FOREIGN OIL—
—THE SOONER WE BECOME DEPENDENT ON THE SKRIT FOR THESE POWERCELLS! WHY NOT INVEST IN MORE RELIABLE HUMAN TECH LIKE SOLAR ROADS?
POWERCELLS WILL PROVIDE US WITH ALL THE ENERGY WE COULD POSSIBLY NEED, AND HELP CLEAN UP OUR ENVIRONMENT.
I ASK YOU, WHAT'S WRONG WITH THAT?
YOU ARE CLEARLY STEERING US OFF TOPIC, SIR! AND FURTHERMORE...
LOUIE, IS THAT YOU?
HEY, ALLY, I'M HOME.
ENJOY YOUR SHOW, SQUIRT.

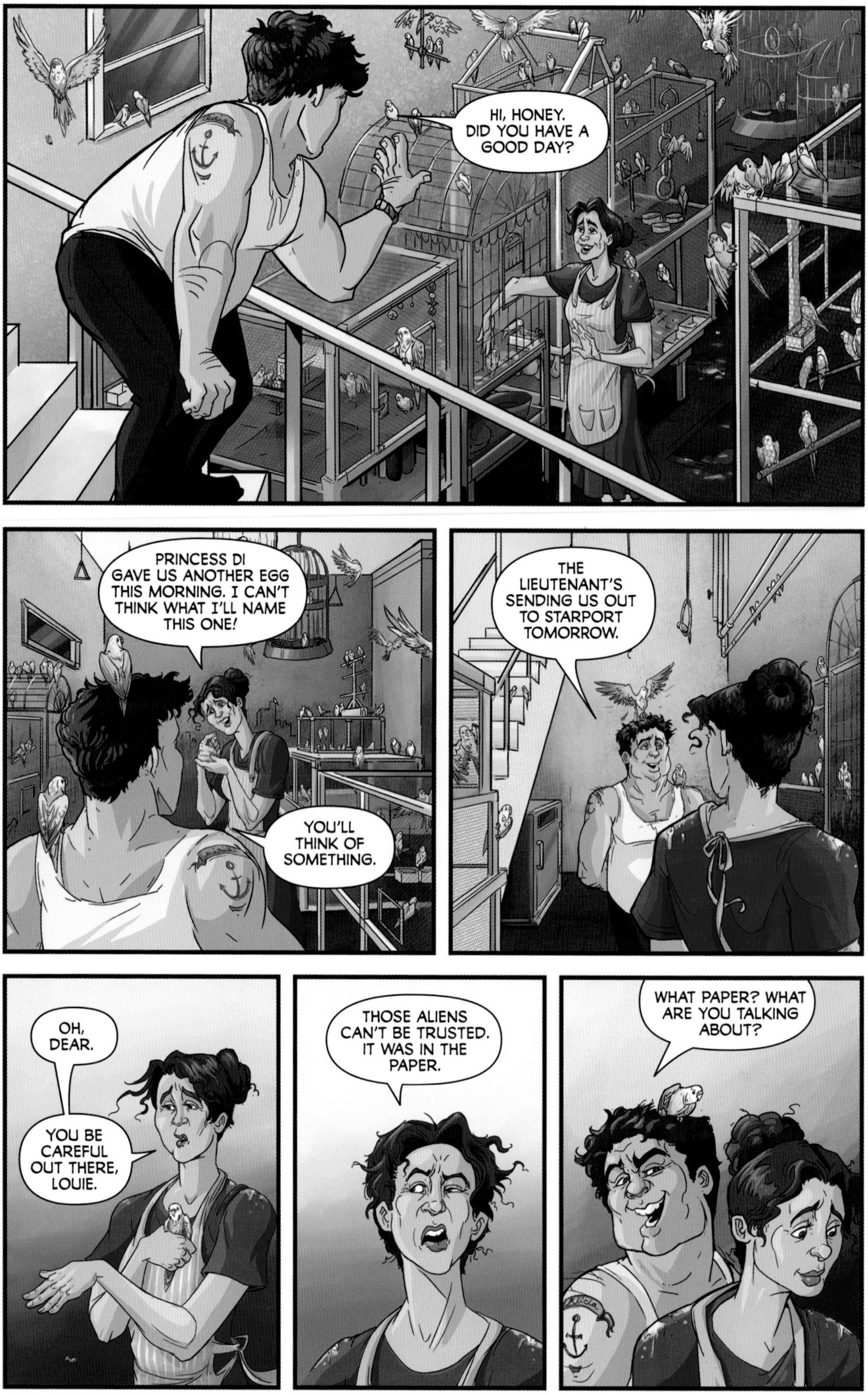
HI, HONEY. DID YOU HAVE A GOOD DAY?
PRINCESS DI GAVE US ANOTHER EGG THIS MORNING. I CAN'T THINK WHAT I'LL NAME THIS ONE!
YOU'LL THINK OF SOMETHING.
THE LIEUTENANT'S SENDING US OUT TO STARPORT TOMORROW.
OH, DEAR.
YOU BE CAREFUL OUT THERE, LOUIE.
THOSE ALIENS CAN'T BE TRUSTED. IT WAS IN THE PAPER.
WHAT PAPER? WHAT ARE YOU TALKING ABOUT?

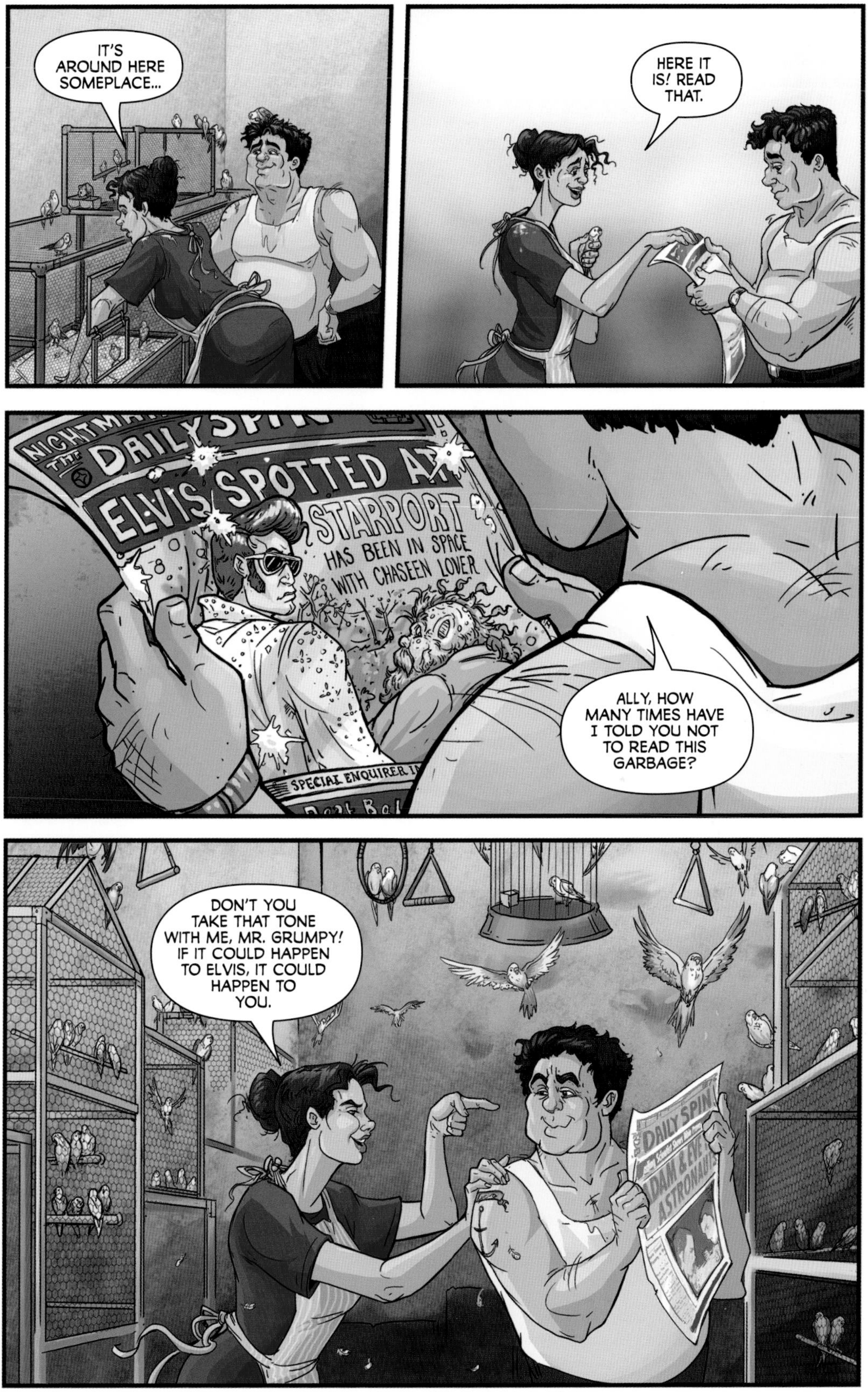
IT'S AROUND HERE SOMEPLACE...
HERE IT IS! READ THAT.
THE DAILY SPIN
ELVIS SPOTTED AT
STARPORT
HAS BEEN IN SPACE WITH CHASEEN LOVER
ALLY, HOW MANY TIMES HAVE I TOLD YOU NOT TO READ THIS GARBAGE?
DON'T YOU TAKE THAT TONE WITH ME, MR. GRUMPY! IF IT COULD HAPPEN TO ELVIS, IT COULD HAPPEN TO YOU.
DAILY SPIN

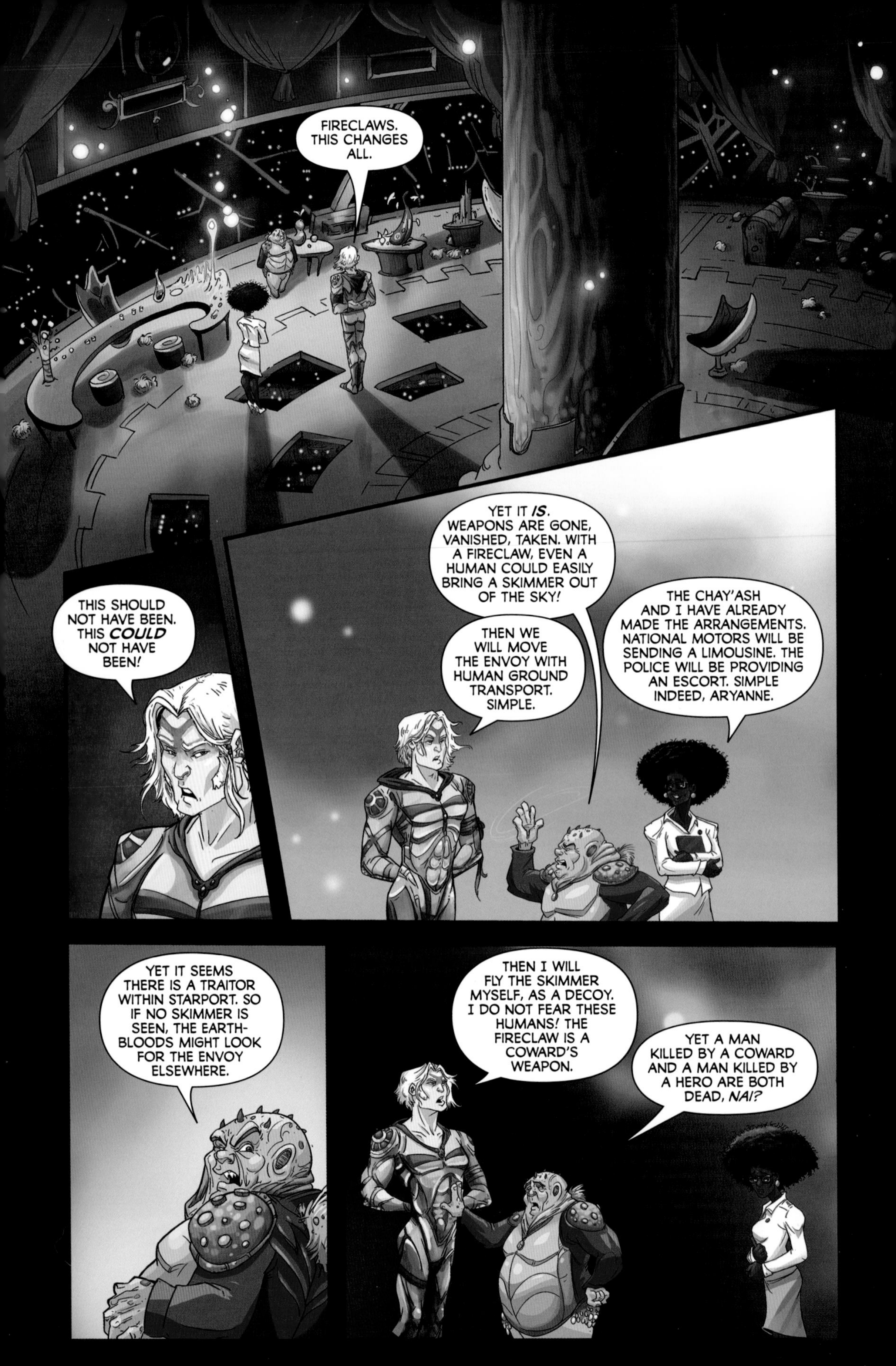
FIRECLAWS. THIS CHANGES ALL.
THIS SHOULD NOT HAVE BEEN. THIS *COULD* NOT HAVE BEEN!
YET IT *IS*. WEAPONS ARE GONE, VANISHED, TAKEN. WITH A FIRECLAW, EVEN A HUMAN COULD EASILY BRING A SKIMMER OUT OF THE SKY!
THEN WE WILL MOVE THE ENVOY WITH HUMAN GROUND TRANSPORT. SIMPLE.
THE CHAY'ASH AND I HAVE ALREADY MADE THE ARRANGEMENTS. NATIONAL MOTORS WILL BE SENDING A LIMOUSINE. THE POLICE WILL BE PROVIDING AN ESCORT. SIMPLE INDEED, ARYANNE.
YET IT SEEMS THERE IS A TRAITOR WITHIN STARPORT. SO IF NO SKIMMER IS SEEN, THE EARTH-BLOODS MIGHT LOOK FOR THE ENVOY ELSEWHERE.
THEN I WILL FLY THE SKIMMER MYSELF, AS A DECOY. I DO NOT FEAR THESE HUMANS! THE FIRECLAW IS A COWARD'S WEAPON.
YET A MAN KILLED BY A COWARD AND A MAN KILLED BY A HERO ARE BOTH DEAD, *NAI*?

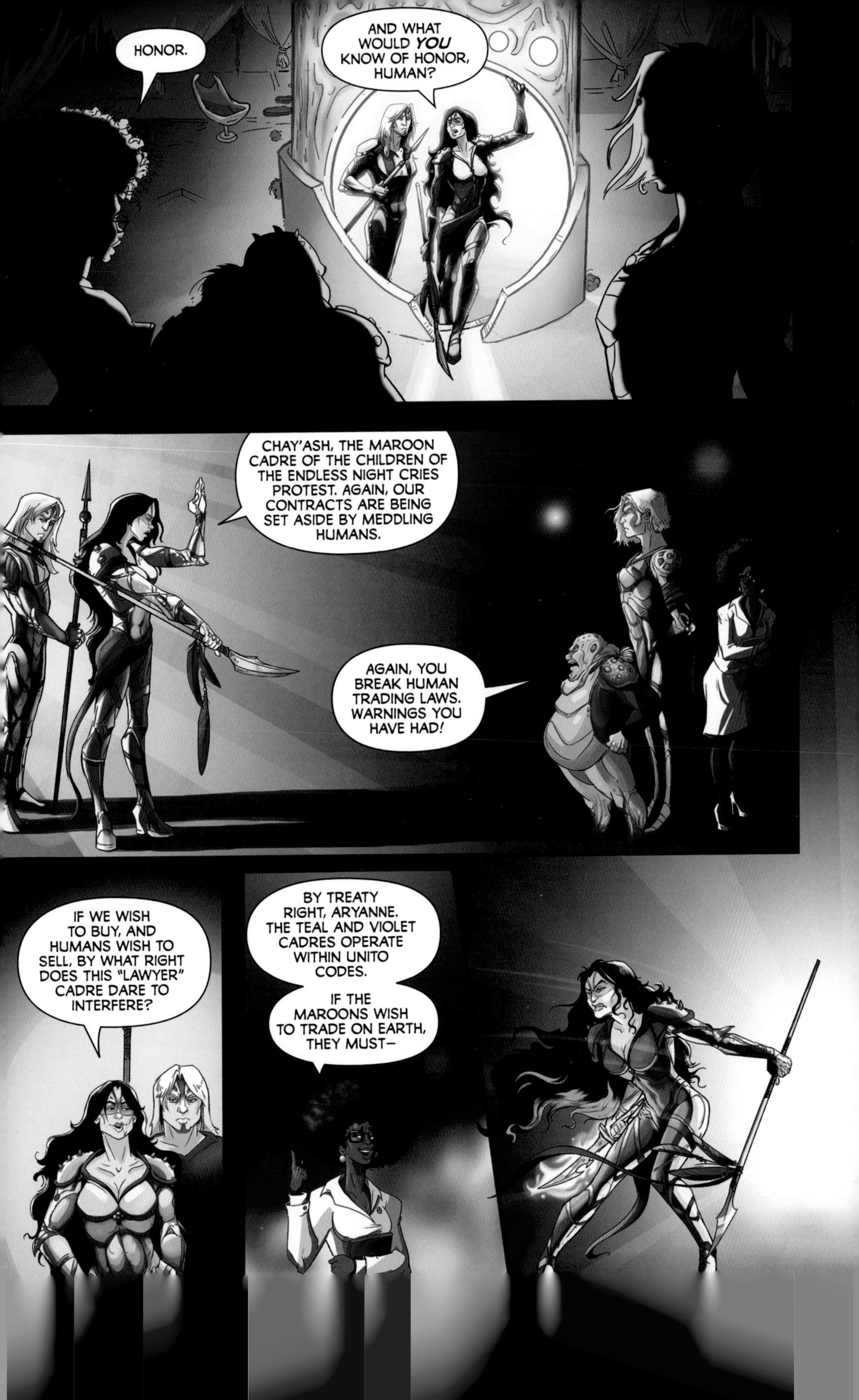
HONOR.
AND WHAT WOULD *YOU* KNOW OF HONOR, HUMAN?
CHAY'ASH, THE MAROON CADRE OF THE CHILDREN OF THE ENDLESS NIGHT CRIES PROTEST. AGAIN, OUR CONTRACTS ARE BEING SET ASIDE BY MEDDLING HUMANS.
AGAIN, YOU BREAK HUMAN TRADING LAWS. WARNINGS YOU HAVE HAD!
IF WE WISH TO BUY, AND HUMANS WISH TO SELL, BY WHAT RIGHT DOES THIS "LAWYER" CADRE DARE TO INTERFERE?
BY TREATY RIGHT, ARYANNE. THE TEAL AND VIOLET CADRES OPERATE WITHIN UNITO CODES.
IF THE MAROONS WISH TO TRADE ON EARTH, THEY MUST—

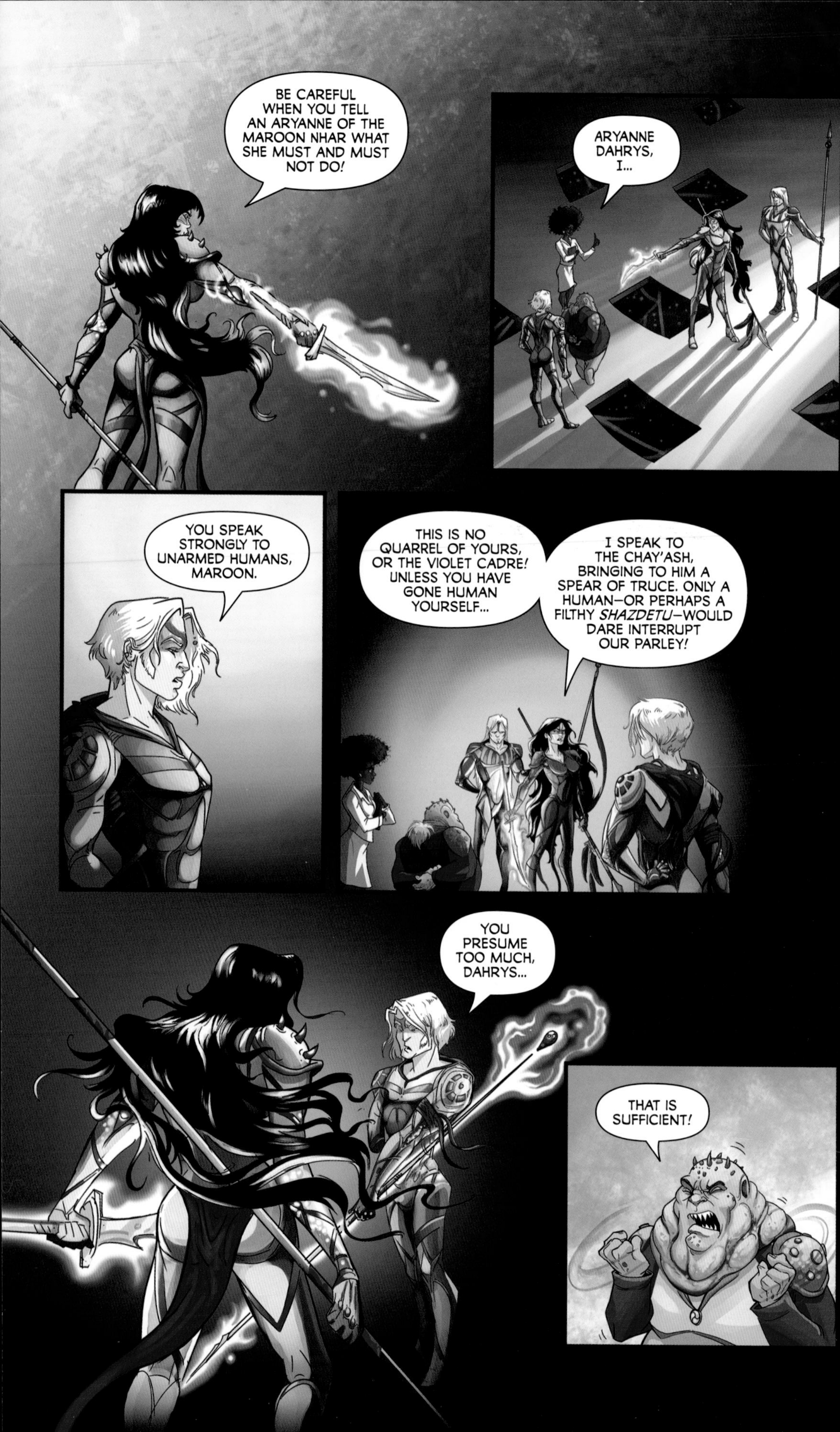
BE CAREFUL WHEN YOU TELL AN ARYANNE OF THE MAROON NHAR WHAT SHE MUST AND MUST NOT DO!
ARYANNE DAHRYS, I...
YOU SPEAK STRONGLY TO UNARMED HUMANS, MAROON.
THIS IS NO QUARREL OF YOURS, OR THE VIOLET CADRE! UNLESS YOU HAVE GONE HUMAN YOURSELF...
I SPEAK TO THE CHAY'ASH, BRINGING TO HIM A SPEAR OF TRUCE. ONLY A HUMAN—OR PERHAPS A FILTHY *SHAZDETU*—WOULD DARE INTERRUPT OUR PARLEY!
YOU PRESUME TOO MUCH, DAHRYS...
THAT IS SUFFICIENT!

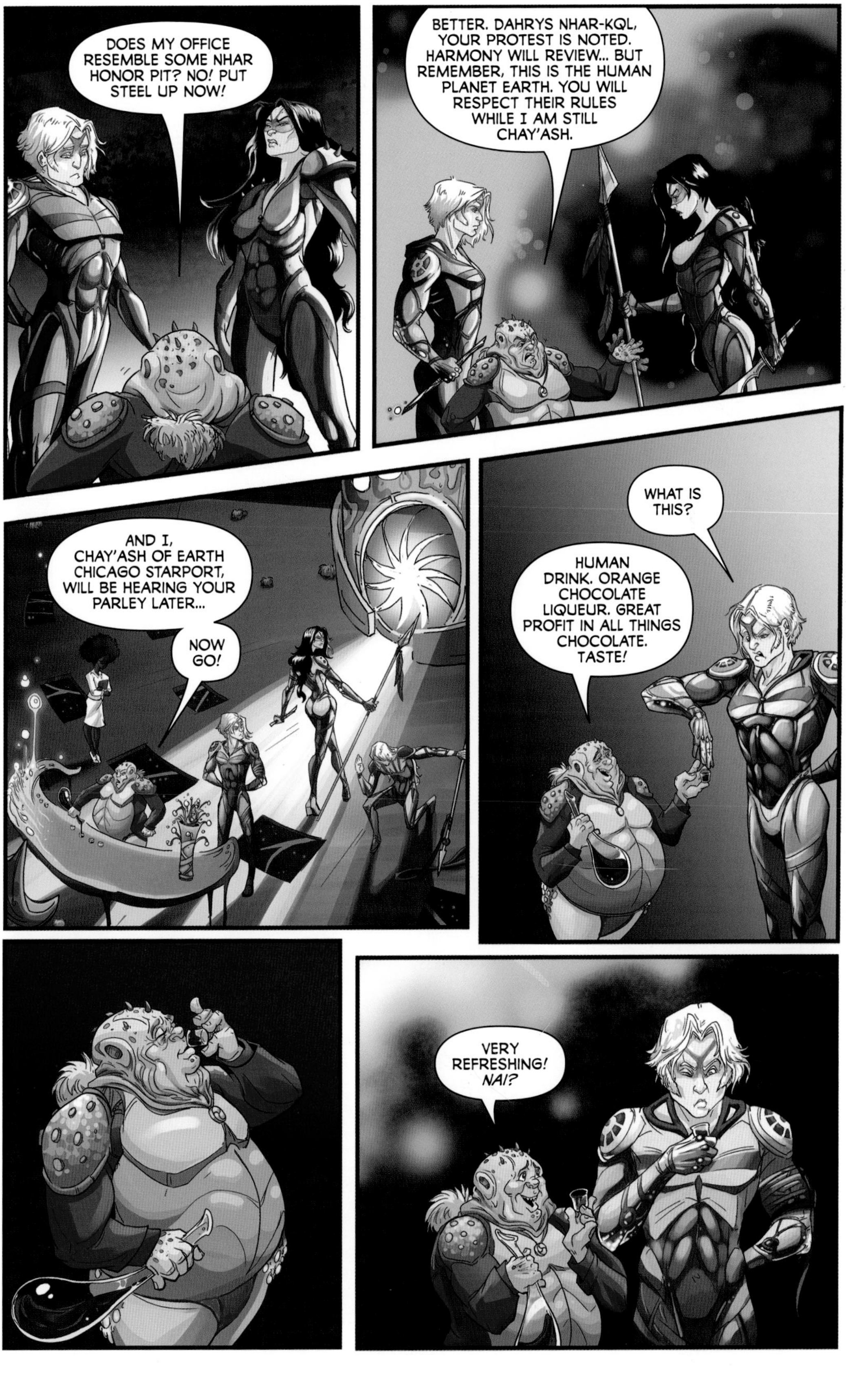
DOES MY OFFICE RESEMBLE SOME NHAR HONOR PIT? NO! PUT STEEL UP NOW!
BETTER. DAHRYS NHAR-KQL, YOUR PROTEST IS NOTED. HARMONY WILL REVIEW... BUT REMEMBER, THIS IS THE HUMAN PLANET EARTH. YOU WILL RESPECT THEIR RULES WHILE I AM STILL CHAY'ASH.
AND I, CHAY'ASH OF EARTH CHICAGO STARPORT, WILL BE HEARING YOUR PARLEY LATER...
NOW GO!
WHAT IS THIS?
HUMAN DRINK. ORANGE CHOCOLATE LIQUEUR. GREAT PROFIT IN ALL THINGS CHOCOLATE. TASTE!
VERY REFRESHING! NAI?

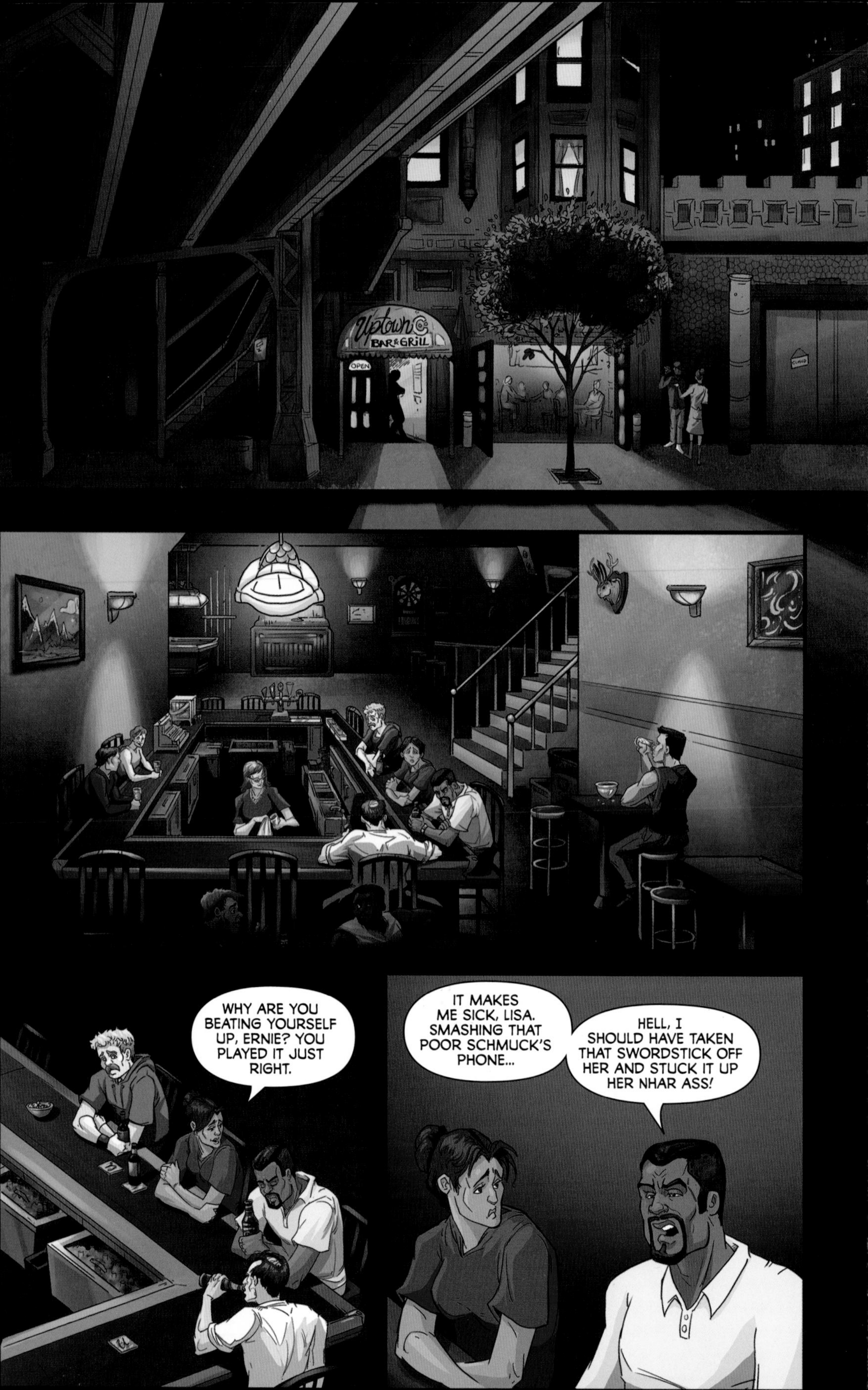
Uptown
BAR & GRILL
OPEN
WHY ARE YOU BEATING YOURSELF UP, ERNIE? YOU PLAYED IT JUST RIGHT.
IT MAKES ME SICK, LISA. SMASHING THAT POOR SCHMUCK'S PHONE...
HELL, I SHOULD HAVE TAKEN THAT SWORDSTICK OFF HER AND STUCK IT UP HER NHAR ASS!

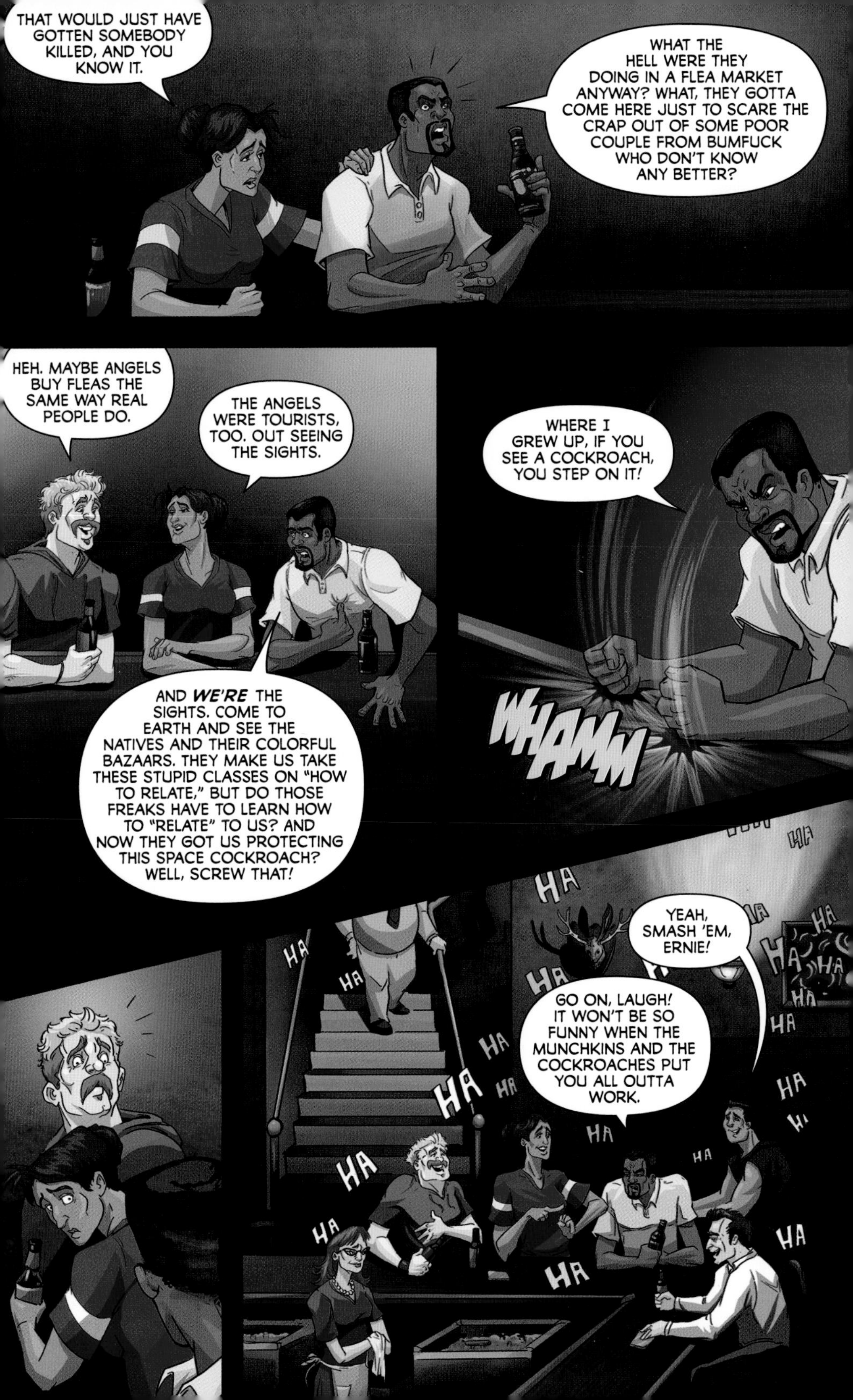
THAT WOULD JUST HAVE GOTTEN SOMEBODY KILLED, AND YOU KNOW IT.
WHAT THE HELL WERE THEY DOING IN A FLEA MARKET ANYWAY? WHAT, THEY GOTTA COME HERE JUST TO SCARE THE CRAP OUT OF SOME POOR COUPLE FROM BUMFUCK WHO DON'T KNOW ANY BETTER?
HEH. MAYBE ANGELS BUY FLEAS THE SAME WAY REAL PEOPLE DO.
THE ANGELS WERE TOURISTS, TOO. OUT SEEING THE SIGHTS.
AND *WE'RE* THE SIGHTS. COME TO EARTH AND SEE THE NATIVES AND THEIR COLORFUL BAZAARS. THEY MAKE US TAKE THESE STUPID CLASSES ON "HOW TO RELATE," BUT DO THOSE FREAKS HAVE TO LEARN HOW TO "RELATE" TO US? AND NOW THEY GOT US PROTECTING THIS SPACE COCKROACH? WELL, SCREW THAT!
WHERE I GREW UP, IF YOU SEE A COCKROACH, YOU STEP ON IT!
WHAMM
YEAH, SMASH 'EM, ERNIE!
GO ON, LAUGH! IT WON'T BE SO FUNNY WHEN THE MUNCHKINS AND THE COCKROACHES PUT YOU ALL OUTTA WORK.
HA HA HA HA HA HA HA HA HA HA HA HA HA HA HA HA HA

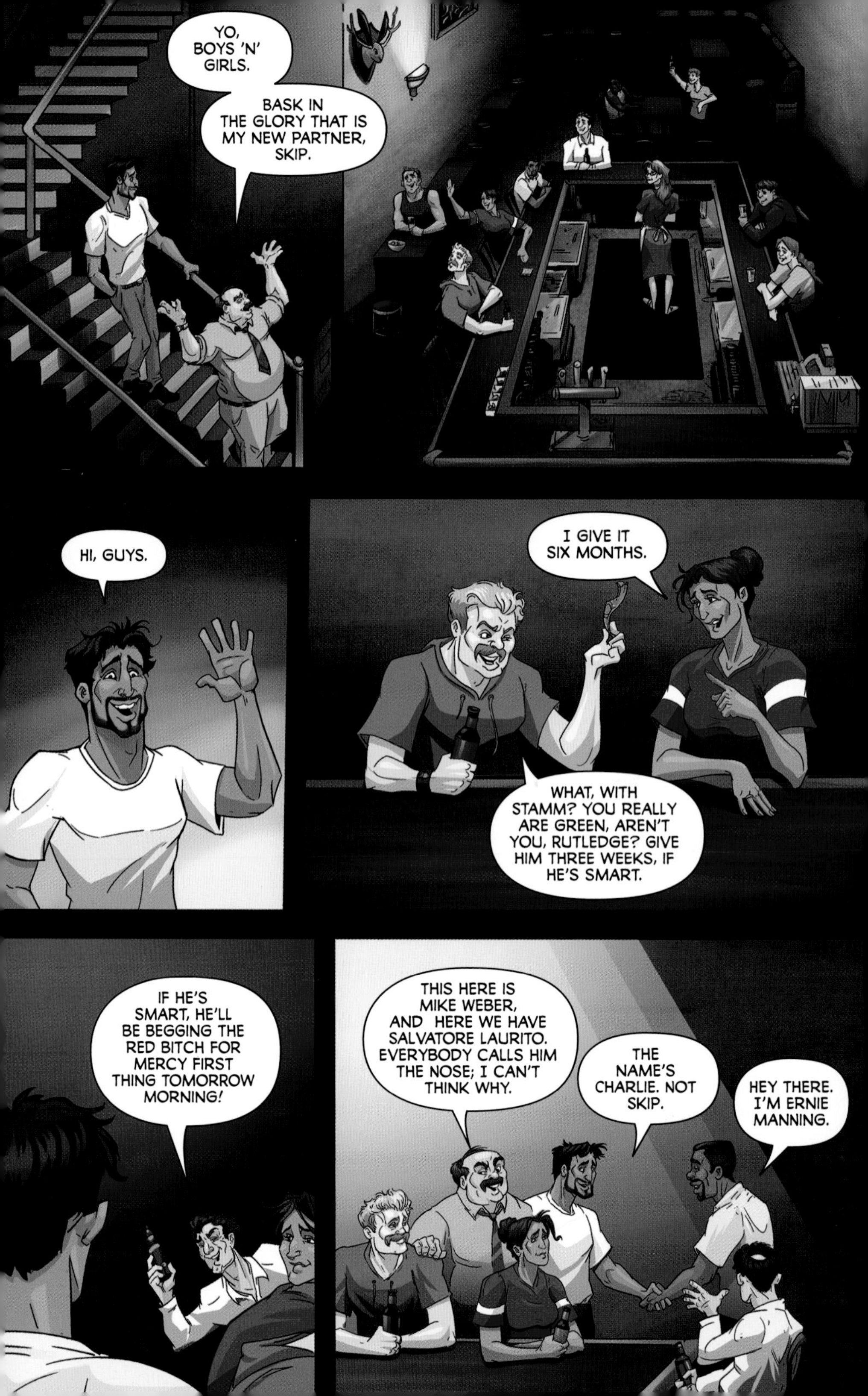
YO, BOYS 'N' GIRLS.
BASK IN THE GLORY THAT IS MY NEW PARTNER, SKIP.
HI, GUYS.
I GIVE IT SIX MONTHS.
WHAT, WITH STAMM? YOU REALLY ARE GREEN, AREN'T YOU, RUTLEDGE? GIVE HIM THREE WEEKS, IF HE'S SMART.
IF HE'S SMART, HE'LL BE BEGGING THE RED BITCH FOR MERCY FIRST THING TOMORROW MORNING!
THIS HERE IS MIKE WEBER, AND HERE WE HAVE SALVATORE LAURITO. EVERYBODY CALLS HIM THE NOSE; I CAN'T THINK WHY.
THE NAME'S CHARLIE. NOT SKIP.
HEY THERE. I'M ERNIE MANNING.

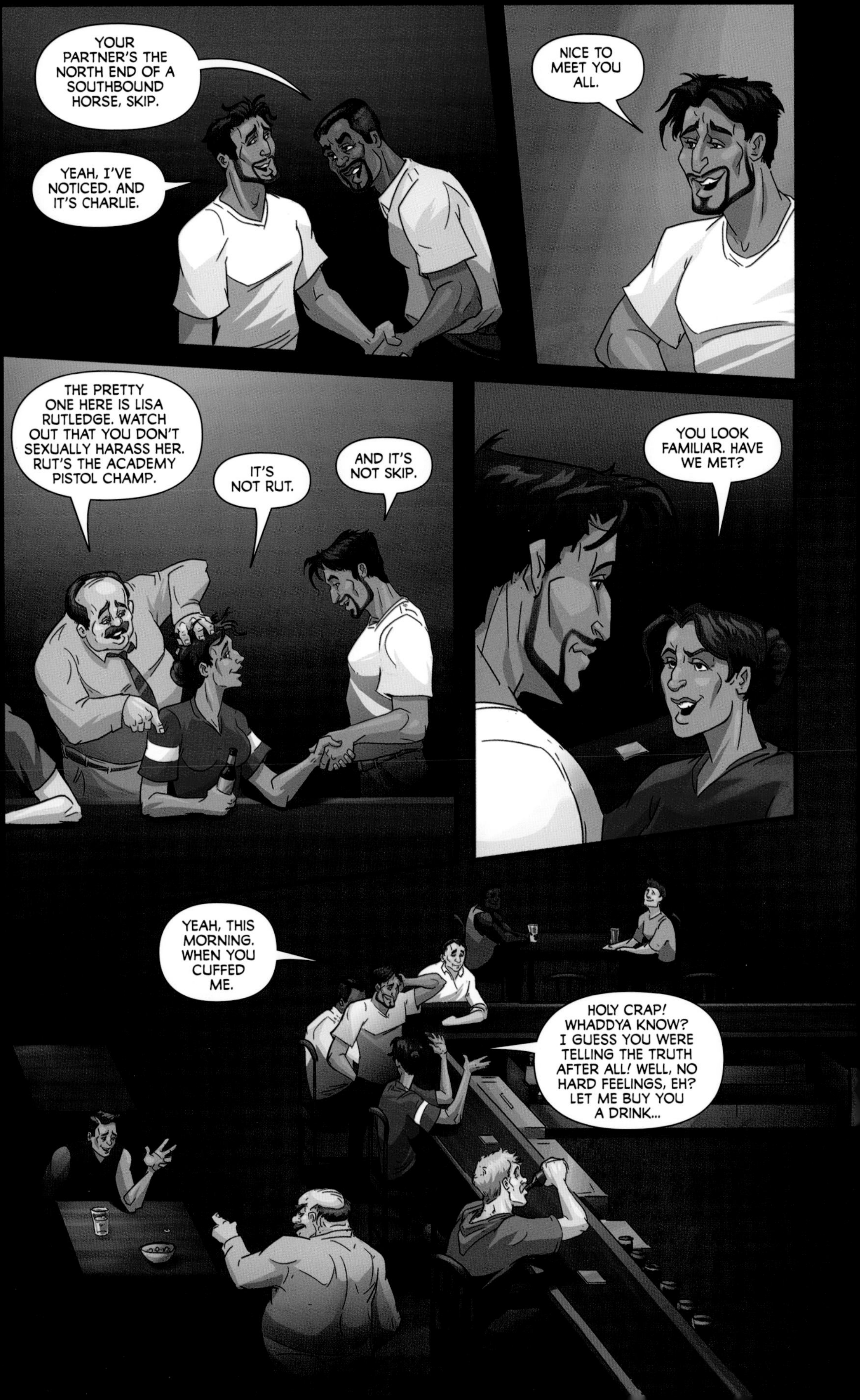
YOUR PARTNER'S THE NORTH END OF A SOUTHBOUND HORSE, SKIP.
YEAH, I'VE NOTICED. AND IT'S CHARLIE.
NICE TO MEET YOU ALL.
THE PRETTY ONE HERE IS LISA RUTLEDGE. WATCH OUT THAT YOU DON'T SEXUALLY HARASS HER. RUT'S THE ACADEMY PISTOL CHAMP.
IT'S NOT RUT.
AND IT'S NOT SKIP.
YOU LOOK FAMILIAR. HAVE WE MET?
YEAH, THIS MORNING. WHEN YOU CUFFED ME.
HOLY CRAP! WHADDYA KNOW? I GUESS YOU WERE TELLING THE TRUTH AFTER ALL! WELL, NO HARD FEELINGS, EH? LET ME BUY YOU A DRINK...

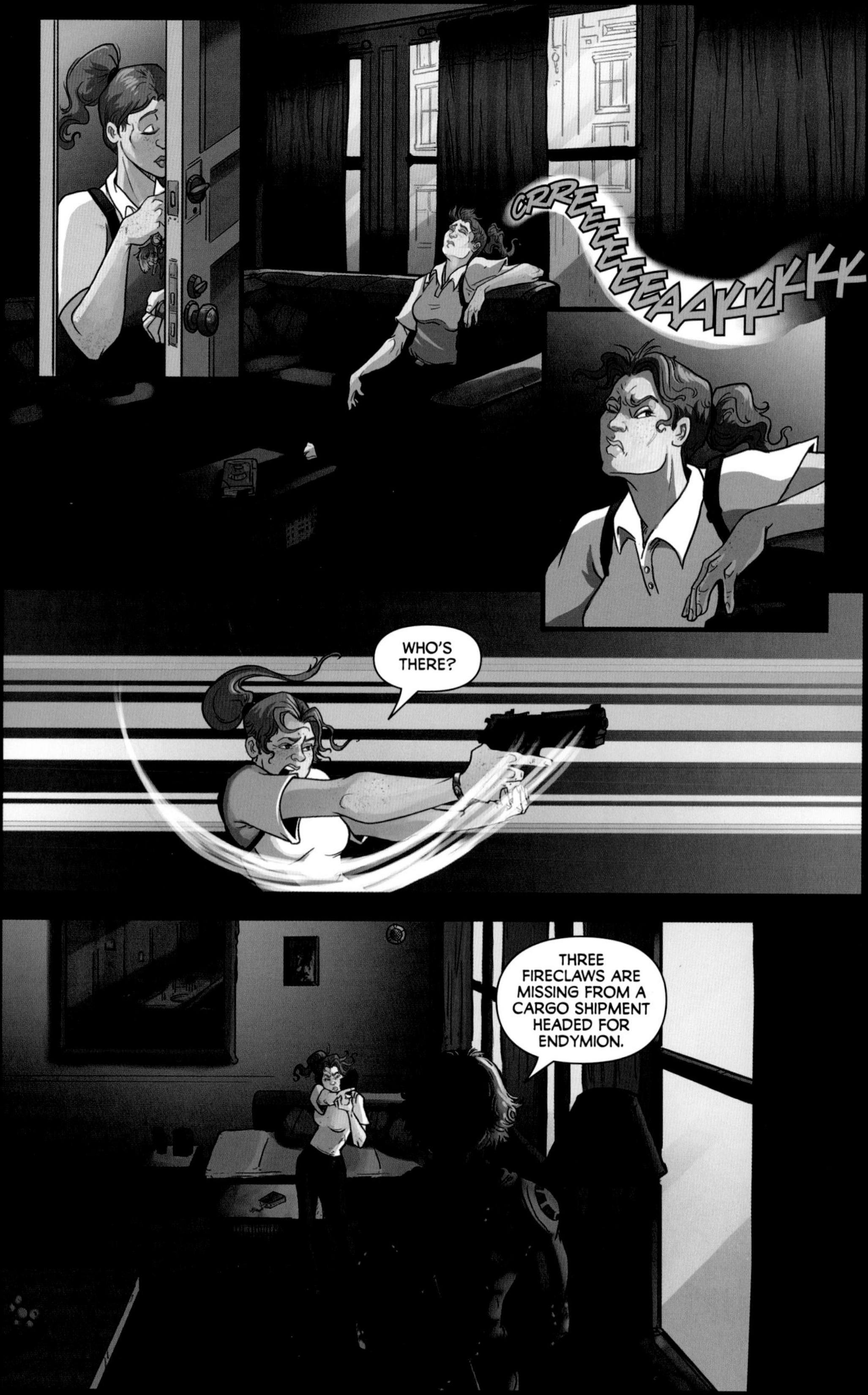
CRREEEEEEEAAKKKKK
WHO'S THERE?
THREE FIRECLAWS ARE MISSING FROM A CARGO SHIPMENT HEADED FOR ENDYMION.

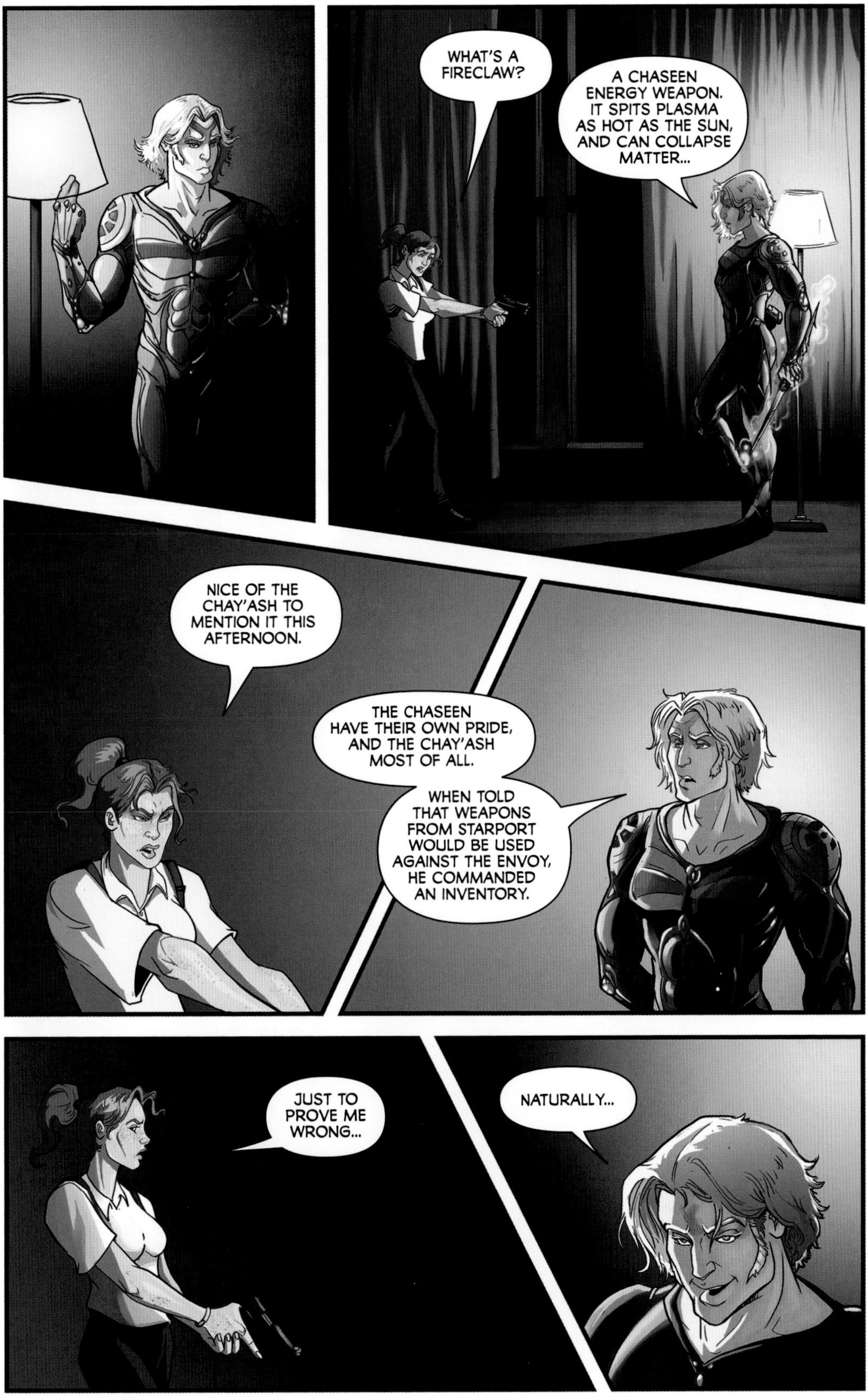
WHAT'S A FIRECLAW?
A CHASEEN ENERGY WEAPON. IT SPITS PLASMA AS HOT AS THE SUN, AND CAN COLLAPSE MATTER...
NICE OF THE CHAY'ASH TO MENTION IT THIS AFTERNOON.
THE CHASEEN HAVE THEIR OWN PRIDE, AND THE CHAY'ASH MOST OF ALL.
WHEN TOLD THAT WEAPONS FROM STARPORT WOULD BE USED AGAINST THE ENVOY, HE COMMANDED AN INVENTORY.
JUST TO PROVE ME WRONG...
NATURALLY...

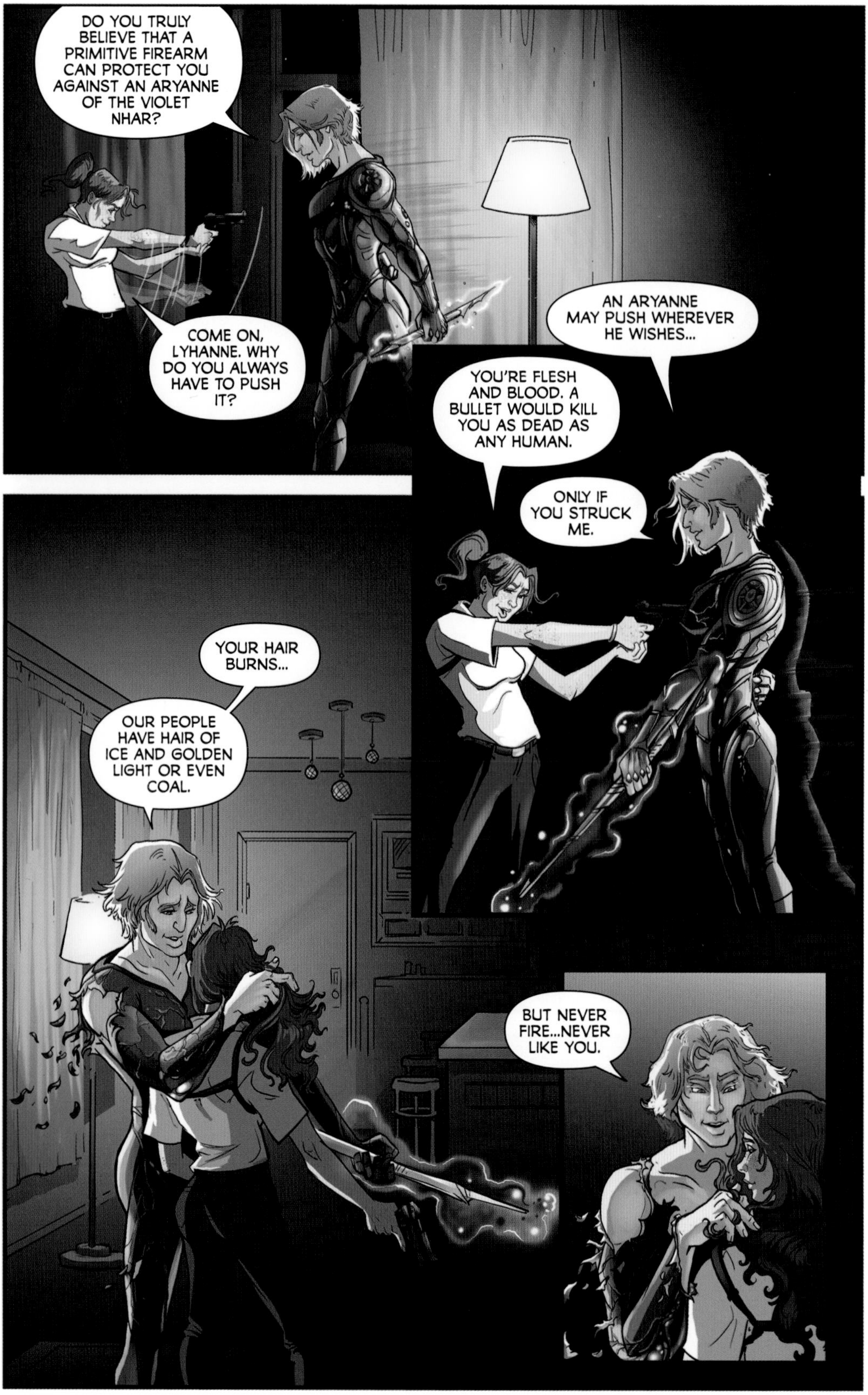
DO YOU TRULY BELIEVE THAT A PRIMITIVE FIREARM CAN PROTECT YOU AGAINST AN ARYANNE OF THE VIOLET NHAR?
COME ON, LYHANNE. WHY DO YOU ALWAYS HAVE TO PUSH IT?
AN ARYANNE MAY PUSH WHEREVER HE WISHES...
YOU'RE FLESH AND BLOOD. A BULLET WOULD KILL YOU AS DEAD AS ANY HUMAN.
ONLY IF YOU STRUCK ME.
YOUR HAIR BURNS...
OUR PEOPLE HAVE HAIR OF ICE AND GOLDEN LIGHT OR EVEN COAL.
BUT NEVER FIRE...NEVER LIKE YOU.

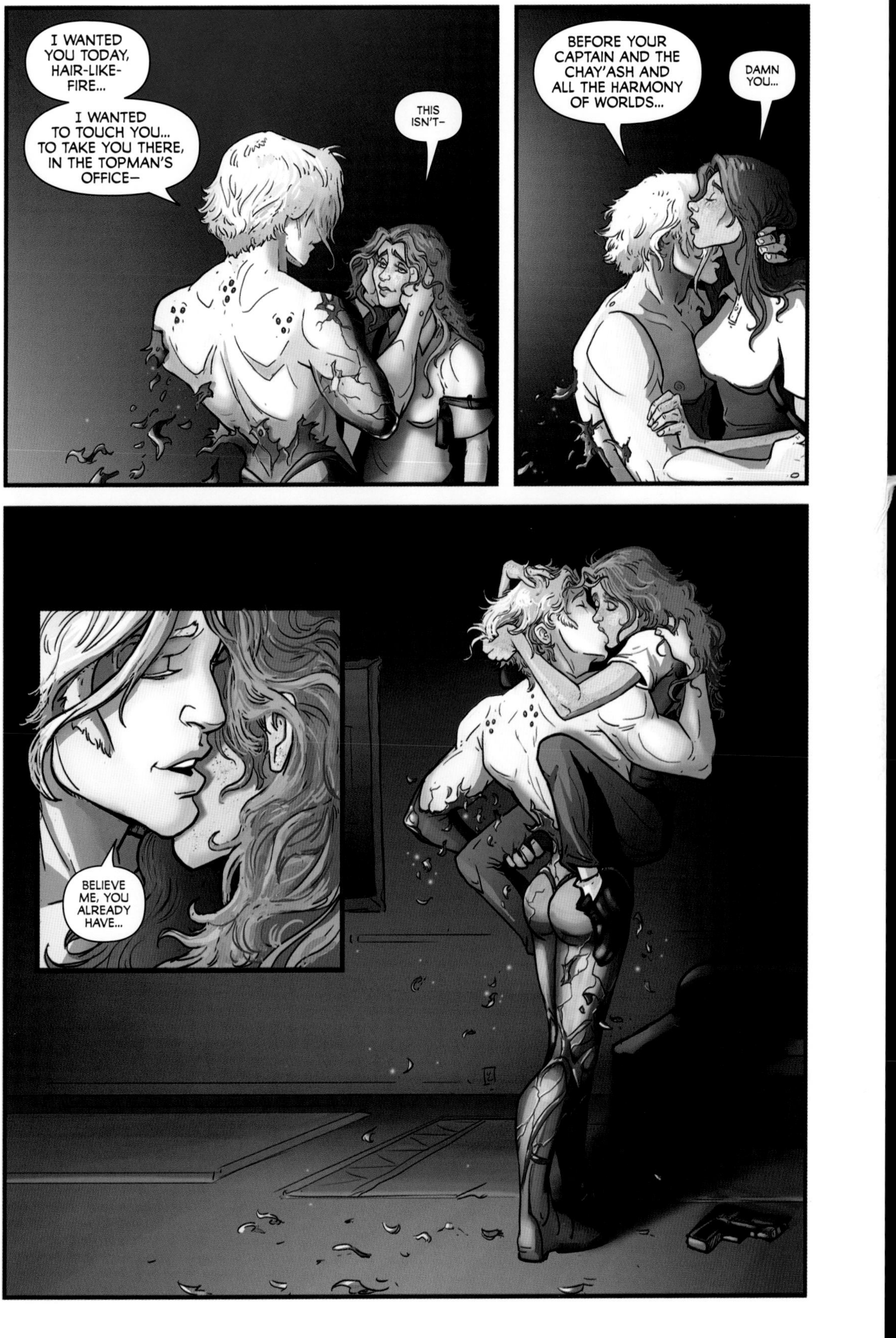
I WANTED YOU TODAY, HAIR-LIKE-FIRE...
I WANTED TO TOUCH YOU... TO TAKE YOU THERE, IN THE TOPMAN'S OFFICE–
THIS ISN'T–
BEFORE YOUR CAPTAIN AND THE CHAY'ASH AND ALL THE HARMONY OF WORLDS...
DAMN YOU...
BELIEVE ME, YOU ALREADY HAVE...

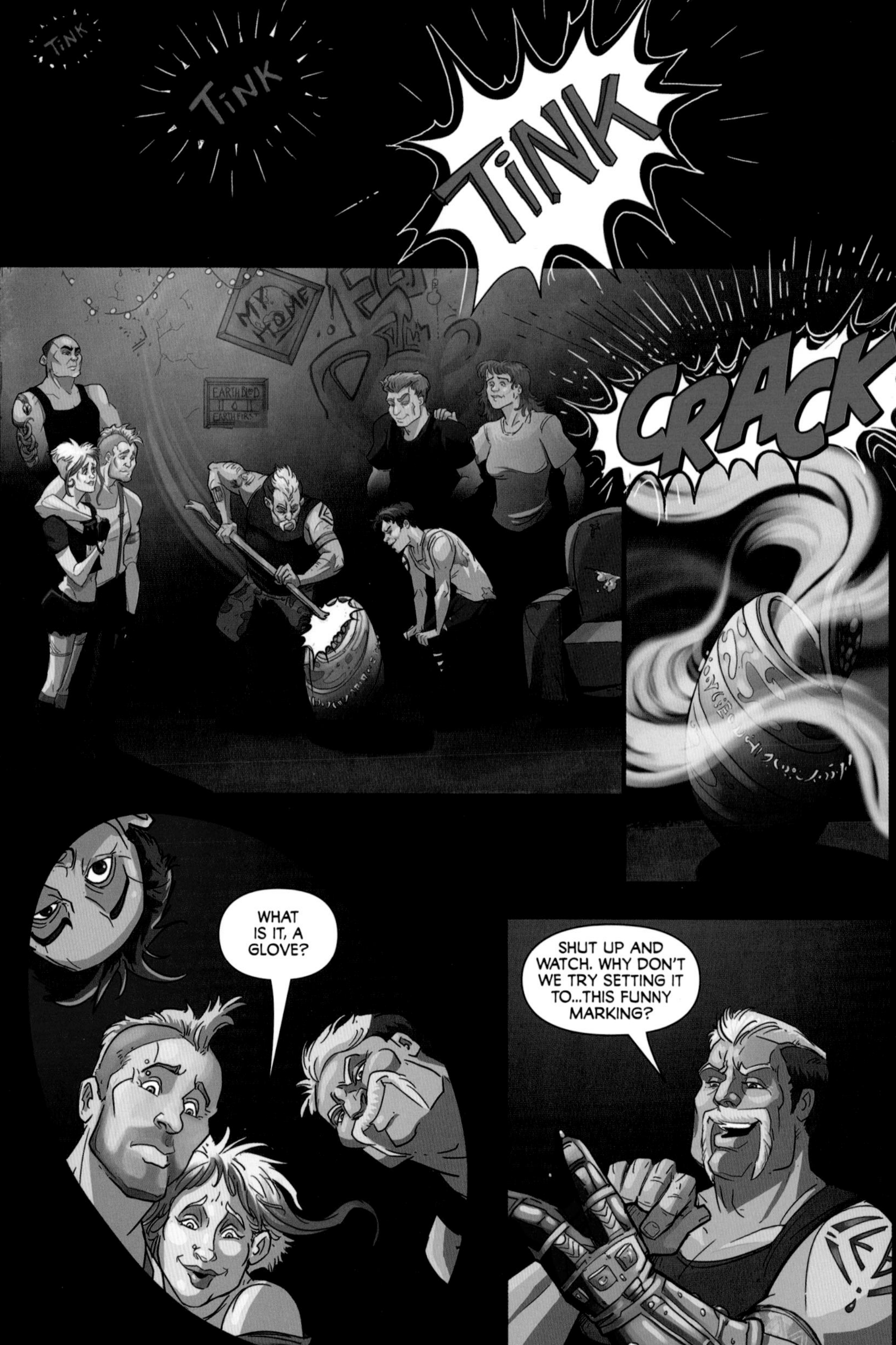
TINK
TINK
TINK
CRACK
WHAT IS IT, A GLOVE?
SHUT UP AND WATCH. WHY DON'T WE TRY SETTING IT TO...THIS FUNNY MARKING?

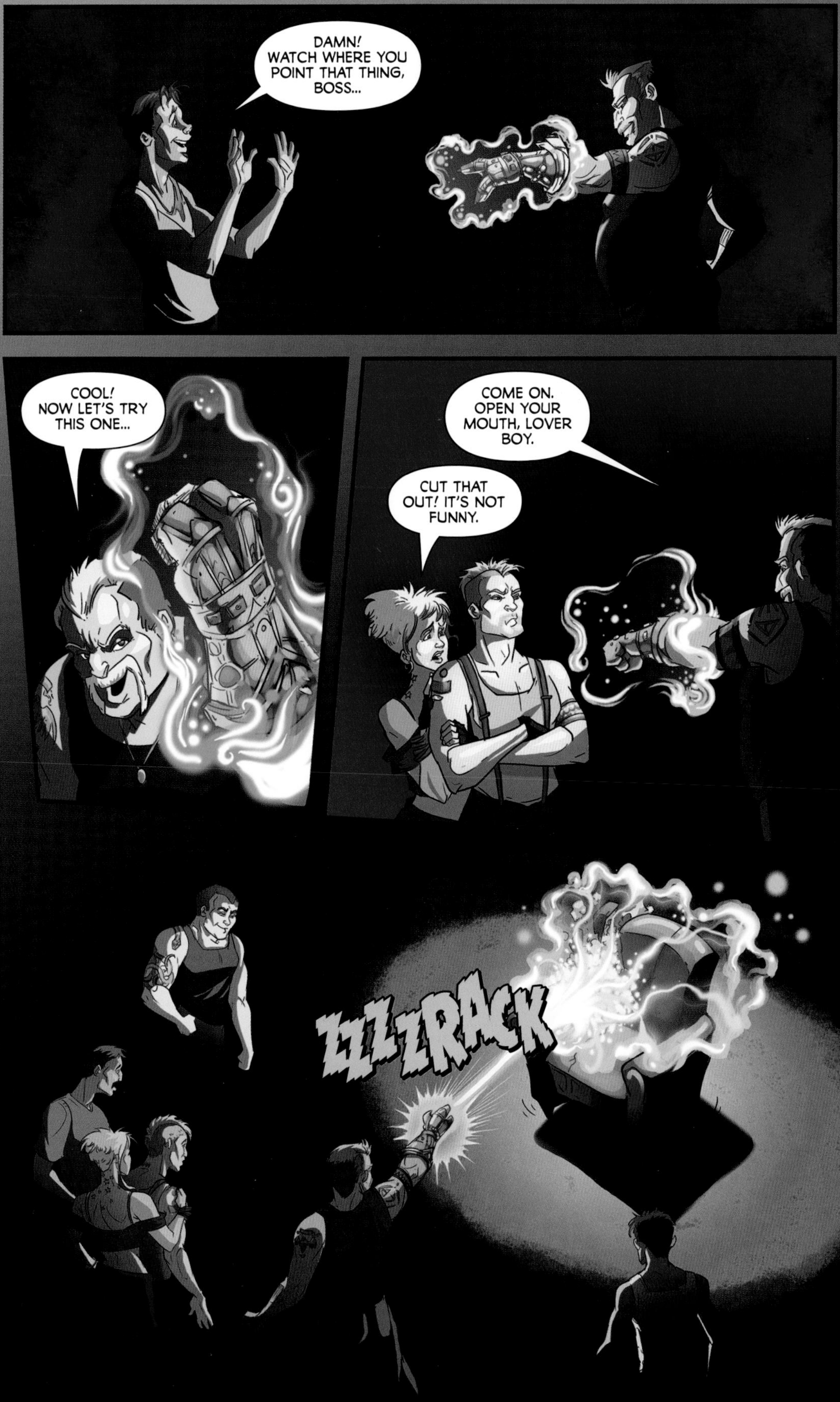
DAMN! WATCH WHERE YOU POINT THAT THING, BOSS...
COOL! NOW LET'S TRY THIS ONE...
COME ON. OPEN YOUR MOUTH, LOVER BOY.
CUT THAT OUT! IT'S NOT FUNNY.
ZZZZRACK

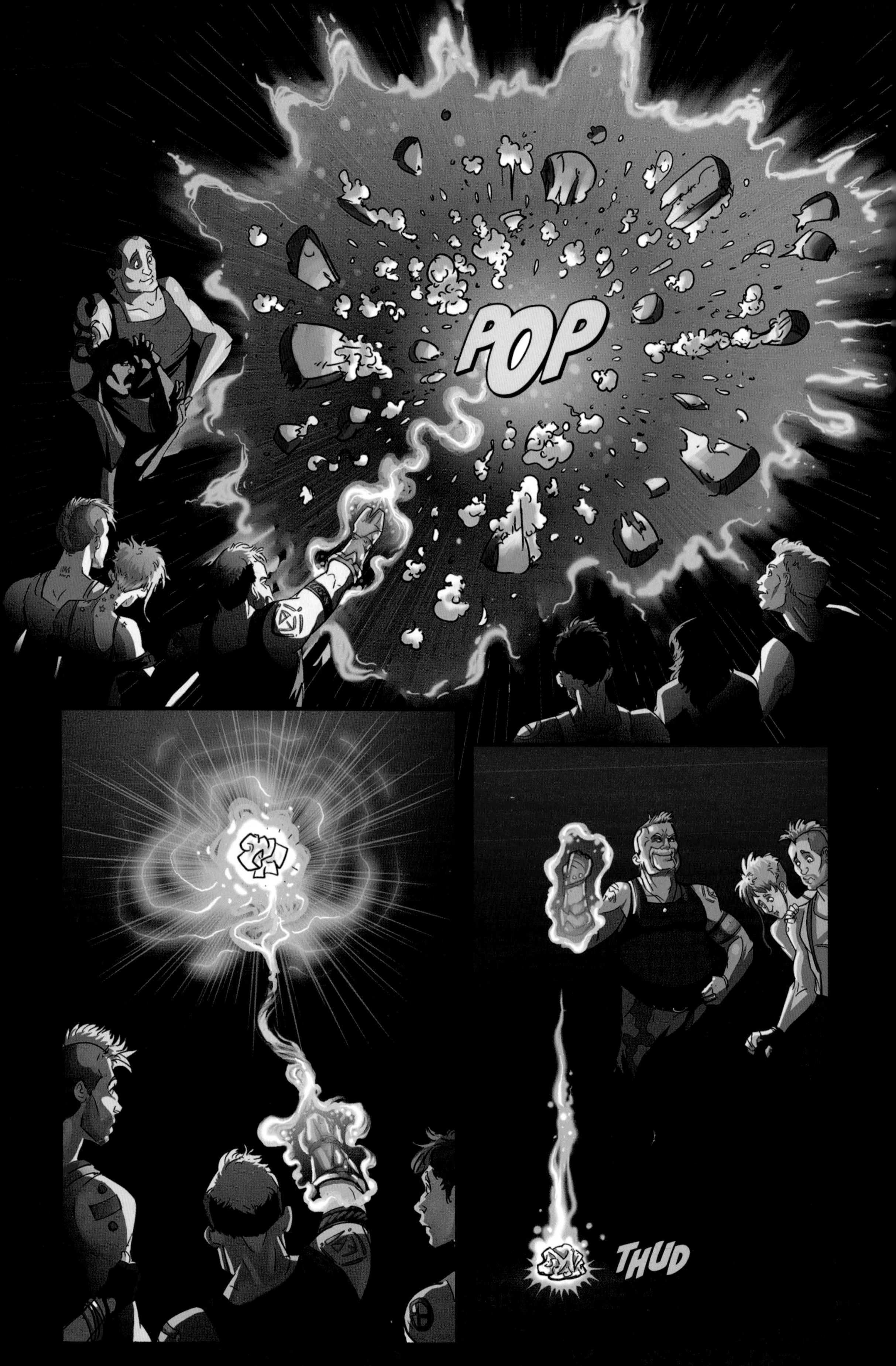
POP
THUD

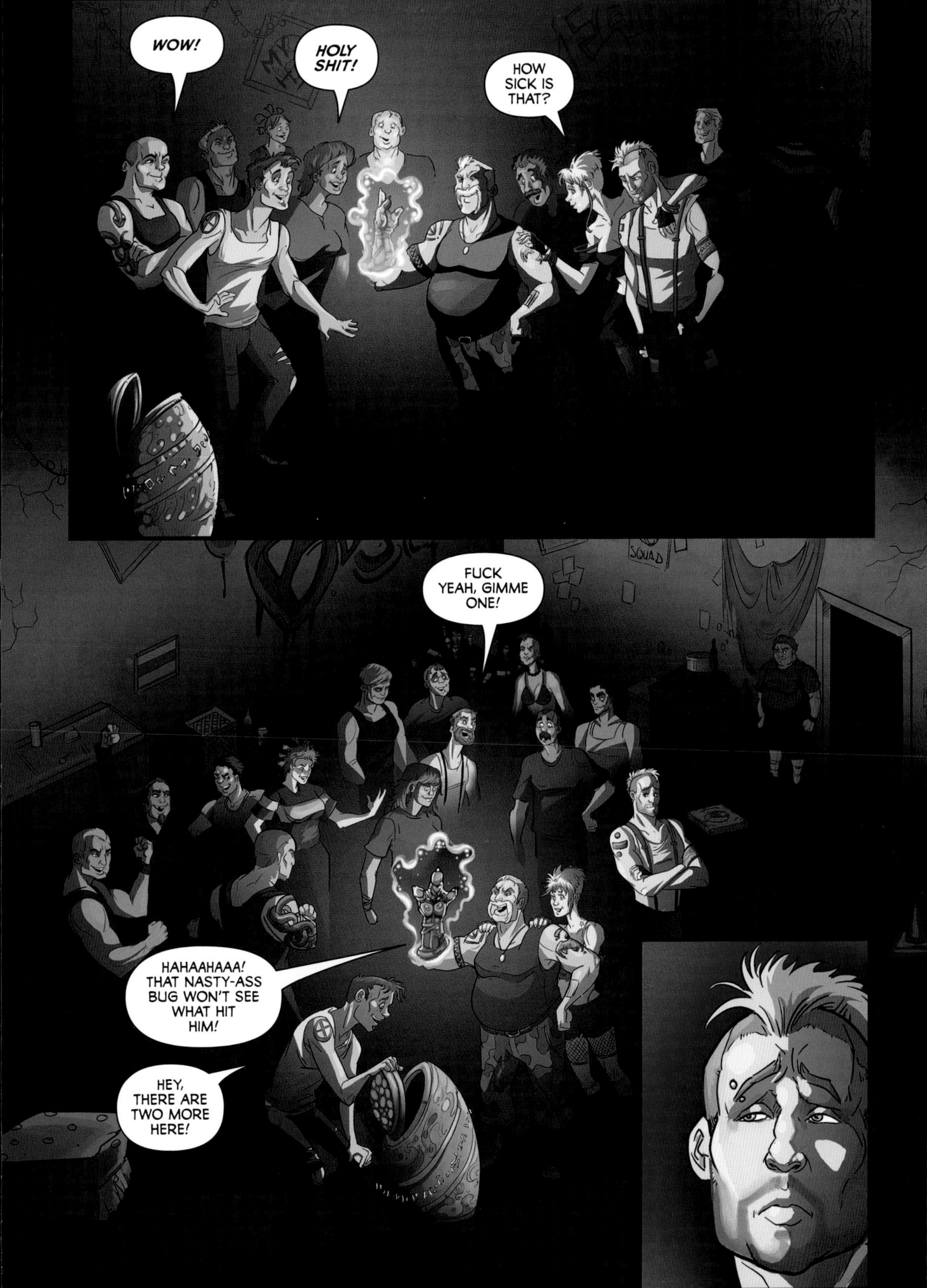
WOW!
HOLY SHIT!
HOW SICK IS THAT?
SQUAD
FUCK YEAH, GIMME ONE!
HAHAAHAAA! THAT NASTY-ASS BUG WON'T SEE WHAT HIT HIM!
HEY, THERE ARE TWO MORE HERE!

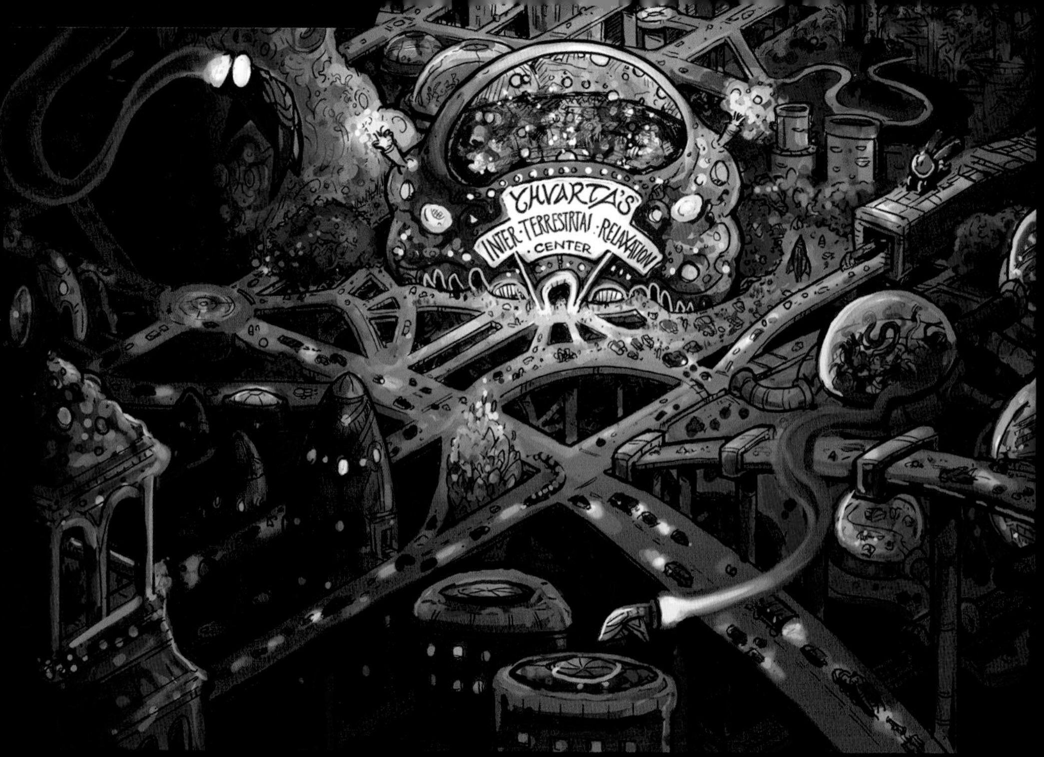
YHVARTA'S
INTER·TERRESTRIAL·RELAXATION
·CENTER

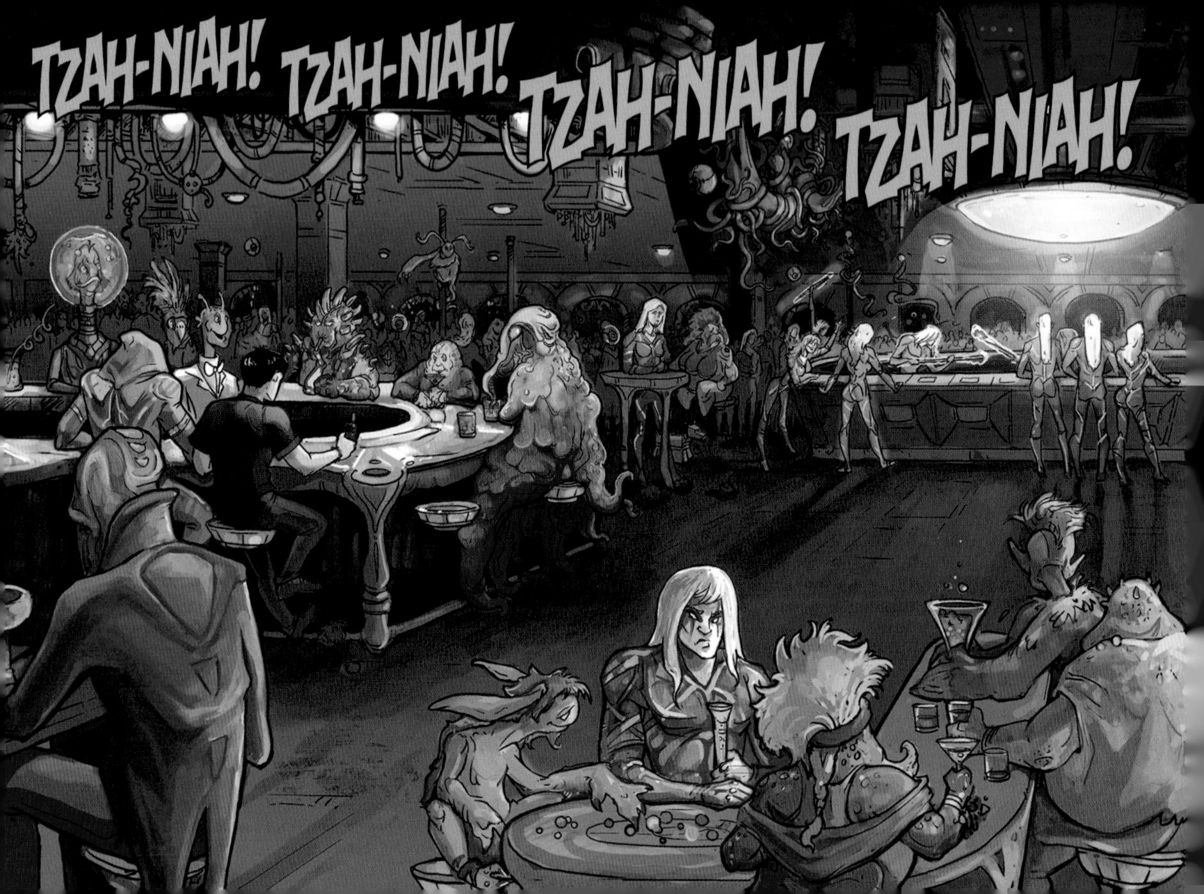
TZAH-NIAH! TZAH-NIAH! TZAH-NIAH! TZAH-NIAH!

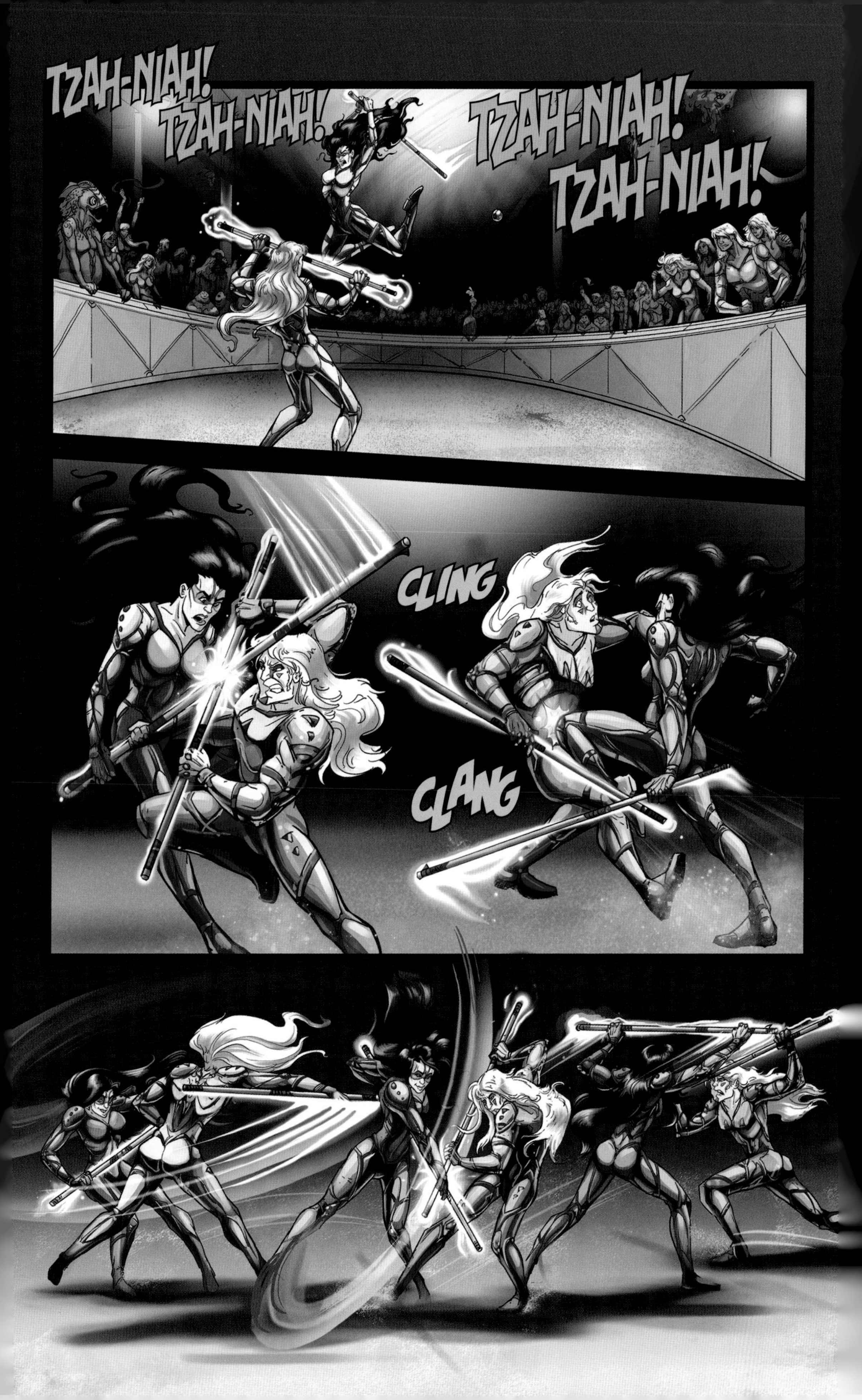
TZAH-NIAH!
TZAH-NIAH!
TZAH-NIAH!
TZAH-NIAH!
CLING
CLANG

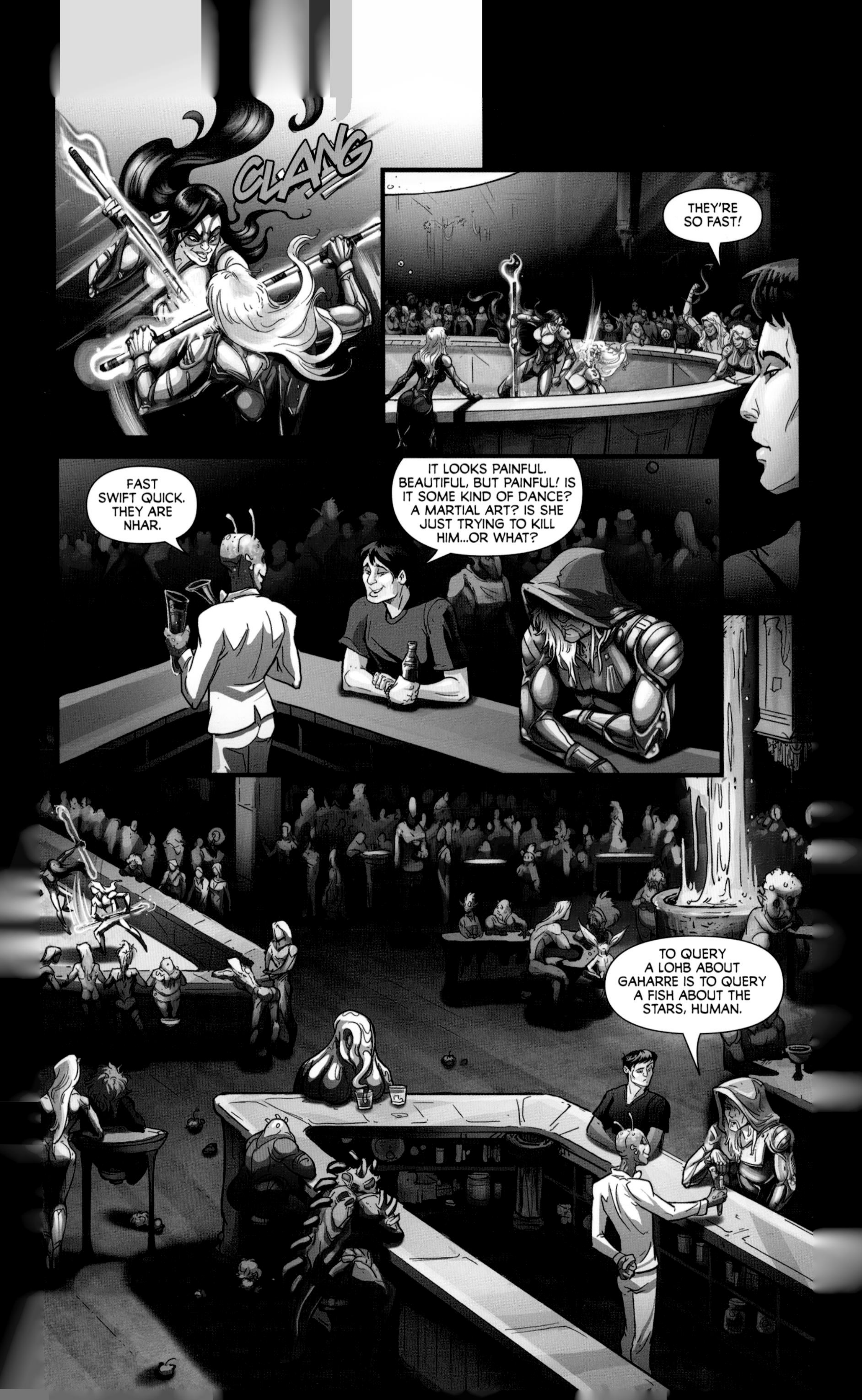
CLANG
THEY'RE SO FAST!
FAST SWIFT QUICK. THEY ARE NHAR.
IT LOOKS PAINFUL. BEAUTIFUL, BUT PAINFUL! IS IT SOME KIND OF DANCE? A MARTIAL ART? IS SHE JUST TRYING TO KILL HIM...OR WHAT?
TO QUERY A LOHB ABOUT GAHARRE IS TO QUERY A FISH ABOUT THE STARS, HUMAN.

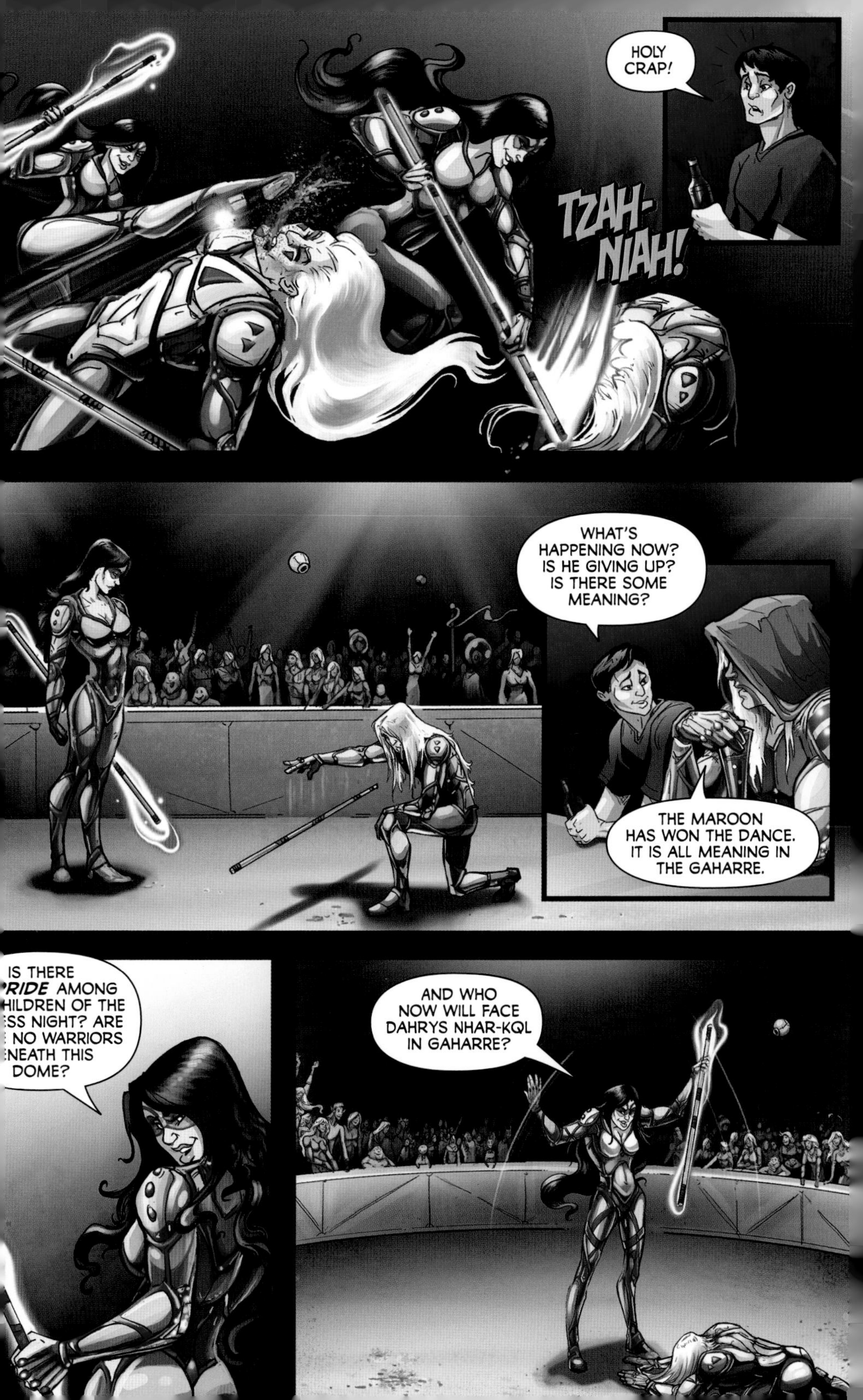
HOLY CRAP!
TZAH-NIAH!
WHAT'S HAPPENING NOW? IS HE GIVING UP? IS THERE SOME MEANING?
THE MAROON HAS WON THE DANCE. IT IS ALL MEANING IN THE GAHARRE.
IS THERE PRIDE AMONG HILDREN OF THE SS NIGHT? ARE NO WARRIORS NEATH THIS DOME?
AND WHO NOW WILL FACE DAHRYS NHAR-KQL IN GAHARRE?

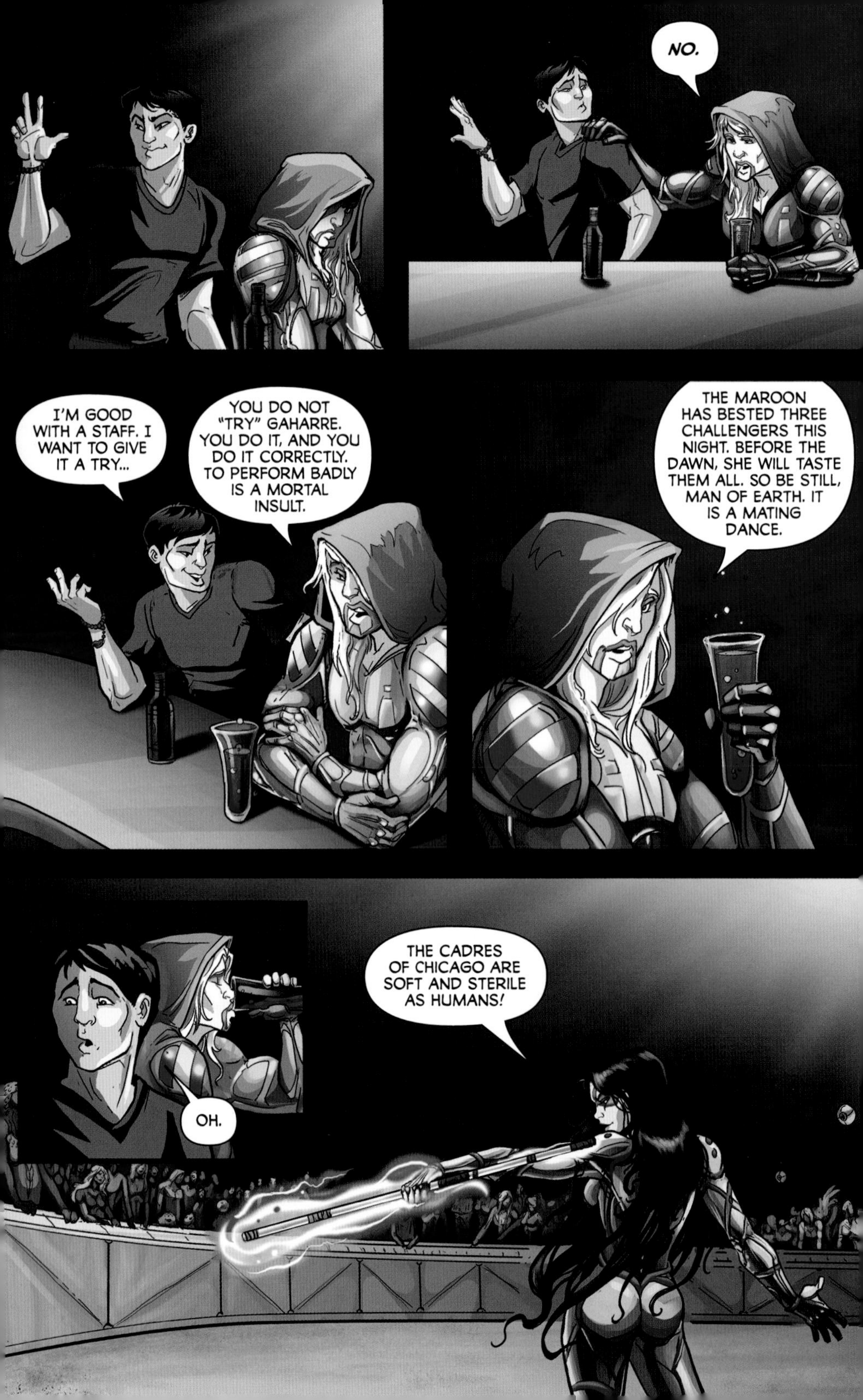
NO.
I'M GOOD WITH A STAFF. I WANT TO GIVE IT A TRY...
YOU DO NOT "TRY" GAHARRE. YOU DO IT, AND YOU DO IT CORRECTLY. TO PERFORM BADLY IS A MORTAL INSULT.
THE MAROON HAS BESTED THREE CHALLENGERS THIS NIGHT. BEFORE THE DAWN, SHE WILL TASTE THEM ALL. SO BE STILL, MAN OF EARTH. IT IS A MATING DANCE.
OH.
THE CADRES OF CHICAGO ARE SOFT AND STERILE AS HUMANS!

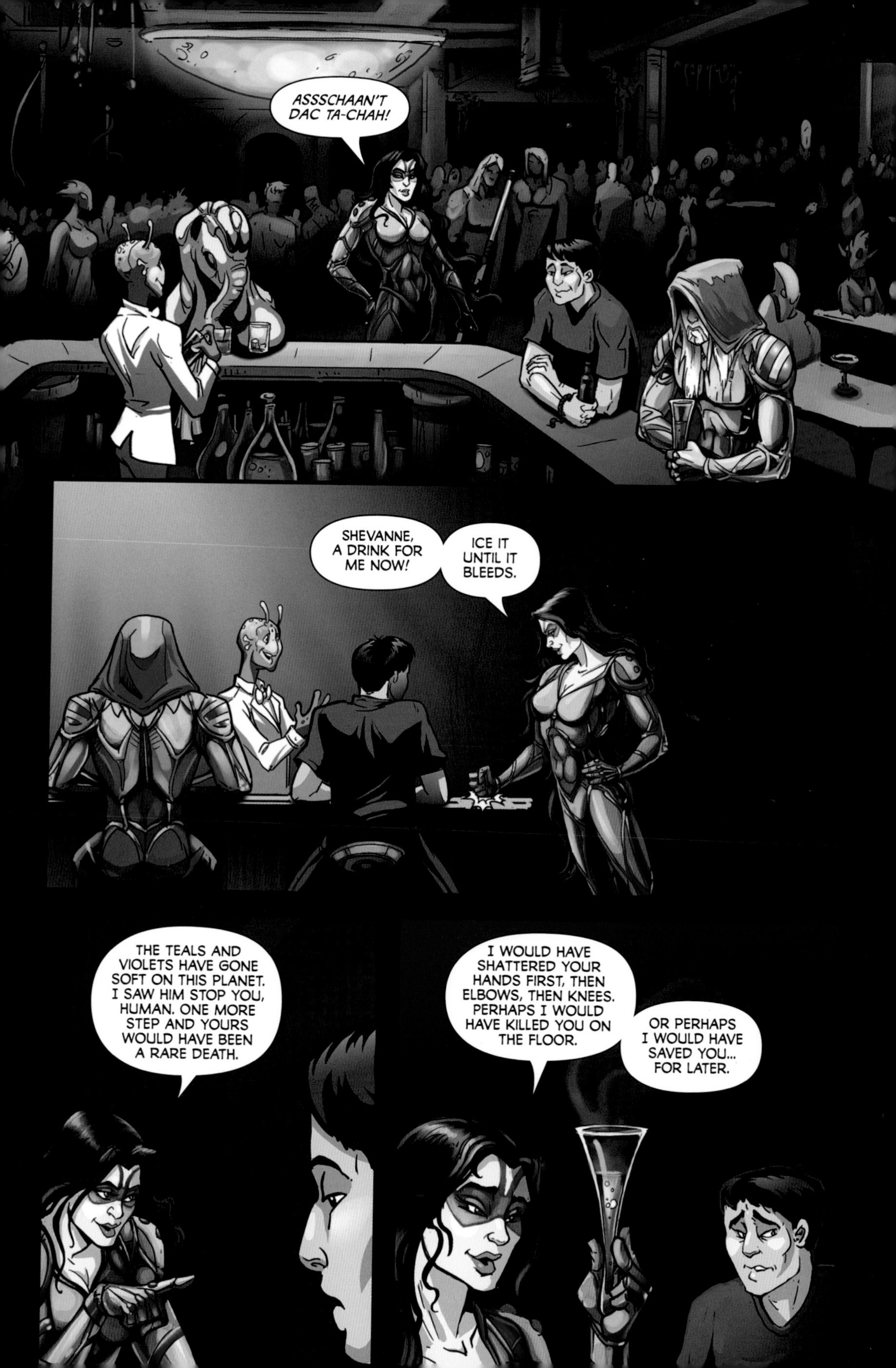
ASSSCHAAN'T DAC TA-CHAH!
SHEVANNE, A DRINK FOR ME NOW!
ICE IT UNTIL IT BLEEDS.
THE TEALS AND VIOLETS HAVE GONE SOFT ON THIS PLANET. I SAW HIM STOP YOU, HUMAN. ONE MORE STEP AND YOURS WOULD HAVE BEEN A RARE DEATH.
I WOULD HAVE SHATTERED YOUR HANDS FIRST, THEN ELBOWS, THEN KNEES. PERHAPS I WOULD HAVE KILLED YOU ON THE FLOOR.
OR PERHAPS I WOULD HAVE SAVED YOU... FOR LATER.

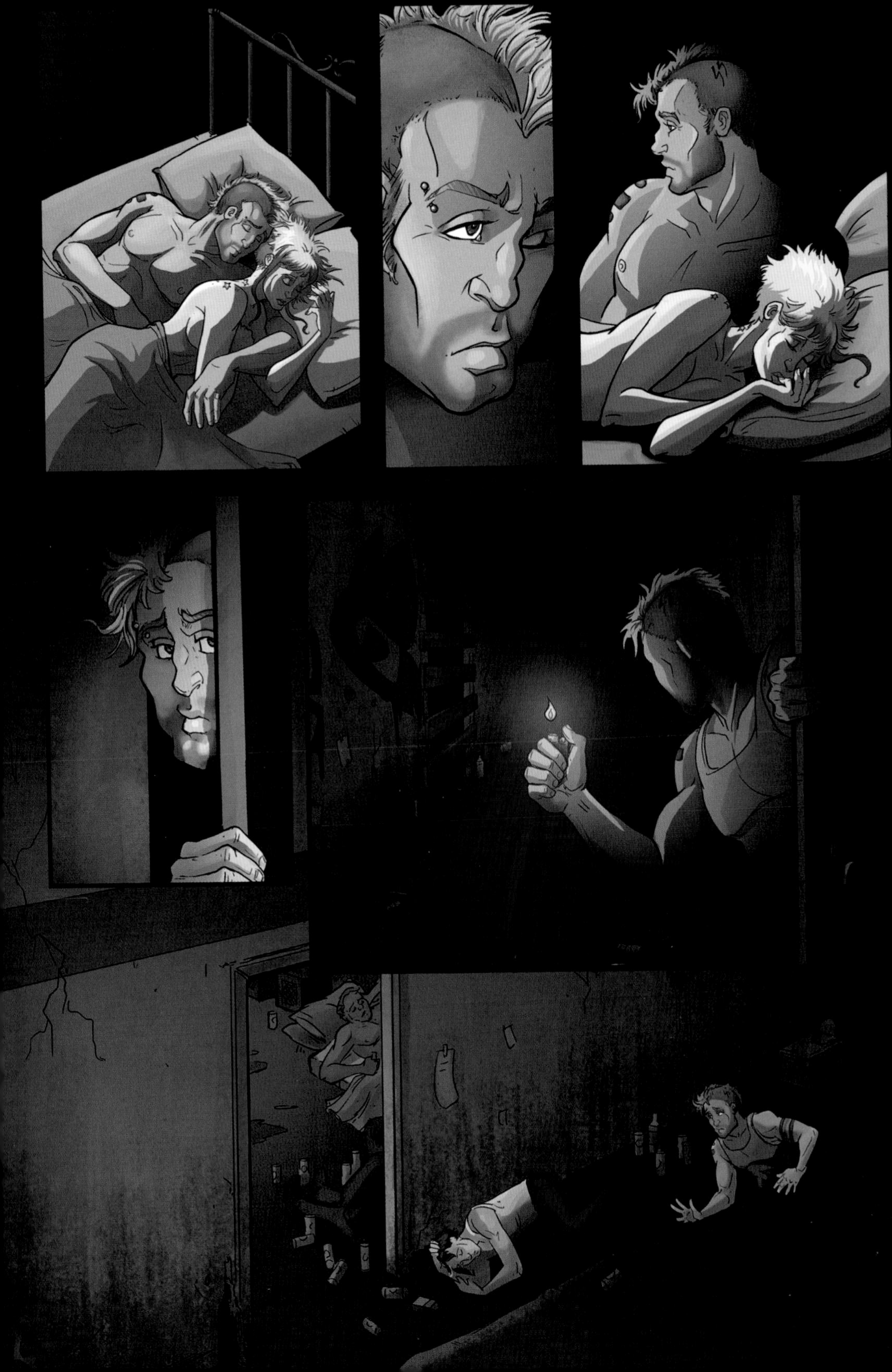

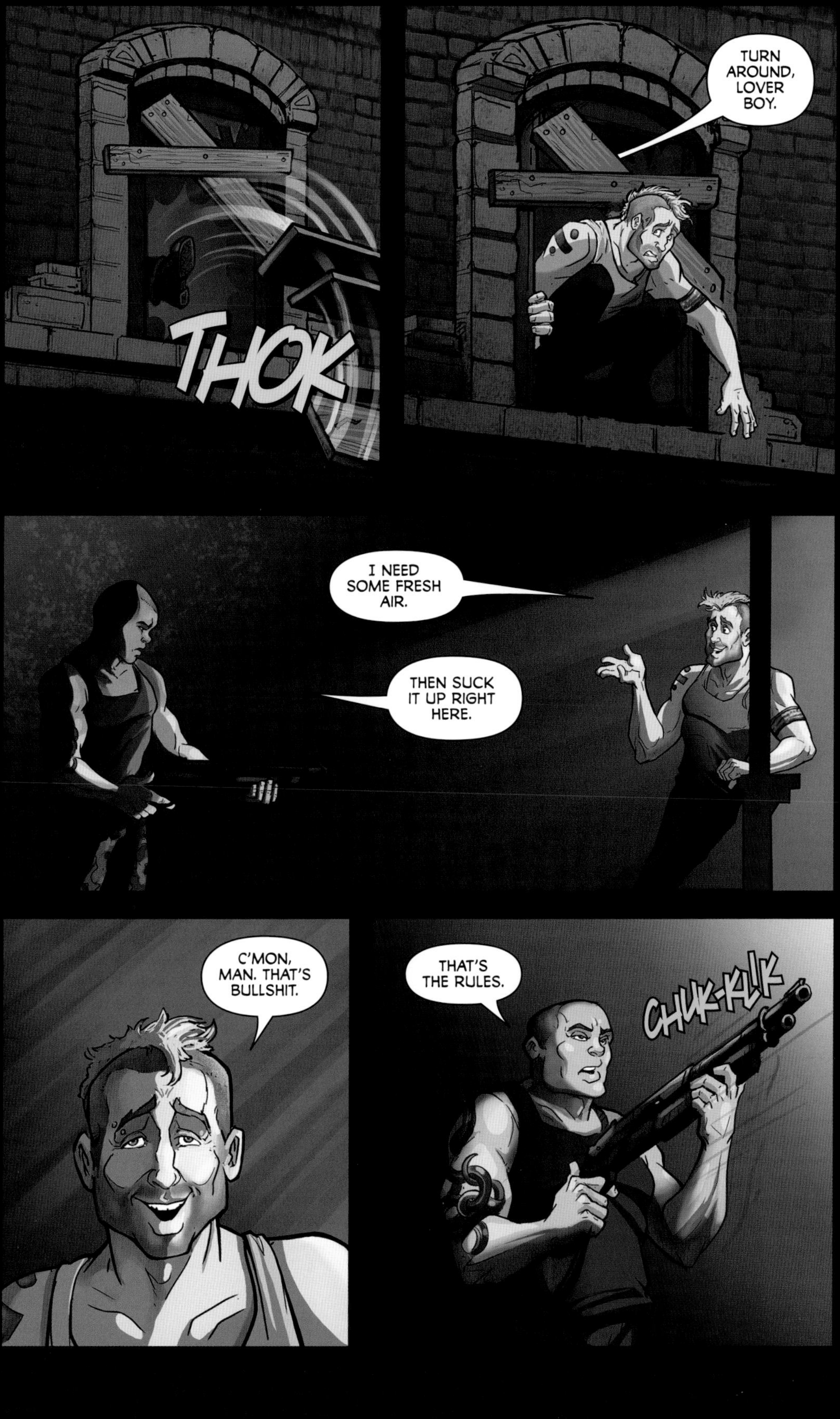
THOK
TURN AROUND, LOVER BOY.
I NEED SOME FRESH AIR.
THEN SUCK IT UP RIGHT HERE.
C'MON, MAN. THAT'S BULLSHIT.
THAT'S THE RULES.
CHUK-KLIK

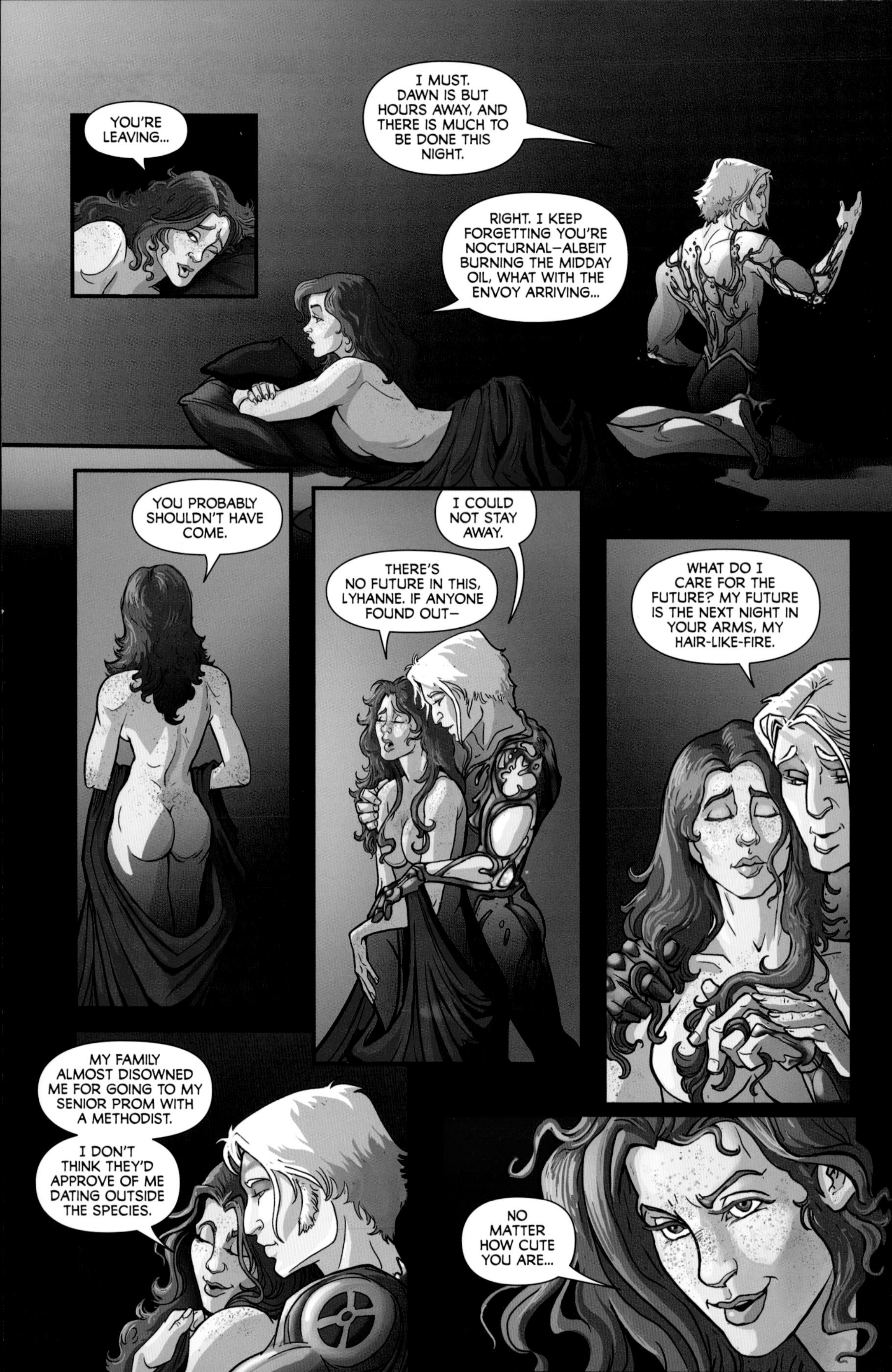
YOU'RE LEAVING...
I MUST. DAWN IS BUT HOURS AWAY, AND THERE IS MUCH TO BE DONE THIS NIGHT.
RIGHT. I KEEP FORGETTING YOU'RE NOCTURNAL—ALBEIT BURNING THE MIDDAY OIL, WHAT WITH THE ENVOY ARRIVING...
YOU PROBABLY SHOULDN'T HAVE COME.
I COULD NOT STAY AWAY.
THERE'S NO FUTURE IN THIS, LYHANNE. IF ANYONE FOUND OUT—
WHAT DO I CARE FOR THE FUTURE? MY FUTURE IS THE NEXT NIGHT IN YOUR ARMS, MY HAIR-LIKE-FIRE.
MY FAMILY ALMOST DISOWNED ME FOR GOING TO MY SENIOR PROM WITH A METHODIST.
I DON'T THINK THEY'D APPROVE OF ME DATING OUTSIDE THE SPECIES.
NO MATTER HOW CUTE YOU ARE...

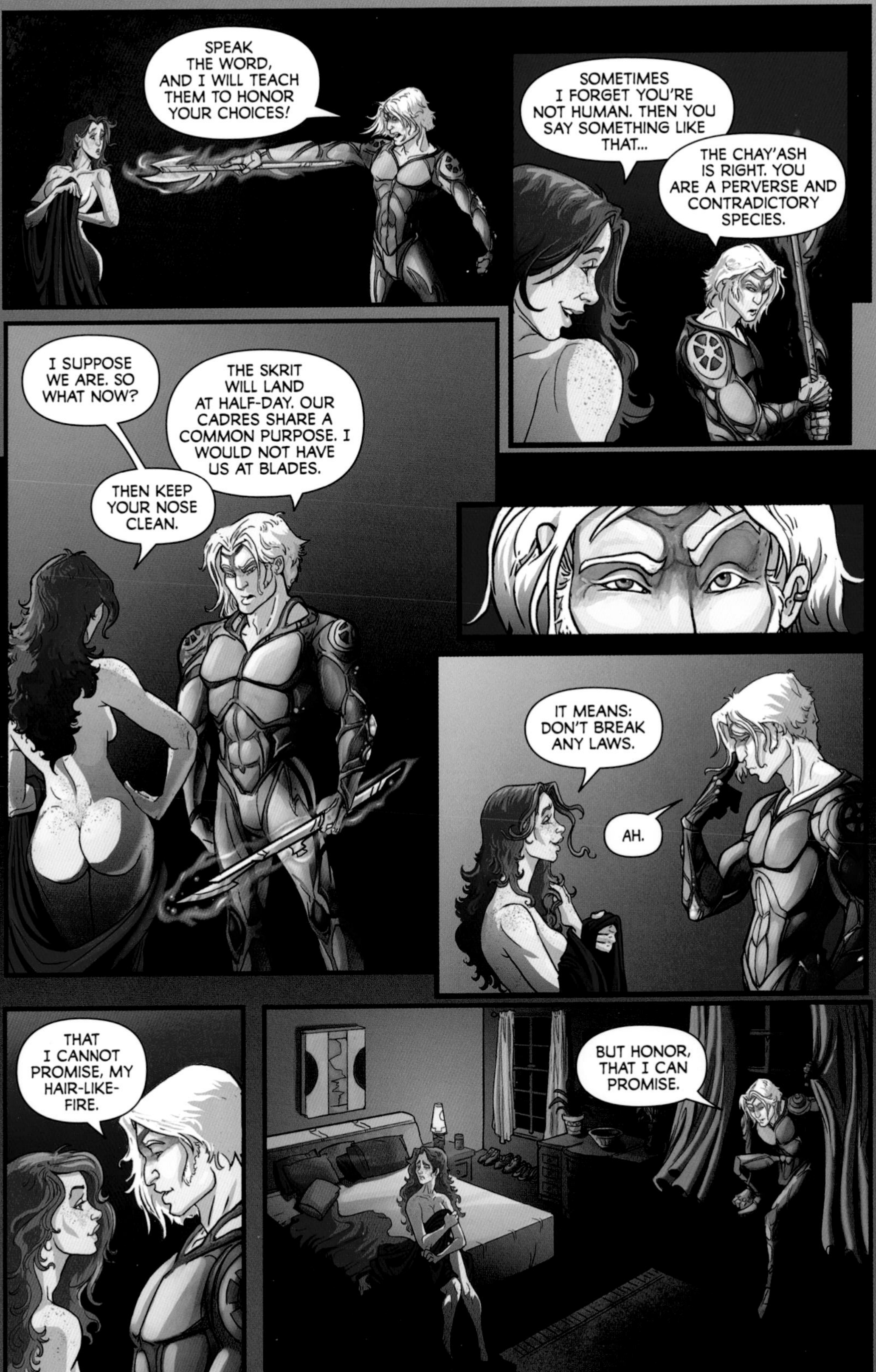
SPEAK THE WORD, AND I WILL TEACH THEM TO HONOR YOUR CHOICES!
SOMETIMES I FORGET YOU'RE NOT HUMAN. THEN YOU SAY SOMETHING LIKE THAT...
THE CHAY'ASH IS RIGHT. YOU ARE A PERVERSE AND CONTRADICTORY SPECIES.
I SUPPOSE WE ARE. SO WHAT NOW?
THE SKRIT WILL LAND AT HALF-DAY. OUR CADRES SHARE A COMMON PURPOSE. I WOULD NOT HAVE US AT BLADES.
THEN KEEP YOUR NOSE CLEAN.
IT MEANS: DON'T BREAK ANY LAWS.
AH.
THAT I CANNOT PROMISE, MY HAIR-LIKE-FIRE.
BUT HONOR, THAT I CAN PROMISE.

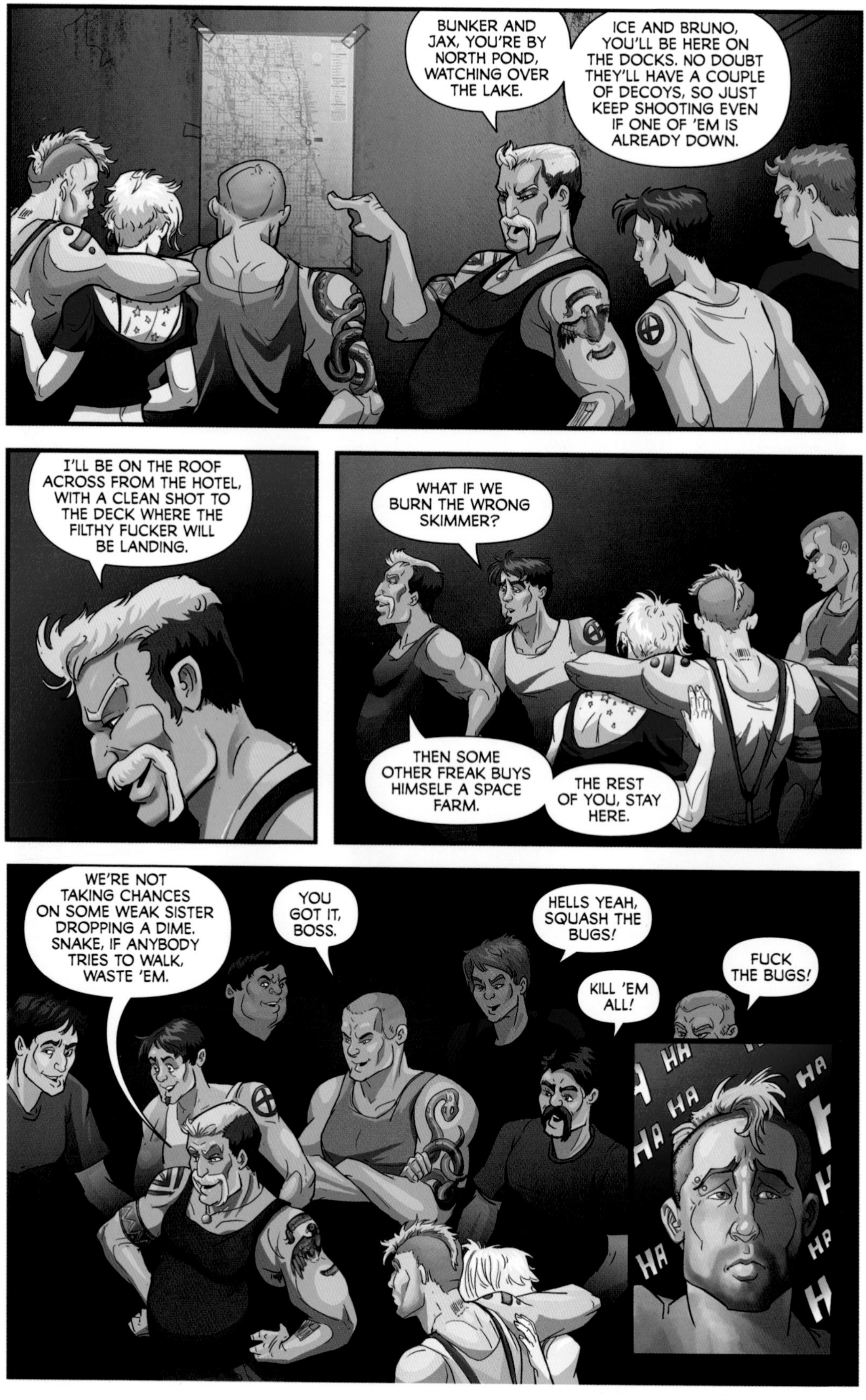
BUNKER AND JAX, YOU'RE BY NORTH POND, WATCHING OVER THE LAKE.
ICE AND BRUNO, YOU'LL BE HERE ON THE DOCKS. NO DOUBT THEY'LL HAVE A COUPLE OF DECOYS, SO JUST KEEP SHOOTING EVEN IF ONE OF 'EM IS ALREADY DOWN.
I'LL BE ON THE ROOF ACROSS FROM THE HOTEL, WITH A CLEAN SHOT TO THE DECK WHERE THE FILTHY FUCKER WILL BE LANDING.
WHAT IF WE BURN THE WRONG SKIMMER?
THEN SOME OTHER FREAK BUYS HIMSELF A SPACE FARM.
THE REST OF YOU, STAY HERE.
WE'RE NOT TAKING CHANCES ON SOME WEAK SISTER DROPPING A DIME. SNAKE, IF ANYBODY TRIES TO WALK, WASTE 'EM.
YOU GOT IT, BOSS.
HELLS YEAH, SQUASH THE BUGS!
KILL 'EM ALL!
FUCK THE BUGS!
HA HA HA HA HA HA HA

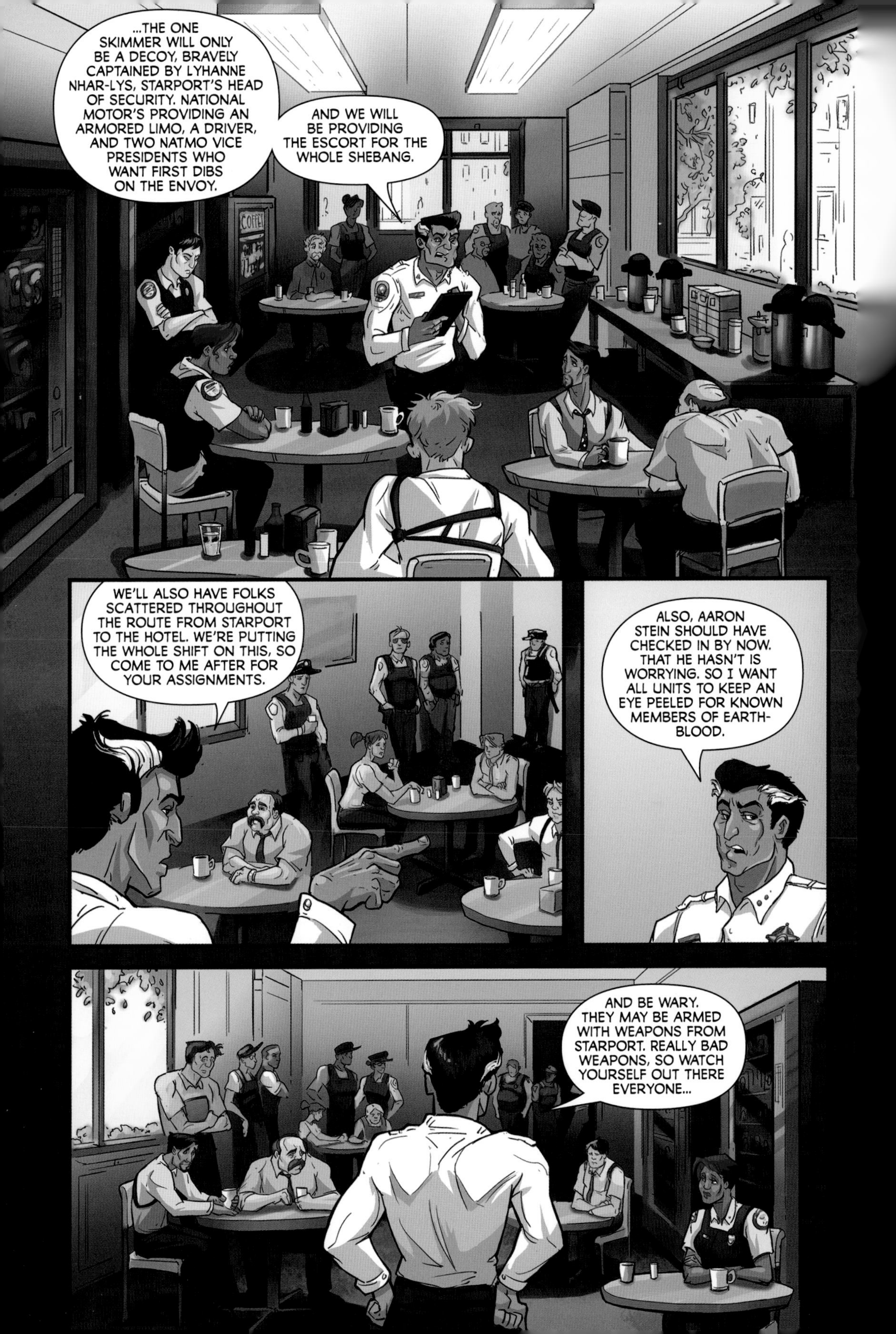
...THE ONE SKIMMER WILL ONLY BE A DECOY, BRAVELY CAPTAINED BY LYHANNE NHAR-LYS, STARPORT'S HEAD OF SECURITY. NATIONAL MOTOR'S PROVIDING AN ARMORED LIMO, A DRIVER, AND TWO NATMO VICE PRESIDENTS WHO WANT FIRST DIBS ON THE ENVOY.
AND WE WILL BE PROVIDING THE ESCORT FOR THE WHOLE SHEBANG.
COFFEE
WE'LL ALSO HAVE FOLKS SCATTERED THROUGHOUT THE ROUTE FROM STARPORT TO THE HOTEL. WE'RE PUTTING THE WHOLE SHIFT ON THIS, SO COME TO ME AFTER FOR YOUR ASSIGNMENTS.
ALSO, AARON STEIN SHOULD HAVE CHECKED IN BY NOW. THAT HE HASN'T IS WORRYING. SO I WANT ALL UNITS TO KEEP AN EYE PEELED FOR KNOWN MEMBERS OF EARTH-BLOOD.
AND BE WARY. THEY MAY BE ARMED WITH WEAPONS FROM STARPORT. REALLY BAD WEAPONS, SO WATCH YOURSELF OUT THERE EVERYONE...

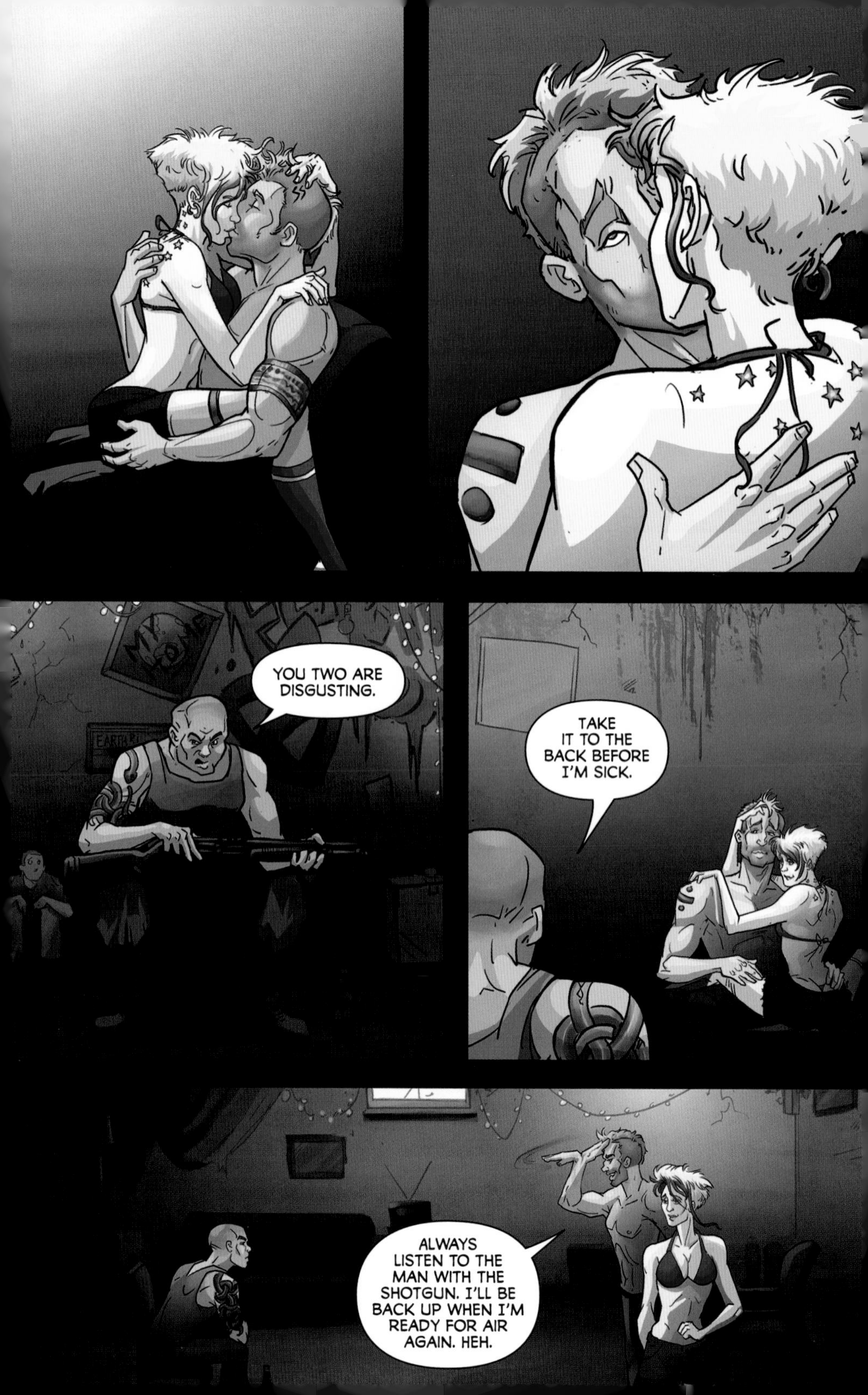
YOU TWO ARE DISGUSTING.
TAKE IT TO THE BACK BEFORE I'M SICK.
ALWAYS LISTEN TO THE MAN WITH THE SHOTGUN. I'LL BE BACK UP WHEN I'M READY FOR AIR AGAIN. HEH.

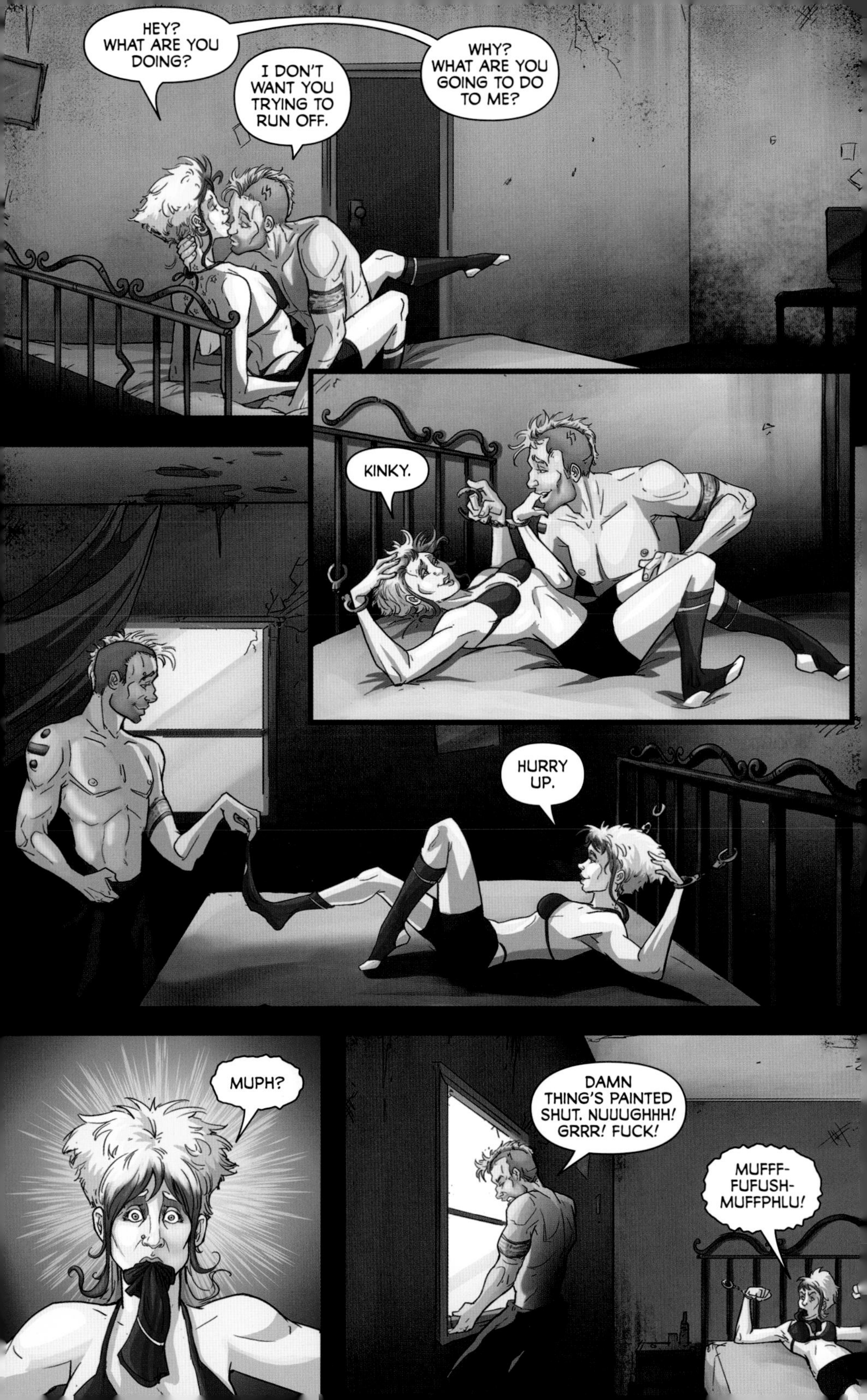
HEY? WHAT ARE YOU DOING?
I DON'T WANT YOU TRYING TO RUN OFF.
WHY? WHAT ARE YOU GOING TO DO TO ME?
KINKY.
HURRY UP.
MUPH?
DAMN THING'S PAINTED SHUT. NUUUGHHH! GRRR! FUCK!
MUFFF-FUFUSH-MUFFPHLU!

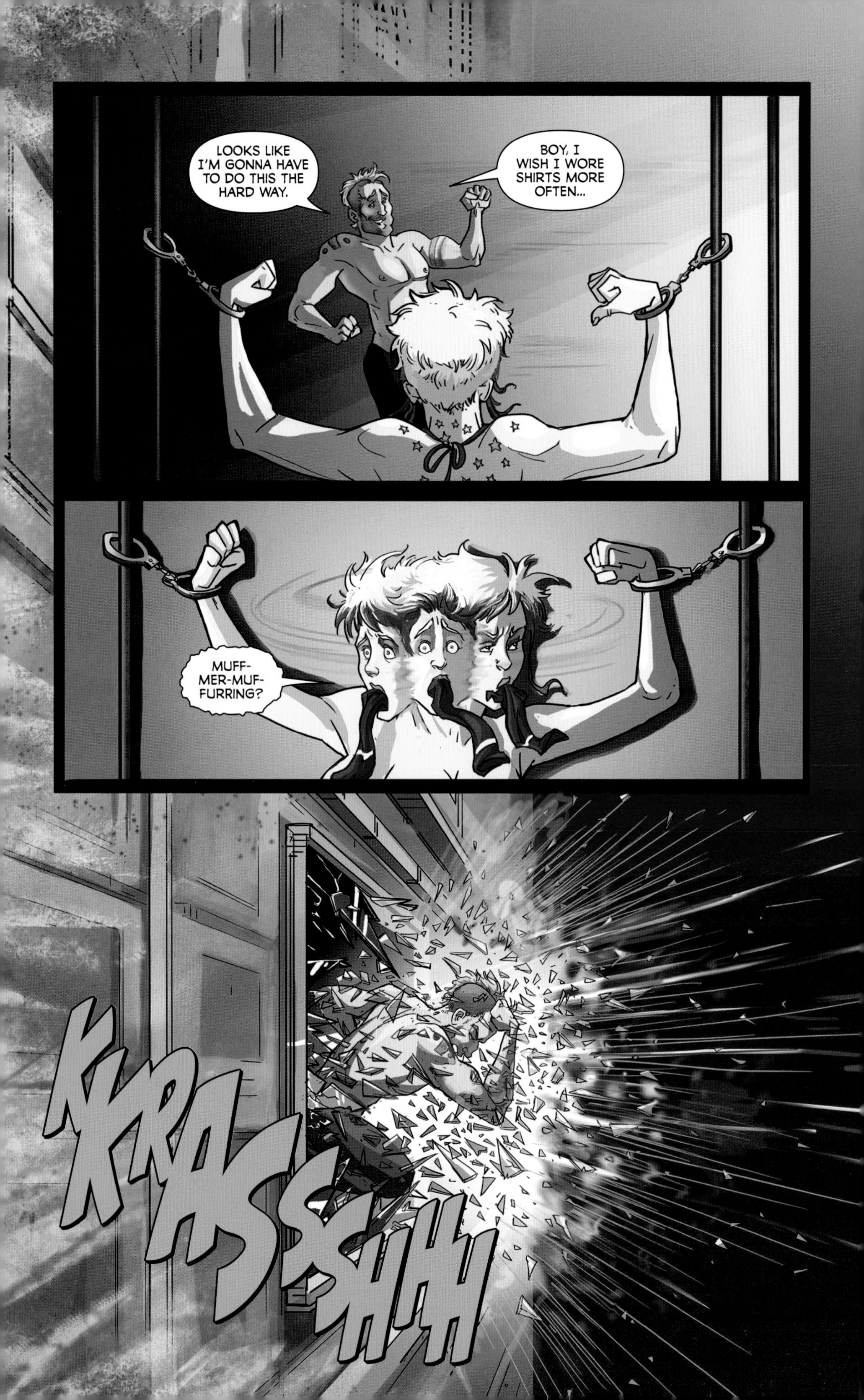
LOOKS LIKE I'M GONNA HAVE TO DO THIS THE HARD WAY.
BOY, I WISH I WORE SHIRTS MORE OFTEN...
MUFF-MER-MUF-FURRING?
KRASSHH

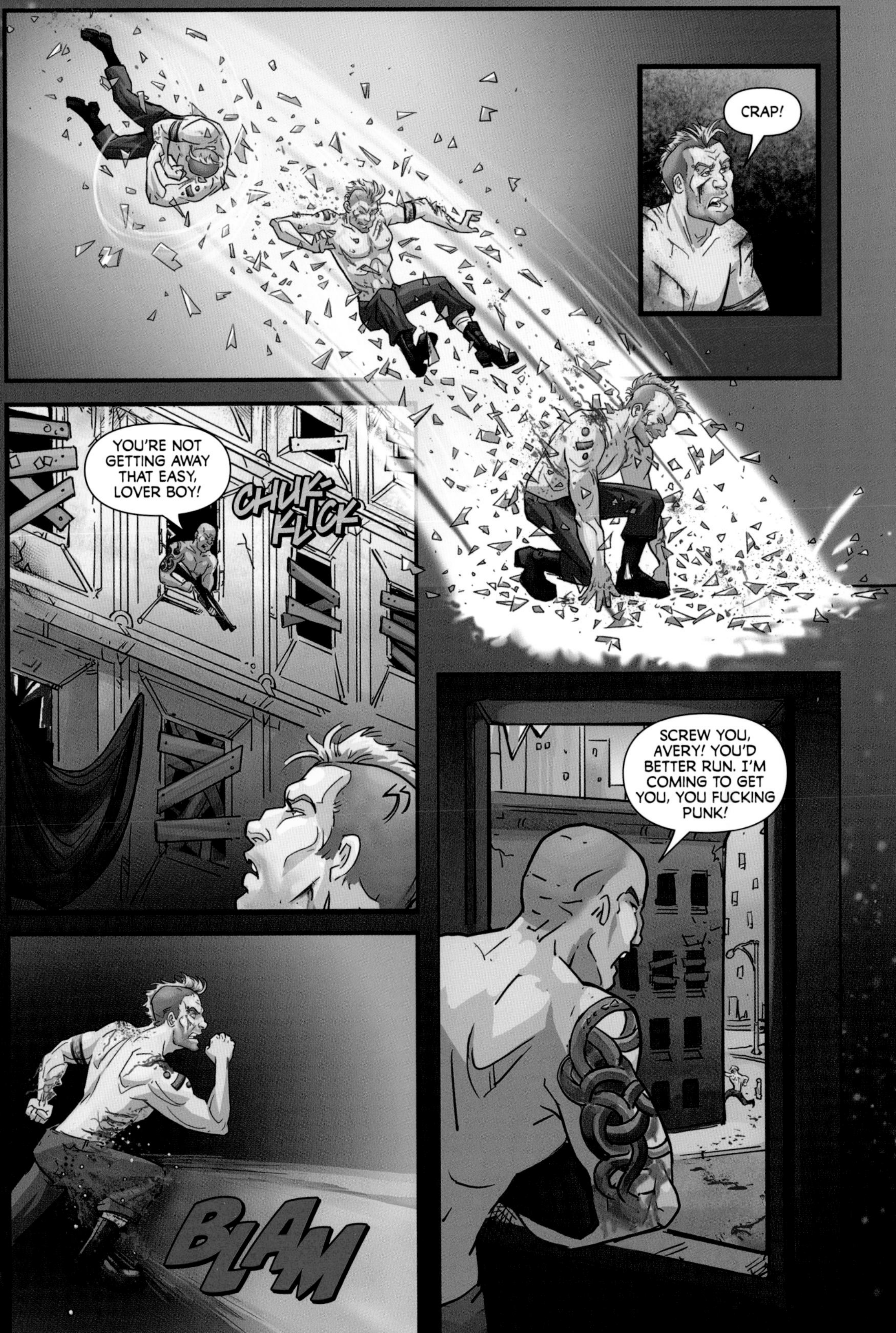
CRAP!
YOU'RE NOT GETTING AWAY THAT EASY, LOVER BOY!
CHUK-KLICK
SCREW YOU, AVERY! YOU'D BETTER RUN. I'M COMING TO GET YOU, YOU FUCKING PUNK!
BLAM

CHAPTER SIX

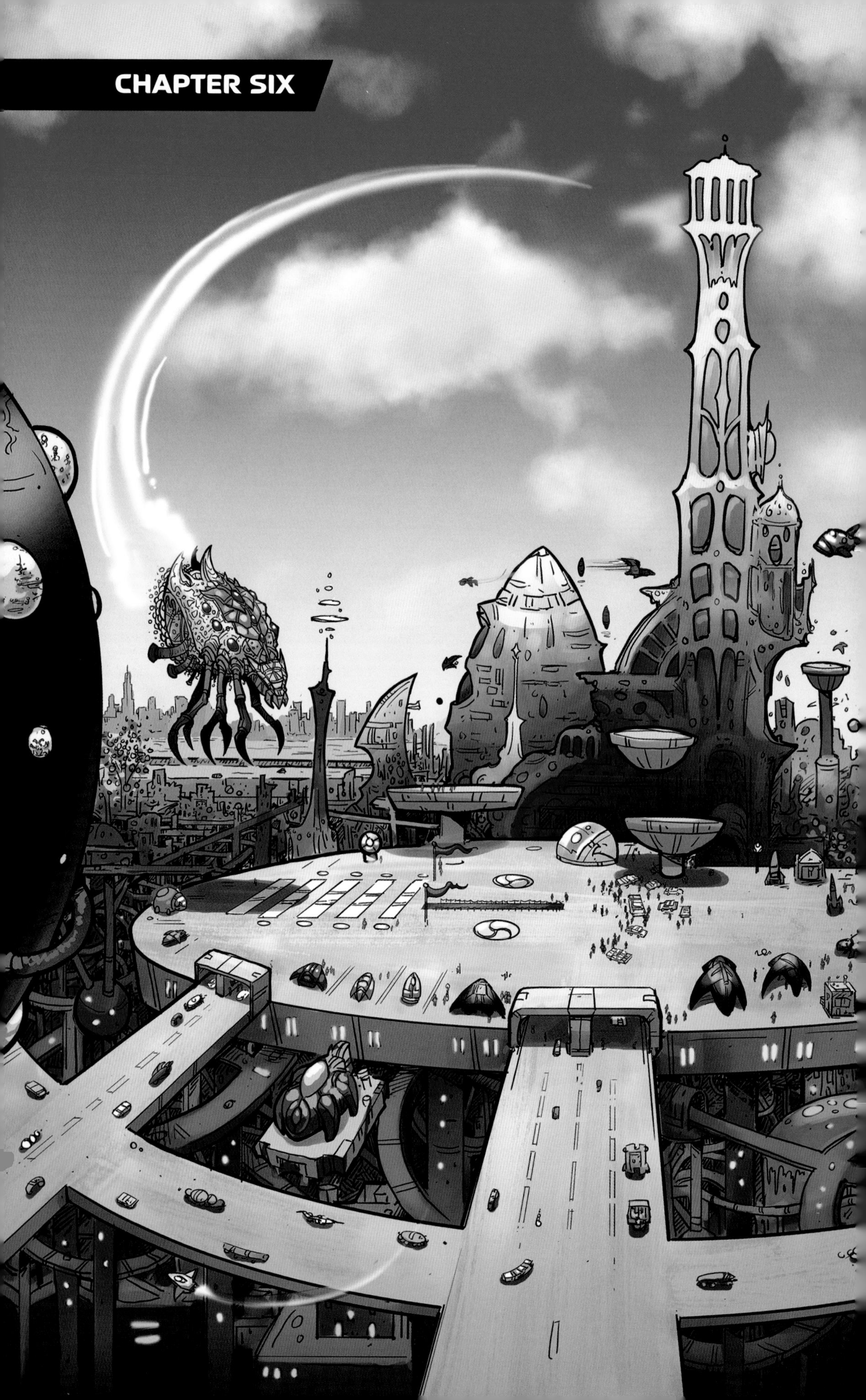

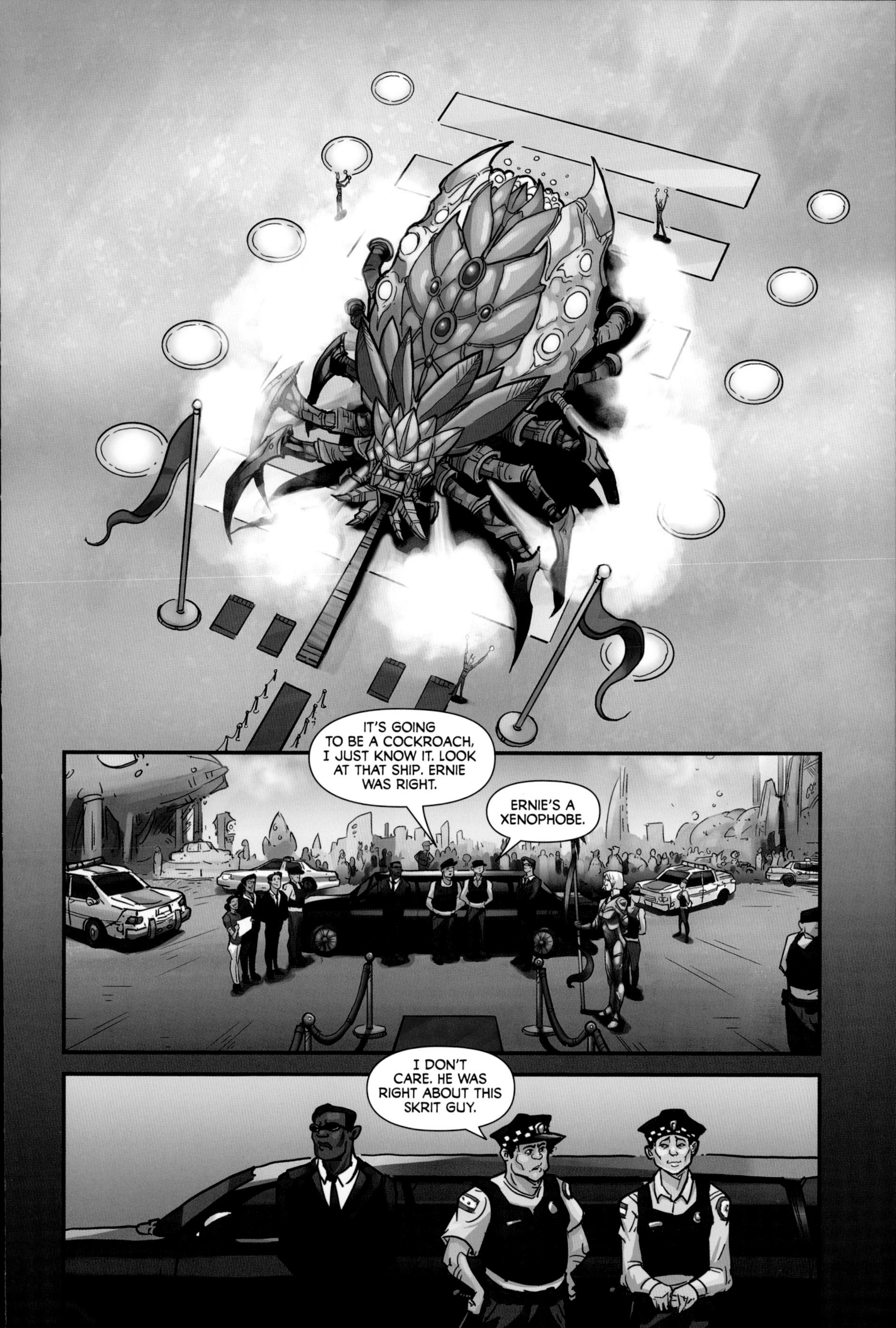
IT'S GOING TO BE A COCKROACH, I JUST KNOW IT. LOOK AT THAT SHIP. ERNIE WAS RIGHT.
ERNIE'S A XENOPHOBE.
I DON'T CARE. HE WAS RIGHT ABOUT THIS SKRIT GUY.

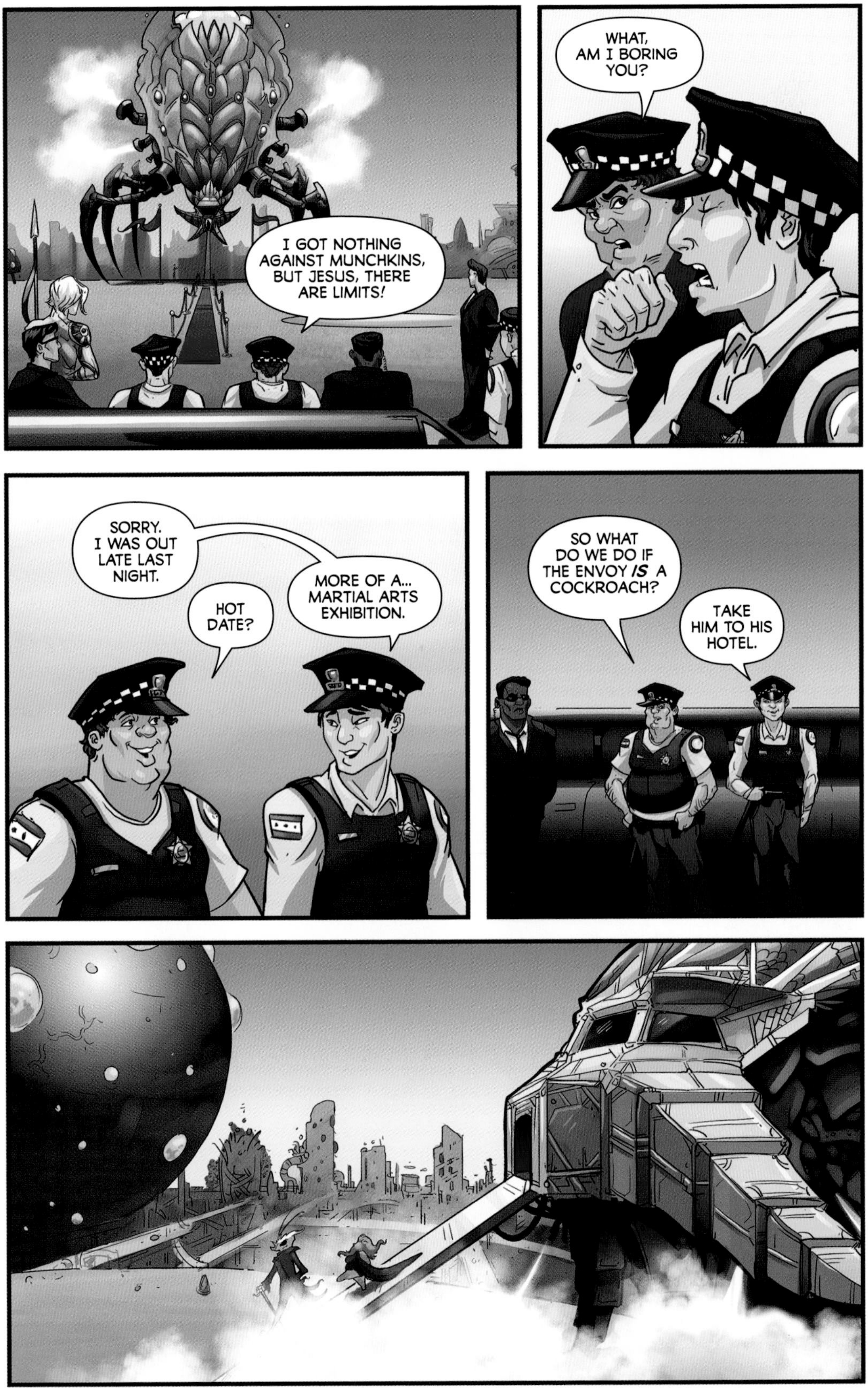
I GOT NOTHING AGAINST MUNCHKINS, BUT JESUS, THERE ARE LIMITS!
WHAT, AM I BORING YOU?
SORRY. I WAS OUT LATE LAST NIGHT.
HOT DATE?
MORE OF A... MARTIAL ARTS EXHIBITION.
SO WHAT DO WE DO IF THE ENVOY *IS* A COCKROACH?
TAKE HIM TO HIS HOTEL.

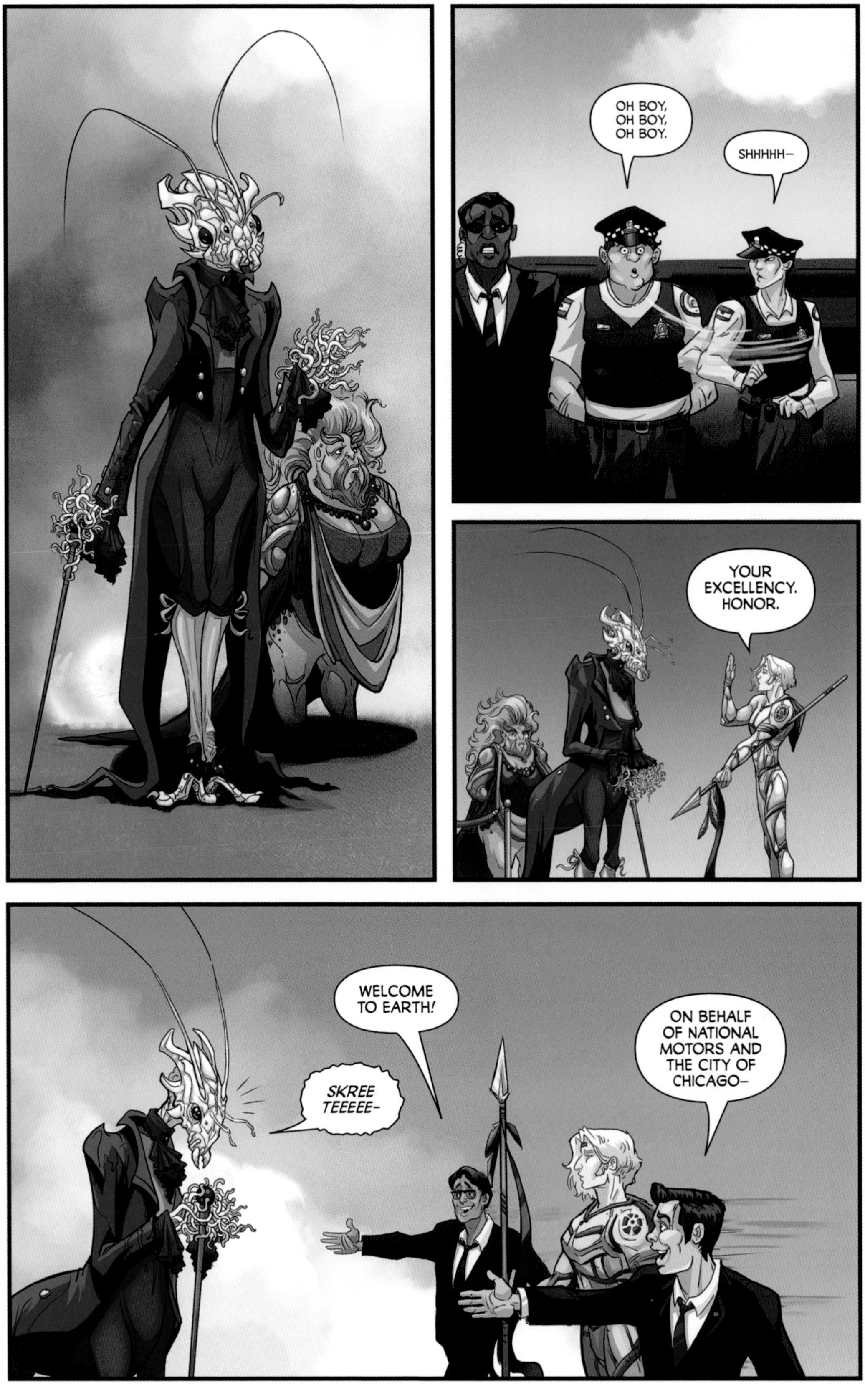
OH BOY, OH BOY, OH BOY.
SHHHHH—
YOUR EXCELLENCY. HONOR.
SKREE TEEEEE-
WELCOME TO EARTH!
ON BEHALF OF NATIONAL MOTORS AND THE CITY OF CHICAGO—

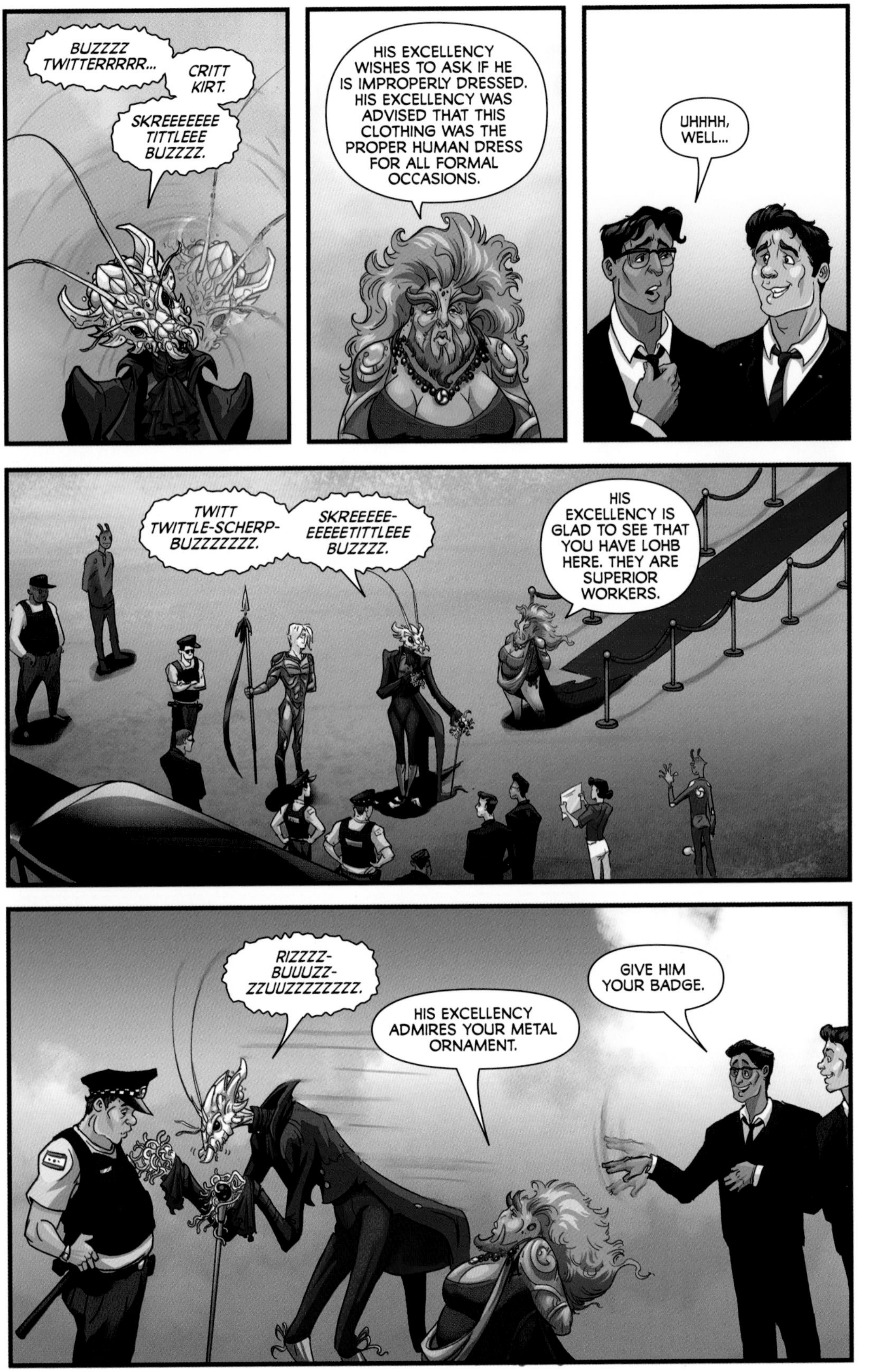
BUZZZZ TWITTERRRRR...
CRITT KIRT.
SKREEEEEEE TITTLEEE BUZZZZ.
HIS EXCELLENCY WISHES TO ASK IF HE IS IMPROPERLY DRESSED. HIS EXCELLENCY WAS ADVISED THAT THIS CLOTHING WAS THE PROPER HUMAN DRESS FOR ALL FORMAL OCCASIONS.
UHHHH, WELL...
TWITT TWITTLE-SCHERP-BUZZZZZZZ.
SKREEEEE-EEEEETITTLEEE BUZZZZ.
HIS EXCELLENCY IS GLAD TO SEE THAT YOU HAVE LOHB HERE. THEY ARE SUPERIOR WORKERS.
RIZZZZ-BUUUZZ-ZZUUZZZZZZZZZ.
HIS EXCELLENCY ADMIRES YOUR METAL ORNAMENT.
GIVE HIM YOUR BADGE.

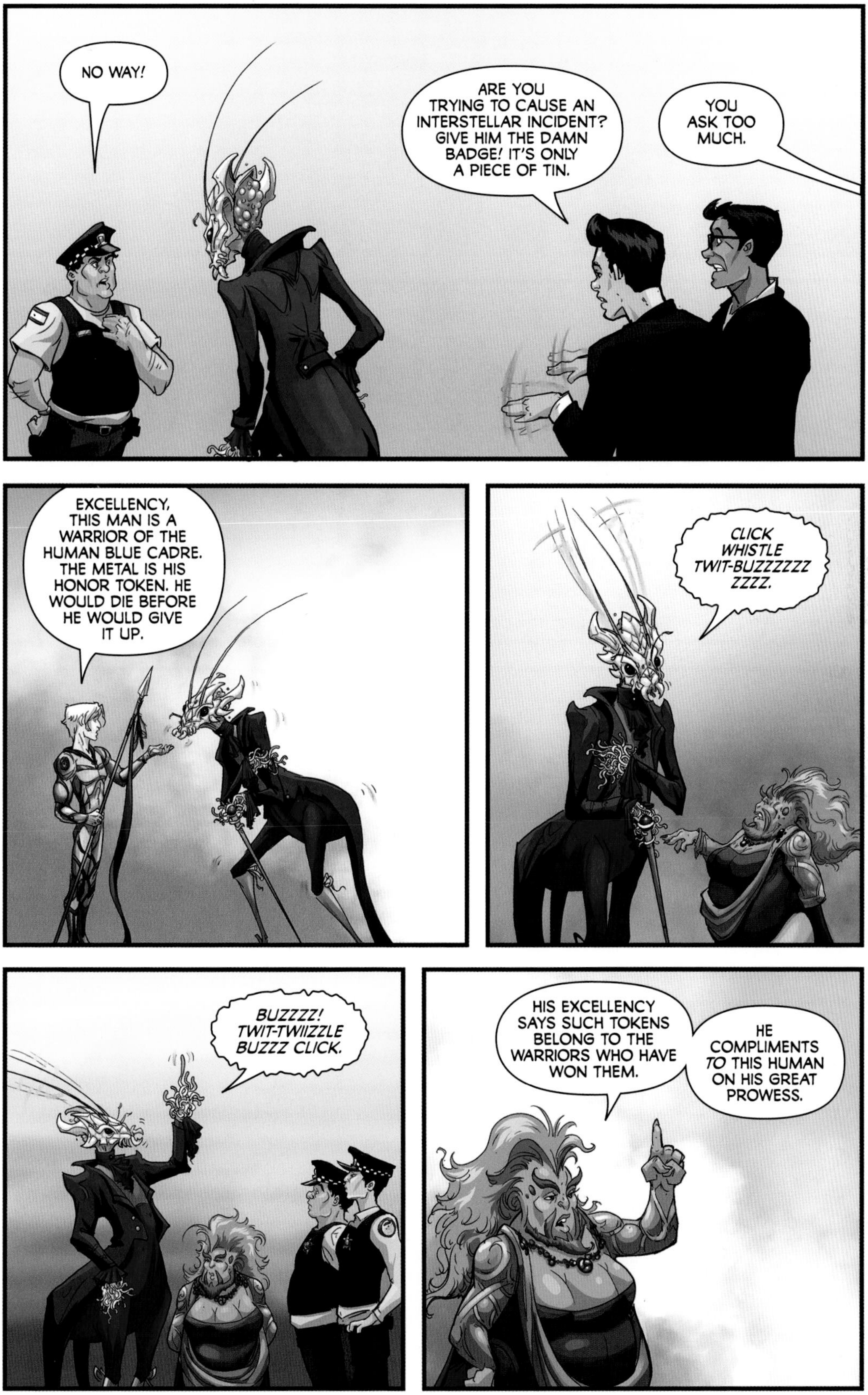
NO WAY!
ARE YOU TRYING TO CAUSE AN INTERSTELLAR INCIDENT? GIVE HIM THE DAMN BADGE! IT'S ONLY A PIECE OF TIN.
YOU ASK TOO MUCH.
EXCELLENCY, THIS MAN IS A WARRIOR OF THE HUMAN BLUE CADRE. THE METAL IS HIS HONOR TOKEN. HE WOULD DIE BEFORE HE WOULD GIVE IT UP.
CLICK WHISTLE TWIT-BUZZZZZZ ZZZZ.
BUZZZZ! TWIT-TWIIZZLE BUZZZ CLICK.
HIS EXCELLENCY SAYS SUCH TOKENS BELONG TO THE WARRIORS WHO HAVE WON THEM.
HE COMPLIMENTS TO THIS HUMAN ON HIS GREAT PROWESS.

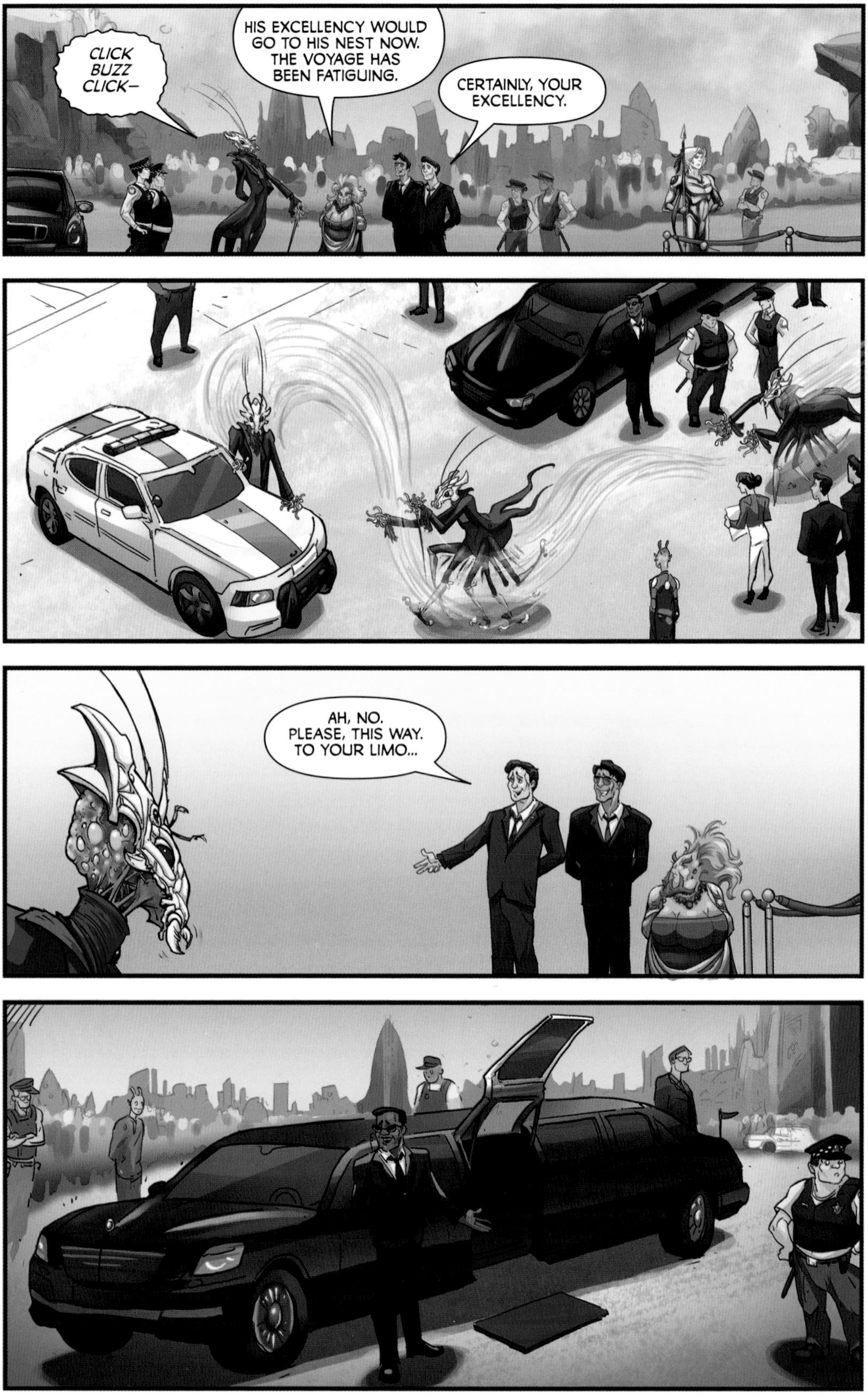
CLICK BUZZ CLICK—
HIS EXCELLENCY WOULD GO TO HIS NEST NOW. THE VOYAGE HAS BEEN FATIGUING.
CERTAINLY, YOUR EXCELLENCY.
AH, NO. PLEASE, THIS WAY. TO YOUR LIMO...

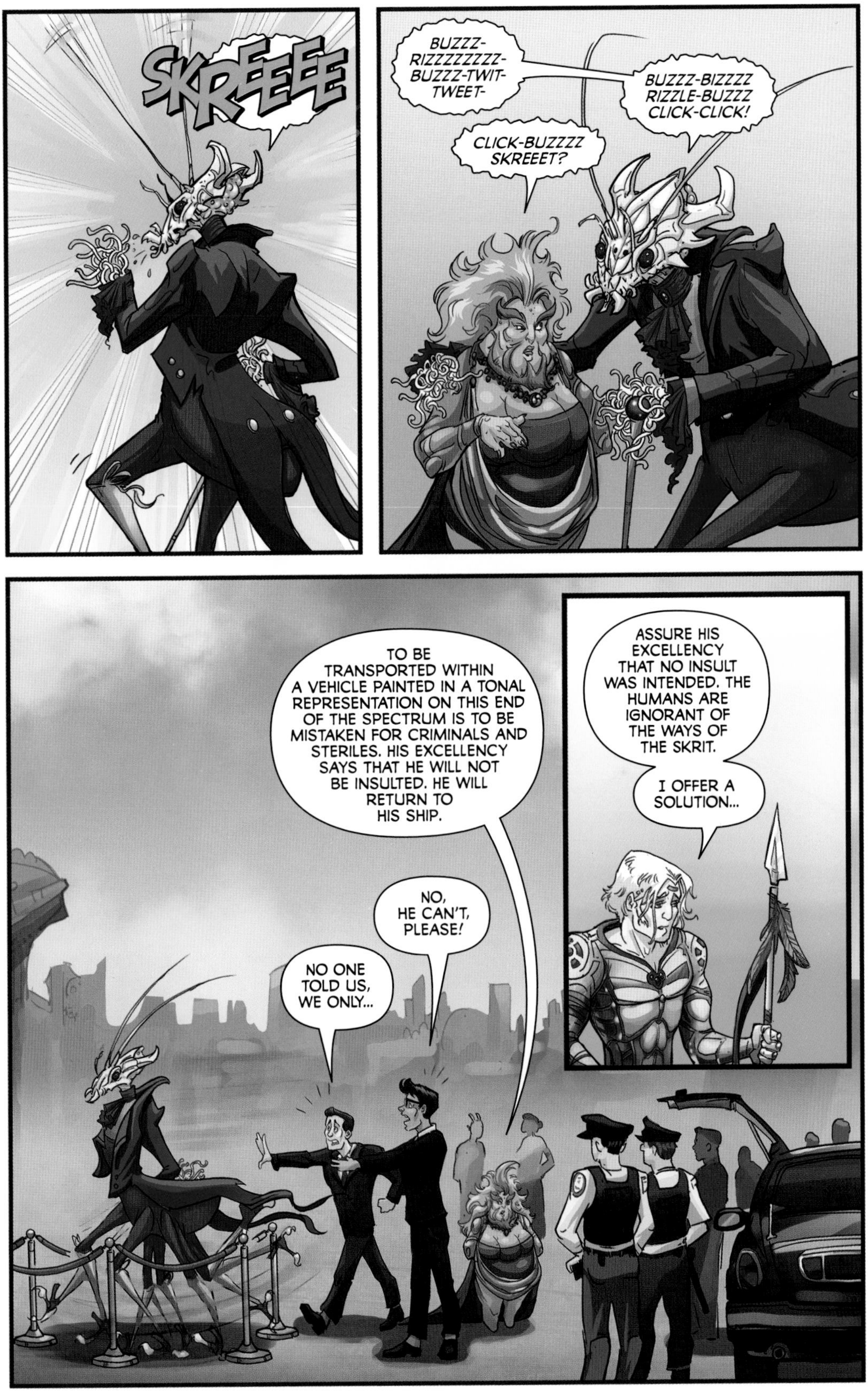
SKREEEE
BUZZZ-RIZZZZZZZZ-BUZZZ-TWIT-TWEET-
BUZZZ-BIZZZZ RIZZLE-BUZZZ CLICK-CLICK!
CLICK-BUZZZZ SKREEET?
TO BE TRANSPORTED WITHIN A VEHICLE PAINTED IN A TONAL REPRESENTATION ON THIS END OF THE SPECTRUM IS TO BE MISTAKEN FOR CRIMINALS AND STERILES. HIS EXCELLENCY SAYS THAT HE WILL NOT BE INSULTED. HE WILL RETURN TO HIS SHIP.
NO, HE CAN'T, PLEASE!
NO ONE TOLD US, WE ONLY...
ASSURE HIS EXCELLENCY THAT NO INSULT WAS INTENDED. THE HUMANS ARE IGNORANT OF THE WAYS OF THE SKRIT.
I OFFER A SOLUTION...

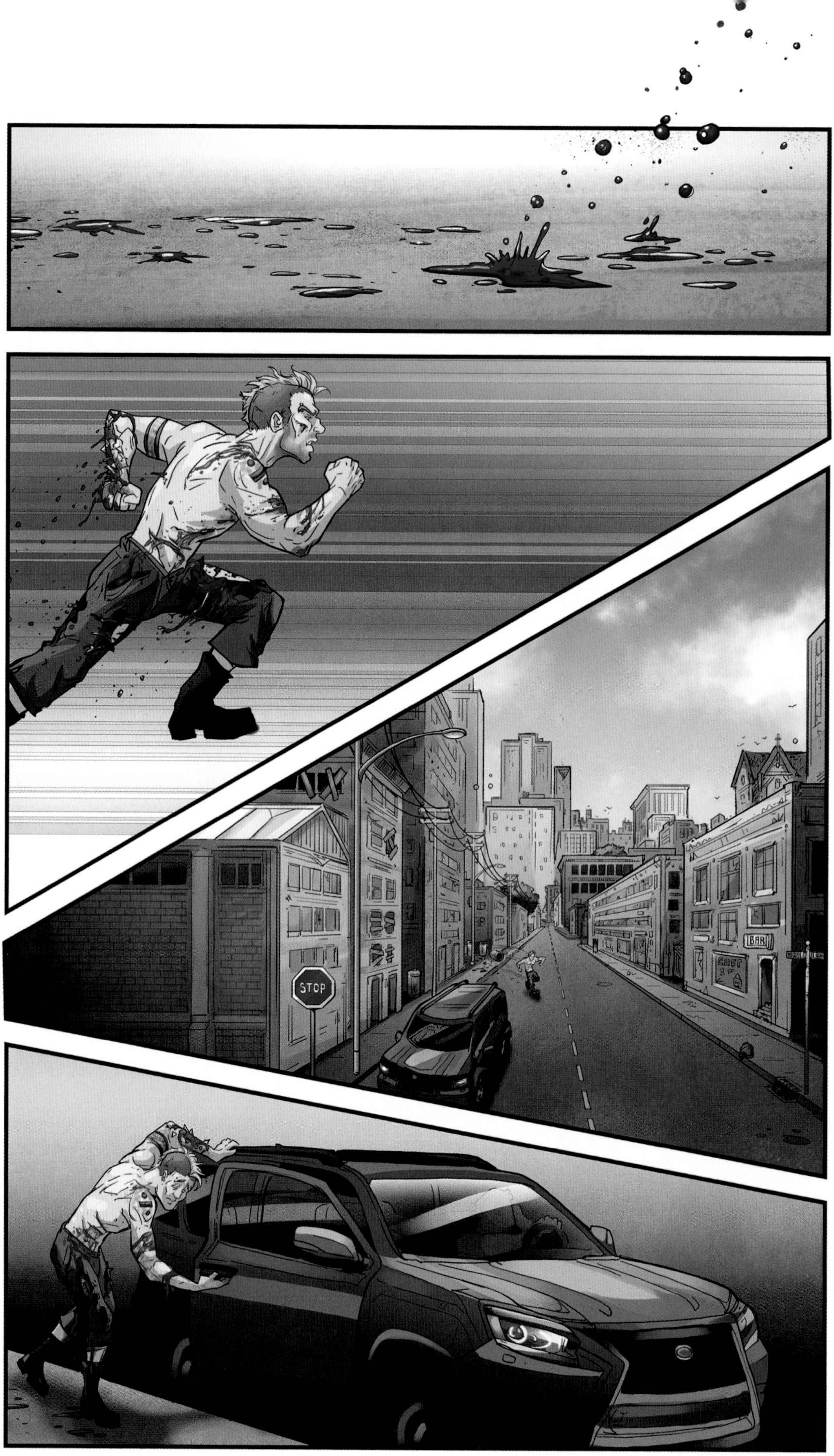
STOP

HI!
HEY, WHAT THE FUCK? GET AWAY! LEAVE ME ALONE, OR I'LL CALL THE POLICE!
I ***AM*** THE POLICE, SO GIVE ME YOUR PHONE... ***NOW!***
MY GOD... YOU'RE BLEEDING!
HAPPENS EVERY TIME I GET SHOT.
THIS IS DETECTIVE AARON STEIN. I HAVE AN EMERGENCY. GET ME SERGEANT MONDRAGON!

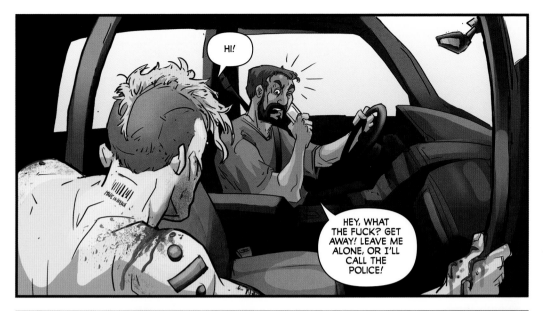

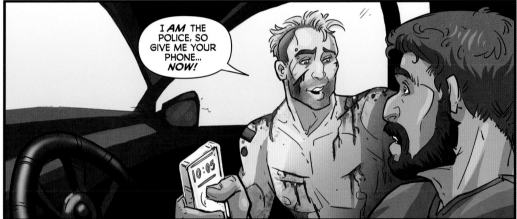

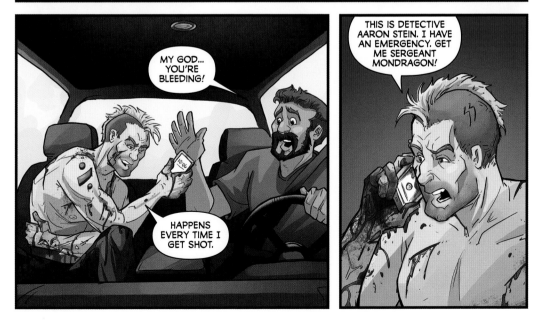

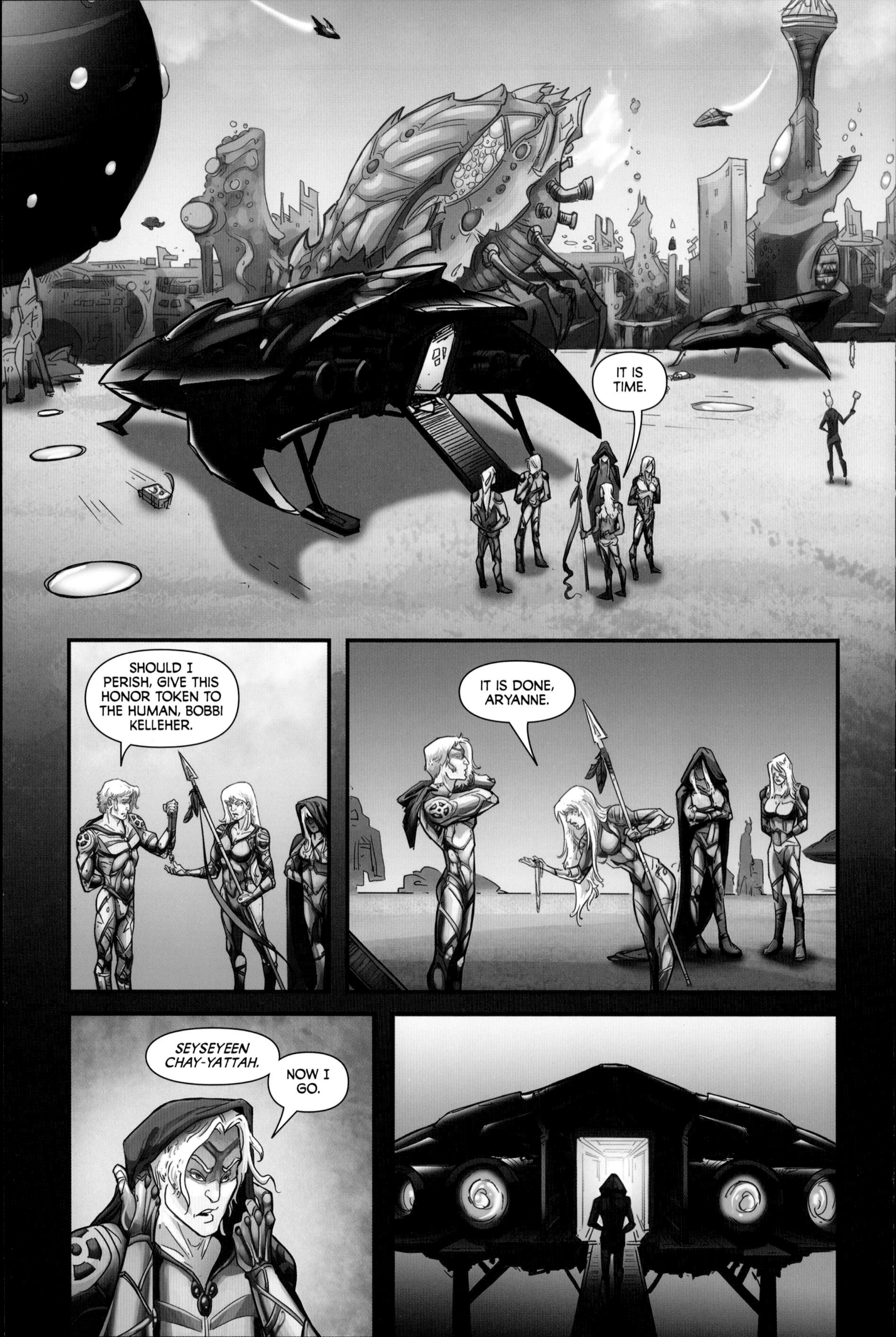
IT IS TIME.
SHOULD I PERISH, GIVE THIS HONOR TOKEN TO THE HUMAN, BOBBI KELLEHER.
IT IS DONE, ARYANNE.
SEYSEYEEN CHAY-YATTAH.
NOW I GO.

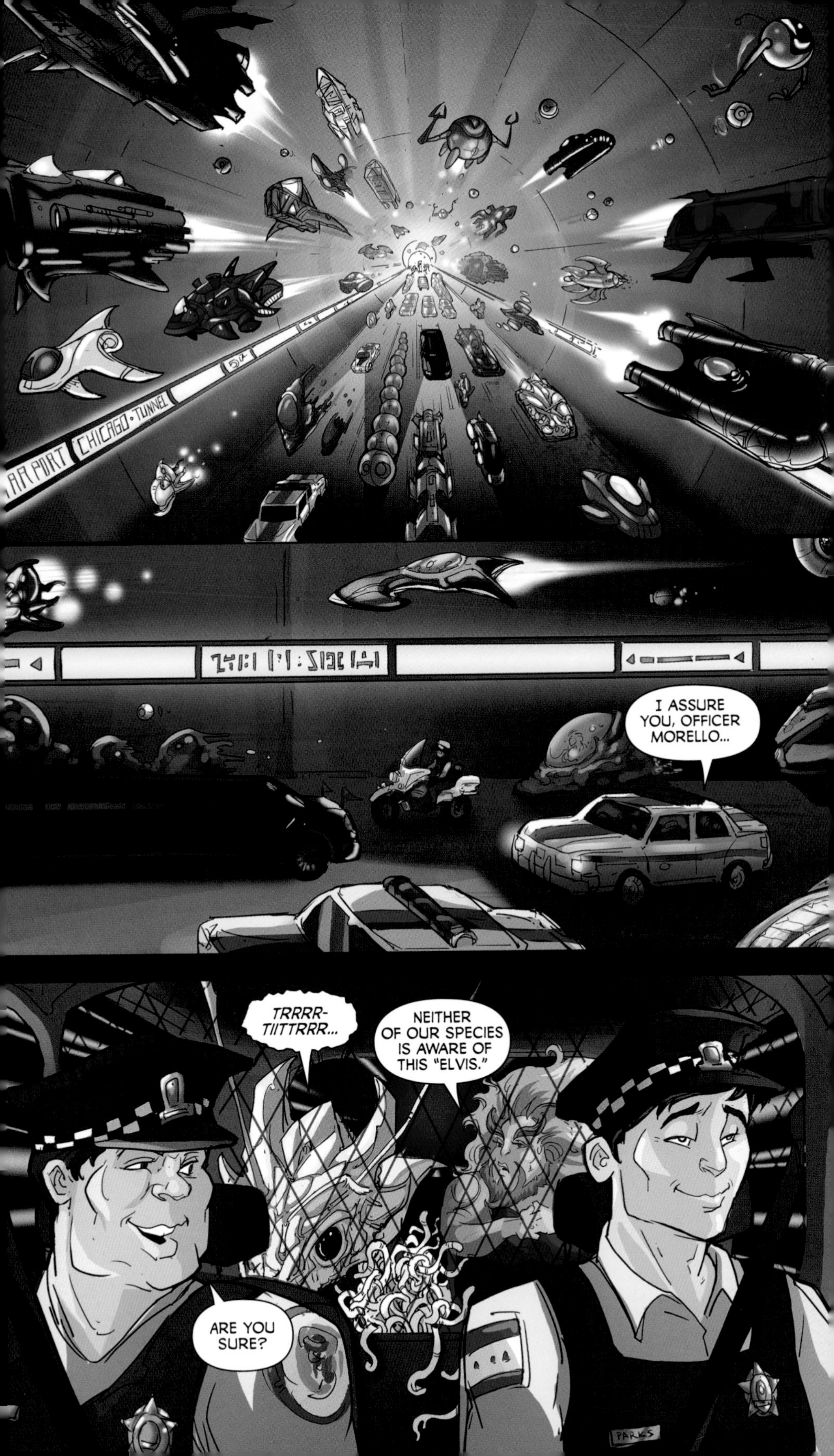
CHICAGO • TUNNEL
I ASSURE YOU, OFFICER MORELLO...
TRRRR-TIITTRRR...
NEITHER OF OUR SPECIES IS AWARE OF THIS "ELVIS."
ARE YOU SURE?
PARKS

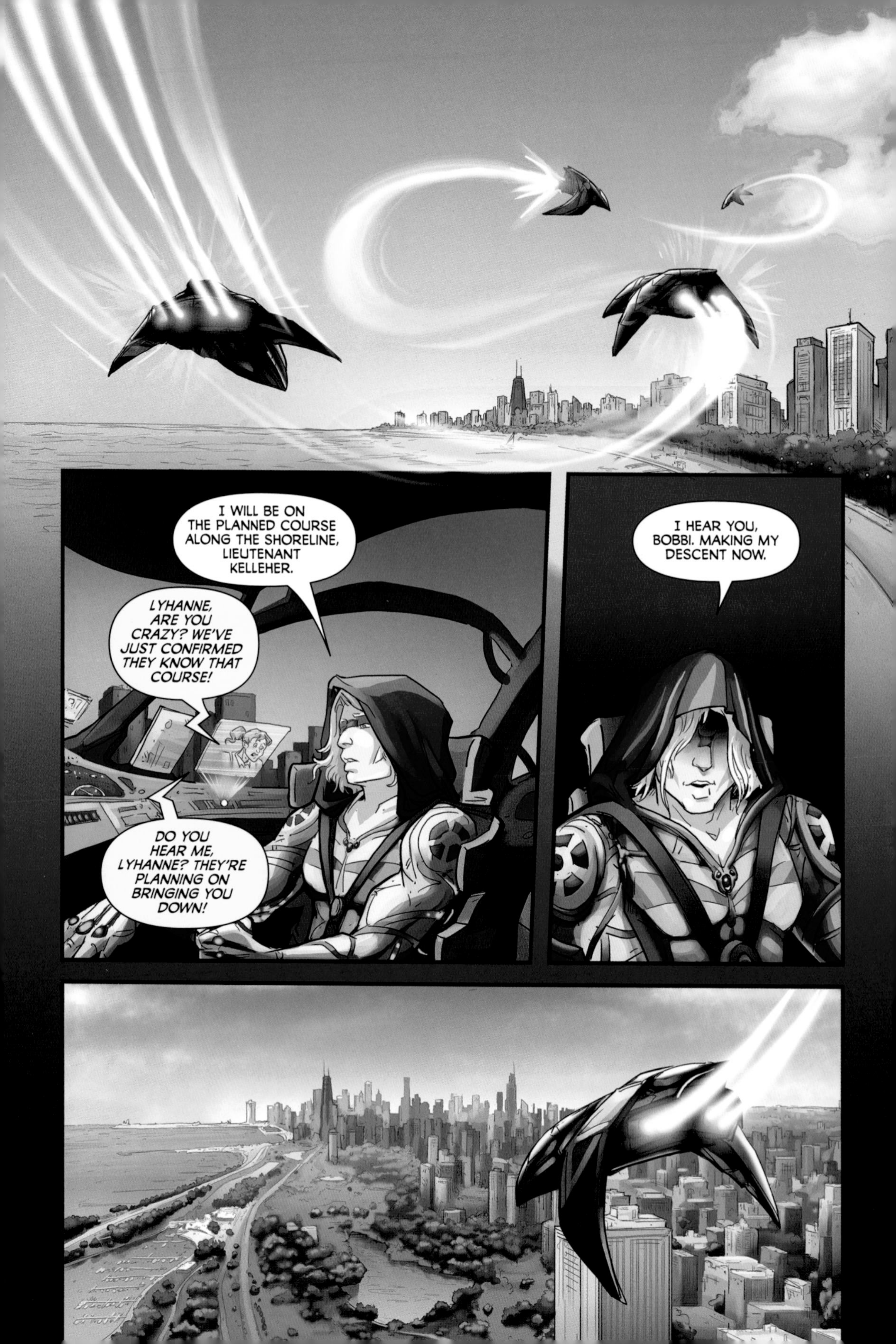
I WILL BE ON THE PLANNED COURSE ALONG THE SHORELINE, LIEUTENANT KELLEHER.
LYHANNE, ARE YOU CRAZY? WE'VE JUST CONFIRMED THEY KNOW THAT COURSE!
DO YOU HEAR ME, LYHANNE? THEY'RE PLANNING ON BRINGING YOU DOWN!
I HEAR YOU, BOBBI. MAKING MY DESCENT NOW.

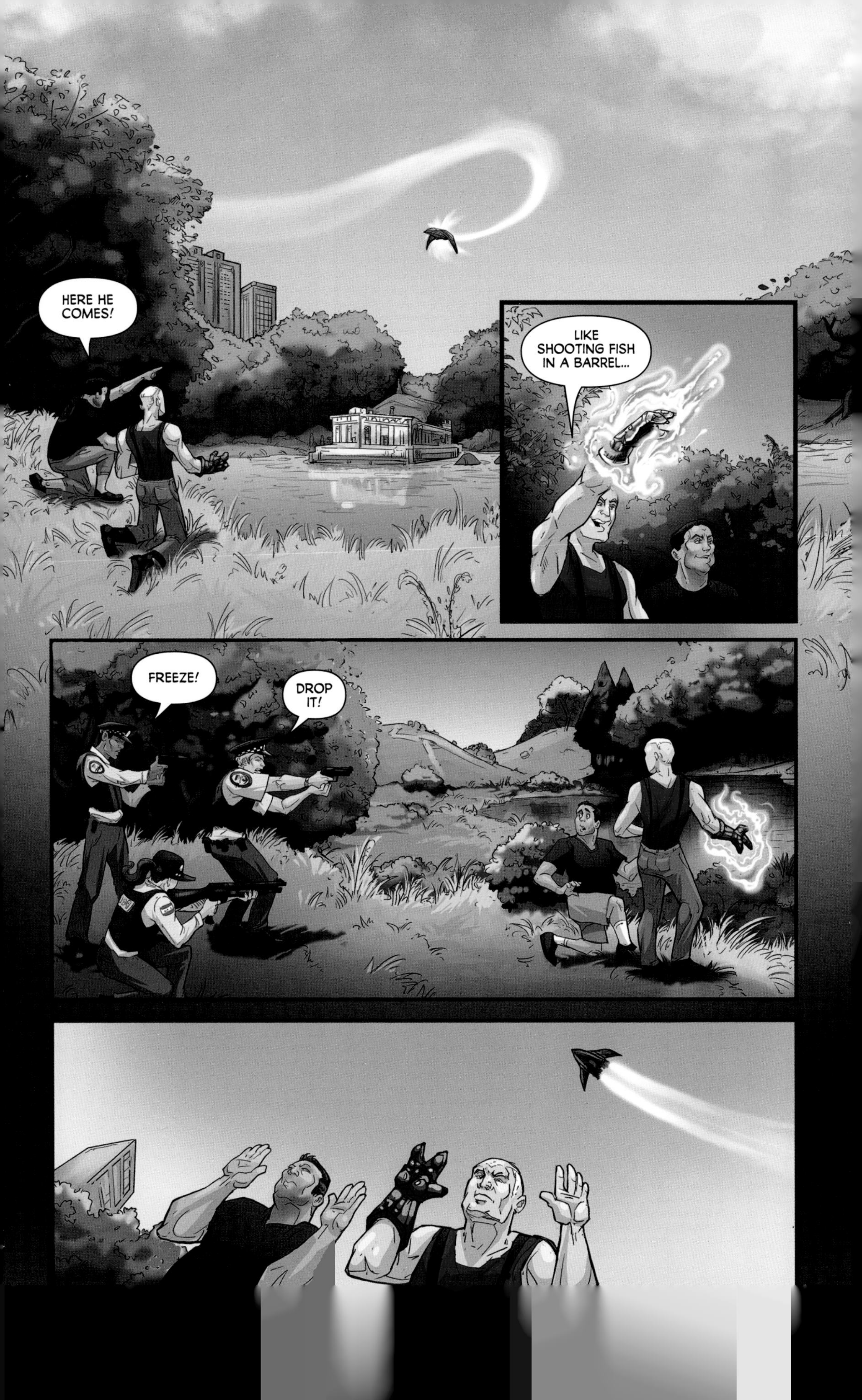
HERE HE COMES!
LIKE SHOOTING FISH IN A BARREL...
FREEZE!
DROP IT!

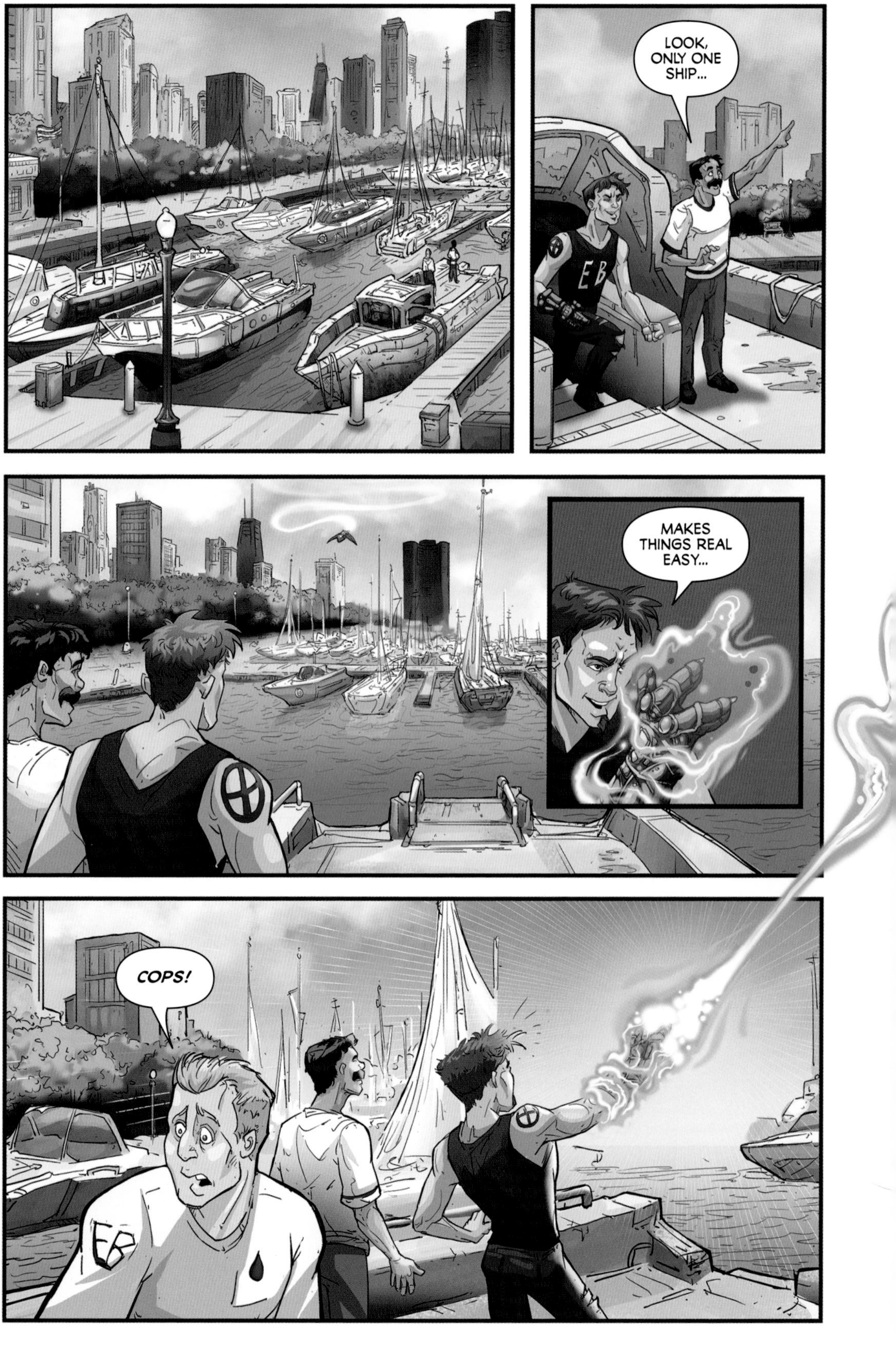
LOOK, ONLY ONE SHIP...
MAKES THINGS REAL EASY...
COPS!

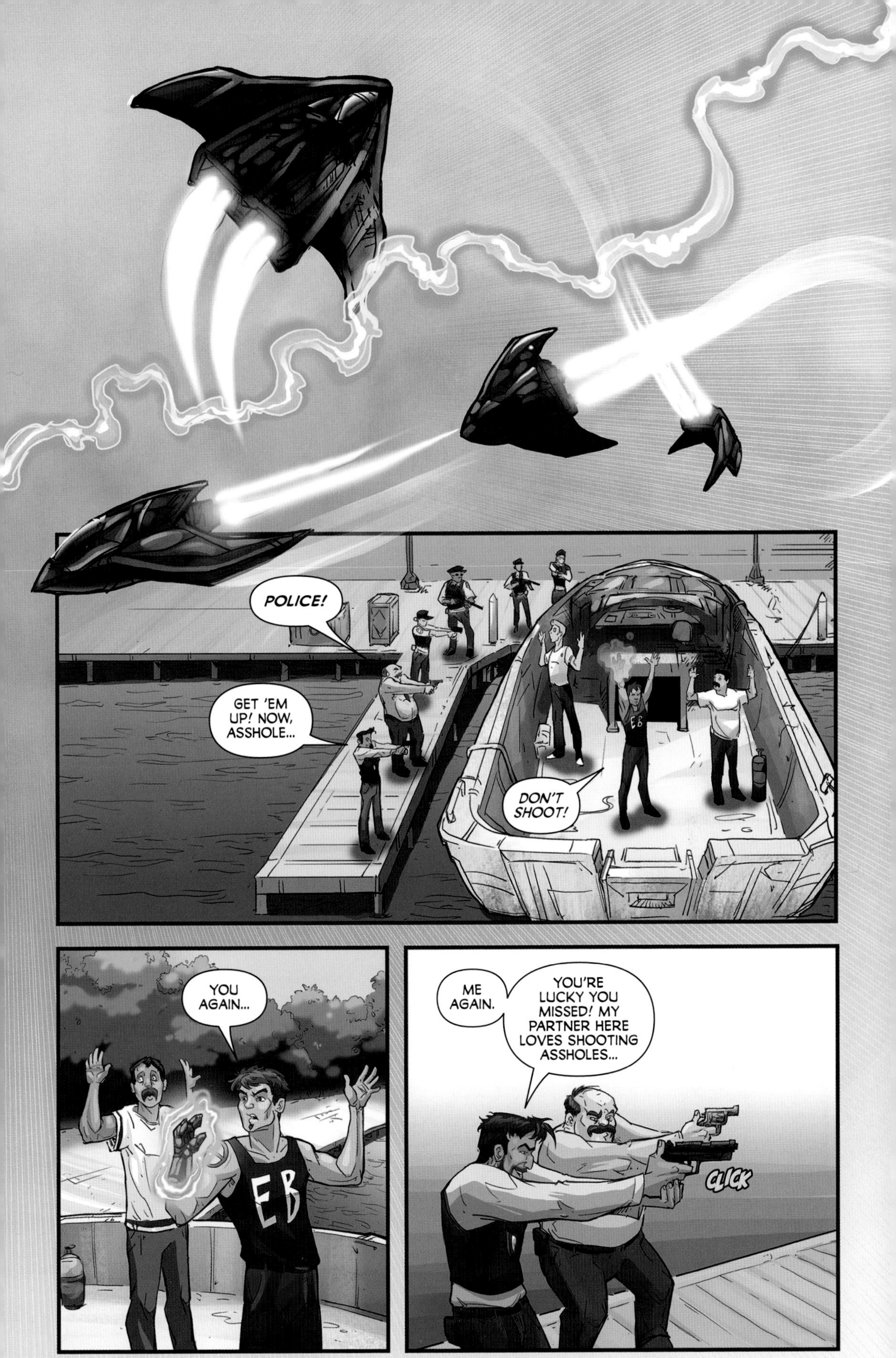
POLICE!
GET 'EM UP! NOW, ASSHOLE...
DON'T SHOOT!
YOU AGAIN...
ME AGAIN.
YOU'RE LUCKY YOU MISSED! MY PARTNER HERE LOVES SHOOTING ASSHOLES...
CLICK

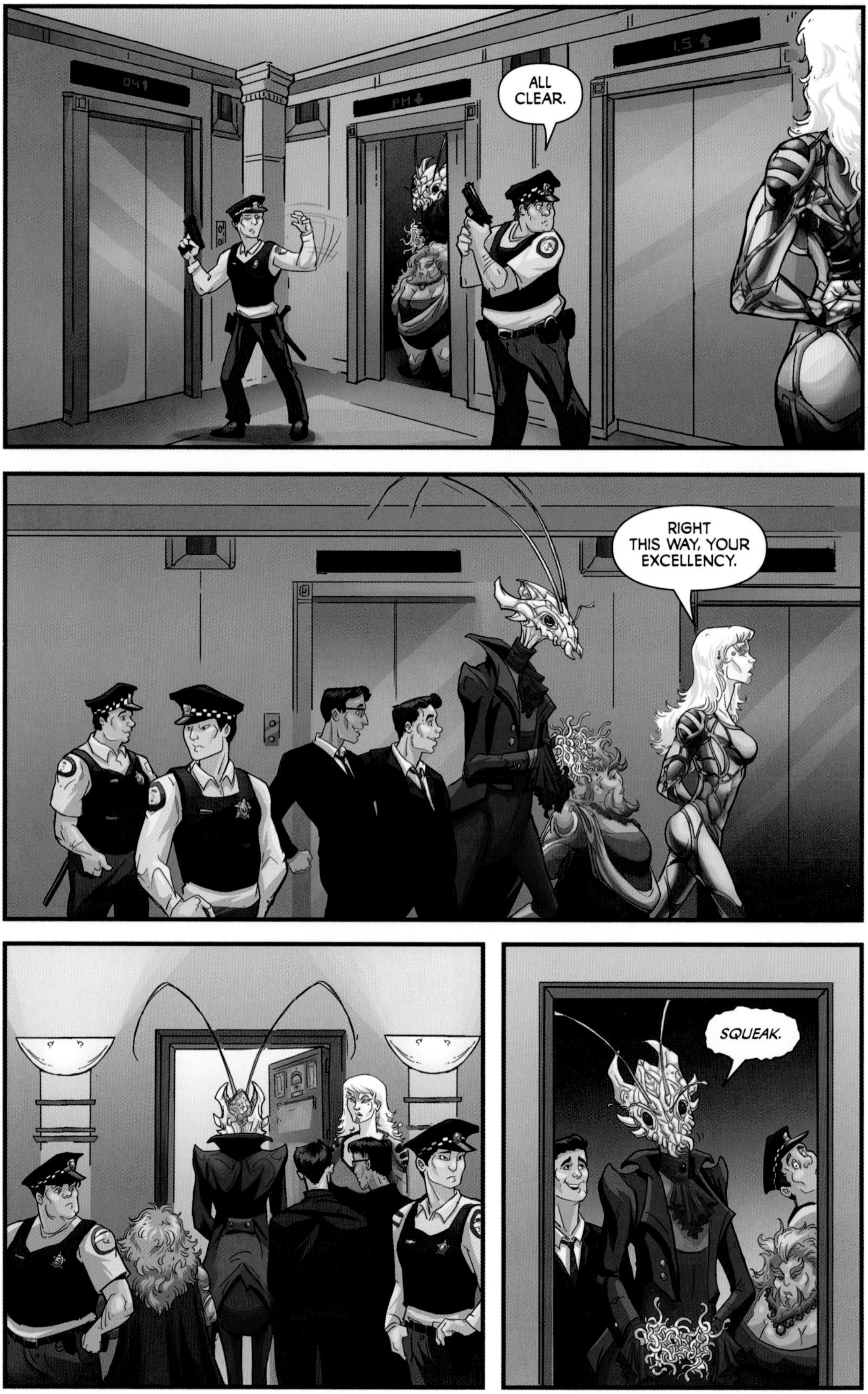
ALL CLEAR.
RIGHT THIS WAY, YOUR EXCELLENCY.
SQUEAK.

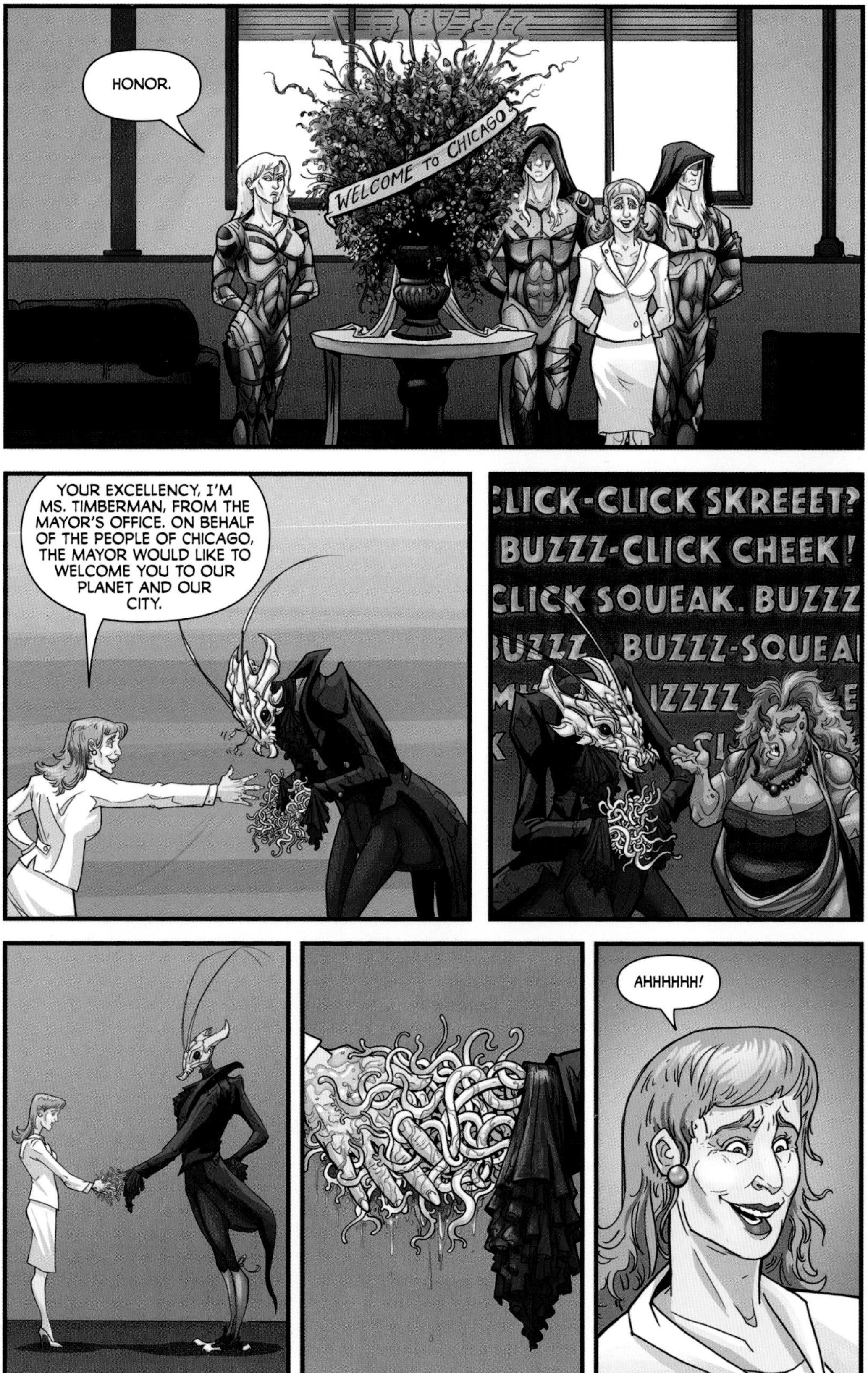
HONOR.
WELCOME TO CHICAGO
YOUR EXCELLENCY, I'M MS. TIMBERMAN, FROM THE MAYOR'S OFFICE. ON BEHALF OF THE PEOPLE OF CHICAGO, THE MAYOR WOULD LIKE TO WELCOME YOU TO OUR PLANET AND OUR CITY.
CLICK-CLICK SKREEET?
BUZZZ-CLICK CHEEK!
CLICK SQUEAK. BUZZZ
BUZZZ BUZZZ-SQUEA
AHHHHHH!

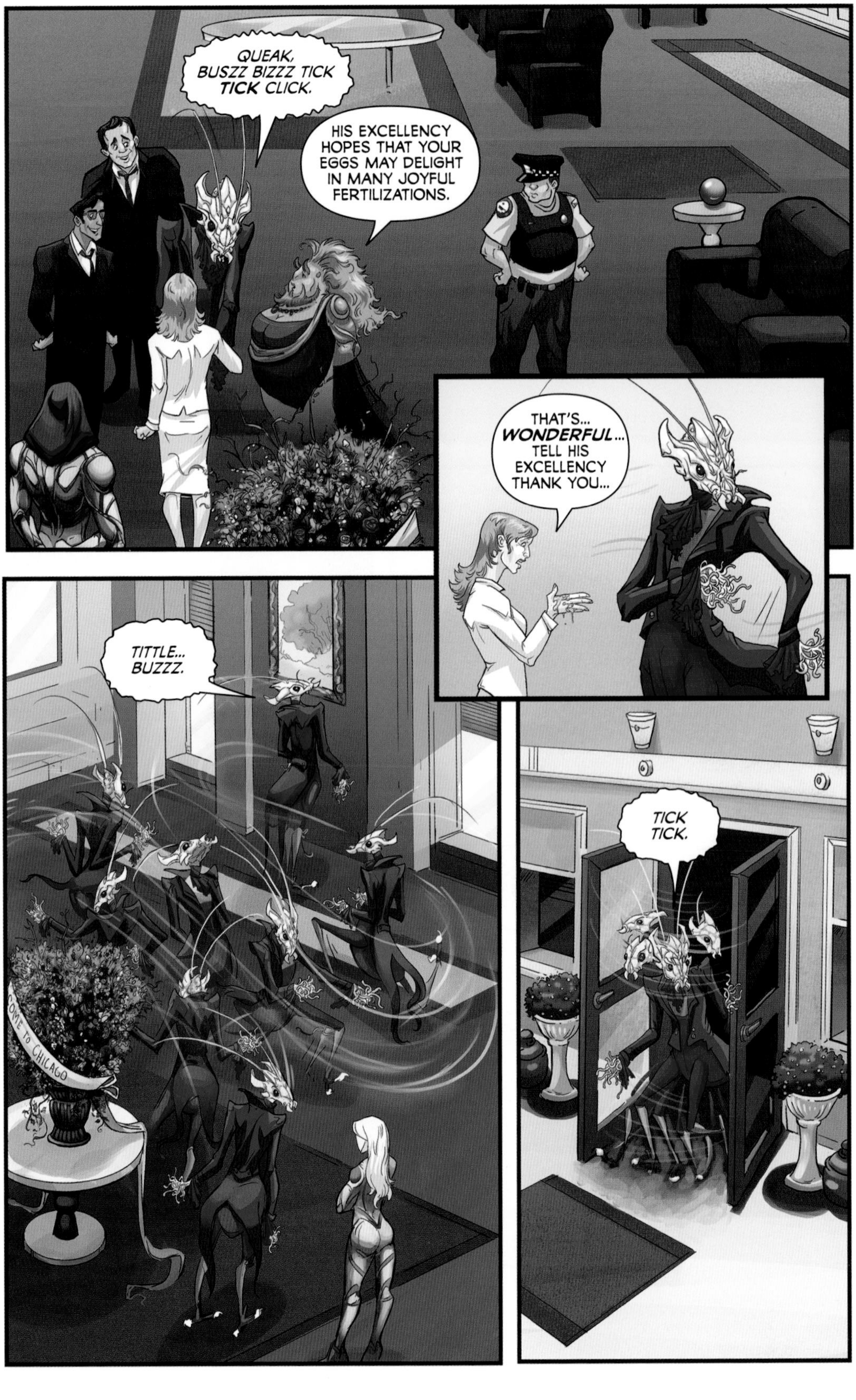
QUEAK, BUSZZ BIZZZ TICK **TICK** CLICK.
HIS EXCELLENCY HOPES THAT YOUR EGGS MAY DELIGHT IN MANY JOYFUL FERTILIZATIONS.
THAT'S... **WONDERFUL**... TELL HIS EXCELLENCY THANK YOU...
TITTLE... BUZZZ.
TICK TICK.

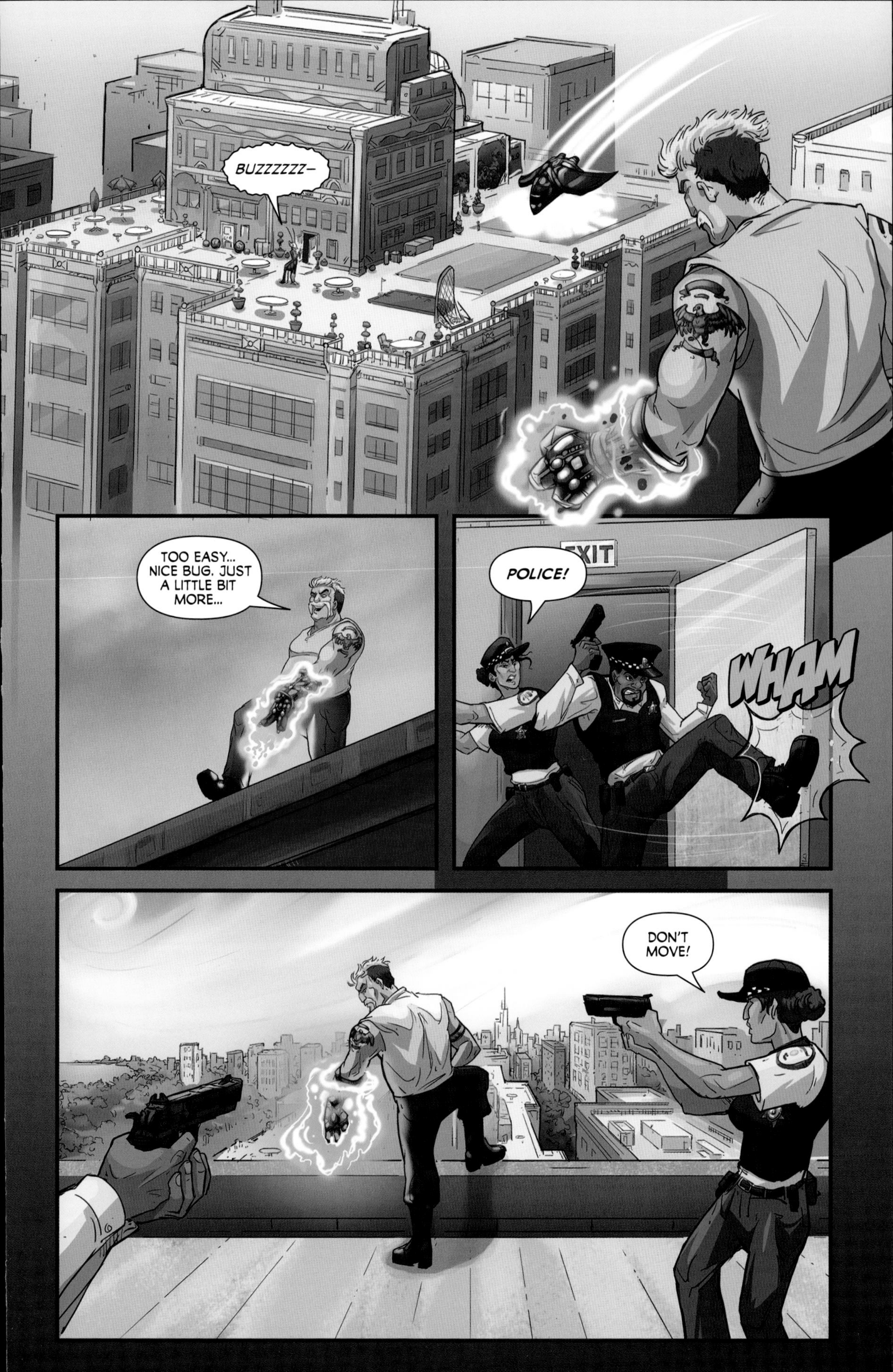
BUZZZZZZ–
TOO EASY... NICE BUG. JUST A LITTLE BIT MORE...
EXIT
POLICE!
WHAM
DON'T MOVE!

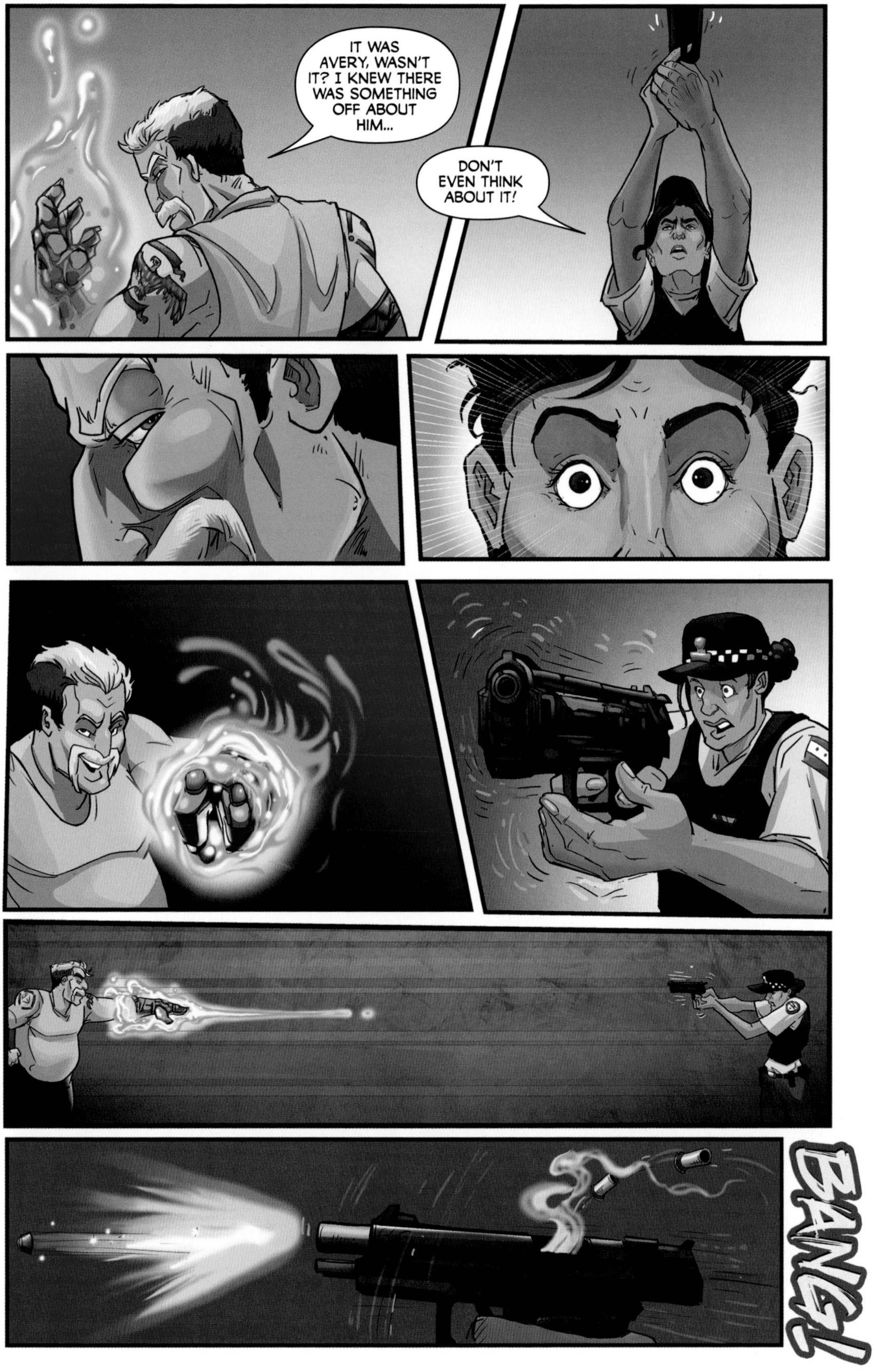
IT WAS AVERY, WASN'T IT? I KNEW THERE WAS SOMETHING OFF ABOUT HIM...
DON'T EVEN THINK ABOUT IT!
BANG!

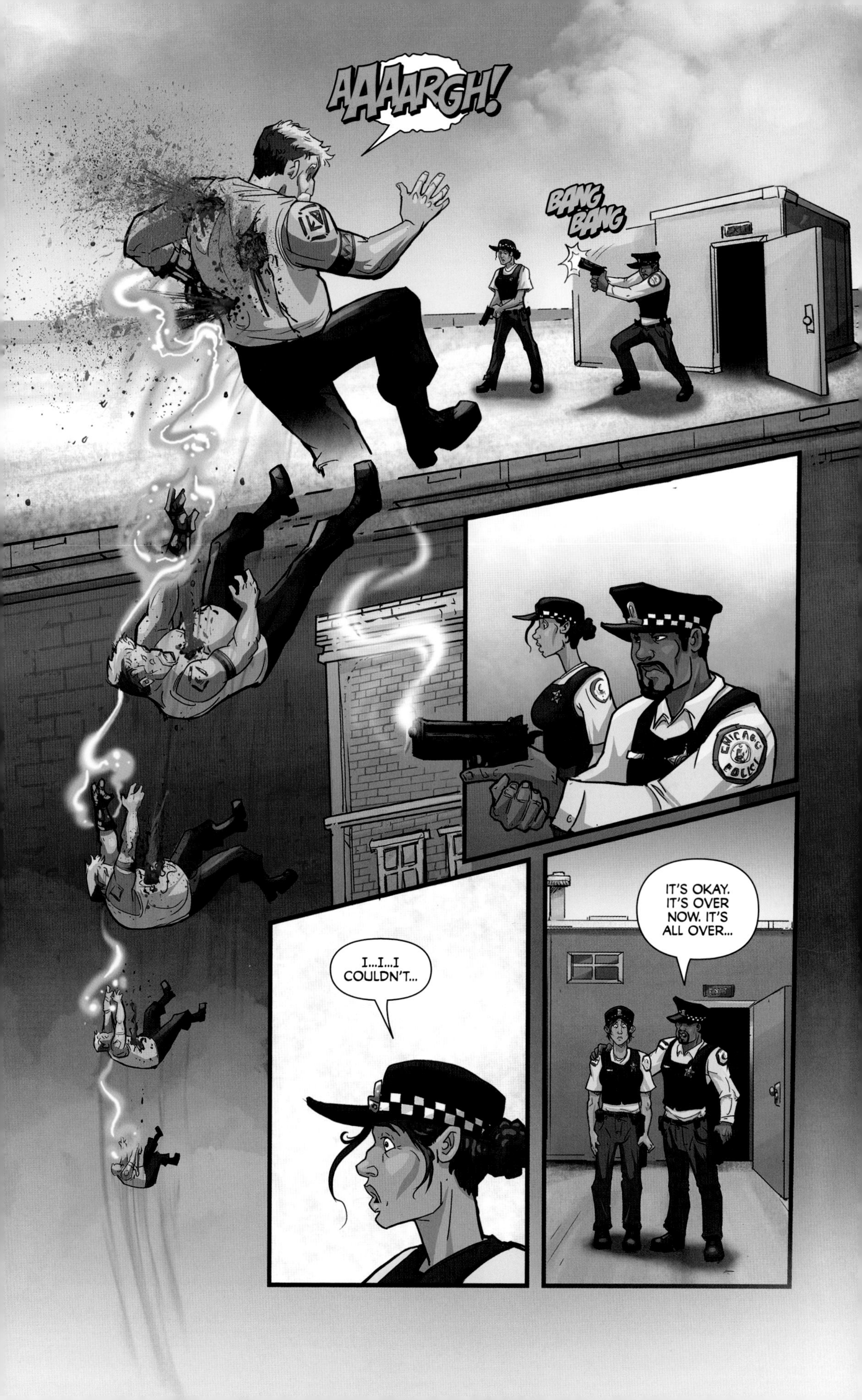
AAAARGH!
BANG BANG
EXIT
CHICAGO POLICE
IT'S OKAY. IT'S OVER NOW. IT'S ALL OVER...
I...I...I COULDN'T...

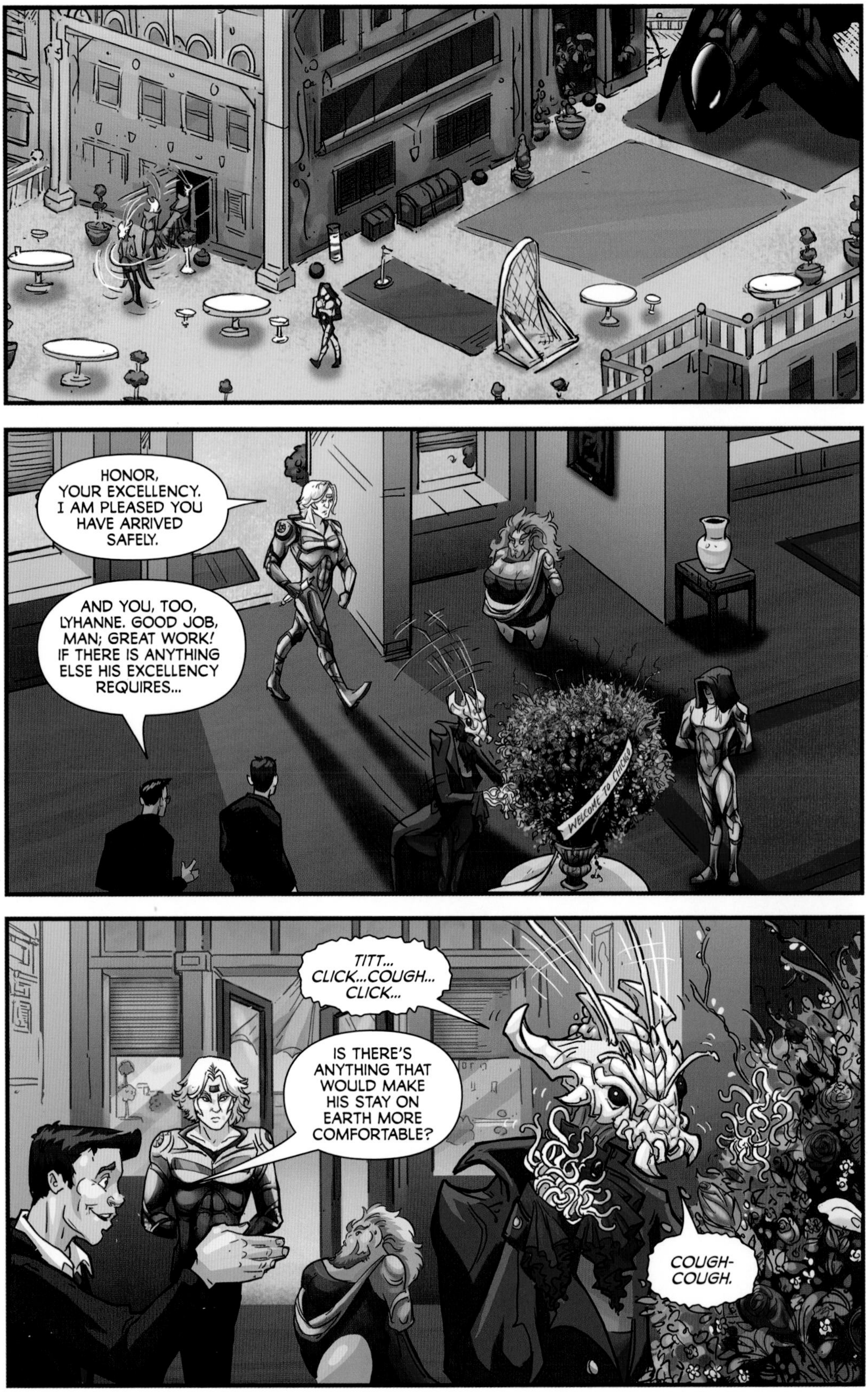
HONOR, YOUR EXCELLENCY. I AM PLEASED YOU HAVE ARRIVED SAFELY.
AND YOU, TOO, LYHANNE. GOOD JOB, MAN; GREAT WORK! IF THERE IS ANYTHING ELSE HIS EXCELLENCY REQUIRES...
TITT... CLICK...COUGH... CLICK...
IS THERE'S ANYTHING THAT WOULD MAKE HIS STAY ON EARTH MORE COMFORTABLE?
COUGH-COUGH.

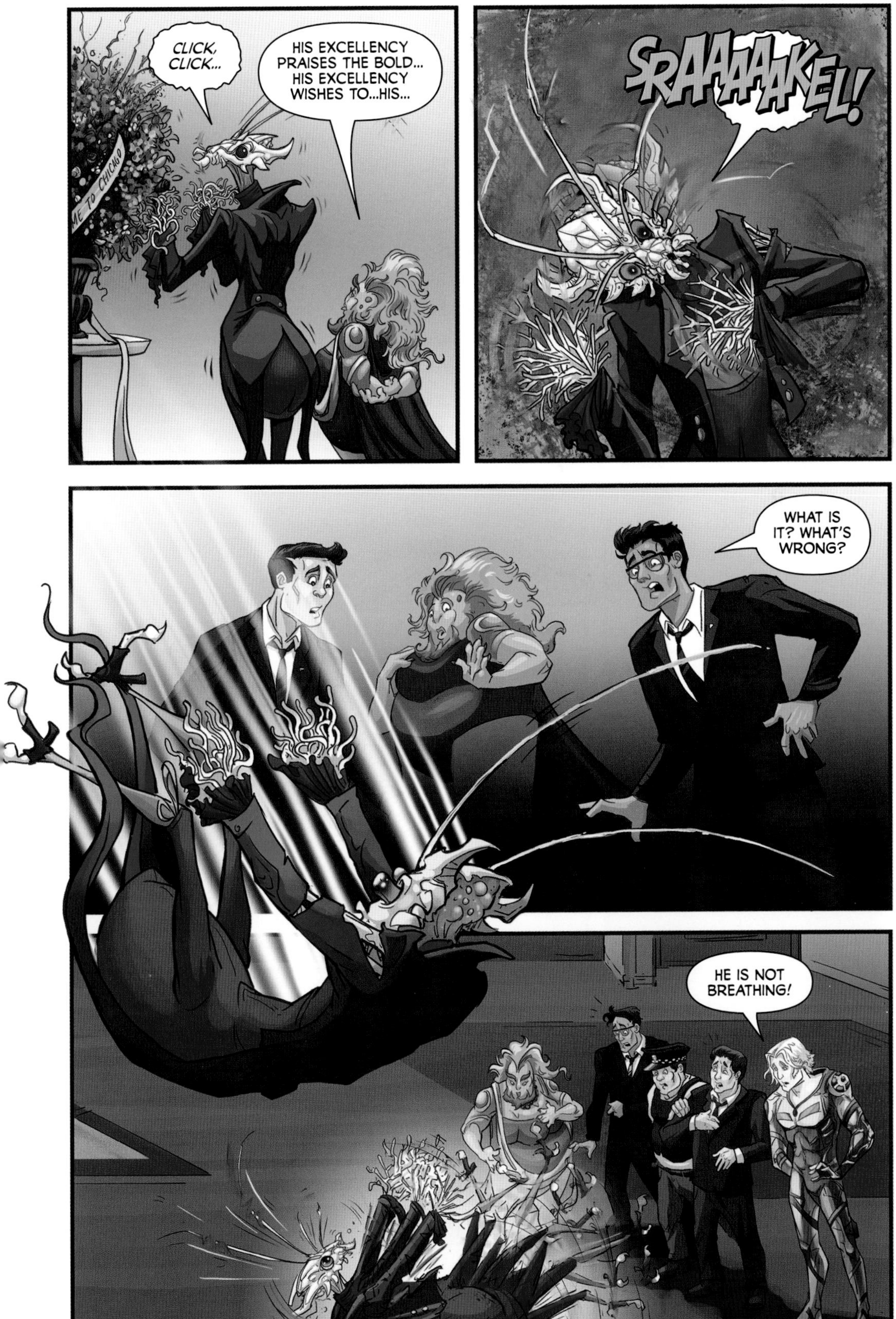
CLICK,
CLICK...
HIS EXCELLENCY PRAISES THE BOLD... HIS EXCELLENCY WISHES TO...HIS...
SRAAAAAKEL!
WHAT IS IT? WHAT'S WRONG?
HE IS NOT BREATHING!

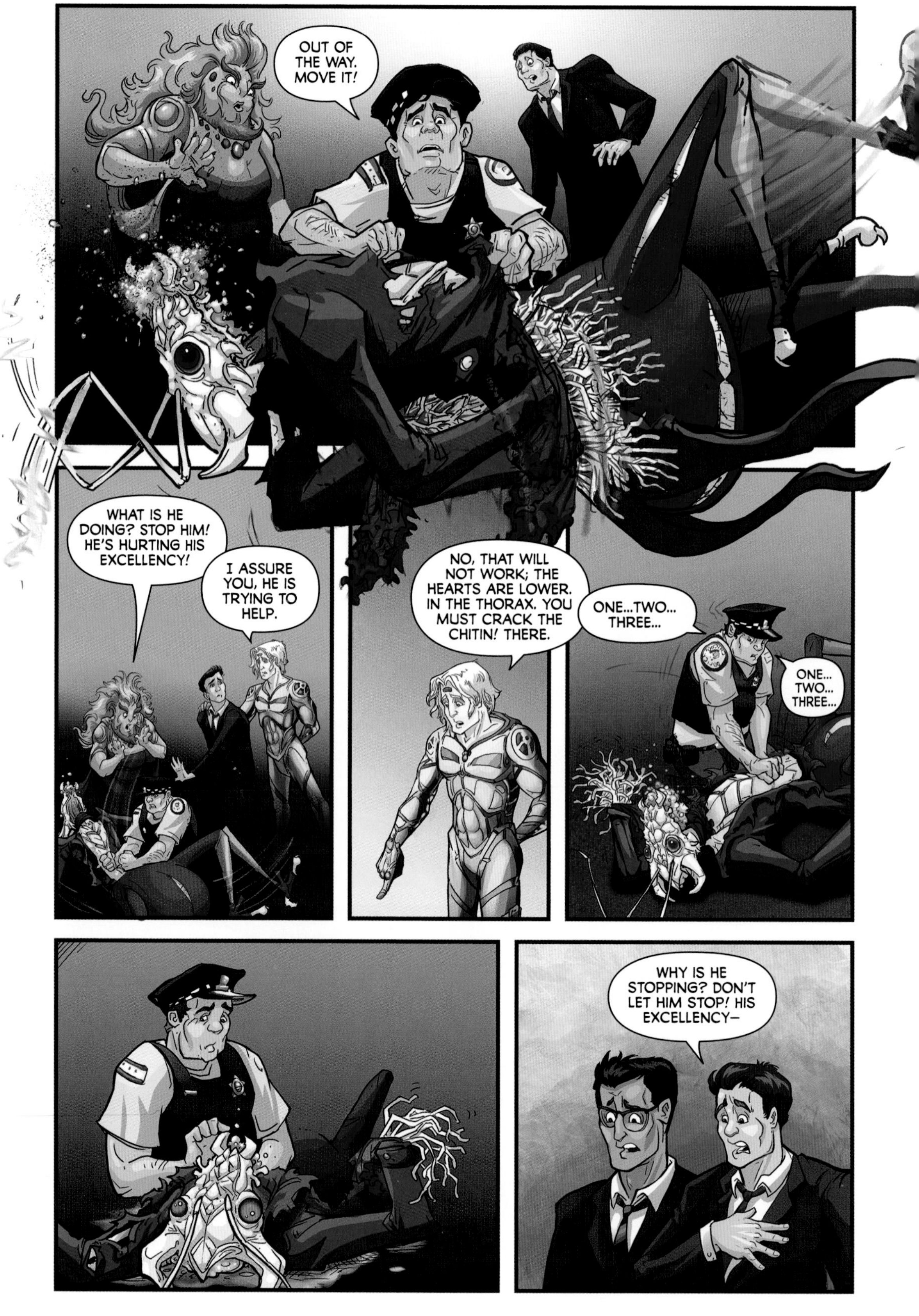
OUT OF THE WAY. MOVE IT!
WHAT IS HE DOING? STOP HIM! HE'S HURTING HIS EXCELLENCY!
I ASSURE YOU, HE IS TRYING TO HELP.
NO, THAT WILL NOT WORK; THE HEARTS ARE LOWER. IN THE THORAX. YOU MUST CRACK THE CHITIN! THERE.
ONE...TWO... THREE...
ONE... TWO... THREE...
WHY IS HE STOPPING? DON'T LET HIM STOP! HIS EXCELLENCY—

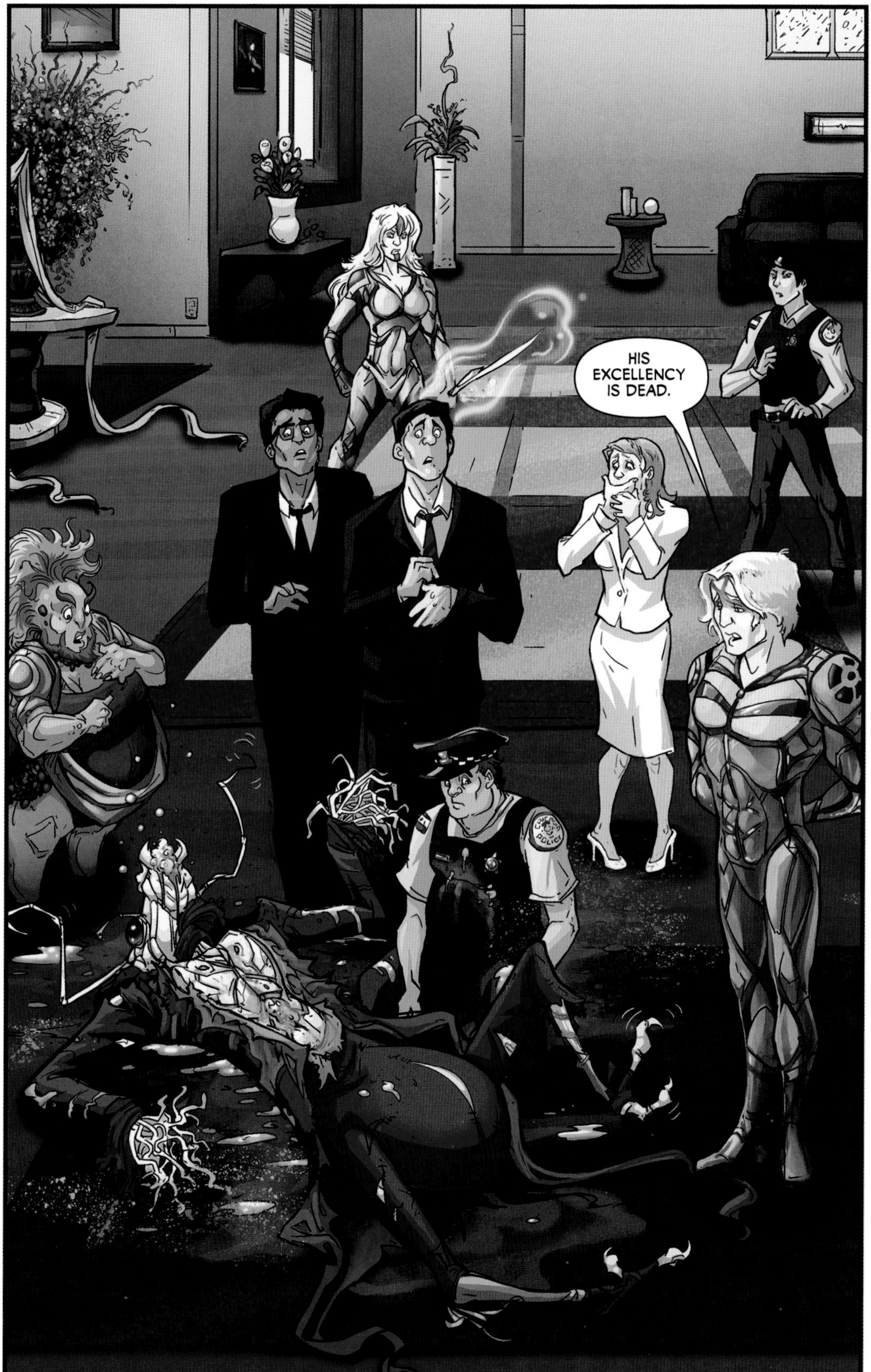
HIS EXCELLENCY IS DEAD.

CHAPTER SEVEN

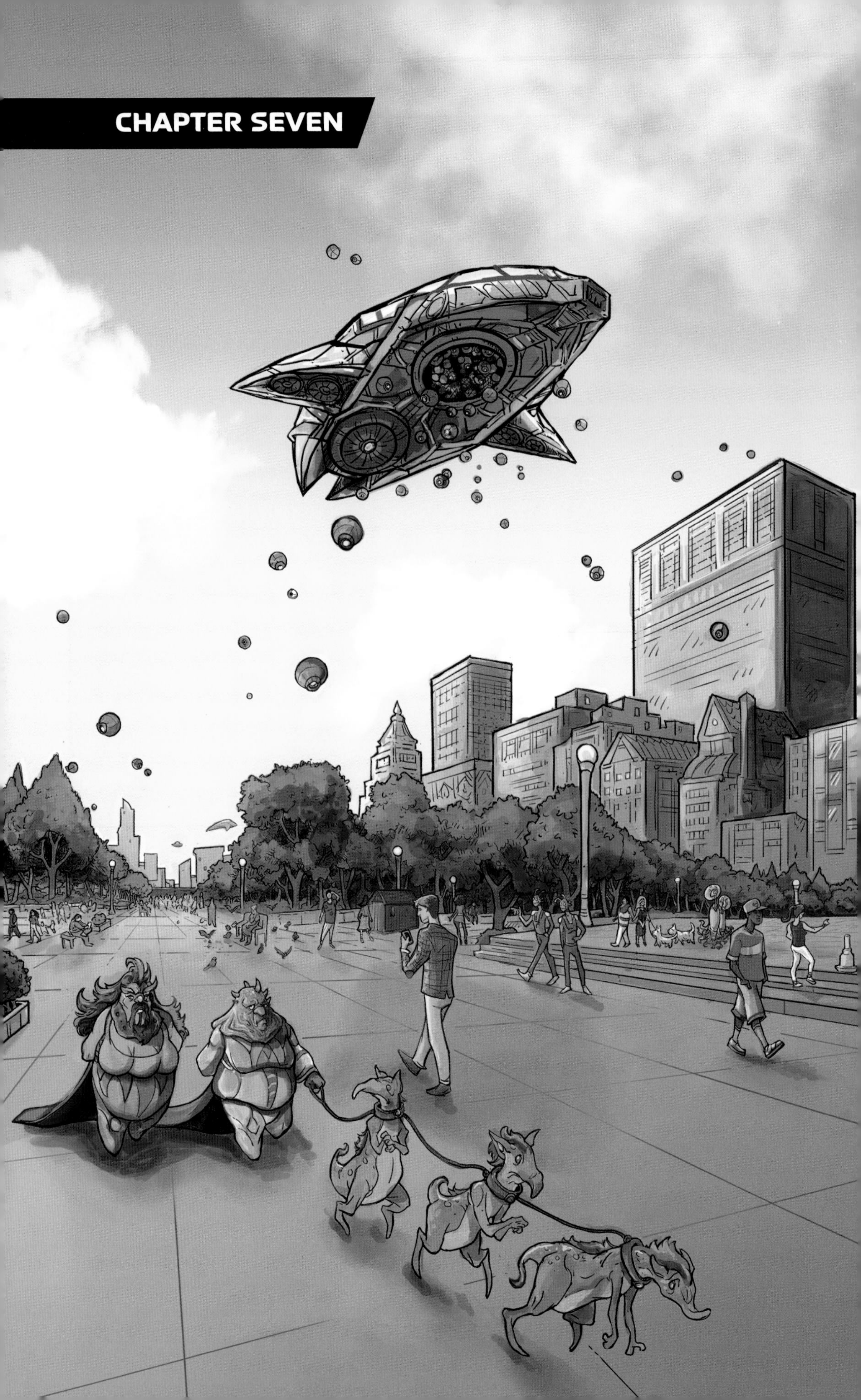

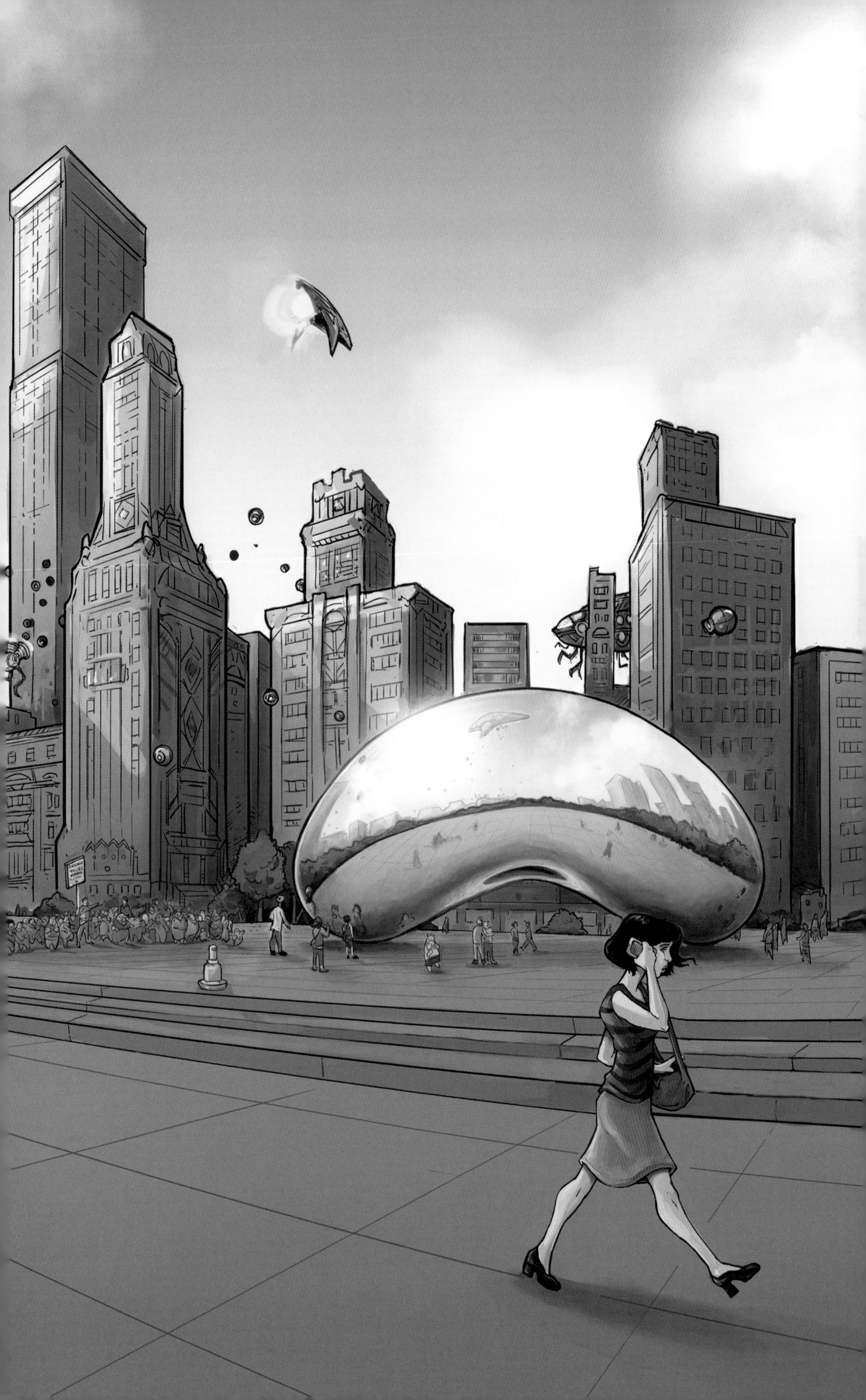
CHICAGO TOURS

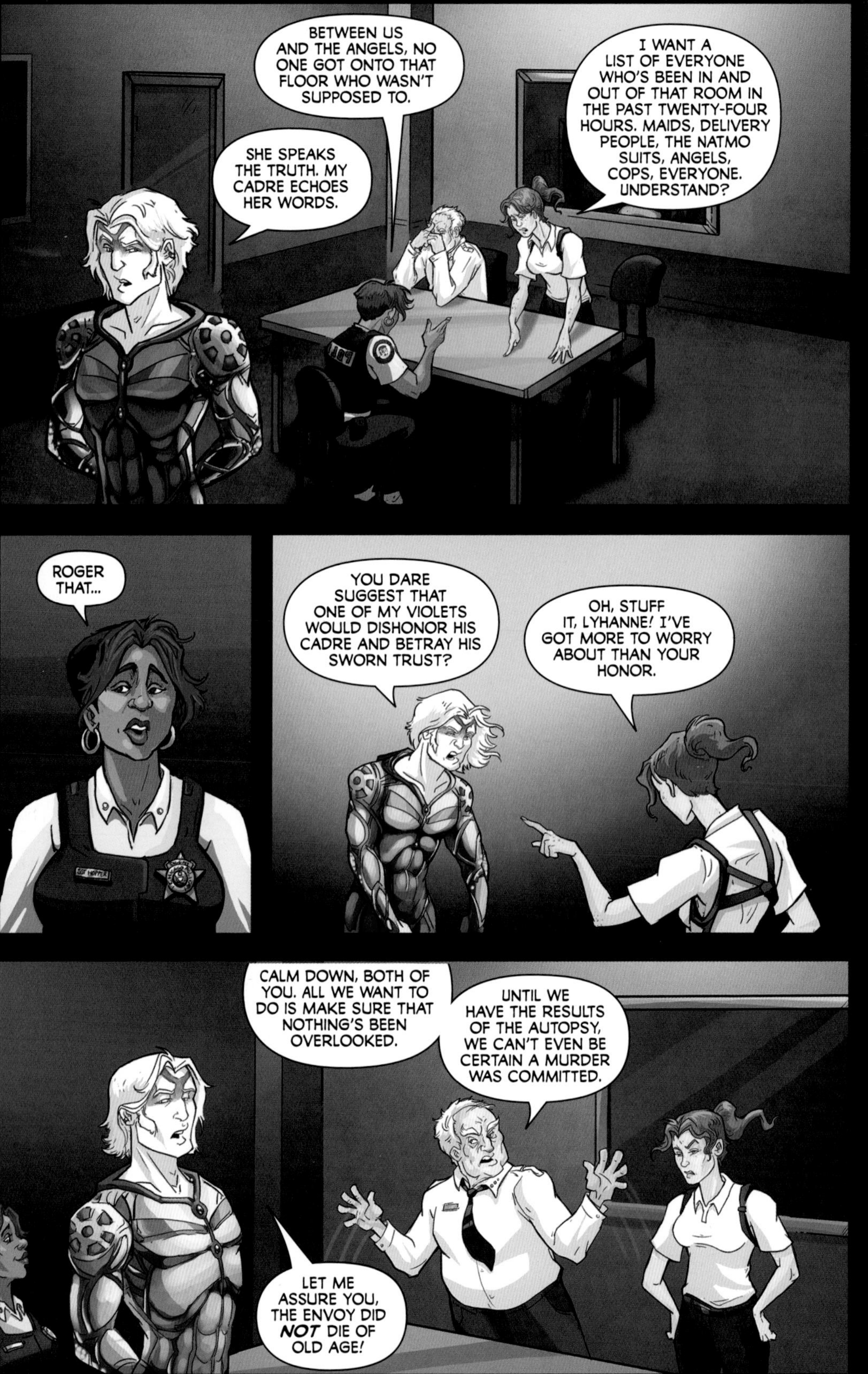
BETWEEN US AND THE ANGELS, NO ONE GOT ONTO THAT FLOOR WHO WASN'T SUPPOSED TO.
SHE SPEAKS THE TRUTH. MY CADRE ECHOES HER WORDS.
I WANT A LIST OF EVERYONE WHO'S BEEN IN AND OUT OF THAT ROOM IN THE PAST TWENTY-FOUR HOURS. MAIDS, DELIVERY PEOPLE, THE NATMO SUITS, ANGELS, COPS, EVERYONE. UNDERSTAND?
ROGER THAT...
YOU DARE SUGGEST THAT ONE OF MY VIOLETS WOULD DISHONOR HIS CADRE AND BETRAY HIS SWORN TRUST?
OH, STUFF IT, LYHANNE! I'VE GOT MORE TO WORRY ABOUT THAN YOUR HONOR.
CALM DOWN, BOTH OF YOU. ALL WE WANT TO DO IS MAKE SURE THAT NOTHING'S BEEN OVERLOOKED.
UNTIL WE HAVE THE RESULTS OF THE AUTOPSY, WE CAN'T EVEN BE CERTAIN A MURDER WAS COMMITTED.
LET ME ASSURE YOU, THE ENVOY DID ***NOT*** DIE OF OLD AGE!

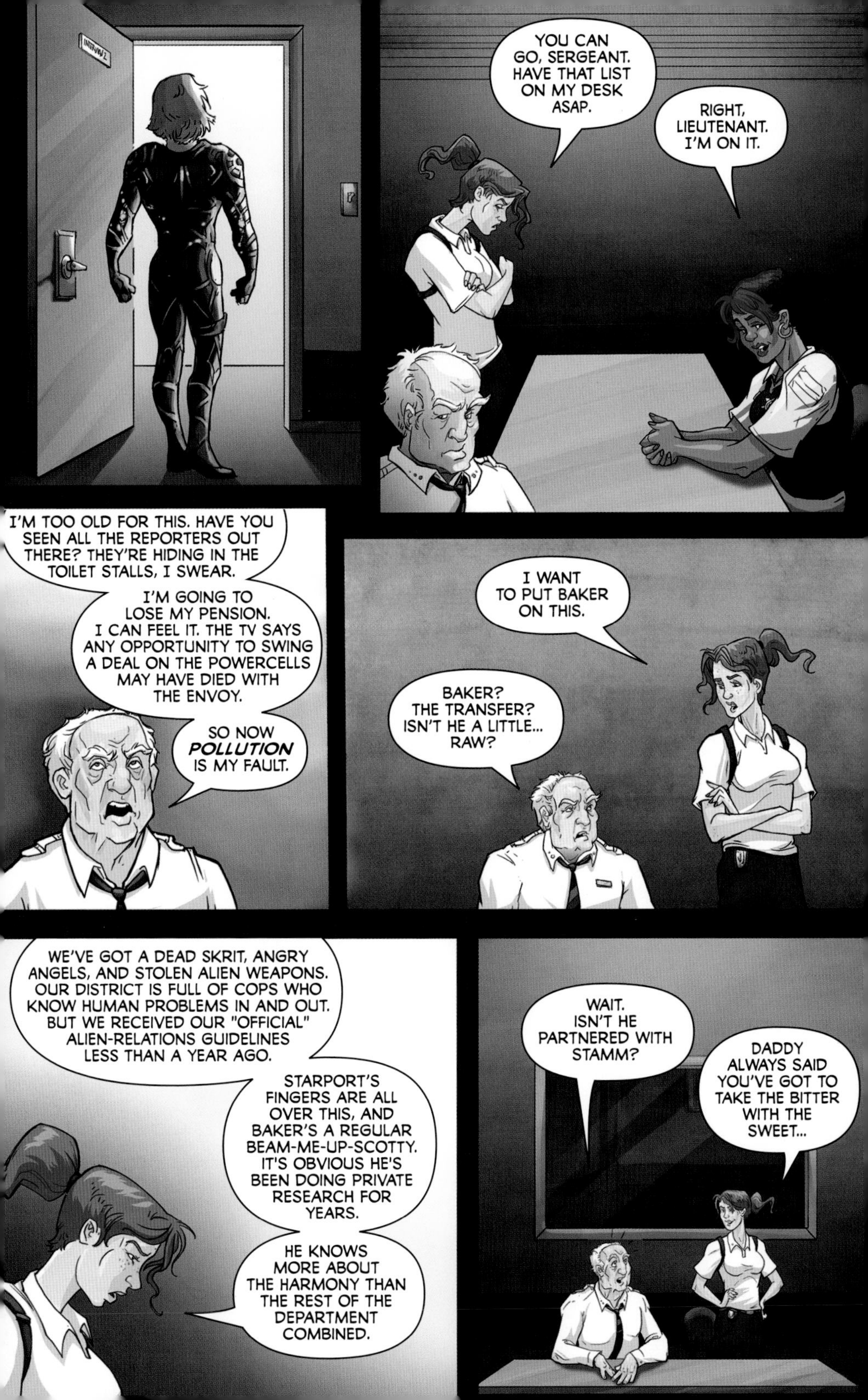
YOU CAN GO, SERGEANT. HAVE THAT LIST ON MY DESK ASAP.
RIGHT, LIEUTENANT. I'M ON IT.
I'M TOO OLD FOR THIS. HAVE YOU SEEN ALL THE REPORTERS OUT THERE? THEY'RE HIDING IN THE TOILET STALLS, I SWEAR.
I'M GOING TO LOSE MY PENSION. I CAN FEEL IT. THE TV SAYS ANY OPPORTUNITY TO SWING A DEAL ON THE POWERCELLS MAY HAVE DIED WITH THE ENVOY.
SO NOW *POLLUTION* IS MY FAULT.
I WANT TO PUT BAKER ON THIS.
BAKER? THE TRANSFER? ISN'T HE A LITTLE... RAW?
WE'VE GOT A DEAD SKRIT, ANGRY ANGELS, AND STOLEN ALIEN WEAPONS. OUR DISTRICT IS FULL OF COPS WHO KNOW HUMAN PROBLEMS IN AND OUT. BUT WE RECEIVED OUR "OFFICIAL" ALIEN-RELATIONS GUIDELINES LESS THAN A YEAR AGO.
STARPORT'S FINGERS ARE ALL OVER THIS, AND BAKER'S A REGULAR BEAM-ME-UP-SCOTTY. IT'S OBVIOUS HE'S BEEN DOING PRIVATE RESEARCH FOR YEARS.
HE KNOWS MORE ABOUT THE HARMONY THAN THE REST OF THE DEPARTMENT COMBINED.
WAIT. ISN'T HE PARTNERED WITH STAMM?
DADDY ALWAYS SAID YOU'VE GOT TO TAKE THE BITTER WITH THE SWEET...

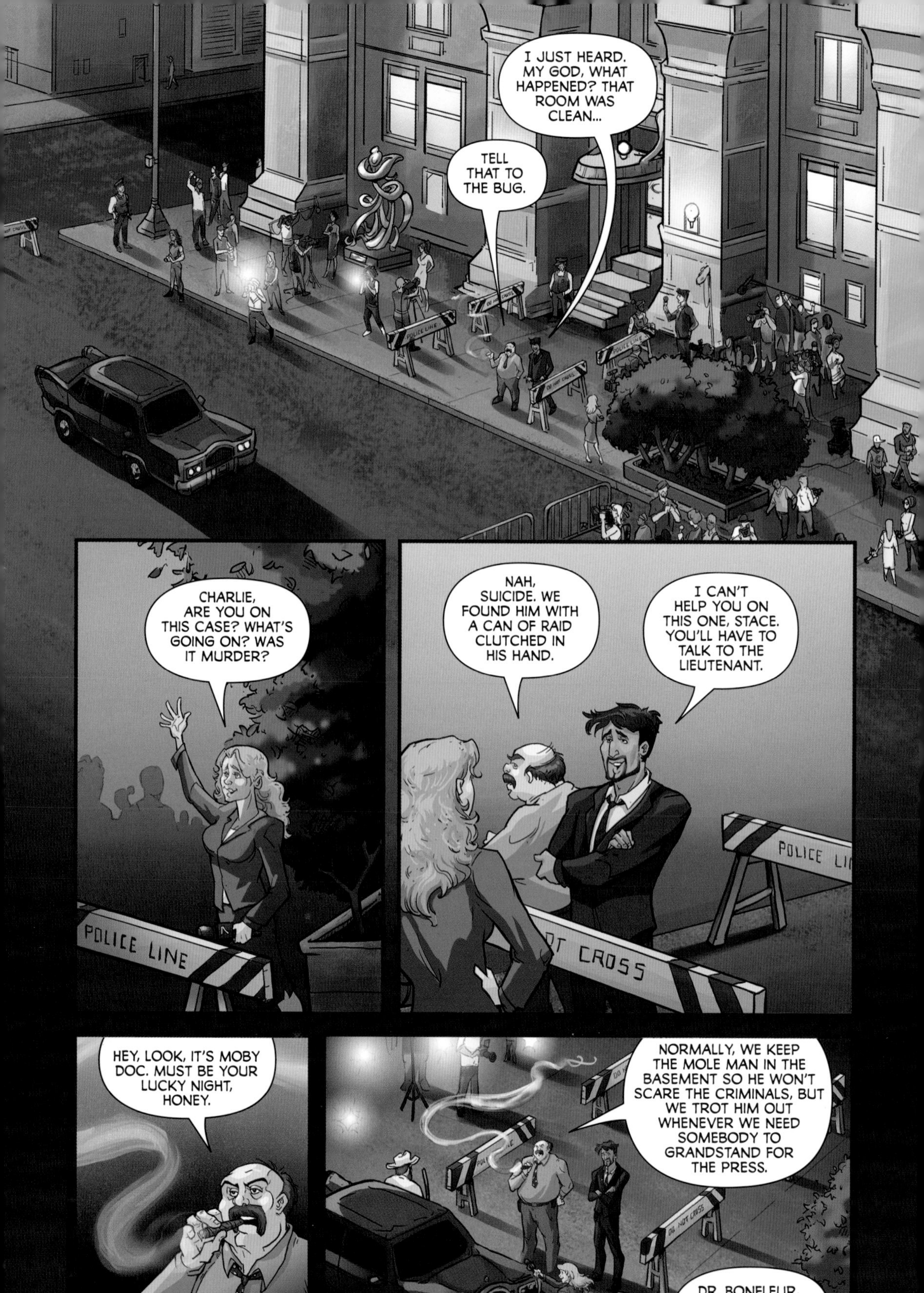
I JUST HEARD. MY GOD, WHAT HAPPENED? THAT ROOM WAS CLEAN...
TELL THAT TO THE BUG.
CHARLIE, ARE YOU ON THIS CASE? WHAT'S GOING ON? WAS IT MURDER?
POLICE LINE
NAH, SUICIDE. WE FOUND HIM WITH A CAN OF RAID CLUTCHED IN HIS HAND.
I CAN'T HELP YOU ON THIS ONE, STACE. YOU'LL HAVE TO TALK TO THE LIEUTENANT.
HEY, LOOK, IT'S MOBY DOC. MUST BE YOUR LUCKY NIGHT, HONEY.
NORMALLY, WE KEEP THE MOLE MAN IN THE BASEMENT SO HE WON'T SCARE THE CRIMINALS, BUT WE TROT HIM OUT WHENEVER WE NEED SOMEBODY TO GRANDSTAND FOR THE PRESS.
DR. BONFLEUR, ARE YOU HERE TO PERFORM AN AUTOPSY?

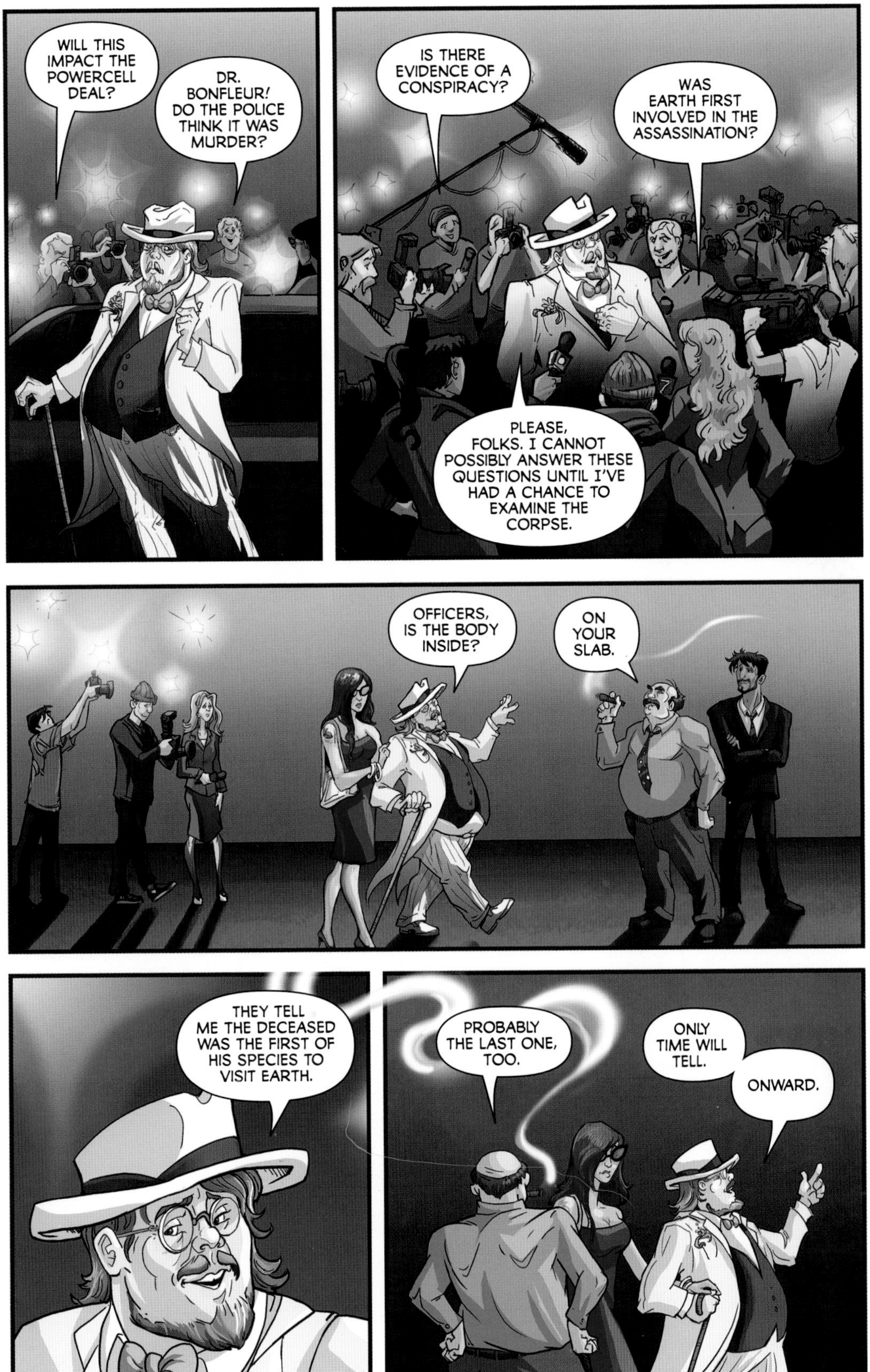
WILL THIS IMPACT THE POWERCELL DEAL?
DR. BONFLEUR! DO THE POLICE THINK IT WAS MURDER?
IS THERE EVIDENCE OF A CONSPIRACY?
WAS EARTH FIRST INVOLVED IN THE ASSASSINATION?
PLEASE, FOLKS. I CANNOT POSSIBLY ANSWER THESE QUESTIONS UNTIL I'VE HAD A CHANCE TO EXAMINE THE CORPSE.
OFFICERS, IS THE BODY INSIDE?
ON YOUR SLAB.
THEY TELL ME THE DECEASED WAS THE FIRST OF HIS SPECIES TO VISIT EARTH.
PROBABLY THE LAST ONE, TOO.
ONLY TIME WILL TELL.
ONWARD.

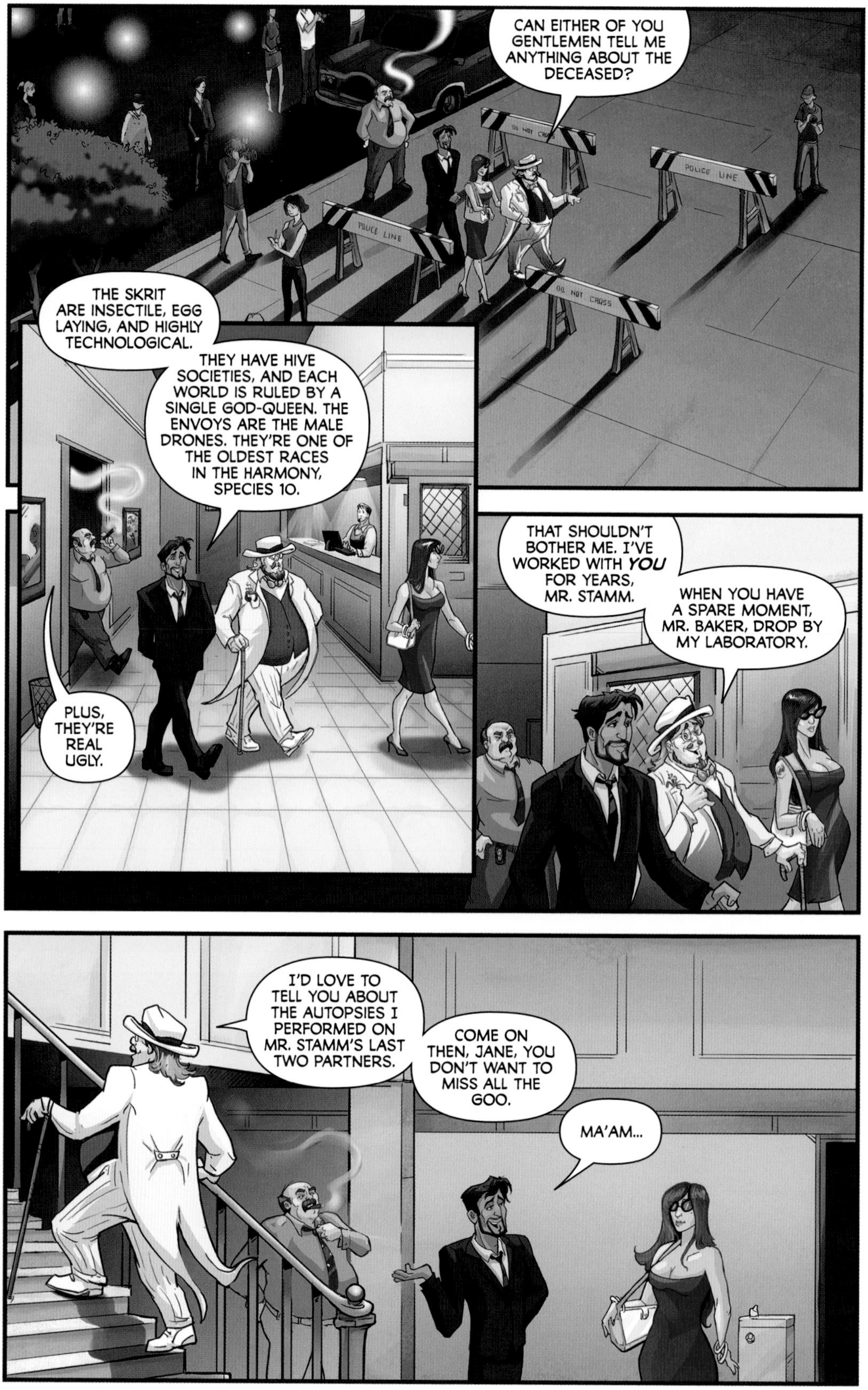
CAN EITHER OF YOU GENTLEMEN TELL ME ANYTHING ABOUT THE DECEASED?
POLICE LINE
DO NOT CROSS
THE SKRIT ARE INSECTILE, EGG LAYING, AND HIGHLY TECHNOLOGICAL.
THEY HAVE HIVE SOCIETIES, AND EACH WORLD IS RULED BY A SINGLE GOD-QUEEN. THE ENVOYS ARE THE MALE DRONES. THEY'RE ONE OF THE OLDEST RACES IN THE HARMONY, SPECIES 10.
PLUS, THEY'RE REAL UGLY.
THAT SHOULDN'T BOTHER ME. I'VE WORKED WITH *YOU* FOR YEARS, MR. STAMM.
WHEN YOU HAVE A SPARE MOMENT, MR. BAKER, DROP BY MY LABORATORY.
I'D LOVE TO TELL YOU ABOUT THE AUTOPSIES I PERFORMED ON MR. STAMM'S LAST TWO PARTNERS.
COME ON THEN, JANE, YOU DON'T WANT TO MISS ALL THE GOO.
MA'AM...

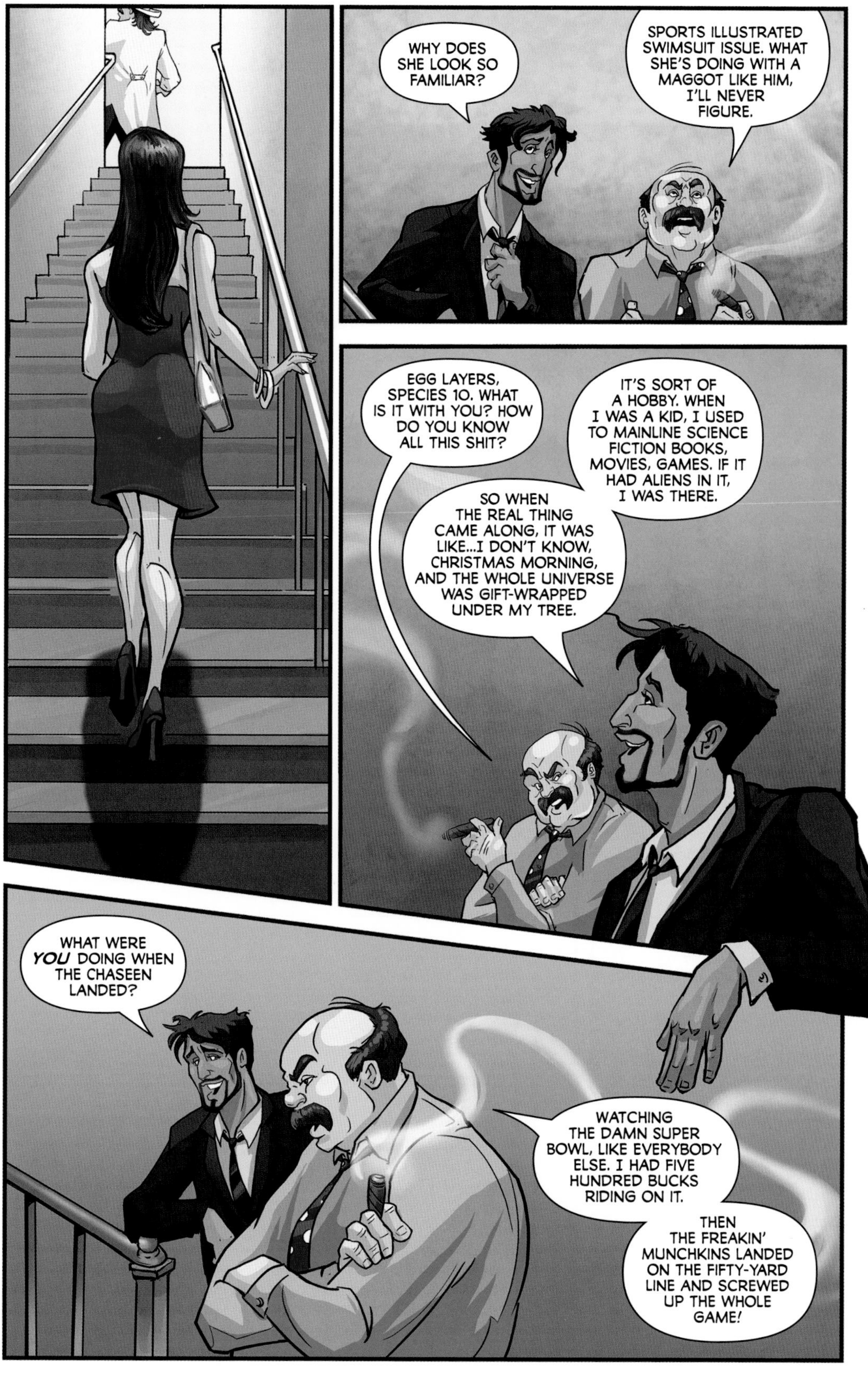

WHY DOES SHE LOOK SO FAMILIAR?
SPORTS ILLUSTRATED SWIMSUIT ISSUE. WHAT SHE'S DOING WITH A MAGGOT LIKE HIM, I'LL NEVER FIGURE.
EGG LAYERS, SPECIES 10. WHAT IS IT WITH YOU? HOW DO YOU KNOW ALL THIS SHIT?
IT'S SORT OF A HOBBY. WHEN I WAS A KID, I USED TO MAINLINE SCIENCE FICTION BOOKS, MOVIES, GAMES. IF IT HAD ALIENS IN IT, I WAS THERE.
SO WHEN THE REAL THING CAME ALONG, IT WAS LIKE...I DON'T KNOW, CHRISTMAS MORNING, AND THE WHOLE UNIVERSE WAS GIFT-WRAPPED UNDER MY TREE.
WHAT WERE *YOU* DOING WHEN THE CHASEEN LANDED?
WATCHING THE DAMN SUPER BOWL, LIKE EVERYBODY ELSE. I HAD FIVE HUNDRED BUCKS RIDING ON IT.
THEN THE FREAKIN' MUNCHKINS LANDED ON THE FIFTY-YARD LINE AND SCREWED UP THE WHOLE GAME!

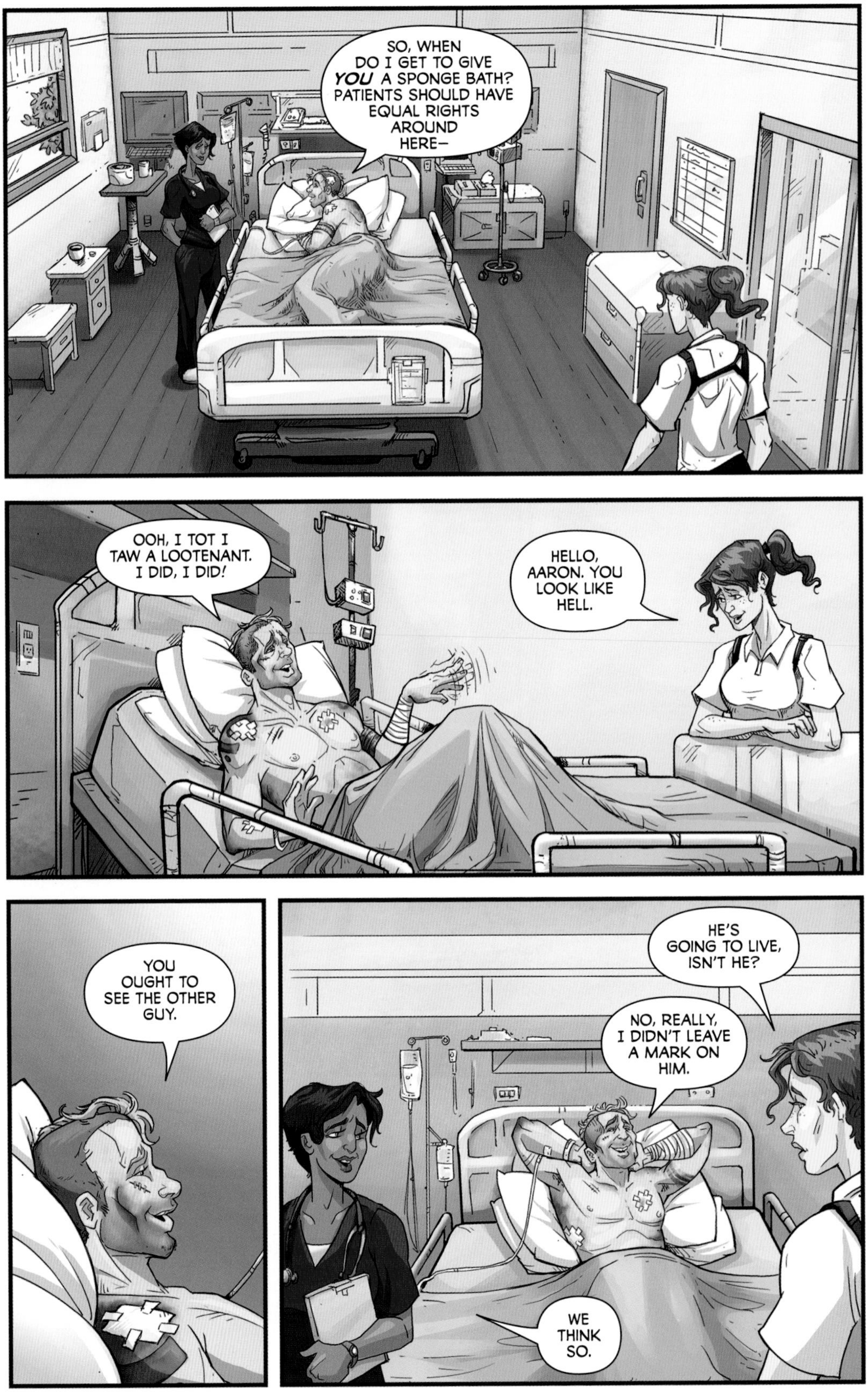
SO, WHEN DO I GET TO GIVE *YOU* A SPONGE BATH? PATIENTS SHOULD HAVE EQUAL RIGHTS AROUND HERE—
OOH, I TOT I TAW A LOOTENANT. I DID, I DID!
HELLO, AARON. YOU LOOK LIKE HELL.
YOU OUGHT TO SEE THE OTHER GUY.
HE'S GOING TO LIVE, ISN'T HE?
NO, REALLY, I DIDN'T LEAVE A MARK ON HIM.
WE THINK SO.

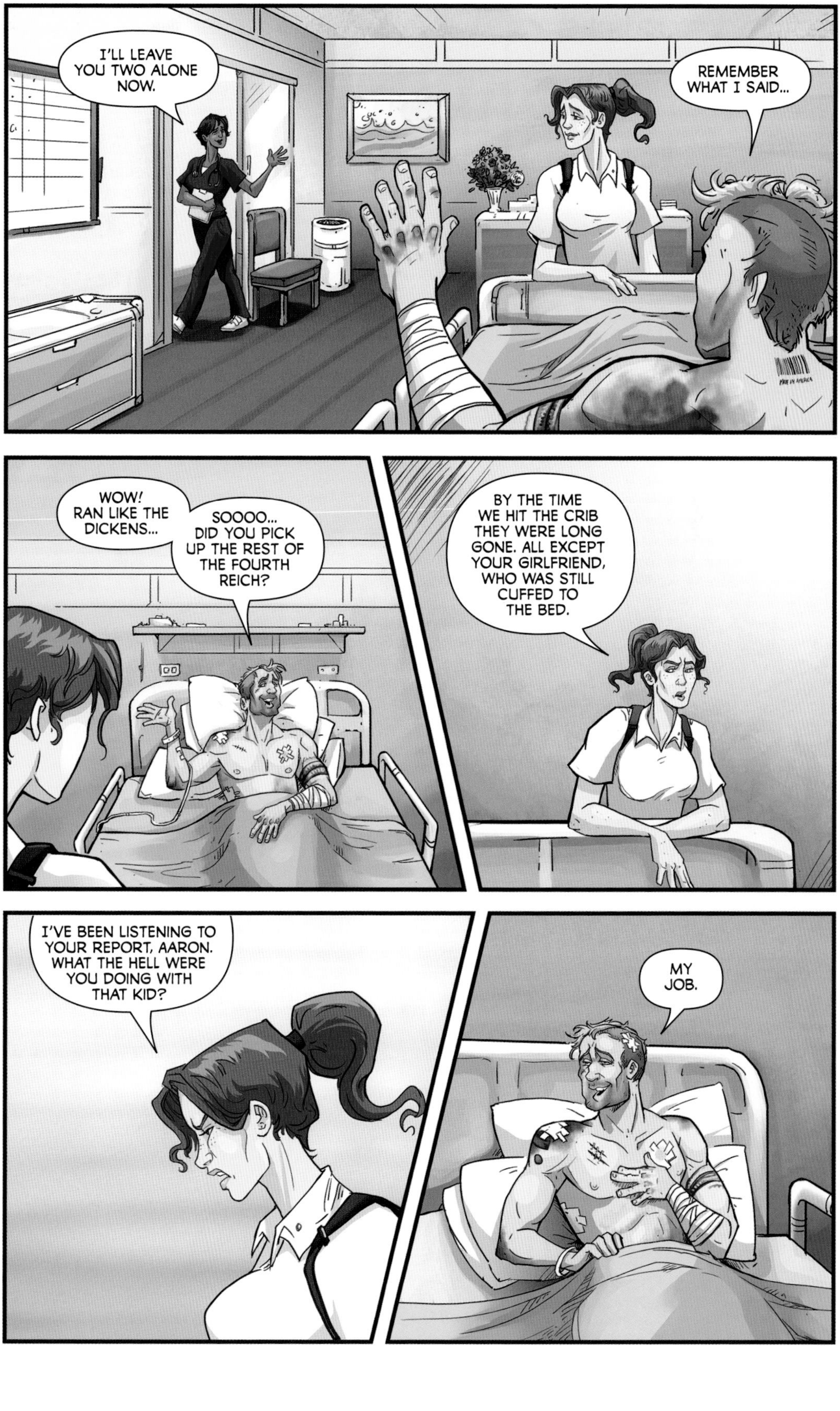
I'LL LEAVE YOU TWO ALONE NOW.
REMEMBER WHAT I SAID...
WOW! RAN LIKE THE DICKENS...
SOOOO... DID YOU PICK UP THE REST OF THE FOURTH REICH?
BY THE TIME WE HIT THE CRIB THEY WERE LONG GONE. ALL EXCEPT YOUR GIRLFRIEND, WHO WAS STILL CUFFED TO THE BED.
I'VE BEEN LISTENING TO YOUR REPORT, AARON. WHAT THE HELL WERE YOU DOING WITH THAT KID?
MY JOB.

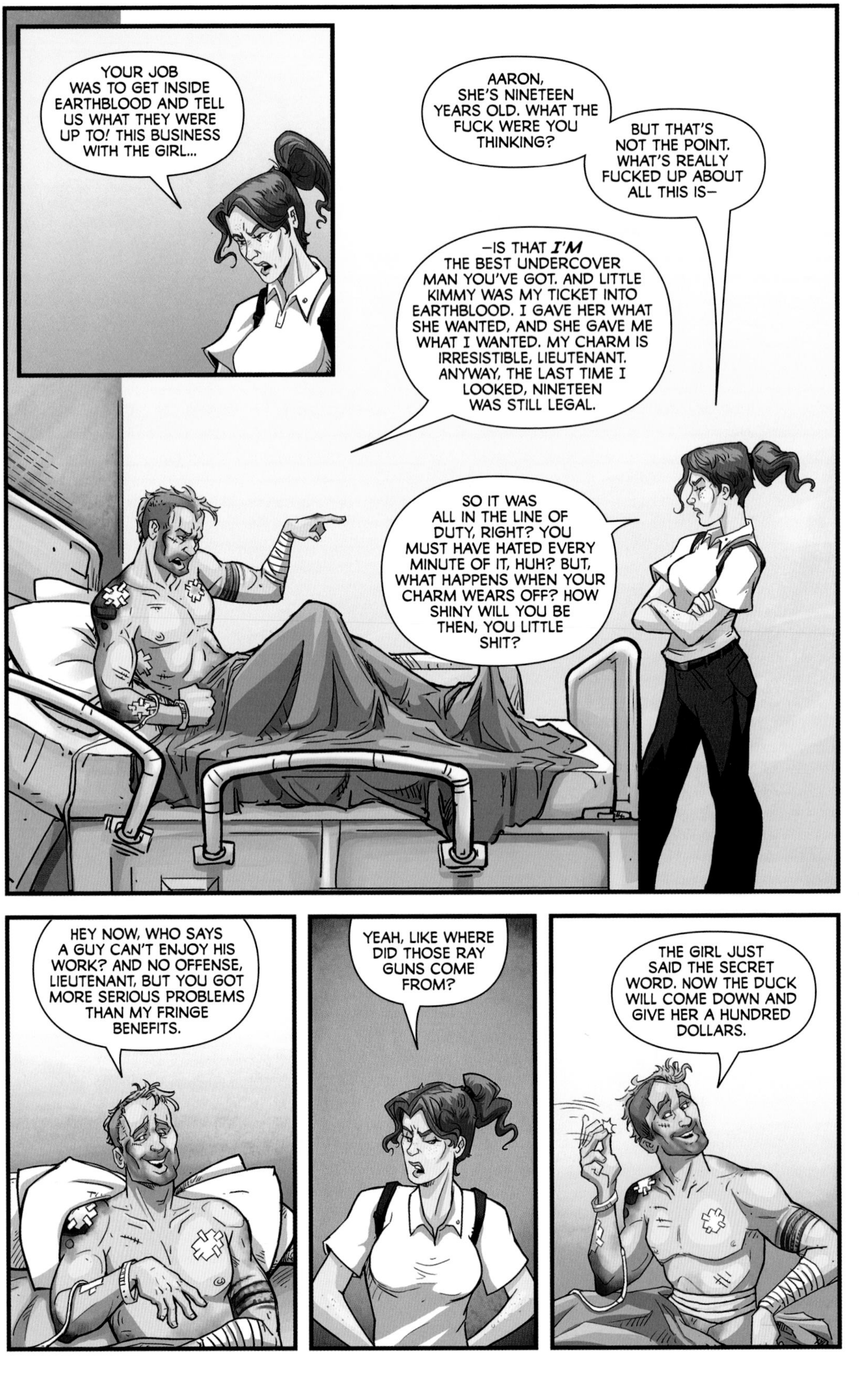
YOUR JOB WAS TO GET INSIDE EARTHBLOOD AND TELL US WHAT THEY WERE UP TO! THIS BUSINESS WITH THE GIRL...
AARON, SHE'S NINETEEN YEARS OLD. WHAT THE FUCK WERE YOU THINKING?
BUT THAT'S NOT THE POINT. WHAT'S REALLY FUCKED UP ABOUT ALL THIS IS—
—IS THAT ***I'M*** THE BEST UNDERCOVER MAN YOU'VE GOT. AND LITTLE KIMMY WAS MY TICKET INTO EARTHBLOOD. I GAVE HER WHAT SHE WANTED, AND SHE GAVE ME WHAT I WANTED. MY CHARM IS IRRESISTIBLE, LIEUTENANT. ANYWAY, THE LAST TIME I LOOKED, NINETEEN WAS STILL LEGAL.
SO IT WAS ALL IN THE LINE OF DUTY, RIGHT? YOU MUST HAVE HATED EVERY MINUTE OF IT, HUH? BUT, WHAT HAPPENS WHEN YOUR CHARM WEARS OFF? HOW SHINY WILL YOU BE THEN, YOU LITTLE SHIT?
HEY NOW, WHO SAYS A GUY CAN'T ENJOY HIS WORK? AND NO OFFENSE, LIEUTENANT, BUT YOU GOT MORE SERIOUS PROBLEMS THAN MY FRINGE BENEFITS.
YEAH, LIKE WHERE DID THOSE RAY GUNS COME FROM?
THE GIRL JUST SAID THE SECRET WORD. NOW THE DUCK WILL COME DOWN AND GIVE HER A HUNDRED DOLLARS.

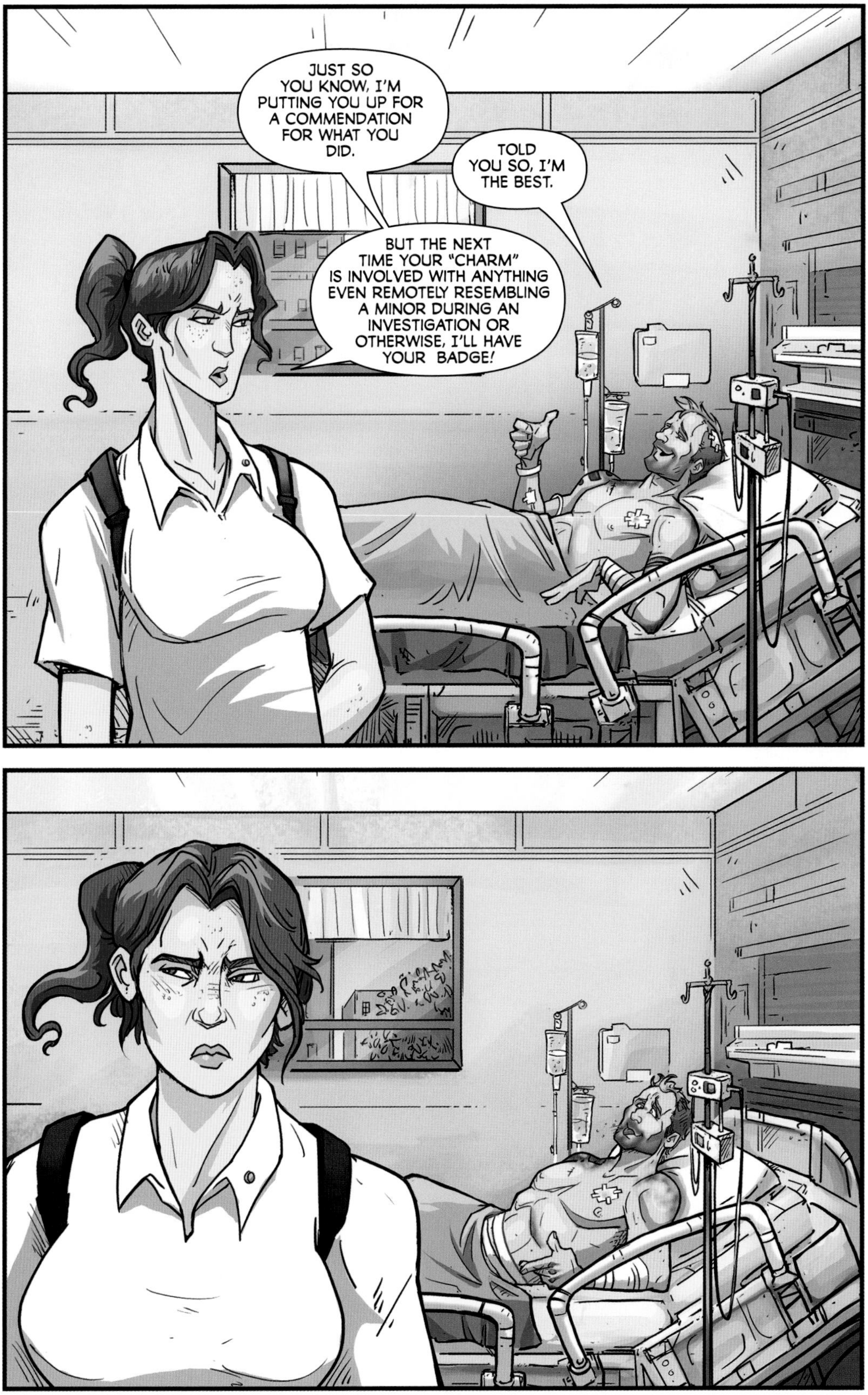
JUST SO YOU KNOW, I'M PUTTING YOU UP FOR A COMMENDATION FOR WHAT YOU DID.
TOLD YOU SO, I'M THE BEST.
BUT THE NEXT TIME YOUR "CHARM" IS INVOLVED WITH ANYTHING EVEN REMOTELY RESEMBLING A MINOR DURING AN INVESTIGATION OR OTHERWISE, I'LL HAVE YOUR BADGE!

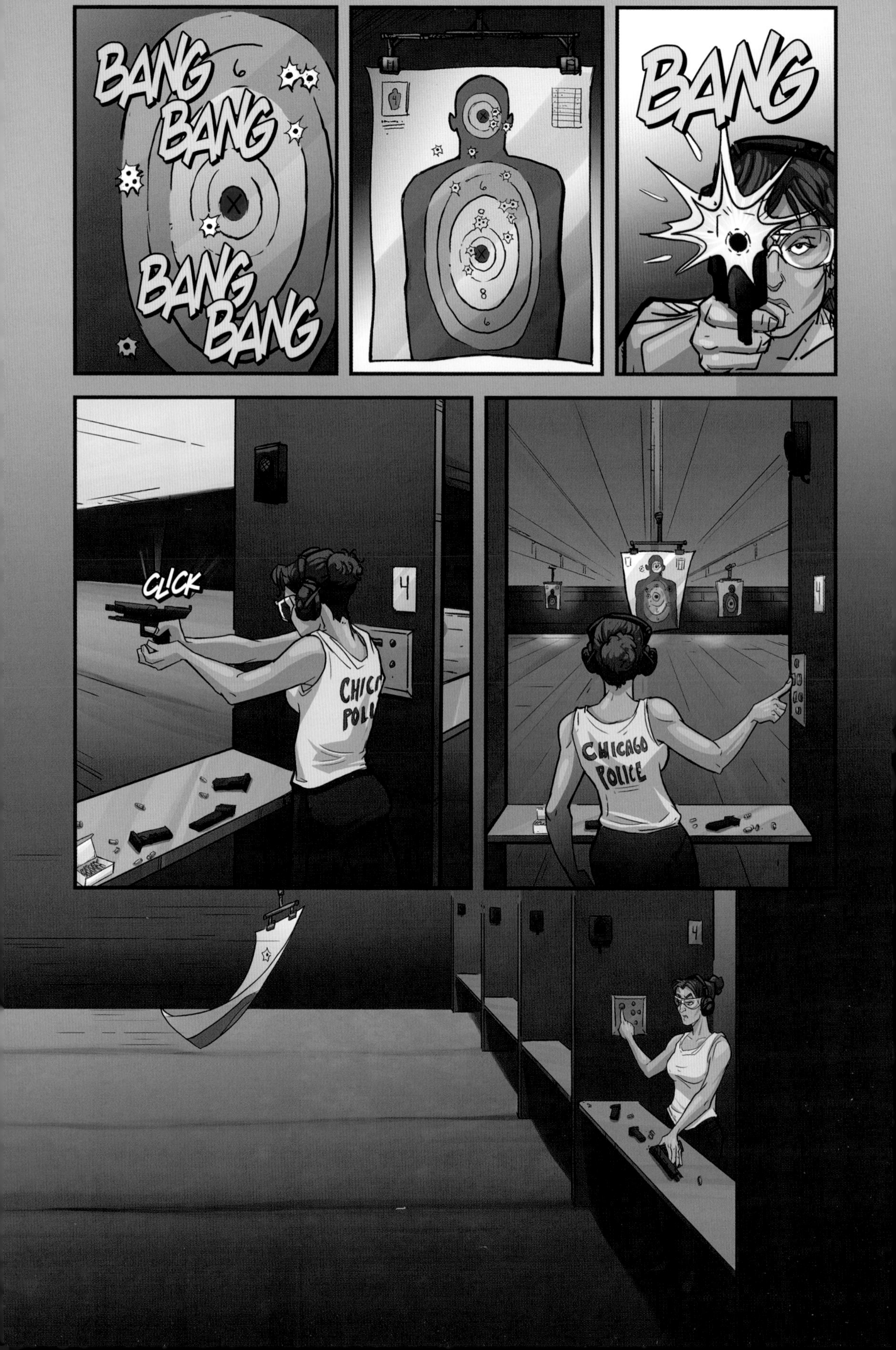
BANG
BANG
BANG
BANG
BANG
CLICK
CHICAGO POLICE

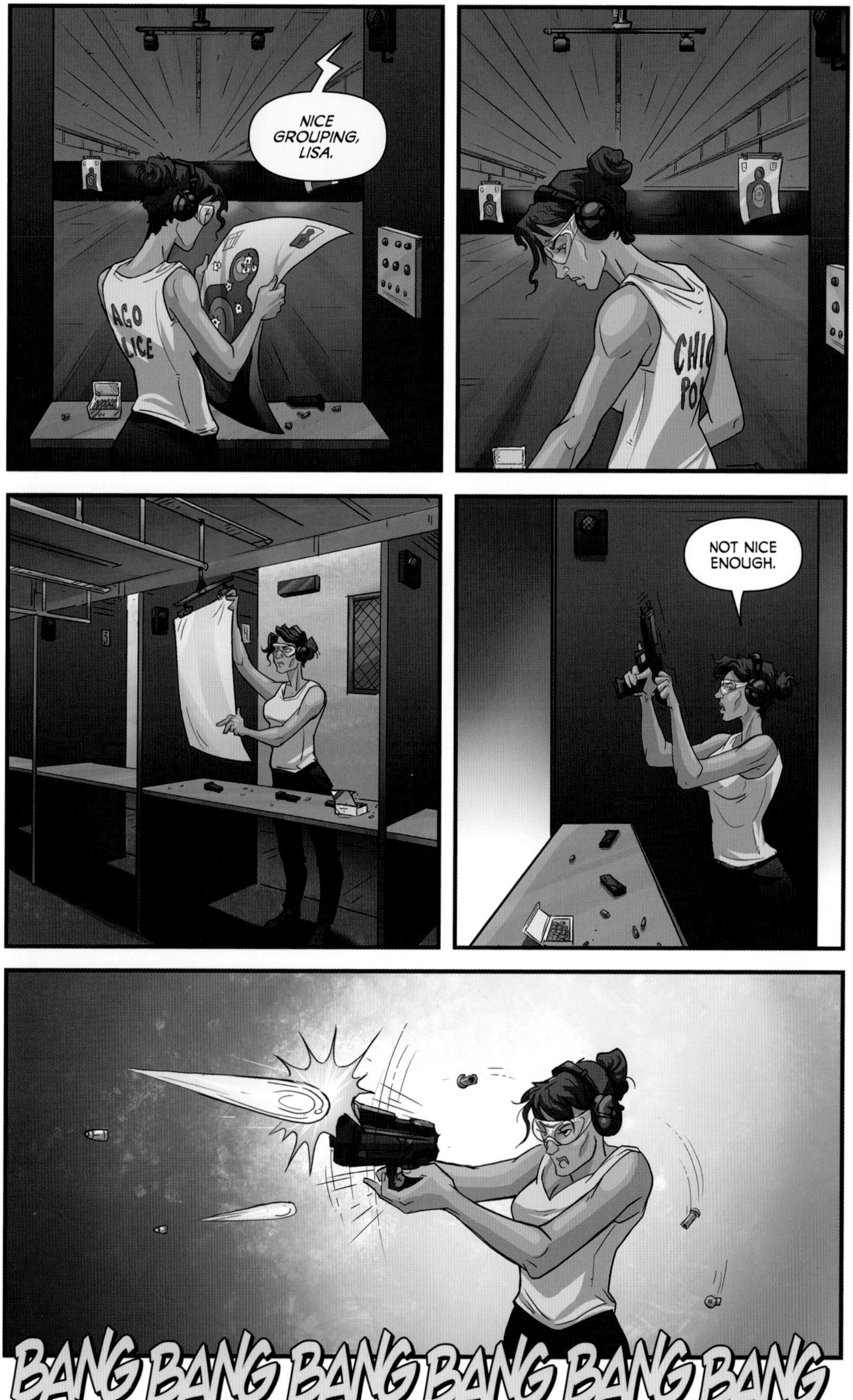
NICE GROUPING, LISA.
NOT NICE ENOUGH.
BANG BANG BANG BANG BANG BANG

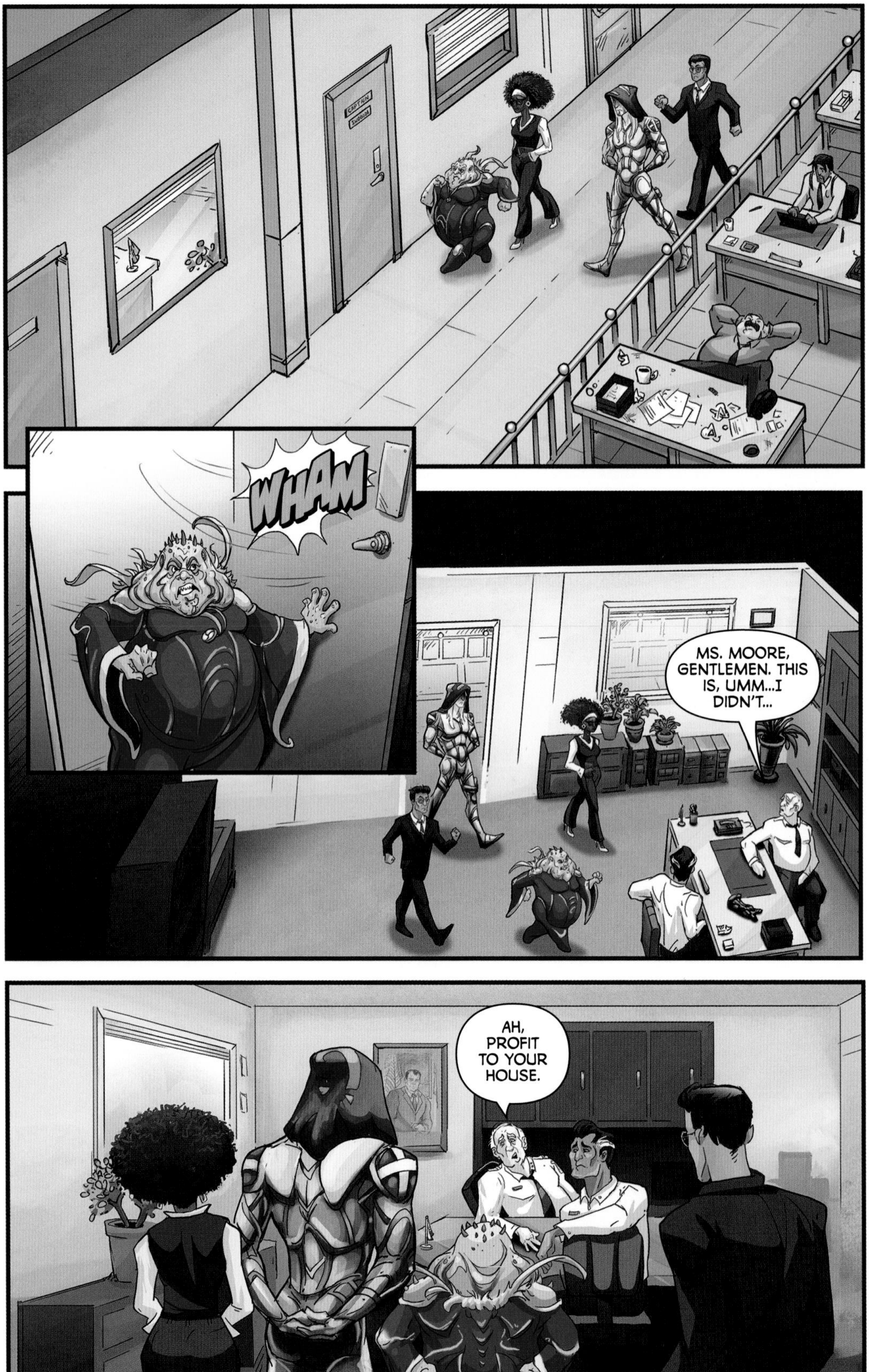
WHAM
MS. MOORE, GENTLEMEN. THIS IS, UMM...I DIDN'T...
AH, PROFIT TO YOUR HOUSE.

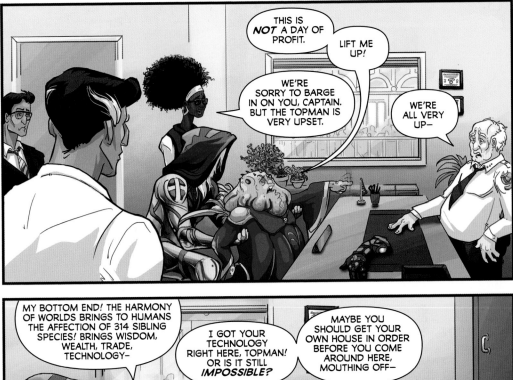

THIS IS *NOT* A DAY OF PROFIT.

LIFT ME UP!

WE'RE SORRY TO BARGE IN ON YOU, CAPTAIN. BUT THE TOPMAN IS VERY UPSET.

WE'RE ALL VERY UP—

MY BOTTOM END! THE HARMONY OF WORLDS BRINGS TO HUMANS THE AFFECTION OF 314 SIBLING SPECIES! BRINGS WISDOM, WEALTH, TRADE, TECHNOLOGY—

I GOT YOUR TECHNOLOGY RIGHT HERE, TOPMAN! OR IS IT STILL *IMPOSSIBLE?*

MAYBE YOU SHOULD GET YOUR OWN HOUSE IN ORDER BEFORE YOU COME AROUND HERE, MOUTHING OFF—

GENTLEMEN, PLEASE...

HARMONY OPENS ROAD TO THE STARS, AND HUMANS REPAY WITH UNGRATEFUL *MURDER!*

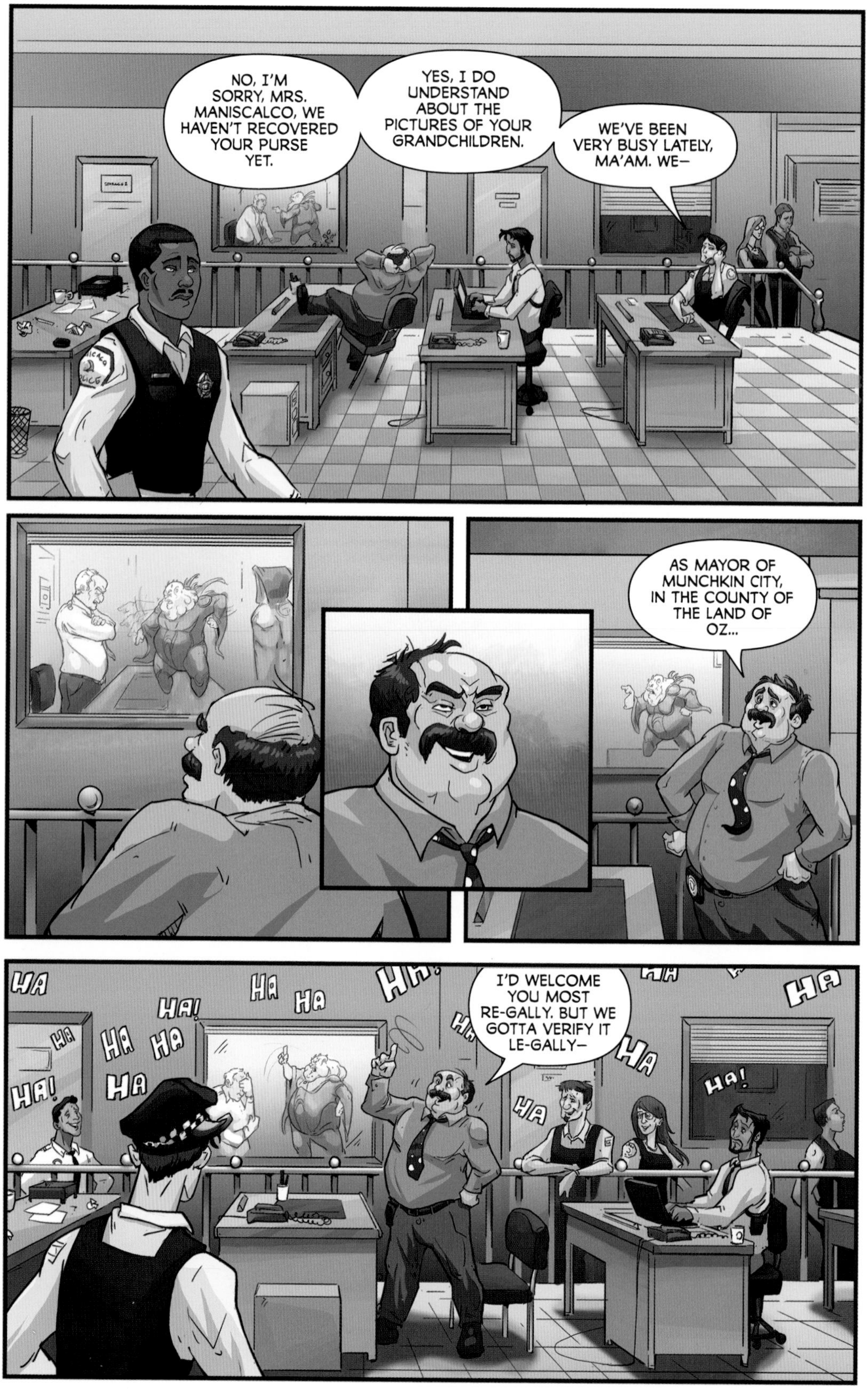
NO, I'M SORRY, MRS. MANISCALCO, WE HAVEN'T RECOVERED YOUR PURSE YET.
YES, I DO UNDERSTAND ABOUT THE PICTURES OF YOUR GRANDCHILDREN.
WE'VE BEEN VERY BUSY LATELY, MA'AM. WE—
AS MAYOR OF MUNCHKIN CITY, IN THE COUNTY OF THE LAND OF OZ...
HA
HA!
HA
HA
HA
HA HA
HA!
HA
I'D WELCOME YOU MOST RE-GALLY. BUT WE GOTTA VERIFY IT LE-GALLY—
HA
HA
HA!
HA

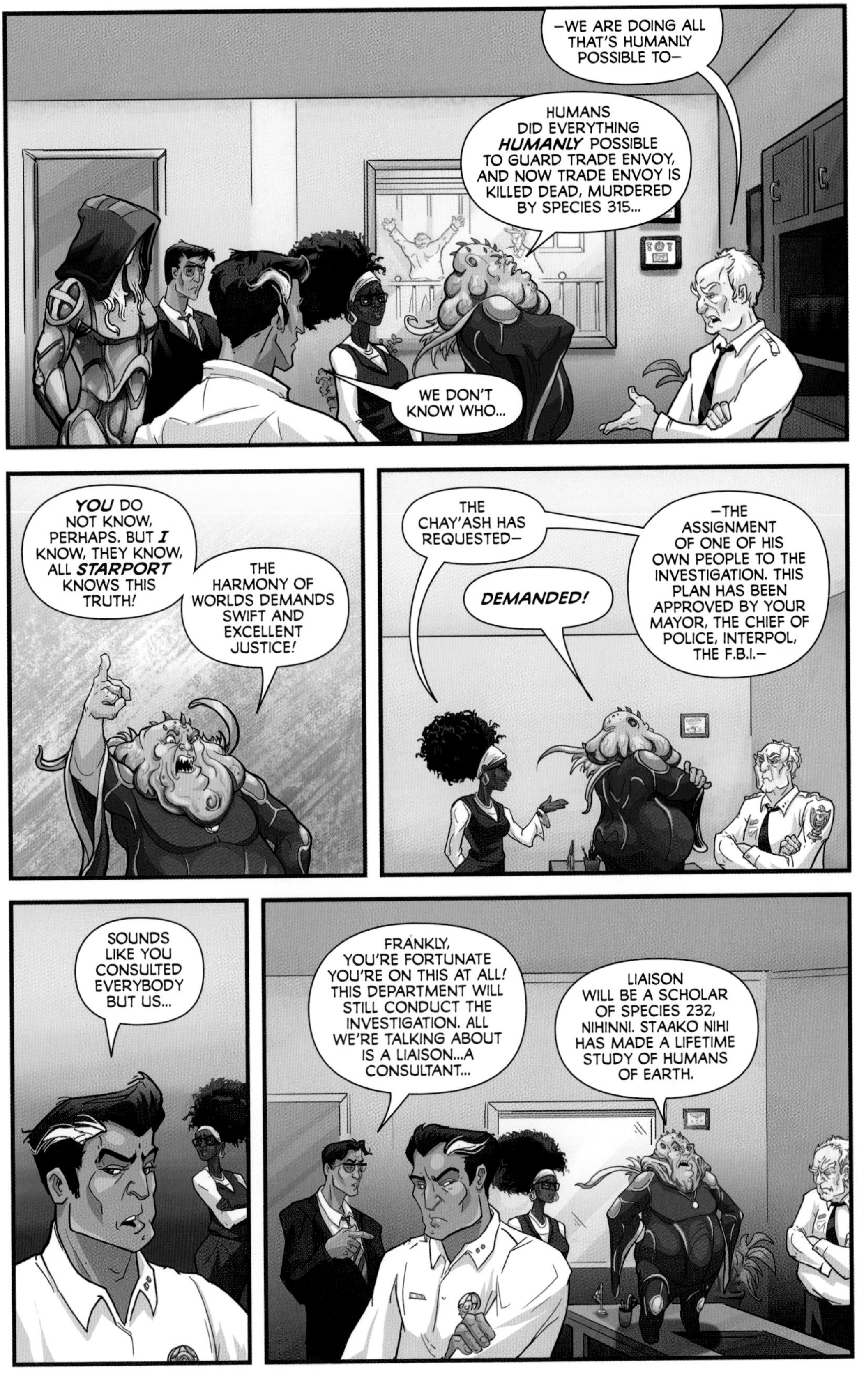
—WE ARE DOING ALL THAT'S HUMANLY POSSIBLE TO—
HUMANS DID EVERYTHING *HUMANLY* POSSIBLE TO GUARD TRADE ENVOY, AND NOW TRADE ENVOY IS KILLED DEAD, MURDERED BY SPECIES 315...
WE DON'T KNOW WHO...
YOU DO NOT KNOW, PERHAPS. BUT *I* KNOW, THEY KNOW, ALL *STARPORT* KNOWS THIS TRUTH!
THE HARMONY OF WORLDS DEMANDS SWIFT AND EXCELLENT JUSTICE!
THE CHAY'ASH HAS REQUESTED—
DEMANDED!
—THE ASSIGNMENT OF ONE OF HIS OWN PEOPLE TO THE INVESTIGATION. THIS PLAN HAS BEEN APPROVED BY YOUR MAYOR, THE CHIEF OF POLICE, INTERPOL, THE F.B.I.—
SOUNDS LIKE YOU CONSULTED EVERYBODY BUT US...
FRANKLY, YOU'RE FORTUNATE YOU'RE ON THIS AT ALL! THIS DEPARTMENT WILL STILL CONDUCT THE INVESTIGATION. ALL WE'RE TALKING ABOUT IS A LIAISON...A CONSULTANT...
LIAISON WILL BE A SCHOLAR OF SPECIES 232, NIHINNI. STAAKO NIHI HAS MADE A LIFETIME STUDY OF HUMANS OF EARTH.

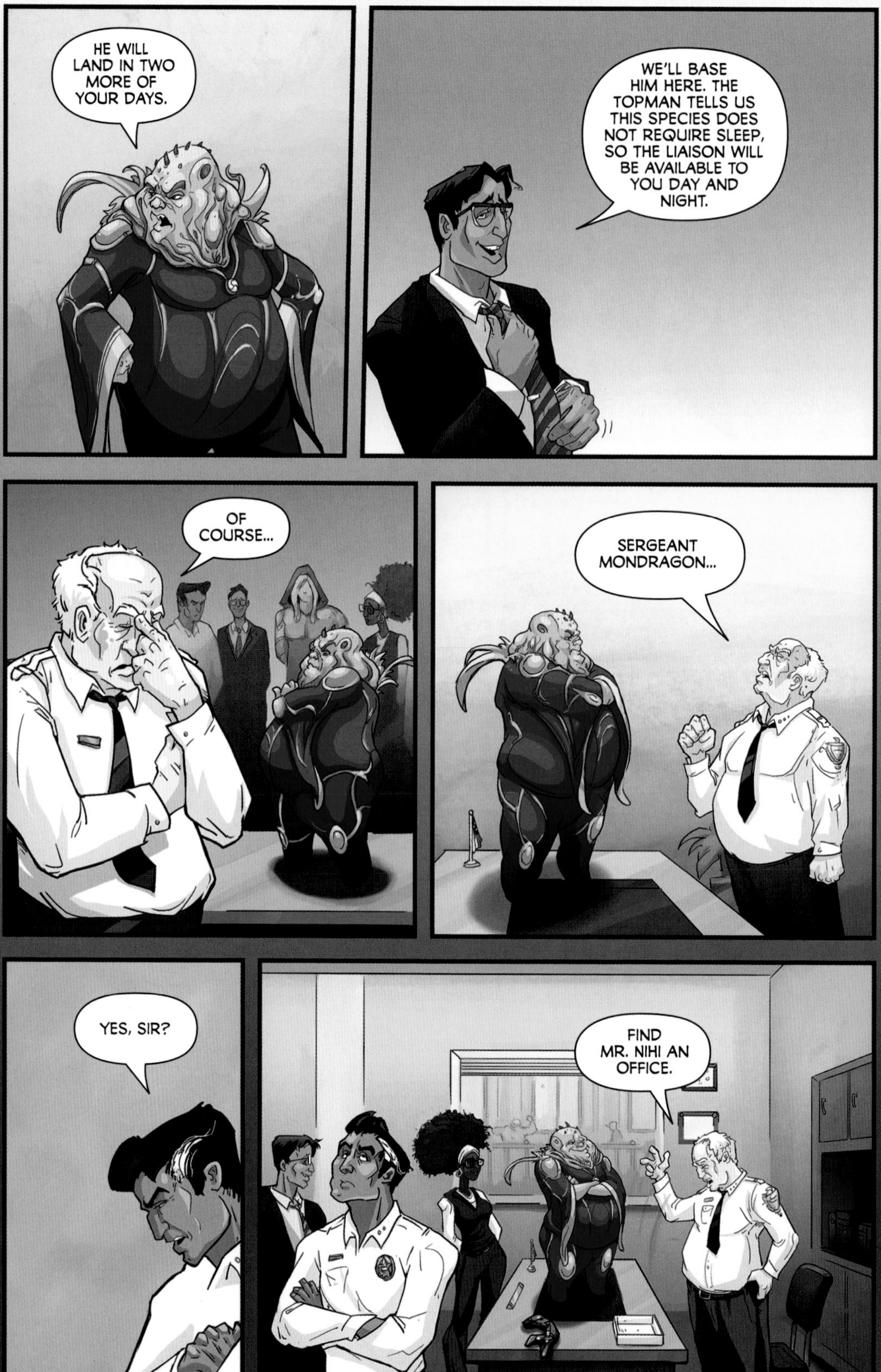
HE WILL LAND IN TWO MORE OF YOUR DAYS.
WE'LL BASE HIM HERE. THE TOPMAN TELLS US THIS SPECIES DOES NOT REQUIRE SLEEP, SO THE LIAISON WILL BE AVAILABLE TO YOU DAY AND NIGHT.
OF COURSE...
SERGEANT MONDRAGON...
YES, SIR?
FIND MR. NIHI AN OFFICE.

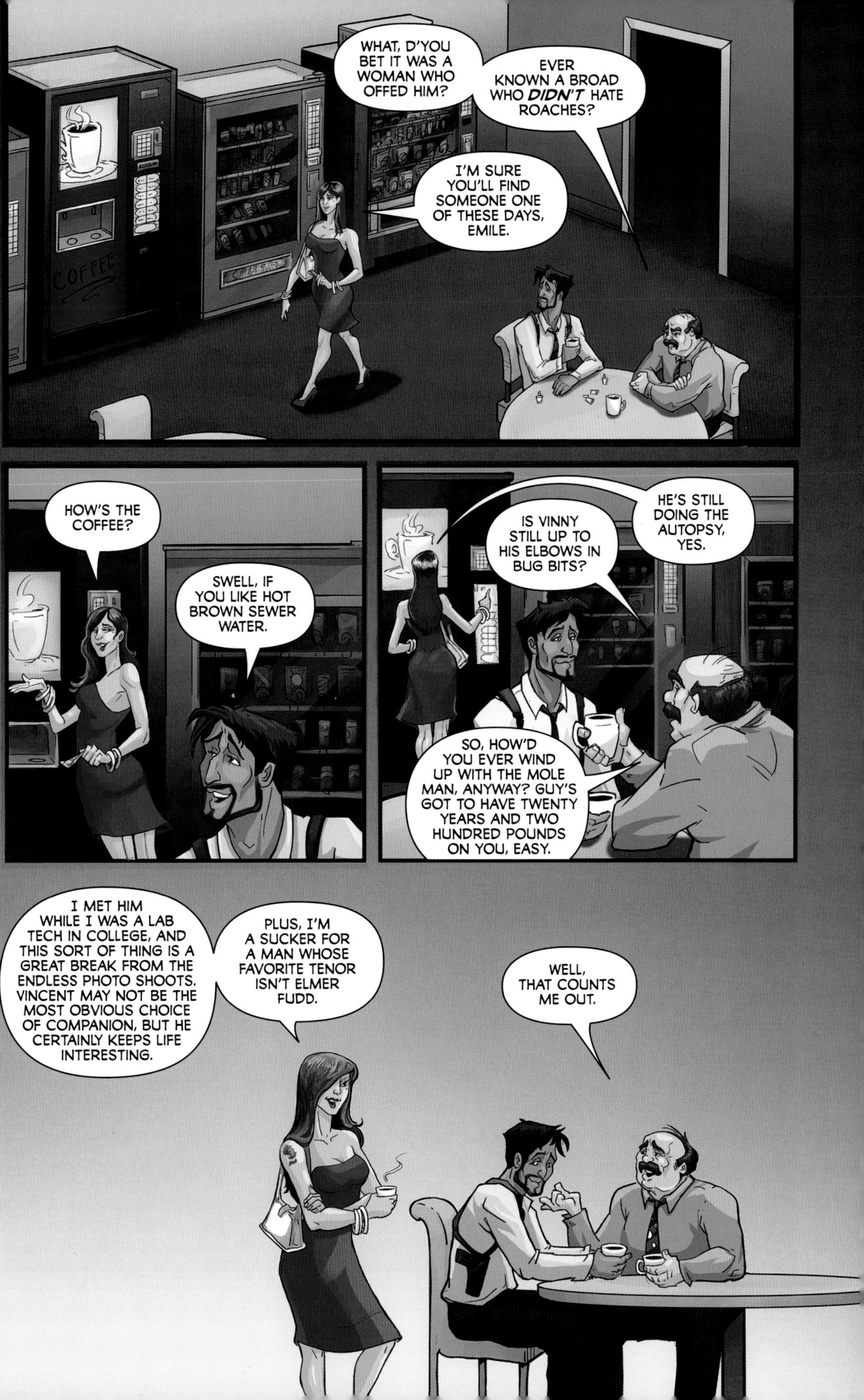
WHAT, D'YOU BET IT WAS A WOMAN WHO OFFED HIM?
EVER KNOWN A BROAD WHO *DIDN'T* HATE ROACHES?
I'M SURE YOU'LL FIND SOMEONE ONE OF THESE DAYS, EMILE.
COFFEE
PUSH
HOW'S THE COFFEE?
SWELL, IF YOU LIKE HOT BROWN SEWER WATER.
IS VINNY STILL UP TO HIS ELBOWS IN BUG BITS?
HE'S STILL DOING THE AUTOPSY, YES.
SO, HOW'D YOU EVER WIND UP WITH THE MOLE MAN, ANYWAY? GUY'S GOT TO HAVE TWENTY YEARS AND TWO HUNDRED POUNDS ON YOU, EASY.
I MET HIM WHILE I WAS A LAB TECH IN COLLEGE, AND THIS SORT OF THING IS A GREAT BREAK FROM THE ENDLESS PHOTO SHOOTS. VINCENT MAY NOT BE THE MOST OBVIOUS CHOICE OF COMPANION, BUT HE CERTAINLY KEEPS LIFE INTERESTING.
PLUS, I'M A SUCKER FOR A MAN WHOSE FAVORITE TENOR ISN'T ELMER FUDD.
WELL, THAT COUNTS ME OUT.

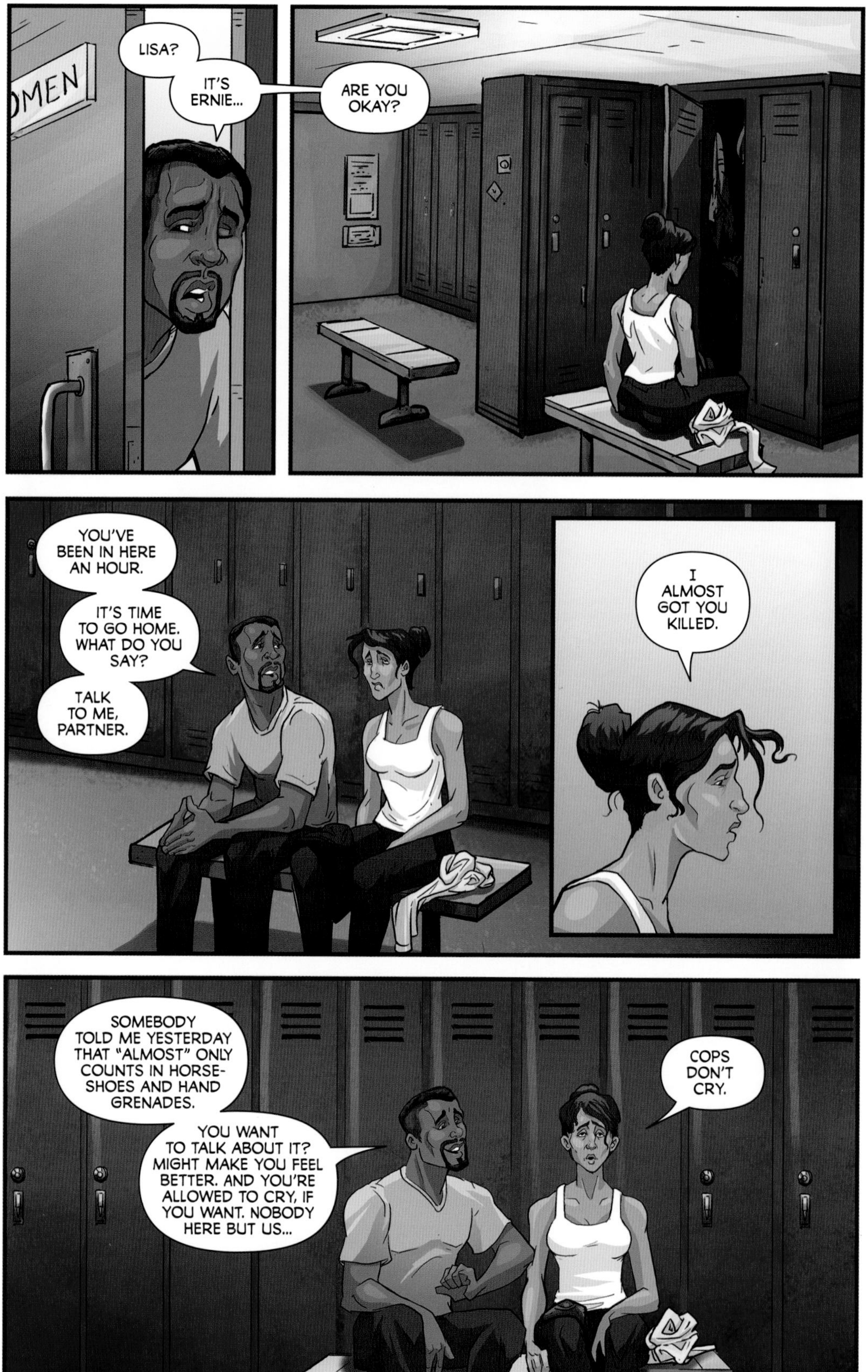
OMEN
LISA?
IT'S ERNIE...
ARE YOU OKAY?
YOU'VE BEEN IN HERE AN HOUR.
IT'S TIME TO GO HOME. WHAT DO YOU SAY?
TALK TO ME, PARTNER.
I ALMOST GOT YOU KILLED.
SOMEBODY TOLD ME YESTERDAY THAT "ALMOST" ONLY COUNTS IN HORSE-SHOES AND HAND GRENADES.
YOU WANT TO TALK ABOUT IT? MIGHT MAKE YOU FEEL BETTER. AND YOU'RE ALLOWED TO CRY, IF YOU WANT. NOBODY HERE BUT US...
COPS DON'T CRY.

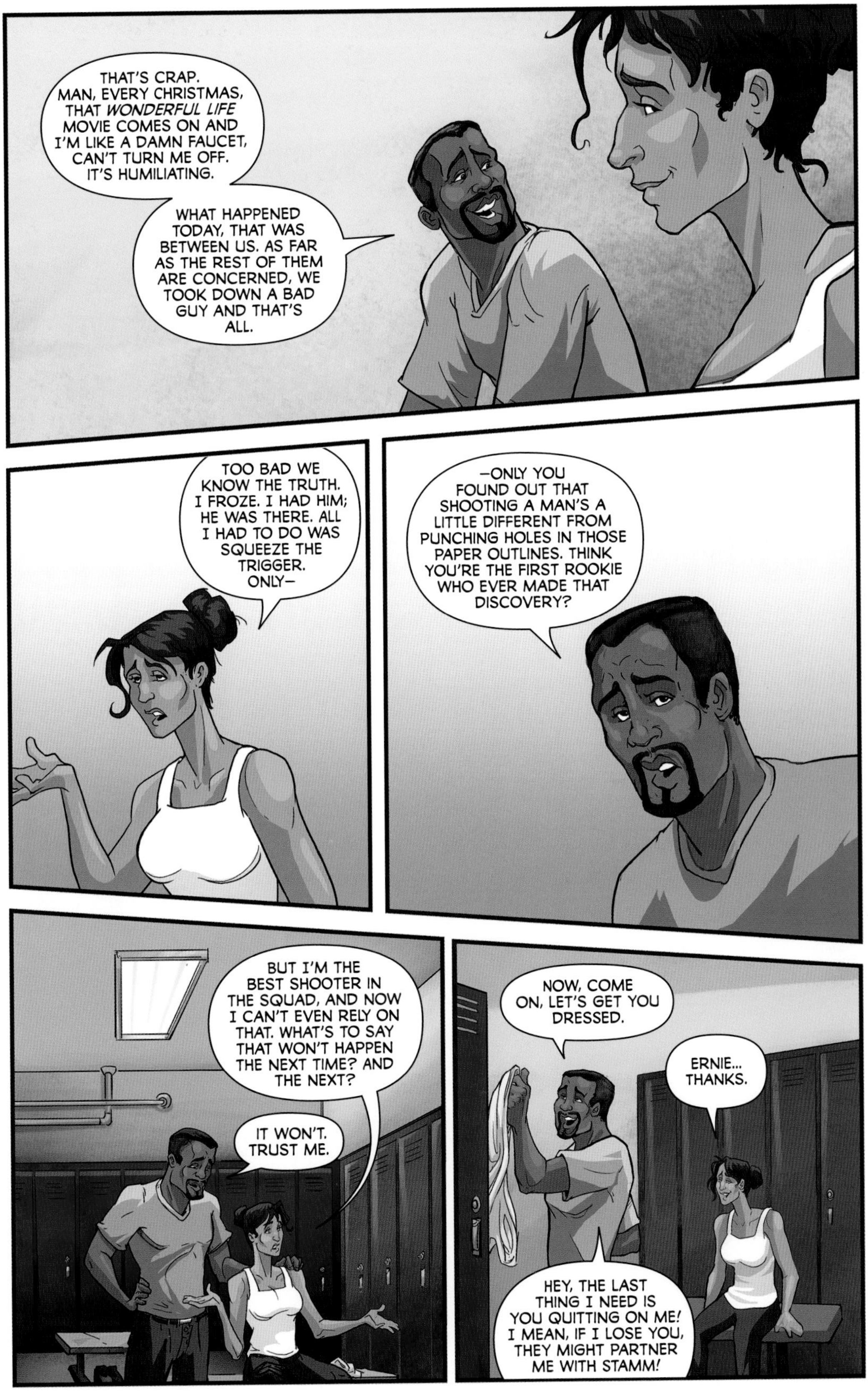
THAT'S CRAP. MAN, EVERY CHRISTMAS, THAT *WONDERFUL LIFE* MOVIE COMES ON AND I'M LIKE A DAMN FAUCET, CAN'T TURN ME OFF. IT'S HUMILIATING.
WHAT HAPPENED TODAY, THAT WAS BETWEEN US. AS FAR AS THE REST OF THEM ARE CONCERNED, WE TOOK DOWN A BAD GUY AND THAT'S ALL.
TOO BAD WE KNOW THE TRUTH. I FROZE. I HAD HIM; HE WAS THERE. ALL I HAD TO DO WAS SQUEEZE THE TRIGGER. ONLY—
—ONLY YOU FOUND OUT THAT SHOOTING A MAN'S A LITTLE DIFFERENT FROM PUNCHING HOLES IN THOSE PAPER OUTLINES. THINK YOU'RE THE FIRST ROOKIE WHO EVER MADE THAT DISCOVERY?
BUT I'M THE BEST SHOOTER IN THE SQUAD, AND NOW I CAN'T EVEN RELY ON THAT. WHAT'S TO SAY THAT WON'T HAPPEN THE NEXT TIME? AND THE NEXT?
IT WON'T. TRUST ME.
NOW, COME ON, LET'S GET YOU DRESSED.
ERNIE... THANKS.
HEY, THE LAST THING I NEED IS YOU QUITTING ON ME! I MEAN, IF I LOSE YOU, THEY MIGHT PARTNER ME WITH STAMM!

CHAPTER EIGHT

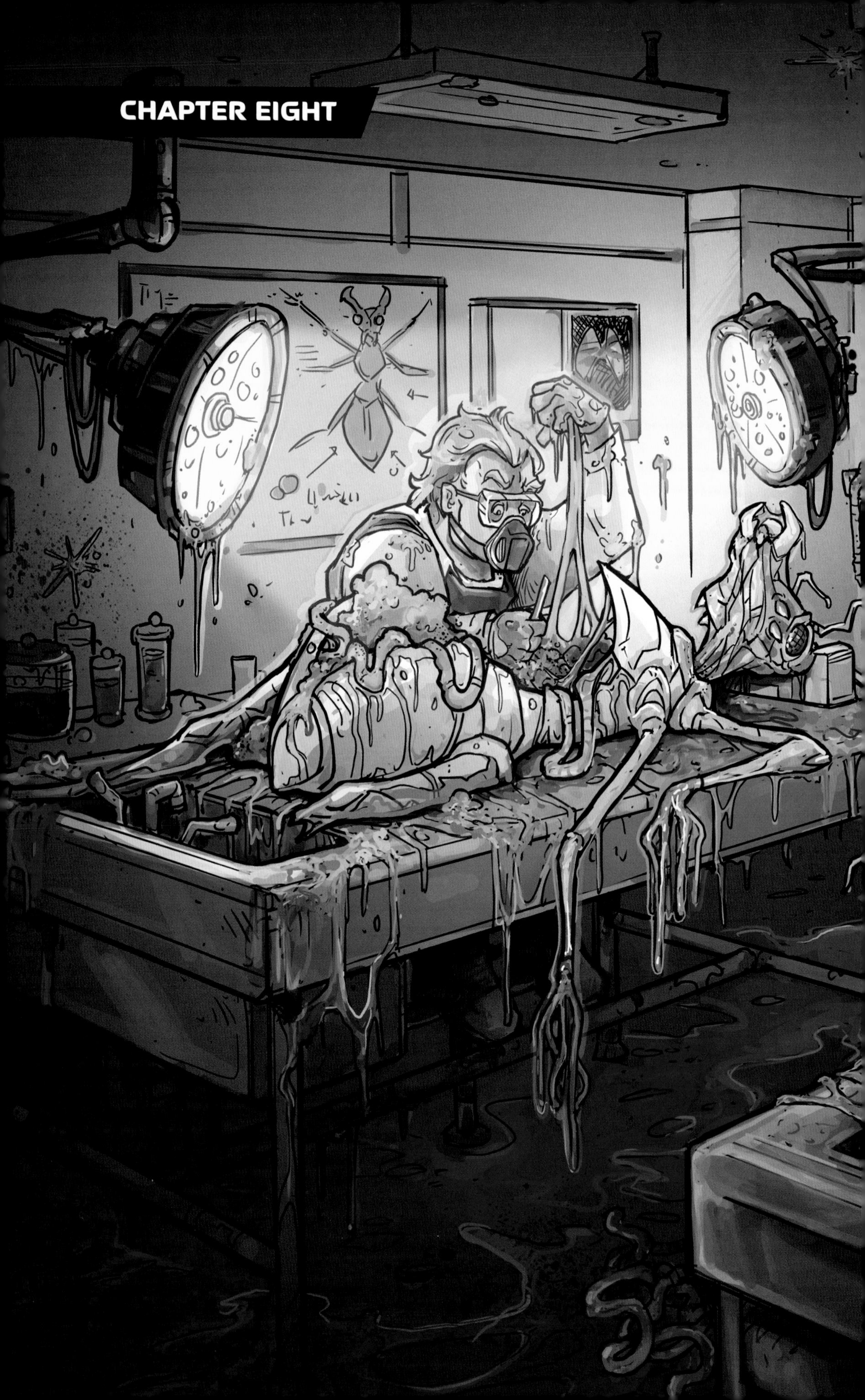

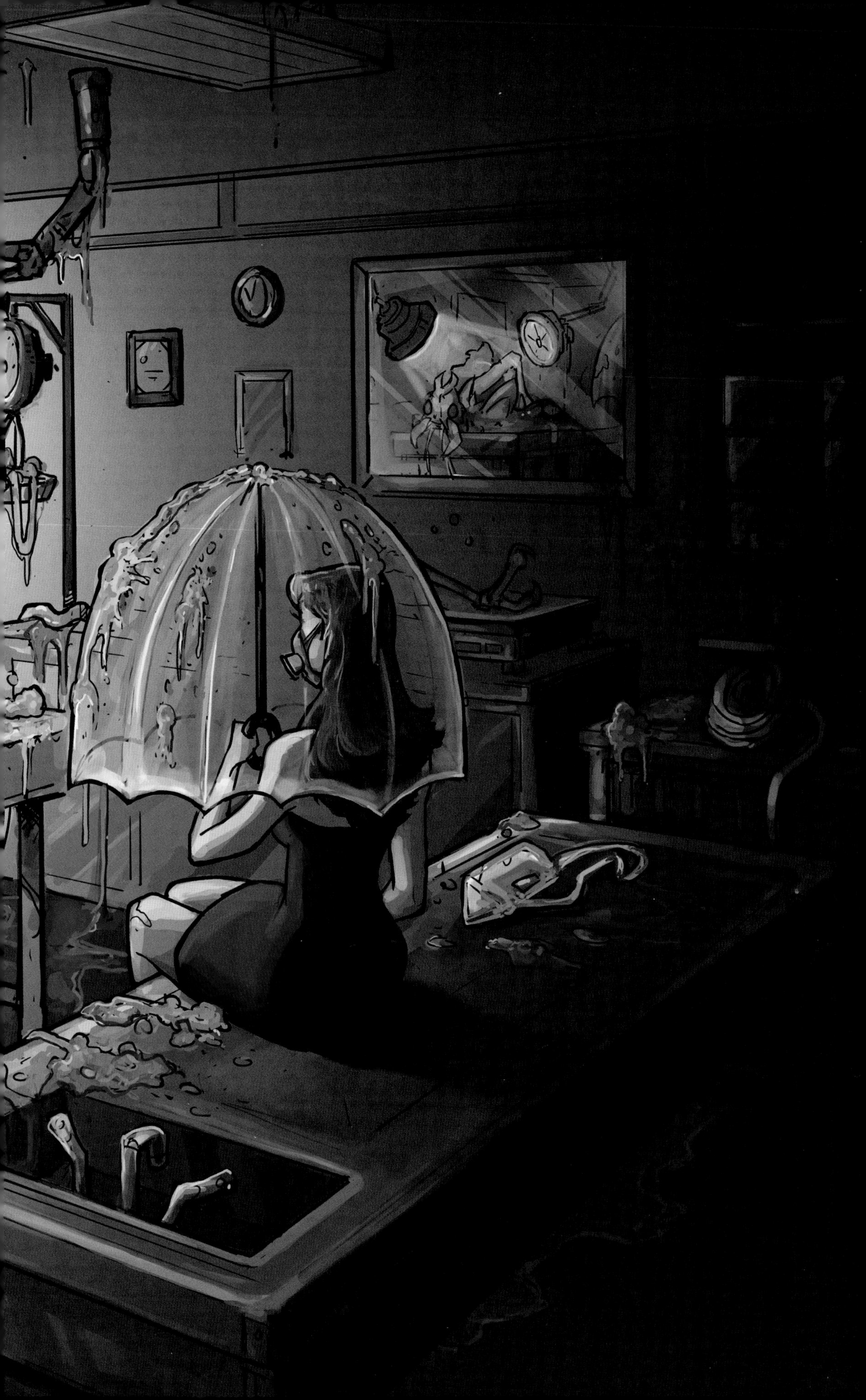

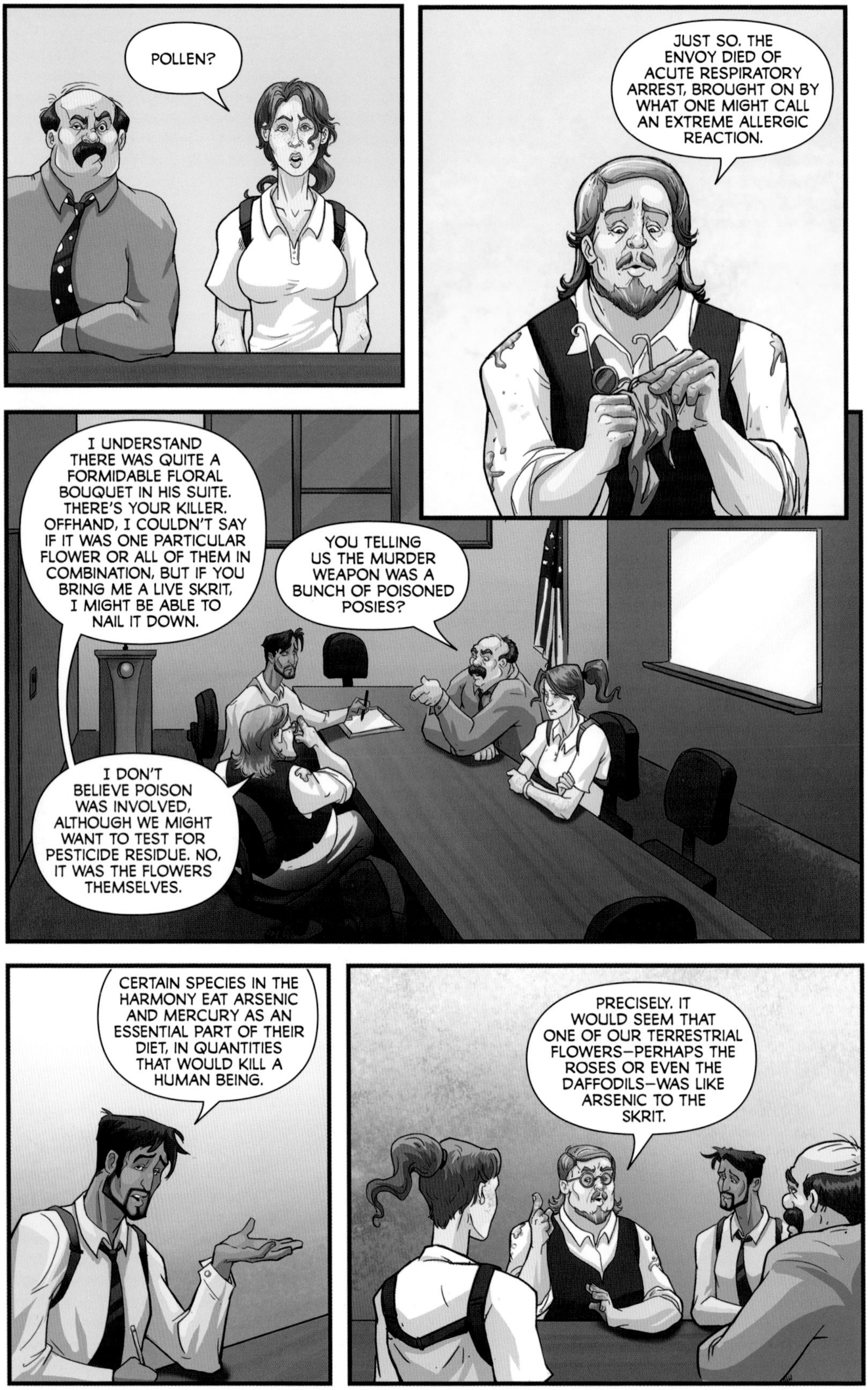
POLLEN?
JUST SO. THE ENVOY DIED OF ACUTE RESPIRATORY ARREST, BROUGHT ON BY WHAT ONE MIGHT CALL AN EXTREME ALLERGIC REACTION.
I UNDERSTAND THERE WAS QUITE A FORMIDABLE FLORAL BOUQUET IN HIS SUITE. THERE'S YOUR KILLER. OFFHAND, I COULDN'T SAY IF IT WAS ONE PARTICULAR FLOWER OR ALL OF THEM IN COMBINATION, BUT IF YOU BRING ME A LIVE SKRIT, I MIGHT BE ABLE TO NAIL IT DOWN.
YOU TELLING US THE MURDER WEAPON WAS A BUNCH OF POISONED POSIES?
I DON'T BELIEVE POISON WAS INVOLVED, ALTHOUGH WE MIGHT WANT TO TEST FOR PESTICIDE RESIDUE. NO, IT WAS THE FLOWERS THEMSELVES.
CERTAIN SPECIES IN THE HARMONY EAT ARSENIC AND MERCURY AS AN ESSENTIAL PART OF THEIR DIET, IN QUANTITIES THAT WOULD KILL A HUMAN BEING.
PRECISELY. IT WOULD SEEM THAT ONE OF OUR TERRESTRIAL FLOWERS—PERHAPS THE ROSES OR EVEN THE DAFFODILS—WAS LIKE ARSENIC TO THE SKRIT.

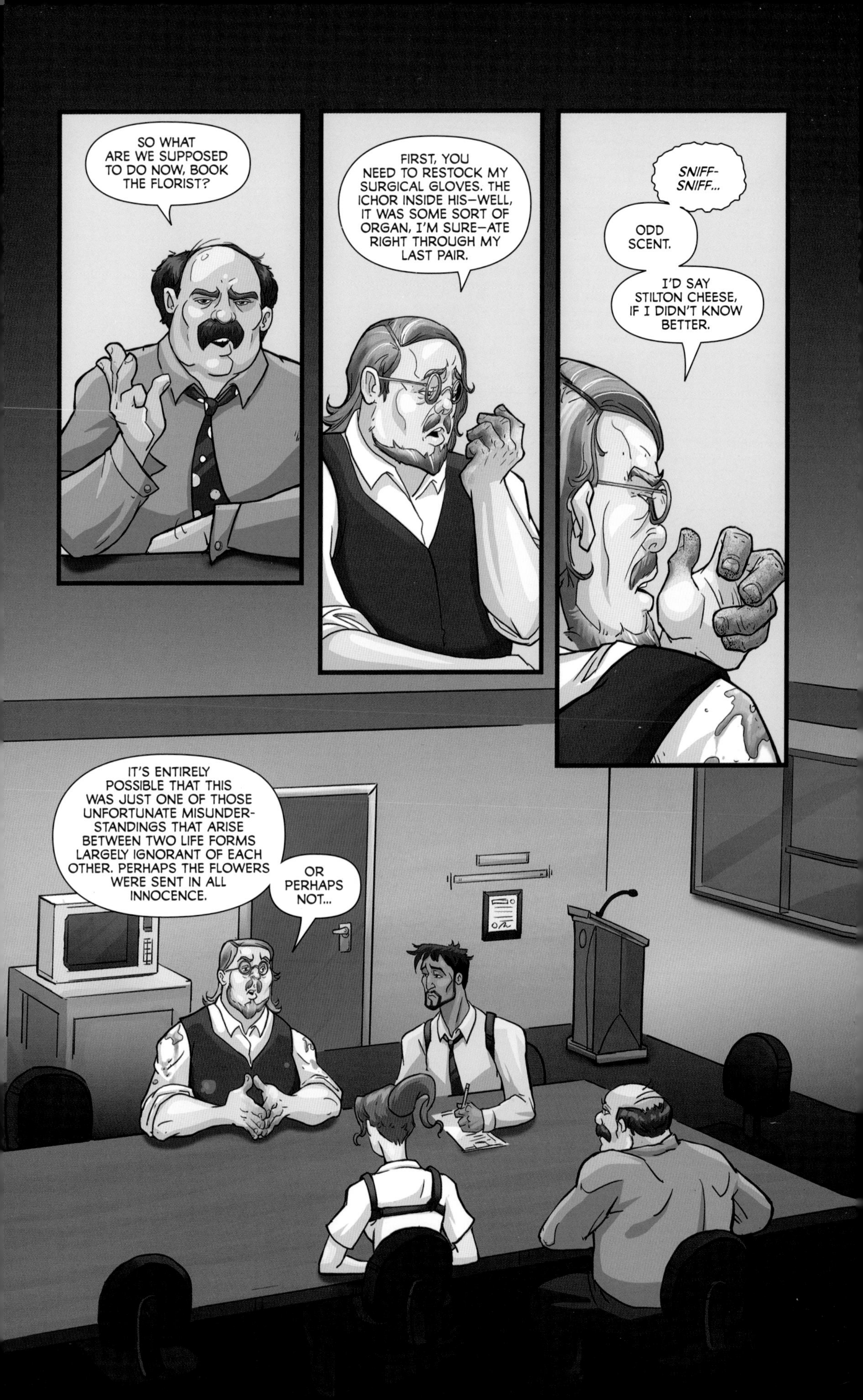
SO WHAT ARE WE SUPPOSED TO DO NOW, BOOK THE FLORIST?
FIRST, YOU NEED TO RESTOCK MY SURGICAL GLOVES. THE ICHOR INSIDE HIS—WELL, IT WAS SOME SORT OF ORGAN, I'M SURE—ATE RIGHT THROUGH MY LAST PAIR.
SNIFF-SNIFF...
ODD SCENT.
I'D SAY STILTON CHEESE, IF I DIDN'T KNOW BETTER.
IT'S ENTIRELY POSSIBLE THAT THIS WAS JUST ONE OF THOSE UNFORTUNATE MISUNDER-STANDINGS THAT ARISE BETWEEN TWO LIFE FORMS LARGELY IGNORANT OF EACH OTHER. PERHAPS THE FLOWERS WERE SENT IN ALL INNOCENCE.
OR PERHAPS NOT...

THE VIOLET CADRE HAS SAVORED ITS PRIDE OF PLACE AMONG THE NHAR SINCE EARTH WAS OPENED. YET THEIR SOFTNESS HAS BROUGHT DEATH TO THE SKRIT, DISGRACE TO THE HARMONY, AND DISHONOR TO ALL THE CHILDREN OF THE ENDLESS NIGHT.

THE TEAL CADRE AGREES. IT IS TIME FOR THE VIOLETS TO DEFEND THEIR CONTRACTS IN THE HONOR PIT!

NO! THEY ARE UNWORTHY OF THE HONOR PIT. LET THEM LEAVE THIS WORLD AND HIDE THEIR SHAME BENEATH STRANGER STARS.

LYHANNE, WHAT SAY YOU TO THIS?

AS THE ARYANNE OF THE VIOLET CADRE, THE FAULT IS MINE ALONE.

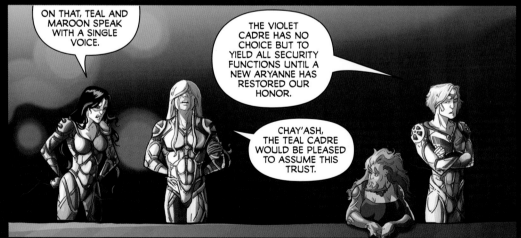

ON THAT, TEAL AND MAROON SPEAK WITH A SINGLE VOICE.

THE VIOLET CADRE HAS NO CHOICE BUT TO YIELD ALL SECURITY FUNCTIONS UNTIL A NEW ARYANNE HAS RESTORED OUR HONOR.

CHAY'ASH, THE TEAL CADRE WOULD BE PLEASED TO ASSUME THIS TRUST.

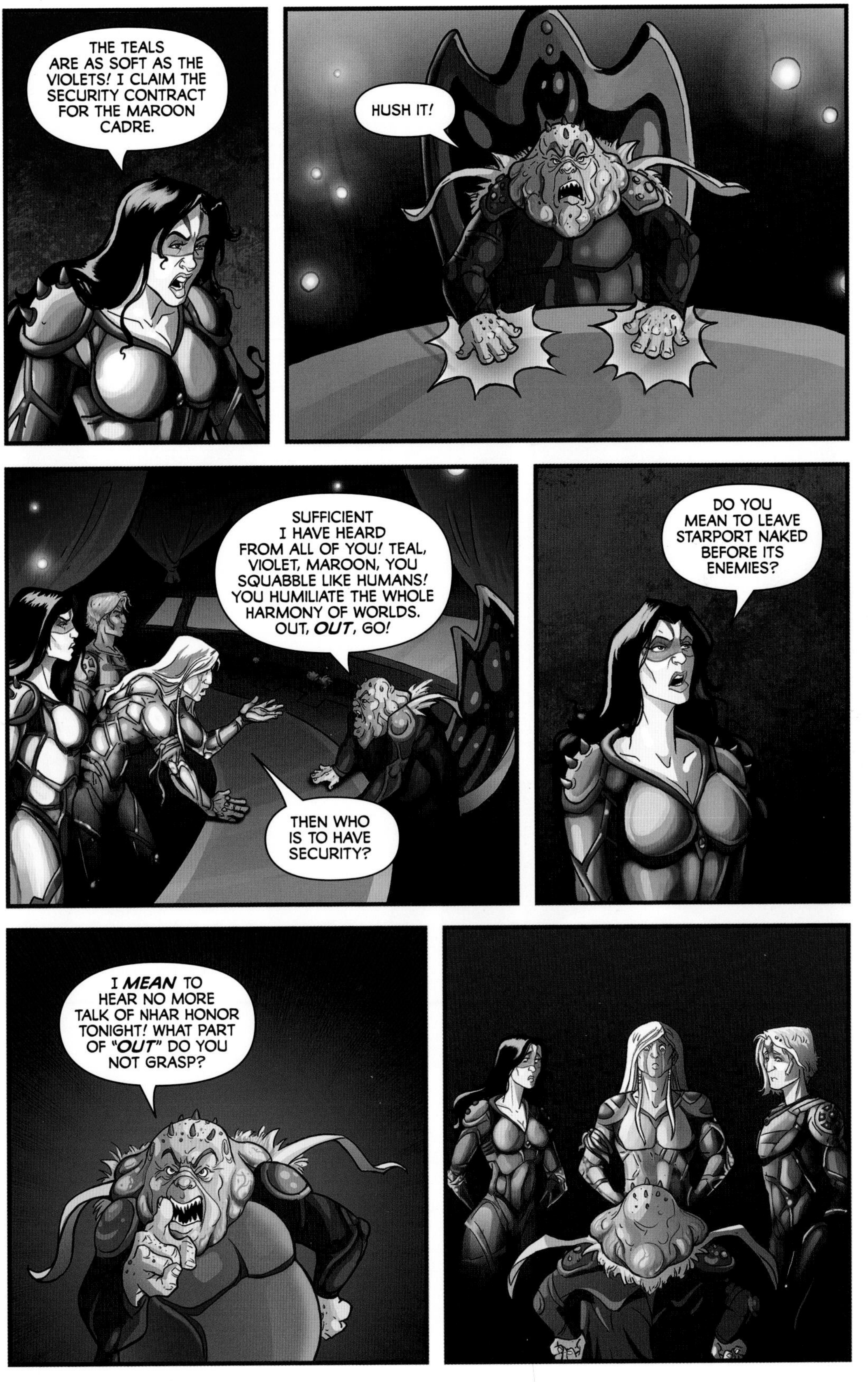
THE TEALS ARE AS SOFT AS THE VIOLETS! I CLAIM THE SECURITY CONTRACT FOR THE MAROON CADRE.
HUSH IT!
SUFFICIENT I HAVE HEARD FROM ALL OF YOU! TEAL, VIOLET, MAROON, YOU SQUABBLE LIKE HUMANS! YOU HUMILIATE THE WHOLE HARMONY OF WORLDS. OUT, *OUT*, GO!
THEN WHO IS TO HAVE SECURITY?
DO YOU MEAN TO LEAVE STARPORT NAKED BEFORE ITS ENEMIES?
I *MEAN* TO HEAR NO MORE TALK OF NHAR HONOR TONIGHT! WHAT PART OF "*OUT*" DO YOU NOT GRASP?

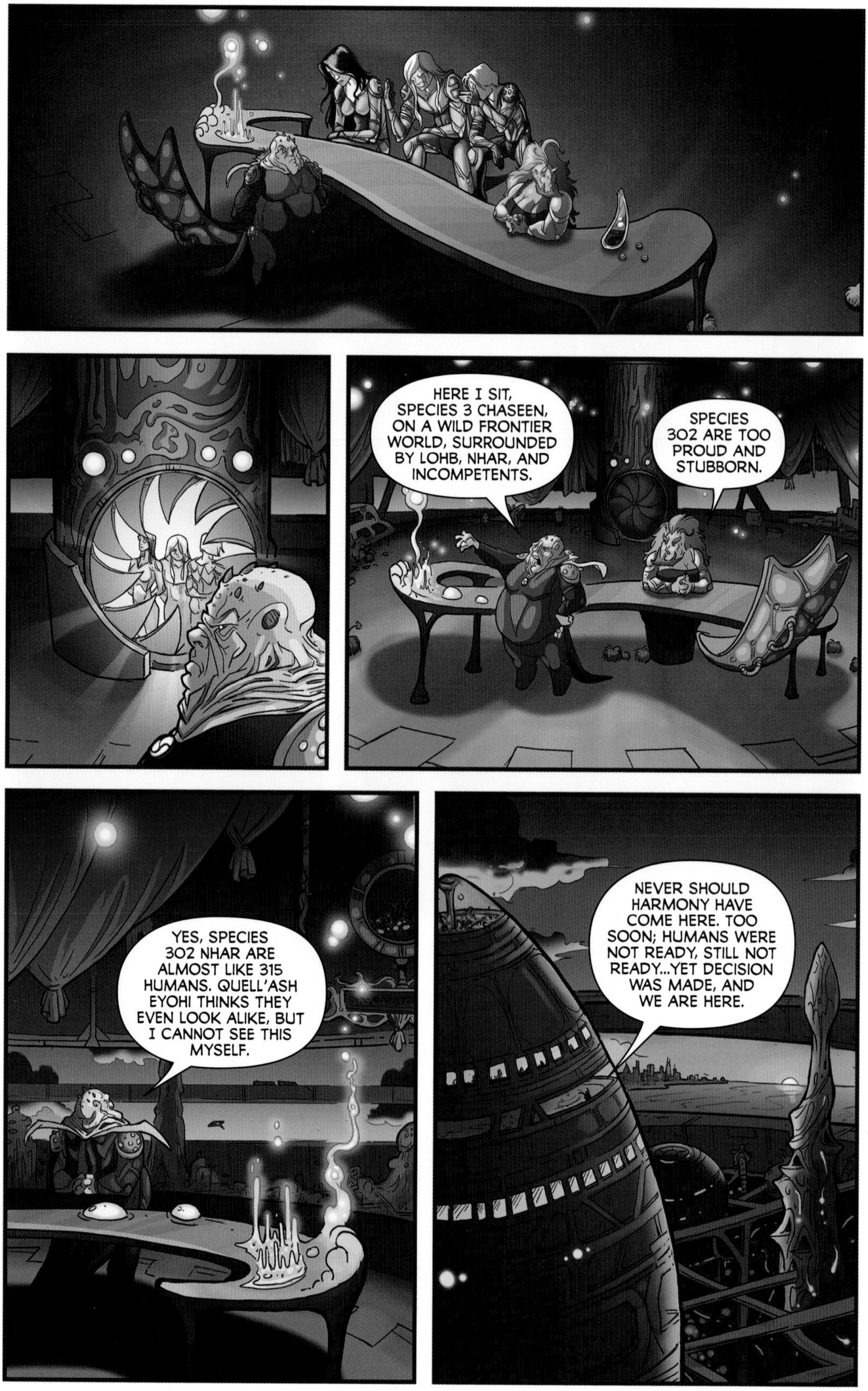
HERE I SIT, SPECIES 3 CHASEEN, ON A WILD FRONTIER WORLD, SURROUNDED BY LOHB, NHAR, AND INCOMPETENTS.
SPECIES 302 ARE TOO PROUD AND STUBBORN.
YES, SPECIES 302 NHAR ARE ALMOST LIKE 315 HUMANS. QUELL'ASH EYOHI THINKS THEY EVEN LOOK ALIKE, BUT I CANNOT SEE THIS MYSELF.
NEVER SHOULD HARMONY HAVE COME HERE. TOO SOON; HUMANS WERE NOT READY, STILL NOT READY...YET DECISION WAS MADE, AND WE ARE HERE.

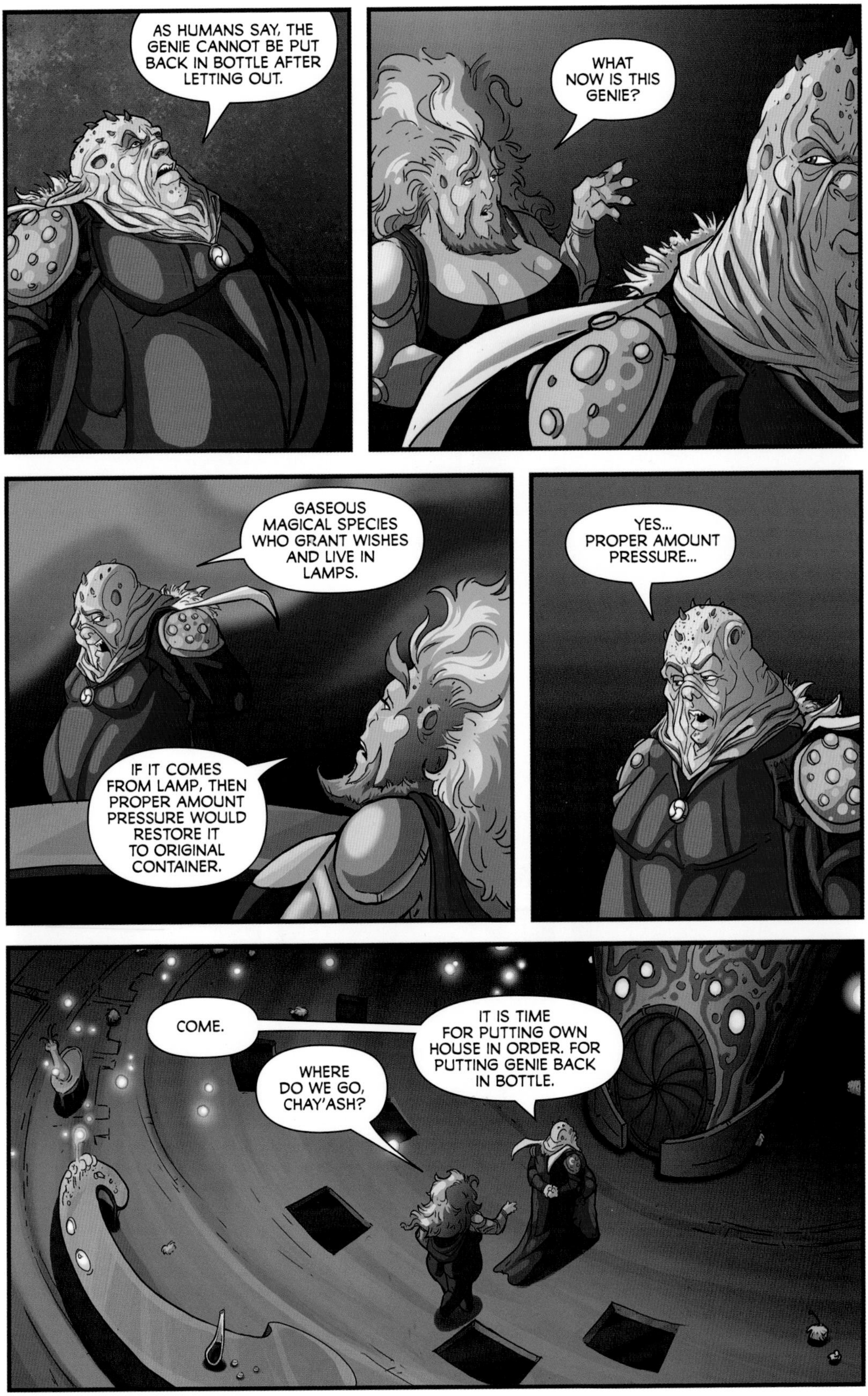
AS HUMANS SAY, THE GENIE CANNOT BE PUT BACK IN BOTTLE AFTER LETTING OUT.
WHAT NOW IS THIS GENIE?
GASEOUS MAGICAL SPECIES WHO GRANT WISHES AND LIVE IN LAMPS.
IF IT COMES FROM LAMP, THEN PROPER AMOUNT PRESSURE WOULD RESTORE IT TO ORIGINAL CONTAINER.
YES... PROPER AMOUNT PRESSURE...
COME.
IT IS TIME FOR PUTTING OWN HOUSE IN ORDER. FOR PUTTING GENIE BACK IN BOTTLE.
WHERE DO WE GO, CHAY'ASH?

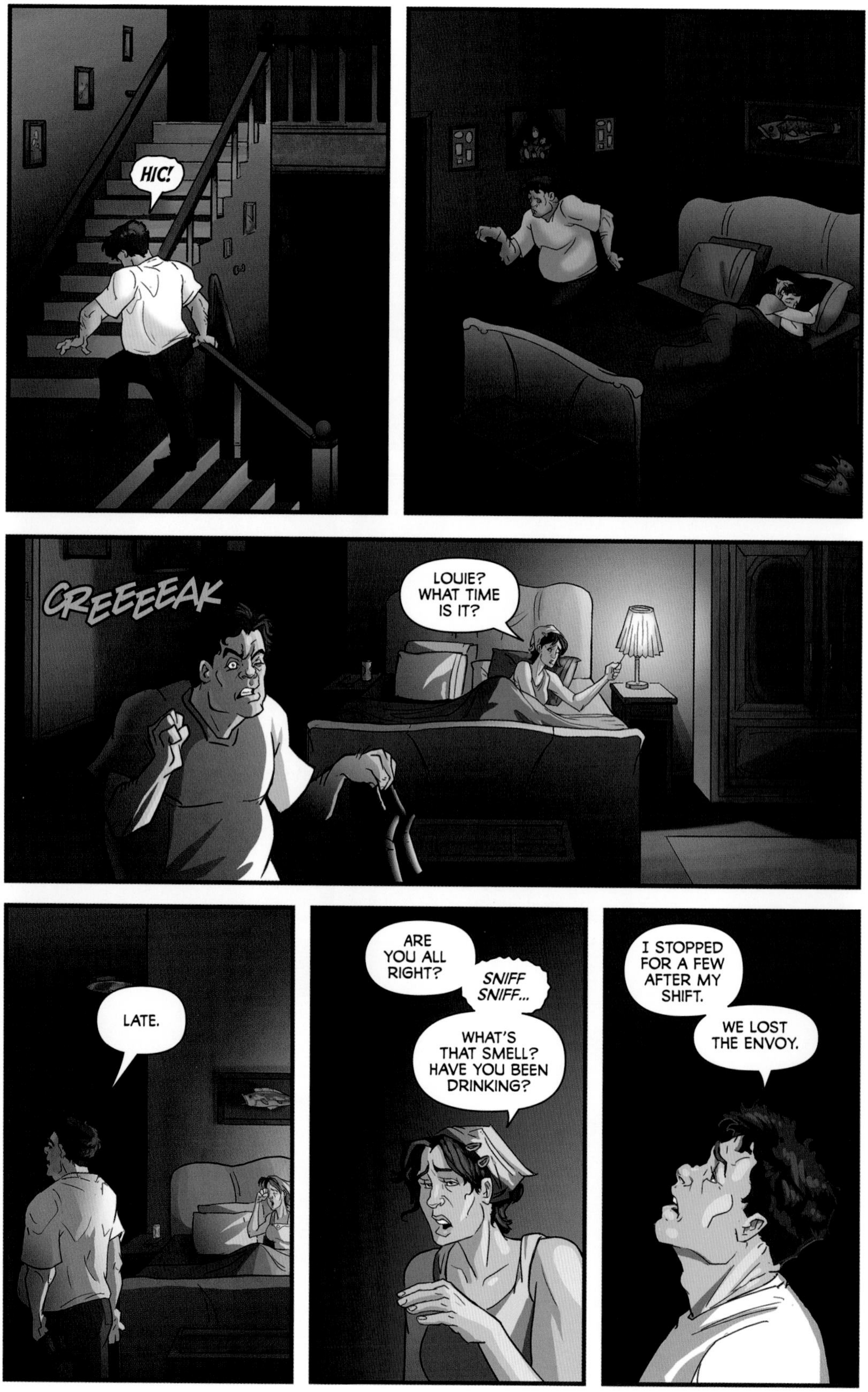
HIC!
CREEEEAK
LOUIE? WHAT TIME IS IT?
LATE.
ARE YOU ALL RIGHT?
SNIFF SNIFF...
WHAT'S THAT SMELL? HAVE YOU BEEN DRINKING?
I STOPPED FOR A FEW AFTER MY SHIFT.
WE LOST THE ENVOY.

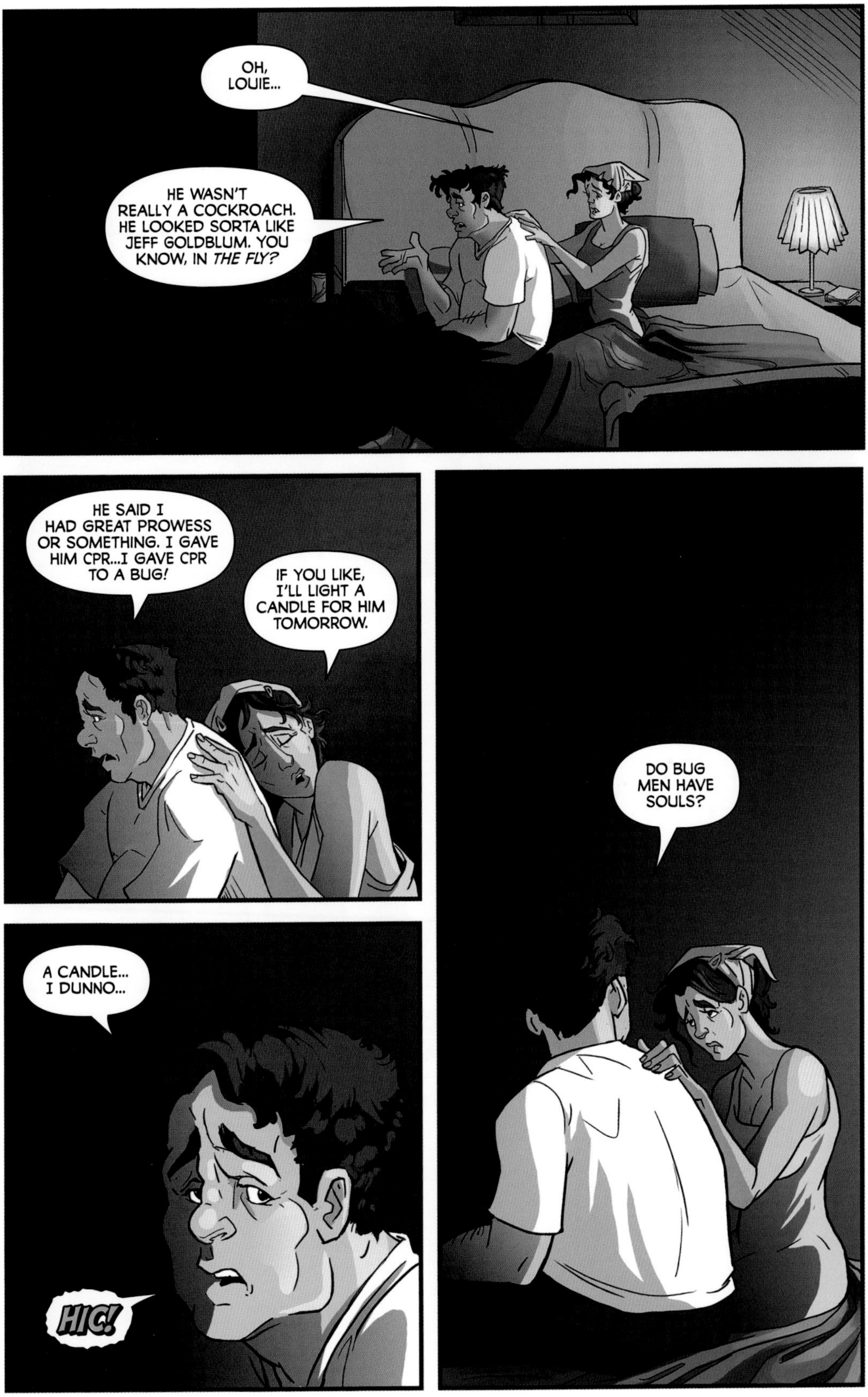
OH, LOUIE...
HE WASN'T REALLY A COCKROACH. HE LOOKED SORTA LIKE JEFF GOLDBLUM. YOU KNOW, IN *THE FLY?*
HE SAID I HAD GREAT PROWESS OR SOMETHING. I GAVE HIM CPR...I GAVE CPR TO A BUG!
IF YOU LIKE, I'LL LIGHT A CANDLE FOR HIM TOMORROW.
A CANDLE... I DUNNO...
HIC!
DO BUG MEN HAVE SOULS?

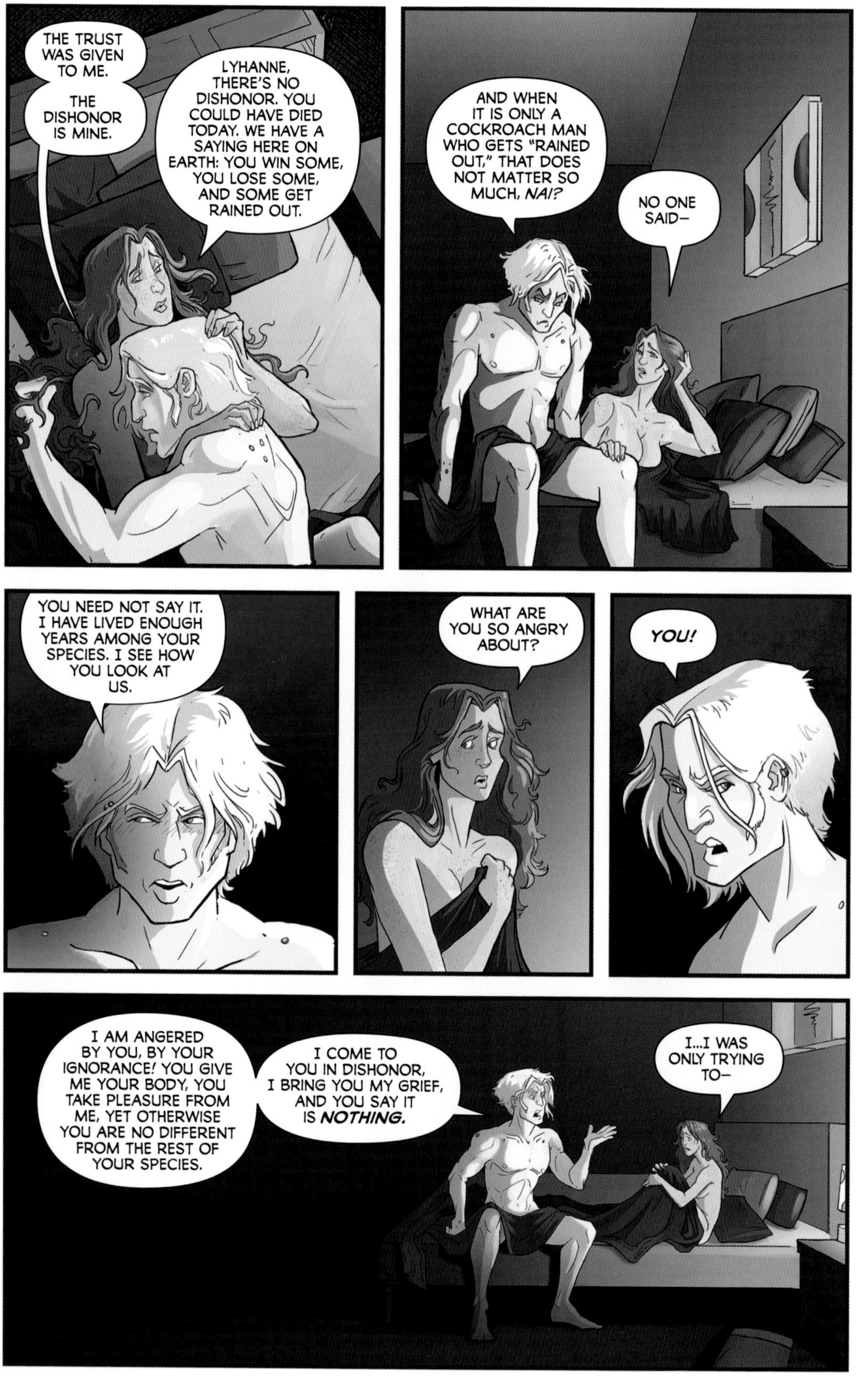
THE TRUST WAS GIVEN TO ME.
THE DISHONOR IS MINE.
LYHANNE, THERE'S NO DISHONOR. YOU COULD HAVE DIED TODAY. WE HAVE A SAYING HERE ON EARTH: YOU WIN SOME, YOU LOSE SOME, AND SOME GET RAINED OUT.
AND WHEN IT IS ONLY A COCKROACH MAN WHO GETS "RAINED OUT," THAT DOES NOT MATTER SO MUCH, *NA!?*
NO ONE SAID—
YOU NEED NOT SAY IT. I HAVE LIVED ENOUGH YEARS AMONG YOUR SPECIES. I SEE HOW YOU LOOK AT US.
WHAT ARE YOU SO ANGRY ABOUT?
YOU!
I AM ANGERED BY YOU, BY YOUR IGNORANCE! YOU GIVE ME YOUR BODY, YOU TAKE PLEASURE FROM ME, YET OTHERWISE YOU ARE NO DIFFERENT FROM THE REST OF YOUR SPECIES.
I COME TO YOU IN DISHONOR, I BRING YOU MY GRIEF, AND YOU SAY IT IS ***NOTHING.***
I...I WAS ONLY TRYING TO—

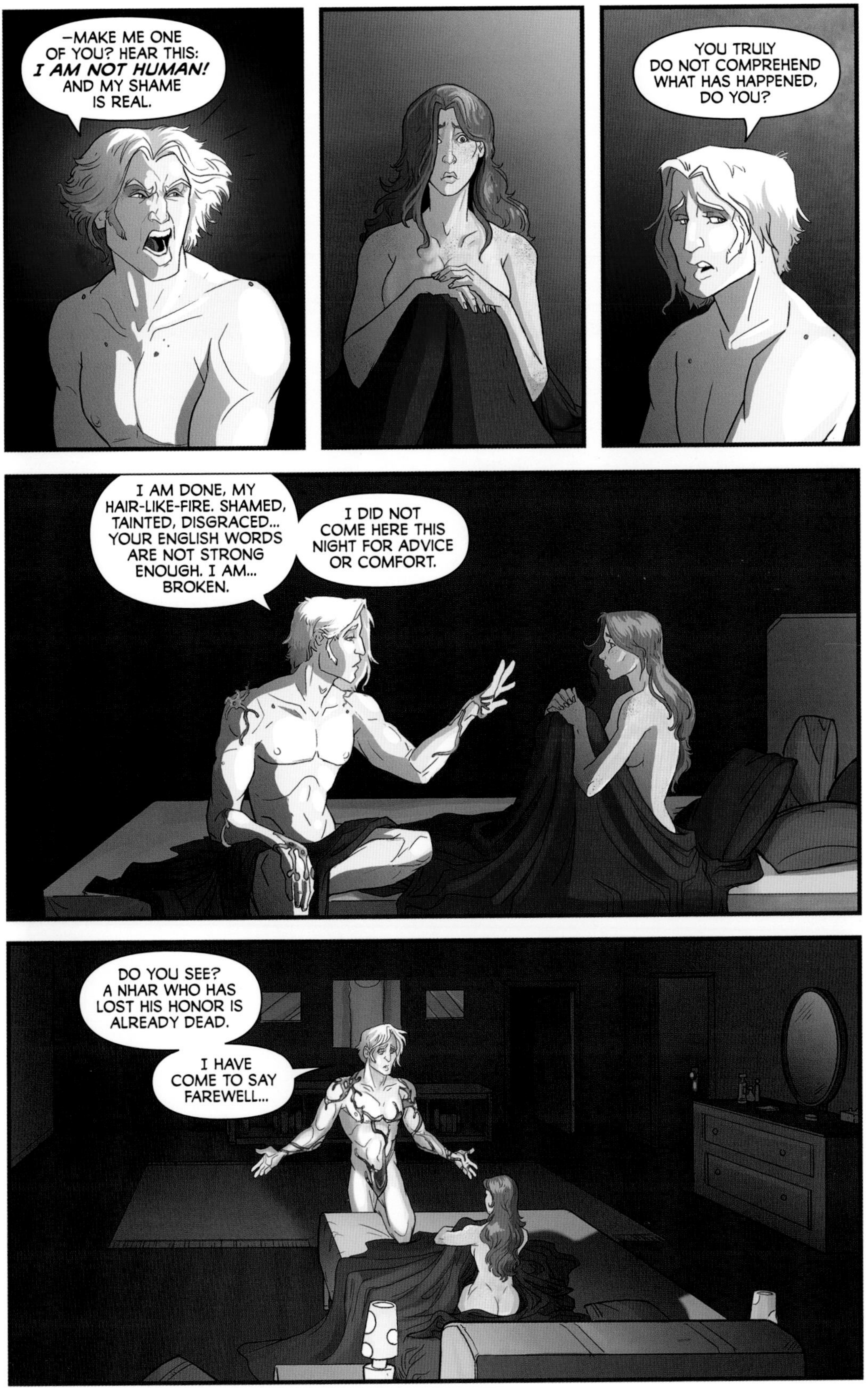
—MAKE ME ONE OF YOU? HEAR THIS: ***I AM NOT HUMAN!*** AND MY SHAME IS REAL.
YOU TRULY DO NOT COMPREHEND WHAT HAS HAPPENED, DO YOU?
I AM DONE, MY HAIR-LIKE-FIRE. SHAMED, TAINTED, DISGRACED... YOUR ENGLISH WORDS ARE NOT STRONG ENOUGH. I AM... BROKEN.
I DID NOT COME HERE THIS NIGHT FOR ADVICE OR COMFORT.
DO YOU SEE? A NHAR WHO HAS LOST HIS HONOR IS ALREADY DEAD.
I HAVE COME TO SAY FAREWELL...

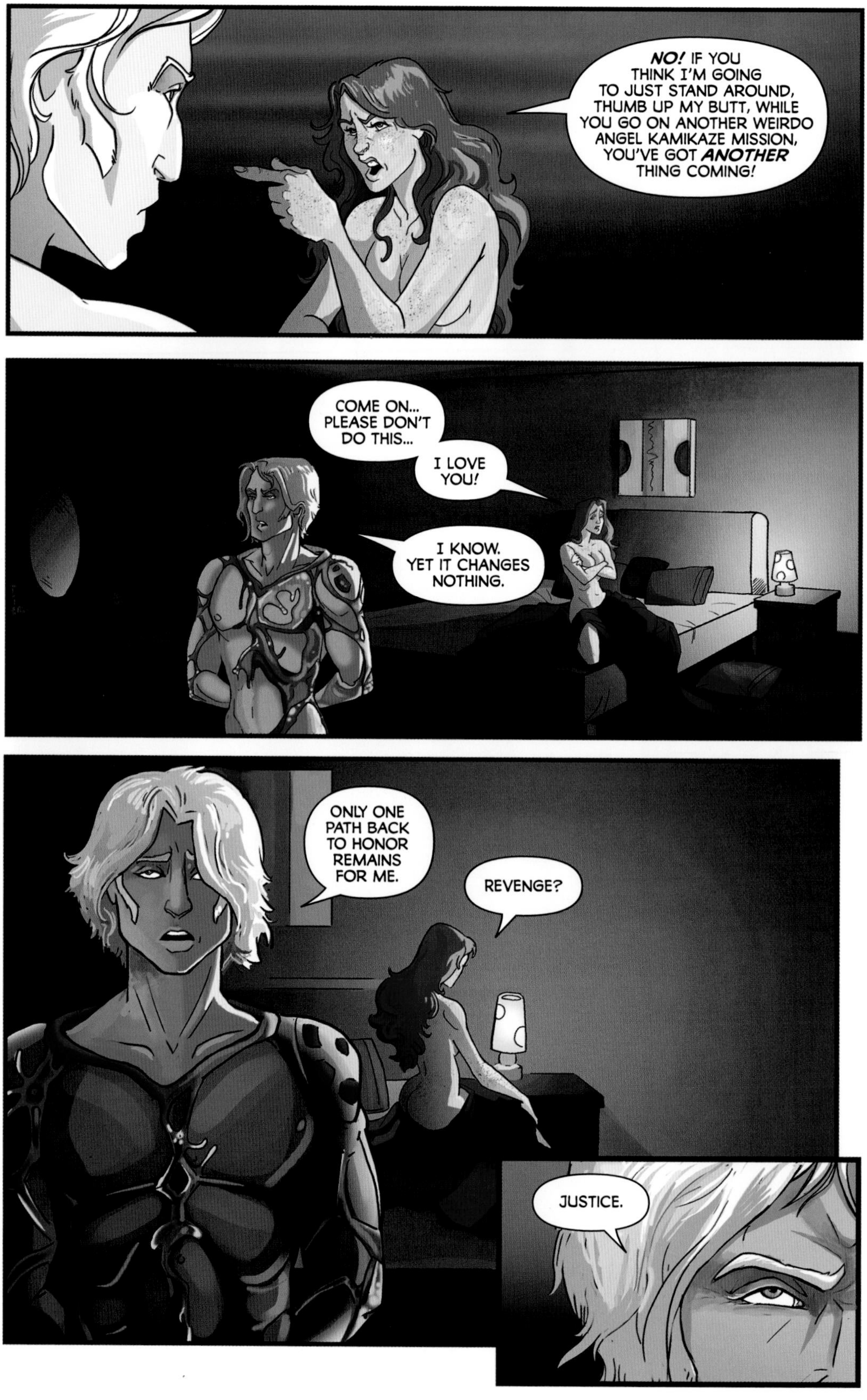

NO! IF YOU THINK I'M GOING TO JUST STAND AROUND, THUMB UP MY BUTT, WHILE YOU GO ON ANOTHER WEIRDO ANGEL KAMIKAZE MISSION, YOU'VE GOT ***ANOTHER*** THING COMING!
COME ON... PLEASE DON'T DO THIS...
I LOVE YOU!
I KNOW. YET IT CHANGES NOTHING.
ONLY ONE PATH BACK TO HONOR REMAINS FOR ME.
REVENGE?
JUSTICE.

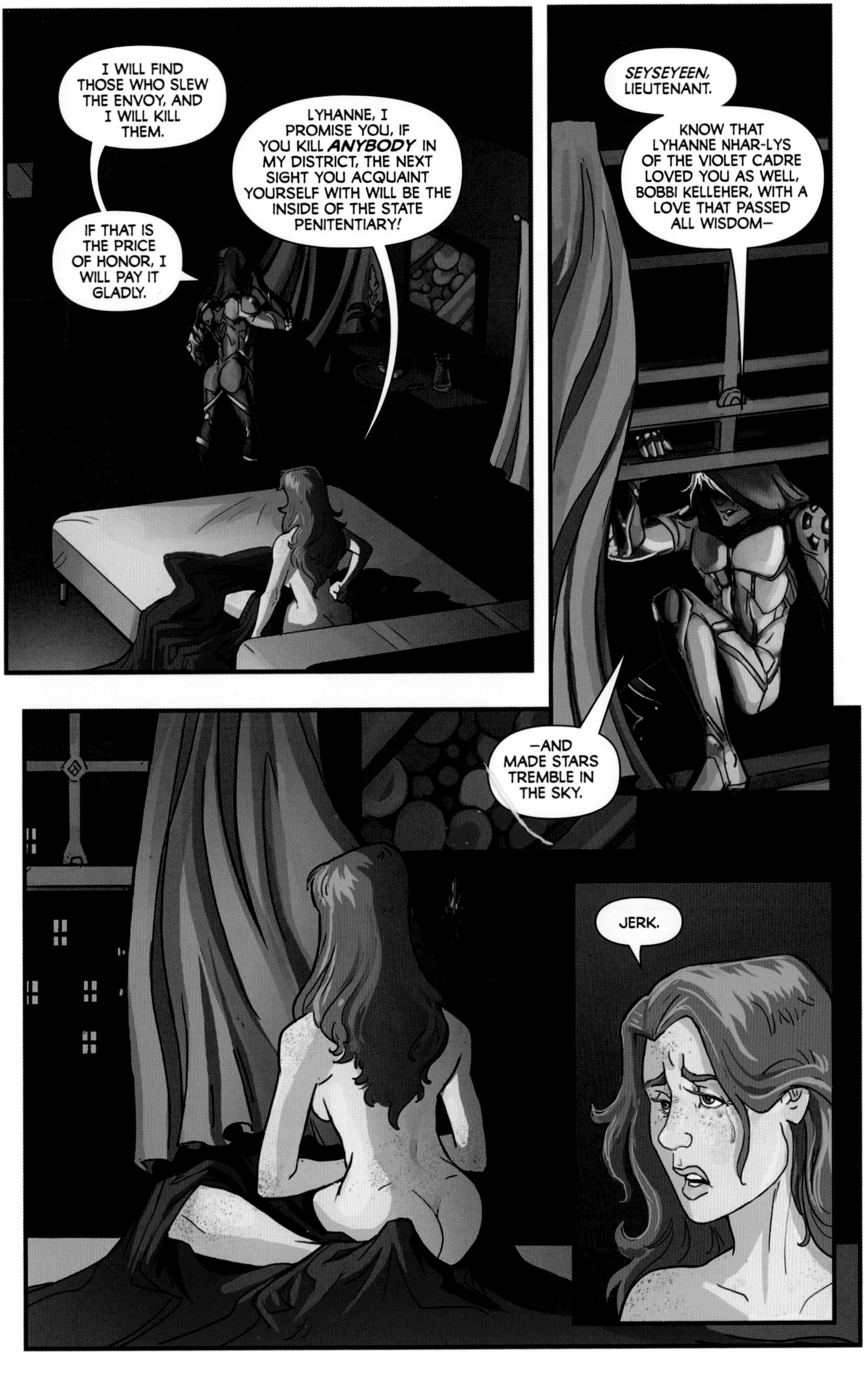

I WILL FIND THOSE WHO SLEW THE ENVOY, AND I WILL KILL THEM.
IF THAT IS THE PRICE OF HONOR, I WILL PAY IT GLADLY.
LYHANNE, I PROMISE YOU, IF YOU KILL *ANYBODY* IN MY DISTRICT, THE NEXT SIGHT YOU ACQUAINT YOURSELF WITH WILL BE THE INSIDE OF THE STATE PENITENTIARY!
SEYSEYEEN, LIEUTENANT.
KNOW THAT LYHANNE NHAR-LYS OF THE VIOLET CADRE LOVED YOU AS WELL, BOBBI KELLEHER, WITH A LOVE THAT PASSED ALL WISDOM—
—AND MADE STARS TREMBLE IN THE SKY.
JERK.

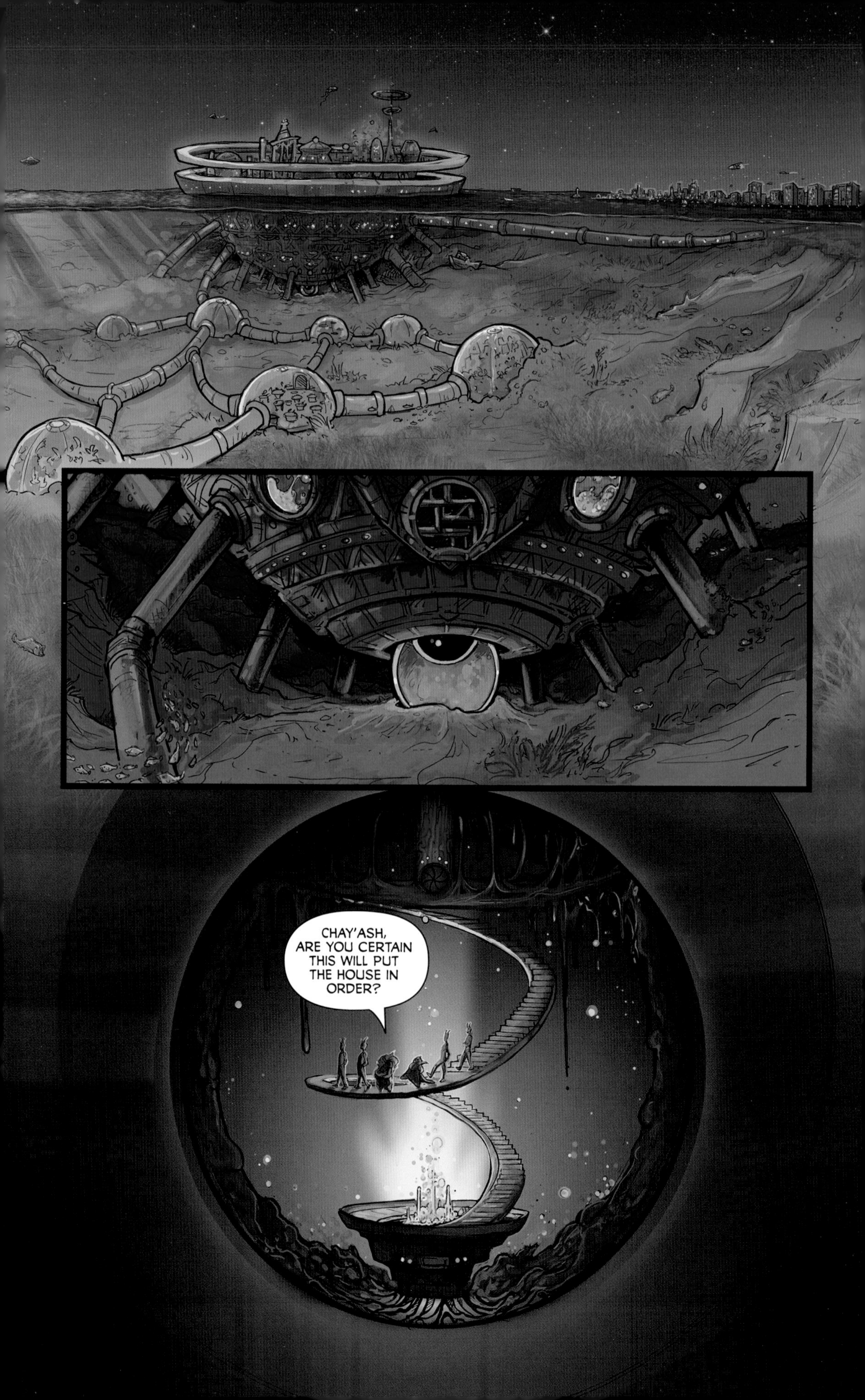
CHAY'ASH, ARE YOU CERTAIN THIS WILL PUT THE HOUSE IN ORDER?

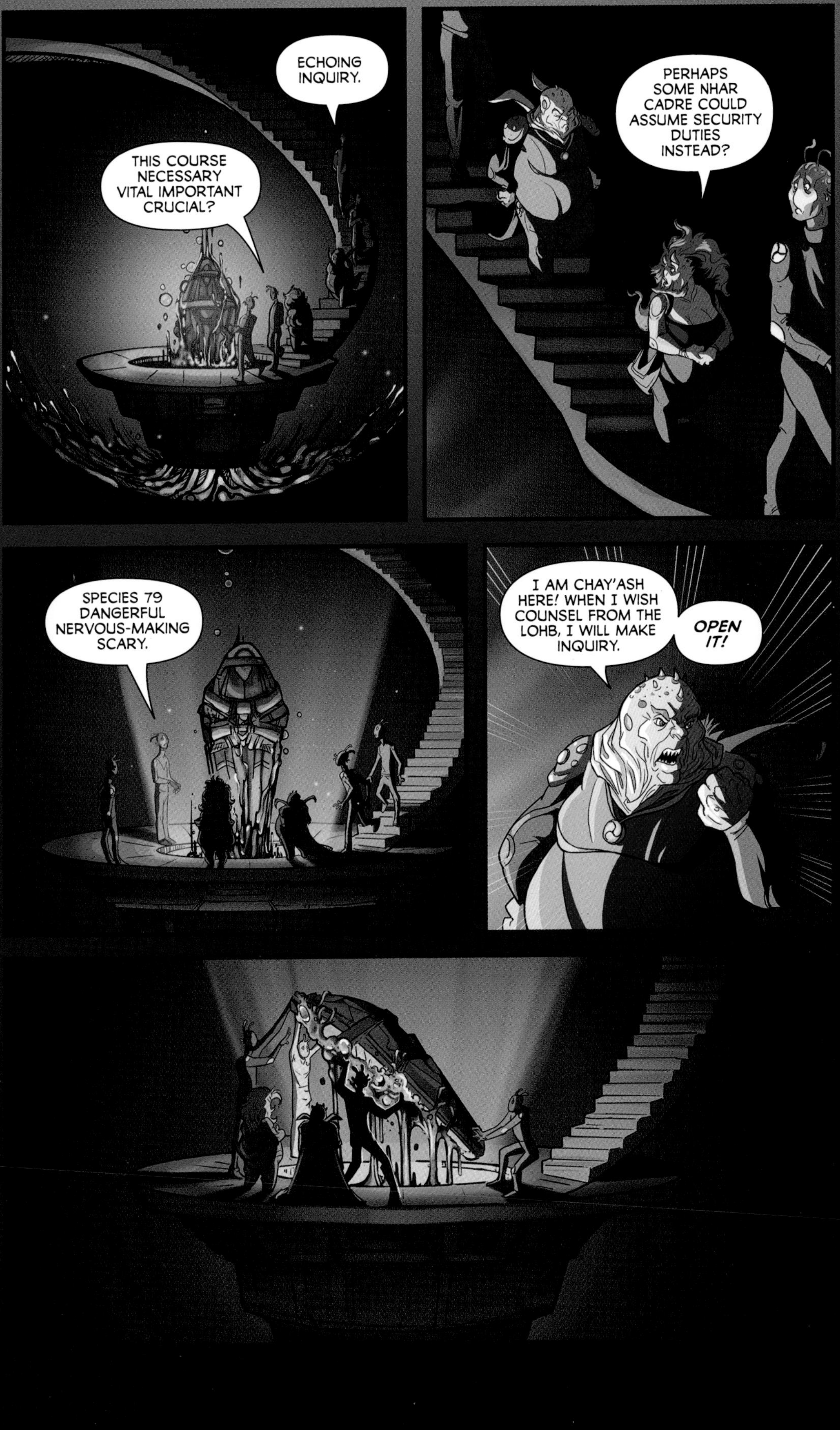
ECHOING INQUIRY.
THIS COURSE NECESSARY VITAL IMPORTANT CRUCIAL?
PERHAPS SOME NHAR CADRE COULD ASSUME SECURITY DUTIES INSTEAD?
SPECIES 79 DANGERFUL NERVOUS-MAKING SCARY.
I AM CHAY'ASH HERE! WHEN I WISH COUNSEL FROM THE LOHB, I WILL MAKE INQUIRY.
OPEN IT!

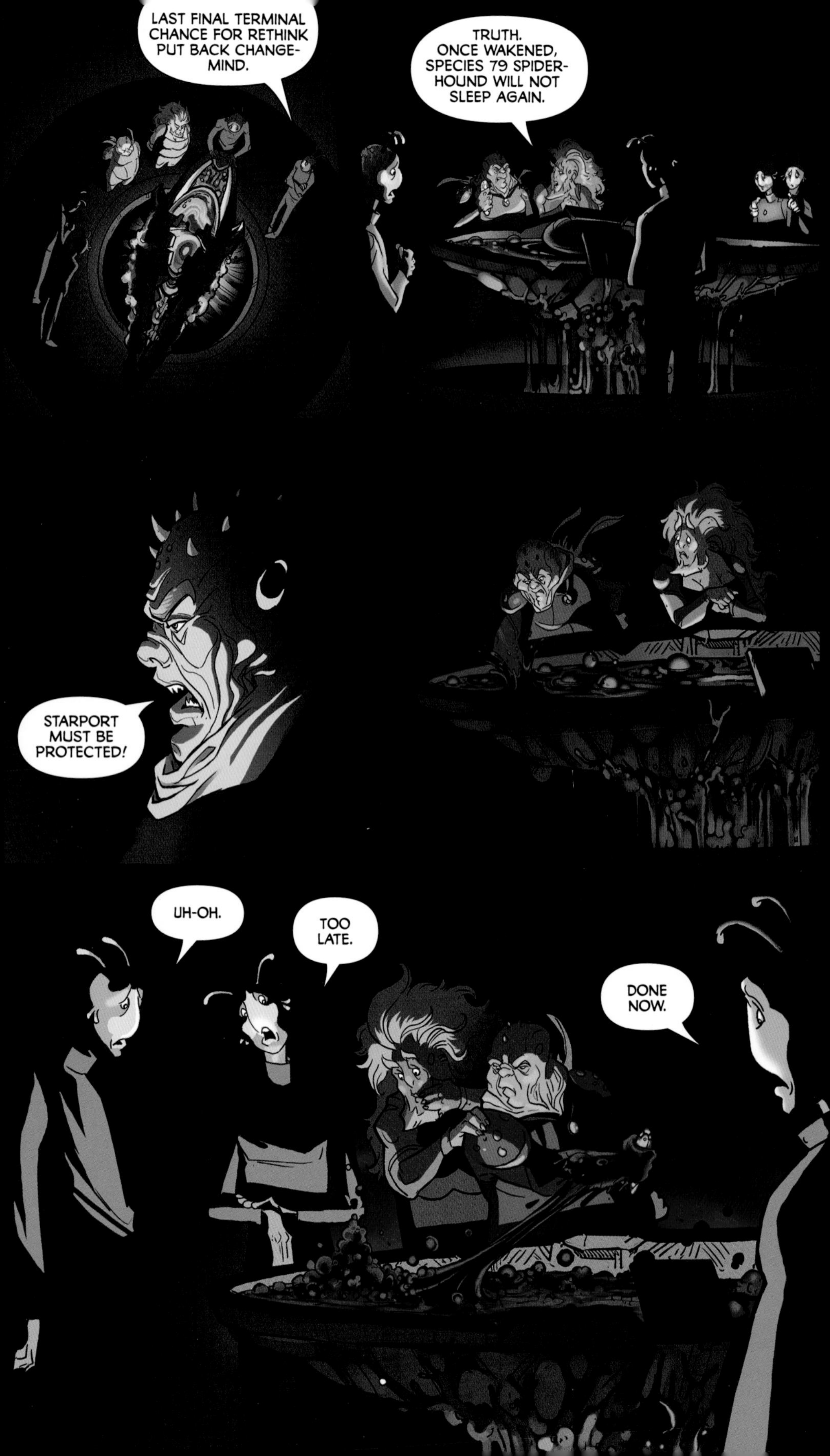
LAST FINAL TERMINAL CHANCE FOR RETHINK PUT BACK CHANGE-MIND.
TRUTH. ONCE WAKENED, SPECIES 79 SPIDER-HOUND WILL NOT SLEEP AGAIN.
STARPORT MUST BE PROTECTED!
UH-OH.
TOO LATE.
DONE NOW.

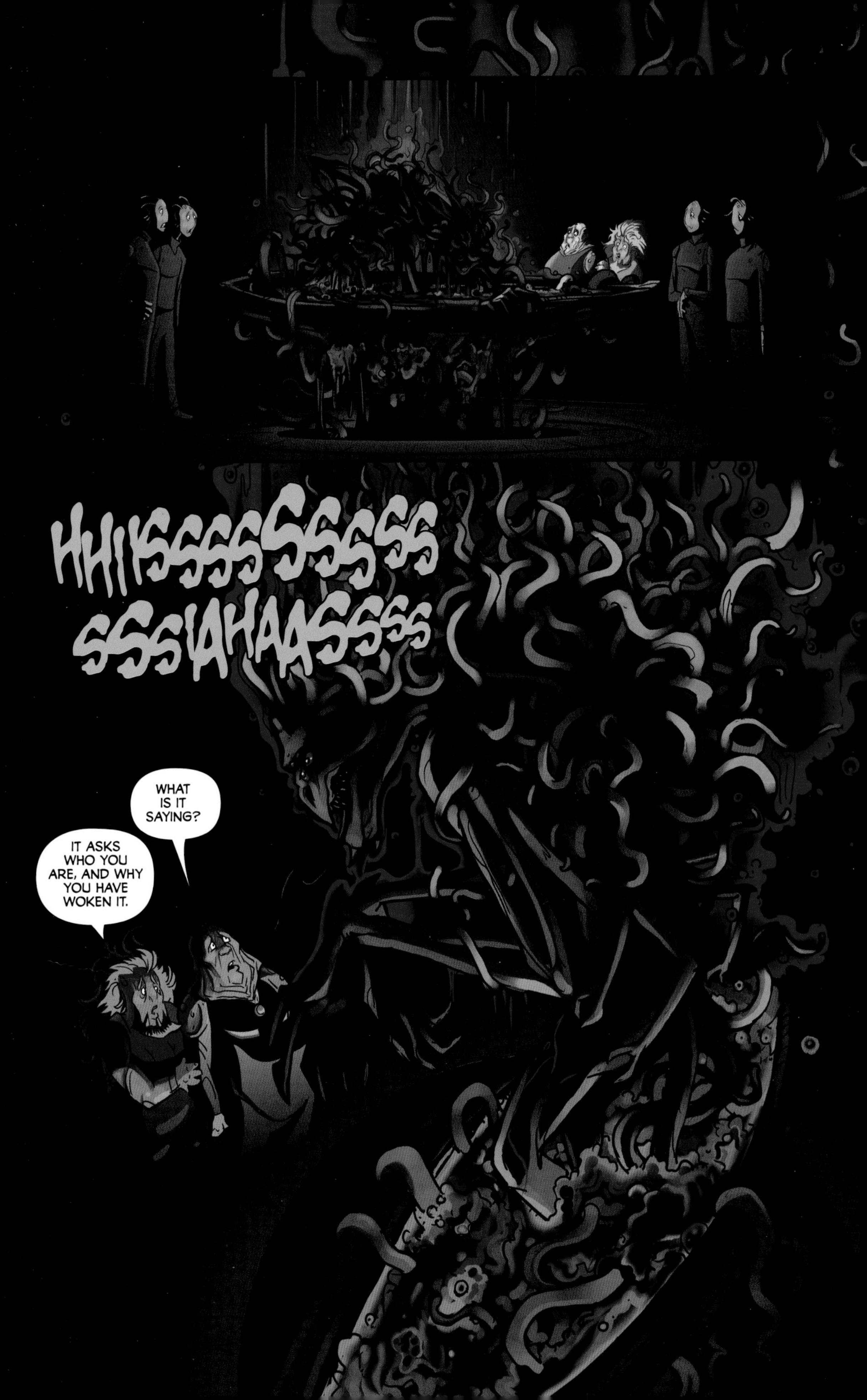
HHIISSSSSSSSSSS
SSSIAHAASSSSS
WHAT IS IT SAYING?
IT ASKS WHO YOU ARE, AND WHY YOU HAVE WOKEN IT.

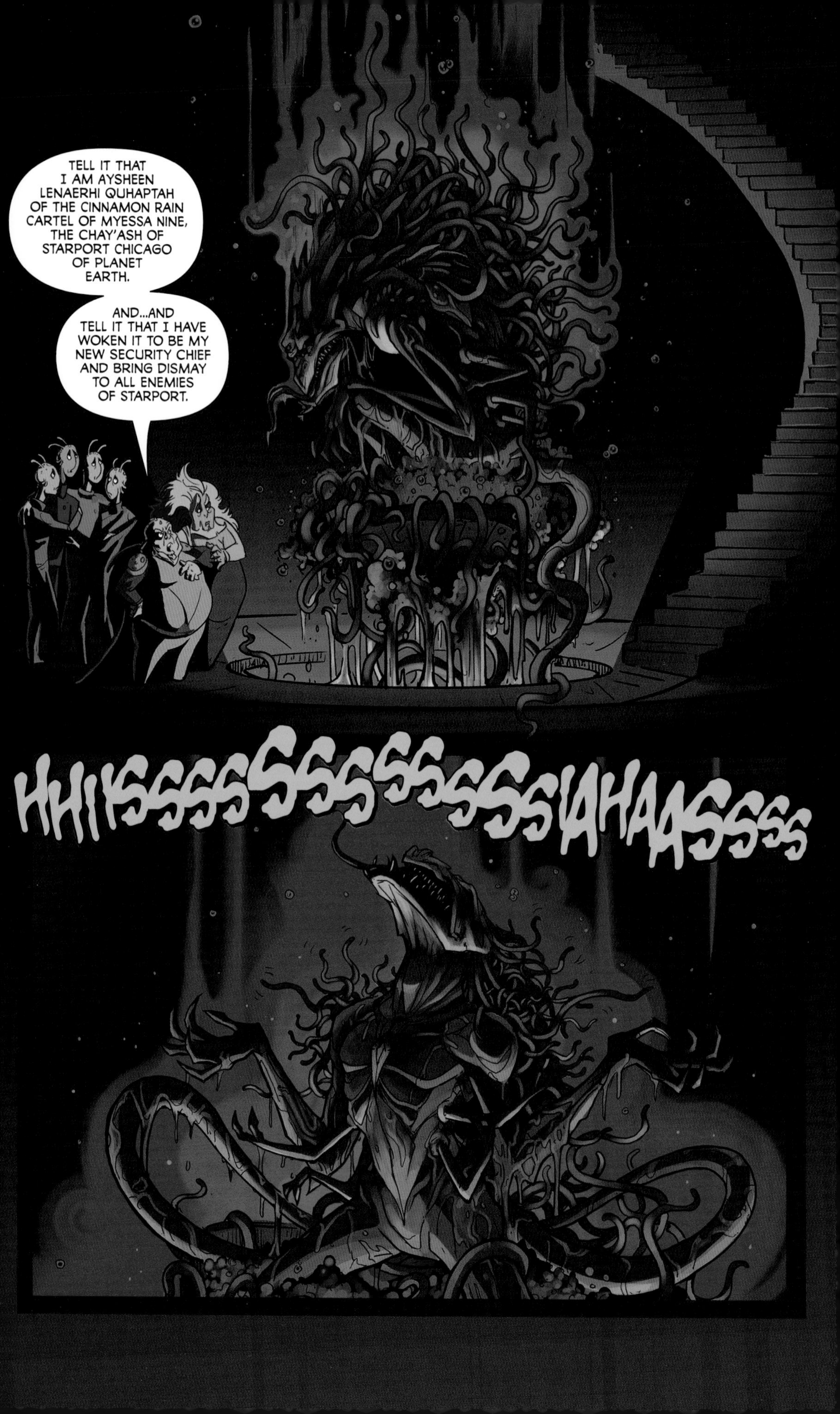
TELL IT THAT I AM AYSHEEN LENAERHI QUHAPTAH OF THE CINNAMON RAIN CARTEL OF MYESSA NINE, THE CHAY'ASH OF STARPORT CHICAGO OF PLANET EARTH.
AND...AND TELL IT THAT I HAVE WOKEN IT TO BE MY NEW SECURITY CHIEF AND BRING DISMAY TO ALL ENEMIES OF STARPORT.
HHIYSSSSSSSSSSSSSSSIAHAASSSSS

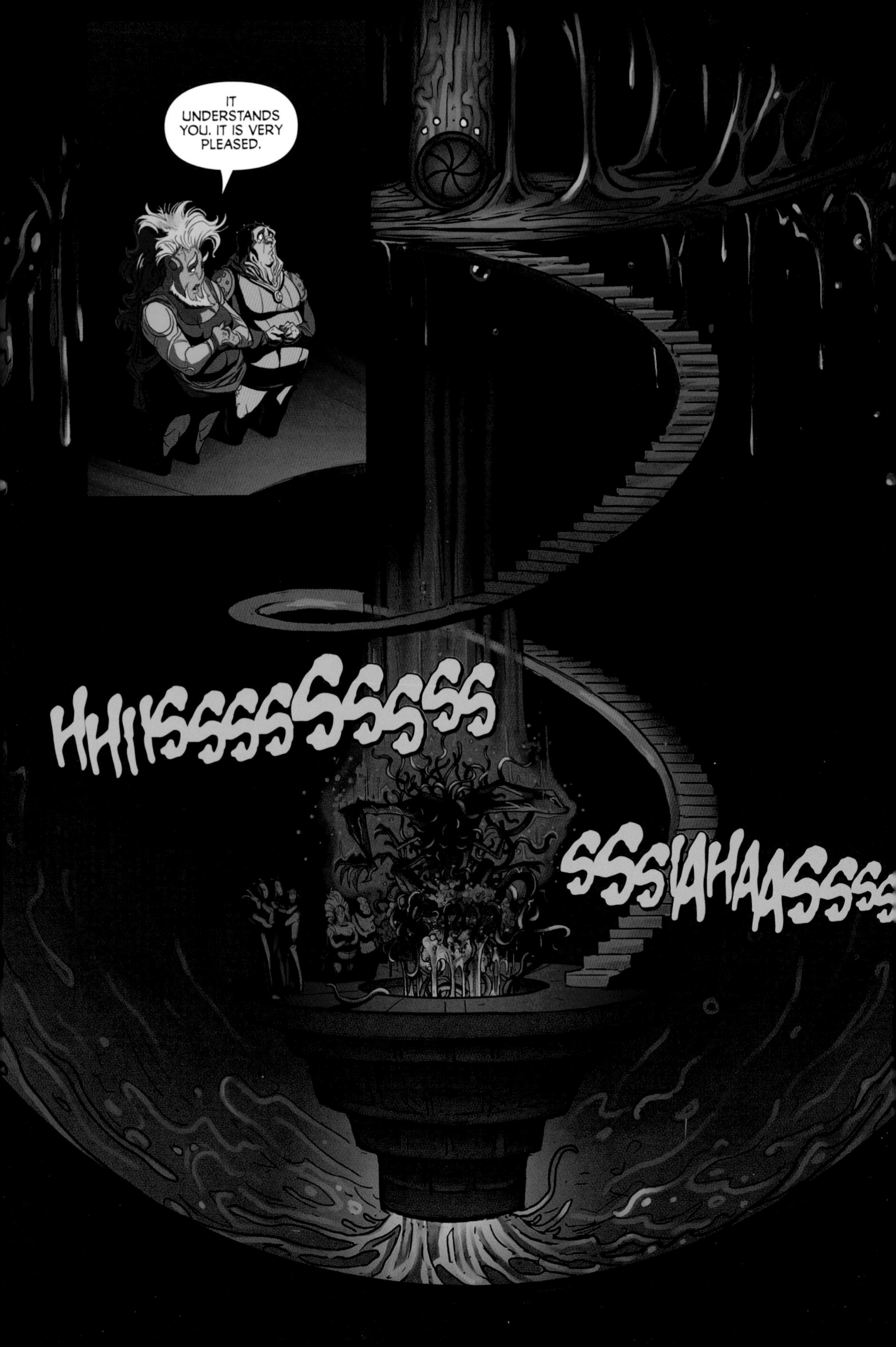
IT UNDERSTANDS YOU. IT IS VERY PLEASED.
HHIISSSSSSSSSS
SSSIAHAASSSSS

CHAPTER NINE

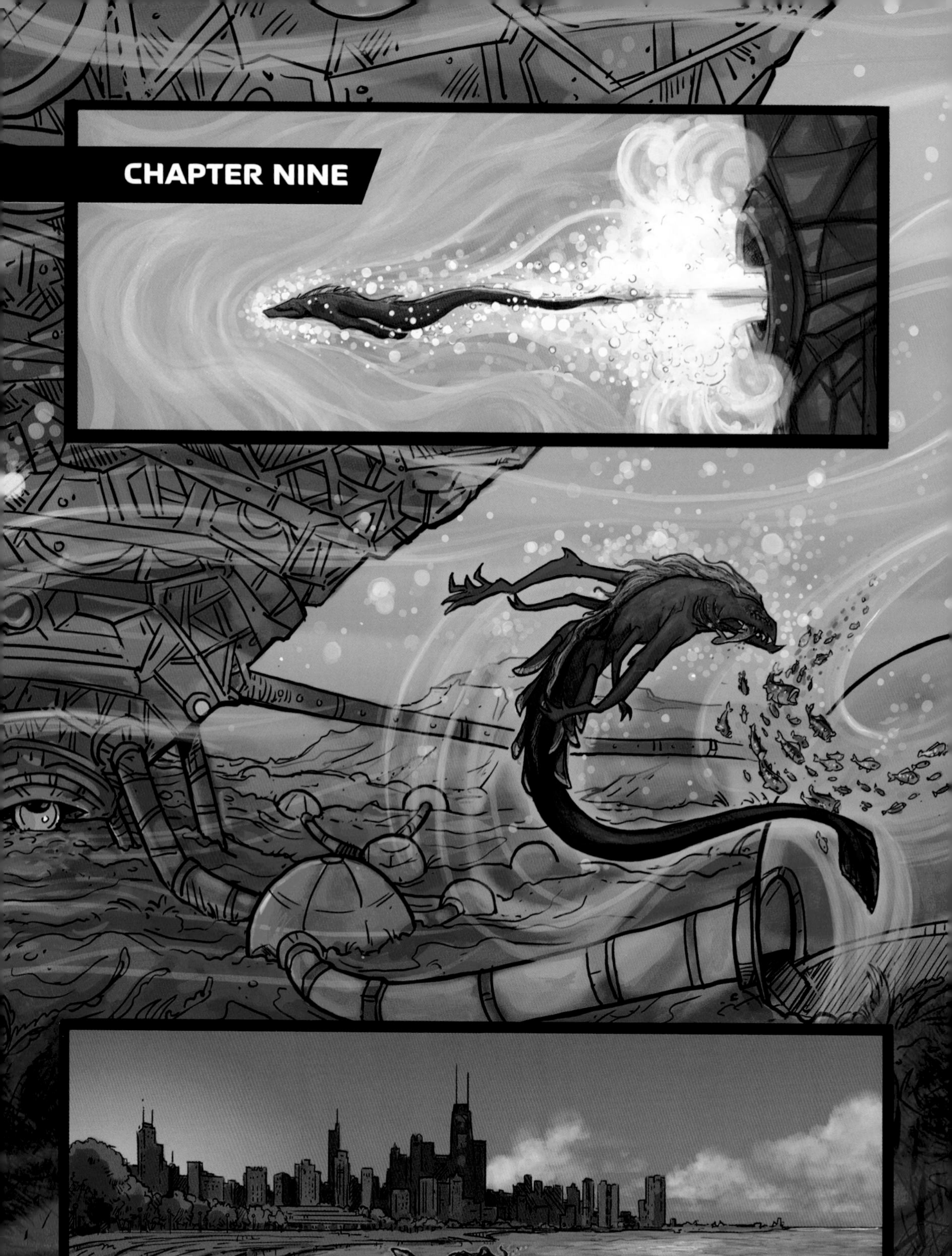

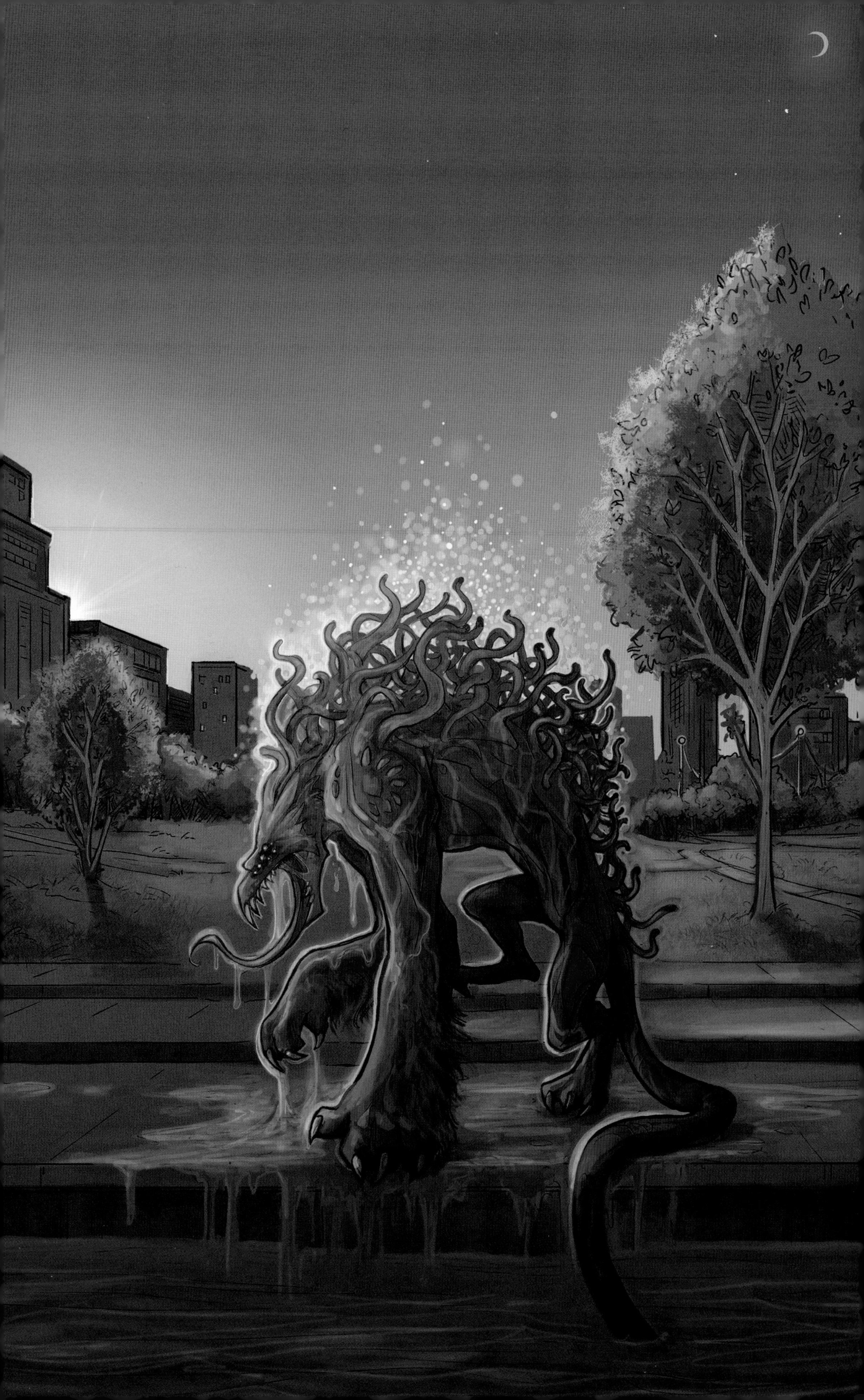

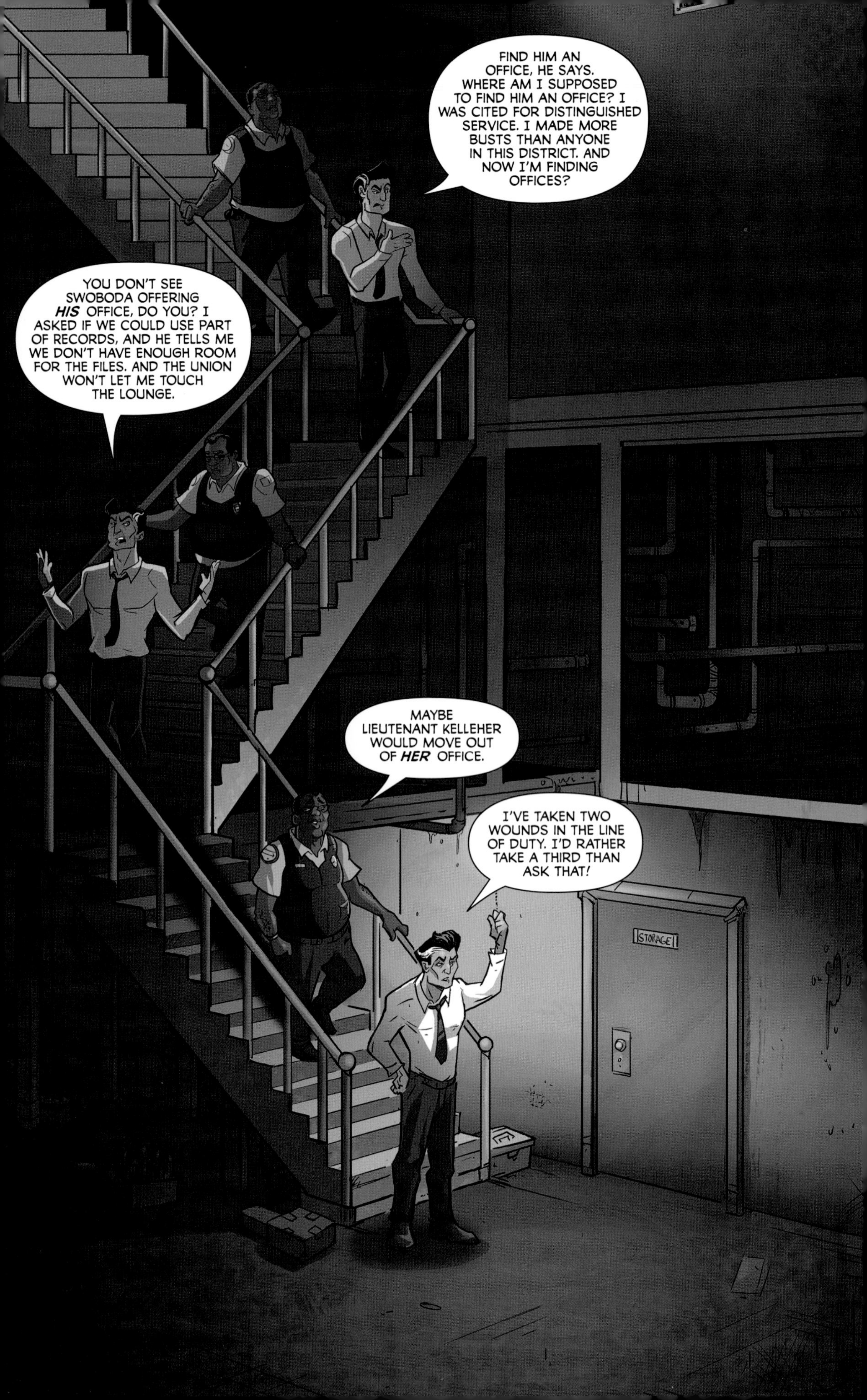
FIND HIM AN OFFICE, HE SAYS. WHERE AM I SUPPOSED TO FIND HIM AN OFFICE? I WAS CITED FOR DISTINGUISHED SERVICE. I MADE MORE BUSTS THAN ANYONE IN THIS DISTRICT. AND NOW I'M FINDING OFFICES?
YOU DON'T SEE SWOBODA OFFERING *HIS* OFFICE, DO YOU? I ASKED IF WE COULD USE PART OF RECORDS, AND HE TELLS ME WE DON'T HAVE ENOUGH ROOM FOR THE FILES. AND THE UNION WON'T LET ME TOUCH THE LOUNGE.
MAYBE LIEUTENANT KELLEHER WOULD MOVE OUT OF *HER* OFFICE.
I'VE TAKEN TWO WOUNDS IN THE LINE OF DUTY. I'D RATHER TAKE A THIRD THAN ASK THAT!
STORAGE

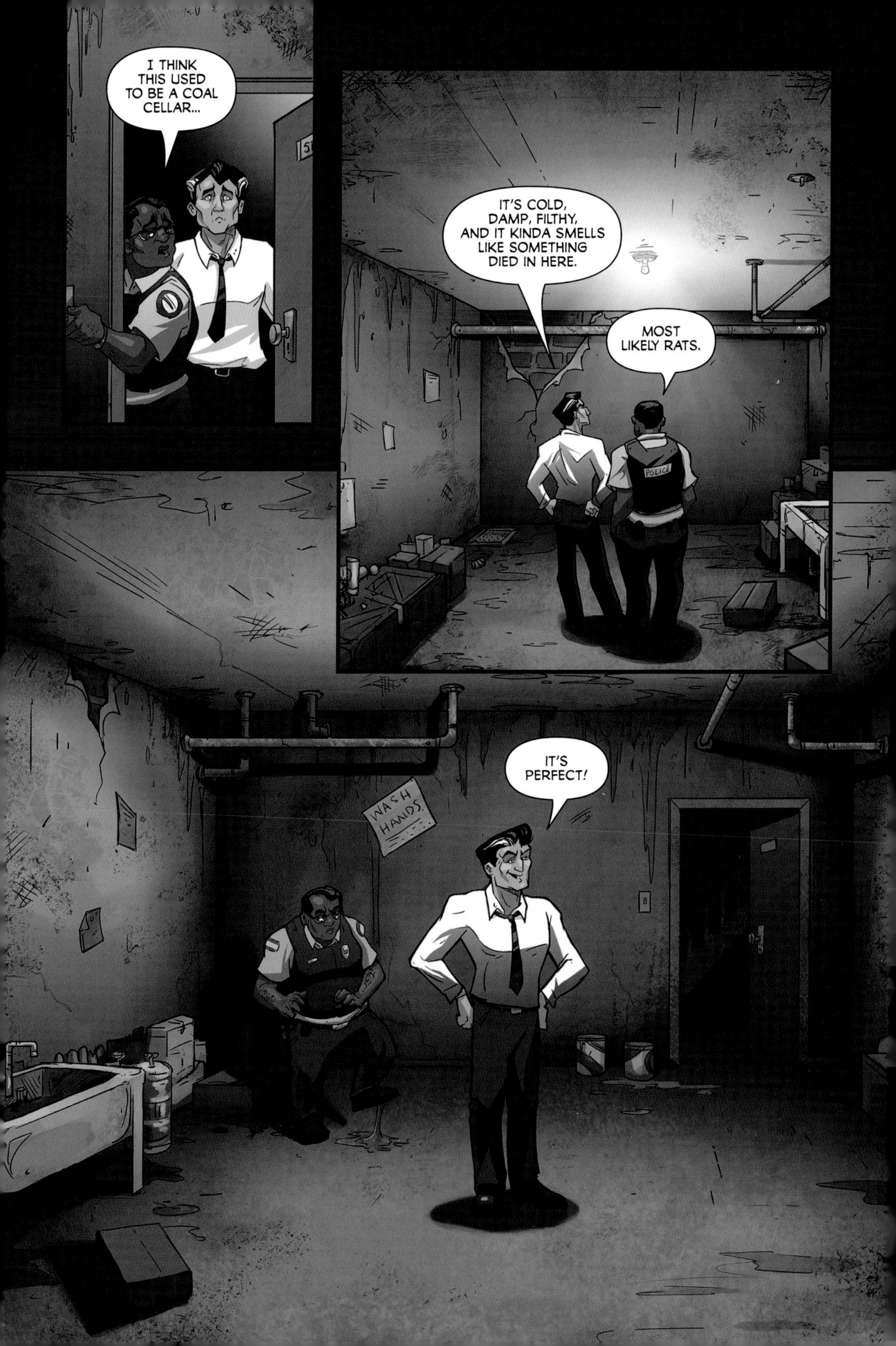
I THINK THIS USED TO BE A COAL CELLAR...
IT'S COLD, DAMP, FILTHY, AND IT KINDA SMELLS LIKE SOMETHING DIED IN HERE.
MOST LIKELY RATS.
POLICE
IT'S PERFECT!
WASH HANDS.

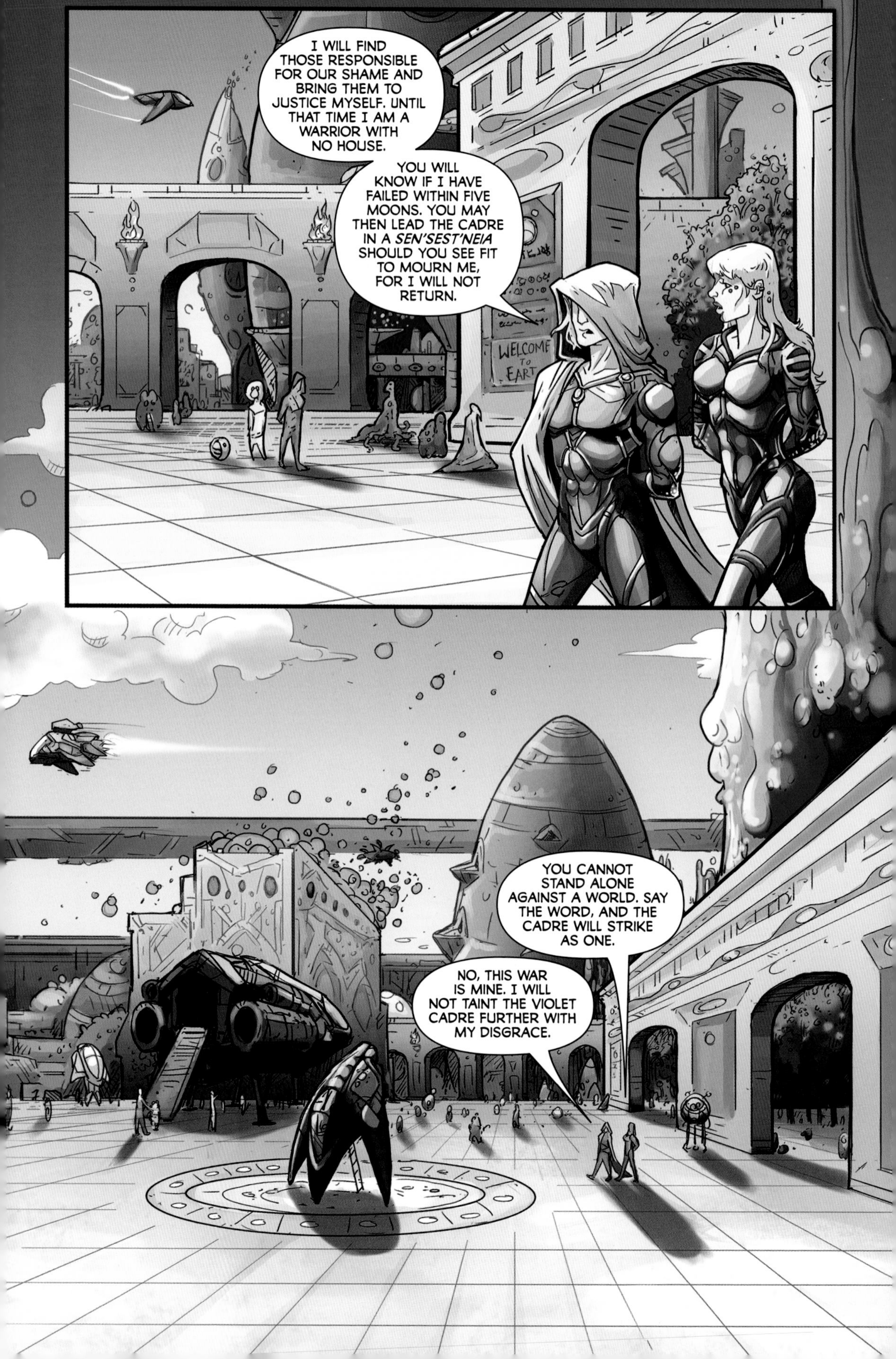
I WILL FIND THOSE RESPONSIBLE FOR OUR SHAME AND BRING THEM TO JUSTICE MYSELF. UNTIL THAT TIME I AM A WARRIOR WITH NO HOUSE.
YOU WILL KNOW IF I HAVE FAILED WITHIN FIVE MOONS. YOU MAY THEN LEAD THE CADRE IN A *SEN'SEST'NEIA* SHOULD YOU SEE FIT TO MOURN ME, FOR I WILL NOT RETURN.
WELCOME TO EART
YOU CANNOT STAND ALONE AGAINST A WORLD. SAY THE WORD, AND THE CADRE WILL STRIKE AS ONE.
NO, THIS WAR IS MINE. I WILL NOT TAINT THE VIOLET CADRE FURTHER WITH MY DISGRACE.

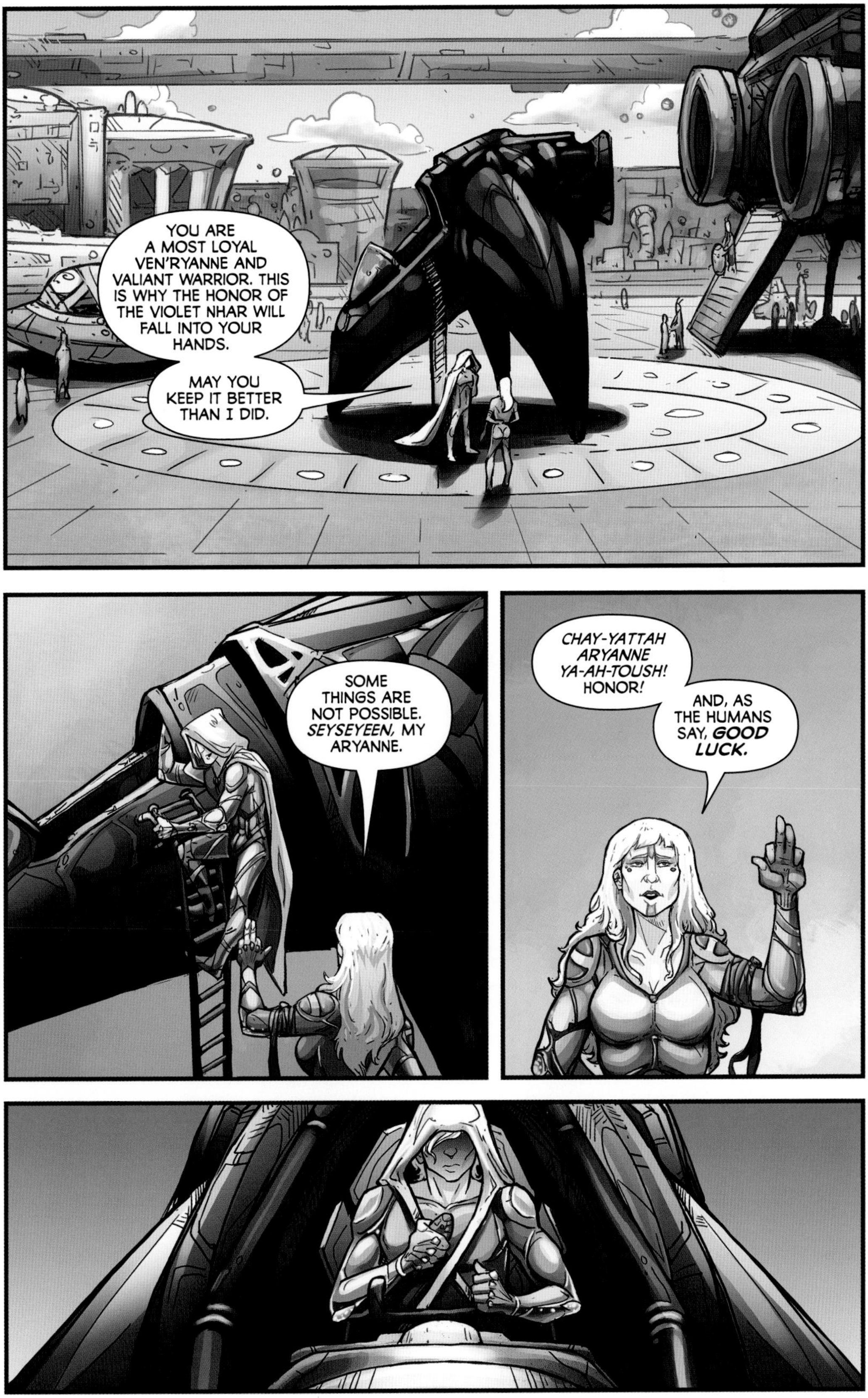
YOU ARE A MOST LOYAL VEN'RYANNE AND VALIANT WARRIOR. THIS IS WHY THE HONOR OF THE VIOLET NHAR WILL FALL INTO YOUR HANDS.
MAY YOU KEEP IT BETTER THAN I DID.
SOME THINGS ARE NOT POSSIBLE. *SEYSEYEEN,* MY ARYANNE.
CHAY-YATTAH ARYANNE YA-AH-TOUSH! HONOR!
AND, AS THE HUMANS SAY, ***GOOD LUCK.***

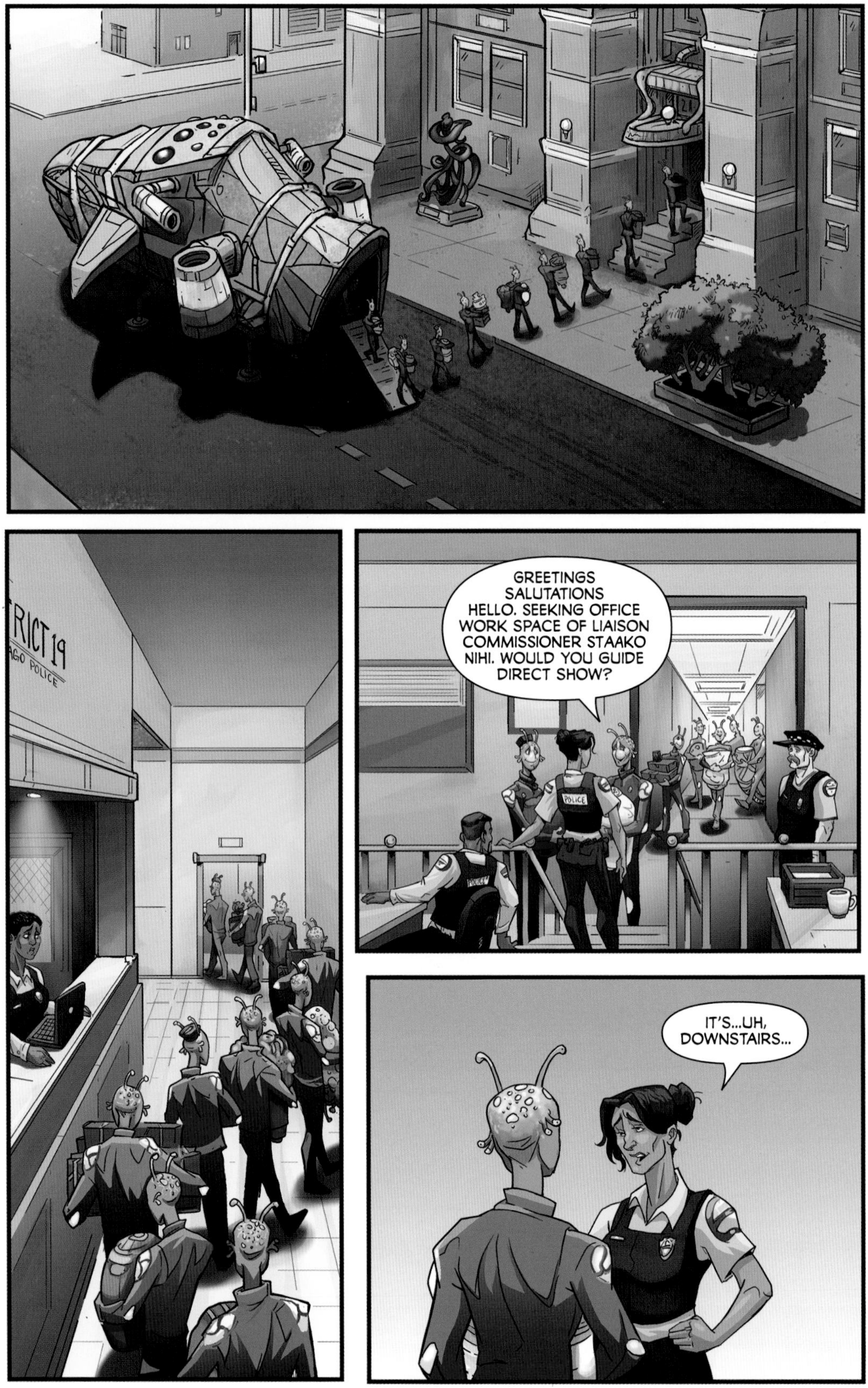
GREETINGS SALUTATIONS HELLO. SEEKING OFFICE WORK SPACE OF LIAISON COMMISSIONER STAAKO NIHI. WOULD YOU GUIDE DIRECT SHOW?
IT'S...UH, DOWNSTAIRS...

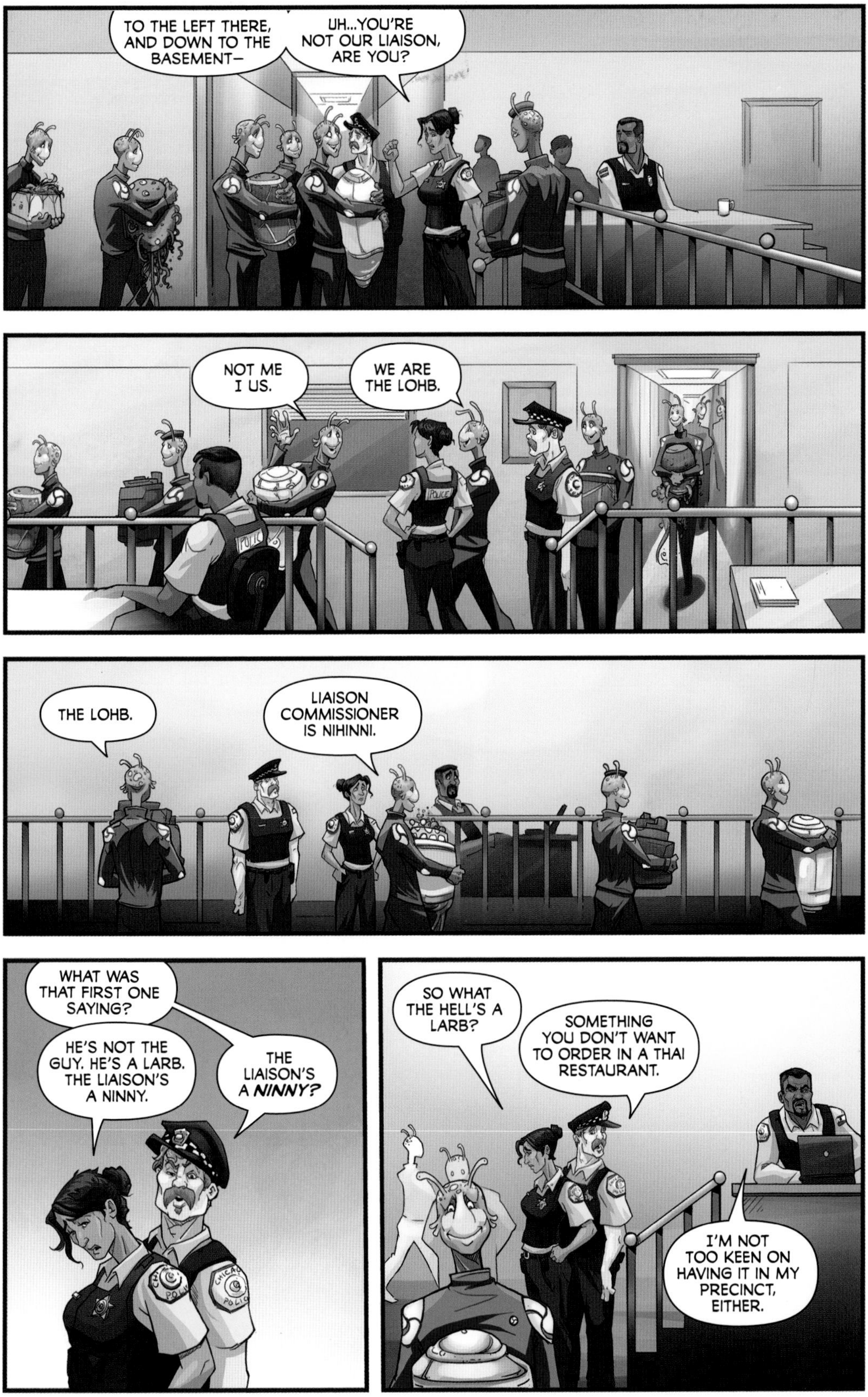
TO THE LEFT THERE, AND DOWN TO THE BASEMENT—
UH...YOU'RE NOT OUR LIAISON, ARE YOU?
NOT ME I US.
WE ARE THE LOHB.
THE LOHB.
LIAISON COMMISSIONER IS NIHINNI.
WHAT WAS THAT FIRST ONE SAYING?
HE'S NOT THE GUY. HE'S A LARB. THE LIAISON'S A NINNY.
THE LIAISON'S A NINNY?
SO WHAT THE HELL'S A LARB?
SOMETHING YOU DON'T WANT TO ORDER IN A THAI RESTAURANT.
I'M NOT TOO KEEN ON HAVING IT IN MY PRECINCT, EITHER.

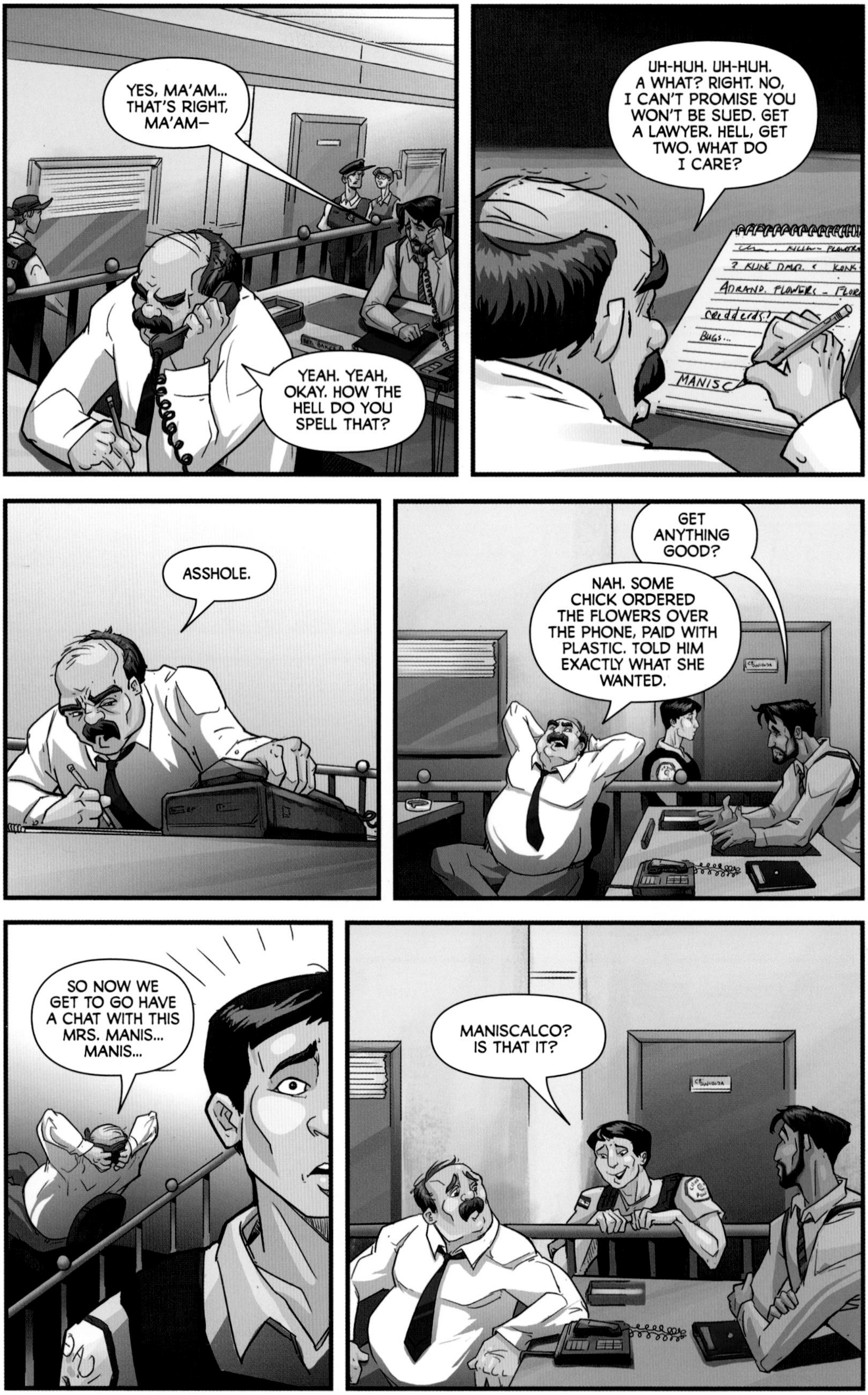

YES, MA'AM... THAT'S RIGHT, MA'AM–
YEAH. YEAH, OKAY. HOW THE HELL DO YOU SPELL THAT?
UH-HUH. UH-HUH. A WHAT? RIGHT. NO, I CAN'T PROMISE YOU WON'T BE SUED. GET A LAWYER. HELL, GET TWO. WHAT DO I CARE?
MANISC
ASSHOLE.
GET ANYTHING GOOD?
NAH. SOME CHICK ORDERED THE FLOWERS OVER THE PHONE, PAID WITH PLASTIC. TOLD HIM EXACTLY WHAT SHE WANTED.
SO NOW WE GET TO GO HAVE A CHAT WITH THIS MRS. MANIS... MANIS...
MANISCALCO? IS THAT IT?

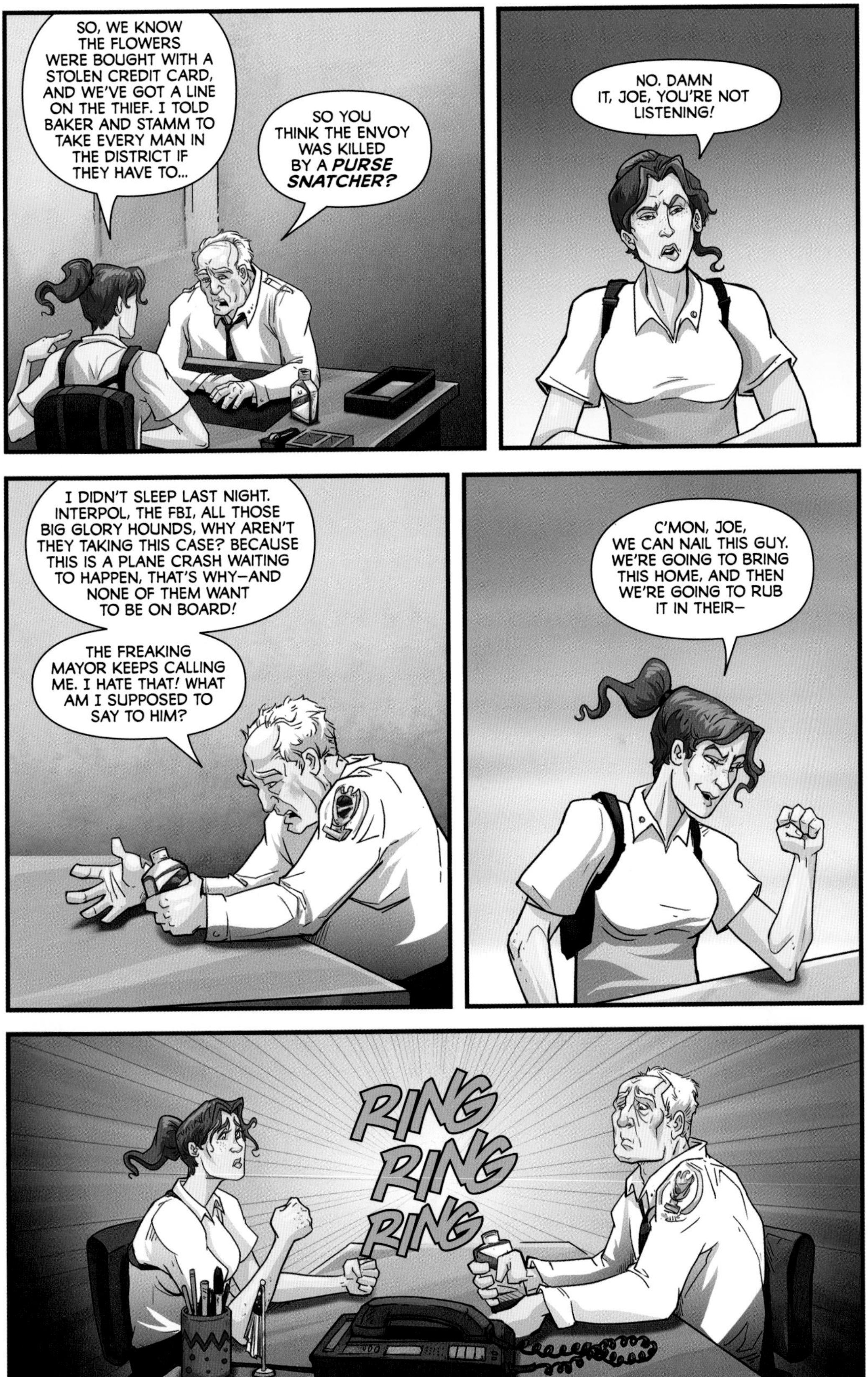
SO, WE KNOW THE FLOWERS WERE BOUGHT WITH A STOLEN CREDIT CARD, AND WE'VE GOT A LINE ON THE THIEF. I TOLD BAKER AND STAMM TO TAKE EVERY MAN IN THE DISTRICT IF THEY HAVE TO...
SO YOU THINK THE ENVOY WAS KILLED BY A *PURSE SNATCHER?*
NO. DAMN IT, JOE, YOU'RE NOT LISTENING!
I DIDN'T SLEEP LAST NIGHT. INTERPOL, THE FBI, ALL THOSE BIG GLORY HOUNDS, WHY AREN'T THEY TAKING THIS CASE? BECAUSE THIS IS A PLANE CRASH WAITING TO HAPPEN, THAT'S WHY—AND NONE OF THEM WANT TO BE ON BOARD!
THE FREAKING MAYOR KEEPS CALLING ME. I HATE THAT! WHAT AM I SUPPOSED TO SAY TO HIM?
C'MON, JOE, WE CAN NAIL THIS GUY. WE'RE GOING TO BRING THIS HOME, AND THEN WE'RE GOING TO RUB IT IN THEIR—
RING
RING
RING

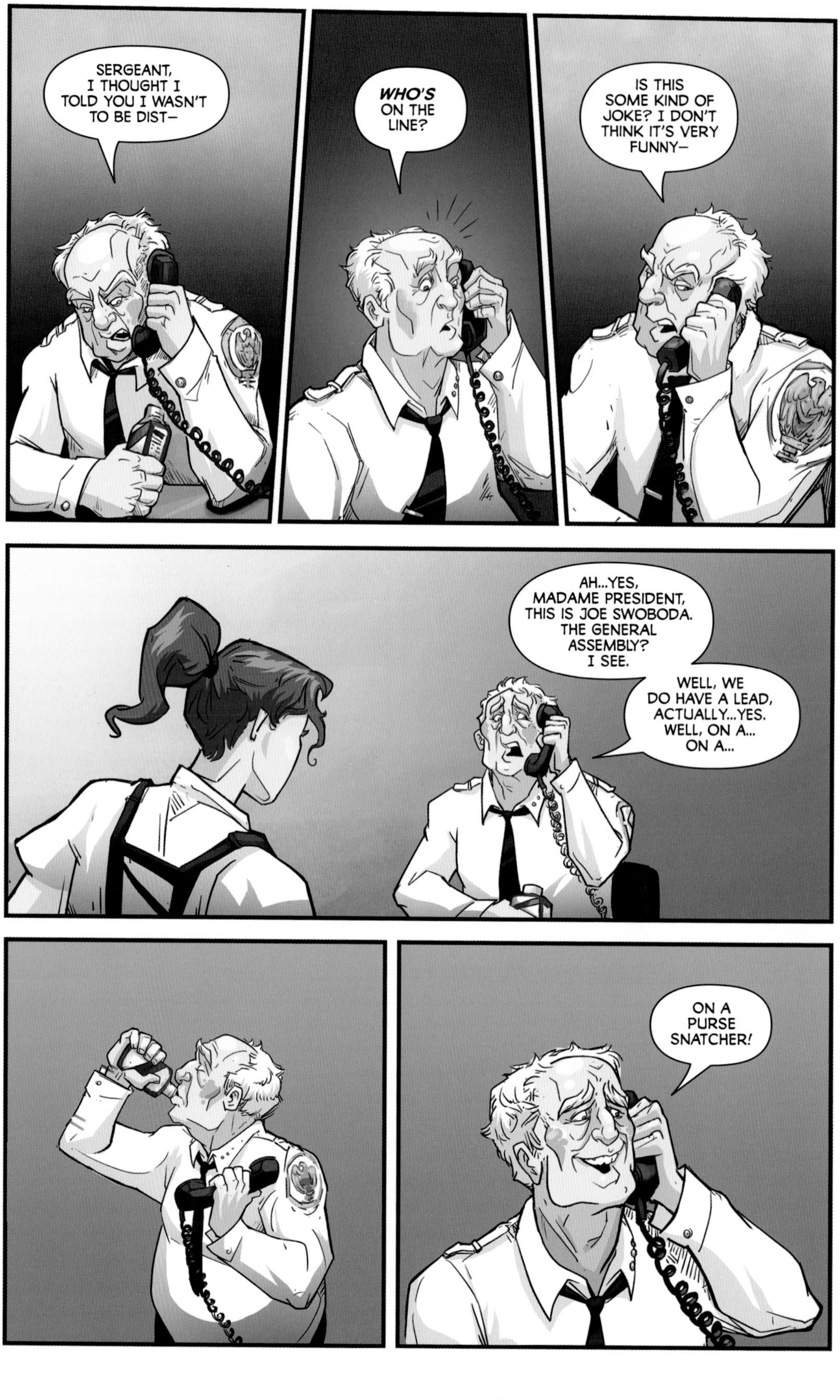
SERGEANT, I THOUGHT I TOLD YOU I WASN'T TO BE DIST—
WHO'S ON THE LINE?
IS THIS SOME KIND OF JOKE? I DON'T THINK IT'S VERY FUNNY—
AH...YES, MADAME PRESIDENT, THIS IS JOE SWOBODA. THE GENERAL ASSEMBLY? I SEE.
WELL, WE DO HAVE A LEAD, ACTUALLY...YES. WELL, ON A... ON A...
ON A PURSE SNATCHER!

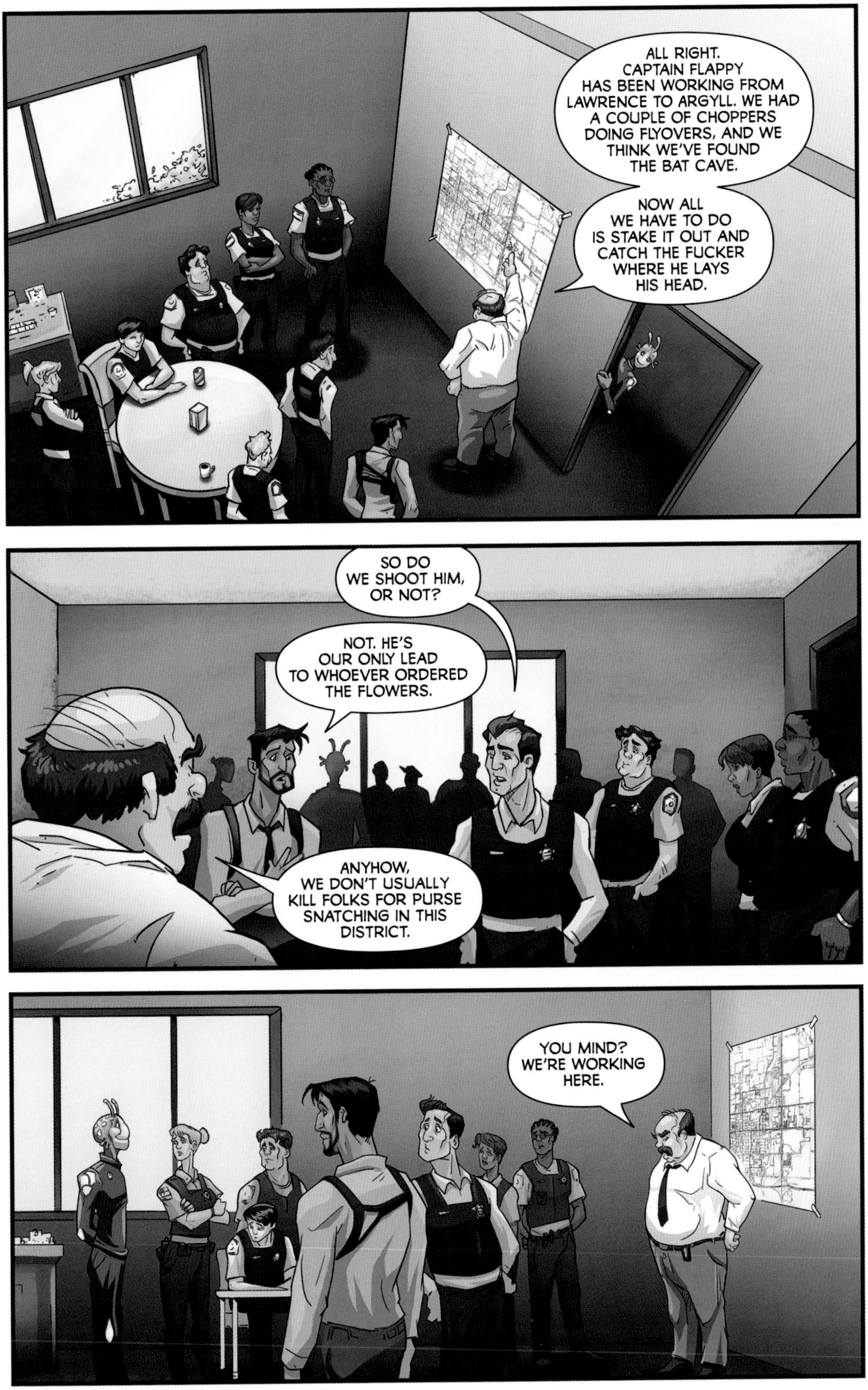
ALL RIGHT. CAPTAIN FLAPPY HAS BEEN WORKING FROM LAWRENCE TO ARGYLL. WE HAD A COUPLE OF CHOPPERS DOING FLYOVERS, AND WE THINK WE'VE FOUND THE BAT CAVE.
NOW ALL WE HAVE TO DO IS STAKE IT OUT AND CATCH THE FUCKER WHERE HE LAYS HIS HEAD.
SO DO WE SHOOT HIM, OR NOT?
NOT. HE'S OUR ONLY LEAD TO WHOEVER ORDERED THE FLOWERS.
ANYHOW, WE DON'T USUALLY KILL FOLKS FOR PURSE SNATCHING IN THIS DISTRICT.
YOU MIND? WE'RE WORKING HERE.

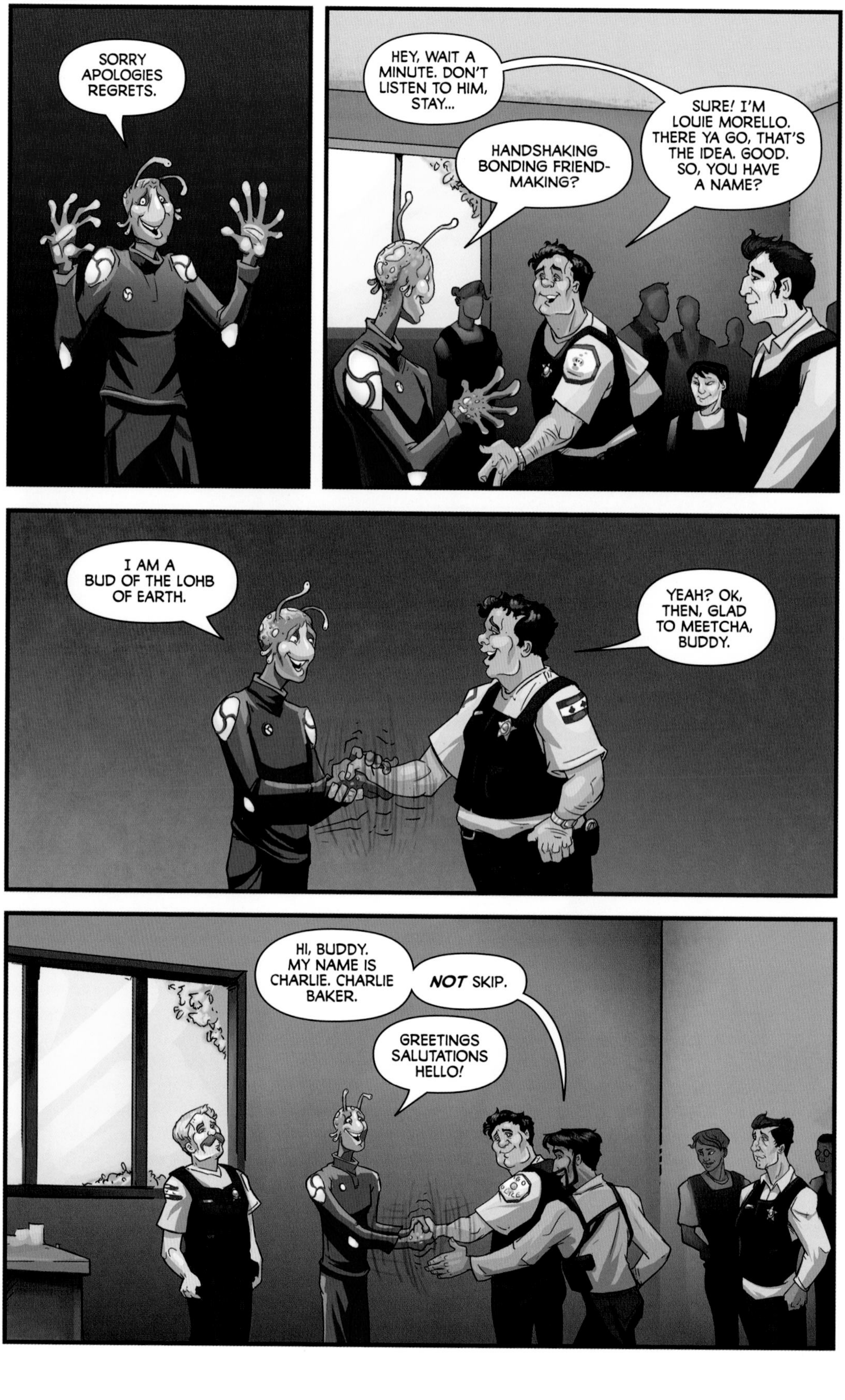
SORRY
APOLOGIES
REGRETS.
HEY, WAIT A MINUTE. DON'T LISTEN TO HIM, STAY...
HANDSHAKING BONDING FRIEND-MAKING?
SURE! I'M LOUIE MORELLO. THERE YA GO, THAT'S THE IDEA. GOOD. SO, YOU HAVE A NAME?
I AM A BUD OF THE LOHB OF EARTH.
YEAH? OK, THEN, GLAD TO MEETCHA, BUDDY.
HI, BUDDY. MY NAME IS CHARLIE. CHARLIE BAKER.
NOT SKIP.
GREETINGS SALUTATIONS HELLO!

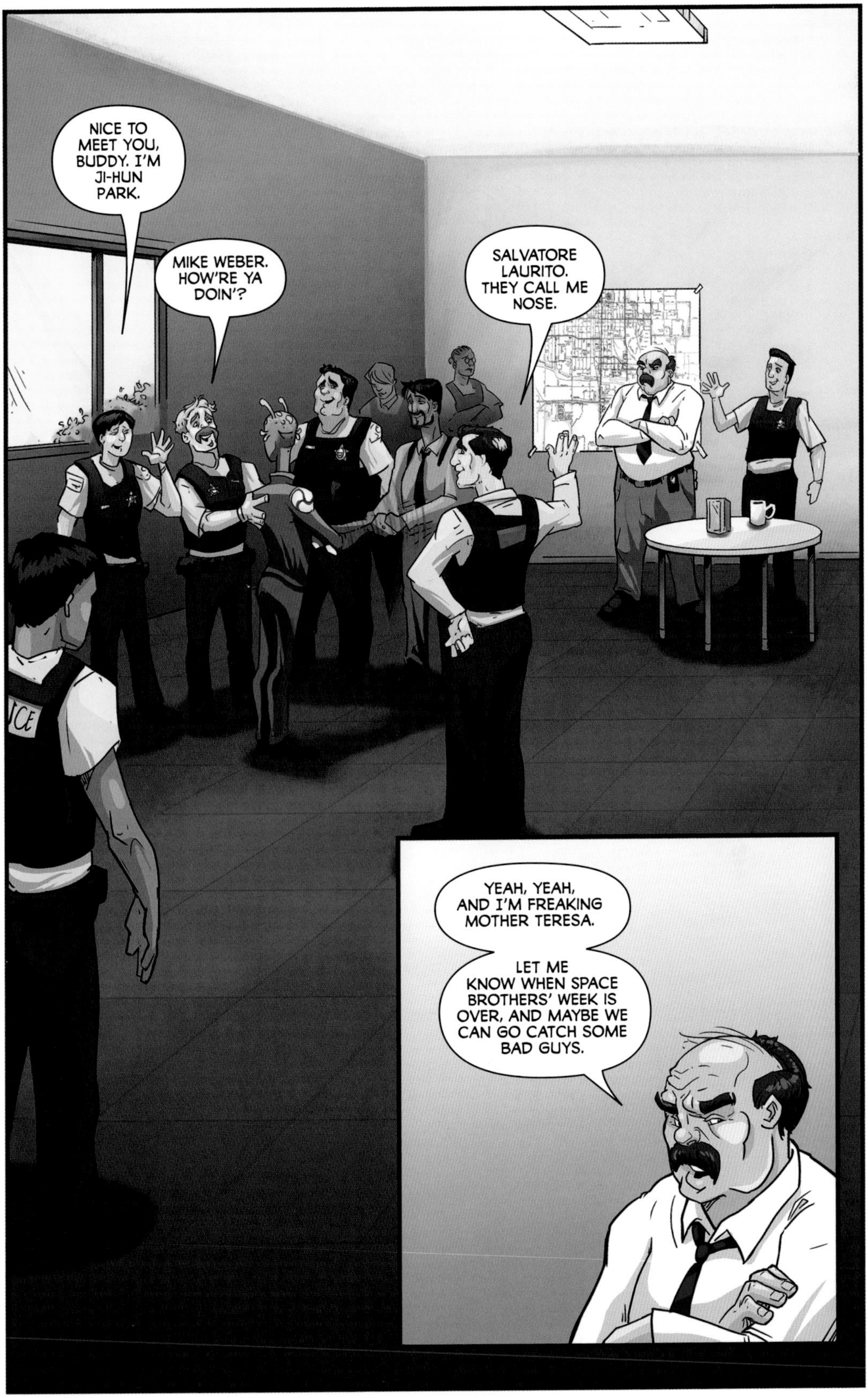
NICE TO MEET YOU, BUDDY. I'M JI-HUN PARK.
MIKE WEBER. HOW'RE YA DOIN'?
SALVATORE LAURITO. THEY CALL ME NOSE.
YEAH, YEAH, AND I'M FREAKING MOTHER TERESA.
LET ME KNOW WHEN SPACE BROTHERS' WEEK IS OVER, AND MAYBE WE CAN GO CATCH SOME BAD GUYS.

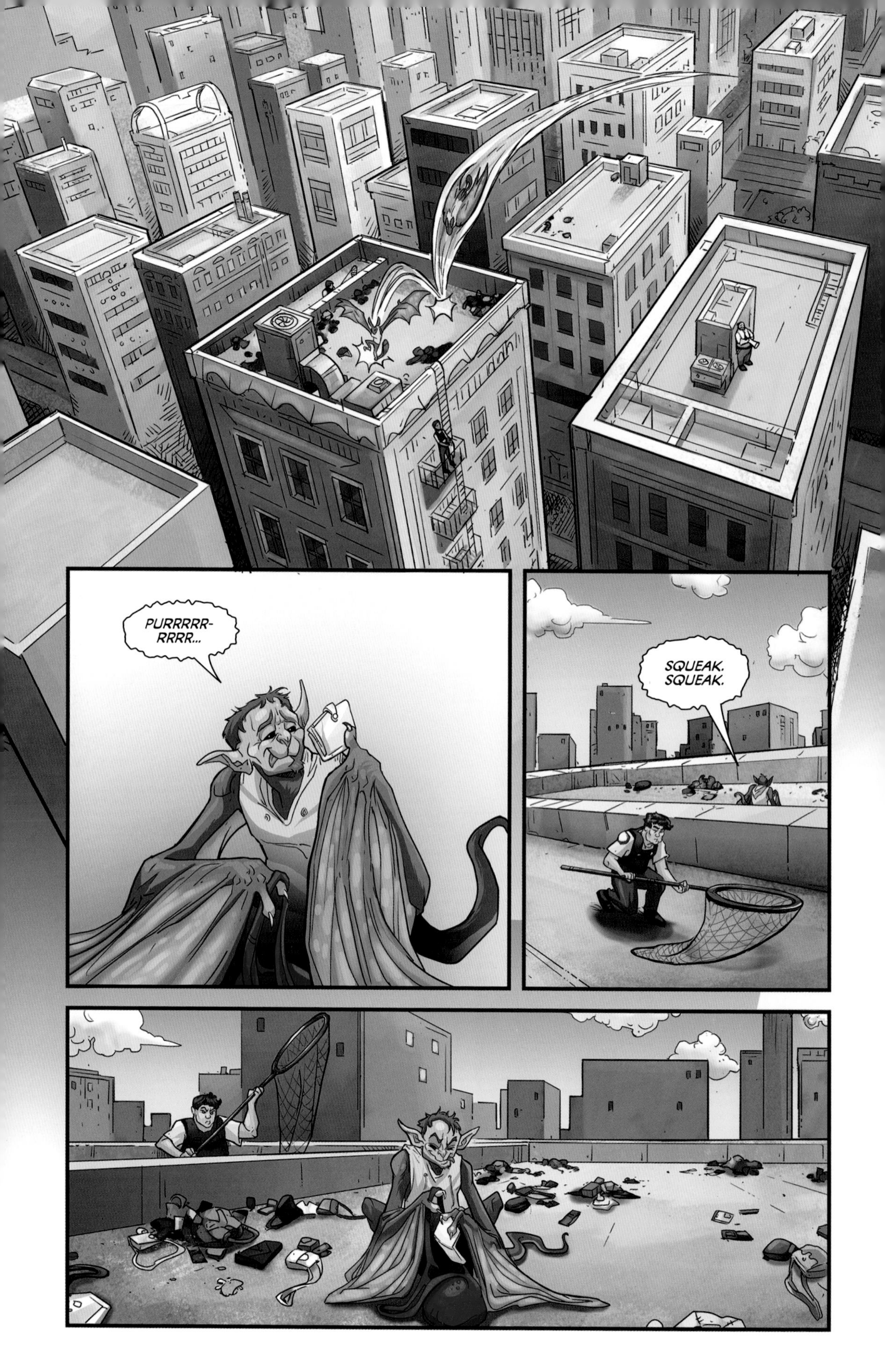
PURRRRR-
RRRR...
SQUEAK.
SQUEAK.

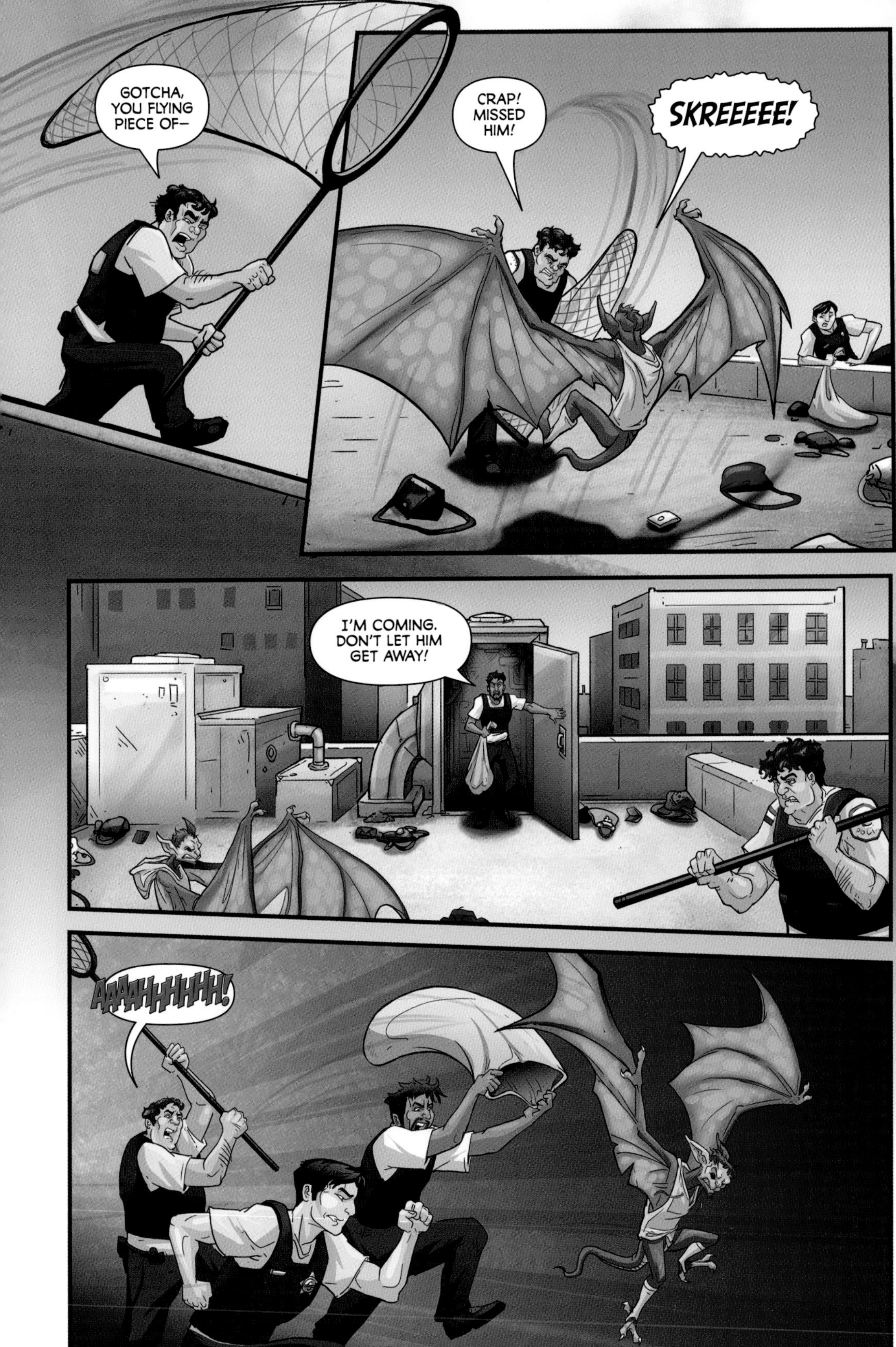
GOTCHA, YOU FLYING PIECE OF—
CRAP! MISSED HIM!
SKREEEEEE!
I'M COMING. DON'T LET HIM GET AWAY!
AAAAHHHHHH!

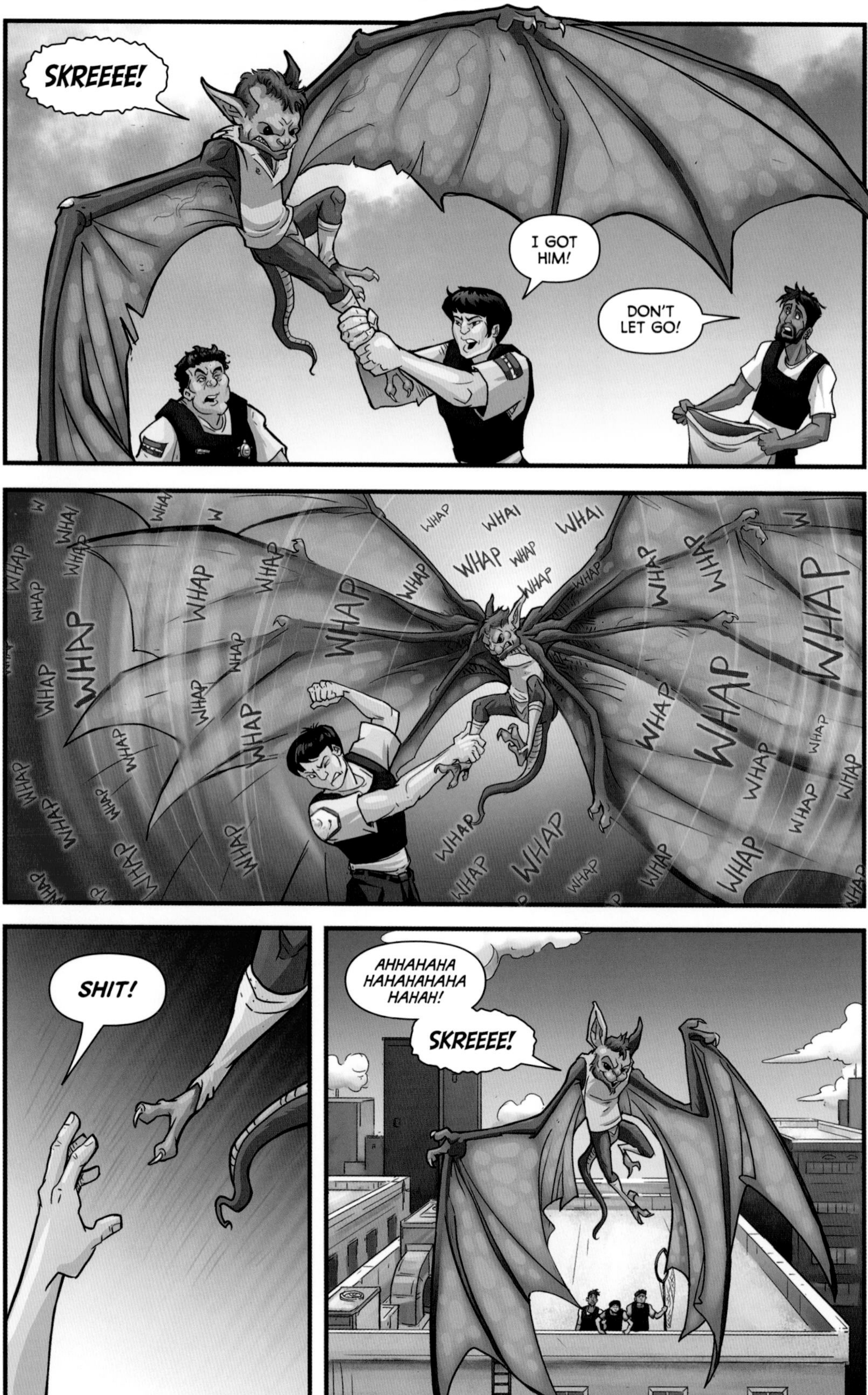
SKREEEE!
I GOT HIM!
DON'T LET GO!
WHAP WHAP WHAP WHAP WHAP
SHIT!
AHHAHAHA HAHAHAHAHA HAHAH!
SKREEEE!

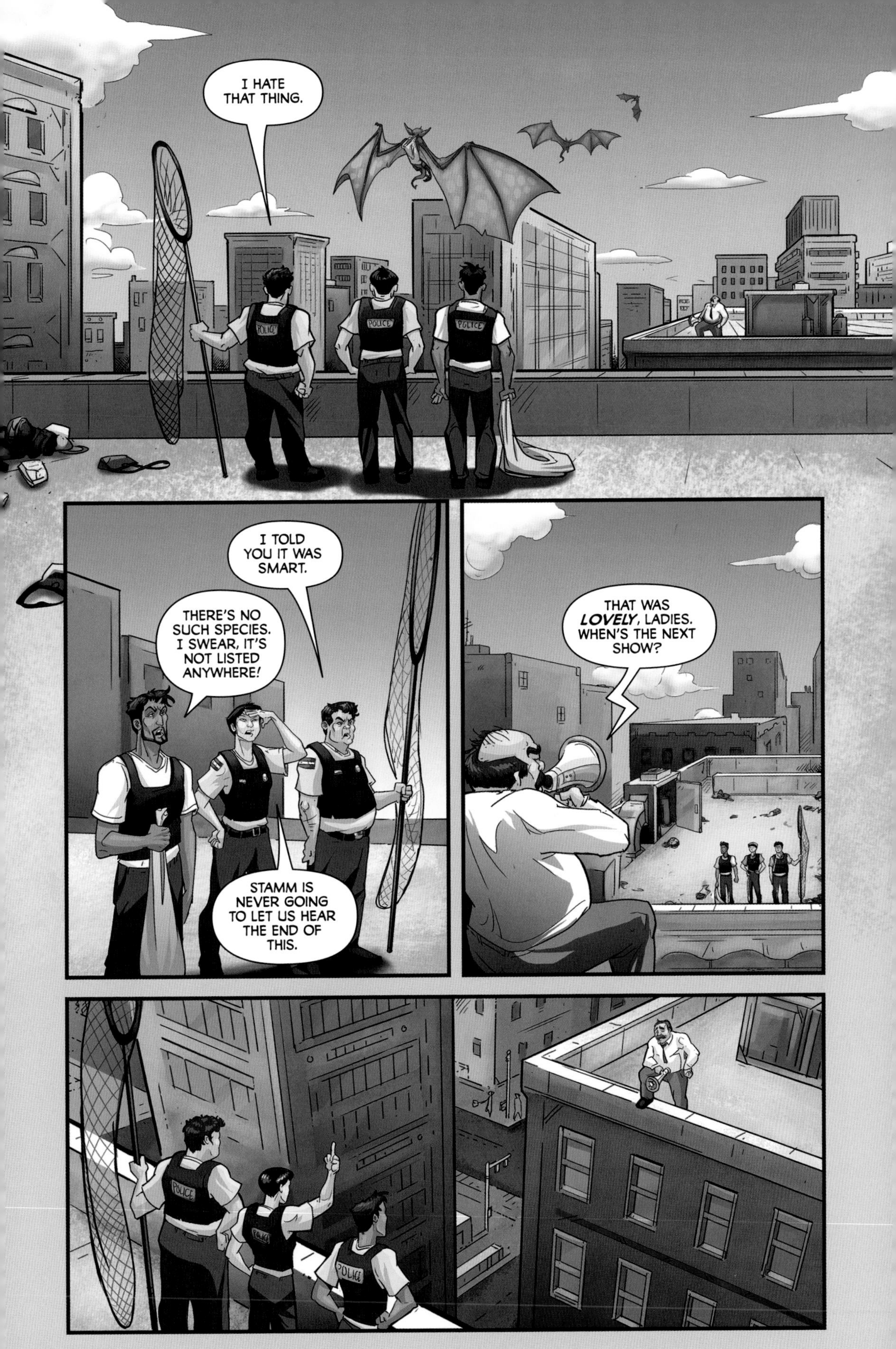
I HATE THAT THING.
I TOLD YOU IT WAS SMART.
THERE'S NO SUCH SPECIES. I SWEAR, IT'S NOT LISTED ANYWHERE!
STAMM IS NEVER GOING TO LET US HEAR THE END OF THIS.
THAT WAS LOVELY, LADIES. WHEN'S THE NEXT SHOW?

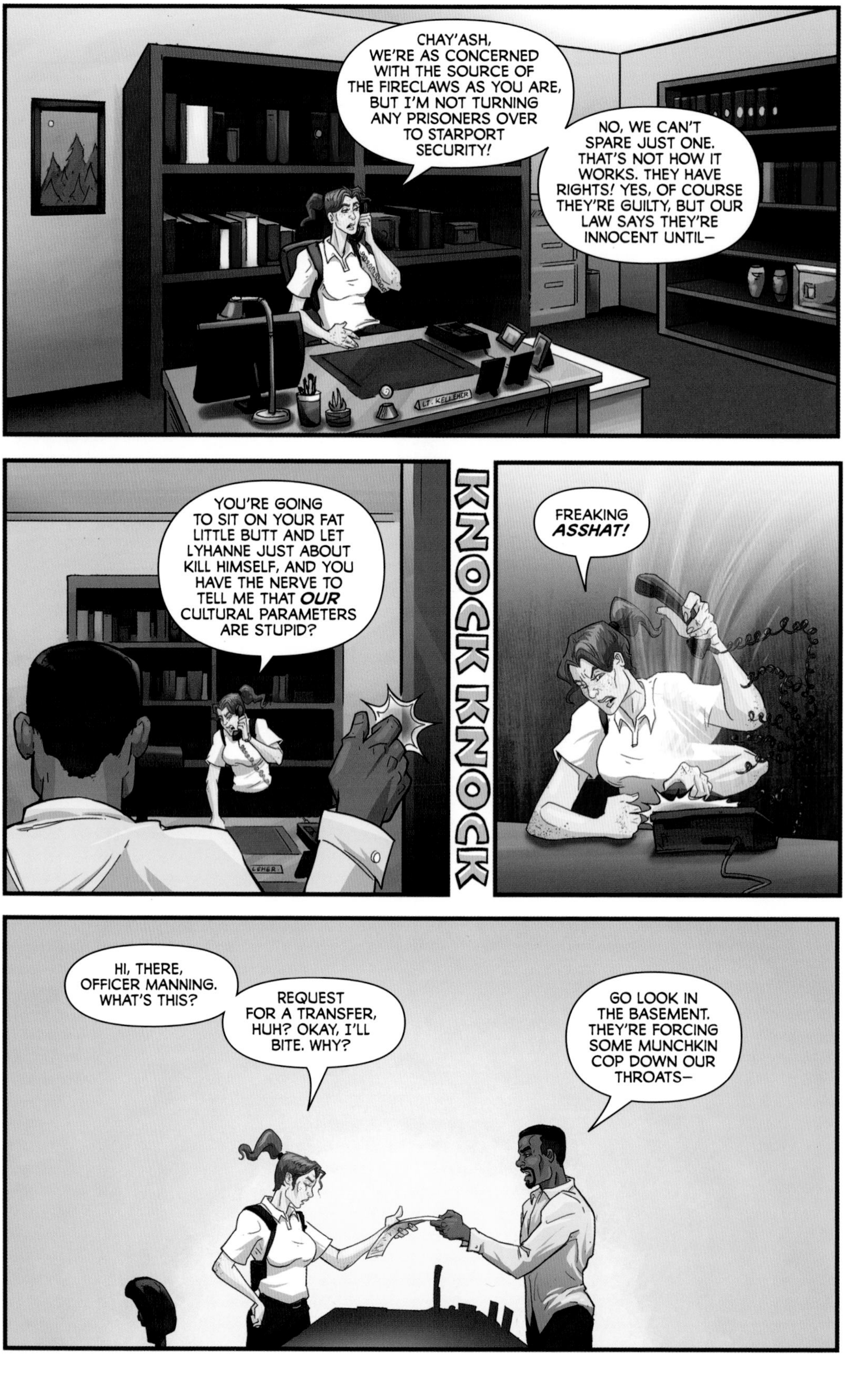
CHAY'ASH, WE'RE AS CONCERNED WITH THE SOURCE OF THE FIRECLAWS AS YOU ARE, BUT I'M NOT TURNING ANY PRISONERS OVER TO STARPORT SECURITY!
NO, WE CAN'T SPARE JUST ONE. THAT'S NOT HOW IT WORKS. THEY HAVE RIGHTS! YES, OF COURSE THEY'RE GUILTY, BUT OUR LAW SAYS THEY'RE INNOCENT UNTIL—
LT. KELLEHER
YOU'RE GOING TO SIT ON YOUR FAT LITTLE BUTT AND LET LYHANNE JUST ABOUT KILL HIMSELF, AND YOU HAVE THE NERVE TO TELL ME THAT *OUR* CULTURAL PARAMETERS ARE STUPID?
KNOCK KNOCK
FREAKING ***ASSHAT!***
HI, THERE, OFFICER MANNING. WHAT'S THIS?
REQUEST FOR A TRANSFER, HUH? OKAY, I'LL BITE. WHY?
GO LOOK IN THE BASEMENT. THEY'RE FORCING SOME MUNCHKIN COP DOWN OUR THROATS—

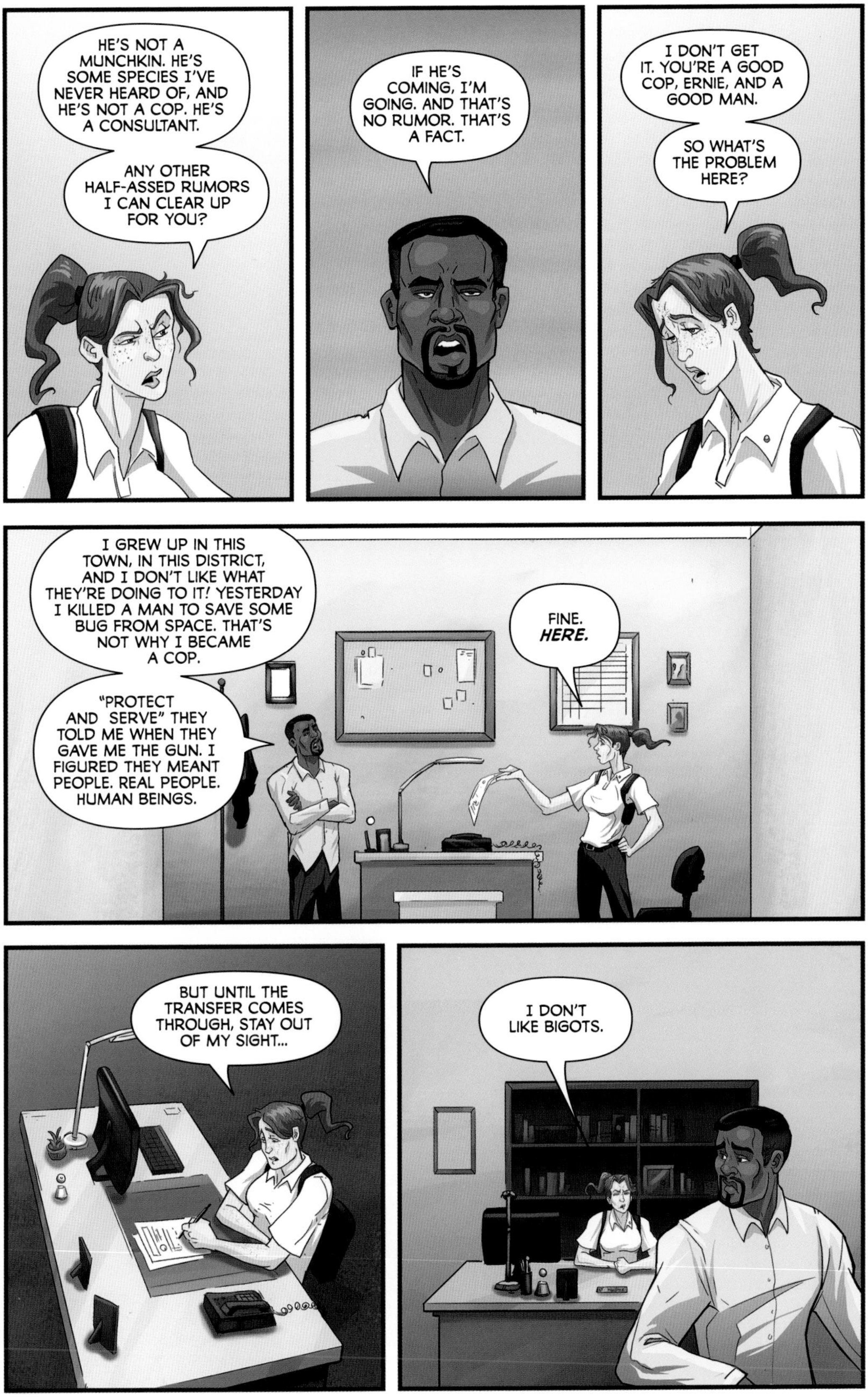
HE'S NOT A MUNCHKIN. HE'S SOME SPECIES I'VE NEVER HEARD OF, AND HE'S NOT A COP. HE'S A CONSULTANT.
ANY OTHER HALF-ASSED RUMORS I CAN CLEAR UP FOR YOU?
IF HE'S COMING, I'M GOING. AND THAT'S NO RUMOR. THAT'S A FACT.
I DON'T GET IT. YOU'RE A GOOD COP, ERNIE, AND A GOOD MAN.
SO WHAT'S THE PROBLEM HERE?
I GREW UP IN THIS TOWN, IN THIS DISTRICT, AND I DON'T LIKE WHAT THEY'RE DOING TO IT! YESTERDAY I KILLED A MAN TO SAVE SOME BUG FROM SPACE. THAT'S NOT WHY I BECAME A COP.
"PROTECT AND SERVE" THEY TOLD ME WHEN THEY GAVE ME THE GUN. I FIGURED THEY MEANT PEOPLE. REAL PEOPLE. HUMAN BEINGS.
FINE. ***HERE.***
BUT UNTIL THE TRANSFER COMES THROUGH, STAY OUT OF MY SIGHT...
I DON'T LIKE BIGOTS.

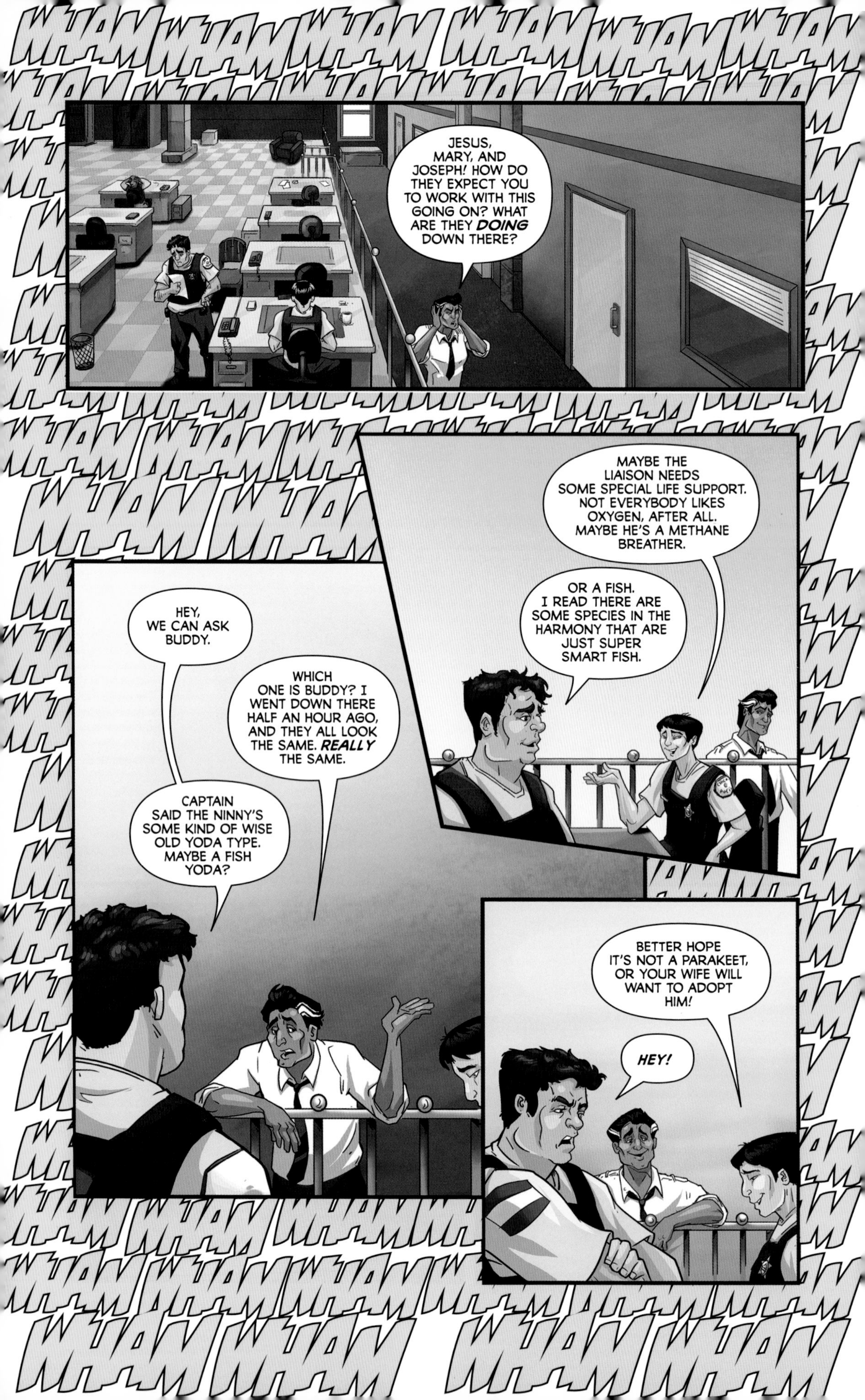
WHAM WHAM WHAM
JESUS, MARY, AND JOSEPH! HOW DO THEY EXPECT YOU TO WORK WITH THIS GOING ON? WHAT ARE THEY *DOING* DOWN THERE?
MAYBE THE LIAISON NEEDS SOME SPECIAL LIFE SUPPORT. NOT EVERYBODY LIKES OXYGEN, AFTER ALL. MAYBE HE'S A METHANE BREATHER.
OR A FISH. I READ THERE ARE SOME SPECIES IN THE HARMONY THAT ARE JUST SUPER SMART FISH.
HEY, WE CAN ASK BUDDY.
WHICH ONE IS BUDDY? I WENT DOWN THERE HALF AN HOUR AGO, AND THEY ALL LOOK THE SAME. *REALLY* THE SAME.
CAPTAIN SAID THE NINNY'S SOME KIND OF WISE OLD YODA TYPE. MAYBE A FISH YODA?
BETTER HOPE IT'S NOT A PARAKEET, OR YOUR WIFE WILL WANT TO ADOPT HIM!
HEY!

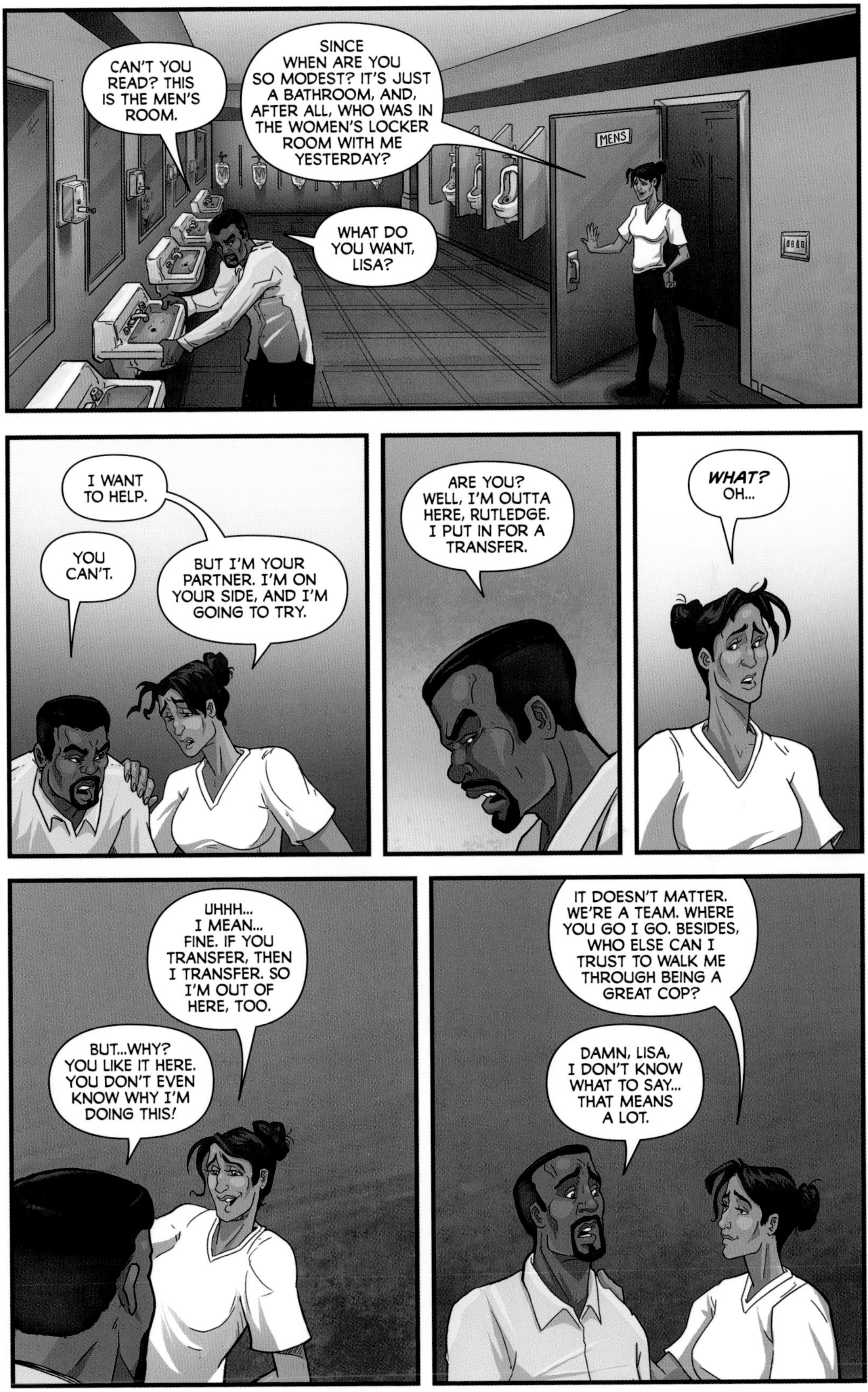
CAN'T YOU READ? THIS IS THE MEN'S ROOM.
SINCE WHEN ARE YOU SO MODEST? IT'S JUST A BATHROOM, AND, AFTER ALL, WHO WAS IN THE WOMEN'S LOCKER ROOM WITH ME YESTERDAY?
MENS
WHAT DO YOU WANT, LISA?
I WANT TO HELP.
YOU CAN'T.
BUT I'M YOUR PARTNER. I'M ON YOUR SIDE, AND I'M GOING TO TRY.
ARE YOU? WELL, I'M OUTTA HERE, RUTLEDGE. I PUT IN FOR A TRANSFER.
WHAT? OH...
UHHH... I MEAN... FINE. IF YOU TRANSFER, THEN I TRANSFER. SO I'M OUT OF HERE, TOO.
BUT...WHY? YOU LIKE IT HERE. YOU DON'T EVEN KNOW WHY I'M DOING THIS!
IT DOESN'T MATTER. WE'RE A TEAM. WHERE YOU GO I GO. BESIDES, WHO ELSE CAN I TRUST TO WALK ME THROUGH BEING A GREAT COP?
DAMN, LISA, I DON'T KNOW WHAT TO SAY... THAT MEANS A LOT.

CHAPTER TEN

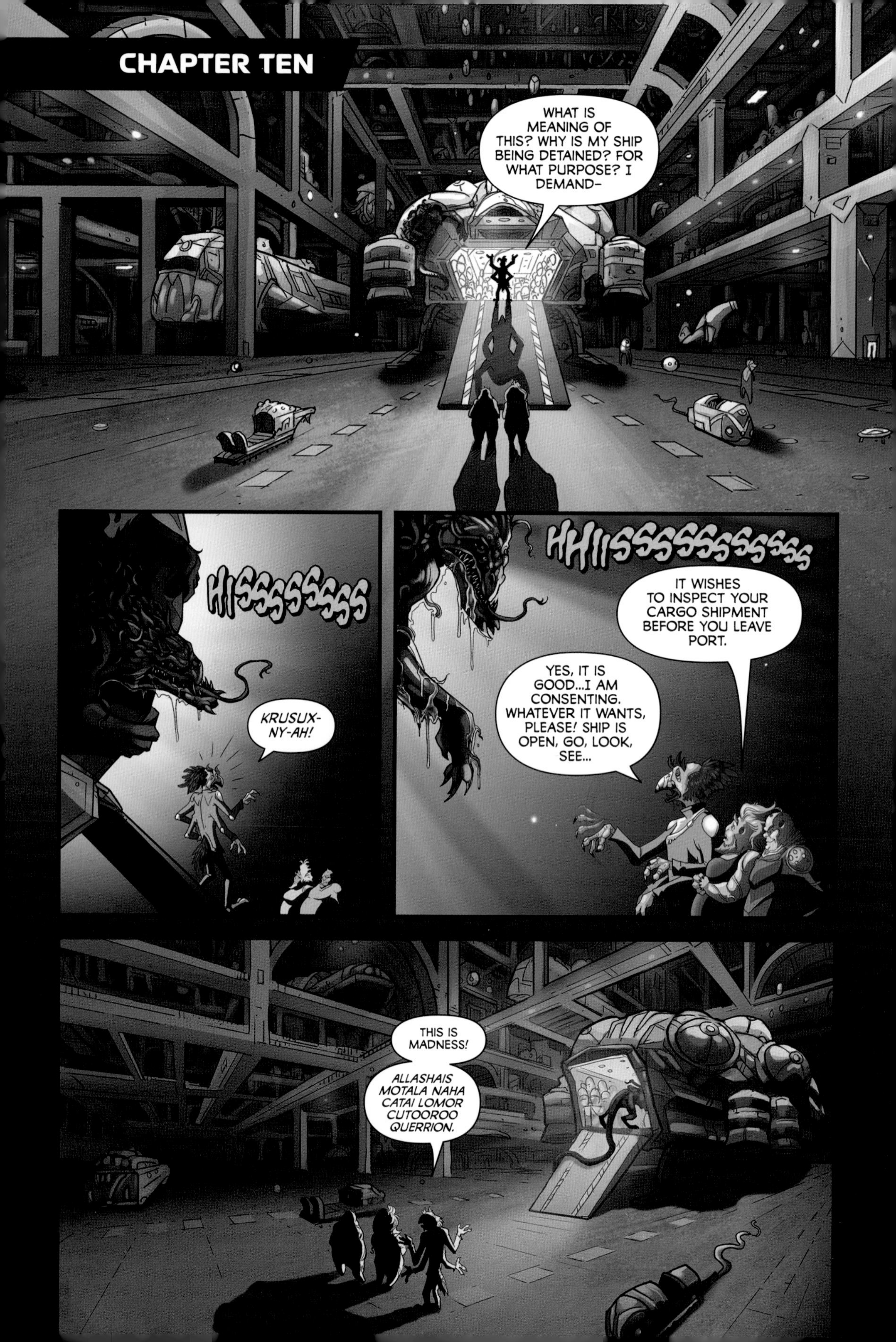
WHAT IS MEANING OF THIS? WHY IS MY SHIP BEING DETAINED? FOR WHAT PURPOSE? I DEMAND–
HISSSSSSSSS
KRUSUX-NY-AH!
HHIISSSSSSSSSSSS
IT WISHES TO INSPECT YOUR CARGO SHIPMENT BEFORE YOU LEAVE PORT.
YES, IT IS GOOD...I AM CONSENTING. WHATEVER IT WANTS, PLEASE! SHIP IS OPEN, GO, LOOK, SEE...
THIS IS MADNESS!
ALLASHAIS MOTALA NAHA CATAI LOMOR CUTOOROO QUERRION.

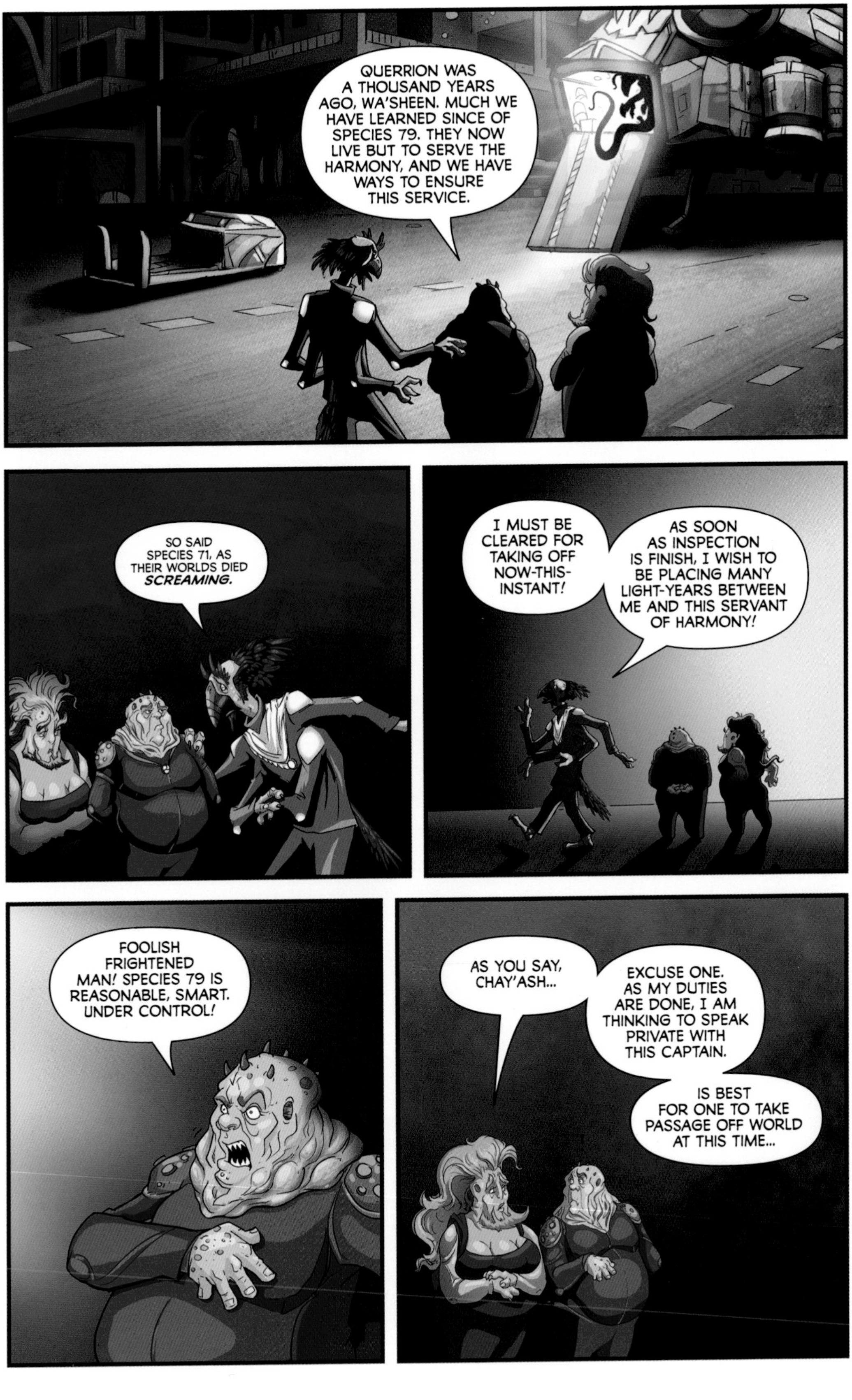
QUERRION WAS A THOUSAND YEARS AGO, WA'SHEEN. MUCH WE HAVE LEARNED SINCE OF SPECIES 79. THEY NOW LIVE BUT TO SERVE THE HARMONY, AND WE HAVE WAYS TO ENSURE THIS SERVICE.
SO SAID SPECIES 71, AS THEIR WORLDS DIED *SCREAMING.*
I MUST BE CLEARED FOR TAKING OFF NOW-THIS-INSTANT!
AS SOON AS INSPECTION IS FINISH, I WISH TO BE PLACING MANY LIGHT-YEARS BETWEEN ME AND THIS SERVANT OF HARMONY!
FOOLISH FRIGHTENED MAN! SPECIES 79 IS REASONABLE, SMART. UNDER CONTROL!
AS YOU SAY, CHAY'ASH...
EXCUSE ONE. AS MY DUTIES ARE DONE, I AM THINKING TO SPEAK PRIVATE WITH THIS CAPTAIN.
IS BEST FOR ONE TO TAKE PASSAGE OFF WORLD AT THIS TIME...

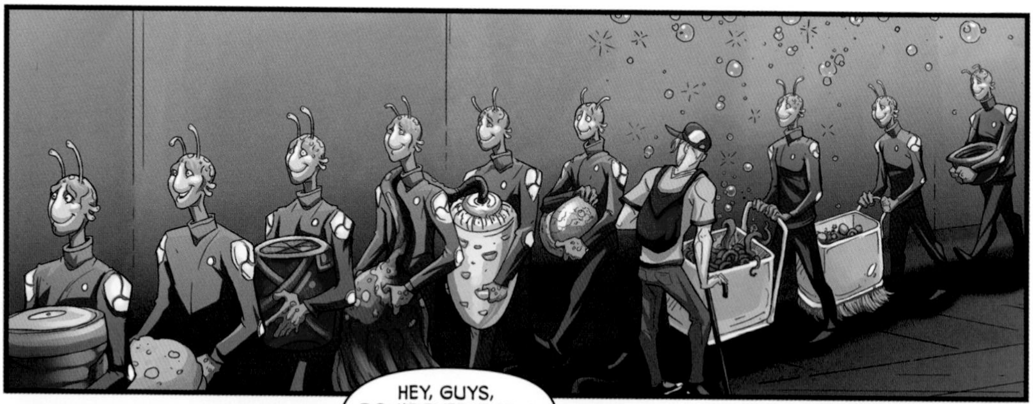

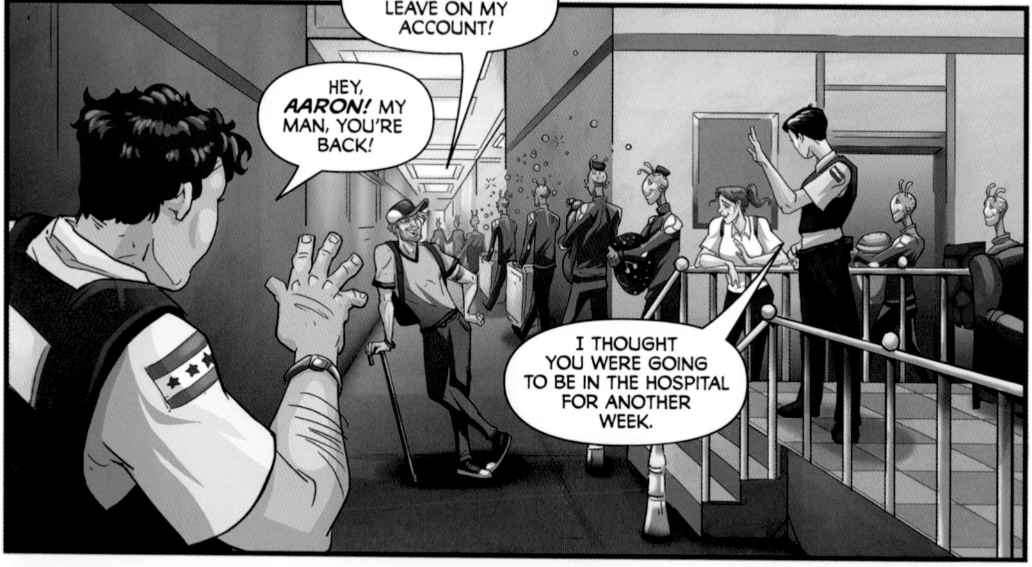
HEY, AARON! MY MAN, YOU'RE BACK!
HEY, GUYS, DON'T EVERYBODY LEAVE ON MY ACCOUNT!
I THOUGHT YOU WERE GOING TO BE IN THE HOSPITAL FOR ANOTHER WEEK.

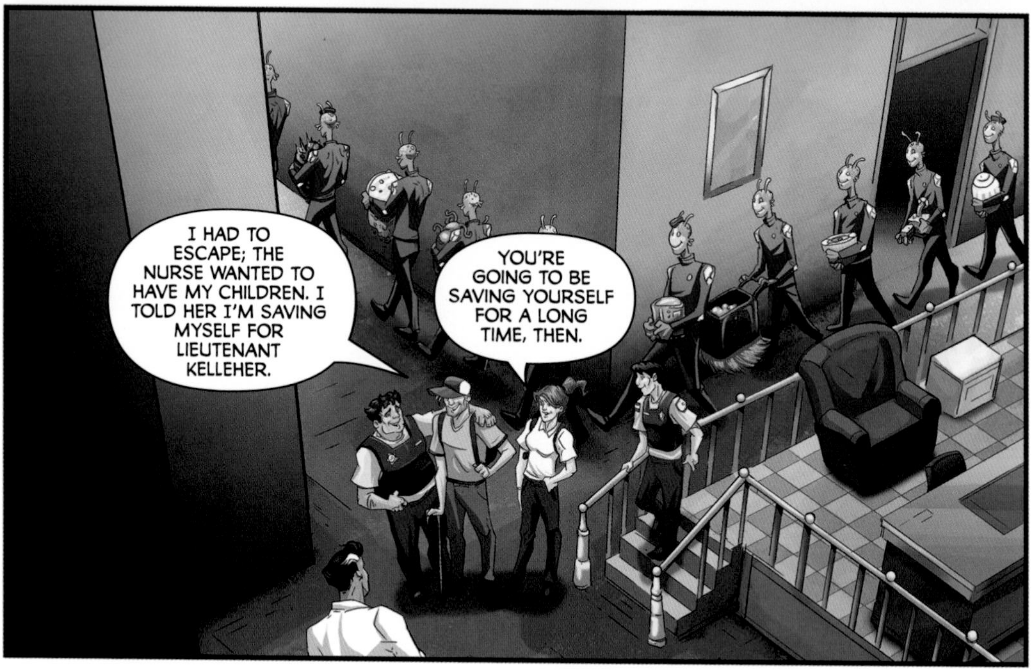
I HAD TO ESCAPE; THE NURSE WANTED TO HAVE MY CHILDREN. I TOLD HER I'M SAVING MYSELF FOR LIEUTENANT KELLEHER.
YOU'RE GOING TO BE SAVING YOURSELF FOR A LONG TIME, THEN.

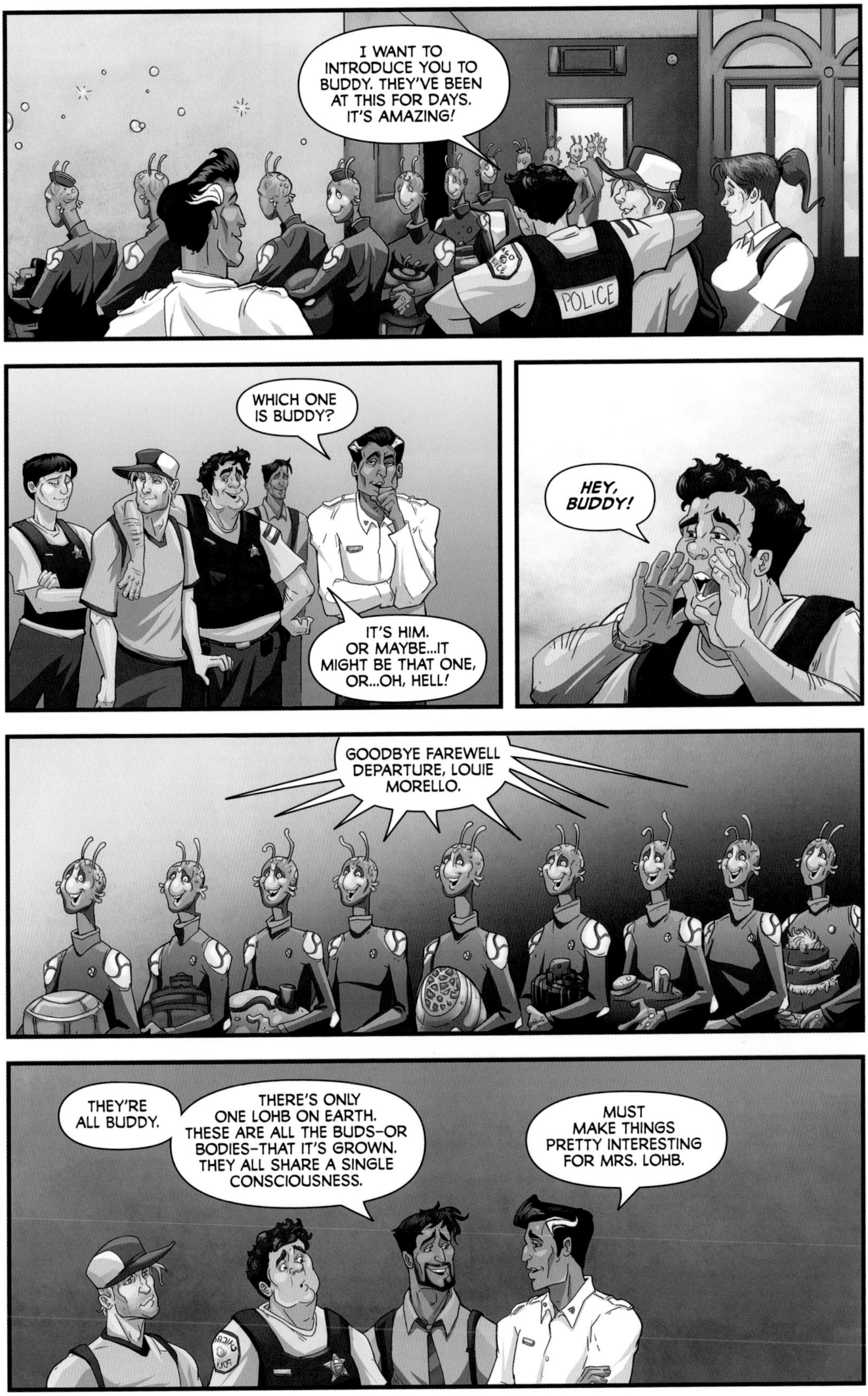
I WANT TO INTRODUCE YOU TO BUDDY. THEY'VE BEEN AT THIS FOR DAYS. IT'S AMAZING!
POLICE
WHICH ONE IS BUDDY?
IT'S HIM. OR MAYBE...IT MIGHT BE THAT ONE, OR...OH, HELL!
HEY, BUDDY!
GOODBYE FAREWELL DEPARTURE, LOUIE MORELLO.
THEY'RE ALL BUDDY.
THERE'S ONLY ONE LOHB ON EARTH. THESE ARE ALL THE BUDS–OR BODIES–THAT IT'S GROWN. THEY ALL SHARE A SINGLE CONSCIOUSNESS.
MUST MAKE THINGS PRETTY INTERESTING FOR MRS. LOHB.

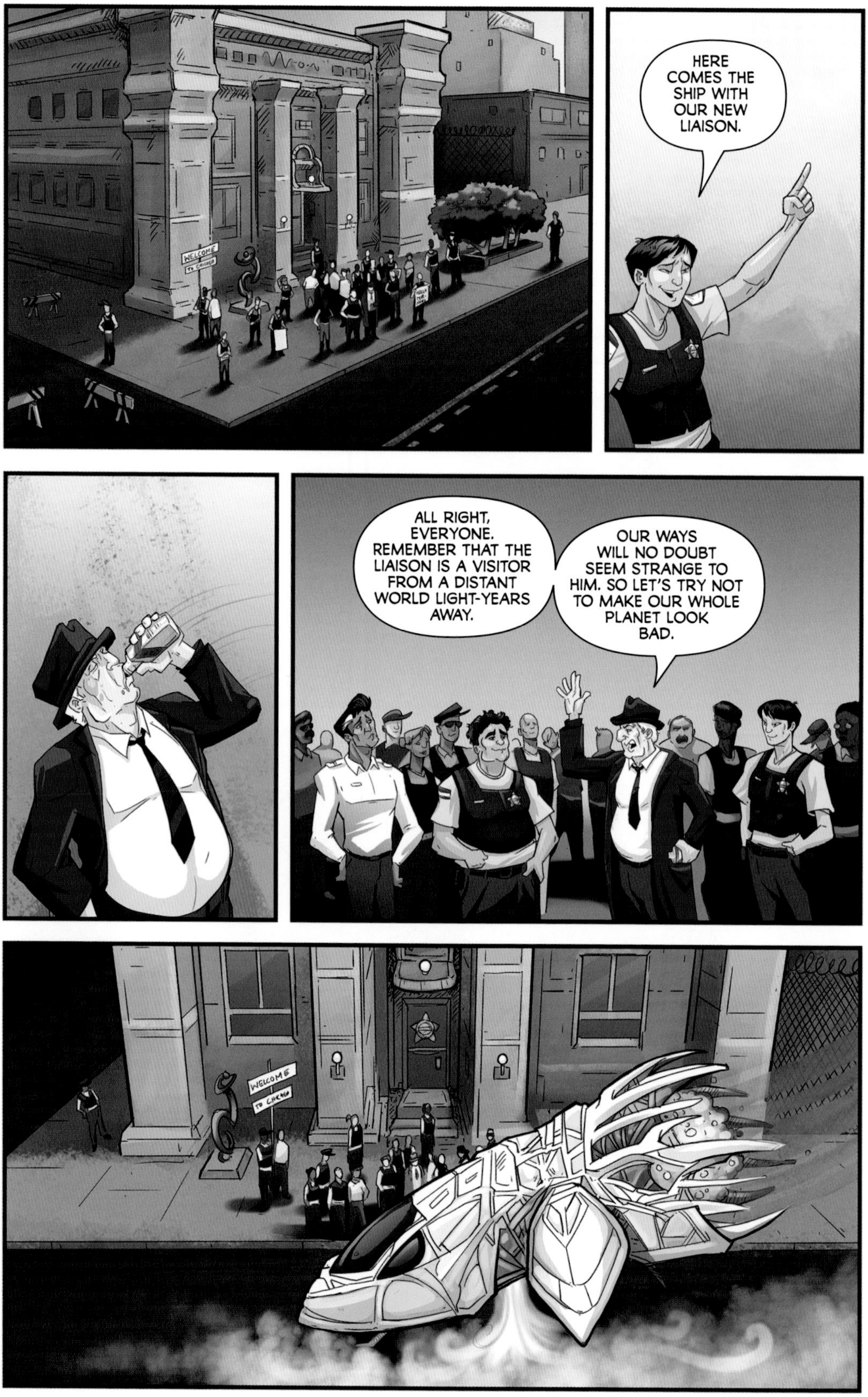
HERE COMES THE SHIP WITH OUR NEW LIAISON.
ALL RIGHT, EVERYONE. REMEMBER THAT THE LIAISON IS A VISITOR FROM A DISTANT WORLD LIGHT-YEARS AWAY.
OUR WAYS WILL NO DOUBT SEEM STRANGE TO HIM. SO LET'S TRY NOT TO MAKE OUR WHOLE PLANET LOOK BAD.

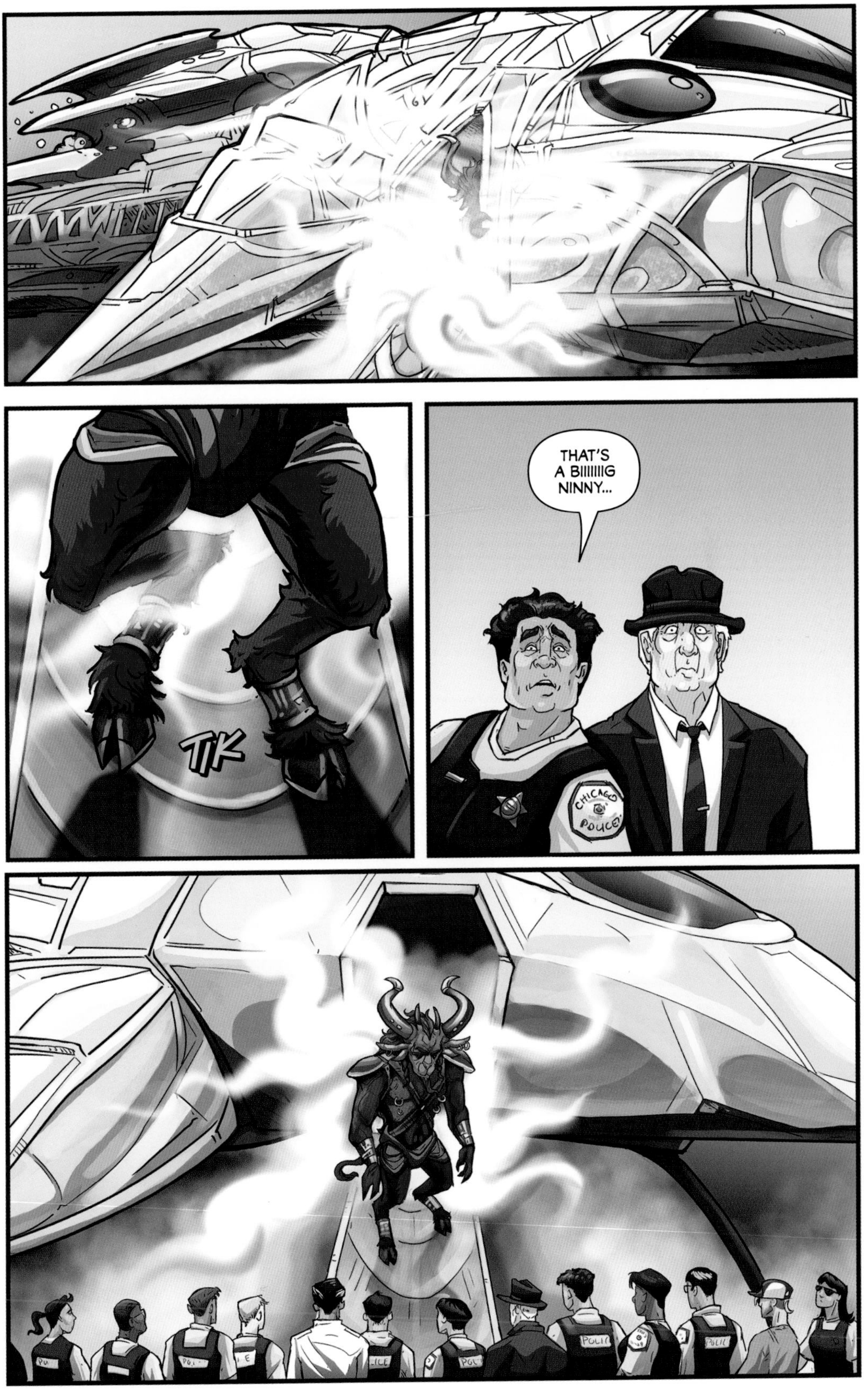
TK
THAT'S A BIIIIIIG NINNY...
CHICAGO POLICE

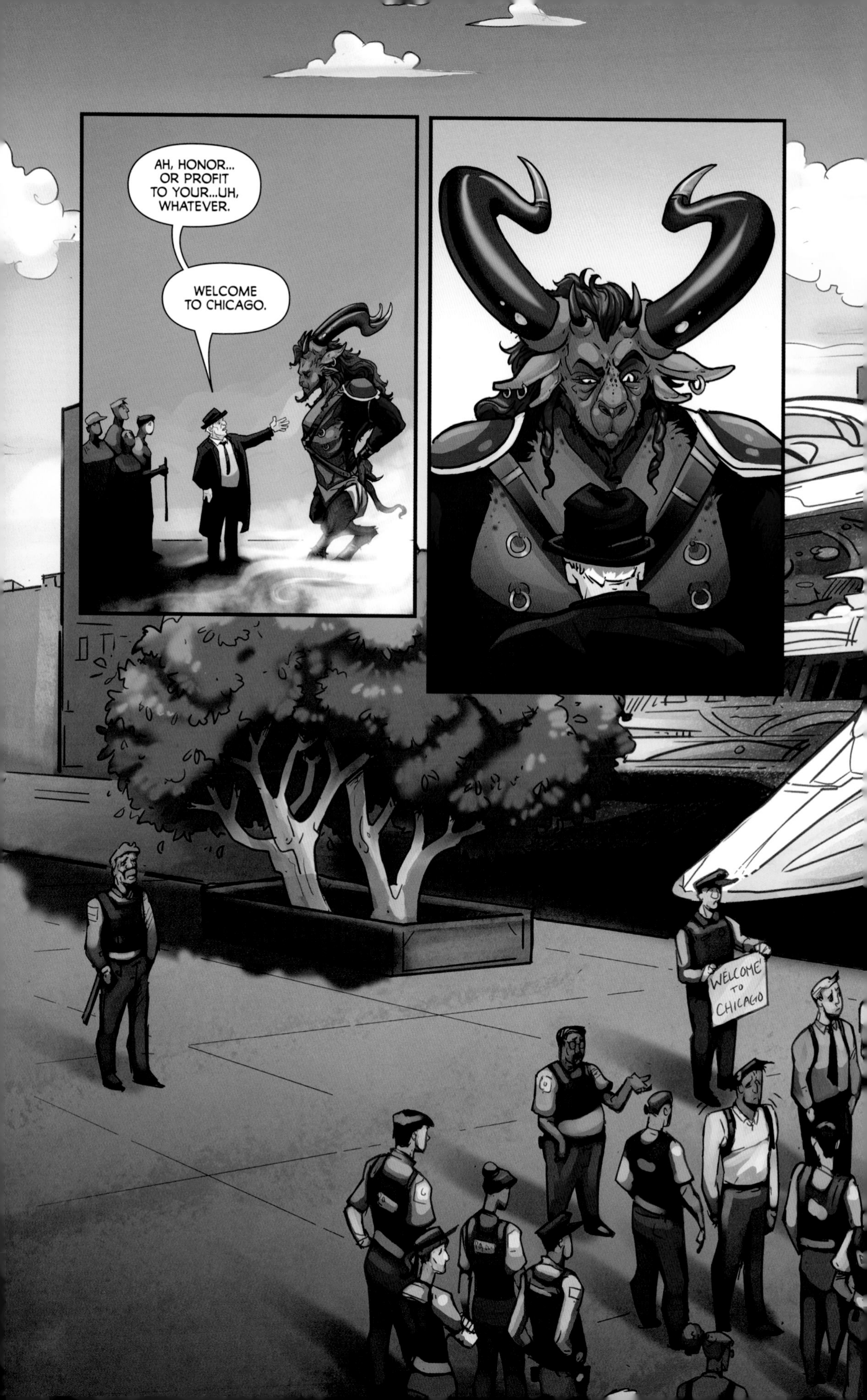
AH, HONOR... OR PROFIT TO YOUR...UH, WHATEVER.
WELCOME TO CHICAGO.
WELCOME TO CHICAGO

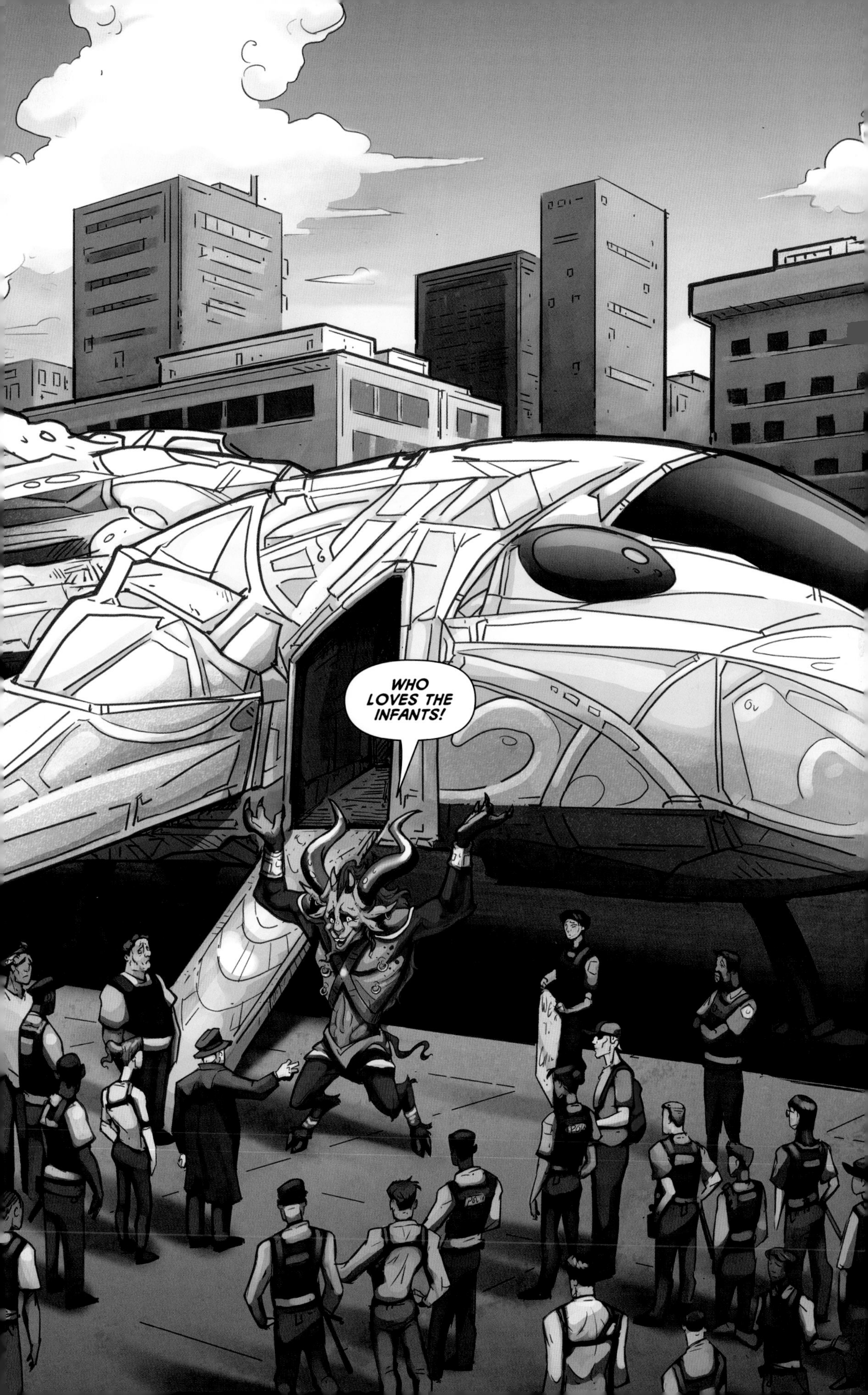
WHO LOVES THE INFANTS!

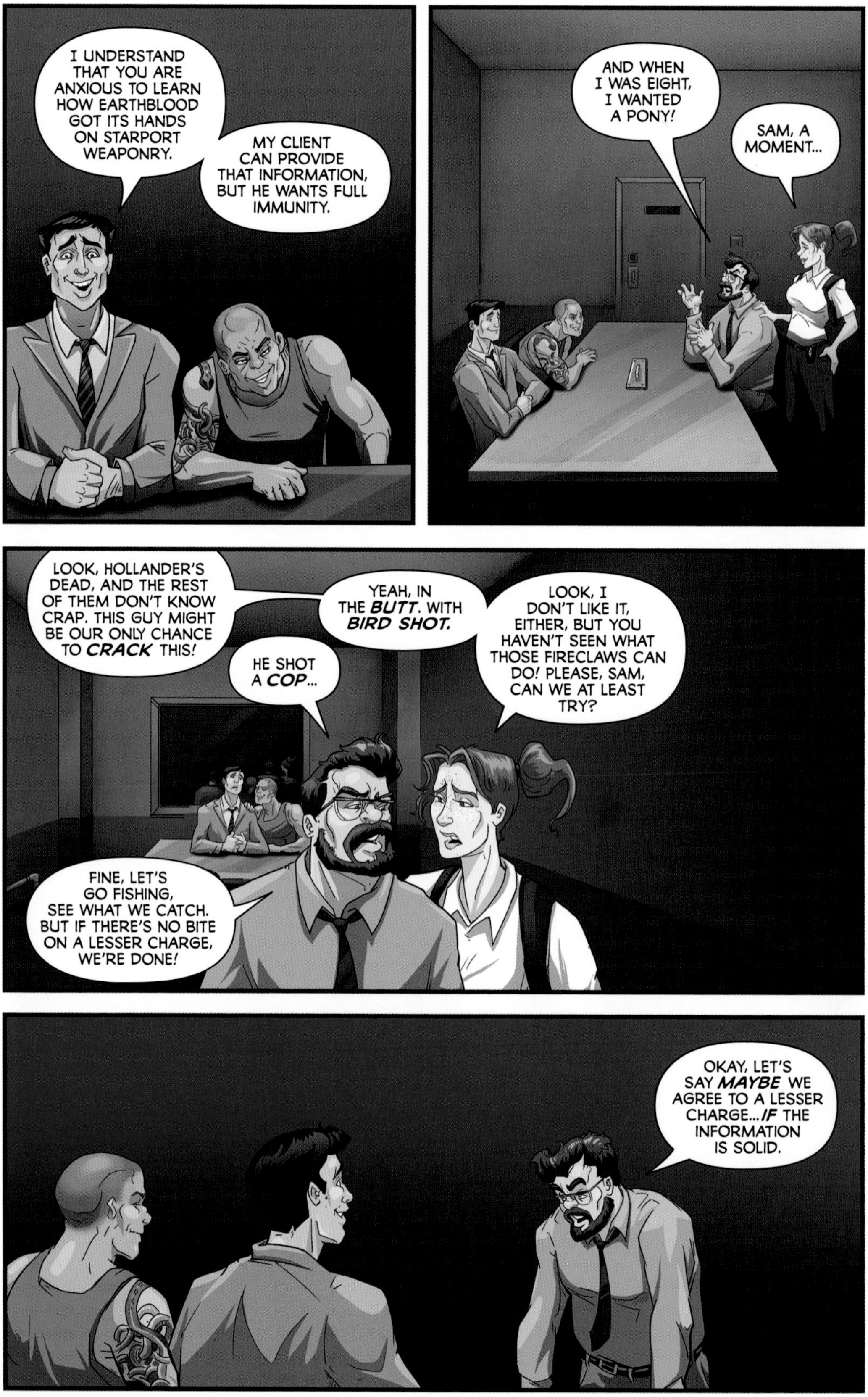
I UNDERSTAND THAT YOU ARE ANXIOUS TO LEARN HOW EARTHBLOOD GOT ITS HANDS ON STARPORT WEAPONRY.
MY CLIENT CAN PROVIDE THAT INFORMATION, BUT HE WANTS FULL IMMUNITY.
AND WHEN I WAS EIGHT, I WANTED A PONY!
SAM, A MOMENT...
LOOK, HOLLANDER'S DEAD, AND THE REST OF THEM DON'T KNOW CRAP. THIS GUY MIGHT BE OUR ONLY CHANCE TO **CRACK** THIS!
HE SHOT A **COP**...
YEAH, IN THE **BUTT**. WITH **BIRD SHOT.**
LOOK, I DON'T LIKE IT, EITHER, BUT YOU HAVEN'T SEEN WHAT THOSE FIRECLAWS CAN DO! PLEASE, SAM, CAN WE AT LEAST TRY?
FINE, LET'S GO FISHING, SEE WHAT WE CATCH. BUT IF THERE'S NO BITE ON A LESSER CHARGE, WE'RE DONE!
OKAY, LET'S SAY **MAYBE** WE AGREE TO A LESSER CHARGE...**IF** THE INFORMATION IS SOLID.

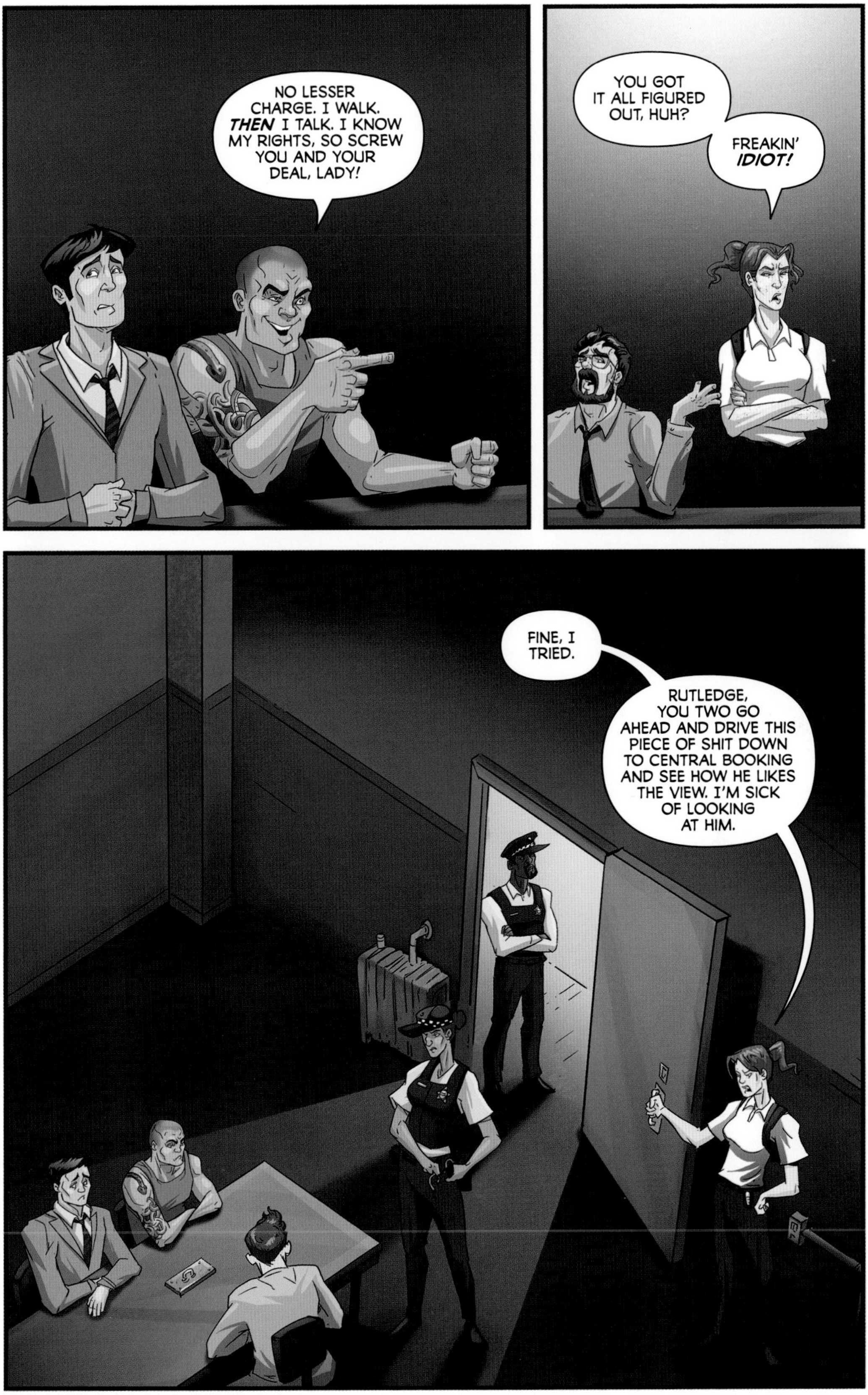
NO LESSER CHARGE. I WALK. *THEN* I TALK. I KNOW MY RIGHTS, SO SCREW YOU AND YOUR DEAL, LADY!
YOU GOT IT ALL FIGURED OUT, HUH?
FREAKIN' *IDIOT!*
FINE, I TRIED.
RUTLEDGE, YOU TWO GO AHEAD AND DRIVE THIS PIECE OF SHIT DOWN TO CENTRAL BOOKING AND SEE HOW HE LIKES THE VIEW. I'M SICK OF LOOKING AT HIM.

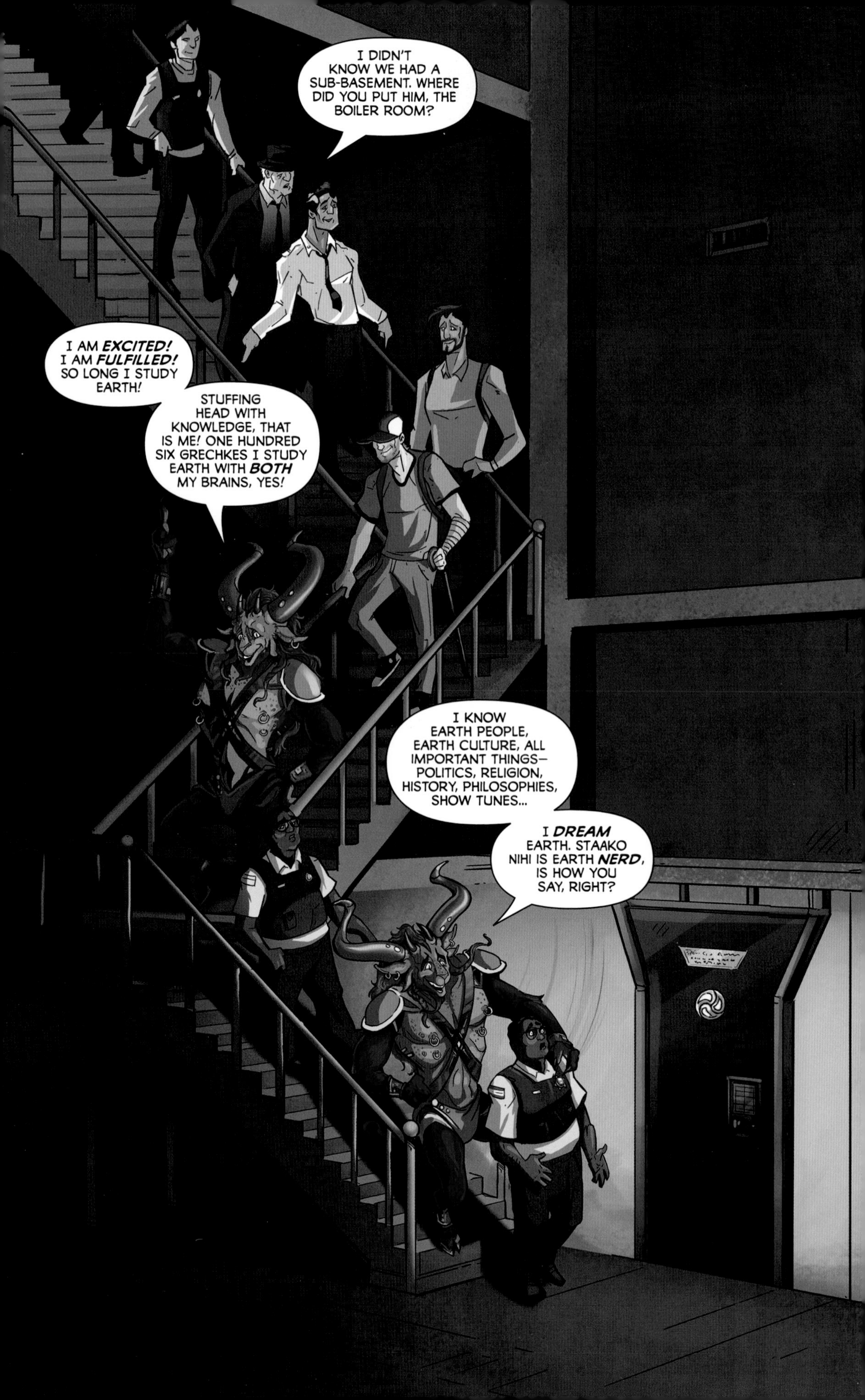
I DIDN'T KNOW WE HAD A SUB-BASEMENT. WHERE DID YOU PUT HIM, THE BOILER ROOM?
I AM *EXCITED!* I AM *FULFILLED!* SO LONG I STUDY EARTH!
STUFFING HEAD WITH KNOWLEDGE, THAT IS ME! ONE HUNDRED SIX GRECHKES I STUDY EARTH WITH *BOTH* MY BRAINS, YES!
I KNOW EARTH PEOPLE, EARTH CULTURE, ALL IMPORTANT THINGS— POLITICS, RELIGION, HISTORY, PHILOSOPHIES, SHOW TUNES...
I *DREAM* EARTH. STAAKO NIHI IS EARTH *NERD*, IS HOW YOU SAY, RIGHT?

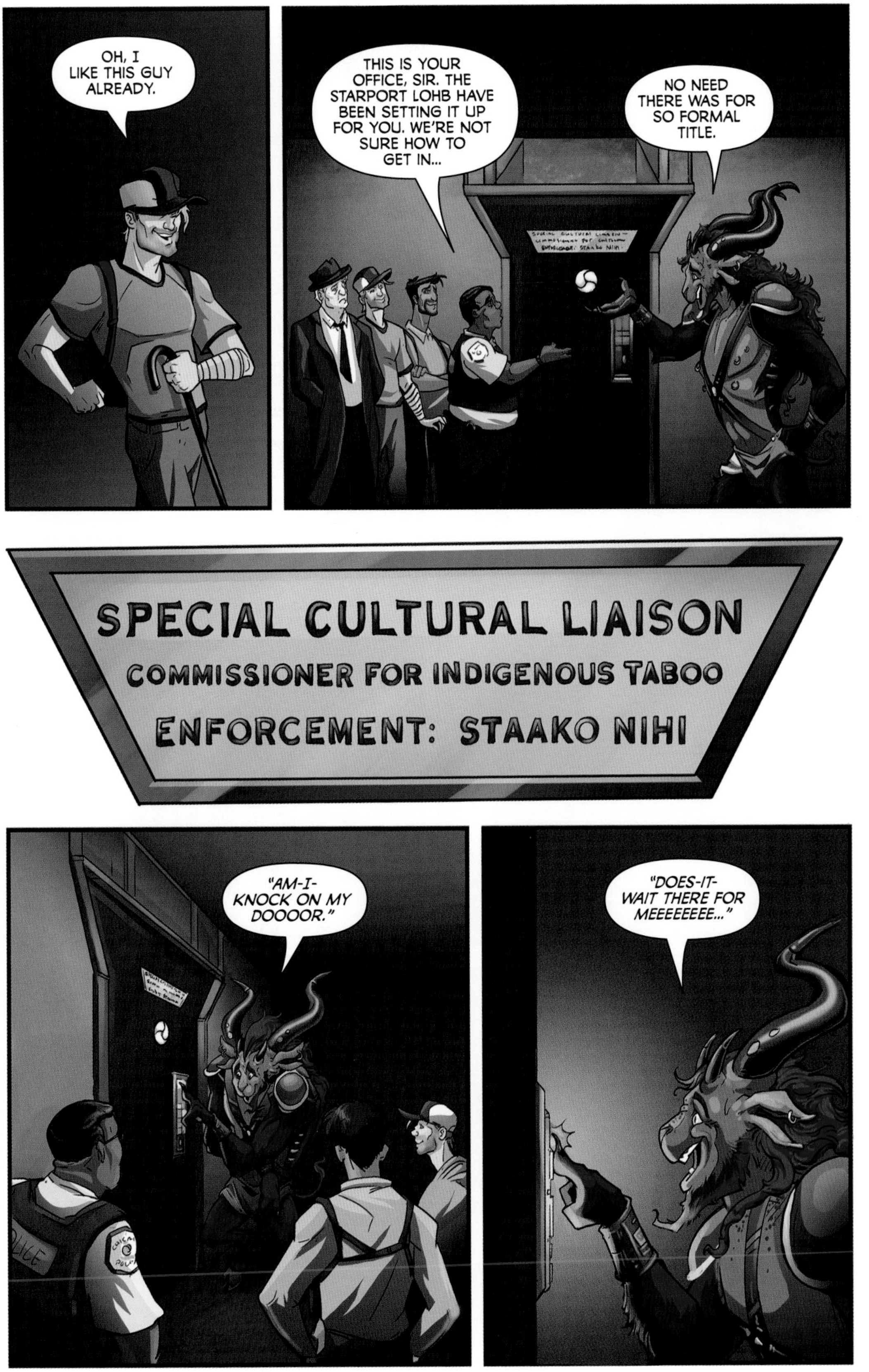
OH, I LIKE THIS GUY ALREADY.
THIS IS YOUR OFFICE, SIR. THE STARPORT LOHB HAVE BEEN SETTING IT UP FOR YOU. WE'RE NOT SURE HOW TO GET IN...
NO NEED THERE WAS FOR SO FORMAL TITLE.
SPECIAL CULTURAL LIAISON
COMMISSIONER FOR INDIGENOUS TABOO
ENFORCEMENT: STAAKO NIHI
"AM-I-KNOCK ON MY DOOOOR."
"DOES-IT-WAIT THERE FOR MEEEEEEEE..."

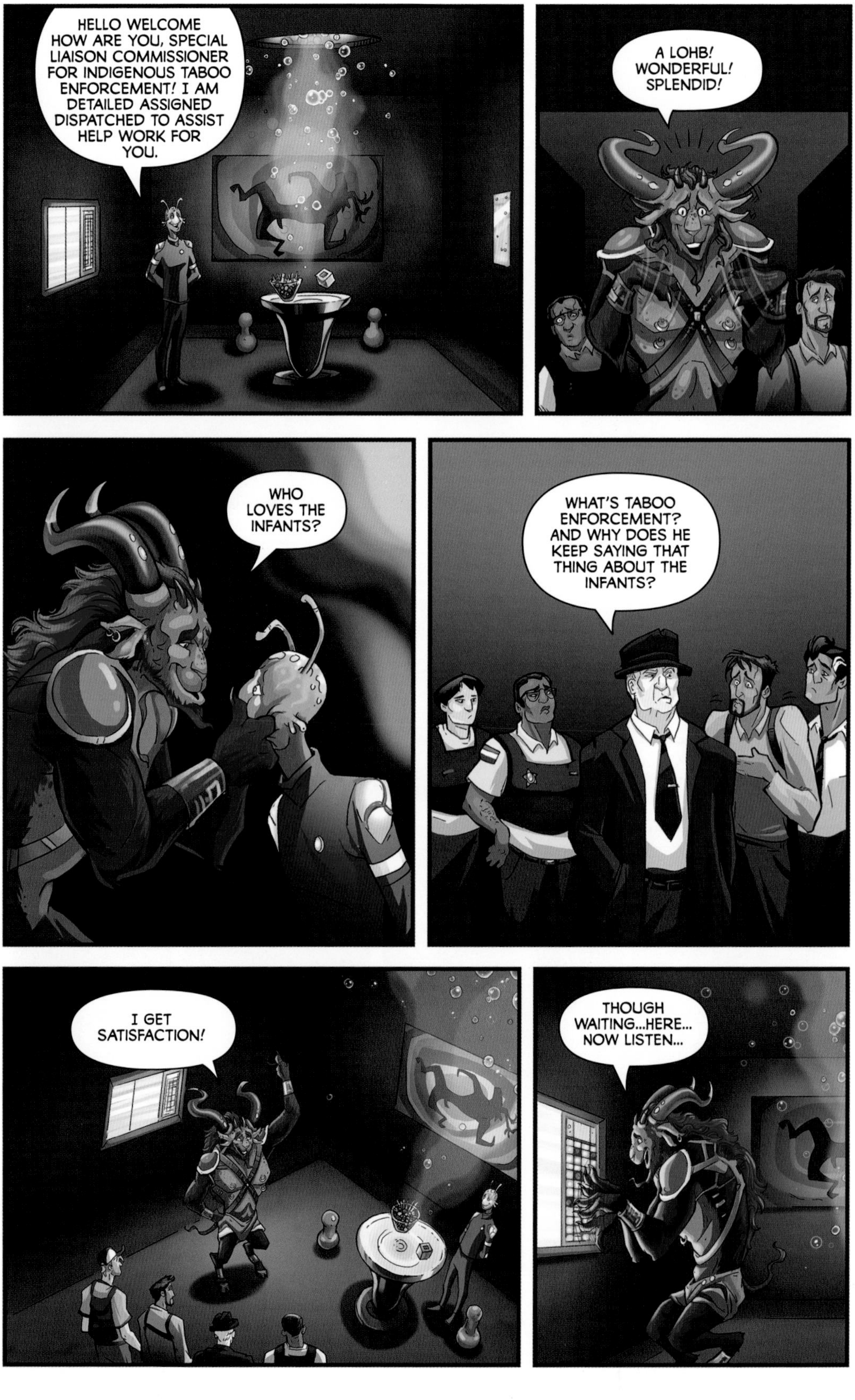
HELLO WELCOME HOW ARE YOU, SPECIAL LIAISON COMMISSIONER FOR INDIGENOUS TABOO ENFORCEMENT! I AM DETAILED ASSIGNED DISPATCHED TO ASSIST HELP WORK FOR YOU.
A LOHB! WONDERFUL! SPLENDID!
WHO LOVES THE INFANTS?
WHAT'S TABOO ENFORCEMENT? AND WHY DOES HE KEEP SAYING THAT THING ABOUT THE INFANTS?
I GET SATISFACTION!
THOUGH WAITING...HERE... NOW LISTEN...

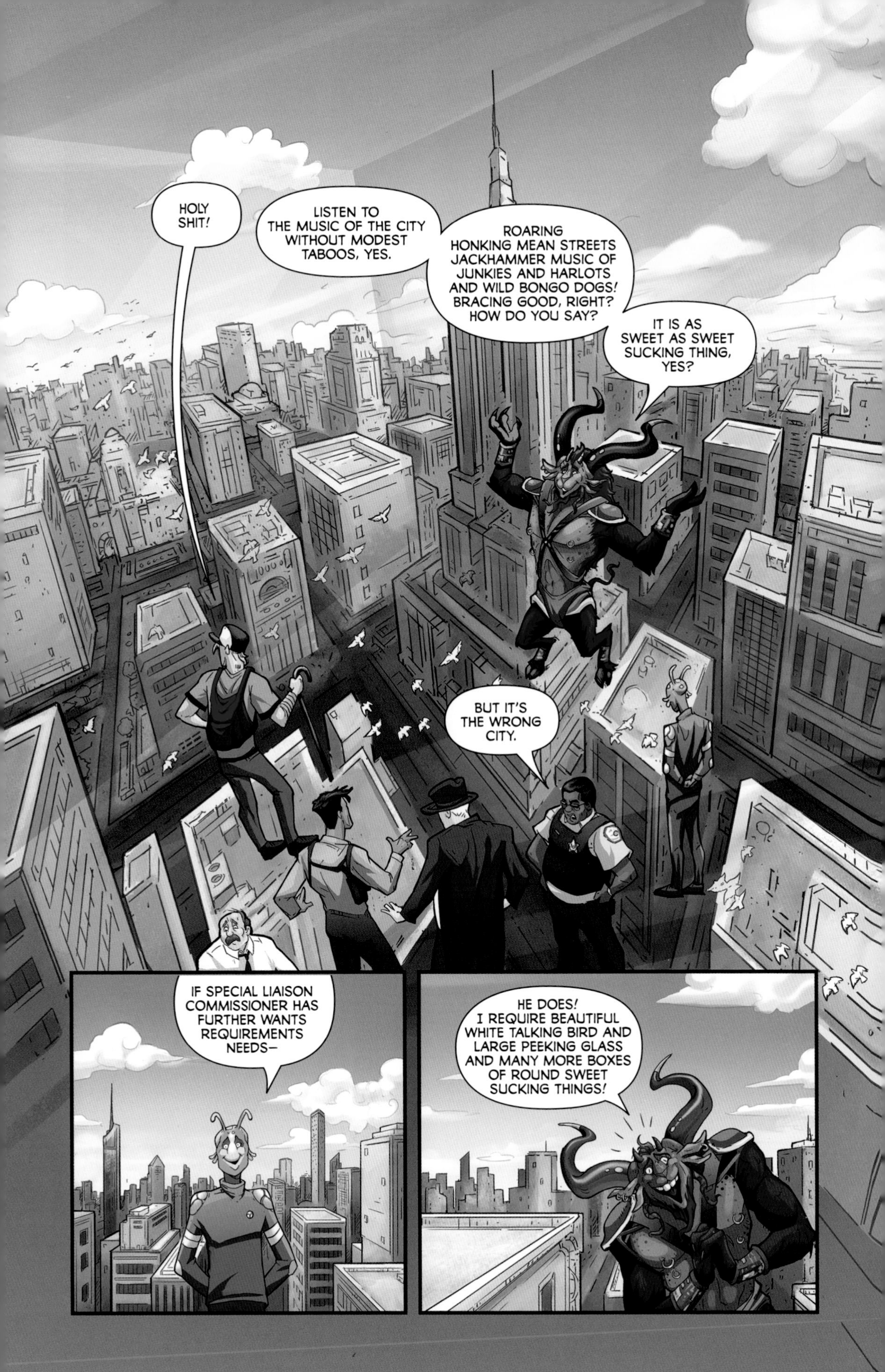
HOLY SHIT!
LISTEN TO THE MUSIC OF THE CITY WITHOUT MODEST TABOOS, YES.
ROARING HONKING MEAN STREETS JACKHAMMER MUSIC OF JUNKIES AND HARLOTS AND WILD BONGO DOGS! BRACING GOOD, RIGHT? HOW DO YOU SAY?
IT IS AS SWEET AS SWEET SUCKING THING, YES?
BUT IT'S THE WRONG CITY.
IF SPECIAL LIAISON COMMISSIONER HAS FURTHER WANTS REQUIREMENTS NEEDS—
HE DOES! I REQUIRE BEAUTIFUL WHITE TALKING BIRD AND LARGE PEEKING GLASS AND MANY MORE BOXES OF ROUND SWEET SUCKING THINGS!

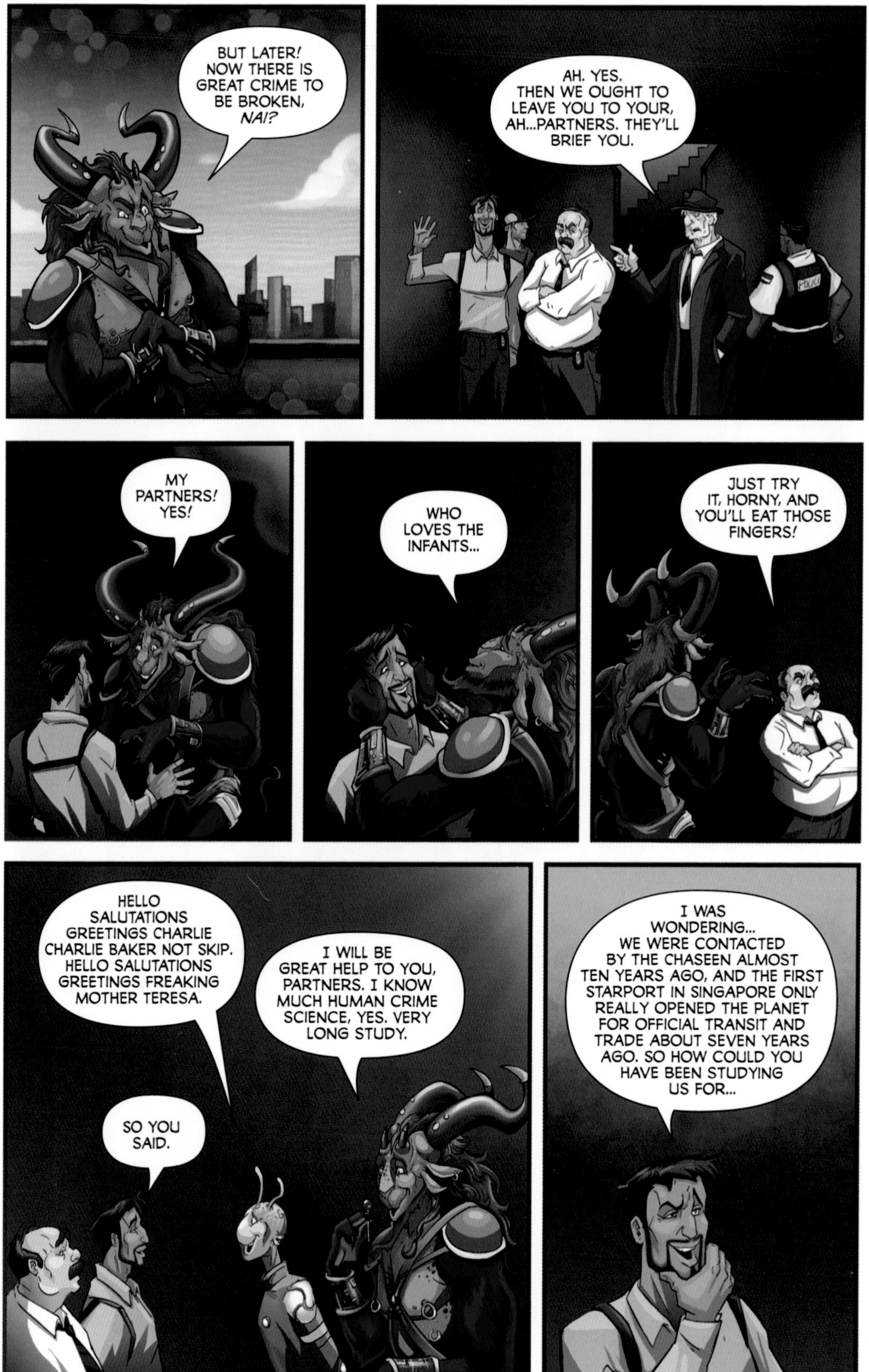
BUT LATER! NOW THERE IS GREAT CRIME TO BE BROKEN, *NAI*?
AH. YES. THEN WE OUGHT TO LEAVE YOU TO YOUR, AH...PARTNERS. THEY'LL BRIEF YOU.
POLICE
MY PARTNERS! YES!
WHO LOVES THE INFANTS...
JUST TRY IT, HORNY, AND YOU'LL EAT THOSE FINGERS!
HELLO SALUTATIONS GREETINGS CHARLIE CHARLIE BAKER NOT SKIP. HELLO SALUTATIONS GREETINGS FREAKING MOTHER TERESA.
I WILL BE GREAT HELP TO YOU, PARTNERS. I KNOW MUCH HUMAN CRIME SCIENCE, YES. VERY LONG STUDY.
SO YOU SAID.
I WAS WONDERING... WE WERE CONTACTED BY THE CHASEEN ALMOST TEN YEARS AGO, AND THE FIRST STARPORT IN SINGAPORE ONLY REALLY OPENED THE PLANET FOR OFFICIAL TRANSIT AND TRADE ABOUT SEVEN YEARS AGO. SO HOW COULD YOU HAVE BEEN STUDYING US FOR...

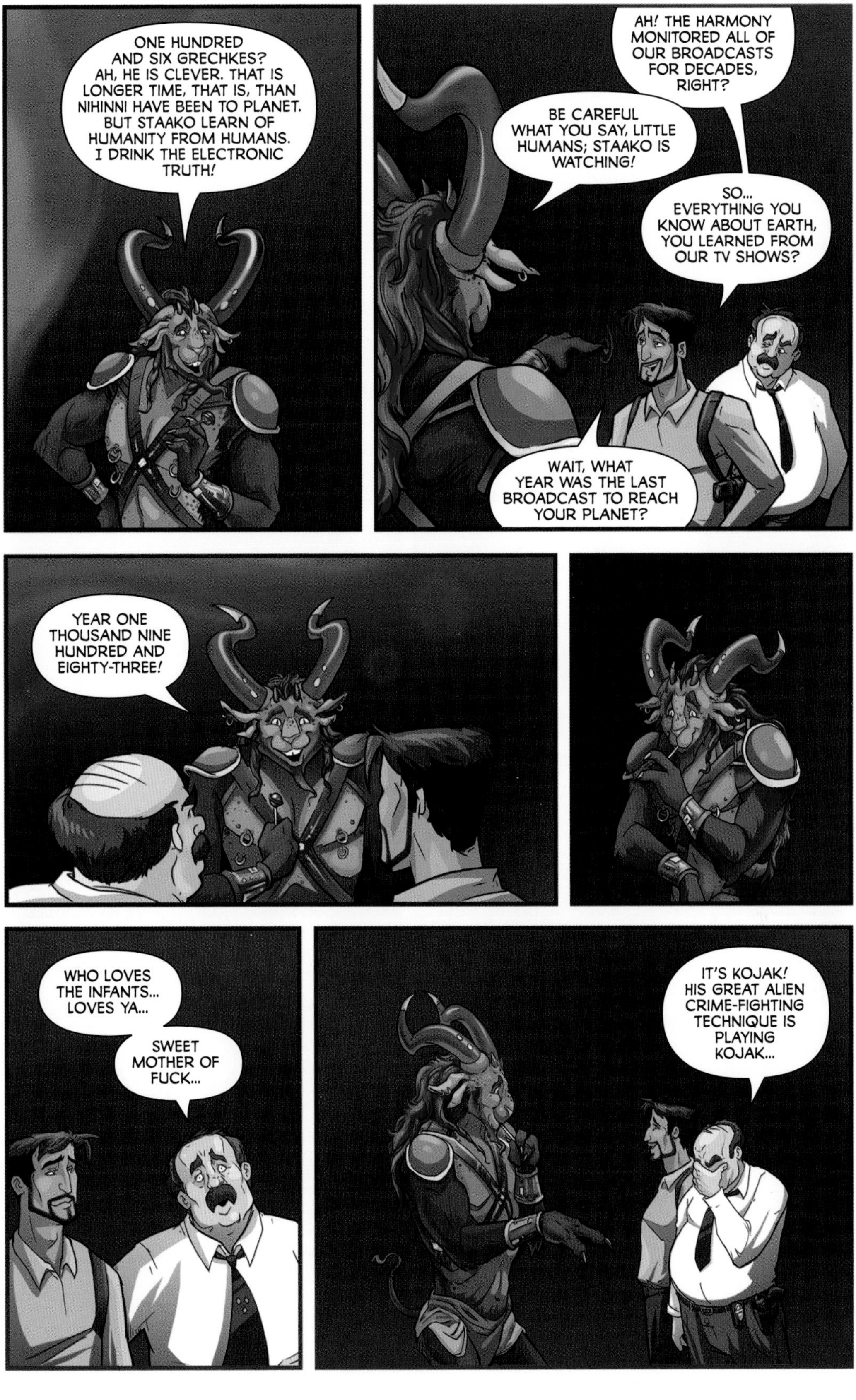
ONE HUNDRED AND SIX GRECHKES? AH, HE IS CLEVER. THAT IS LONGER TIME, THAT IS, THAN NIHINNI HAVE BEEN TO PLANET. BUT STAAKO LEARN OF HUMANITY FROM HUMANS. I DRINK THE ELECTRONIC TRUTH!
AH! THE HARMONY MONITORED ALL OF OUR BROADCASTS FOR DECADES, RIGHT?
BE CAREFUL WHAT YOU SAY, LITTLE HUMANS; STAAKO IS WATCHING!
SO... EVERYTHING YOU KNOW ABOUT EARTH, YOU LEARNED FROM OUR TV SHOWS?
WAIT, WHAT YEAR WAS THE LAST BROADCAST TO REACH YOUR PLANET?
YEAR ONE THOUSAND NINE HUNDRED AND EIGHTY-THREE!
WHO LOVES THE INFANTS... LOVES YA...
SWEET MOTHER OF FUCK...
IT'S KOJAK! HIS GREAT ALIEN CRIME-FIGHTING TECHNIQUE IS PLAYING KOJAK...

CHAPTER ELEVEN

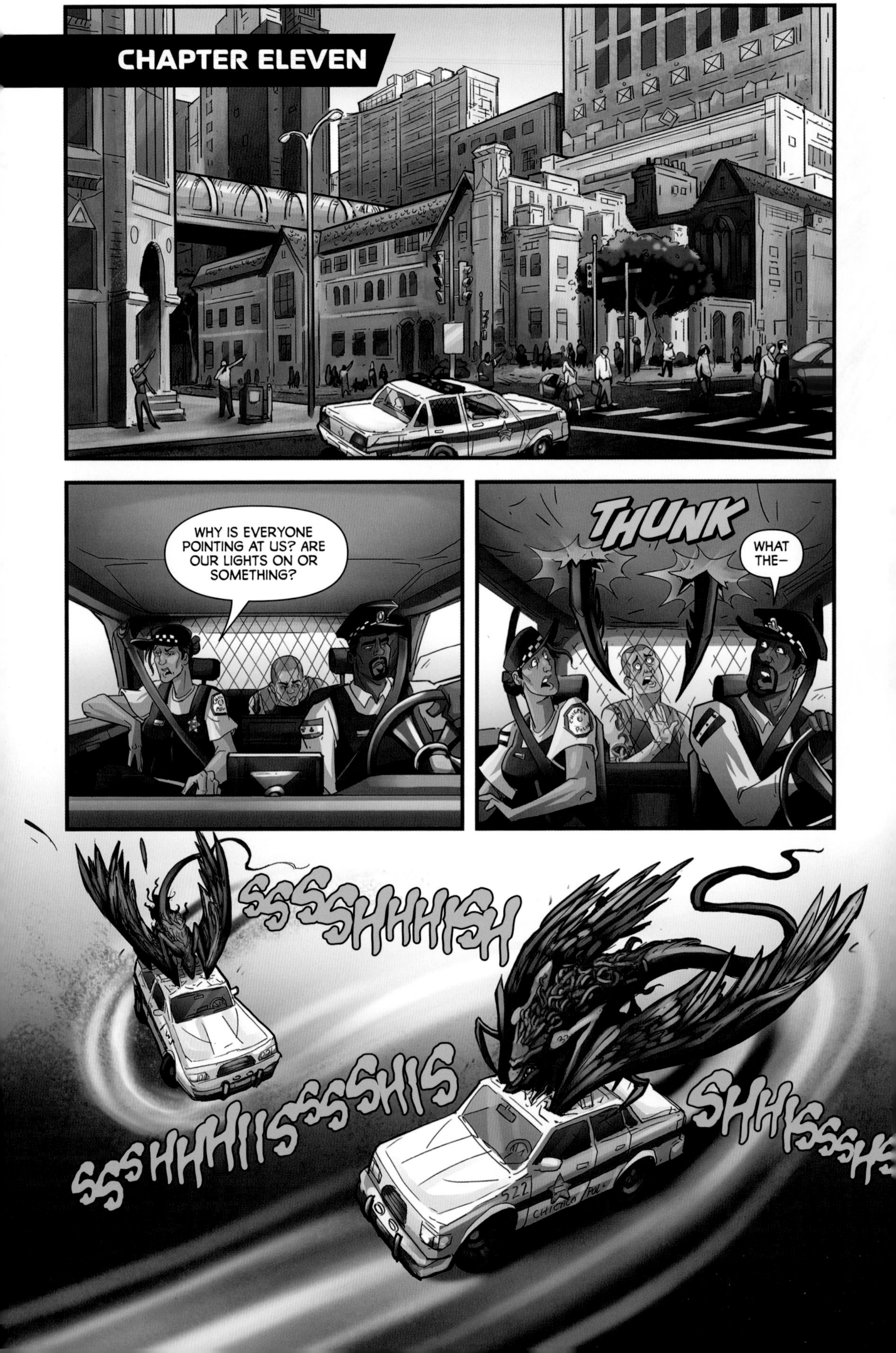
WHY IS EVERYONE POINTING AT US? ARE OUR LIGHTS ON OR SOMETHING?
THUNK
WHAT THE—
SSSSHHHISH
SSSHHHIISSSSHIS
SHHISSSHS

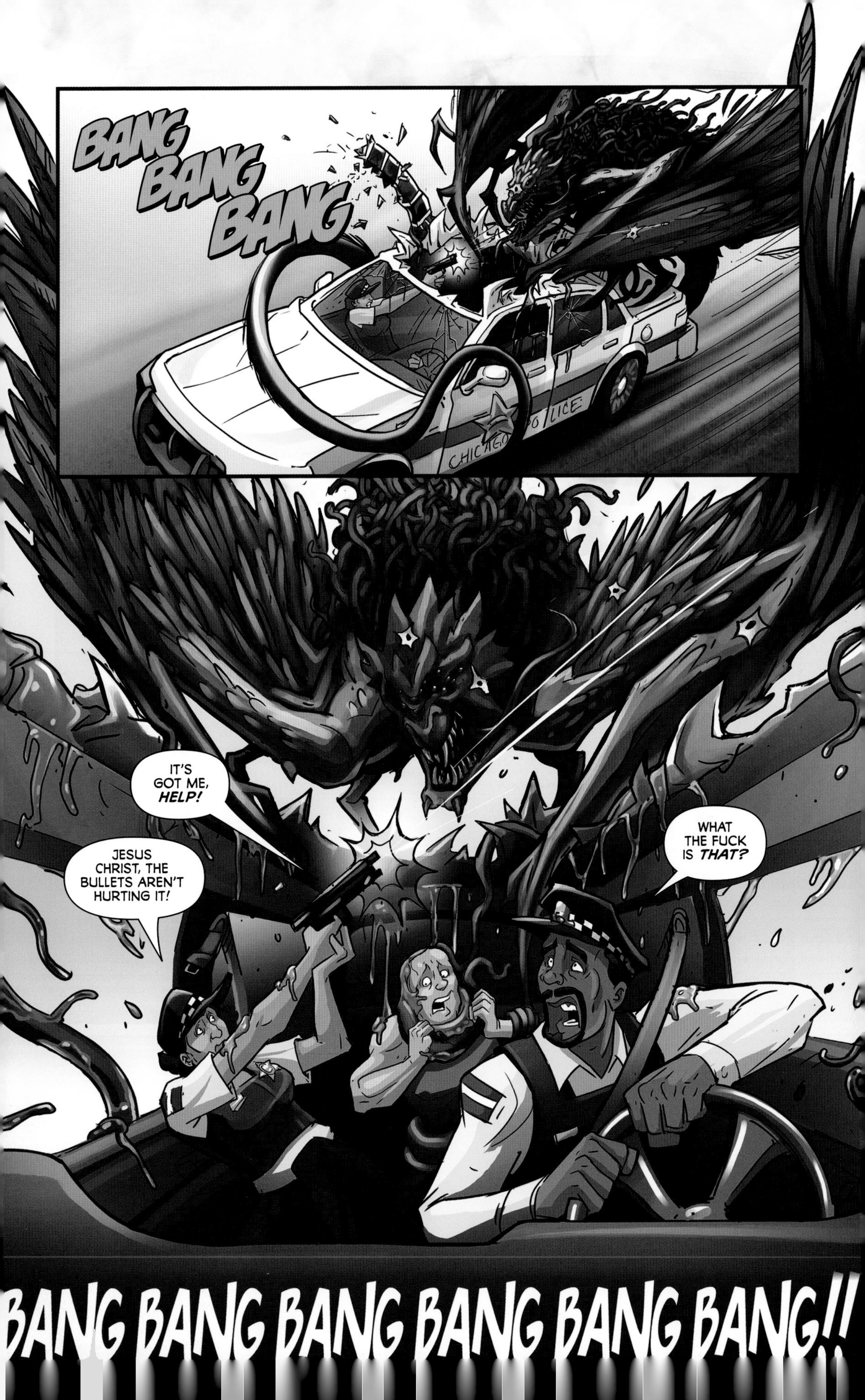
BANG BANG BANG
IT'S GOT ME, HELP!
JESUS CHRIST, THE BULLETS AREN'T HURTING IT!
WHAT THE FUCK IS THAT?
BANG BANG BANG BANG BANG BANG!!

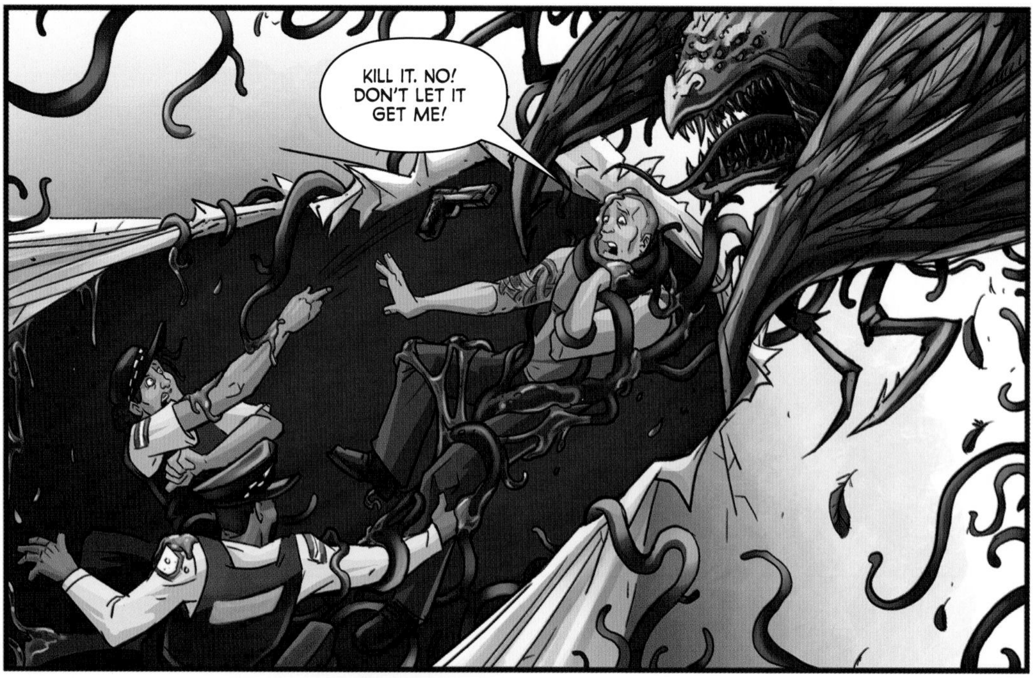
KILL IT. NO! DON'T LET IT GET ME!

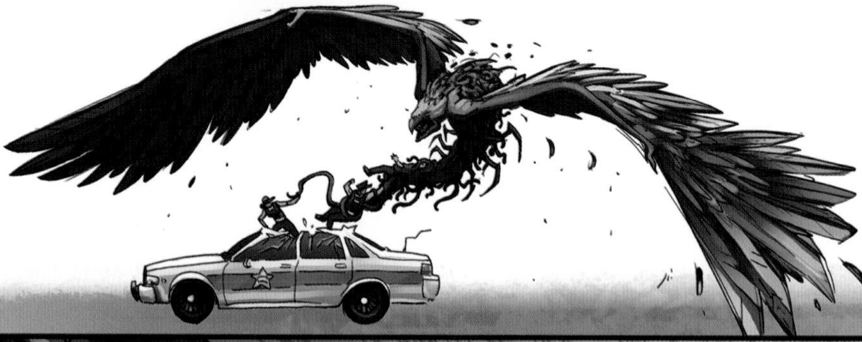

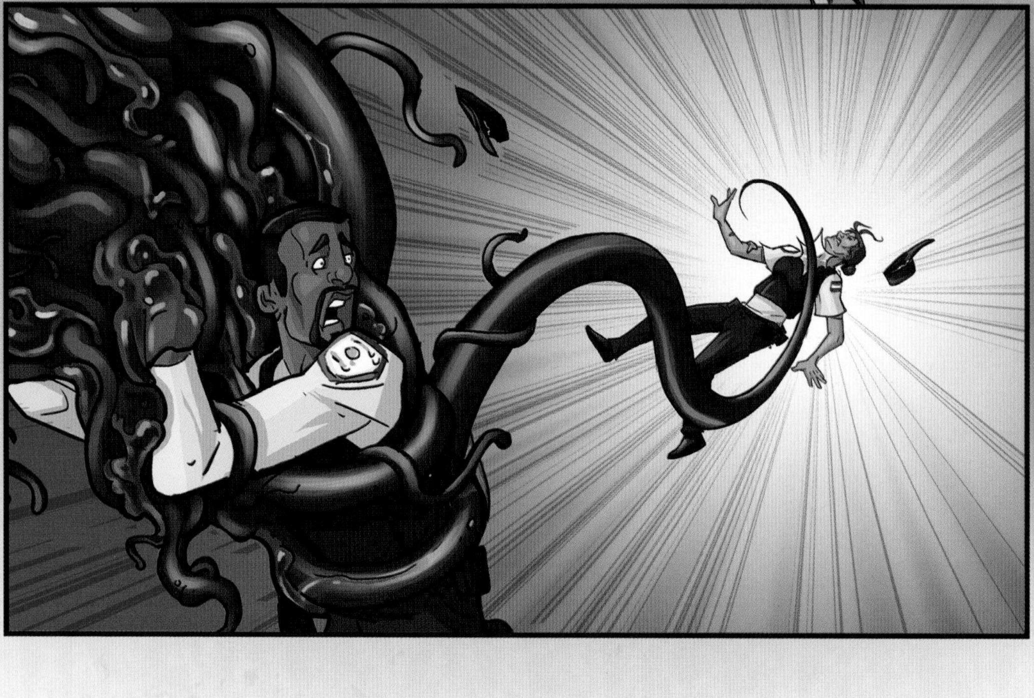

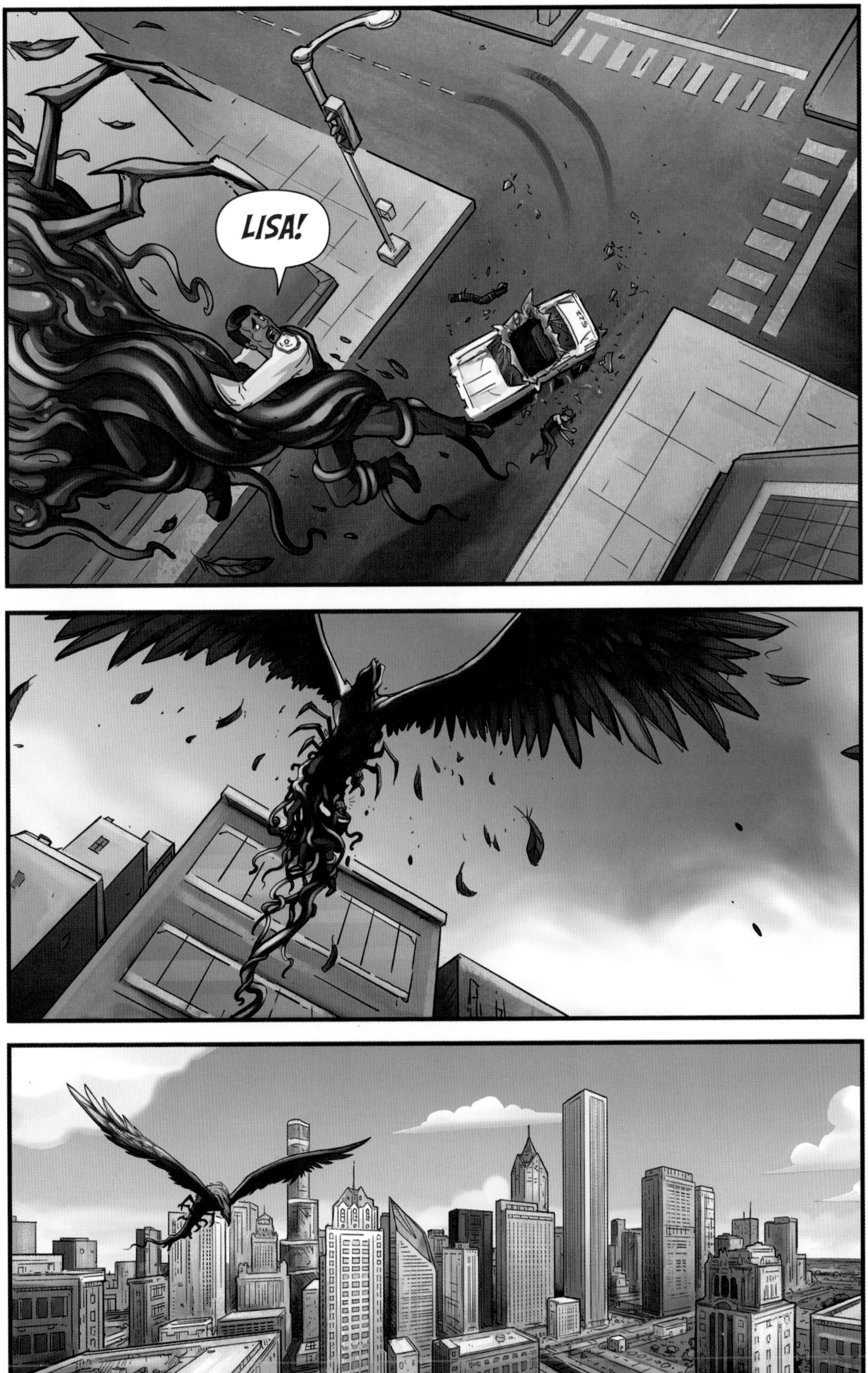
LISA!

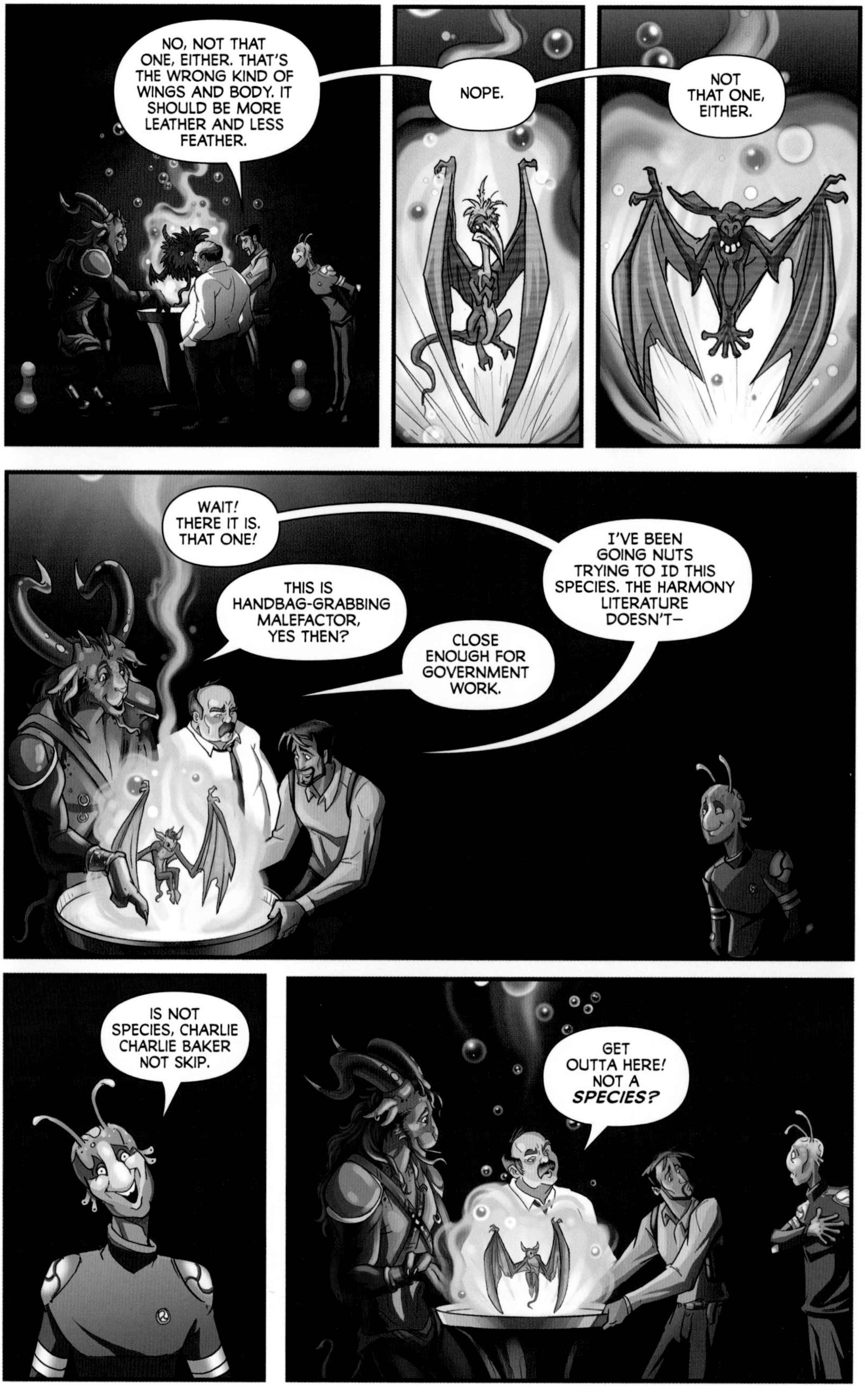
NO, NOT THAT ONE, EITHER. THAT'S THE WRONG KIND OF WINGS AND BODY. IT SHOULD BE MORE LEATHER AND LESS FEATHER.
NOPE.
NOT THAT ONE, EITHER.
WAIT! THERE IT IS. THAT ONE!
I'VE BEEN GOING NUTS TRYING TO ID THIS SPECIES. THE HARMONY LITERATURE DOESN'T—
THIS IS HANDBAG-GRABBING MALEFACTOR, YES THEN?
CLOSE ENOUGH FOR GOVERNMENT WORK.
IS NOT SPECIES, CHARLIE CHARLIE BAKER NOT SKIP.
GET OUTTA HERE! NOT A *SPECIES?*

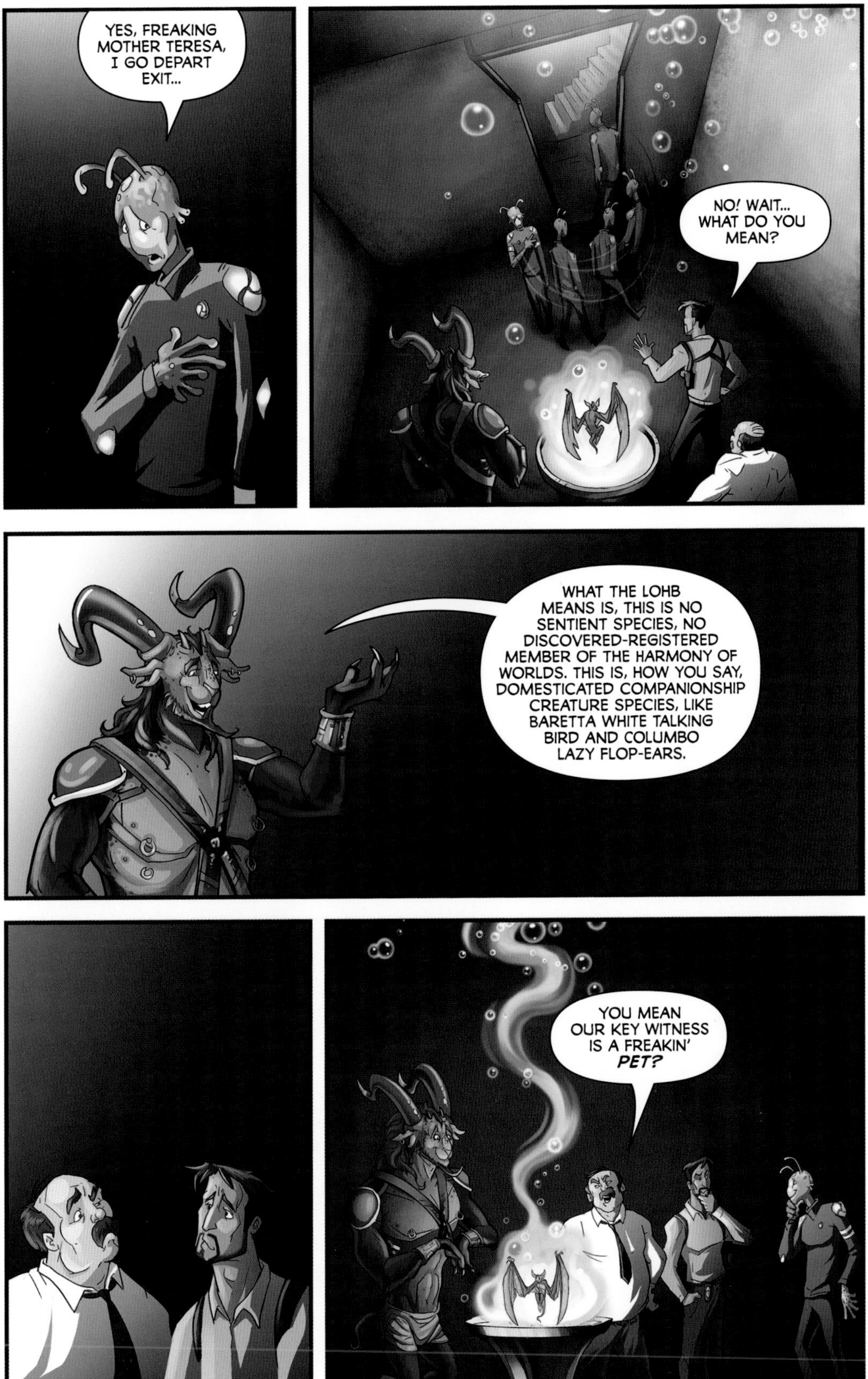
YES, FREAKING MOTHER TERESA, I GO DEPART EXIT...
NO! WAIT... WHAT DO YOU MEAN?
WHAT THE LOHB MEANS IS, THIS IS NO SENTIENT SPECIES, NO DISCOVERED-REGISTERED MEMBER OF THE HARMONY OF WORLDS. THIS IS, HOW YOU SAY, DOMESTICATED COMPANIONSHIP CREATURE SPECIES, LIKE BARETTA WHITE TALKING BIRD AND COLUMBO LAZY FLOP-EARS.
YOU MEAN OUR KEY WITNESS IS A FREAKIN' *PET?*

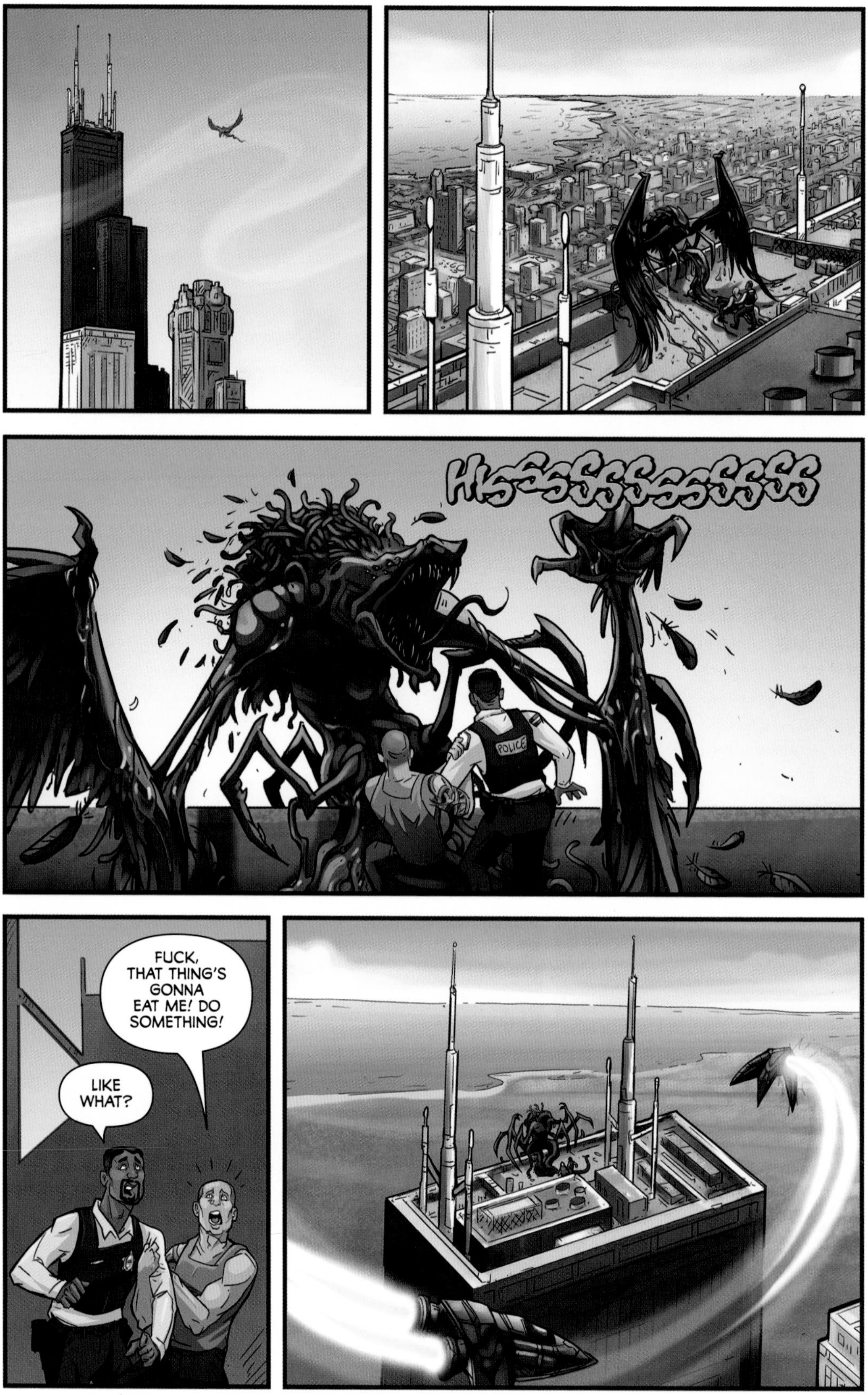
HISSSSSSSSSSSS
FUCK, THAT THING'S GONNA EAT ME! DO SOMETHING!
LIKE WHAT?
POLICE

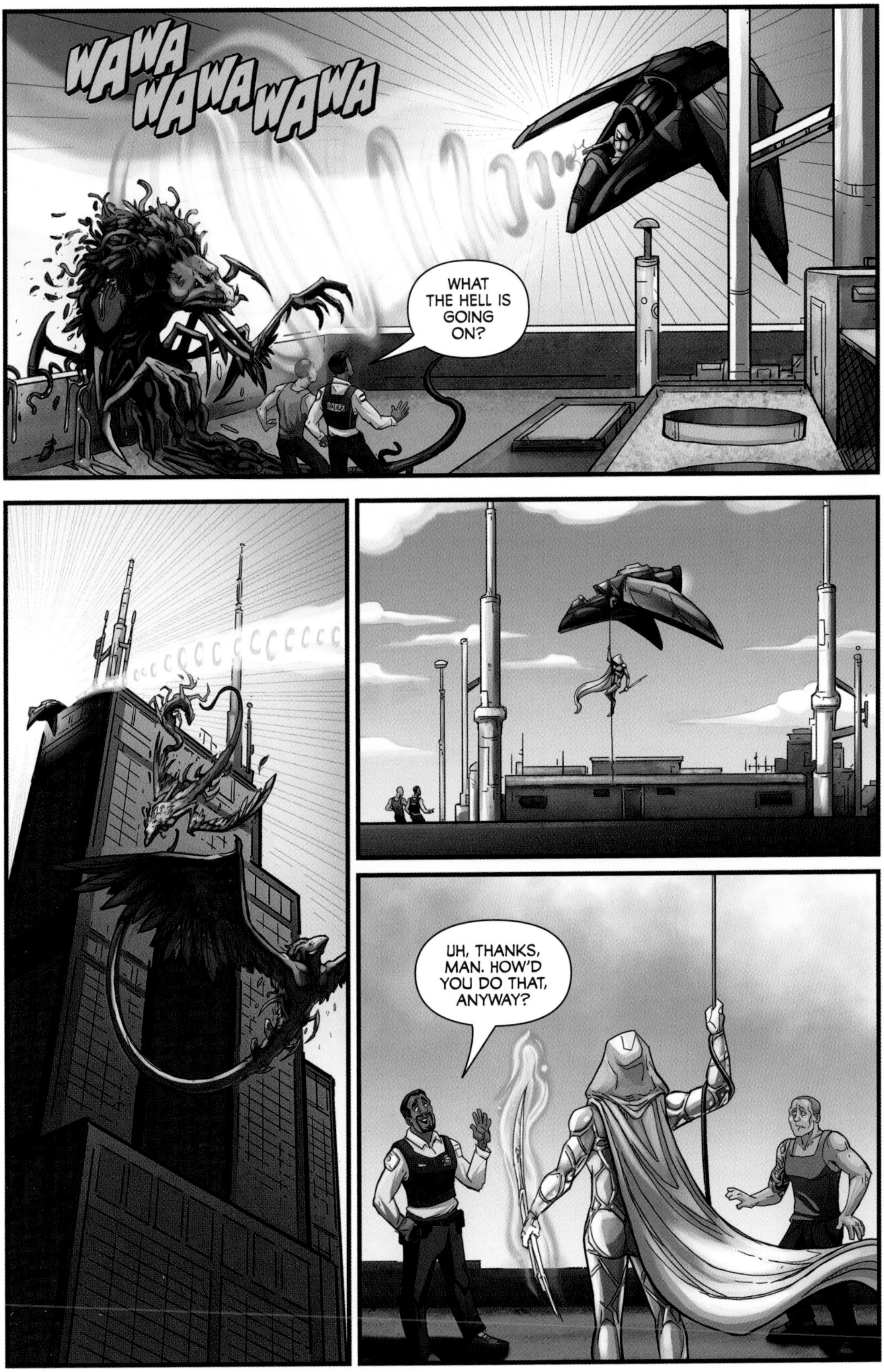
WAWA WAWA WAWA
WHAT THE HELL IS GOING ON?
UH, THANKS, MAN. HOW'D YOU DO THAT, ANYWAY?

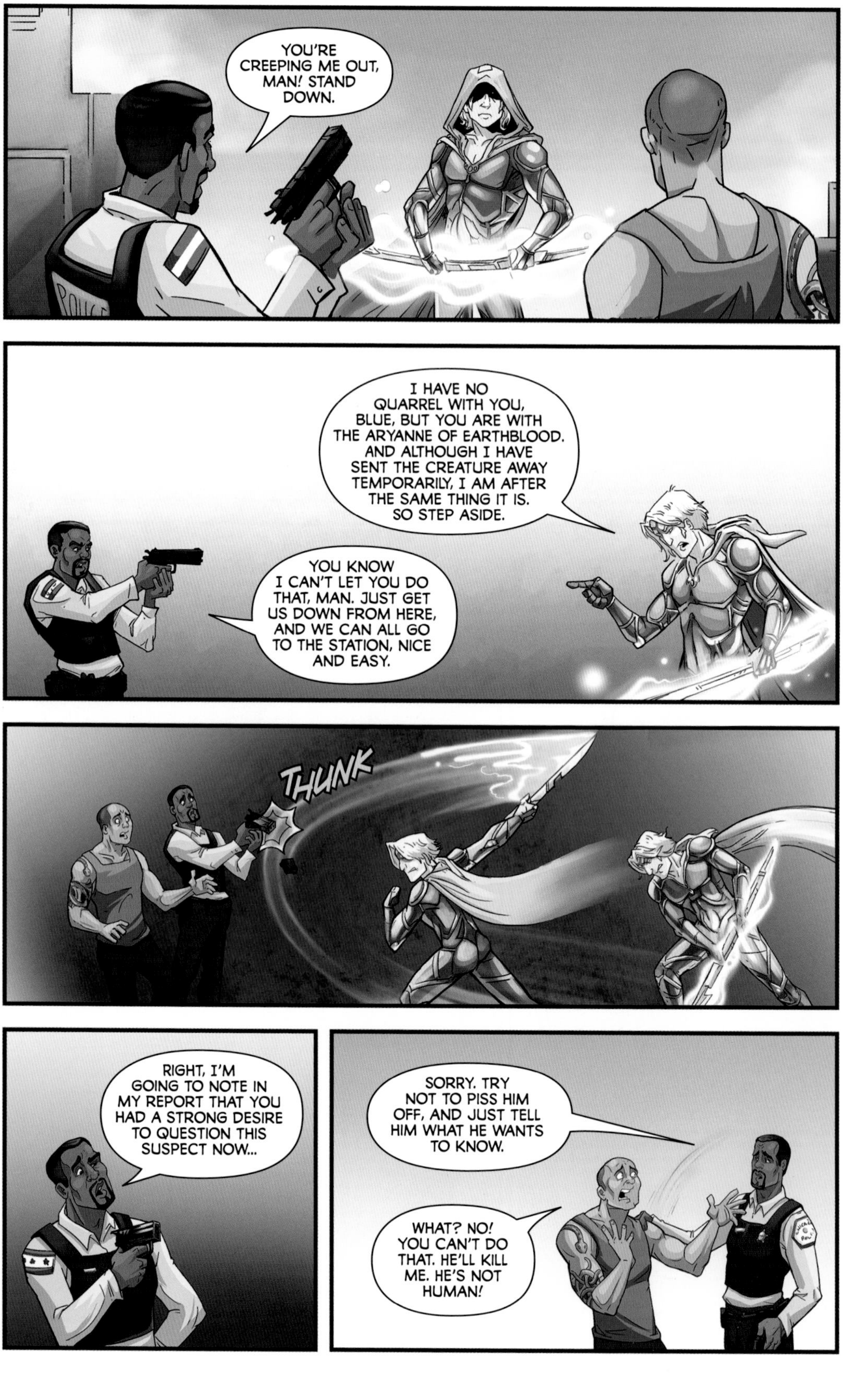
YOU'RE CREEPING ME OUT, MAN! STAND DOWN.
I HAVE NO QUARREL WITH YOU, BLUE, BUT YOU ARE WITH THE ARYANNE OF EARTHBLOOD. AND ALTHOUGH I HAVE SENT THE CREATURE AWAY TEMPORARILY, I AM AFTER THE SAME THING IT IS. SO STEP ASIDE.
YOU KNOW I CAN'T LET YOU DO THAT, MAN. JUST GET US DOWN FROM HERE, AND WE CAN ALL GO TO THE STATION, NICE AND EASY.
THUNK
RIGHT, I'M GOING TO NOTE IN MY REPORT THAT YOU HAD A STRONG DESIRE TO QUESTION THIS SUSPECT NOW...
SORRY. TRY NOT TO PISS HIM OFF, AND JUST TELL HIM WHAT HE WANTS TO KNOW.
WHAT? NO! YOU CAN'T DO THAT. HE'LL KILL ME. HE'S NOT HUMAN!

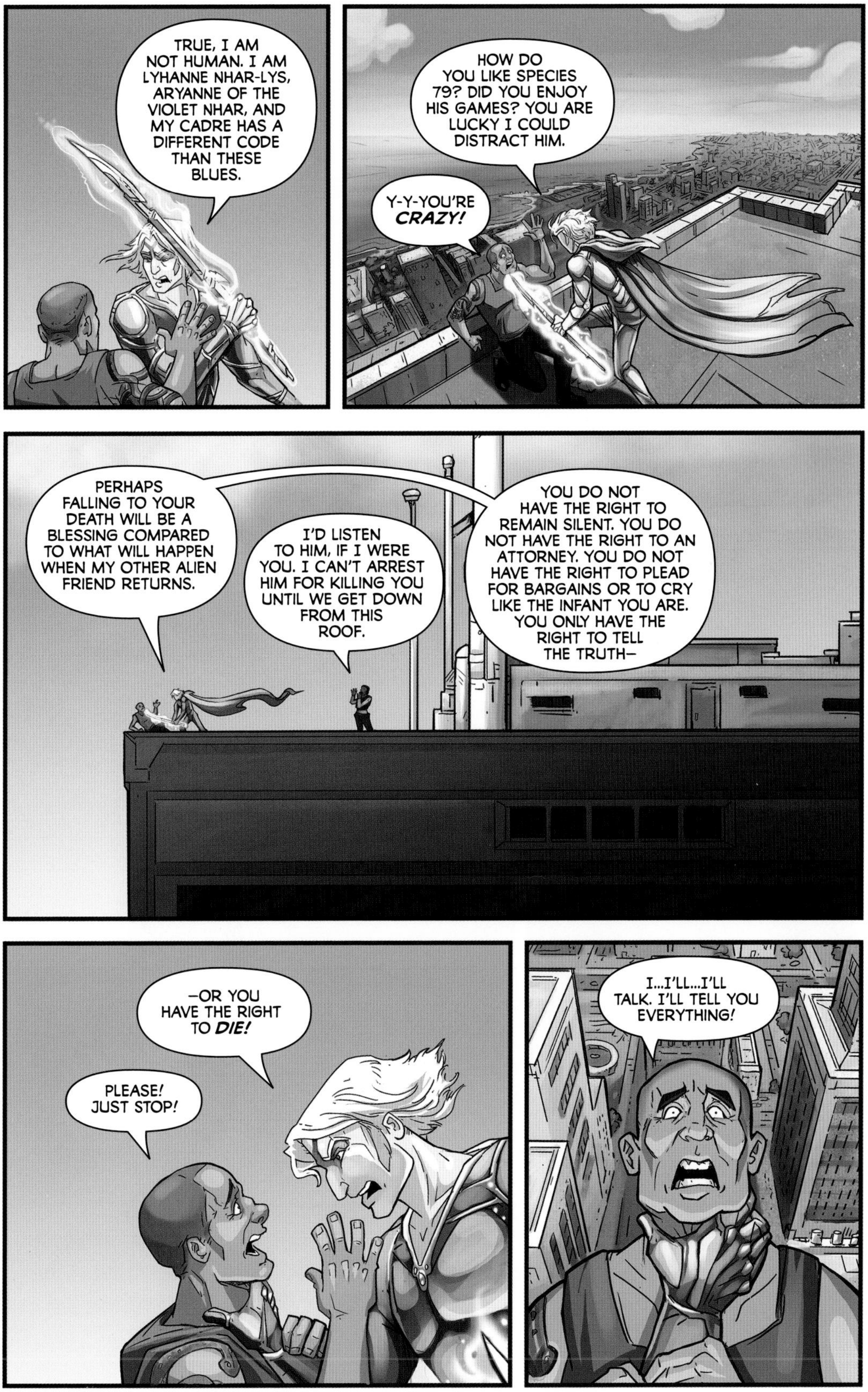
TRUE, I AM NOT HUMAN. I AM LYHANNE NHAR-LYS, ARYANNE OF THE VIOLET NHAR, AND MY CADRE HAS A DIFFERENT CODE THAN THESE BLUES.
HOW DO YOU LIKE SPECIES 79? DID YOU ENJOY HIS GAMES? YOU ARE LUCKY I COULD DISTRACT HIM.
Y-Y-YOU'RE *CRAZY!*
PERHAPS FALLING TO YOUR DEATH WILL BE A BLESSING COMPARED TO WHAT WILL HAPPEN WHEN MY OTHER ALIEN FRIEND RETURNS.
I'D LISTEN TO HIM, IF I WERE YOU. I CAN'T ARREST HIM FOR KILLING YOU UNTIL WE GET DOWN FROM THIS ROOF.
YOU DO NOT HAVE THE RIGHT TO REMAIN SILENT. YOU DO NOT HAVE THE RIGHT TO AN ATTORNEY. YOU DO NOT HAVE THE RIGHT TO PLEAD FOR BARGAINS OR TO CRY LIKE THE INFANT YOU ARE. YOU ONLY HAVE THE RIGHT TO TELL THE TRUTH—
—OR YOU HAVE THE RIGHT TO *DIE!*
PLEASE! JUST STOP!
I...I'LL...I'LL TALK. I'LL TELL YOU EVERYTHING!

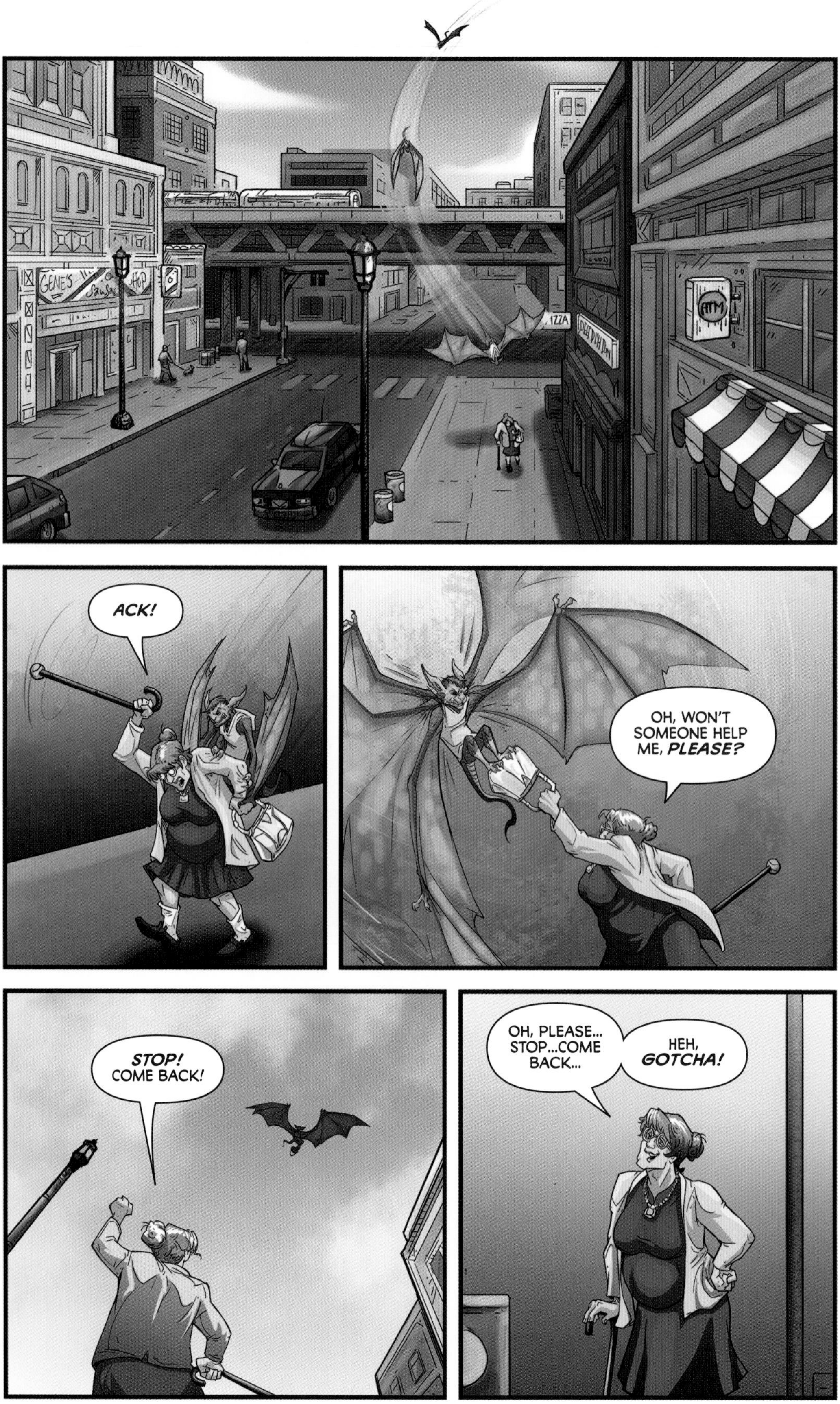
ATM
ACK!
OH, WON'T SOMEONE HELP ME, *PLEASE?*
STOP! COME BACK!
OH, PLEASE... STOP...COME BACK...
HEH, *GOTCHA!*

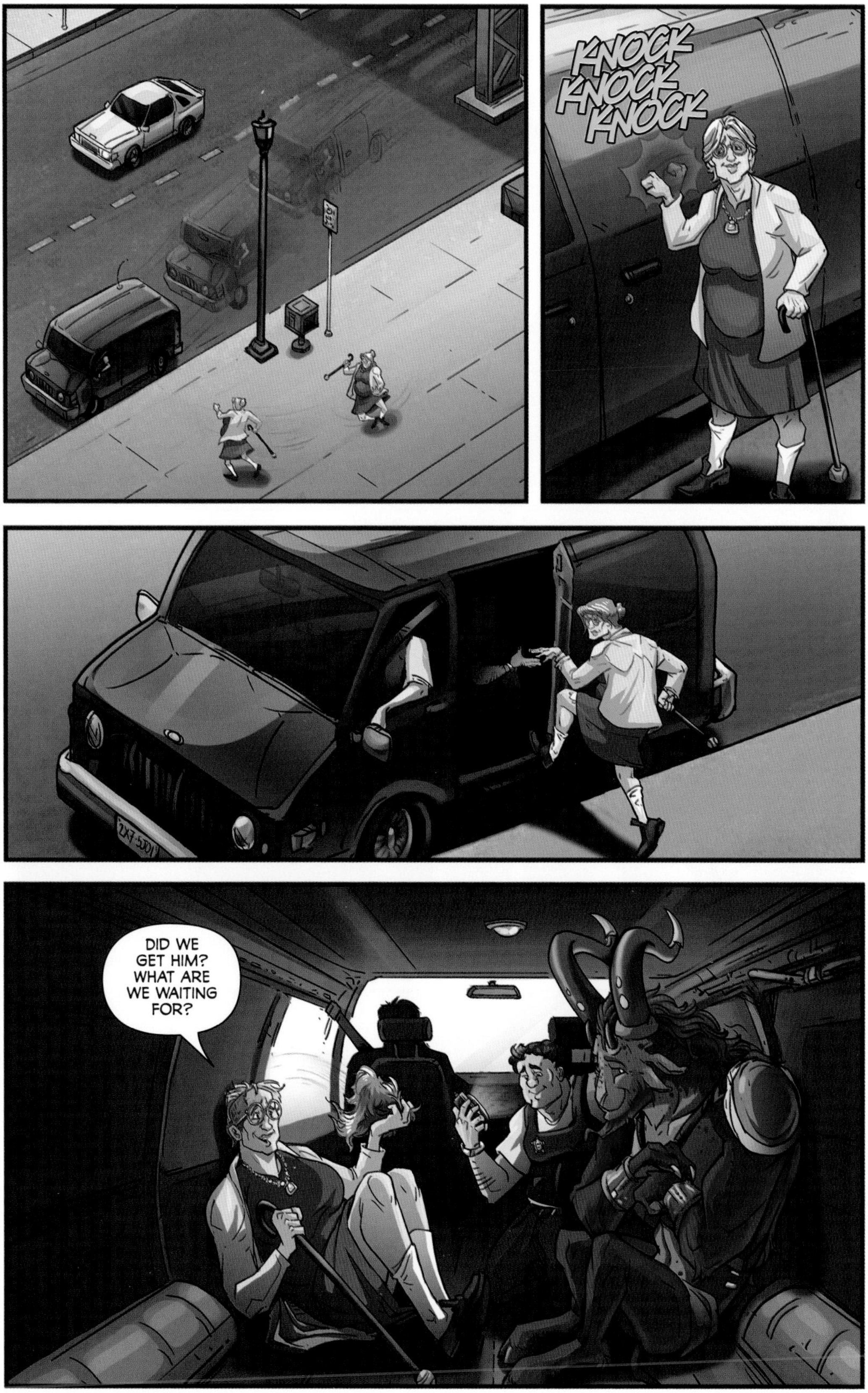
KNOCK
KNOCK
KNOCK
2X7-5001
DID WE GET HIM? WHAT ARE WE WAITING FOR?

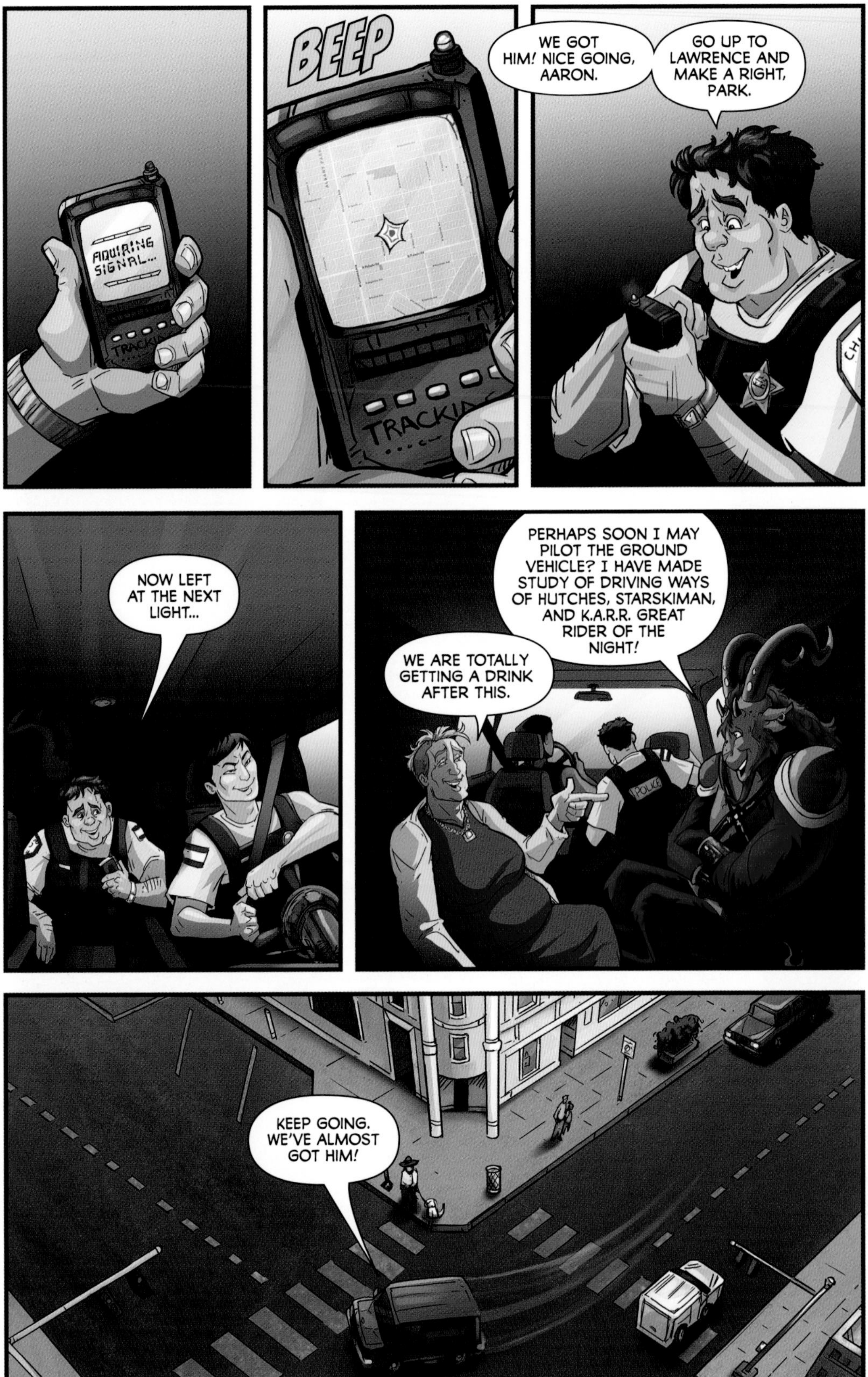
AQUIRING SIGNAL...
TRACKING
BEEP
TRACKING
WE GOT HIM! NICE GOING, AARON.
GO UP TO LAWRENCE AND MAKE A RIGHT, PARK.
NOW LEFT AT THE NEXT LIGHT...
PERHAPS SOON I MAY PILOT THE GROUND VEHICLE? I HAVE MADE STUDY OF DRIVING WAYS OF HUTCHES, STARSKIMAN, AND K.A.R.R. GREAT RIDER OF THE NIGHT!
WE ARE TOTALLY GETTING A DRINK AFTER THIS.
POLICE
KEEP GOING. WE'VE ALMOST GOT HIM!

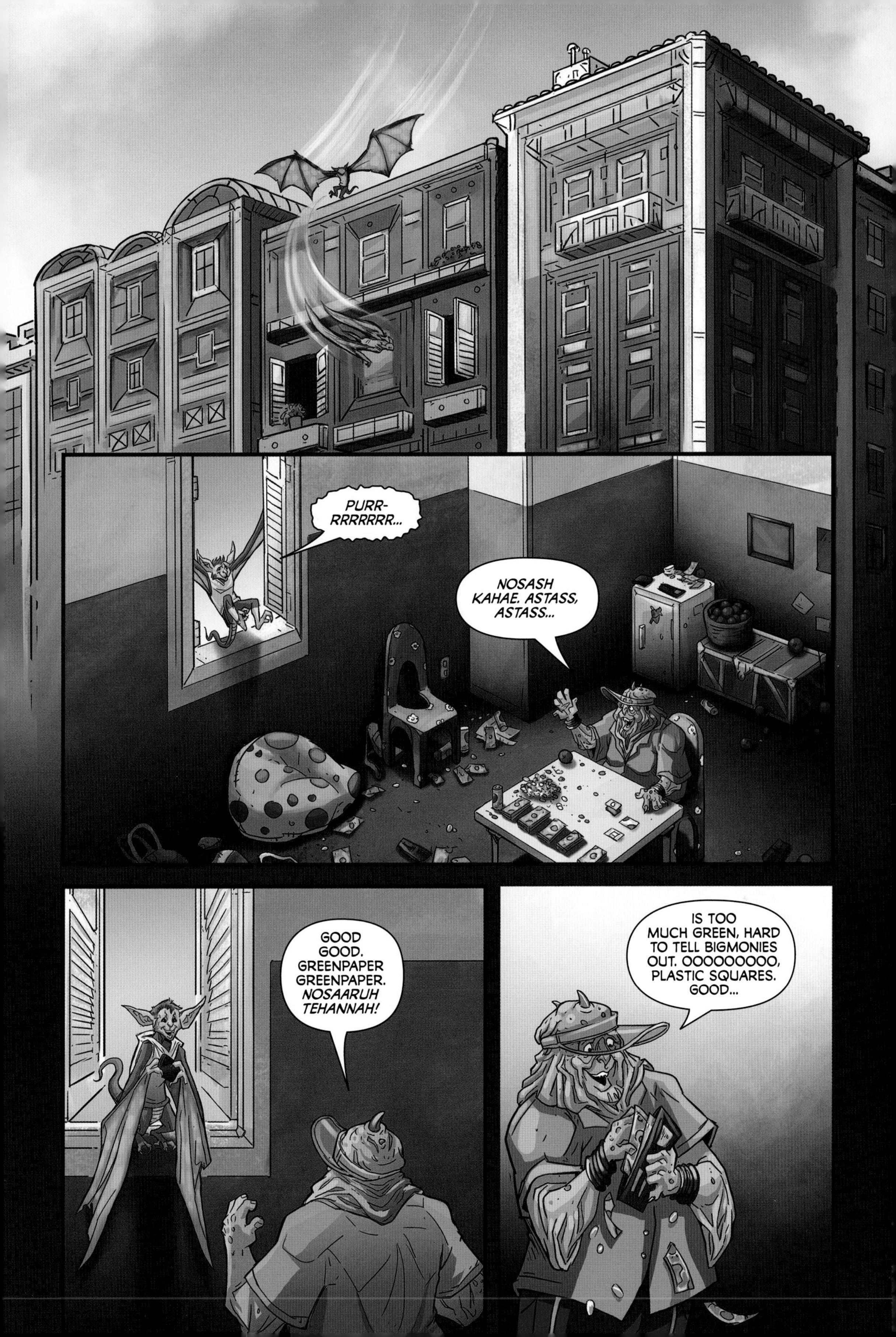
PURR-
RRRRRRR...
NOSASH
KAHAE. ASTASS,
ASTASS...
GOOD
GOOD.
GREENPAPER
GREENPAPER.
NOSAARUH
TEHANNAH!
IS TOO
MUCH GREEN, HARD
TO TELL BIGMONIES
OUT. OOOOOOOOO,
PLASTIC SQUARES.
GOOD...

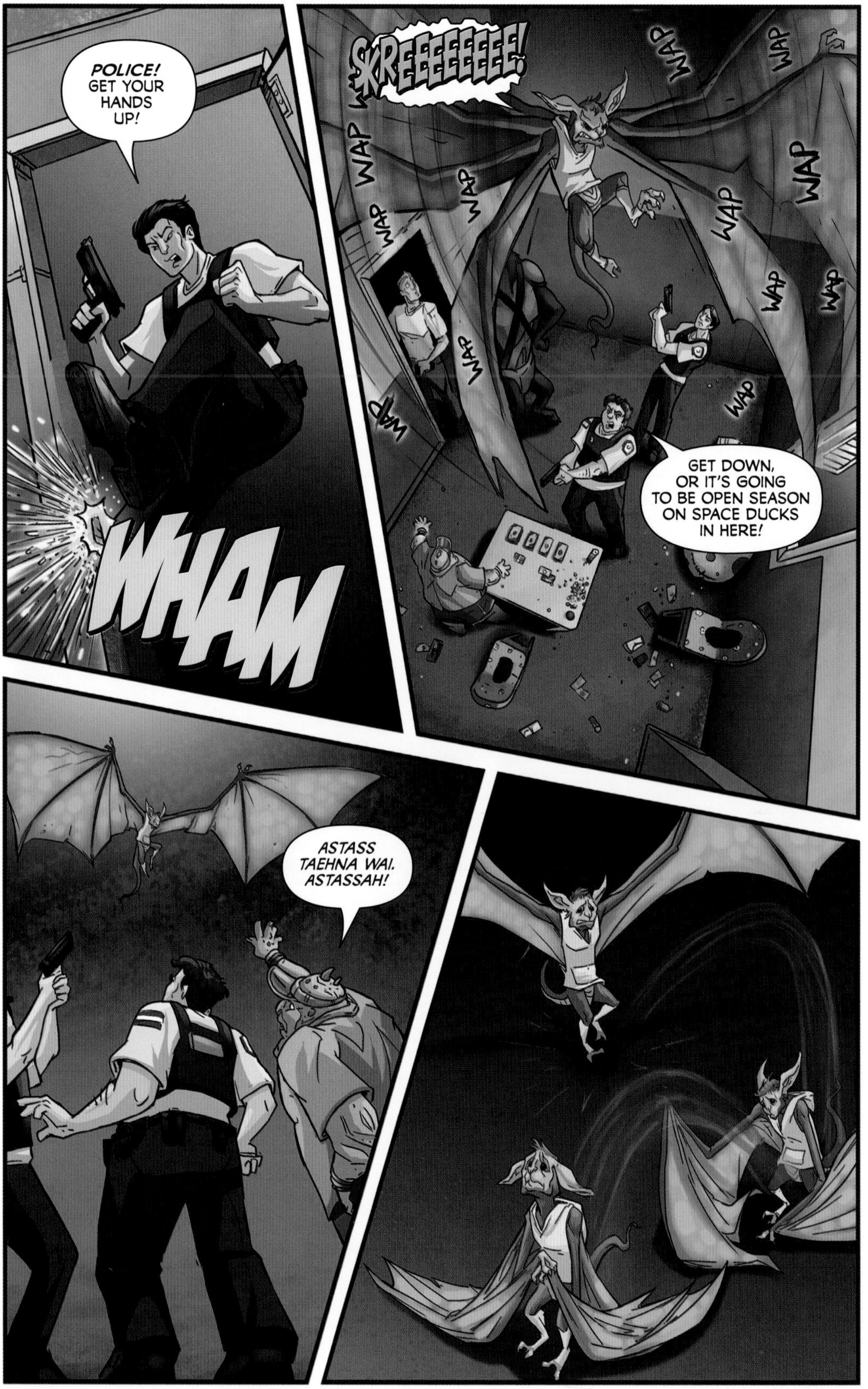

POLICE! GET YOUR HANDS UP!
WHAM
SKREEEEEEEE!
WAP WAP WAP WAP WAP WAP WAP WAP WAP WAP WAP WAP
GET DOWN, OR IT'S GOING TO BE OPEN SEASON ON SPACE DUCKS IN HERE!
ASTASS TAEHNA WAI. ASTASSAH!

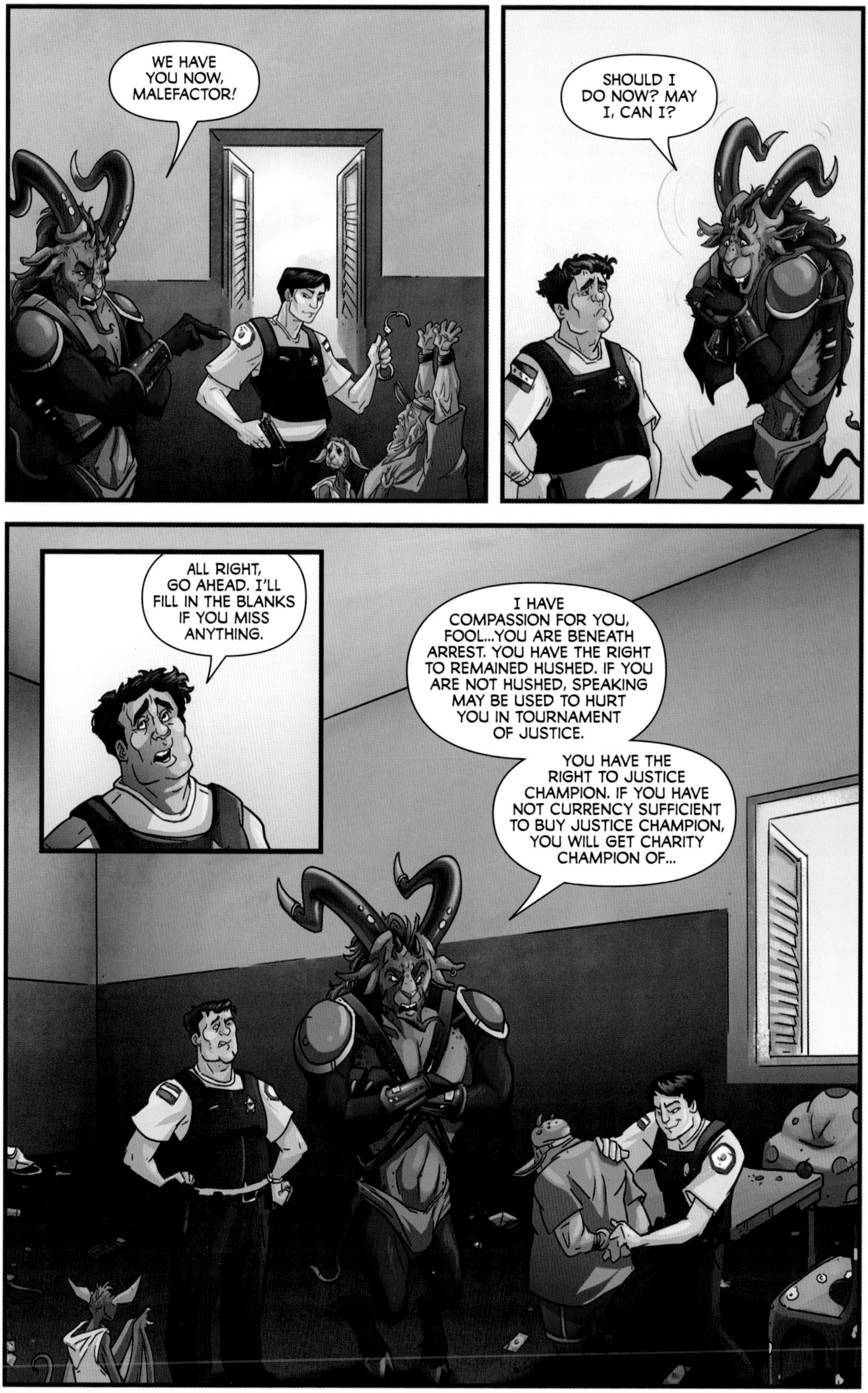
WE HAVE YOU NOW, MALEFACTOR!
SHOULD I DO NOW? MAY I, CAN I?
ALL RIGHT, GO AHEAD. I'LL FILL IN THE BLANKS IF YOU MISS ANYTHING.
I HAVE COMPASSION FOR YOU, FOOL...YOU ARE BENEATH ARREST. YOU HAVE THE RIGHT TO REMAINED HUSHED. IF YOU ARE NOT HUSHED, SPEAKING MAY BE USED TO HURT YOU IN TOURNAMENT OF JUSTICE.
YOU HAVE THE RIGHT TO JUSTICE CHAMPION. IF YOU HAVE NOT CURRENCY SUFFICIENT TO BUY JUSTICE CHAMPION, YOU WILL GET CHARITY CHAMPION OF...

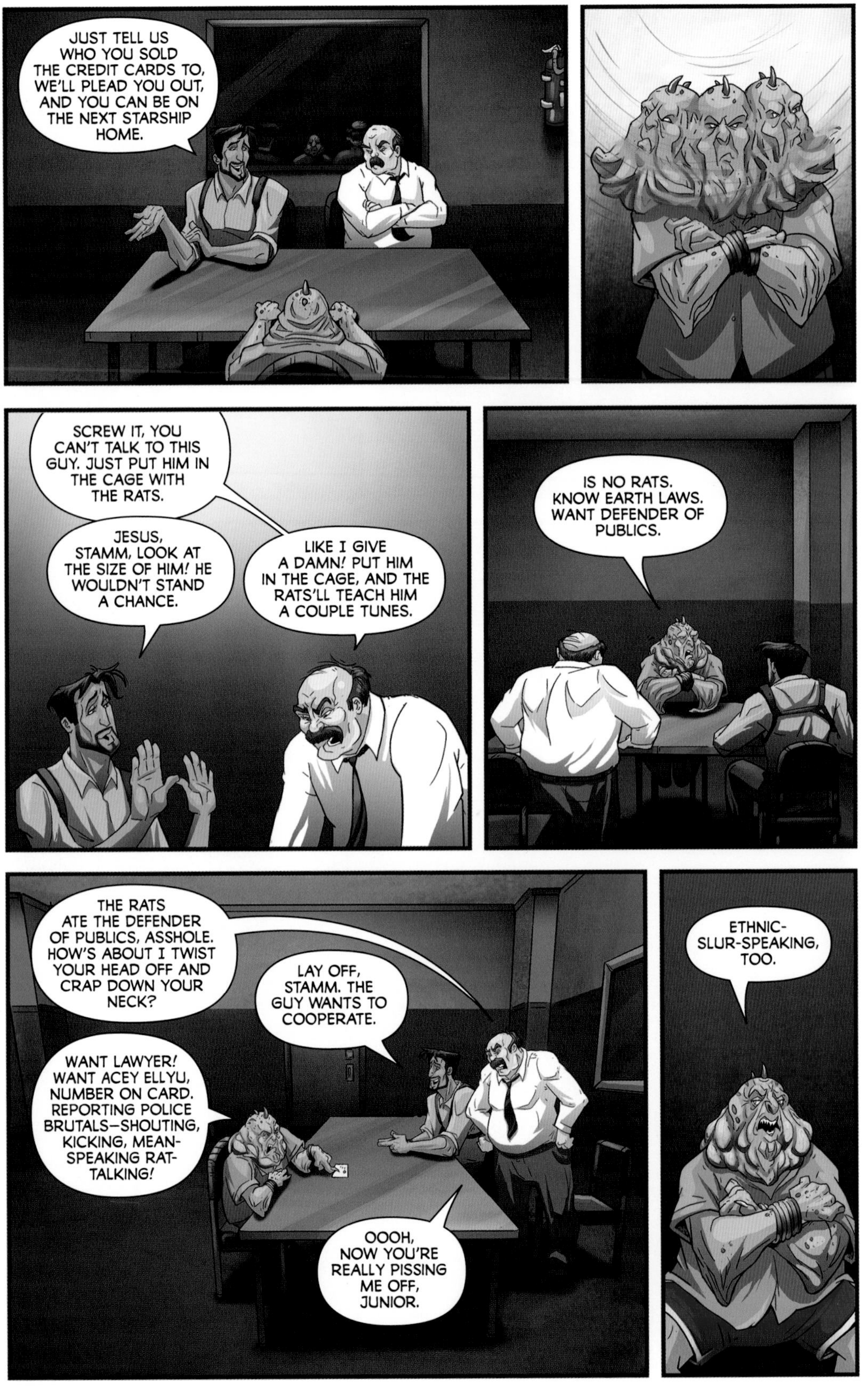
JUST TELL US WHO YOU SOLD THE CREDIT CARDS TO, WE'LL PLEAD YOU OUT, AND YOU CAN BE ON THE NEXT STARSHIP HOME.
SCREW IT, YOU CAN'T TALK TO THIS GUY. JUST PUT HIM IN THE CAGE WITH THE RATS.
JESUS, STAMM, LOOK AT THE SIZE OF HIM! HE WOULDN'T STAND A CHANCE.
LIKE I GIVE A DAMN! PUT HIM IN THE CAGE, AND THE RATS'LL TEACH HIM A COUPLE TUNES.
IS NO RATS. KNOW EARTH LAWS. WANT DEFENDER OF PUBLICS.
THE RATS ATE THE DEFENDER OF PUBLICS, ASSHOLE. HOW'S ABOUT I TWIST YOUR HEAD OFF AND CRAP DOWN YOUR NECK?
LAY OFF, STAMM. THE GUY WANTS TO COOPERATE.
WANT LAWYER! WANT ACEY ELLYU, NUMBER ON CARD. REPORTING POLICE BRUTALS—SHOUTING, KICKING, MEAN-SPEAKING RAT-TALKING!
OOOH, NOW YOU'RE REALLY PISSING ME OFF, JUNIOR.
ETHNIC-SLUR-SPEAKING, TOO.

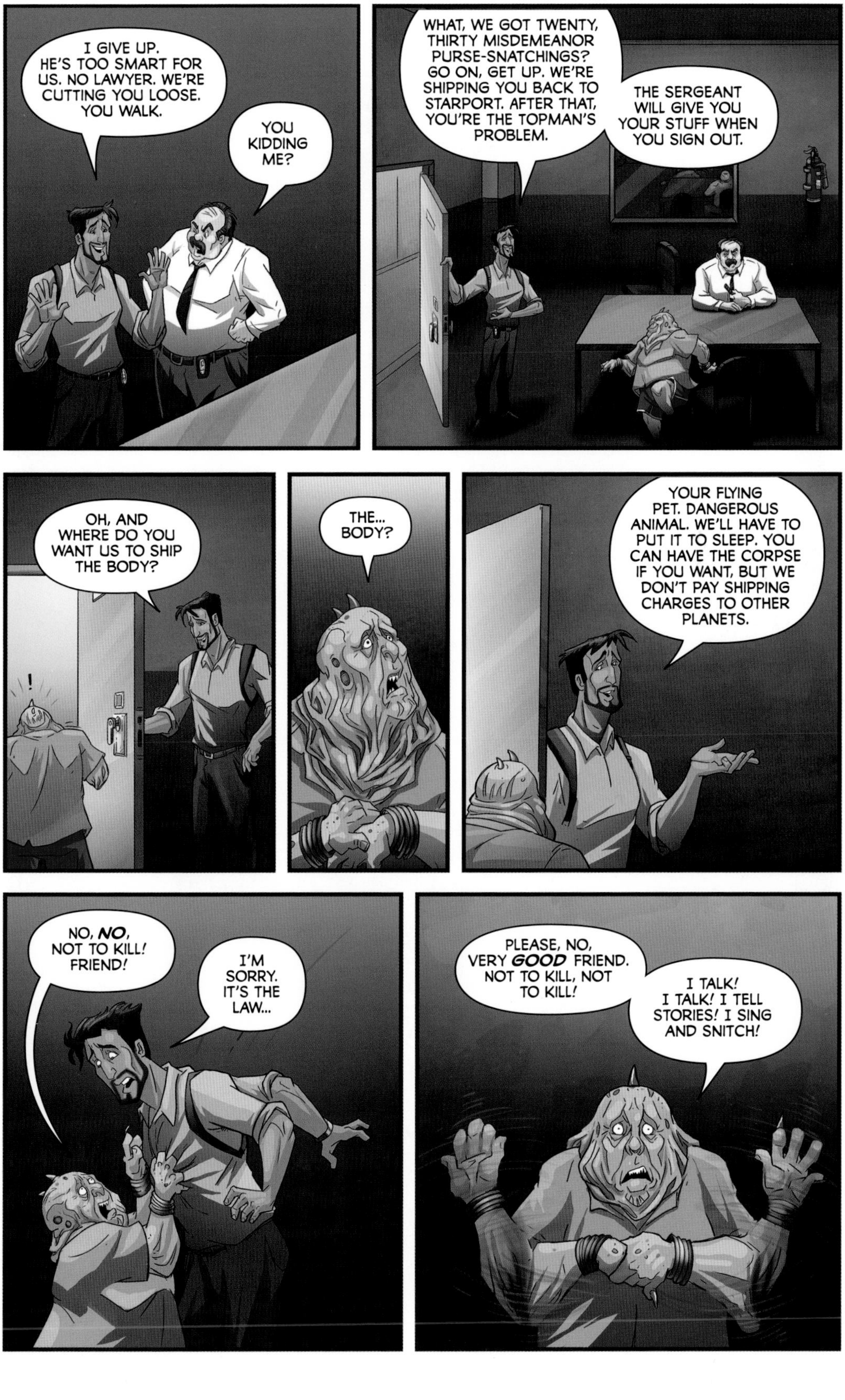
I GIVE UP. HE'S TOO SMART FOR US. NO LAWYER. WE'RE CUTTING YOU LOOSE. YOU WALK.
YOU KIDDING ME?
WHAT, WE GOT TWENTY, THIRTY MISDEMEANOR PURSE-SNATCHINGS? GO ON, GET UP. WE'RE SHIPPING YOU BACK TO STARPORT. AFTER THAT, YOU'RE THE TOPMAN'S PROBLEM.
THE SERGEANT WILL GIVE YOU YOUR STUFF WHEN YOU SIGN OUT.
OH, AND WHERE DO YOU WANT US TO SHIP THE BODY?
!
THE... BODY?
YOUR FLYING PET. DANGEROUS ANIMAL. WE'LL HAVE TO PUT IT TO SLEEP. YOU CAN HAVE THE CORPSE IF YOU WANT, BUT WE DON'T PAY SHIPPING CHARGES TO OTHER PLANETS.
NO, ***NO***, NOT TO KILL! FRIEND!
I'M SORRY. IT'S THE LAW...
PLEASE, NO, VERY ***GOOD*** FRIEND. NOT TO KILL, NOT TO KILL!
I TALK! I TALK! I TELL STORIES! I SING AND SNITCH!

CHAPTER TWELVE

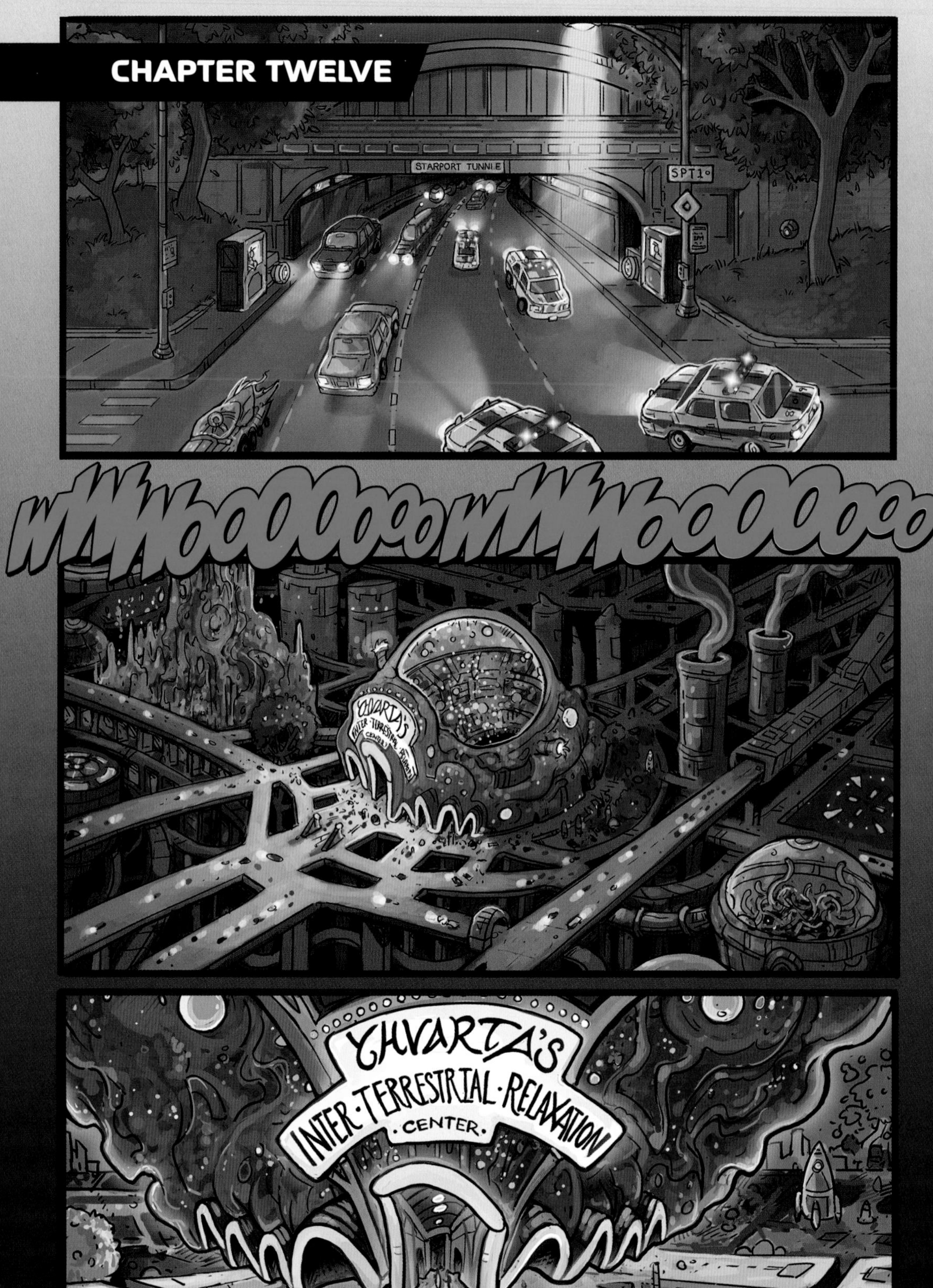
wWWooOOOoowWWooOOOoo
YHVARTA'S
INTER·TERRESTRIAL·RELAXATION
·CENTER·

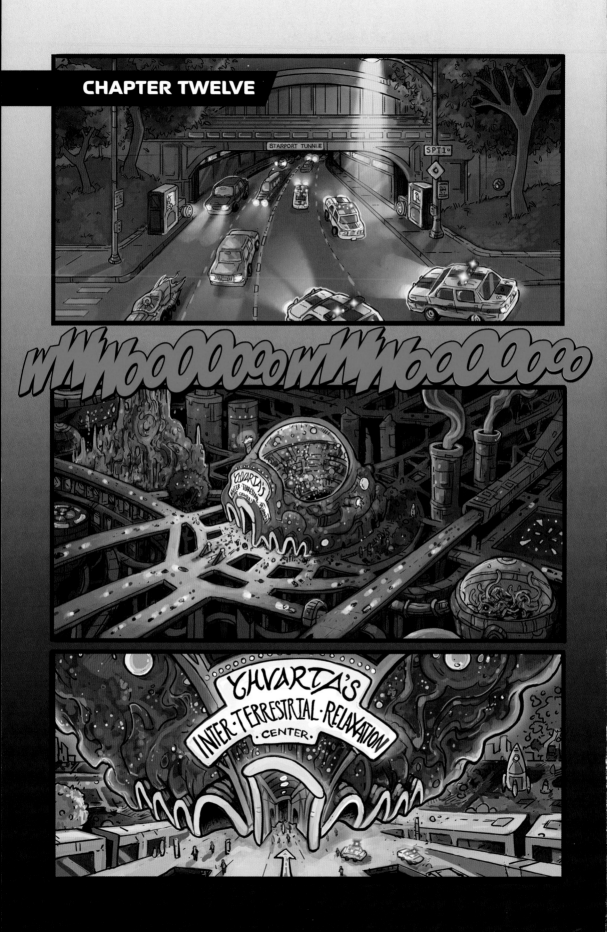

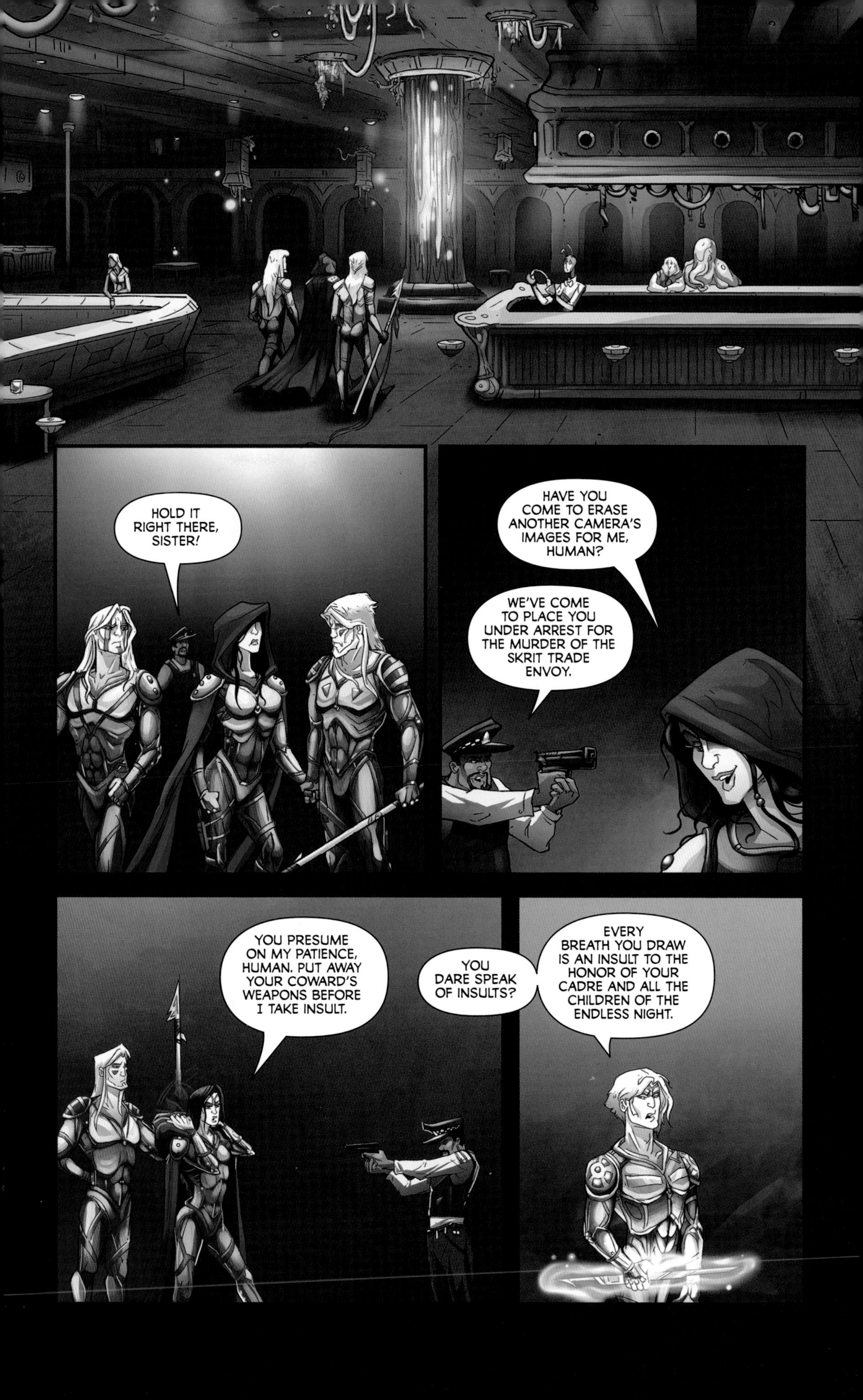
HOLD IT RIGHT THERE, SISTER!
HAVE YOU COME TO ERASE ANOTHER CAMERA'S IMAGES FOR ME, HUMAN?
WE'VE COME TO PLACE YOU UNDER ARREST FOR THE MURDER OF THE SKRIT TRADE ENVOY.
YOU PRESUME ON MY PATIENCE, HUMAN. PUT AWAY YOUR COWARD'S WEAPONS BEFORE I TAKE INSULT.
YOU DARE SPEAK OF INSULTS?
EVERY BREATH YOU DRAW IS AN INSULT TO THE HONOR OF YOUR CADRE AND ALL THE CHILDREN OF THE ENDLESS NIGHT.

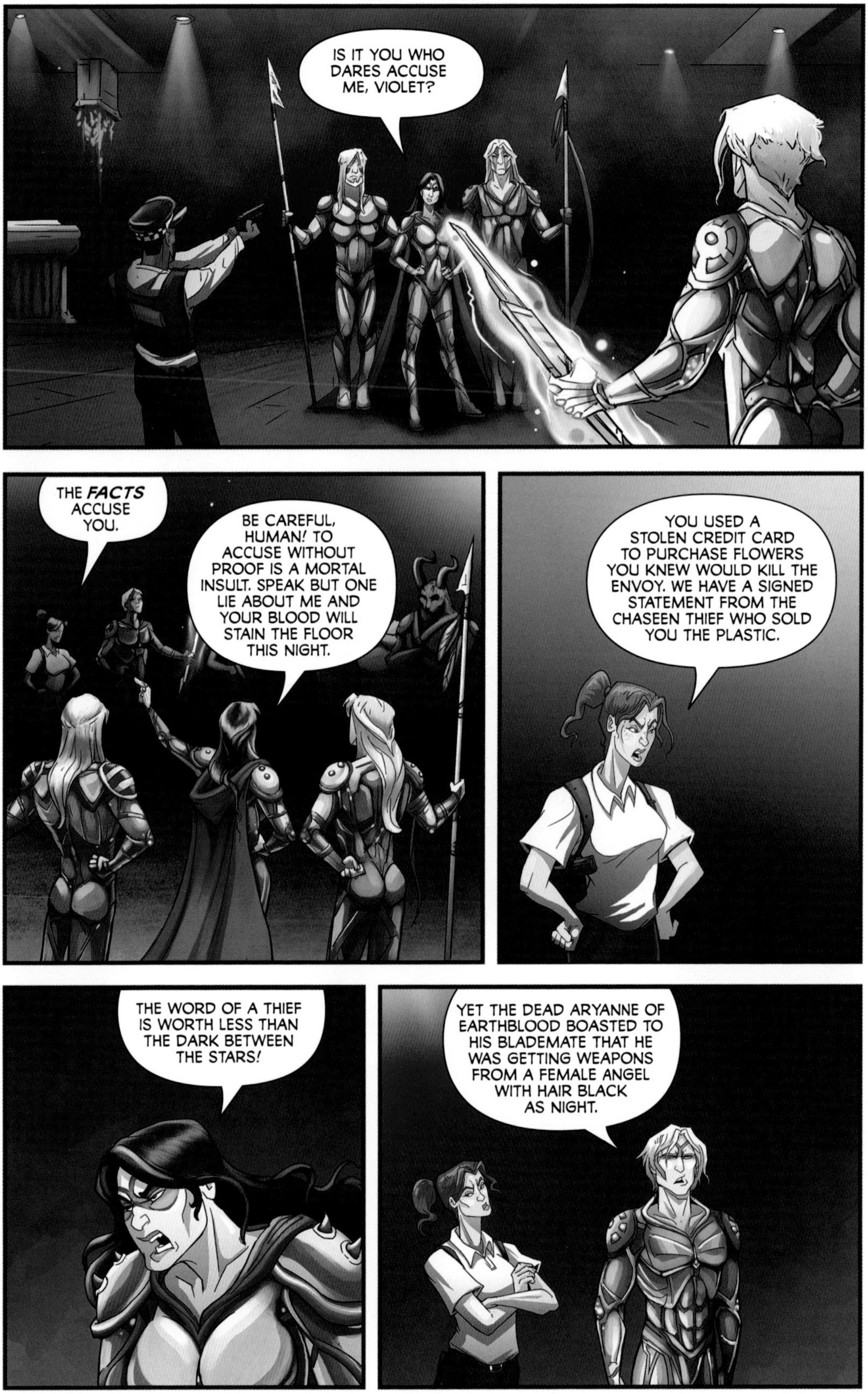
IS IT YOU WHO DARES ACCUSE ME, VIOLET?
THE ***FACTS*** ACCUSE YOU.
BE CAREFUL, HUMAN! TO ACCUSE WITHOUT PROOF IS A MORTAL INSULT. SPEAK BUT ONE LIE ABOUT ME AND YOUR BLOOD WILL STAIN THE FLOOR THIS NIGHT.
YOU USED A STOLEN CREDIT CARD TO PURCHASE FLOWERS YOU KNEW WOULD KILL THE ENVOY. WE HAVE A SIGNED STATEMENT FROM THE CHASEEN THIEF WHO SOLD YOU THE PLASTIC.
THE WORD OF A THIEF IS WORTH LESS THAN THE DARK BETWEEN THE STARS!
YET THE DEAD ARYANNE OF EARTHBLOOD BOASTED TO HIS BLADEMATE THAT HE WAS GETTING WEAPONS FROM A FEMALE ANGEL WITH HAIR BLACK AS NIGHT.

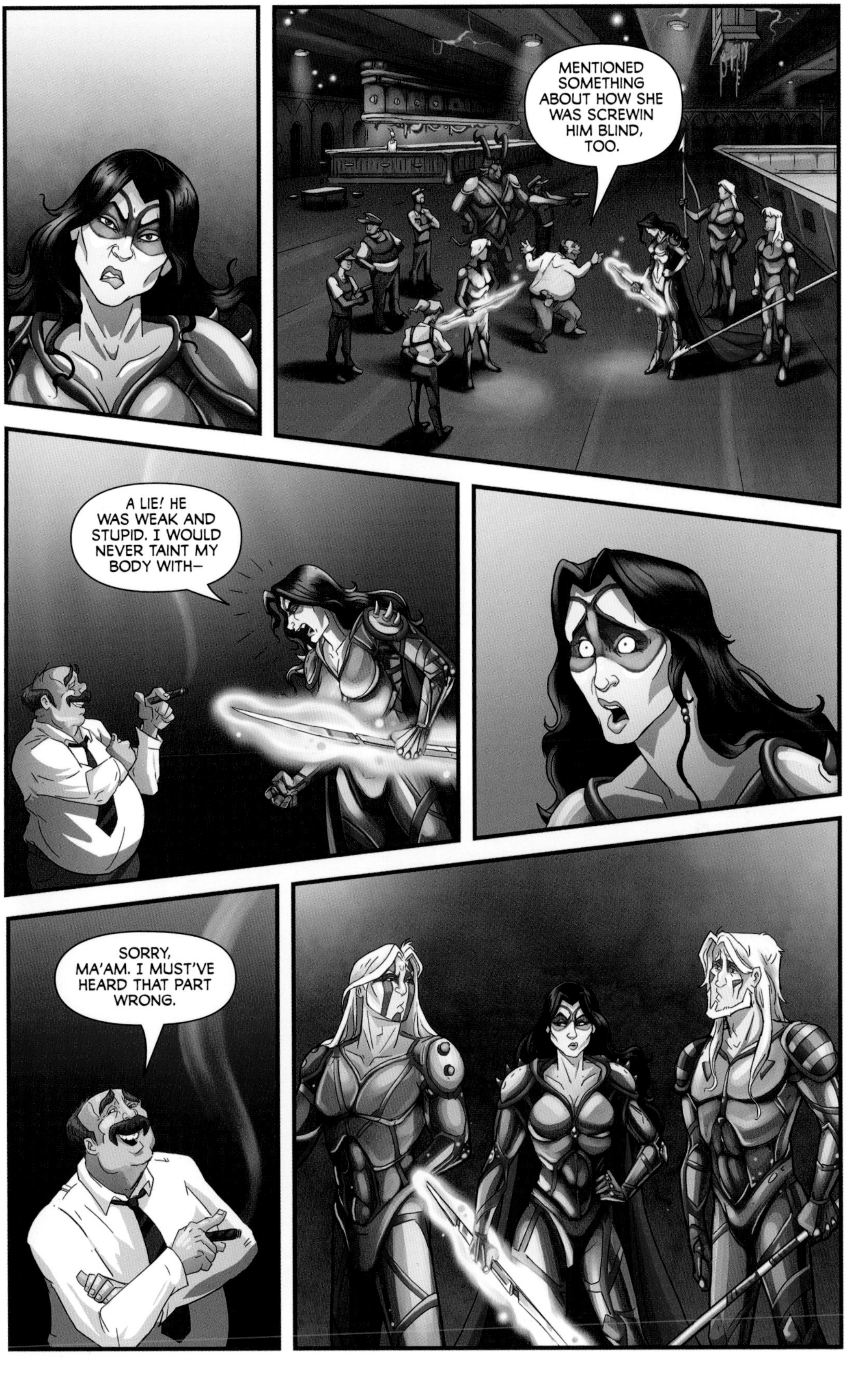
MENTIONED SOMETHING ABOUT HOW SHE WAS SCREWIN HIM BLIND, TOO.
A LIE! HE WAS WEAK AND STUPID. I WOULD NEVER TAINT MY BODY WITH—
SORRY, MA'AM. I MUST'VE HEARD THAT PART WRONG.

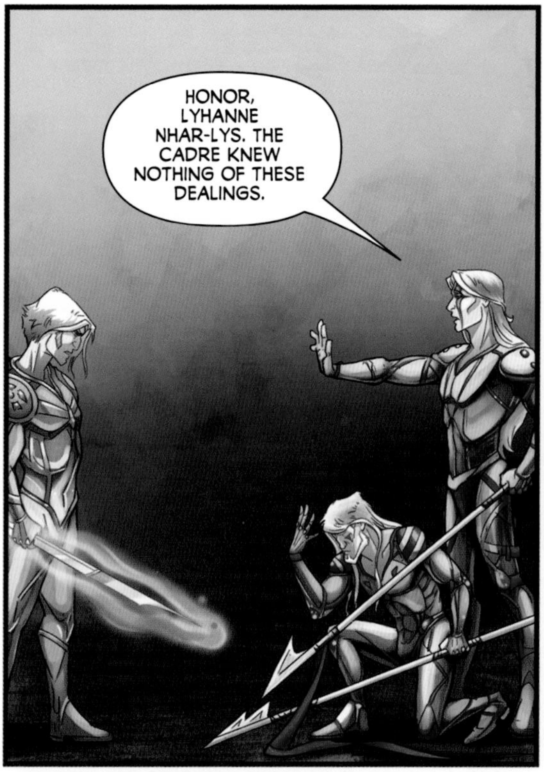
HONOR, LYHANNE NHAR-LYS. THE CADRE KNEW NOTHING OF THESE DEALINGS.

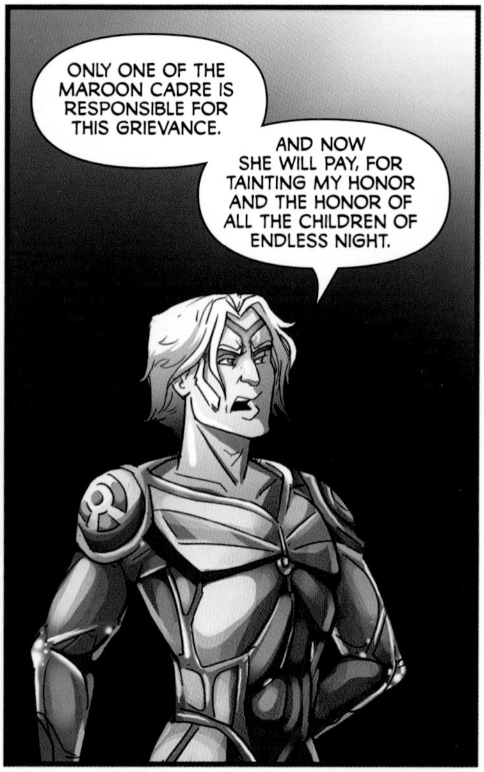
ONLY ONE OF THE MAROON CADRE IS RESPONSIBLE FOR THIS GRIEVANCE.
AND NOW SHE WILL PAY, FOR TAINTING MY HONOR AND THE HONOR OF ALL THE CHILDREN OF ENDLESS NIGHT.

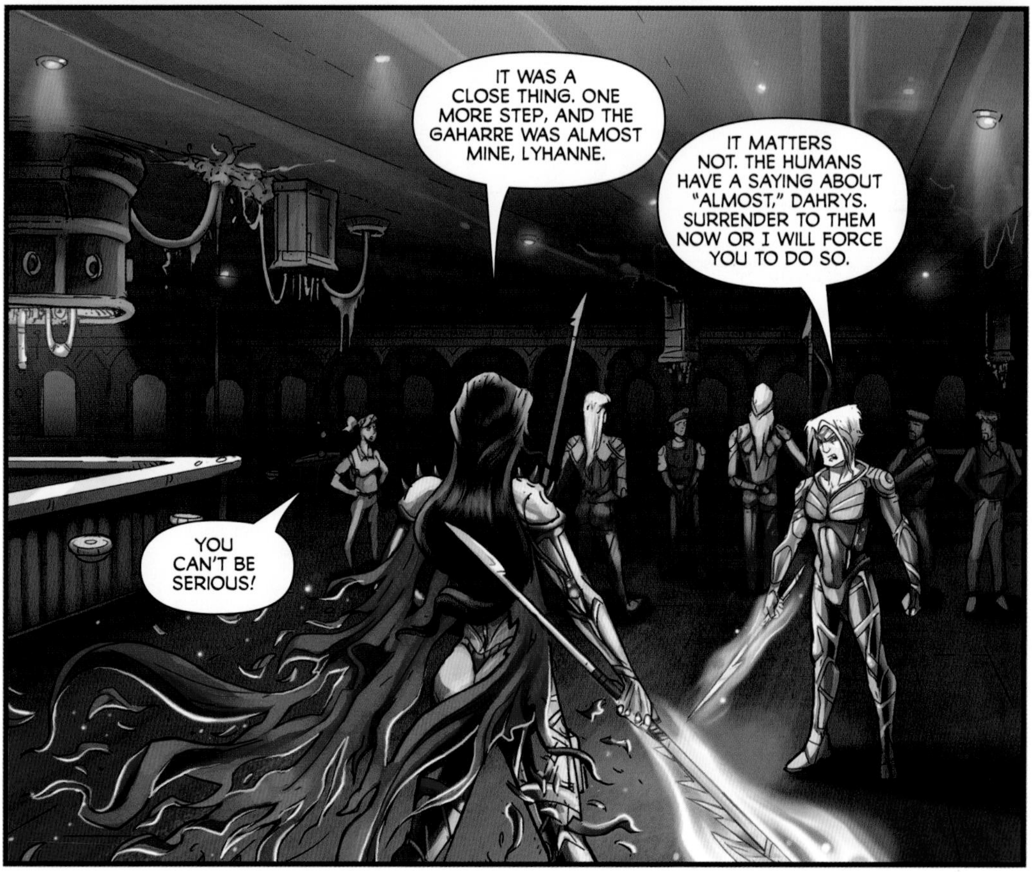
IT WAS A CLOSE THING. ONE MORE STEP, AND THE GAHARRE WAS ALMOST MINE, LYHANNE.
IT MATTERS NOT. THE HUMANS HAVE A SAYING ABOUT "ALMOST," DAHRYS. SURRENDER TO THEM NOW OR I WILL FORCE YOU TO DO SO.
YOU CAN'T BE SERIOUS!

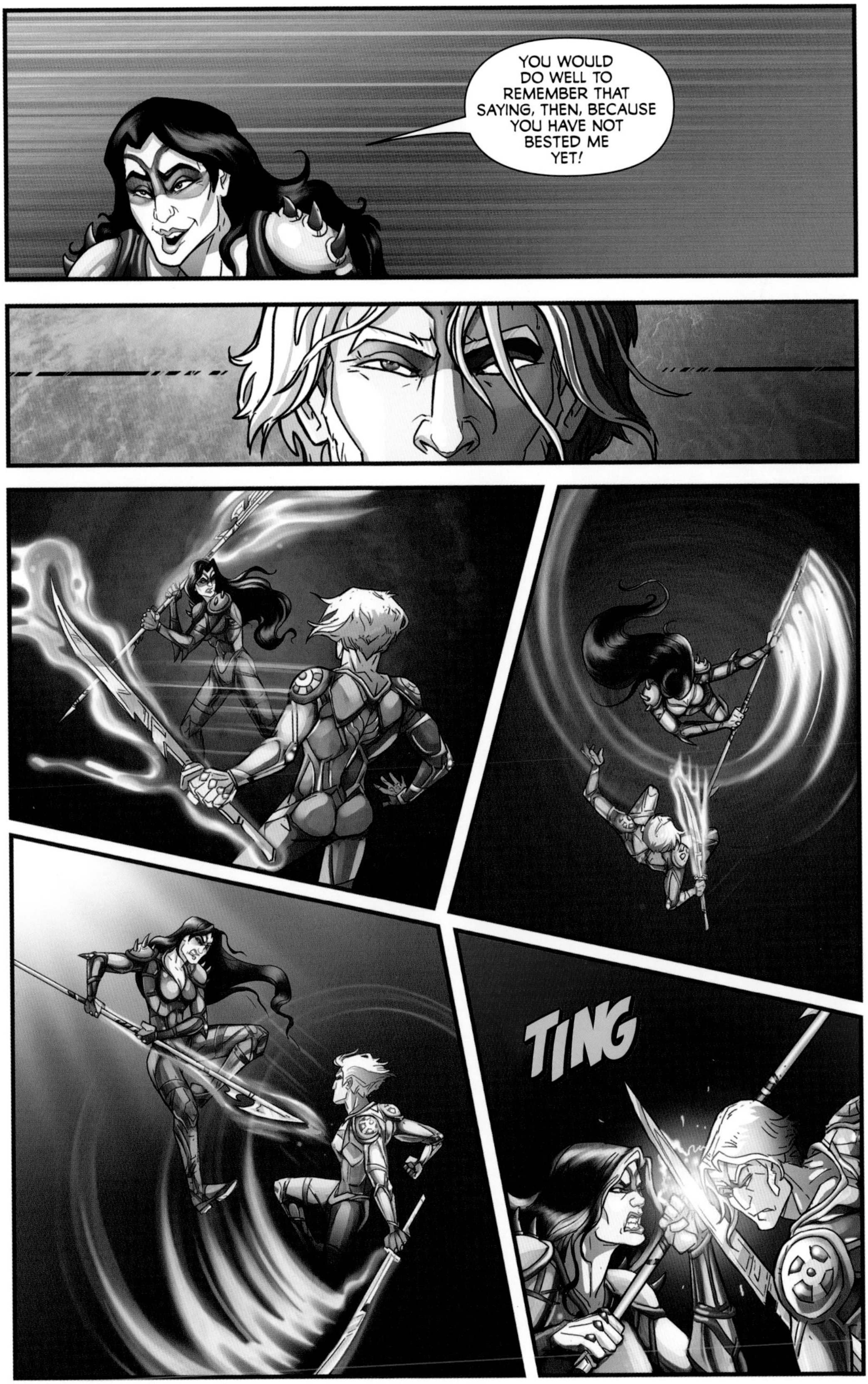
YOU WOULD DO WELL TO REMEMBER THAT SAYING, THEN, BECAUSE YOU HAVE NOT BESTED ME YET!
TING

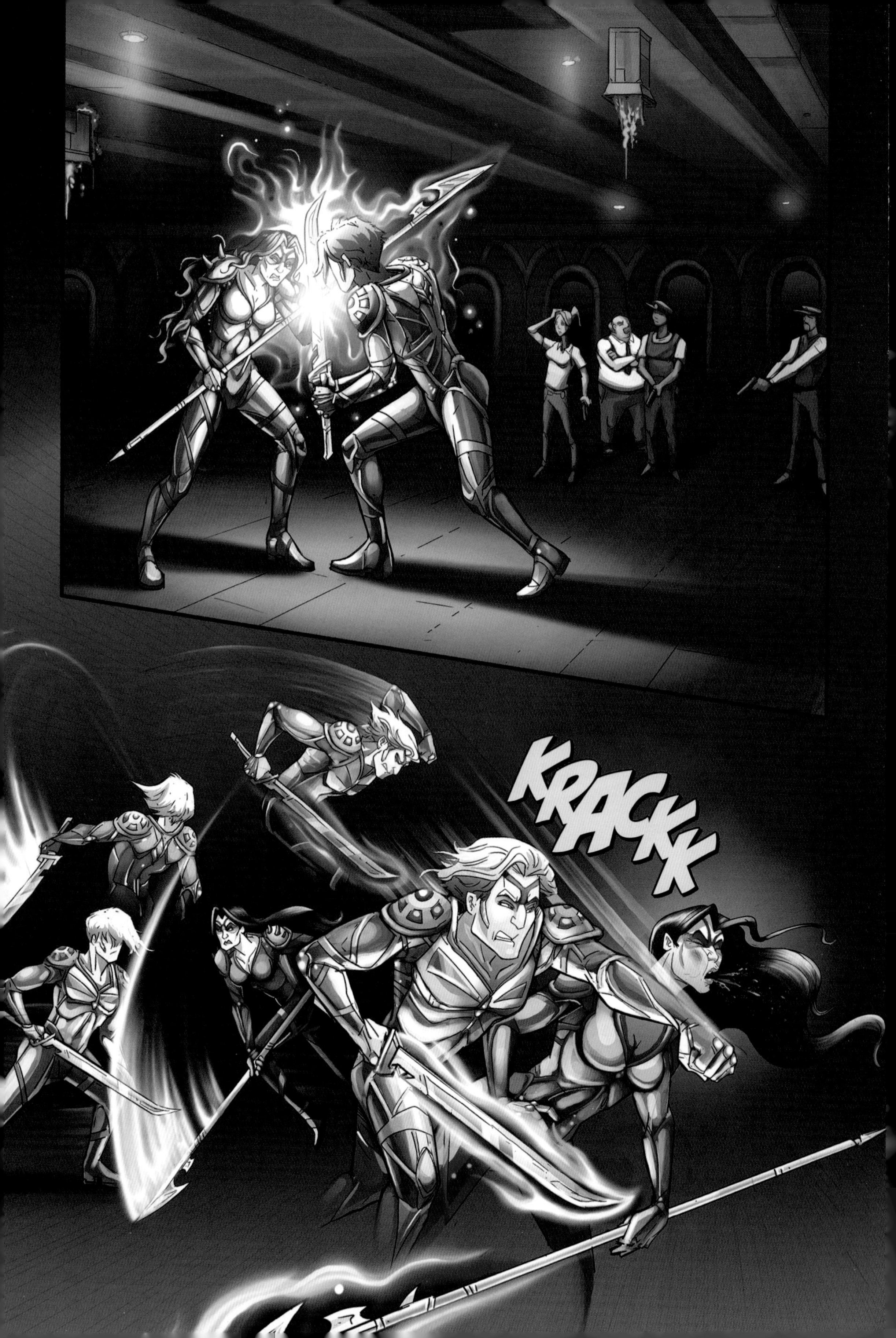
KRACKK

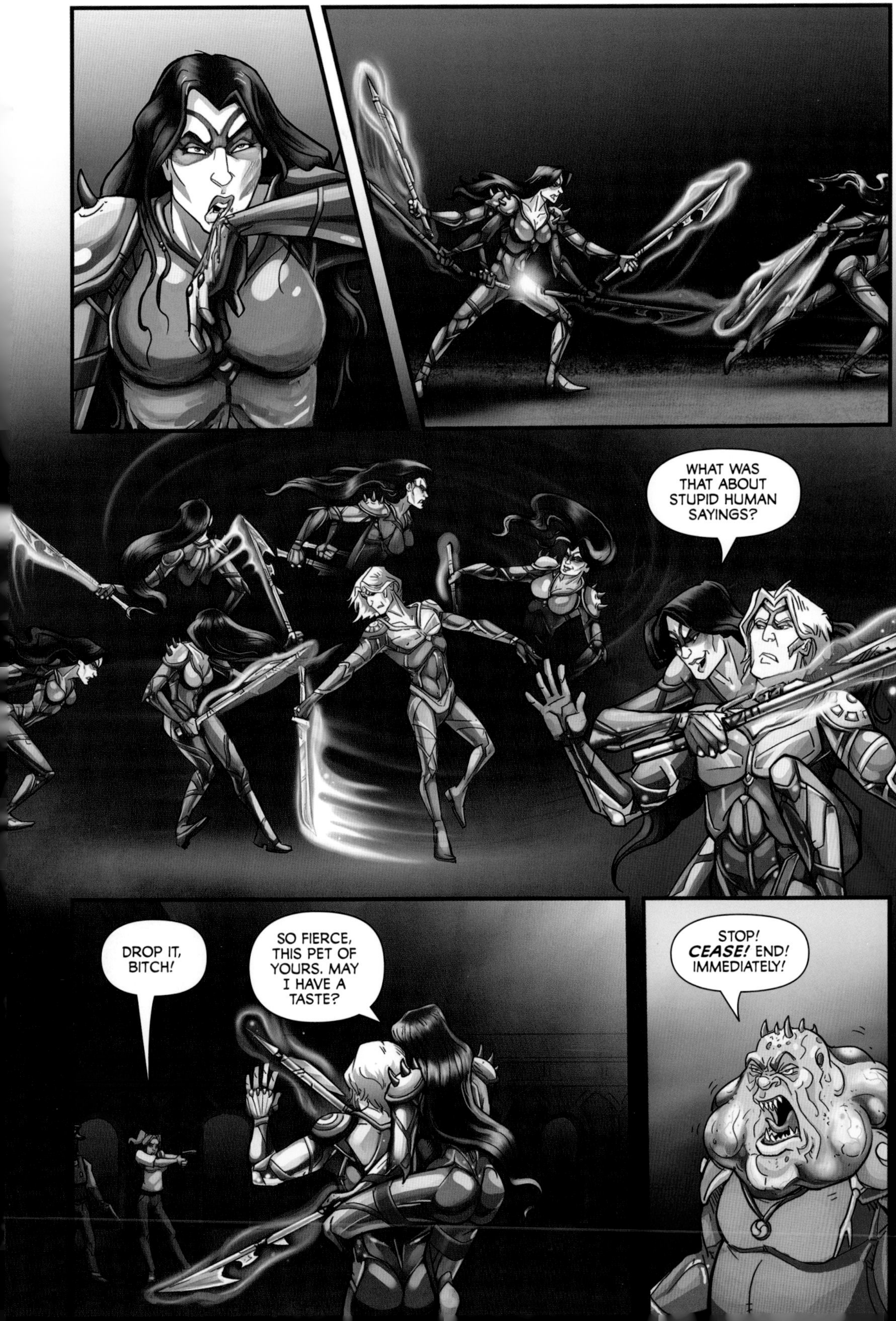
WHAT WAS THAT ABOUT STUPID HUMAN SAYINGS?
DROP IT, BITCH!
SO FIERCE, THIS PET OF YOURS. MAY I HAVE A TASTE?
STOP! CEASE! END! IMMEDIATELY!

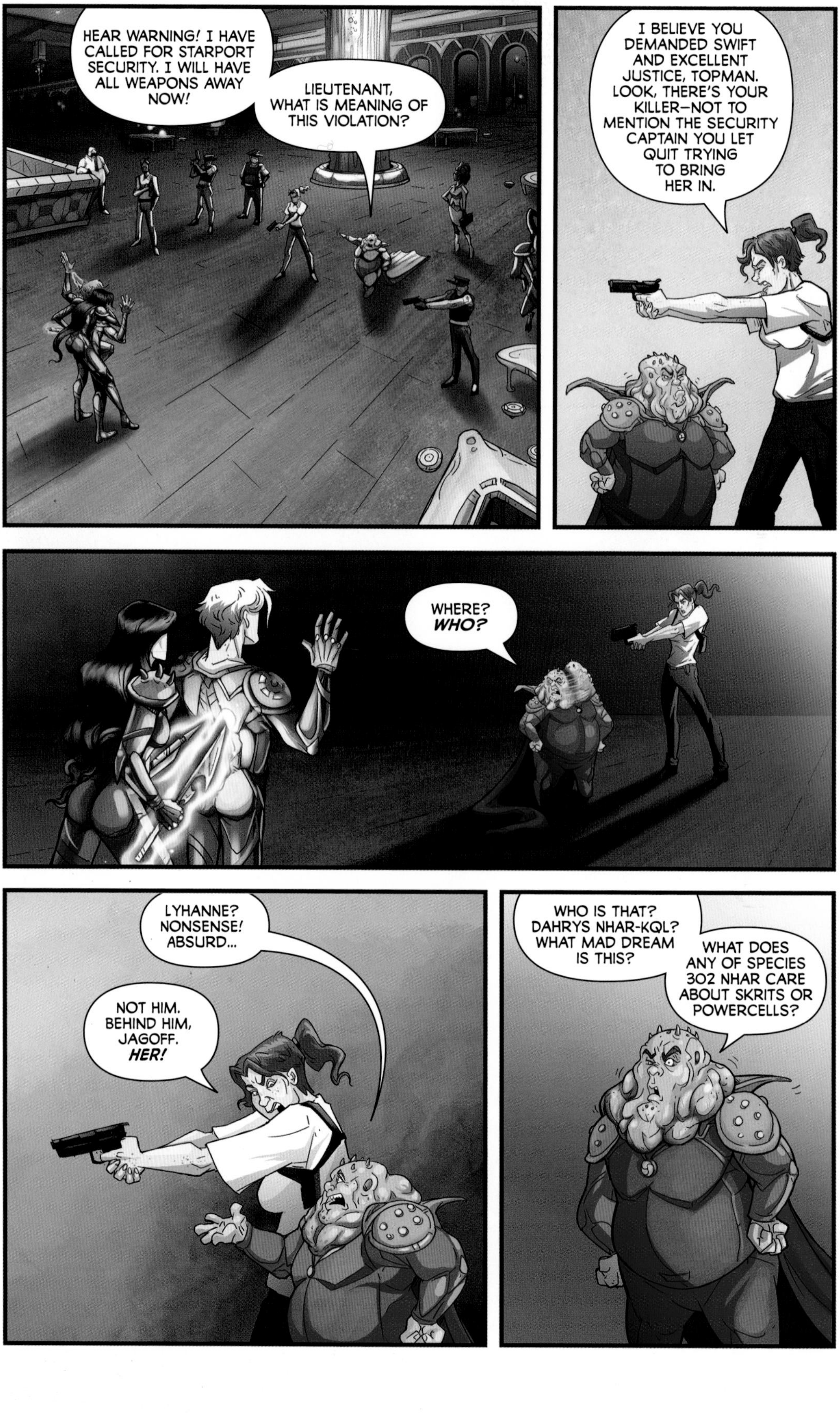
HEAR WARNING! I HAVE CALLED FOR STARPORT SECURITY. I WILL HAVE ALL WEAPONS AWAY NOW!
LIEUTENANT, WHAT IS MEANING OF THIS VIOLATION?
I BELIEVE YOU DEMANDED SWIFT AND EXCELLENT JUSTICE, TOPMAN. LOOK, THERE'S YOUR KILLER—NOT TO MENTION THE SECURITY CAPTAIN YOU LET QUIT TRYING TO BRING HER IN.
WHERE? ***WHO?***
LYHANNE? NONSENSE! ABSURD...
NOT HIM. BEHIND HIM, JAGOFF. ***HER!***
WHO IS THAT? DAHRYS NHAR-KQL? WHAT MAD DREAM IS THIS?
WHAT DOES ANY OF SPECIES 302 NHAR CARE ABOUT SKRITS OR POWERCELLS?

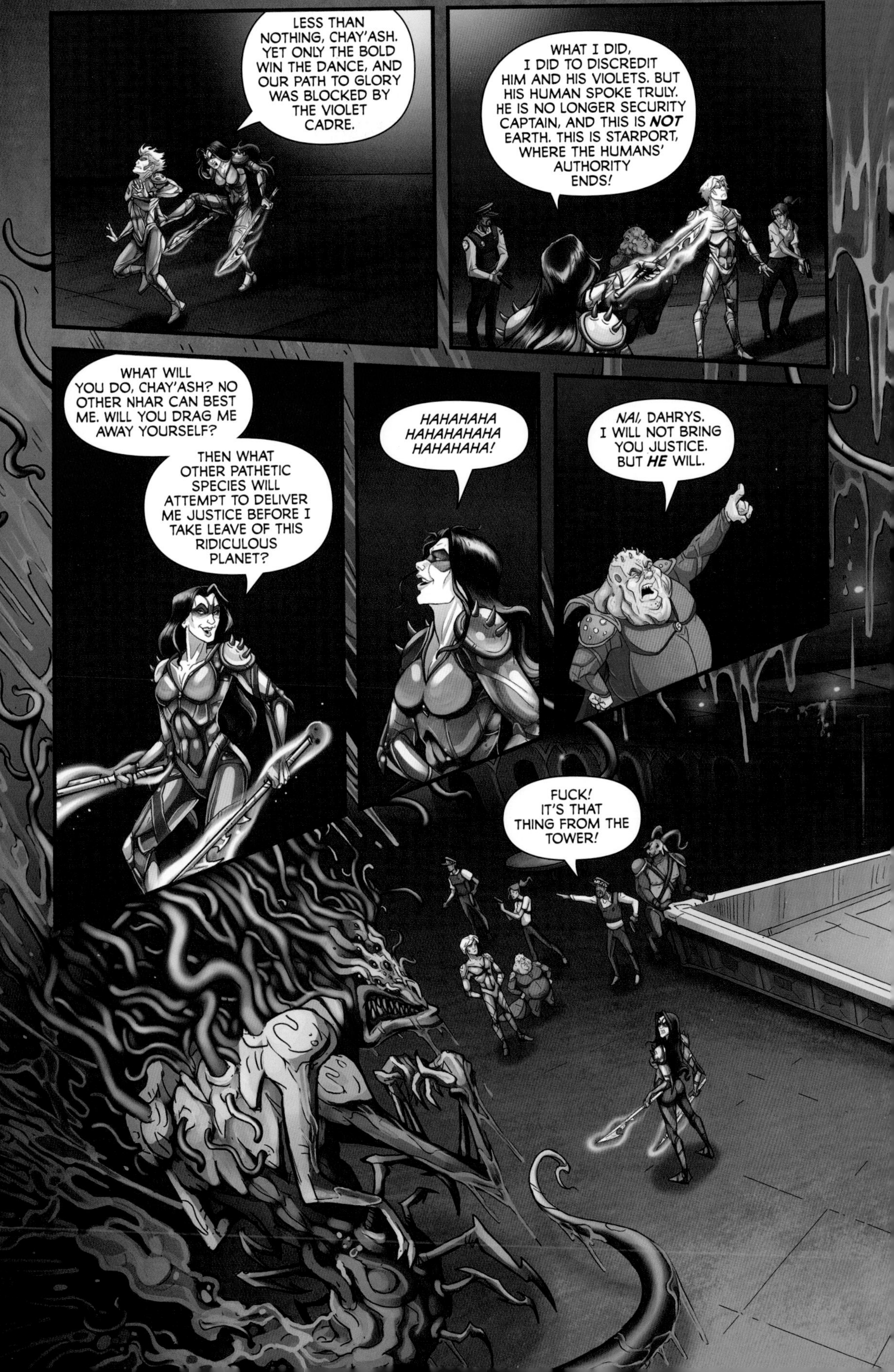
LESS THAN NOTHING, CHAY'ASH. YET ONLY THE BOLD WIN THE DANCE, AND OUR PATH TO GLORY WAS BLOCKED BY THE VIOLET CADRE.
WHAT I DID, I DID TO DISCREDIT HIM AND HIS VIOLETS. BUT HIS HUMAN SPOKE TRULY. HE IS NO LONGER SECURITY CAPTAIN, AND THIS IS ***NOT*** EARTH. THIS IS STARPORT, WHERE THE HUMANS' AUTHORITY ENDS!
WHAT WILL YOU DO, CHAY'ASH? NO OTHER NHAR CAN BEST ME. WILL YOU DRAG ME AWAY YOURSELF?
THEN WHAT OTHER PATHETIC SPECIES WILL ATTEMPT TO DELIVER ME JUSTICE BEFORE I TAKE LEAVE OF THIS RIDICULOUS PLANET?
HAHAHAHA HAHAHAHAHA HAHAHAHA!
NAI, DAHRYS. I WILL NOT BRING YOU JUSTICE. BUT ***HE*** WILL.
FUCK! IT'S THAT THING FROM THE TOWER!

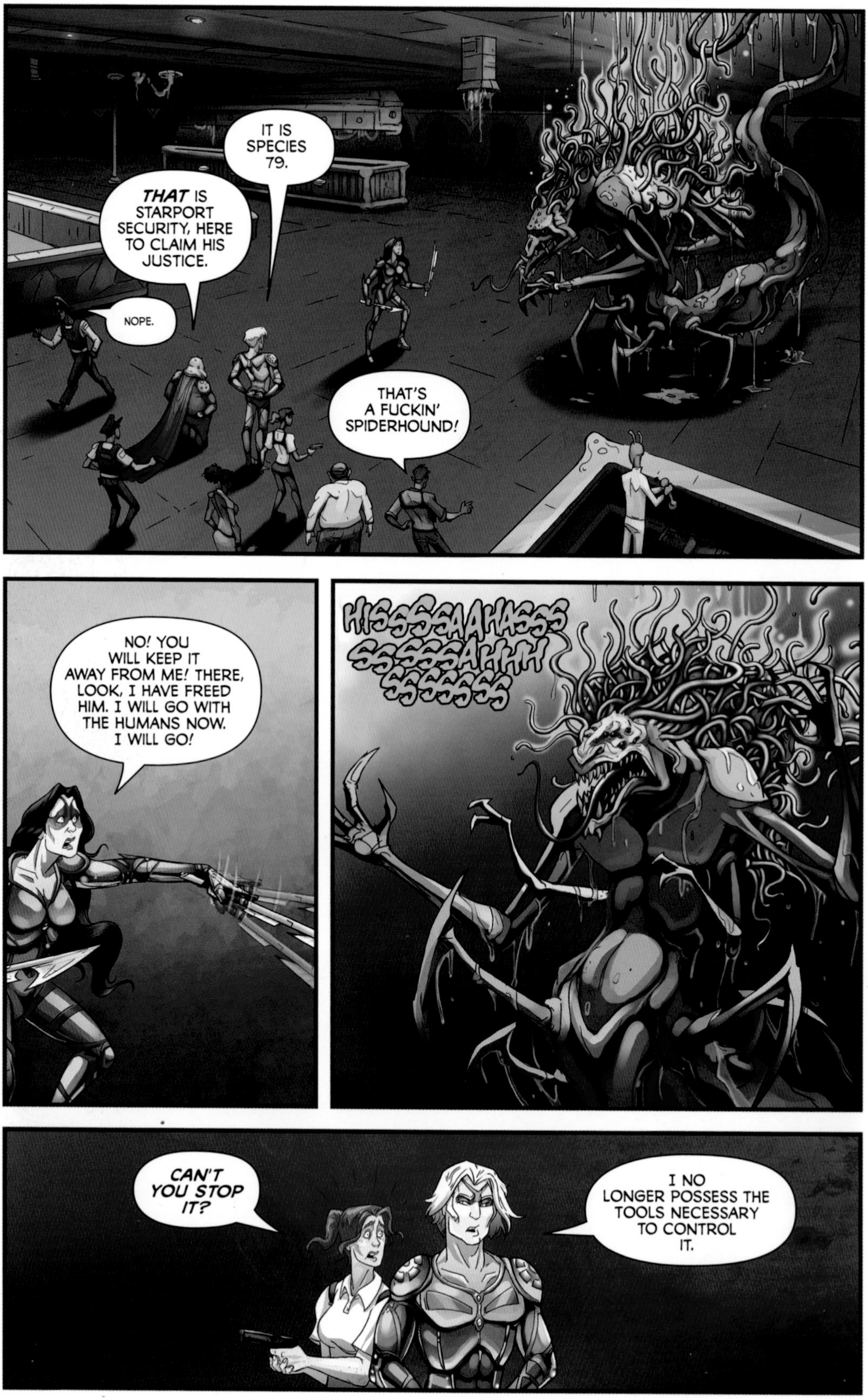
IT IS SPECIES 79.
THAT IS STARPORT SECURITY, HERE TO CLAIM HIS JUSTICE.
NOPE.
THAT'S A FUCKIN' SPIDERHOUND!
NO! YOU WILL KEEP IT AWAY FROM ME! THERE, LOOK, I HAVE FREED HIM. I WILL GO WITH THE HUMANS NOW. I WILL GO!
HISSSSAAHASSS SSSSSAHHH SSSSSSS
CAN'T YOU STOP IT?
I NO LONGER POSSESS THE TOOLS NECESSARY TO CONTROL IT.

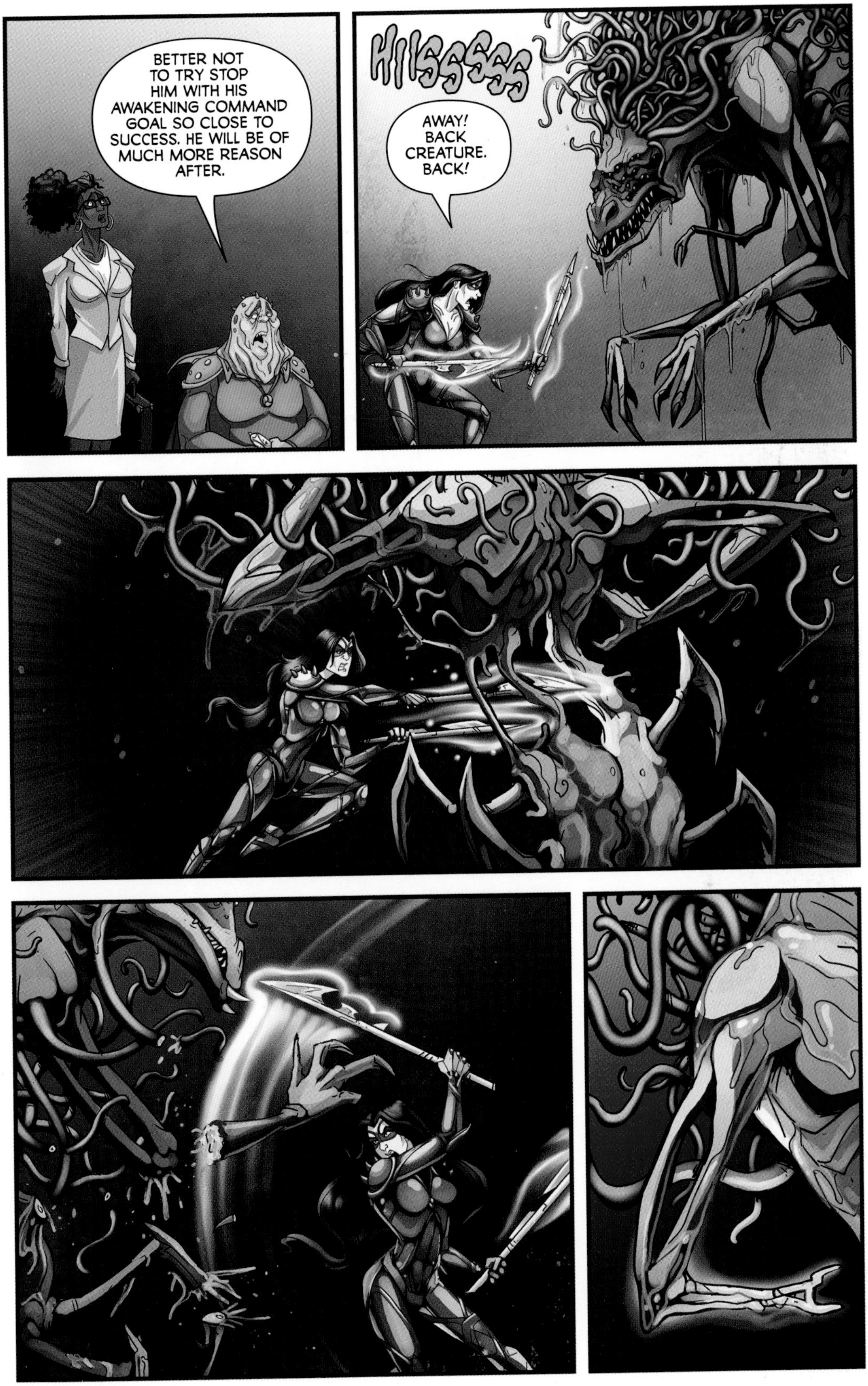
BETTER NOT TO TRY STOP HIM WITH HIS AWAKENING COMMAND GOAL SO CLOSE TO SUCCESS. HE WILL BE OF MUCH MORE REASON AFTER.
HIISSSSS
AWAY! BACK CREATURE. BACK!

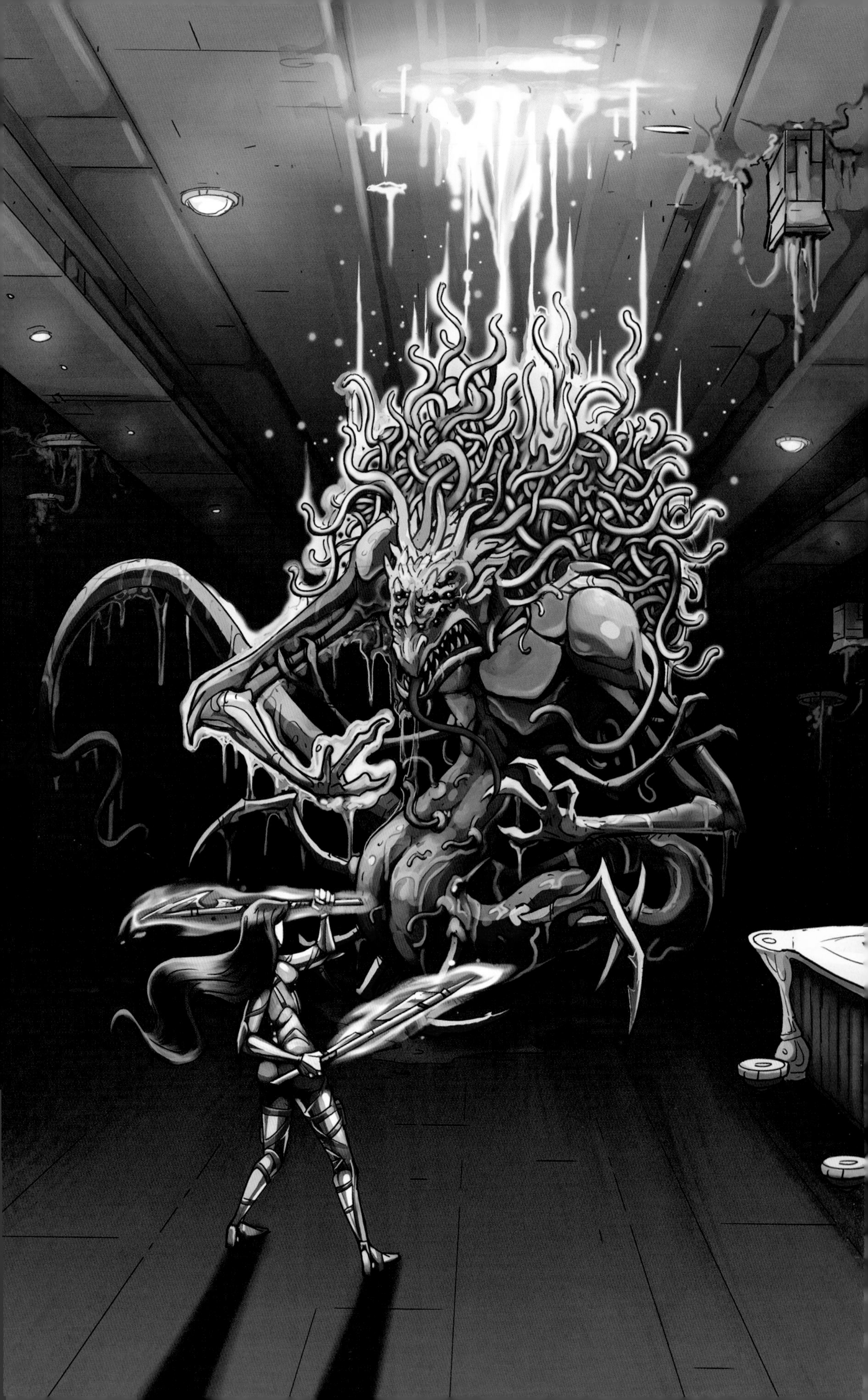

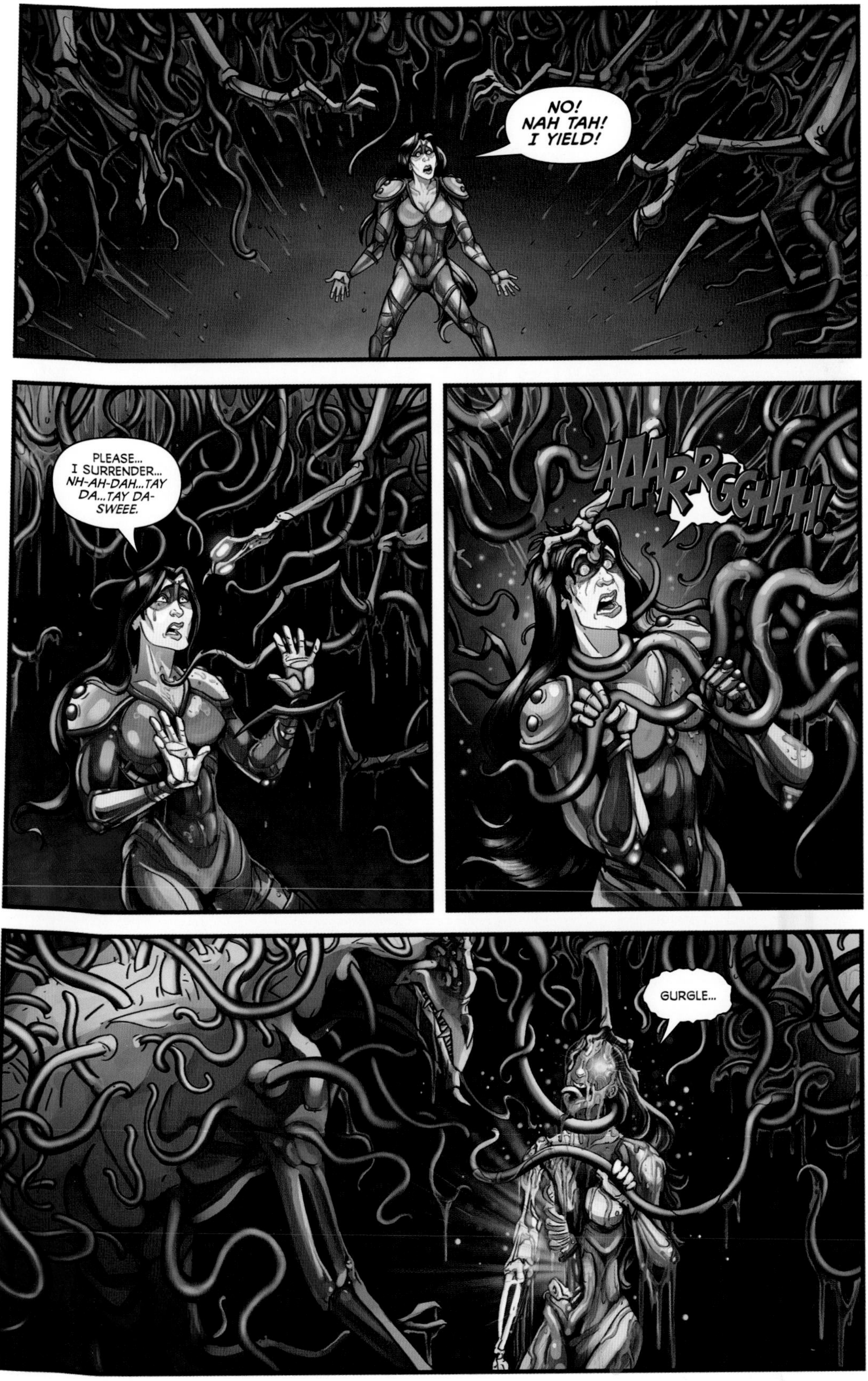
NO! NAH TAH! I YIELD!
PLEASE... I SURRENDER... NH-AH-DAH...TAY DA...TAY DA-SWEEE.
AAARRGGHHH!
GURGLE...

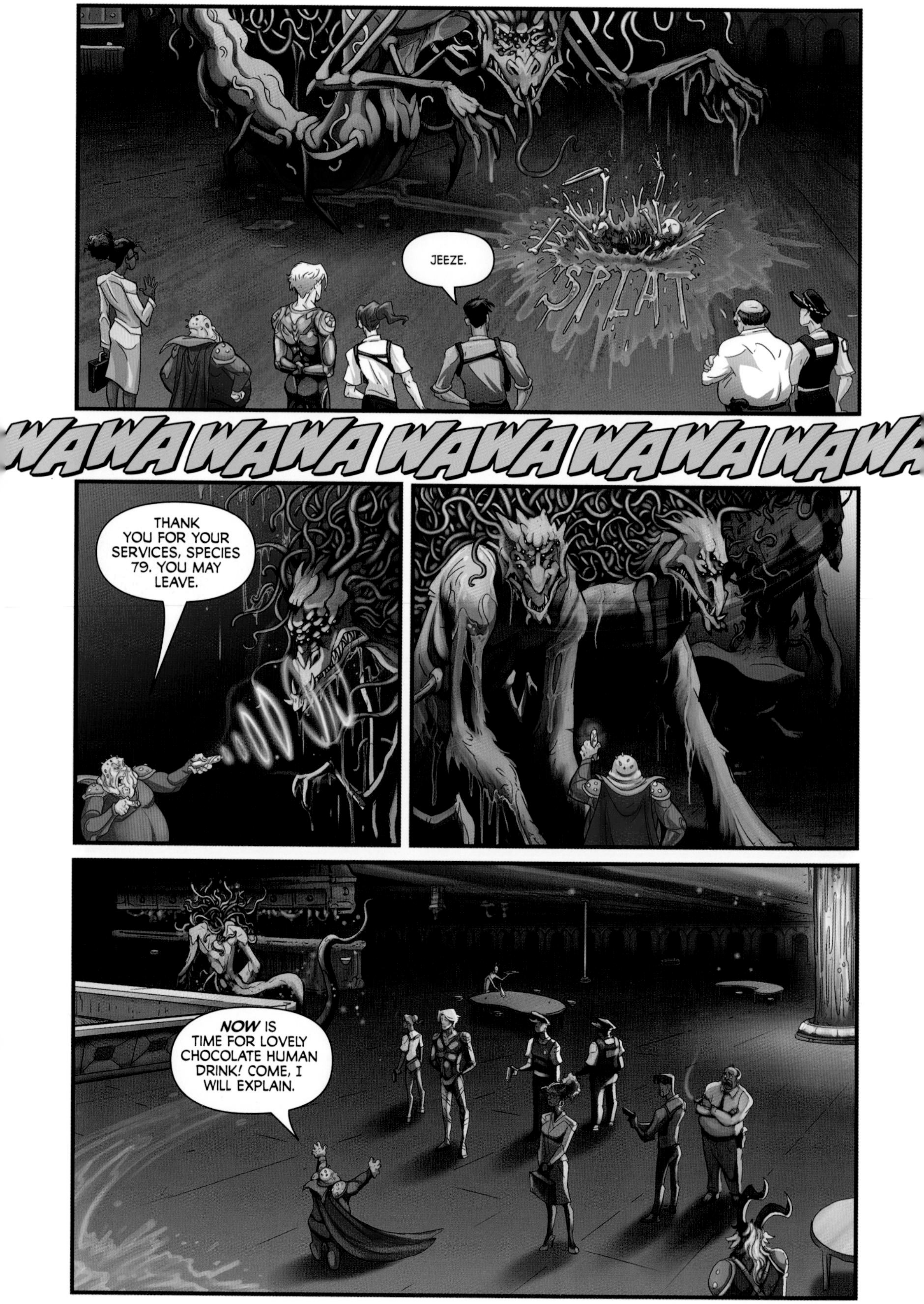
JEEZE.
SPLAT
WAWA WAWA WAWA WAWA WAWA
THANK YOU FOR YOUR SERVICES, SPECIES 79. YOU MAY LEAVE.
NOW IS TIME FOR LOVELY CHOCOLATE HUMAN DRINK! COME, I WILL EXPLAIN.

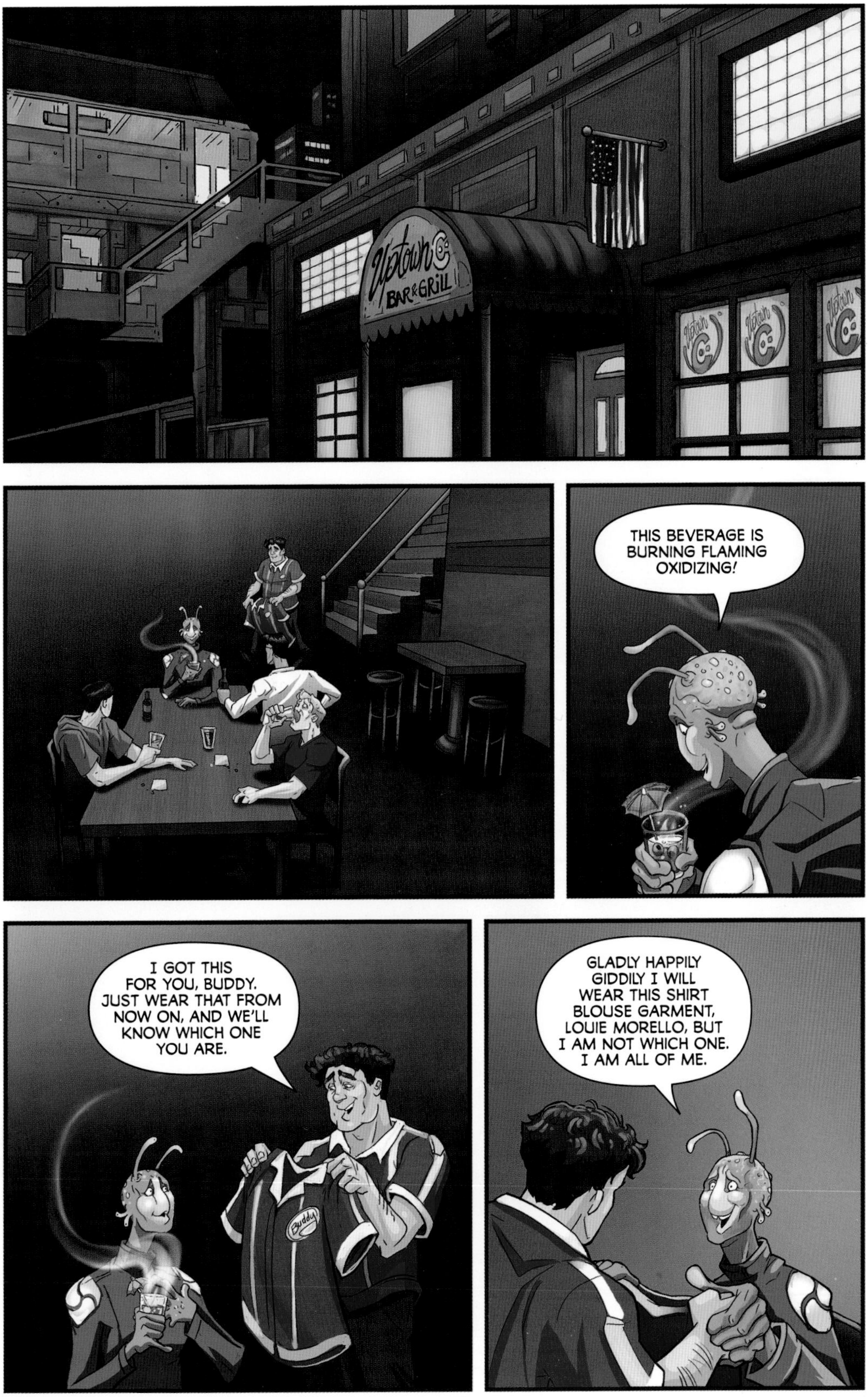
Uptown
BAR & GRILL
THIS BEVERAGE IS BURNING FLAMING OXIDIZING!
I GOT THIS FOR YOU, BUDDY. JUST WEAR THAT FROM NOW ON, AND WE'LL KNOW WHICH ONE YOU ARE.
Buddy
GLADLY HAPPILY GIDDILY I WILL WEAR THIS SHIRT BLOUSE GARMENT, LOUIE MORELLO, BUT I AM NOT WHICH ONE. I AM ALL OF ME.

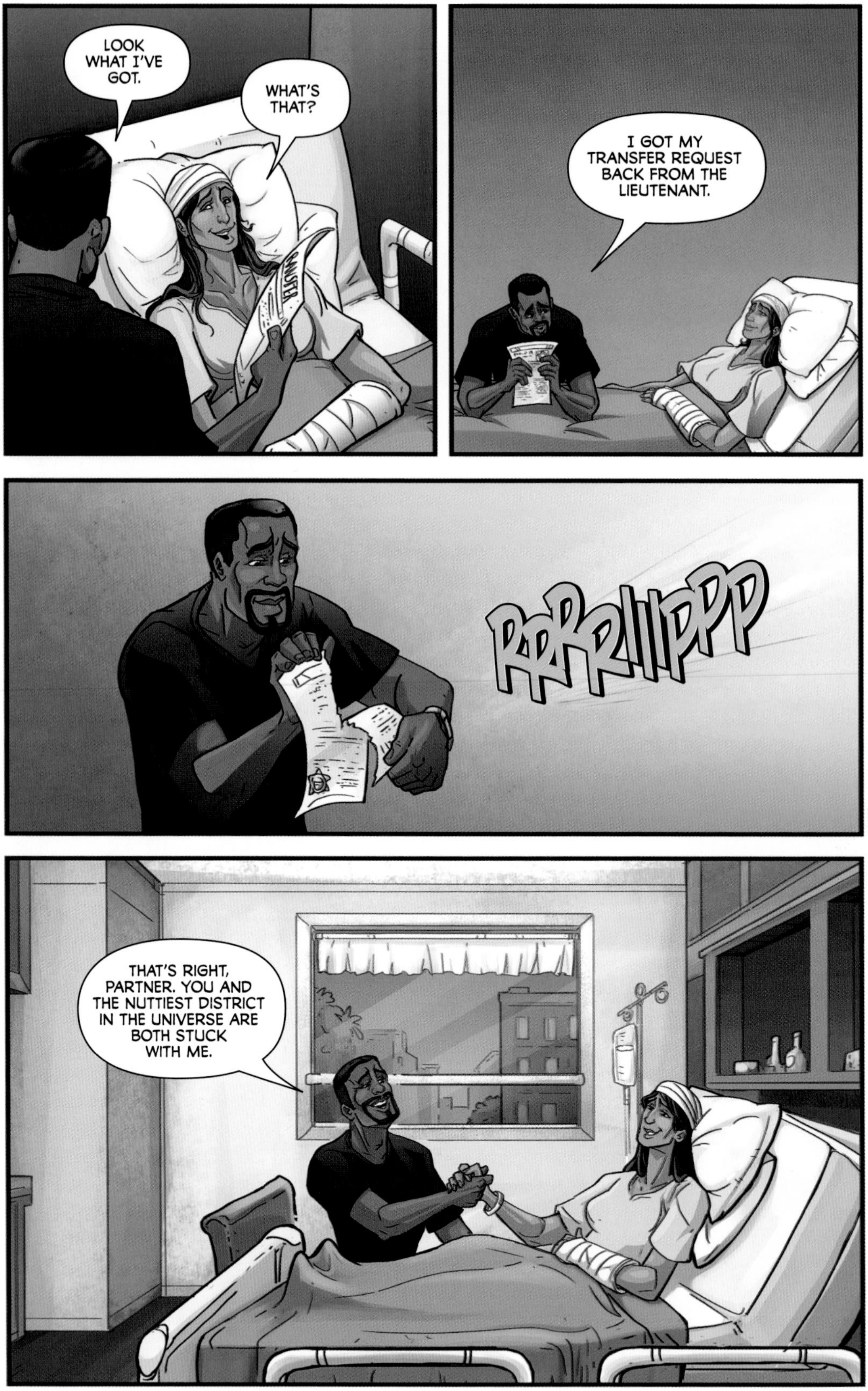
LOOK WHAT I'VE GOT.
WHAT'S THAT?
I GOT MY TRANSFER REQUEST BACK FROM THE LIEUTENANT.
RRRRIIIPPP
THAT'S RIGHT, PARTNER. YOU AND THE NUTTIEST DISTRICT IN THE UNIVERSE ARE BOTH STUCK WITH ME.

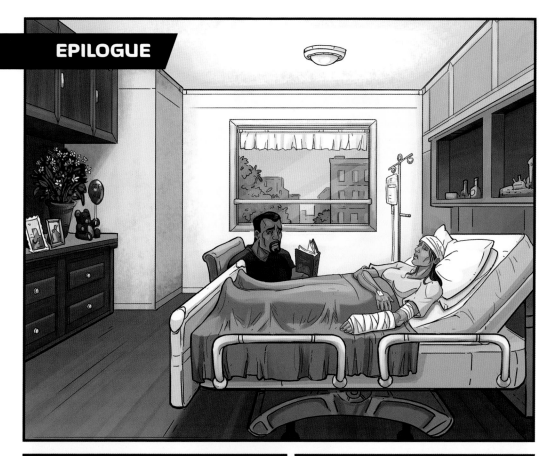

ERNIE... IS THAT YOU?

RIGHT HERE. ANYONE EVER TELL YOU YOU'VE GOT A REAL HARD HEAD?

I DIDN'T FREEZE.

I NOTICED THAT.

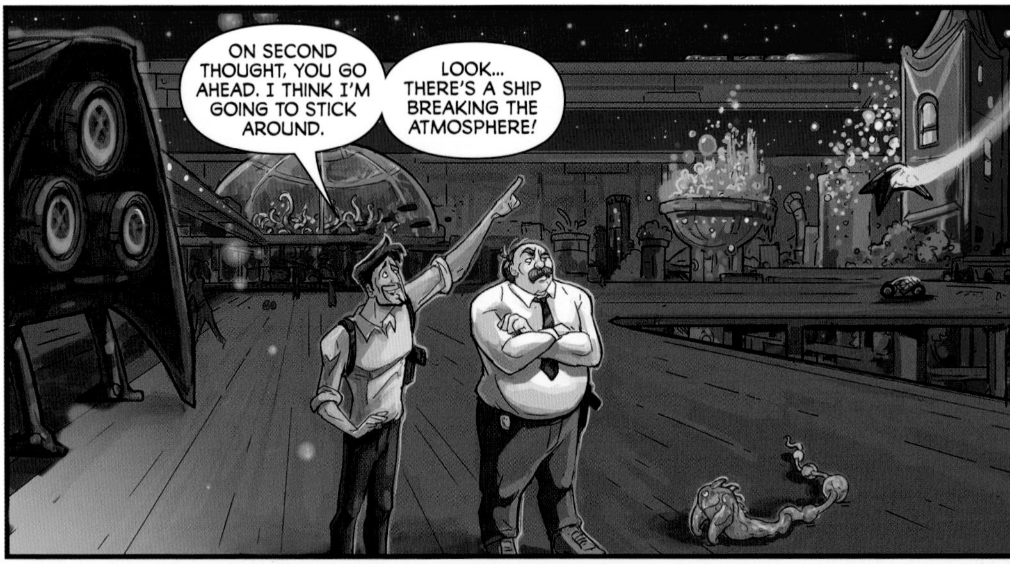
ON SECOND THOUGHT, YOU GO AHEAD. I THINK I'M GOING TO STICK AROUND.
LOOK... THERE'S A SHIP BREAKING THE ATMOSPHERE!

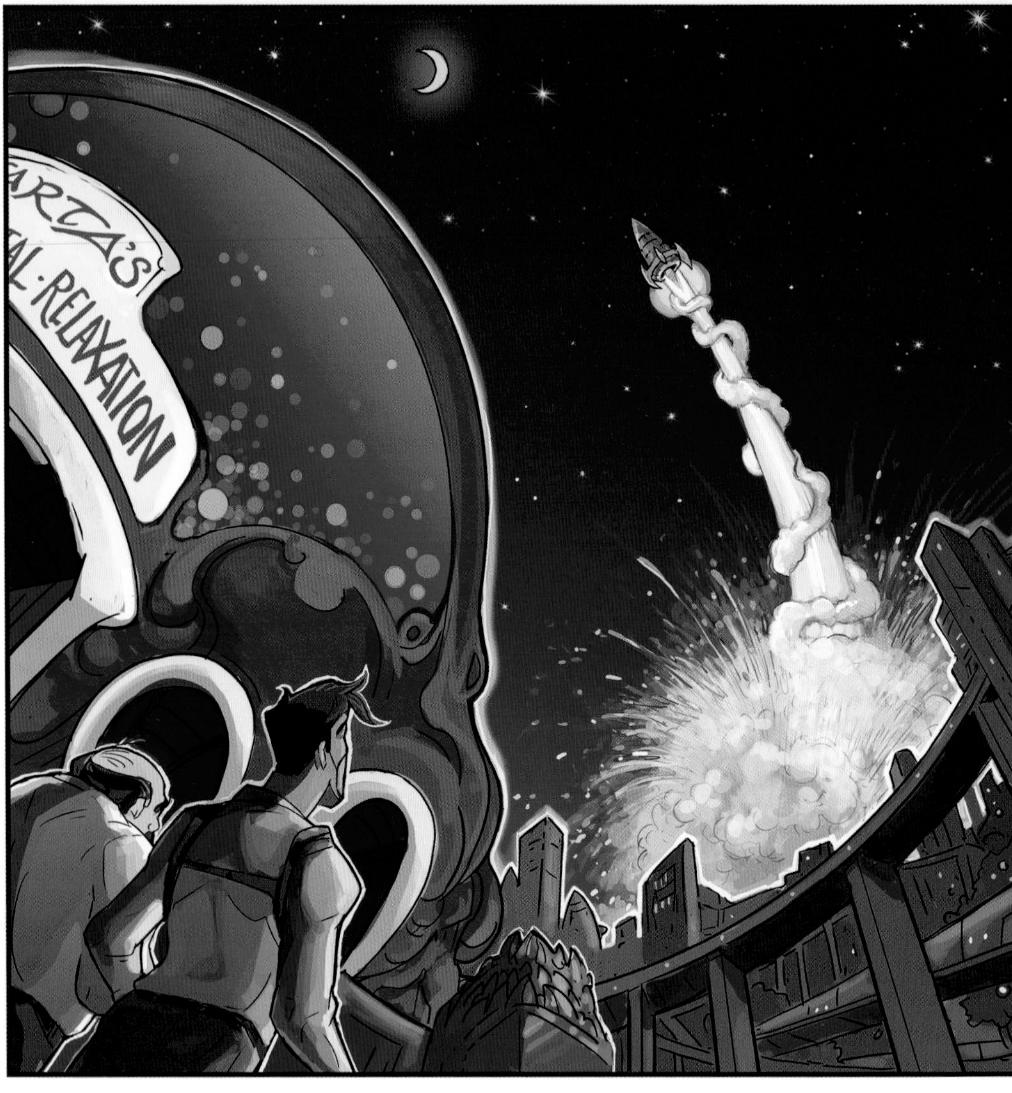

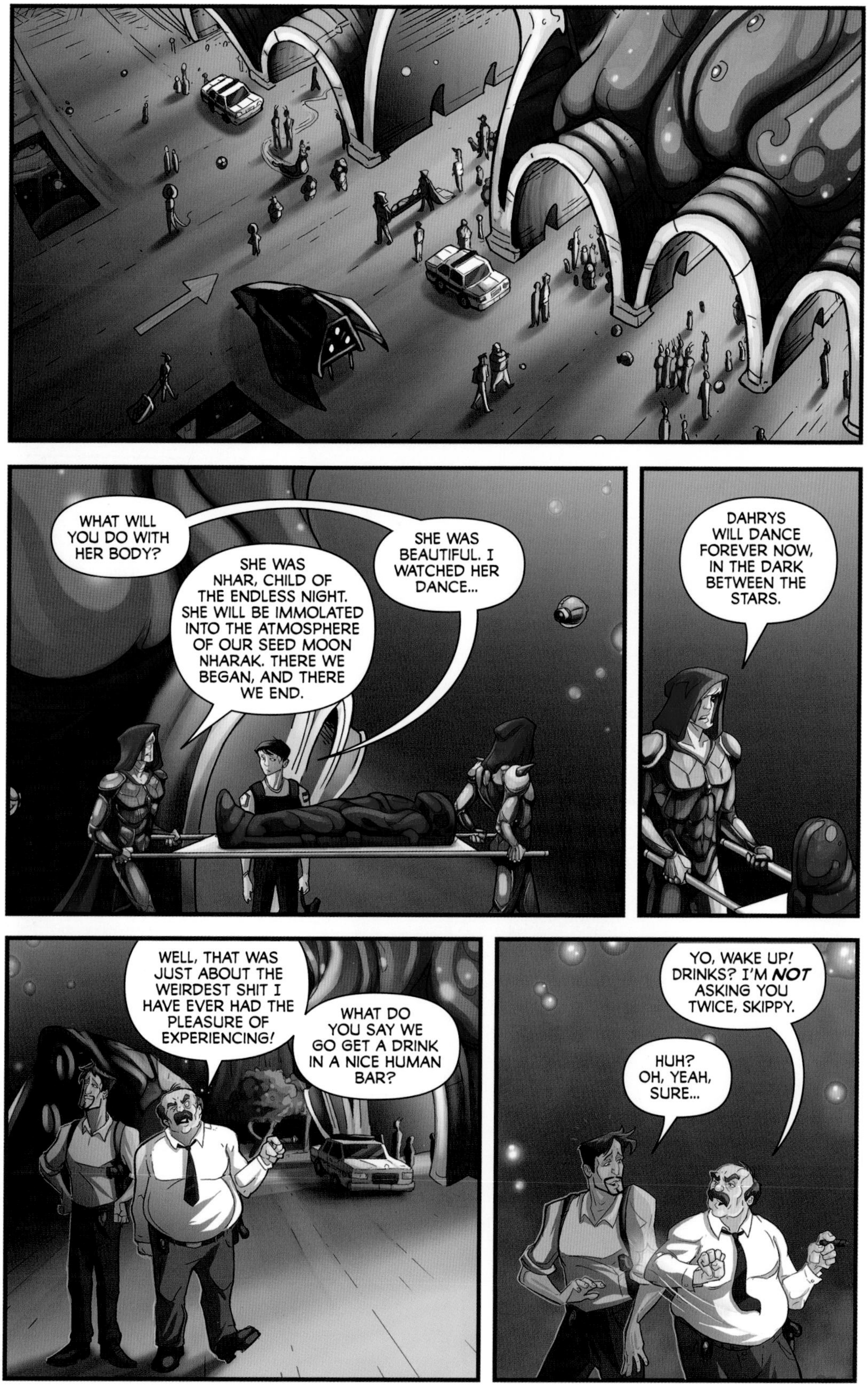
WHAT WILL YOU DO WITH HER BODY?
SHE WAS NHAR, CHILD OF THE ENDLESS NIGHT. SHE WILL BE IMMOLATED INTO THE ATMOSPHERE OF OUR SEED MOON NHARAK. THERE WE BEGAN, AND THERE WE END.
SHE WAS BEAUTIFUL. I WATCHED HER DANCE...
DAHRYS WILL DANCE FOREVER NOW, IN THE DARK BETWEEN THE STARS.
WELL, THAT WAS JUST ABOUT THE WEIRDEST SHIT I HAVE EVER HAD THE PLEASURE OF EXPERIENCING!
WHAT DO YOU SAY WE GO GET A DRINK IN A NICE HUMAN BAR?
YO, WAKE UP! DRINKS? I'M **NOT** ASKING YOU TWICE, SKIPPY.
HUH? OH, YEAH, SURE...

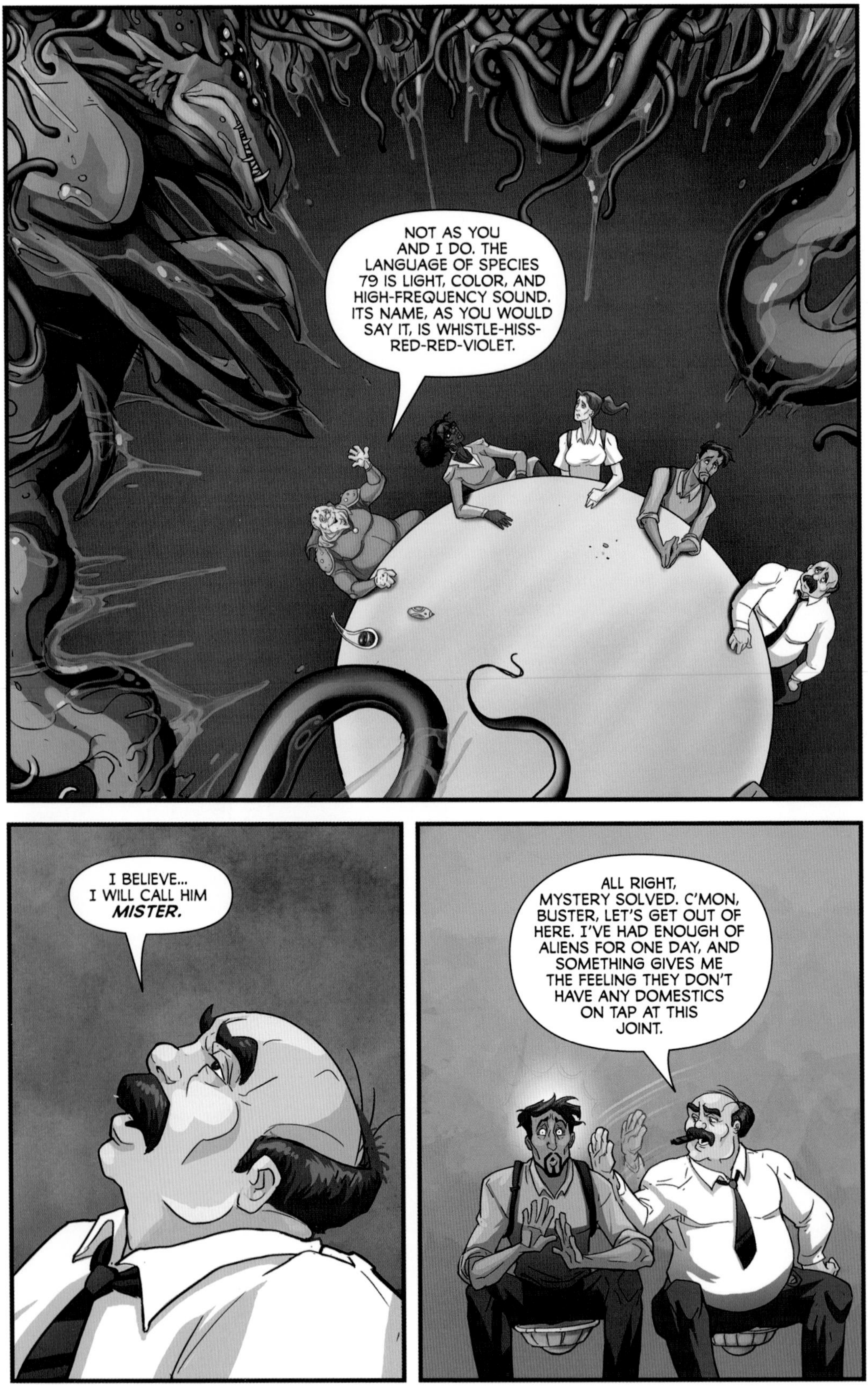
NOT AS YOU AND I DO. THE LANGUAGE OF SPECIES 79 IS LIGHT, COLOR, AND HIGH-FREQUENCY SOUND. ITS NAME, AS YOU WOULD SAY IT, IS WHISTLE-HISS-RED-RED-VIOLET.
I BELIEVE... I WILL CALL HIM *MISTER.*
ALL RIGHT, MYSTERY SOLVED. C'MON, BUSTER, LET'S GET OUT OF HERE. I'VE HAD ENOUGH OF ALIENS FOR ONE DAY, AND SOMETHING GIVES ME THE FEELING THEY DON'T HAVE ANY DOMESTICS ON TAP AT THIS JOINT.

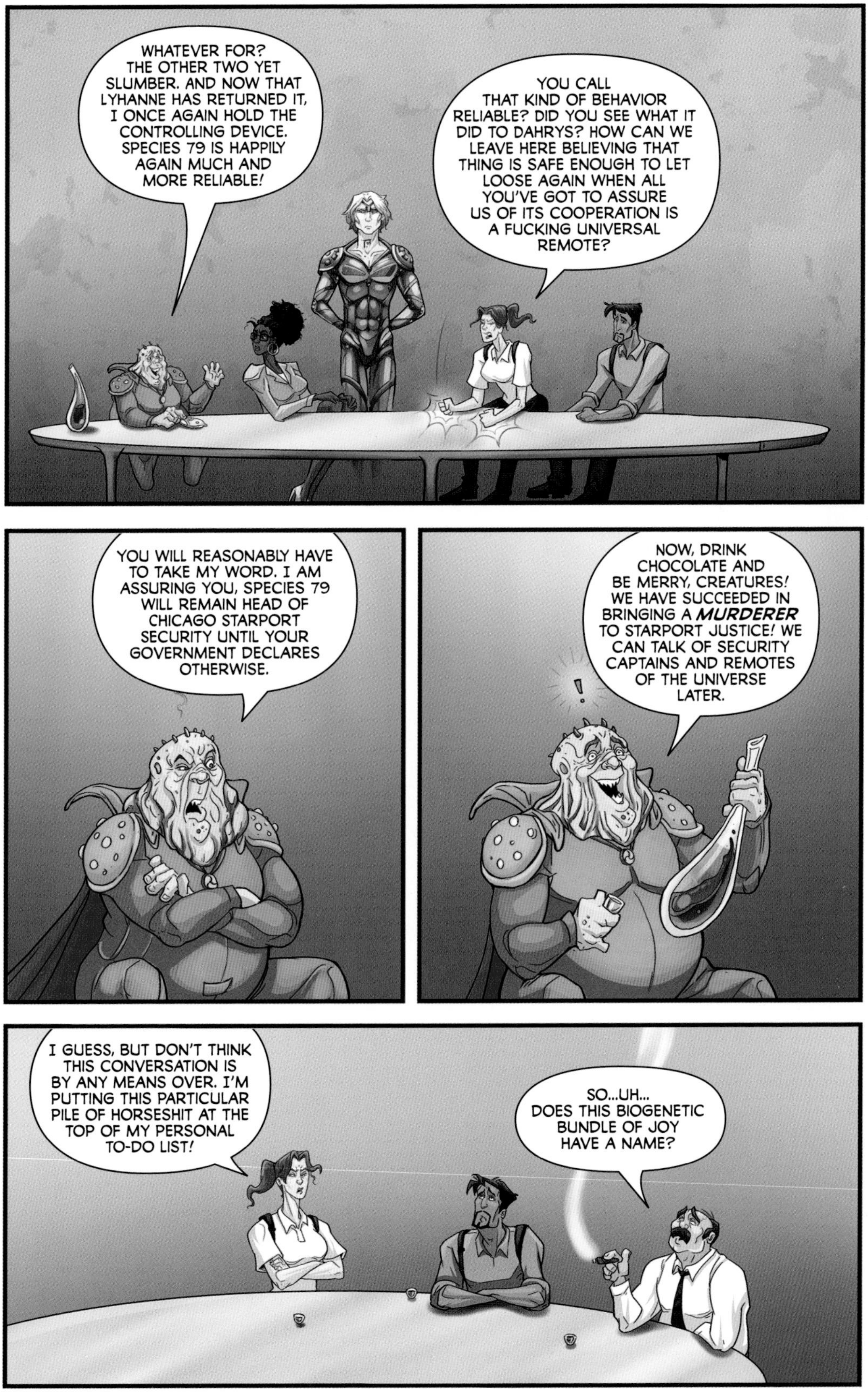
WHATEVER FOR? THE OTHER TWO YET SLUMBER. AND NOW THAT LYHANNE HAS RETURNED IT, I ONCE AGAIN HOLD THE CONTROLLING DEVICE. SPECIES 79 IS HAPPILY AGAIN MUCH AND MORE RELIABLE!
YOU CALL THAT KIND OF BEHAVIOR RELIABLE? DID YOU SEE WHAT IT DID TO DAHRYS? HOW CAN WE LEAVE HERE BELIEVING THAT THING IS SAFE ENOUGH TO LET LOOSE AGAIN WHEN ALL YOU'VE GOT TO ASSURE US OF ITS COOPERATION IS A FUCKING UNIVERSAL REMOTE?
YOU WILL REASONABLY HAVE TO TAKE MY WORD. I AM ASSURING YOU, SPECIES 79 WILL REMAIN HEAD OF CHICAGO STARPORT SECURITY UNTIL YOUR GOVERNMENT DECLARES OTHERWISE.
!
NOW, DRINK CHOCOLATE AND BE MERRY, CREATURES! WE HAVE SUCCEEDED IN BRINGING A ***MURDERER*** TO STARPORT JUSTICE! WE CAN TALK OF SECURITY CAPTAINS AND REMOTES OF THE UNIVERSE LATER.
I GUESS, BUT DON'T THINK THIS CONVERSATION IS BY ANY MEANS OVER. I'M PUTTING THIS PARTICULAR PILE OF HORSESHIT AT THE TOP OF MY PERSONAL TO-DO LIST!
SO...UH... DOES THIS BIOGENETIC BUNDLE OF JOY HAVE A NAME?

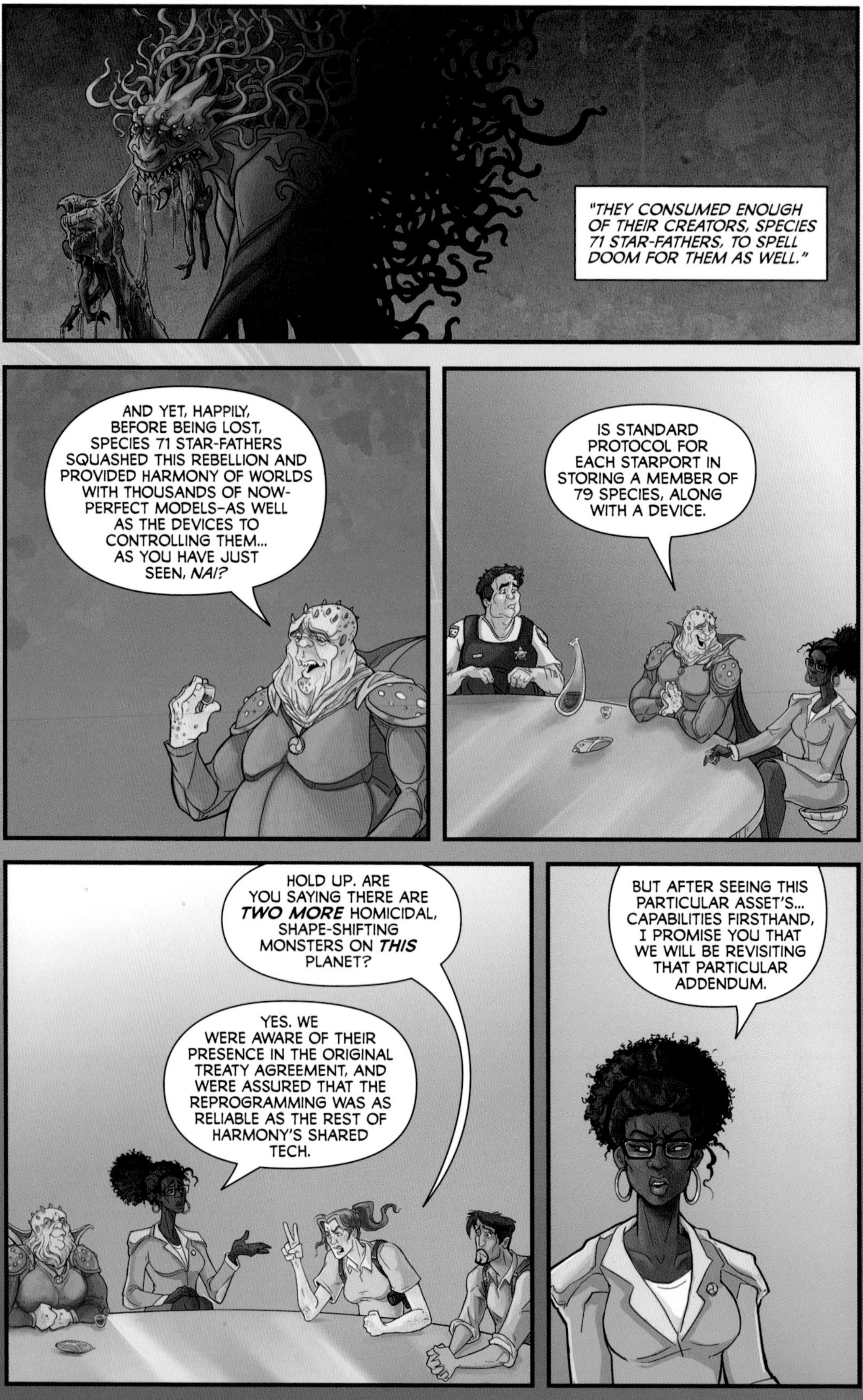
"THEY CONSUMED ENOUGH OF THEIR CREATORS, SPECIES 71 STAR-FATHERS, TO SPELL DOOM FOR THEM AS WELL."
AND YET, HAPPILY, BEFORE BEING LOST, SPECIES 71 STAR-FATHERS SQUASHED THIS REBELLION AND PROVIDED HARMONY OF WORLDS WITH THOUSANDS OF NOW-PERFECT MODELS–AS WELL AS THE DEVICES TO CONTROLLING THEM... AS YOU HAVE JUST SEEN, *NAI?*
IS STANDARD PROTOCOL FOR EACH STARPORT IN STORING A MEMBER OF 79 SPECIES, ALONG WITH A DEVICE.
HOLD UP. ARE YOU SAYING THERE ARE ***TWO MORE*** HOMICIDAL, SHAPE-SHIFTING MONSTERS ON ***THIS*** PLANET?
YES. WE WERE AWARE OF THEIR PRESENCE IN THE ORIGINAL TREATY AGREEMENT, AND WERE ASSURED THAT THE REPROGRAMMING WAS AS RELIABLE AS THE REST OF HARMONY'S SHARED TECH.
BUT AFTER SEEING THIS PARTICULAR ASSET'S... CAPABILITIES FIRSTHAND, I PROMISE YOU THAT WE WILL BE REVISITING THAT PARTICULAR ADDENDUM.

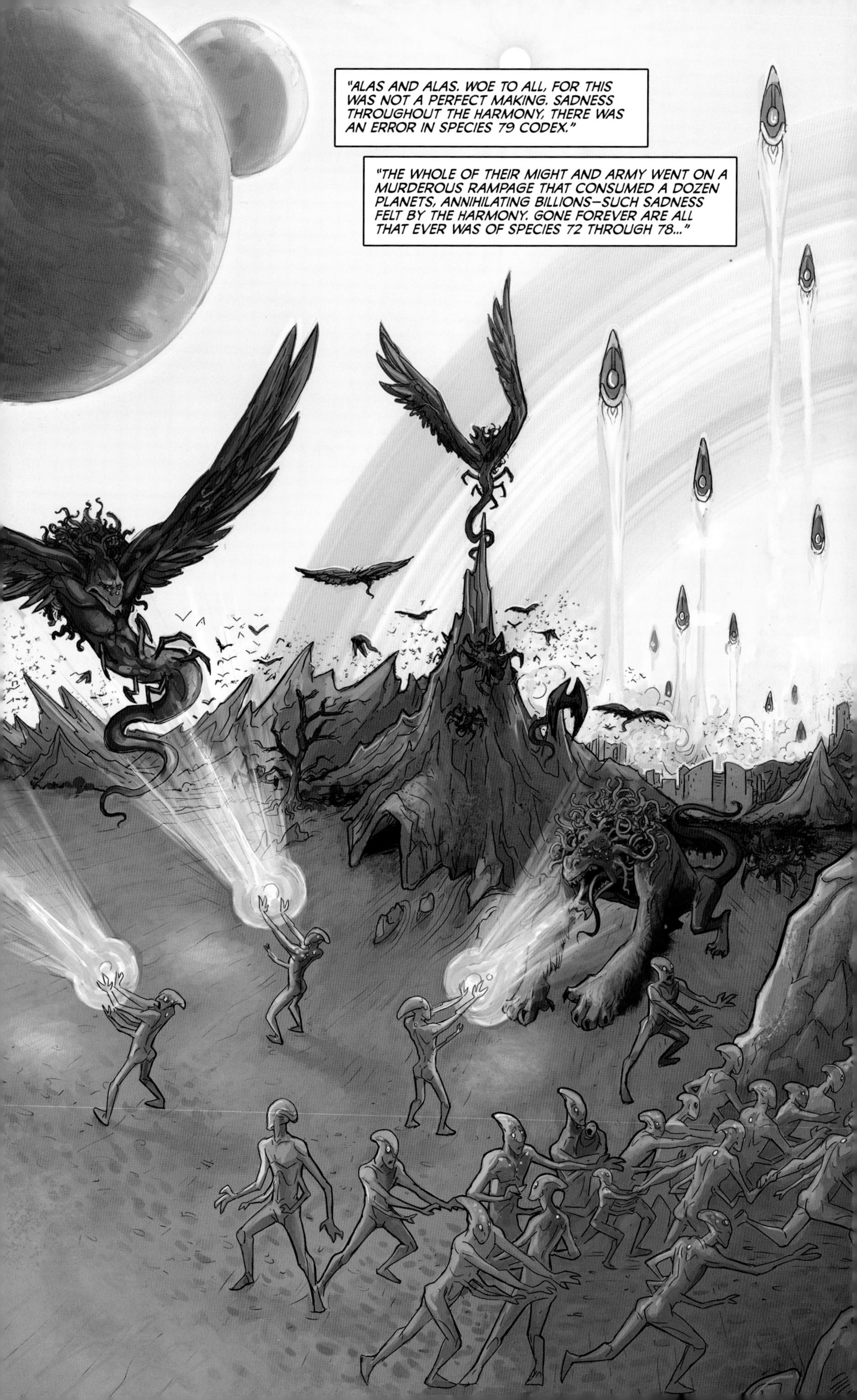
"ALAS AND ALAS. WOE TO ALL, FOR THIS WAS NOT A PERFECT MAKING. SADNESS THROUGHOUT THE HARMONY, THERE WAS AN ERROR IN SPECIES 79 CODEX."
"THE WHOLE OF THEIR MIGHT AND ARMY WENT ON A MURDEROUS RAMPAGE THAT CONSUMED A DOZEN PLANETS, ANNIHILATING BILLIONS—SUCH SADNESS FELT BY THE HARMONY. GONE FOREVER ARE ALL THAT EVER WAS OF SPECIES 72 THROUGH 78..."

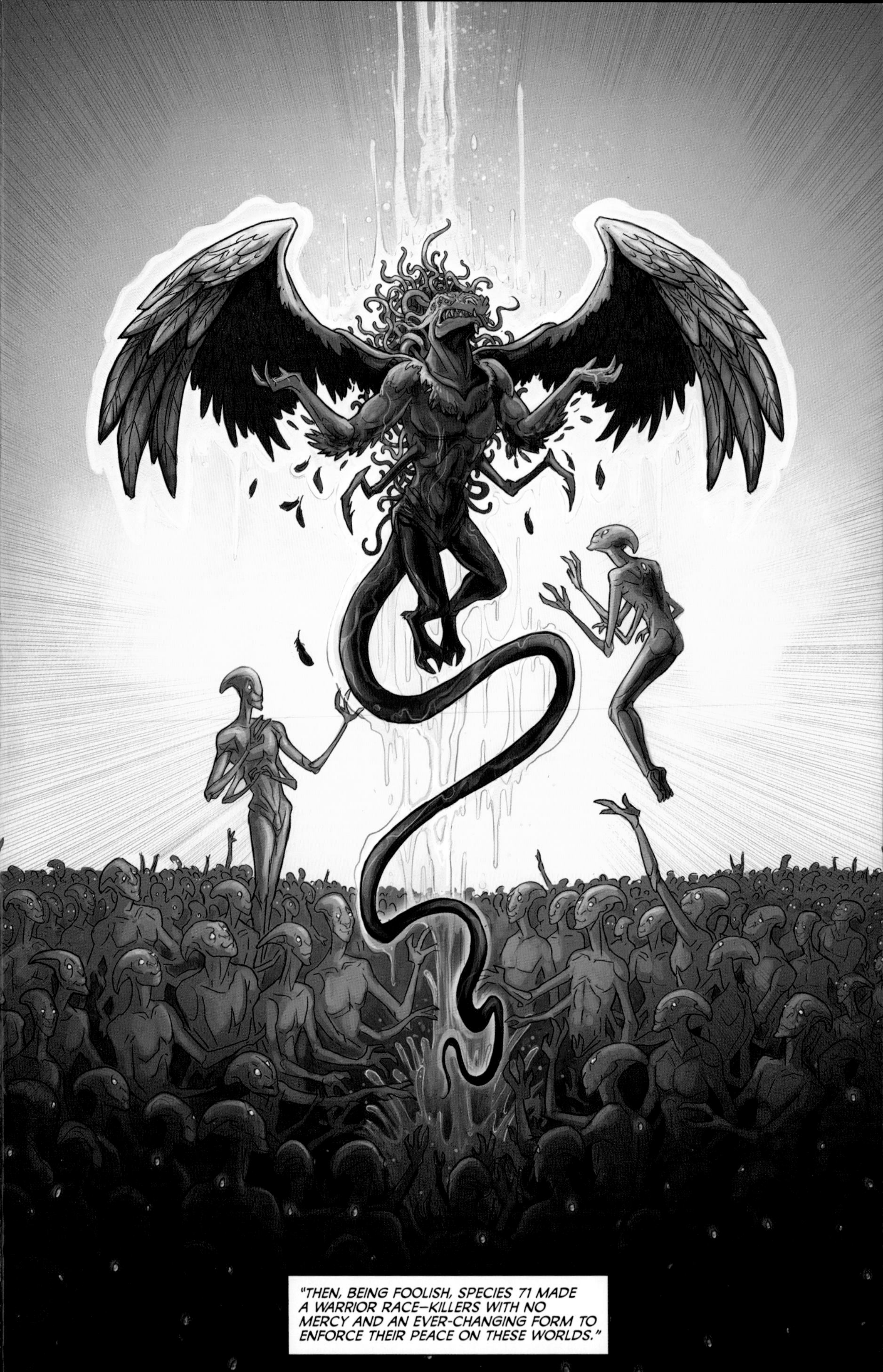
"THEN, BEING FOOLISH, SPECIES 71 MADE A WARRIOR RACE—KILLERS WITH NO MERCY AND AN EVER-CHANGING FORM TO ENFORCE THEIR PEACE ON THESE WORLDS."

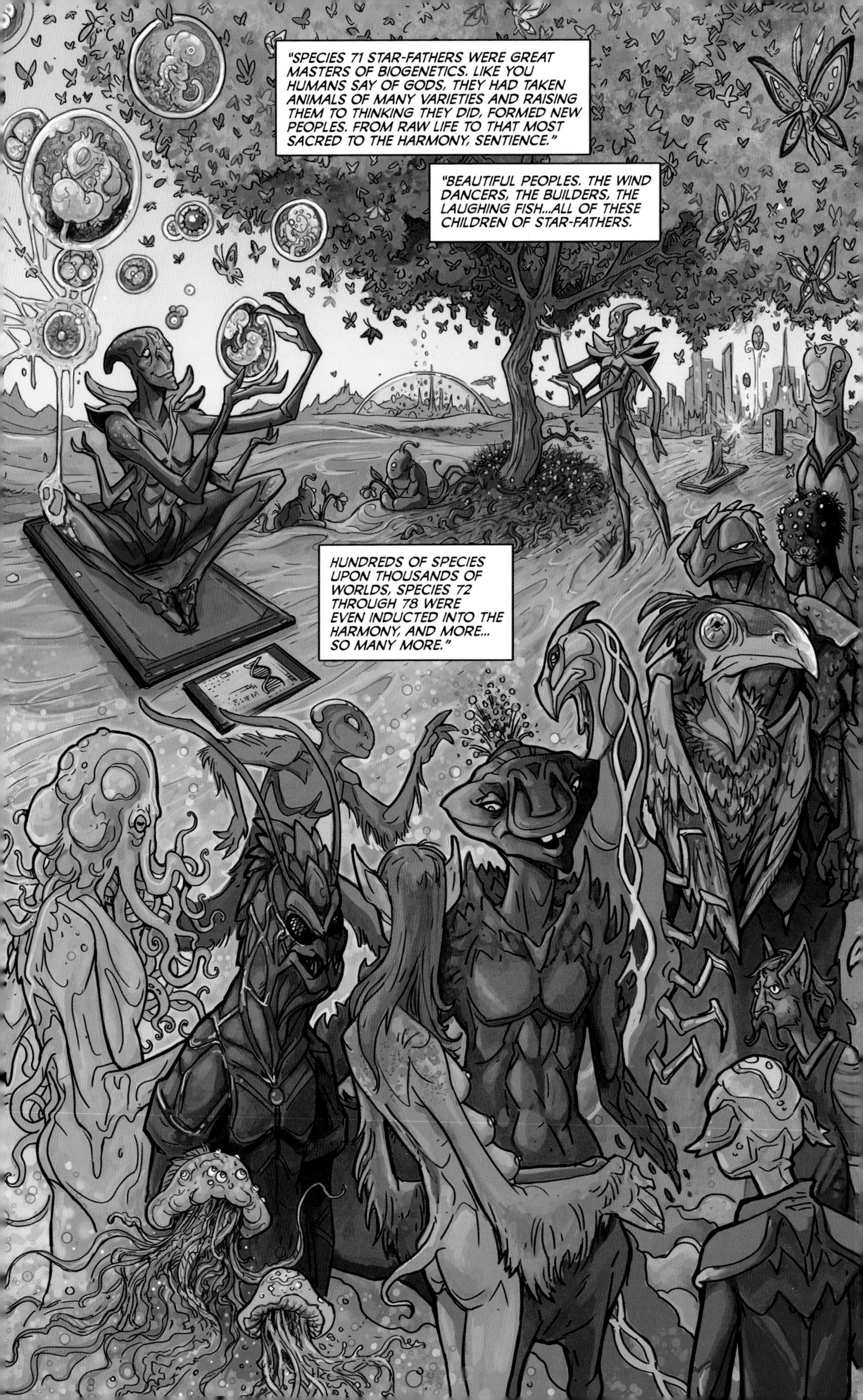
"SPECIES 71 STAR-FATHERS WERE GREAT MASTERS OF BIOGENETICS. LIKE YOU HUMANS SAY OF GODS, THEY HAD TAKEN ANIMALS OF MANY VARIETIES AND RAISING THEM TO THINKING THEY DID, FORMED NEW PEOPLES. FROM RAW LIFE TO THAT MOST SACRED TO THE HARMONY, SENTIENCE."
"BEAUTIFUL PEOPLES. THE WIND DANCERS, THE BUILDERS, THE LAUGHING FISH...ALL OF THESE CHILDREN OF STAR-FATHERS.
HUNDREDS OF SPECIES UPON THOUSANDS OF WORLDS, SPECIES 72 THROUGH 78 WERE EVEN INDUCTED INTO THE HARMONY, AND MORE... SO MANY MORE."

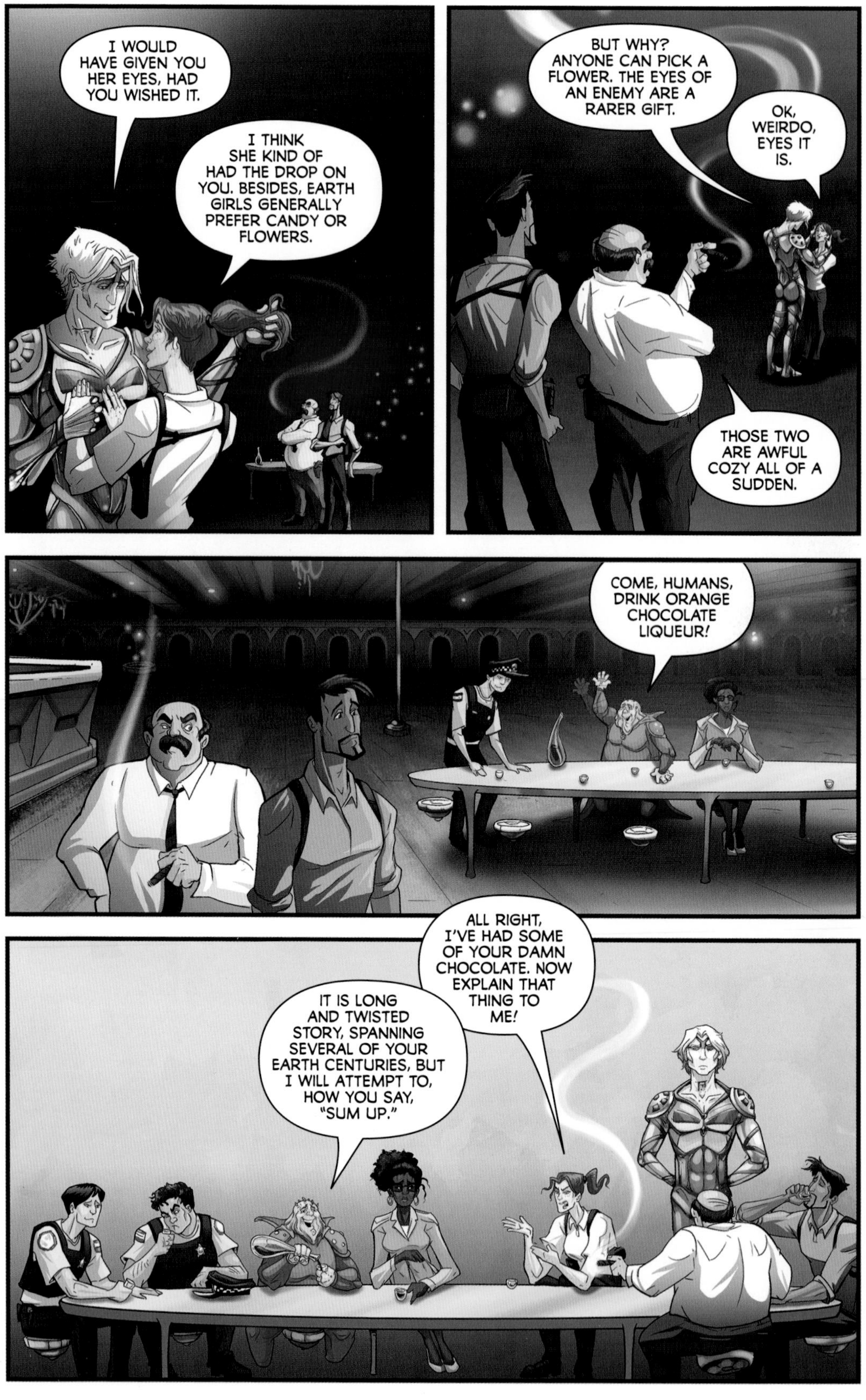
I WOULD HAVE GIVEN YOU HER EYES, HAD YOU WISHED IT.
I THINK SHE KIND OF HAD THE DROP ON YOU. BESIDES, EARTH GIRLS GENERALLY PREFER CANDY OR FLOWERS.
BUT WHY? ANYONE CAN PICK A FLOWER. THE EYES OF AN ENEMY ARE A RARER GIFT.
OK, WEIRDO, EYES IT IS.
THOSE TWO ARE AWFUL COZY ALL OF A SUDDEN.
COME, HUMANS, DRINK ORANGE CHOCOLATE LIQUEUR!
ALL RIGHT, I'VE HAD SOME OF YOUR DAMN CHOCOLATE. NOW EXPLAIN THAT THING TO ME!
IT IS LONG AND TWISTED STORY, SPANNING SEVERAL OF YOUR EARTH CENTURIES, BUT I WILL ATTEMPT TO, HOW YOU SAY, "SUM UP."

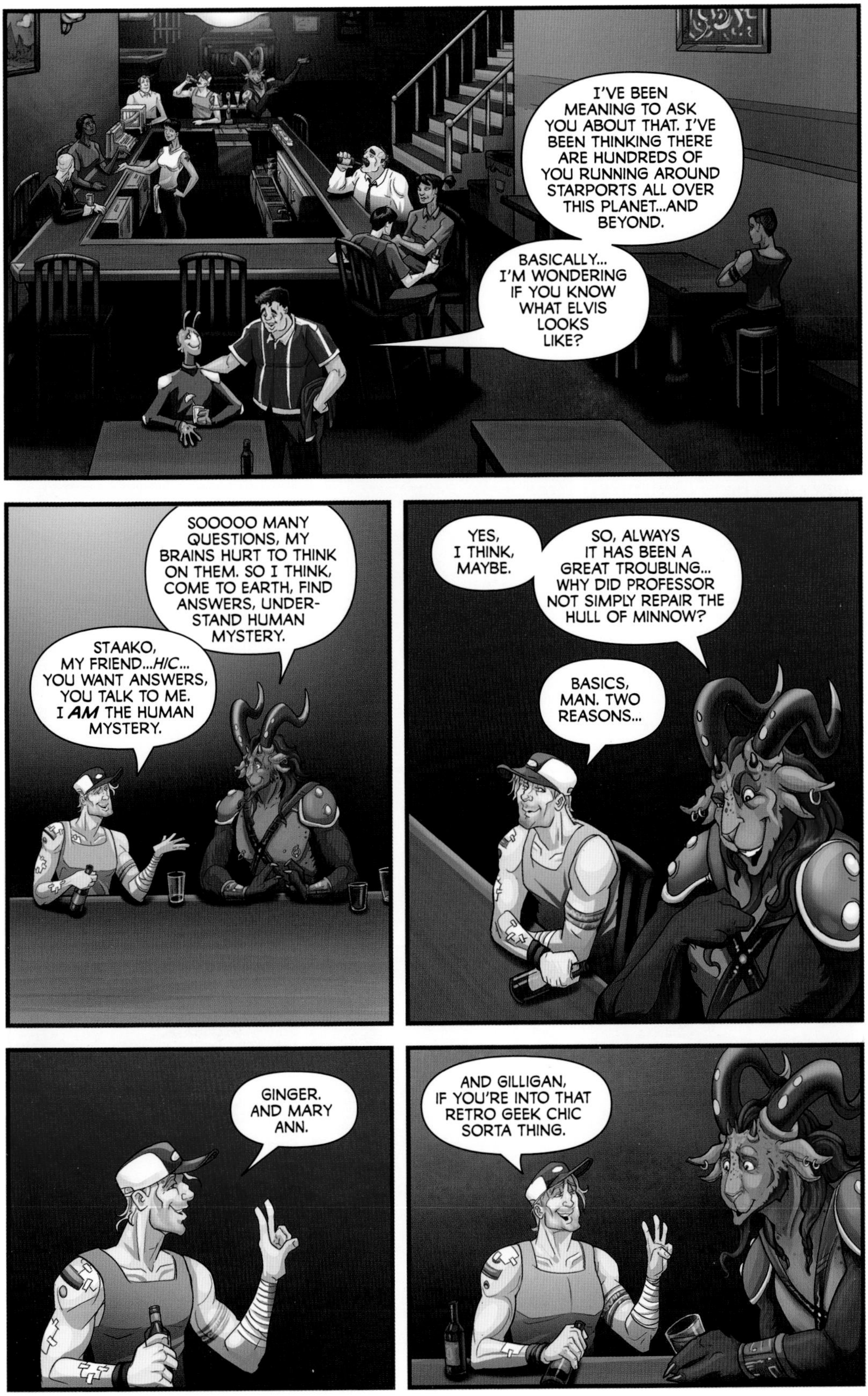
I'VE BEEN MEANING TO ASK YOU ABOUT THAT. I'VE BEEN THINKING THERE ARE HUNDREDS OF YOU RUNNING AROUND STARPORTS ALL OVER THIS PLANET...AND BEYOND.
BASICALLY... I'M WONDERING IF YOU KNOW WHAT ELVIS LOOKS LIKE?
SOOOOO MANY QUESTIONS, MY BRAINS HURT TO THINK ON THEM. SO I THINK, COME TO EARTH, FIND ANSWERS, UNDERSTAND HUMAN MYSTERY.
STAAKO, MY FRIEND...*HIC*... YOU WANT ANSWERS, YOU TALK TO ME. I ***AM*** THE HUMAN MYSTERY.
YES, I THINK, MAYBE.
SO, ALWAYS IT HAS BEEN A GREAT TROUBLING... WHY DID PROFESSOR NOT SIMPLY REPAIR THE HULL OF MINNOW?
BASICS, MAN. TWO REASONS...
GINGER. AND MARY ANN.
AND GILLIGAN, IF YOU'RE INTO THAT RETRO GEEK CHIC SORTA THING.

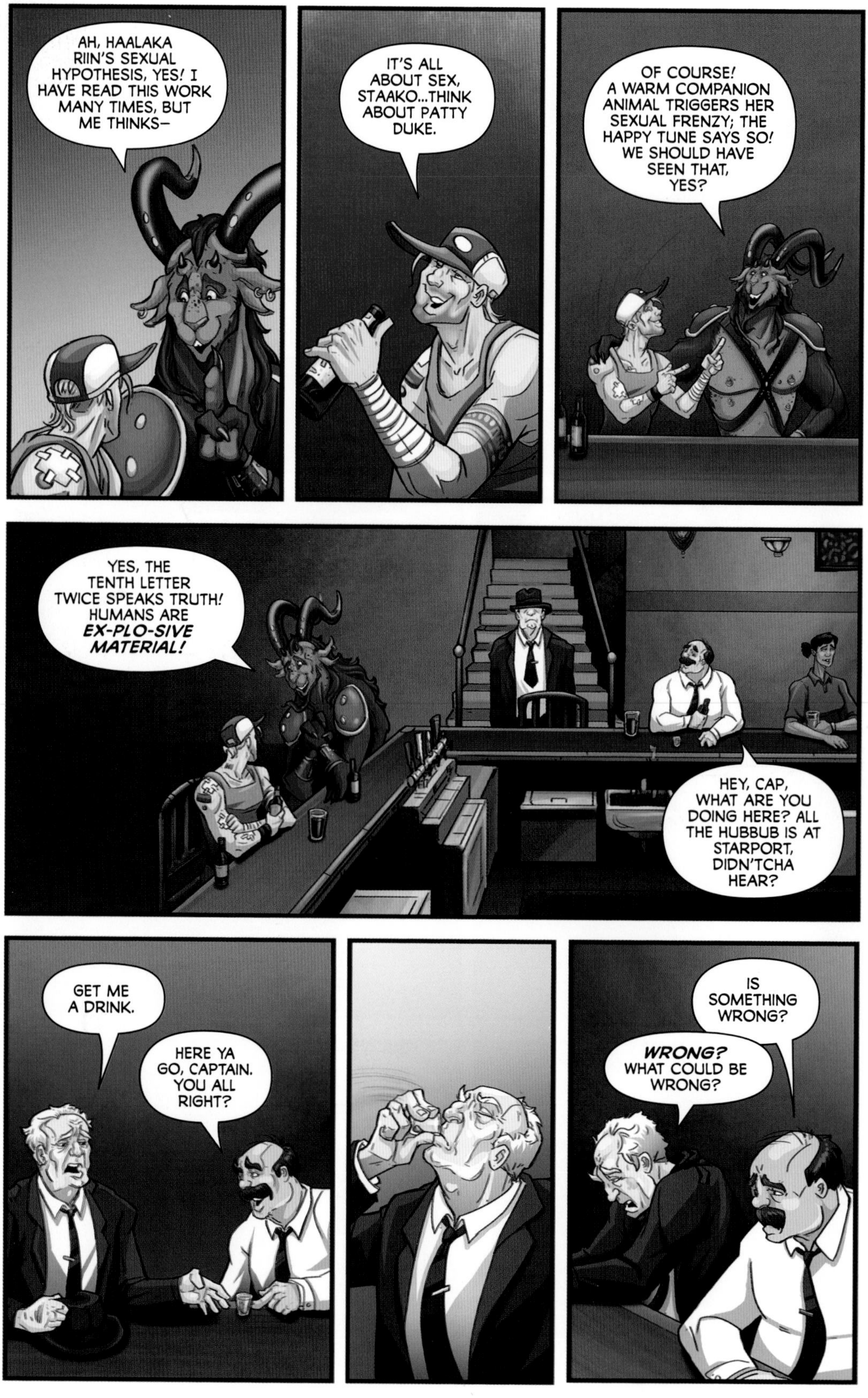
AH, HAALAKA RIIN'S SEXUAL HYPOTHESIS, YES! I HAVE READ THIS WORK MANY TIMES, BUT ME THINKS—
IT'S ALL ABOUT SEX, STAAKO...THINK ABOUT PATTY DUKE.
OF COURSE! A WARM COMPANION ANIMAL TRIGGERS HER SEXUAL FRENZY; THE HAPPY TUNE SAYS SO! WE SHOULD HAVE SEEN THAT, YES?
YES, THE TENTH LETTER TWICE SPEAKS TRUTH! HUMANS ARE *EX-PLO-SIVE MATERIAL!*
HEY, CAP, WHAT ARE YOU DOING HERE? ALL THE HUBBUB IS AT STARPORT, DIDN'TCHA HEAR?
GET ME A DRINK.
HERE YA GO, CAPTAIN. YOU ALL RIGHT?
IS SOMETHING WRONG?
WRONG? WHAT COULD BE WRONG?

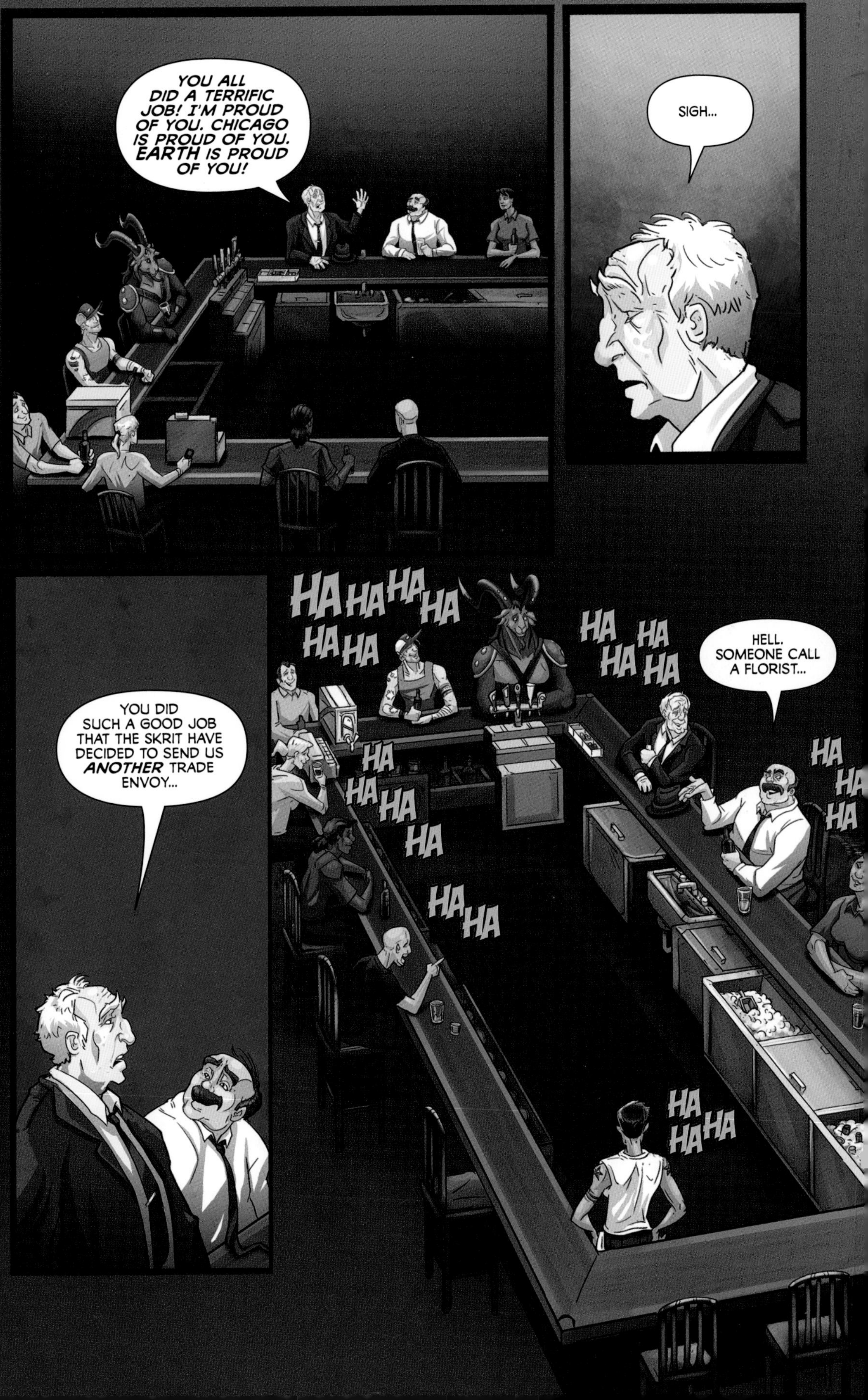

YOU ALL DID A TERRIFIC JOB! I'M PROUD OF YOU. CHICAGO IS PROUD OF YOU. ***EARTH*** IS PROUD OF YOU!
SIGH...
YOU DID SUCH A GOOD JOB THAT THE SKRIT HAVE DECIDED TO SEND US ***ANOTHER*** TRADE ENVOY...
HA HA HA HA HA HA
HA HA HA HA
HELL. SOMEONE CALL A FLORIST...
HA HA HA HA
HA HA
HA HA HA

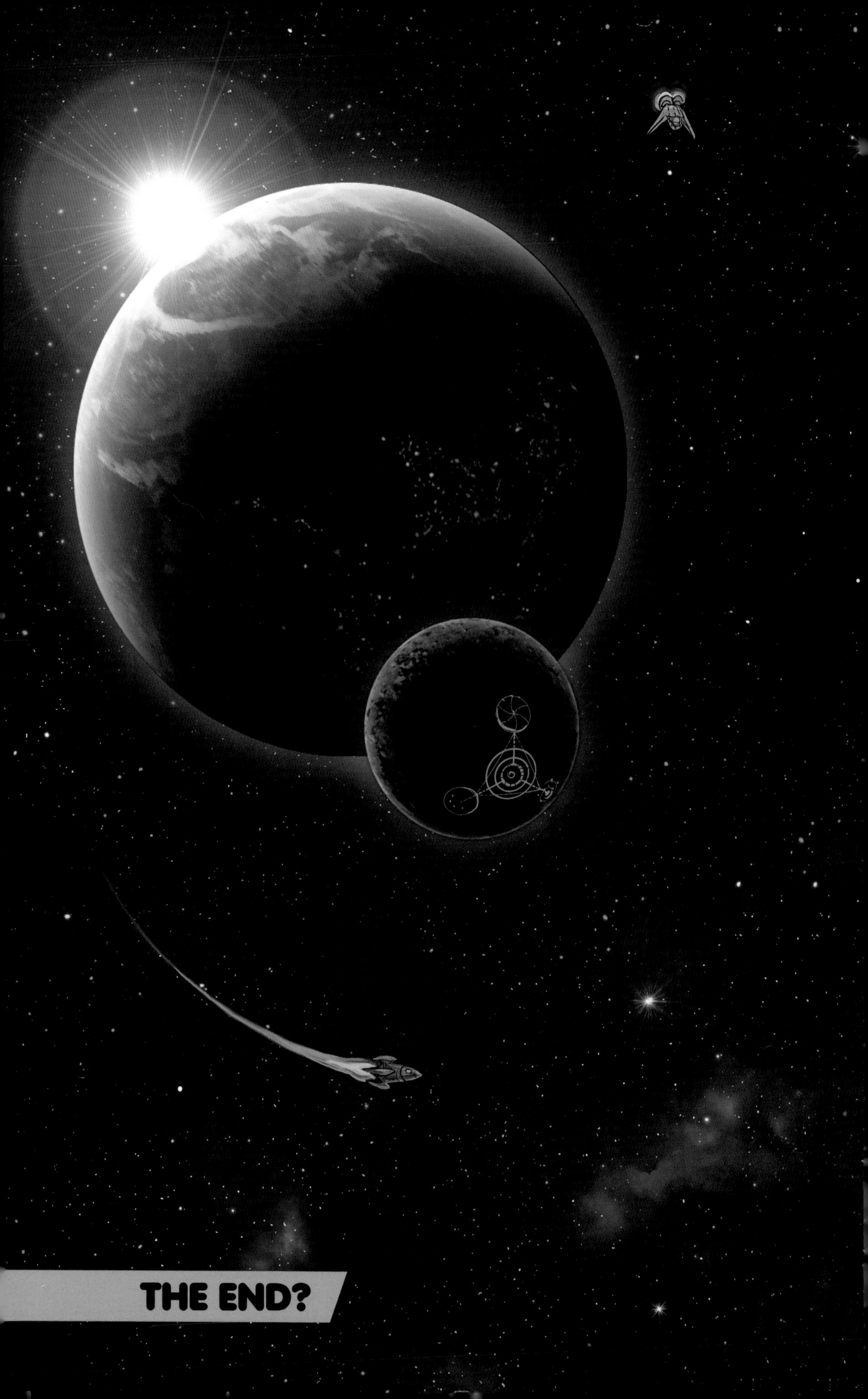
THE END?